ISBN 978-0-276-44450-0

www.readersdigest.co.uk

Published in the United Kingdom by Vivat Direct Limited (t/a Reader's Digest),
157 Edgware Road, London W2 2HR

and in Canada
www.rd.ca

The Reader's Digest Association (Canada) ULC, 1100 René-Lévesque Blvd. West, Montréal,
Québec, H3B 5H5 Canada

# of love & life

Three novels selected and condensed
by Reader's Digest

Reader's
Digest

The Reader's Digest Association Inc., London, Montreal

CONTENTS

The Legacy

Katherine Webb

My characters all have their secrets—from the world, from each other, and in some cases even from themselves. What I've tried to show is that when you make a mistake, however huge and frightening it may be, the chances are that unless you face it and deal with the aftermath, you will never be free of it.

As my first published novel, this story and these characters will always hold a special place in my heart. It's a story about love, loss, regret and redemption; I hope that you enjoy reading it as much as I enjoyed writing it!

Katherine

Prologue

1905

GRADUALLY, CAROLINE returned to her senses. The numbness inside her head receded and she became aware of myriad thoughts, too fast for her to grasp. Unsteadily, she got to her feet. The child was still there, on the bed. A slick of fear washed down her spine. Part of her had been hoping that somehow he would have gone, or never have been there at all. He had pulled himself to the far side of the bed, struggling to crawl on the slippery-soft counterpane. He had grown so big. In another place, in another life, he would have been a warrior. His hair was mid-night black. The baby peered over the bed and then turned his head to look at Caroline. Her eyes swam with tears. He was real; he was here, in her bed chamber at Storton Manor.

Her shame was a cloud she could not see through. She had no idea what to do. Long minutes passed, until she thought she heard a foot-step in the hallway outside the door. It sent her heart lurching, so all she knew, in the end, was that the baby couldn't stay there. Not on the bed, not in her room, not in the manor house. He just could not, and neither must any of the servants, or her husband, know that he ever had been.

Wiping her face, Caroline went around the bed and picked the boy up, too ashamed to look into his eyes. They were black too, she knew. As black and inscrutable as ink spots. She lay him down and took off all his clothes, even though they were coarsely made, in case they could somehow lead back to her. She cast them into the grate, where they oozed smoke on the embers of the morning's fire. Then she looked around, at a loss, before her eyes lit on the embroidered pillowcase at the head of the bed. Caroline stripped the pillow bare and put the struggling baby into the case. She did this tenderly, her hands aware of her love for the child even if her mind could not encompass it. But she did not use it to wrap him in. Instead she turned it into a sack and carried the baby out in it like a poacher might carry rabbits. Tears wet her face, but she could not pause, she could not let herself love him again.

Outside it was raining heavily. Caroline crossed the lawn feeling the eyes of the house upon her. Once safely out of sight beneath the trees she gasped for breath, her knuckles white where they gripped the pillowcase shut. Inside, the child was fidgeting but he did not cry out. Rain ran through her hair and dripped from her chin. But it will never wash me clean, she told herself with quiet despair. There was a pond, she knew. A dew pond, at the far side of the grounds. It was deep and shaded, ready to hide any secret cast into it. She held her breath as the thought of it rose in her mind. It turned her cold. No, I cannot, she pleaded, silently. I cannot. She had taken so much from him already.

She walked farther, not in the direction of the pond but away from the house, praying for some other option to present itself. When it did, Caroline staggered with relief. There was a covered wagon, parked in a green clearing where the woods met the lane. Thin skeins of smoke rose from a metal chimney pipe in the roof. Tinkers, she thought, with a flare of desperate hope in her chest. They would find him, take him, move away with him. She would never have to see him again. But he would be cared for. He would have a life.

Now the baby began to cry as rain soaked through the pillowcase. Hurriedly, Caroline hoisted the sack back onto her shoulder and made her way through the trees to the other side of the clearing, farther away from the house so that the trail would not point in that direction. It would seem, she hoped, that somebody coming along the lane from the south had left the child. She put him among the knotted roots of a large beech tree, where it was fairly dry, and backed away as his cries grew louder. Take him and be gone, she implored silently.

She stumbled back into the woods as quickly and quietly as she could, and the baby's cries followed her for a while before finally falling out of earshot. When they did, her steps faltered. She stood still, swaying, torn between continuing forward and going back. I will never hear him again, she told herself, but there was no relief in this, in the end. It could not be any other way, but a chill spread through the heart of her. There would be no getting away from what she had done, she knew then, no forgetting it. It sat inside her like a canker, and just as there was no going back, she was no longer sure that she could go on either. Her hand went to her midriff, to where she knew a child lay nestled. She let it feel the warmth of her hand, as if to prove to this child that she was still living, and feeling, and would love it. Then she made her way slowly back to the house, where she would realise, hours too late, that having carefully stripped the baby she had then left him to be found in the fine, embroidered pillowcase. She pressed her face into her bare pillow and tried to wipe the boy child from her memory.

1

AT LEAST IT'S WINTER. We only ever came here in the summertime, so the place doesn't seem quite the same. It's not as dreadfully familiar, not as overpowering. Storton Manor, grim and bulky, the colour of today's low sky. A Victorian, neo-Gothic pile with stone mullioned windows and peeling woodwork, green with algae. Climbing out of the car, I breathe calmly. Through the windscreen of my tatty white Golf I can see Beth's hands in her lap and the wispy ends of the long rope of her hair. Odd strands of grey snake through it now, and it seems too soon, far too soon. Our hair used to be so bright when we were little. It was the white blonde of young Vikings, a purity of colour that faded with age to this uninspiring, mousy brown. I colour mine now, to cheer it up.

We look less and less like sisters these days. I remember Beth and Dinny with their heads together, whispering: his hair so dark, and hers so fair. I was cramped with jealousy at the time, and now, in my mind's eye, their heads look like yin and yang. As thick as thieves.

The house is ours now, all twelve bedrooms—the soaring ceilings, the grand staircase, the underground rooms where the flagstones are worn smooth from the passage of servile feet. It's all ours, but only if we stay and live here. That's what Meredith always wanted. Meredith—our grandmother, with her spite and her hands in bony fists. She wanted our mother to move us all in years ago, and watch her die. Our mother refused, was duly cut off, and we continued our happy, suburban lives in Reading. If we don't move here it will be sold and the money sent to good causes. So now the house is ours—but only for a little while, because I don't think we can bear to live here.

There's a reason why not. If I try to look right at it, it slips away like vapour. Only a name surfaces: Henry. The boy who disappeared. What I think now, staring up into the dizzying branches; what I think is that I know. I know why we can't live here. I know. I know why Beth won't even get out of the car. I wonder if I shall have to coax her out, the way one must coax her to eat. I scramble back into the car.

Beth is staring at her hands. I don't think she's even looked up yet, looked out at the house. Suddenly I doubt whether I've done the right thing, bringing her here. I fear that I've left it too late, and this fear gives my insides a twist. She is thin these days, so fragile looking. Still my sister, but different now. There's something inside her that I can't fathom.

Maxwell wants her hospitalised again. He told me on the phone, two days ago, and I bit his head off for suggesting it. But I act differently around her now, however hard I try not to. I smile brightly.

'Shall we go in?' I say. 'I could use a stiff drink.' My voice is loud. This solicitude is my way of showing Beth that I know she doesn't want to be back here. But then, with a deep breath, she gets out and strides over to the house as if driven, and I hurry after her.

Inside, the house does seem smaller, as things from childhood will, but it's still huge. This is the first time we've ever arrived here alone, without our parents, and it feels so odd that we mill like sheep.

'Stick the kettle on. I'll dig out some booze and we'll have tipsy coffee.'

'Erica, it's not even lunch time.'

'So what? We're on holiday, aren't we?' Oh, but we're not. I don't know what this is, but it's not a holiday. Beth shakes her head.

'I'll just have tea,' she says, drifting towards the kitchen. Her back is narrow, shoulders pointing sharply through her shirt. I notice them with a jolt of unease—just ten days, since I saw her last, but she is visibly thinner now. I want to squeeze her, to make her be well.

The house is cold and damp, so I press buttons on an ancient panel until I hear things stirring, deep pipes complaining, water seething. There are rank ashes in the fire grates; there are still tissues and a sweetly rotting apple core in the wastepaper basket in the drawing room. Encroaching on Meredith's life like this makes me feel uneasy.

First we have to sort, to make some order of all the layers of possessions. I should feel sad, I suppose, to think of it sold, the line of family history down the years to Beth and me, breaking. But I don't. Perhaps because, by rights, everything should have gone to Henry. That was when it all got broken. I watch Beth for a while, as she lifts lace handkerchiefs out of a drawer and piles them on her knee. She takes them out one by one, studying the patterns, tracing the threads with her fingertips. There's no point to what she's doing. It's one of those things she does that I can't understand.

'I'm going for a walk,' I announce, rising on stiff knees, biting back irritation. Beth jumps as if she'd forgotten I was there.

'Where are you going?'

'For a walk, I just said. I need some fresh air.'

'Well, don't be long,' Beth says. She does this sometimes, as well— talks to me as if I'm a wilful child, as if I might run off. I sigh.

'No. Twenty minutes. Stretch my legs.' I think she knows where.

I follow my feet. The lawn is ragged and lumpy, a choppy sea of broken brown grasses that soak my feet. It all used to be so manicured, so beautiful. I had been thinking that it must have got out of hand since Meredith died. But that's ridiculous. She died a month ago, and the garden shows several seasons of neglect.

I have no idea how she coped before she died—if she coped. Mum and Dad came to see her, every year or so. Beth and I hadn't been for an age. But our absence was understood, I think. We were never pestered to come. Perhaps she would have liked us to, perhaps not. It was hard to tell with Meredith. She was not a sweet grandmother, she was not even maternal. Our great-grandmother, Caroline, was also here while our mother grew up. Another source of discomfort. Our mother left as soon as she could. Meredith died suddenly, of a stroke. One day ageless, an old woman for as long as I can remember; the next day no longer.

Here's the dew pond. It sits in the corner of a large field of closely grazed turf. The field stretches away to the east, woods to the west. It was irresistible on hot July days, this pond; but with the sky this drab it looks like a shallow puddle. I know it's not shallow. In the sunshine the water was a glassy blue. It looked deep but Dinny said it was deeper even than that. I didn't believe him until he dived one day, taking a huge lungful of air and kicking, kicking downwards. I watched his brown body ripple and truncate, watched him continue to kick even when it seemed he should have reached the bottom. He surfaced with a gasp, to find me rapt, astonished.

This pond feeds the stream that runs through the village of Barrow Storton, down the side of this wide hill from the manor house. This pond is etched in my memory; it seems to dominate my childhood. I can see Beth paddling at the edge the first time I swam in it. She stalked to and fro, nervous because she was the eldest, and the banks were steep, and if I drowned it would be her fault. She made me run around and around the garden before she would let me near the house, so

I would be warm and not white, teeth chattering, requiring explanation.

I carry on walking, climbing over the gate into the field. This field, and then another, and then you are on the Wiltshire Downs. On the horizon sits the barrow that gives the village its name, a Bronze Age burial mound for a king whose name has passed out of all remembrance: a low, narrow hump, about the length of two cars, open at one end.

I jump two-footed down the stone steps at the entrance to the barrow and startle a girl inside. She straightens with a gasp and hits her head on the low ceiling.

'Shit! Sorry! I didn't mean to pounce on you like that . . . I didn't know anybody was in here.' I smile. The light from the doorway shines onto her, onto golden bubble curls tied back with a turquoise scarf, onto a young face and an oddly shapeless body. She squints up at me.

'Are you OK?' She doesn't answer me.

She rises, scowls, pushes past me without a word. I realise that her shapelessness is in fact the heaviness of pregnancy. When I emerge from the tomb I look down the slope towards the village but she's not there. She is walking the other way—in the direction I came from, towards the woodlands near the manor house.

Beth and I eat dinner in the study this first night. It is the only one with a TV in it, and we eat pasta from trays on our knees with the evening news to keep us company, because small talk seems to have abandoned us, and big talk is just too big yet. We're not ready. I'm not sure that we ever will be, but there are things I want to ask my sister. I will wait, I will make sure I get the questions right. I hope that, if I ask the right ones, I can make her better. That the truth will set her free.

Beth chases each quill around her bowl before catching it on her fork. She raises the fork to her lips several times before putting it into her mouth. Some of these quills never make it—she knocks them back off the fork, selects an alternative. I see all this in the corner of my eye, just like I see her body starving.

'Do you think it's a good idea? Having Eddie here for Christmas?' she asks me suddenly.

'Of course. Why wouldn't it be? We'll be staying for a while to get things sorted, so we may as well stay for Christmas. Together.' I shrug.

'No, I mean . . . bringing a child here. Into this . . . place.'

'Beth, it's just a house. He'll love it. He doesn't know . . . Well. He'll have a blast—there are so many nooks and crannies to explore.'

'A bit big and empty, though, isn't it? A bit lonely, perhaps?'

'Well, you could tell him to bring a friend. Why don't you? Call him tomorrow. Some of the working parents might be glad of a few extra days' grace before their little home-wreckers reappear, don't you think?'

'Hmm.' Beth rolls her eyes. 'I don't think any of the mothers at that school do anything as common as work for a living.'

'Only riffraff like you?'

'Only riffraff like me,' she agrees, deadpan.

'Ironic, really, since you're the real thing. Blue blood, practically.'

'Hardly. Just as you are.'

'No. I think the nobility skipped a generation in me.' I smile.

Meredith told me this once, when I was ten. Your sister has the Calcott mien, Erica. You, I fear, are all your father. I didn't mind then and I don't mind now. When she turned away I stuck out my tongue, and Mum wagged a finger at me.

Beth rejects it too. She fought with Maxwell—Eddie's father—to allow their son to attend the village primary school, which was tiny and friendly. But Maxwell won the toss when it came to secondary education. Perhaps it was for the best. Eddie boards now, all term long. Beth has weeks and weeks to build herself up, shake a sparkle into her smile.

'We'll fill up the space,' I assure her. 'It won't be like . . .' but I trail off. I'm not sure what I was about to say.

Almost midnight, and Beth and I have retired to our rooms. The same rooms we always took, where we found the same bedspreads, smooth and faded. There's a knock and Beth's face appears around the door.

'Are you OK? I can't sleep,' she whispers.

'I'm fine, Beth, just not sleepy.'

'Oh.' She lingers in the doorway, hesitates. 'It's so strange to be here.' This is not a question. I wait. 'It's all so familiar, and yet wrong too. Why do you think she left us the house?'

'I really don't know. To get at Mum and Uncle Clifford, I imagine. That's the kind of thing Meredith would do,' I sigh. Still Beth hovers, so pretty, so girlish. Right now it's as if no time has passed, as if nothing has changed. She could be twelve again, I could be eight, and she could be leaning in to wake me, to make sure I'm not late for breakfast.

'I think she did it to punish us,' she says softly, and looks stricken.

'No, Beth. We didn't do anything wrong,' I say firmly.

'Didn't we? That summer. No. I suppose not.' She flicks her eyes over me now, puzzled; and I get the feeling she is trying to see something, some truth about me. 'Good night, Rick,' she whispers, using a familiar tomboy truncation of my name, and vanishes from the doorway.

I remember so many things from that summer. The last summer that everything was right, the summer of 1986. I remember Beth being distraught that Wham! were breaking up. I remember watching, on Meredith's tiny television, Sarah Ferguson marry Prince Andrew on the twenty-third of July—that huge dress, making me ache with envy.

I remember reporters and policemen, facing each other on either side of Storton Manor's iron gates. The policemen seemed bored and hot in their uniforms. The reporters milled and fiddled with their equipment, spoke into cameras, into tape recorders, and waited for news. I remember Beth's eyes pinning me as the policeman talked to me about Henry, asked me where we'd been playing, what we'd been doing. I told him, I think, and I felt unwell; and Beth's eyes on me were ragged and wide.

I sleep easily in the end. I dream of the dew pond, of swimming in it and trying to dive down, of needing to fetch something from the bottom but being unable to reach. The cold shock of the water, the awful fear of what my fingers will find at the bottom.

Leaving

1902

I WILL REMAIN STEADFAST, Caroline reminded herself firmly, as she watched her aunt Bathilda covertly through lowered eyelashes. The older woman cleared her plate methodically before speaking again.

'I fear you are making a grave mistake, my dear.'

'So you have said before, Aunt Bathilda.' Caroline kept her voice low and respectful, but still her aunt glared at her.

'I repeat myself, because you do not appear to hear me,' she snapped.

Heat flared in Caroline's cheeks. The dining room at La Fiorentina was excessively bright, closed in behind windows that had steamed opaque with the vapours of hot food.

'I do listen to you, Aunt. I have always listened to you.'

'You listened to me in the past because you had to, as I understand it. In the most important decision you will ever make, you ignore me. Well, I am only glad my poor dear brother is not alive to see how I have failed his only child.' Bathilda heaved a martyr's sigh.

'You have not failed, Aunt,' Caroline murmured, reluctantly.

A waiter cleared their empty plates, brought them the pastry trolley.

Bathilda chose an eclair, cut a large piece and widened her mouth to accommodate it. The floury flesh of her chin folded over her lace collar.

Caroline watched her with distaste. She felt a flare of defiance.

'Mr Massey is a good man, his family is respectable—' she began.

'The man's morals are irrelevant. Corin Massey will make you a common drudge. He will not make you happy,' Bathilda interrupted. 'How could he? He is beneath you. He is far beneath you, in fortune and in manners—in every station of life.'

'You've barely even met him!' Caroline cried. Bathilda shot her a censorious look.

'May I remind you that you, also, have barely even met him? You may be eighteen now, you may be independent from me, but have I earned no respect in raising you? In keeping you and teaching you—'

'You have kept me with the money my parents left. You have done your duty,' Caroline said, a touch bitterly.

'Don't interrupt me. Our name is a good one and would have stood you in good stead here in New York. And yet you choose to wed a . . . farmer. And move away from everything and everyone you know to live in the middle of nowhere. I have indeed failed, that much is clear.'

'But I don't know anybody here, Aunt. Not really. I know only you,' Caroline said, sadly. 'And Corin is not a farmer. He's a cattle rancher, a most successful one. His business—'

'His business? His business should have stayed in the wilderness and not found its way here to prey upon impressionable young girls.'

'I have money enough.' Caroline said defiantly. 'We will not be poor.'

'Not yet, you don't. Not for another two years. We'll see how well you like living on a farmer's income until then. And we'll see how long your wealth lasts once he has his hands upon it and finds his way to the gaming tables!'

'Don't say such things. He is a good man. And he loves me, and . . . and I love him,' Caroline declared, adamantly. He loved her. She let this thought pour through her and could not keep from smiling.

When Corin had proposed to Caroline, he had said that he'd loved her from the first moment of their meeting, which was at a ball a month previously—the Montgomery ball to mark the beginning of Lent. Since her debut, Caroline had envied the enjoyment that other girls seemed to derive from such functions. They danced and they laughed and they chatted with ease. Caroline, when forced to enter the room with Bathilda, found herself always at a disadvantage, always afraid to speak in case she caused her aunt to correct her, or to scold. Corin had changed all that.

Caroline chose her fawn silk gown and her mother's emeralds for the Montgomery ball. The necklace was cool and heavy around her neck. It covered the slender expanse of her decolletage with a glow of gold and a deep glitter that sparked light in her grey eyes.

The room was stuffy and hot. Caroline stood up straight, sipping sour wine that lightened her head. But then Corin appeared in front of her and she barely heard Charlie Montgomery's introduction because she was captured by the newcomer's frank gaze; and when she blushed he did too, and he fumbled his first words to her, saying, 'Hello, how are you?' as though they were two Odd Fellows meeting over a game of whist. He grasped her hand in its embroidered glove as if to shake it, realised his mistake and dropped it abruptly, letting it fall limply into her skirts. At this she blushed more, and dared not look at Bathilda.

'Sorry, miss . . . I, uh . . . won't you excuse me?' he mumbled, inclining his head to them and disappearing into the crowd.

'What an extraordinary young man!' Bathilda exclaimed, scathingly. 'Where on earth did you find him, Charlie?' Charlie Montgomery's black hair was as slick as oilskin, flashing light as he turned his head.

'Oh, don't mind Corin. He's a bit out of practice at all this, that's all. He's a far-off cousin of mine. His people are here in New York but he's lived out west for years now, in Oklahoma Territory. He's back in town for his father's funeral,' Charlie said.

'How extraordinary,' Bathilda said again. 'I never thought that one should have to practise one's manners.' At this Charlie smiled vaguely.

'What happened to his father?' she asked Charlie, surprising herself.

'He was on one of the trains that collided in the Park Avenue Tunnel last month. It was a right old mess,' Charlie said, pulling a face. 'Seventeen dead, it's now reported, and nigh on forty injured.'

'How dreadful!' Caroline breathed. Charlie nodded in agreement.

Bathilda heaved a gentle sigh, as if bored, so Charlie Montgomery excused himself and moved away.

Caroline searched the crowd for the stranger's bronze-coloured hair, and found herself feeling sorry for him—for his bereavement, and for his fumbling of her hand under Bathilda's unforgiving eye. The shocking pain of losing close family was something she could sympathise with. Her parents had died eight years ago when there had been an explosion at a factory as they were travelling home one evening. A wall collapsed and their carriage had been trapped beneath it. Caroline sipped absently at her wine, which had gone warm in her hand.

When Corin appeared at Caroline's side a minute later and asked her for a dance, she accepted mutely, with a startled nod.

They danced a slow waltz. Caroline smiled uncertainly at him, and they did not speak at first.

Then he said, 'You must please excuse me, Miss Fitzpatrick. For before, and for . . . I fear I am not an accomplished dancer. It has been some time since I was lucky enough to attend such a function as this, or to dance with someone so . . . uh . . .'

He hesitated, and she smiled, lowering her gaze as she had been taught. She could feel the heat of his hand in the small of her back, as if there was nothing at all between her skin and his. She felt naked suddenly, wildly disconcerted, but thrilled as well. His face was deeply tanned, and the sun had lingered in the hair of his brows and moustache, tinting them with warm colour. He watched her with light brown eyes, and she thought she saw a startled kind of happiness there.

As the dance ended and he escorted her from the floor, her glove snagged against the roughened skin of his palm. On impulse, she turned his hand over in her own and studied it, pushing her thumb into the callous at the root of each finger, comparing the width of it to her own. Her hand looked like a child's in his, and she drew breath and parted her lips to say this before realising how inappropriate it would be. She felt childlike indeed, and she noticed that he was breathing deeply.

'Are you quite well, Mr Massey?' she asked.

'Yes . . . I'm fine, thank you. It's a little confined in here, isn't it?'

'Come over to the window, you will find the air fresher,' she said, taking his arm to steer him through the crowd.

'Thank you,' Corin said. 'I'm not used to seeing so many people under one roof all at once. It's funny, how quickly and completely a person can become unaccustomed to such things.'

'I have never left New York,' Caroline blurted out. 'That is, only for my family's summerhouse, on the coast . . . I mean to say . . .' but she wasn't sure what she meant to say.

'Would you not like to travel, Miss Fitzpatrick?' he asked, and she began to understand that something had started between them. A negotiation of some kind, a sounding out.

'There you are, my dear.' Bathilda bore down on them. 'Do come along, I want to introduce you to Lady Clemence.' Caroline had no choice but to be led away, though she glanced back over her shoulder and raised her hand in slight salute.

'Don't be ridiculous, girl!' Bathilda broke into her thoughts and returned her to the present, and the lunch table at La Fiorentina. 'You are acting like a lovesick schoolgirl! I, too, have read Mr Wister's novel, and it has clearly filled your head with romantic notions. But you will learn that *The Virginian* is a work of fiction and bears little relation to the reality of it. Did you not also read of the dangers, and the emptiness, and the hardships of the frontier land?'

'It's not like that any more. Corin has told me all about it. He says the land is so beautiful you can see God's hand in every blade of grass.' At this Bathilda snorted inelegantly. 'And Woodward is a thriving town—'

'Woodward? Who has heard of Woodward? What state is it in?'

'I . . . do not know,' Caroline confessed.

'It is in no state at all, that's why you do not know. No state of the Union. It is uncharted land, full of savages and uncouth men of all kinds. Why, I heard there are no ladies to be found west of Dodge City at all—only women of the worst kind. No ladies! Can't you imagine how godless a place it must be?' Bathilda's chest swelled within the confines of her burgundy gown. She was moved, Caroline realised, incredulously. Bathilda was actually moved.

His proposal came a few weeks after the ball. In the interim there had been a skating trip, accompanied by Charlie Montgomery and his sister Diana. Corin called upon her on a Tuesday afternoon, knowing he would find her alone, it being her aunt's custom to play bridge with Lady Atwell on that day. As the maid ushered him into the room, colour poured into Caroline's face and her throat went dry.

'How kind of you to call,' She managed at last, her voice trembling like her hands. 'I trust you are well?'

Instead of replying, Corin turned his hat around in his hands, began to speak but faltered. Caroline watched him in astonishment.

'Won't . . . won't you sit down?' she offered at length. Corin glanced at her and seemed to find some resolve at last.

'No, I won't sit down,' he declared, startling Caroline with the gruffness of his tone. They faced each other for a long moment, at an impasse, then Corin crossed the room in two large strides, took Caroline's face in his hands and kissed her. The press of his mouth was so shocking that Caroline made no move to stop him, or to move away as she knew she ought. She was struck by the unexpected softness of his lips, and the heat of him. She could not breathe, and dizziness confounded her even as a peculiar warm ache began in her stomach.

'Mr . . . Mr Massey . . .' she stammered when he pulled away, still holding her face in his hands and studying her with quiet urgency.

'Caroline . . . come away with me. Marry me,' he said. Caroline could scarcely find the words to answer him.

'Do you . . . do you love me, then?' she asked at last. Her pulse jumped up in panic as she waited for the words she so longed to hear.

'Do you not know? Can't you tell?' he asked, incredulously. 'I have loved you since the first moment I met you. The very first moment,' he murmured. Caroline shut her eyes, overwhelmed with relief. 'You're smiling,' Corin said, brushing his finger over her cheek. 'Does that mean you will marry me, or that you're laughing at me?' He smiled anxiously, and Caroline took his hand in hers, pressed it to her face.

'It means I will marry you, Mr Massey. It means that . . . I want nothing more than to marry you,' she breathed.

'I will make you so happy,' he promised, kissing her again.

Bathilda refused to announce the engagement between her niece and Corin Massey. 'It's hardly to be celebrated,' she said. 'I'm only glad I shan't be here to have to answer questions about it. I will be returning to London, to stay with a cousin of my dear late husband's. There is nothing to tie me here in New York, now.'

'You're going back to London? But . . . when?' Caroline asked. Unhappily, she realised that in spite of the rift between them, her Aunt Bathilda represented her only family, her only home.

'Next month, when the weather is more clement.'

'I see,' Caroline breathed. 'Then we shall not see each other much from now on, I suppose,' she murmured.

'Indeed not, my dear. I will give you my address in London, and of course you must write to me. And I dare say you will find company enough on the farm. There will be other farm wives in the vicinity, I am sure,' she said, smiling faintly. Caroline felt a jolt of fear and did not know whether to run to or from Bathilda.

'You have never shown me love,' she whispered, her voice fearful and tight. 'I do not know why you should be so surprised that I run after it when it is offered to me.' And she left the room before Bathilda could scorn this sentiment.

So Caroline married with nobody to give her away and no family to represent her. She chose a gown of diaphanous white muslin, with a wide yoke of lace ruffles across the bust and crisp frills at the neck and cuffs. Her hair was piled high on her head and held with ivory combs, and pearl drop earrings were her only jewels.

She carried her mother's silk fan on her wrist, fingering it nervously as she travelled to a small church on the Upper East Side. Corin wore a borrowed suit and tie, his hair combed neatly back. He fidgeted with his collar as she began her approach along the aisle, but then he met her anxious gaze, and he smiled and fell still as though naught else mattered. His mother and two elder brothers were in attendance, solemn as the couple made their vows before the minister. Mrs Massey still wore her mourning dress, and although she welcomed her new daughter-in-law, her grief was too fresh for her to feel truly glad.

It was another wet day, and the church was quiet and dark, smelling of damp brick dust and candle wax. Caroline did not mind. Her world had contracted to include nothing but the man in front of her. Caroline felt such a surge of elation that she could not contain it, and it spilled from her in a storm of happy tears that Corin gathered on his fingertips and kissed away. With him she would start her real life at last.

But to his new wife's dismay, Corin packed and made ready to leave New York the following day.

'We will have our wedding night in our home, in the house that I have built for us; not here in a place still sorrowing for my father. I came for a funeral, and I didn't bank on finding a wife,' he smiled, kissing her hands. 'I've got to sort a few things out, get the house ready for your arrival. I want it to be perfect.'

'It will be perfect, Corin,' she assured him, still unused to addressing any man by his first name alone. His kisses burned into her skin, made it hard to breathe. 'Please let me come with you now.'

'Give me a month, that's all, my sweetheart. Follow after me four weeks from today and I will have everything ready. You'll have time to say goodbye to all your friends, and I'll have time to boast to mine that I have married the most beautiful girl in the whole of America,' he said; and so she agreed even though his departure felt like the sky growing dark.

2

MY MOTHER'S BROTHER, my Uncle Clifford, and his wife Mary, want the old linen press from the nursery, the round Queen Anne table from the study and the collection of miniatures that live in a glass-topped display case at the foot of the stairs. Our mother has asked only for any family photographs I can find.

I hope Clifford is sending enough men. The linen press is enormous.

It looms against the far wall of the nursery. I pull stiff, solid piles of linens from the shelves and drop them to the floor. Dust flies and my nose prickles, and Beth appears in the doorway. There is so much of it. It could be decades since some of these piles have been disturbed.

Once I've emptied the press I am not sure what to do with all the piles of linen. It could go to charity, I suppose. I pile it back up against the wall, and as I do my eyes catch on one pattern, one splash of weak colour in all the white. Yellow flowers. Three pillowcases with yellow flowers, embroidered into each corner in silk thread that still catches the light. I run my thumb over the neat stitching. There is something in the back of my mind, something I know I recognise but can't remember. Have I seen them before? The flowers are ragged looking, wild. I can't put a name to them. And there are only three. Four pillowcases with every other set but this one. I drop them back onto a pile.

Clifford and Mary are Henry's parents. Were Henry's parents. They were in Saint Tropez when he disappeared, which the press unfairly made a great deal out of. As if they had left him with strangers. Our parents did it too. We often came here for the school holidays, and for two weeks or even three, most years, Mum and Dad would go away without us. I liked and feared having them gone. Liked it because Meredith never checked up on us much. We felt liberated, we tore about like yahoos. But feared it because, inside the house, Meredith had sole charge of us. We had to be with her. Eat our dinner with her, answer her questions, think up lies. It never occurred to me that I didn't like her. I was too young to think that way. But when Mum got back I flew to her, gathered clammy handfuls of her skirts.

Beth kept me extra close when our parents were away. If she walked ahead, it was with one hand held slightly behind her, long fingers spread, always waiting for me to take hold of them. And if I didn't she would pause, glance over her shoulder, make sure that I was following.

In my head Henry is always bigger than me, older than me. Eleven when I was seven. It seemed an enormous gap at the time. He was a big boy, loud and bossy. He said I had to do what he told me. He buttered Meredith up—she always preferred boys to girls. Henry: dark brown hair, clear blue eyes that he would narrow, make ugly, pale skin that burned across the nose in summer. One of those children, I see him now, who is a grown-up in miniature rather than a child, who you can look at and know, at once, what they will look like as an adult. He wore himself in his face, I think, charmless, obvious. But this is unfair. He never got the chance to prove me wrong, after all.

Eddie still has the face of a child, and I love it. A nondescript boy's face, sharp nose, tufty hair, kneecaps standing proud from skinny shanks in his school shorts. My nephew. He hugs Beth on the platform, a little sheepishly because some of his classmates are on the train behind him, banging on the glass, sticking up their fingers. I wait by the car for them, my hands puckered with cold, grinning as they draw near.

'Hey, Eddie Baby! Edderino! Eddius Maximus!' I call to him, putting my arms around him and squeezing, pulling his feet off the ground.

'Auntie Rick, it's just Ed now,' he protests, with a hint of exasperation.

''Course. Sorry. And you can't call me Auntie—you make me feel a hundred years old! Sling your bag in the back and let's get going,' I say, resisting the urge to tease him. He is eleven now. The same age Henry will always be, and old enough for teasing to matter.

'Is this a new car?'

'New-ish,' I tell him. 'The old Beetle finally died on me. Wait until you see the house, Ed. It's a monster.' But as we pull in and I look at him expectantly, he nods, raises his eyebrows, is not impressed. Then I think the manor might only be the size of one wing of his school—smaller than his friends' houses, perhaps.

'I'm so glad it's school holidays again, darling,' Beth says, taking Eddie's bag from him. He smiles at her sidelong, slightly abashed. He will be taller than her eventually—he reaches her shoulder already.

I tour Eddie around the grounds while Beth settles down with his report card. I take him up to the barrow, skirt the dreary woods, arrive at the dew pond. He has found a long stick somewhere and swishes it, beheading the weeds and dead nettles. It's warmer today, but damp.

'Why's it called a dew pond? Isn't it just a pond?' he asks, smacking the edge with his stick. Ripples fly out across the surface.

'This is where the stream starts. It was dug out a long time ago, to make this pond a kind of reservoir. And dew pond because it traps the dew as well, I suppose.'

'Can you swim in it?'

'We used to—Dinny and your mum and I. Actually, I don't think your mum ever went all the way in. It was always pretty cold.'

'Who's Dinny?'

'Dinny . . . was a boy we used to play with. When we came here as kids. His family lived nearby. So . . .' I trail off. Why should talking about Dinny make me feel so conspicuous? Dinny. 'He was a real adventurer. He built a fabulous tree house one year . . .'

'Can we see it? Is it still there?' he asks.

'We can go and look, if you like,' I offer. Eddie grins, and jogs a few paces ahead, taking aim at a sapling, tackling it with a two-handed blow.

We are closer than many aunts and nephews, Eddie and I. I stayed with him for two months while Beth recovered, while she got help. It was a strained time, a time of keeping going and pretending. We didn't have any big conversations. Eddie was too young. But we shared a time of sadness and anger and confusion. We jarred along, the both of us feeling that way; and that's what makes us close—the knowledge of that time. His father Maxwell and I holding hushed, strangled arguments behind closed doors, not wanting Eddie to hear his father call his mother unfit.

All that remains of the tree house that Dinny built are a few ragged planks, dark and green and slimy looking, like the rotten bones of a shipwreck. 'Well, I guess it's kind of had its day,' I say, sadly.

'You could rebuild it. I'll help, if you want?' Eddie says, to cheer me up.

I smile. 'We could try. It's more of a summer thing though—it'd be a bit cold and mucky up there now, I should think.'

'Why did you stop coming here? To visit Great-Grandma?' What a question for him to ask.

'Oh . . . you know. We just . . . went on holiday with our parents more as we got older. I don't really remember.'

'But you always say you never forget the important things that happen when you're a kid. That's what you told me, when I won that prize for speech and drama.' I had meant it to be a positive thing when I said it. But he won the prize while I was staying with him for those two months, and what we both thought, was that what he would always remember was coming home from school and finding Beth the way he did. I saw the thought fly across his face, shut my eyes, wished I could pull my words back out of the air.

'Well, that just goes to show that it can't have been that big a thing, doesn't it?' I say lightly. 'Come on—there's loads more to see.'

Beth is making mince pies again when we clatter into the kitchen. She started yesterday, in preparation for Eddie's arrival, and shows no sign of stopping. The kitchen table is awash with flour and scraps, empty mincemeat jars. The smell is heavenly. Flushed, she emerges from the Rayburn with another batch. She's filled every tin and biscuit barrel. There are several bags in the ancient freezer in the cellar. I pick two up, pass one to Eddie. The filling scalds my tongue.

'These are fabulous, Beth,' I say, by way of a greeting. She shoots me a small smile, which broadens when it moves to her son. She crosses to kiss his cheek, leaving ghostly flour fingerprints on his sleeves.

'Well done, darling. All your teachers seem very pleased with you,' she tells him. I pick up the report card from the table, blow flour from it and flick through. 'With the possible exception of Miss Wilton . . .' she qualifies.

'What does she teach?' I ask him, as he squirms slightly.

'French,' Eddie mumbles, through a mouthful of pie.

'She says you aren't trying nearly hard enough,' Beth goes on.

'French is just so boring!' he declares.

'Well, just try to pay a bit more attention, OK? French is really important—no, it is!' she insists, when Eddie rolls his eyes. 'When I'm rich and I retire to the south of France, how are you going to cope if you can't speak the language?'

'By shouting and pointing?' he ventures. Beth presses her lips together severely, but then she laughs, a rich, glowing sound I so rarely hear.

'Can I have another mince pie?' Eddie asks, sensing victory.

'Go on. Then go and get in the bath—you're filthy!' Eddie grabs two pies and darts out of the kitchen.

Later, we watch a film, Beth curled with Eddie on the sofa with a huge bowl of popcorn wedged between them. When I glance at her I see that she's hardly following the film. She turns her chin, rests it on the top of Eddie's head, shuts her eyes contentedly, and I feel some of the knots inside me loosen. The weekend passes quickly this way—a trip to the cinema in Devizes, school work at the kitchen table, mince pies, Eddie out in the coach house, or marauding through the deserted stables. Beth is serene, if a little distracted. She stops baking when she runs out of flour, and stands for long moments, watching Eddie through the window with a faint, faraway smile.

'I told you he'd have fun here,' I say. 'Christmas will be excellent.'

On Sunday afternoon, Maxwell arrives to collect his son. I shout for Beth as I open the door to him, and when she does not appear I give Maxwell a tour of the ground floor and make him a coffee. He divorced Beth five years ago, when her depression seemed to be getting worse and her weight plummeted, and he said he just couldn't cope and it was no way to raise a child. So he left her and remarried pretty much straight away—a short, plump, healthy-looking woman called Diane: white teeth, cashmere, perfect nails. Uncomplicated.

'Quite an impressive place,' he says, taking a gulp of the scalding-hot coffee with a loud sound I don't like.

'Yes, I suppose it is,' I agree, leaning against the Rayburn, folding my arms. I found it hard to warm to Maxwell when he was still my brother-in-law. Now, I find it near impossible.

'Needs a lot of work, of course. But huge potential,' he declares. He made his money in property. 'Have you decided what you're going to do with it?'

'No, not yet. Beth and I haven't really talked about it,' I say. A flash of irritation crosses his face.

'Well, this legacy could make the pair of you very wealthy women. Have you thought about converting it into flats? You'd need planning, but that shouldn't be a problem. You could keep an apartment and the freehold for yourselves, and sell the rest off with long leaseholds. You'd make an absolute killing, and keep to the terms of the will.'

'Thanks. I'll mention it to Beth.' My tone is final. Maxwell looks at me with a stern eye but says nothing for a while.

He fixes his eyes on a painting of fruit on the opposite wall, and at length he clears his throat slightly, so I know what he will ask next.

'And how is Beth?'

'She's fine,' I shrug, deliberately vague.

'Come on, Erica. When I saw her last week she was looking very thin again. Is she eating? Has she been acting up at all?' I try not to think about the mince pies. About the hundreds of mince pies.

'Not that I've noticed,' I lie. It's a big lie. She's getting worse again, and though I don't exactly know why, I do know when it started—when she peaked, and started to fall again: it was when Meredith died. When, by dying, she brought this place back into our lives.

'So where is she?'

'I've no idea. Probably in the bathroom,' I shrug.

'Keep an eye on her. I don't want Eddie spending Christmas here if she's going to have one of her episodes. It's just not fair on him.'

'She's not going to have an *episode*. Not unless you try to keep Eddie away from her,' I snap.

'I know you only want to stick up for her, Erica, but this isn't a game. Seeing her at her worst is something that might affect Edward for the rest of his life, and I am not prepared to let that happen! Not again.'

'Look, Maxwell, you can't change the fact that Beth is Eddie's mother. People aren't perfect—Beth's not perfect. But she is a great mother, and she adores Eddie, and if you could just focus on that for a change, instead of crying "sole custody" every time she gets a little bit down . . .'

'*A little bit down* is something of an understatement, though, isn't it, Erica?' he says, and I can only glare at him because he is right. In the pause we hear a noise from outside the room, and exchange an accusatory glance. Eddie is in the hallway, swinging his kit bag awkwardly, left to right. It twists his skinny wrist.

'Edward!' Maxwell calls, smiling broadly and crossing to engulf his son in a brief hug.

It takes me quite some time to find Beth. The house is dark today, like the world outside. I move from door to door, flinging them open, peering in. I find her at last, wedged onto the windowsill in one of the top-floor bedrooms. From there she can see the silver car in the driveway.

'Maxwell's here,' I say, pointlessly. Beth ignores me. 'Eddie's going, Beth. You have to come down and see him off. Come on. And Maxwell wants to speak to you.'

'I don't want to speak to him. I don't want Eddie to go.'

'I know. But it's just for a while. And you can't let Eddie go without saying goodbye.' She rolls her head to glare at me. So tired, she looks. So tired and sad. 'Please, Beth. They're waiting . . . we have to go down.' Beth draws in a breath, unfolds herself from the sill.

'Found her!' My cheerful announcement is too loud. 'This place is big enough to get lost in.' Beth and Maxwell ignore me, but Eddie smiles. I wish Beth would put on a better act sometimes. I could shake her for not showing Maxwell a better front right now.

'Good to see you, Beth. You look well,' Max lies.

'So do you.'

'Look, do you mind if we drop Eddie back next Saturday, rather than the Friday? Only it's Melissa's school carol concert on the Friday night and we'd all like to go together, wouldn't we, Ed?' Eddie shrugs a shoulder and nods at the same time. The poor boy could teach diplomacy. Beth's mouth pinches, her jaw knots. How she hates any mention of Max's new family. But she strives to be reasonable.

'Of course. Of course it's no problem,' she says.

'Great,' Maxwell smiles, a quick, businesslike smile. 'Right, well, let's get on, shall we, Ed?' Maxwell ushers his son towards the door. 'We'll see you on Saturday. Have a good week, the pair of you.'

When the door is shut behind them I turn to Beth, but she won't meet my eye.

'I wish you wouldn't always be so quiet in front of Maxwell!' I burst out. 'Can't you be more . . .' I trail off, at a loss. Beth flings her arms up.

'No, I can't! I know he wants to take Eddie away from me. I can't pretend I don't know, or don't mind!' she cries.

'I know, I know,' I soothe her. 'Eddie will be back soon,' I add. 'You know how much he loves being with you, Beth—he just adores you, and nothing Maxwell ever does will change that.' I grip her shoulders gently, try to coax a smile from her. Beth sighs, folds her arms.

'I know. I just . . . I'm going for a shower,' she says, and turns away.

With Eddie gone, the house is just big and empty again. By silent consensus we have stopped sorting through Meredith's things for now.

'I never thought, before, about what happens to a person's things when they die,' I say as we eat supper. The larder was full of Heinz tinned soups when we arrived but we're getting through them. I'll have to venture out into the village sometime soon.

'What do you mean?'

'Well . . . just that, I've never known anybody to die before. I've never had to deal with the aftermath, to . . .'

'*Deal with the aftermath?* You make it sound like a selfish thing to do, dying. Is that what you think?' Beth's voice is low and intense.

'No! Of course not. I just meant that it's not something you think about, until it happens . . . who'll sort everything out. Where things will go.' I am struggling; the conversation was meant to be flippant.

'What does it matter, Erica?' Beth snaps at me. I stop talking, break off a piece of bread, crumble it between my fingers.

'It doesn't matter,' I say. Sometimes I feel very lonely with Beth.

I never used to, not when we were younger, not before. We didn't antagonise each other much, or argue. Not even when we were shut inside for two whole days, two long sunny days, did we turn on each other. That was Henry's doing, and Meredith's. Meredith forbade us playing with Dinny, told us not to talk to any of his family, after we had innocently announced our new friendship to her at tea time.

We met him at the dew pond, where he was swimming. The day was warm but not hot. His clothes were in a pile on the bank. All of his clothes. Beth took my hand, but we did not run away. Straight away, we wanted to know him—a thin, dark, naked boy, swimming and diving, all by himself. How old was I? Four or five? I'm not sure.

'Who are you?' he asked, treading water. I shuffled closer to Beth.

'That's our grandmother's house,' Beth explained, pointing back at the manor. Dinny paddled a bit closer.

'But who are you?' he smiled, teeth and eyes gleaming.

'Beth!' I whispered urgently. 'He's got no clothes on!'

'Shh!' Beth hushed me, but it was a funny little sound, made buoyant by a giggle.

'Beth, then. And you?' Dinny looked at me. I lifted my chin a little. 'I'm Erica,' I announced, with all the composure I could muster.

Just then a brown and white Jack Russell terrier burst from the woods and bounded over to us, yapping and wagging.

'I'm Nathan Dinsdale and that's Arthur.' He nodded to the dog. After that, I would have followed him anywhere. I longed for a pet. I was so busy playing with the dog that I don't remember how Dinny got out of the pond without Beth seeing him naked. I suspect that he did not.

We kept seeing him, of course, in spite of Meredith's ban, and we usually managed to keep it secret by giving Henry the slip before going down to the camp where Dinny lived with his family, at the edge of the manor's grounds. Henry usually steered clear of it anyway. He didn't want to disobey Meredith, and instead absorbed her contempt for the travellers, nurtured it, let it grow into a hatred of his own.

The time she shut us in our parents had gone away for the weekend. We went into the village with Dinny, to buy sweets and Coke at the shop. I turned and saw Henry. He ducked behind the phone box, but not quickly enough. Dinny said goodbye and wandered off through the trees, giving the house a wide berth.

Meredith was waiting for us on the step when we got back, Henry nowhere to be seen. But I knew how she knew. She grabbed our arms, nails cutting in, bent down, put her livid face close to ours. 'If you play with dogs, you will catch fleas,' she said, the words clipped and bitten. We were towed upstairs, made to bath in water so hot our skin turned red and angry and I wailed and wailed. Beth was silent, furious.

Afterwards, as I lay in bed and snivelled, Beth coached me in a low voice. 'She wants to punish us, by keeping us indoors, so we have to show that we don't care. That we don't mind. Do you understand, Erica? Please don't cry!' she whispered. I nodded, but I was too upset to pay attention to her. It was still broad daylight outside. An August afternoon and we had been put to bed. Confined for the whole weekend.

When our parents got back we told them everything.

Dad said, 'This is too much, Laura. I mean it this time.' I felt a flare of joy, of love for him.

Mum said, 'I'll talk to her.'

At tea time, I overheard them in the kitchen. Mum and Meredith. 'He seems like a nice-enough boy. Quite sensible. I really don't see the harm in it, Mother,' Mum said.

'Don't see the harm? Do you want the girls to start using that dreadful Wiltshire slang? Do you want them to learn how to steal, and to swear? Do you want them to come home lousy and degraded? If so, then indeed, there can be no harm,' Meredith replied, coldly.

'My girls would never steal,' Mum told her firmly. 'And I think degraded is overdoing it, really.'

'I don't, Laura. Perhaps you've forgotten how much trouble those people have caused us over the years?'

'How could I forget?' Mum sighed.

'Well, they are your children, but if you want them to live under my roof, and in my care, then they will have to abide by my rules,' Meredith snapped.

Mum took a deep breath. 'If I hear that they have been locked up inside again, then they won't come here at all any more, and neither will David and I,' she said quietly, but I could hear the tension. Nearly a tremor. Meredith did not reply. I heard her footsteps coming towards me and I bolted out of sight. With the coast clear I went in to my mother, found her washing up with a quiet intensity, eyes bright. I put my arms around her legs, squeezed her tight.

Meredith was never any less averse to us playing with Dinny, but we were never shut in our room again. Mum won on that point, at least.

Monday morning is leaden and wet. The tips of my fingers and toes were chilled when I woke up, and have stayed that way; and now the end of my nose too. I'm in the orangery, on the south side of the house, overlooking a small lawn ringed with gnarled fruit trees. When we were playing too loudly, when we were trying Meredith's patience, we would be sent here, to the small lawn, while the grown-ups sat on the west-facing terrace, drinking iced tea and vodka.

It's earthy and damp in here, a fecund smell, in spite of the season. One of my earliest memories of Henry, who would have been eight or nine: on the small lawn when I was five or so, a hot August day. They set up one of those giant paddling pools for us on the small lawn. So big that there were steps to climb over the side and an expanse of blue plastic sheet inside. The water from the hose came straight from the mains and it was icy on our toasted skin.

Henry climbed in straight away. He picked up the hosepipe and waved it at us, now that the grown-ups had retreated. He sprayed us and would not let us come near. I remember being so desperate to get in. But I did not want to be splashed. Every time I got near, he sprayed me. Then he stopped, and he swore to me that I could enter safely, that he had finished spraying. I made him put the hose down before I climbed in carefully. A second of ecstatic cold on my feet then Henry grabbed me, put my head under his arm, pushed the hose right into my face. Water up my nose, in my eyes, freezing, choking, Beth shouting at him from ringside. I coughed and howled until Mum came looking.

On the workbench I find a trug and some secateurs, and I head out towards the woods. I walk in a loop via the dew pond. I do this most days. Hints of something return to me when I stand here. Wherever I stand around Storton Manor, hints return to me—little snapshots that go with a view, or a smell, or a room. Yellow flowers stitched on a pillowcase. Every step is an aide-mémoire. Here at the pond there is something I should remember. Something I am trying to know.

I head back into the woods, nothing in my trug so far. The ground is choked with leaf fall and brambles. Unseen things move away from me with small rustling sounds. I have to watch my feet to keep from stumbling. But I'm not watching where I'm going and I nearly step on a crouching person. I yelp in surprise. A young man with long dreadlocks and bright, mismatched clothes.

'Sorry! Hello,' I gasp. He stands up, far taller than me, and I see a large bracket fungus by his feet. Yellow and ugly. He was examining it. 'I . . . I don't think you can eat those,' I add, smiling briefly. The man faces me and says nothing. He is lean and rangy. He stands there, watching me, and I feel the pull of unease towing me away from him. Some instinct, perhaps, or something missing from behind his eyes, tells me that all is not as it should be. I take a step back and turn left. He steps to his right to block me. I turn the other way and he follows. My heart beats harder. His silence is unsettling.

'Look, just get out of the bloody way, will you!' I snap, tensely. But he takes a step towards me and I try to step away but my heel catches in a web of brambles and I fall awkwardly, onto my side, feeling the air rush out of my lungs. I turn my head and the tall man is leaning over me. I think about shouting but the house is far behind me and there's no way Beth would hear me. Panic makes me shake, makes the air hard to breathe. Then strong, heavy hands close tightly on my arms.

'Let go! Get off me! Get off!' I shout out wildly.

I hear a second voice and the hands release me, dropping me unceremoniously back into the mulch.

'Harry's no bother. You didn't mean to be a bother, did you, Harry?' the newcomer says, clapping the tall man on the shoulder. I peer up at them from the ground. Harry shakes his head and I see now that he is downcast, troubled, not fierce or lascivious in the slightest. 'He was just trying to help you up,' the other man says, with a hint of rebuke. Harry returns to his close scrutiny of the yellow fungus.

'He just . . . I was just . . . looking for greenery. For the house,' I say, still rattled. 'I thought . . . Well. Nothing really,' I finish. My heart slows slightly and I feel ridiculous. The stranger puts out a hand, pulls me to my feet. 'Thanks,' I mutter.

There's an air rifle angled over his forearm, a dull gleam on the barrel. I glance at my rescuer with a small, embarrassed smile. I find him watching me with an unsettling intensity, and then he smiles.

'Erica?'

'How did you . . . I'm sorry, do I know you?' I say.

'Don't you recognise me?' he says. I look again—a dark mess of hair, held back at the nape of his neck, a broad chest, a slight hook in the nose, straight forehead, straight brows, mouth a straight, determined line. Black eyes that shine. And then the world tips slightly, skews, features fall into place, and something stunningly familiar coalesces.

'Dinny? Is that you?' I gasp, my ribs squeezing in on themselves.

'Nobody's called me Dinny in a long time. It's Nathan, these days.' His smile is not quite sure of itself: pleased, as curious as I am to meet a figure from the past, yet guarded, held back. But his eyes never leave my face. Their gaze is like a spotlight on my every move.

'I can't believe it's really you! How . . . how are you? What are you doing here?' I am amazed. It never occurred to me that Dinny grew up too, that he would ever come back to Barrow Storton. 'You look so different!' My cheeks are burning, as if I have been caught out somehow.

'But you look just the same, Erica. I saw a bit in the paper—about Lady Calcott dying. It made me think of . . . this place. We haven't been back here since my dad died. But suddenly I wanted to come . . .'

'Oh, no . . . I'm so sorry to hear that. About your dad.' Dinny's father, Mickey. Beth and I loved him. He had a huge grin, huge hands, always gave us a penny or a sweet—pulled it out from behind our ears. And Dinny's mum, Maureen, always called Mo. Mickey and Mo. Our code name, to be used whenever Meredith might hear, was that we were going to visit Mickey Mouse.

'It was eight years ago. He went quickly, and he didn't see it coming. I suppose that's the best way to go,' Dinny says calmly.

'I suppose so.'

'What got Lady Calcott in the end?' I notice his tone, a slight bitterness, and that he doesn't commiserate with me on my loss.

'A stroke. She was ninety-nine.' There's a silence. I have so much to say to him I can't think where to start.

'Look, I'm sorry I swore. At . . . Harry. He startled me, that's all,' I say.

'You don't need to be afraid of him, he's harmless,' Dinny assures me, standing so close that I could touch him. Dinny, real and right here again when he was almost a myth, just minutes ago. I almost don't believe it.

'Is he . . . is there something wrong with him?' I ask.

'He's gentle and friendly and he doesn't like to talk. If that means there's something wrong with him, then yes.'

'Oh, I didn't mean anything by it. Anything bad.' My voice is too high. I take a deep breath, let it out.

'And you were looking for . . . holly?'

'Yes—or mistletoe. To decorate the house.' I smile.

'Come on, Harry. Let's show Erica the big holly tree,' Dinny says.

'Thanks,' I say again. Dinny turns ahead of me and I notice a brace of grey squirrels, tied by their tails with string, slung over his back.

'What are the squirrels for?' I ask.

'Dinner,' Dinny replies calmly. He looks around, sees the horror fleet across my face and smiles half a smile. 'I guess squirrel hasn't reached the menus of smart London restaurants yet?'

'Well, some of them, perhaps. Not the ones I eat in, though. How did you know I lived in London?' He turns again, glances at my smart boots, dark jeans, voluminous wool coat. The sharp ends of my fringe.

'Wild guess,' he murmurs.

'Don't you like London?' I ask.

'I've been only once,' Dinny remarks. 'But generally, no. I don't like cities. I like the horizon to be more than ten metres away.'

'Well, I like having things to look at,' I shrug. Dinny doesn't smile, but falls back to walk beside me, his silence almost companionable. I search for ways to fill it. He is not much taller than me, about the same height as Beth. I can see the tie in his hair, a dark red length of leather bootlace, snapped off, knotted tightly. His jeans are muddy at the hems; he wears a T-shirt and a cotton jumper. We walk up a shallow rise.

'Over there,' Dinny says, pointing. I look ahead, see a dark holly tree, twisted and old. Harry has picked up a fallen sprig of it.

I set about cutting some branches—those with the spikiest leaves, the fattest sprays of berries. Dinny watches me, his expression inscrutable.

'How's your mother? Is she here with you?' I ask. I want to hear him talk, I want to hear everything he's done since I saw him last, I want him to be real again, still to be a friend.

'She's well, thanks. She doesn't travel with us any more. When Dad died she gave it up—she said she was getting too old for it, but I think she'd just had enough of the road. She's hitched to a plumber called Keith. They live in West Hatch, just over the way.'

'Oh, well. Give her my best, when you see her next.' At this he frowns slightly and I wonder if I've said the wrong thing.

With my trug full of holly, we walk back through the woods to the clearing where they always camped before. A broad space at the western edge of the copse, surrounded by sheltering trees on three sides, with open fields to the west and a rutted green lane that takes you back to the road. Harry drifts along behind us.

'And you? Are you living here now?' Dinny asks, at length.

'Oh, no. I don't know. Probably not. For Christmas, anyway. We've inherited the house, Beth and I . . .' How pompous I sound.

'Beth's here?' Dinny interrupts, turning to face me.

'Yes, but . . . Yes, she's here.' I was going to say, *But she's different.* 'You should come up to the house and say hello,' I say, knowing that he won't.

There are six vehicles in the camp—more than there used to be. Two minibuses, two camper vans, a big old horse lorry and a converted army ambulance, which Dinny says is his. Coils of smoke shred away from chimney pipes. Harry strides ahead to sit on a stump of wood, picking something up from the ground and setting to work upon it. As we approach, three dogs race over to us. I know this drill. I stand still, let my arms hang, wait for them to reach us, to sniff me, to see me not run.

'Yours?'

'Only two of them—the black and tan belongs to my cousin Patrick. This is Blot,' Dinny scuffs the ears of a vicious-looking black mongrel, toothy and scarred, 'and this is Popeye.' A smaller, gentler dog, a rough brown coat and kind eyes. Popeye licks the fingers Dinny offers to him.

'So . . . um, are you working around here? What do you do?' I fall back on a party stalwart, and Dinny shrugs. For a second I think that perhaps he draws endless benefits, that he steals, sells drugs. But these are Meredith's thoughts, and I'm ashamed to have them.

'Nothing right now. We follow work around the country for most of the year. Farm work, bar work, festivals. This time of year is pretty dead.'

'That must be hard.'

Dinny gives me a quick glance. 'It's fine, Erica,' he tells me mildly. He doesn't ask me what I do. In the short walk to the camp I seem to have used up all the credit a childhood acquaintance afforded me.

'I like your ambulance,' I say, desperate. As I speak, the ambulance door bangs open and a girl climbs awkwardly out. I recognise her at once—the pregnant girl from the barrow. But she can only be fifteen, sixteen. Dinny is the same age as Beth: thirty-five. I look at the girl again and try to make her eighteen, maybe nineteen, but I can't.

The girl with the bubble-curls, a bright natural blonde that you rarely see these days. Her skin is pale and there are blue smudges under her eyes. In a tight, stripy jersey it is very clear how close to term she is. She sees me standing with Dinny and she comes across to us, scowling. I try to smile, to seem comfortable there. She looks fiercer than Blot.

'Who's this?' she demands. She talks to Dinny, not to me.

'Erica, this is Honey. Honey, Erica.'

'Honey? Pleased to meet you. I'm sorry for scaring you, up at the barrow the other day,' I say, in a cheery tone.

Honey gazes at me with tired eyes. 'That was you? You didn't scare me.'

'No, well. Not scare, but . . .' I shrug. She looks at me for a long moment. Palpable relief when she dismisses me, looks back at Dinny.

'The stove's not drawing right,' she says.

Dinny sighs. 'I'll see to it in a minute,' he tells her. She stares at him then goes back inside. I am momentarily dumbstruck by her.

'So . . . when's the due date? Must be soon?' I ask awkwardly, hoping she won't hear me from inside.

'A little after Christmas,' Dinny says, looking across the clearing.

'So close! You must be very excited. Has she got her overnight bag ready and everything? For the hospital?' Dinny shakes his head.

'No hospital. She wants to have it out there, in the woods.'

'In the woods? But . . . it's December! Is she mad?'

'I know it's December, Erica.' he says flatly. 'She's taking the idea of a natural birth about as far as she possibly can.'

'Well, you have a right to choose, too. The father has a right too. First babies can take their time, you know. Beth was in labour for thirty-six hours with Eddie . . .'

'Beth has a baby?'

'Had a baby. He's eleven now. He's coming for Christmas, so you'll probably meet him . . . Eddie. He's a fantastic kid.'

'So she's married?'

'Was married. Not married now,' I say shortly. He has questions about Beth, but none about me.

The first drops of rain land on our hands and faces.

'Well, if Honey wants to talk to somebody about it, maybe she could talk to Beth? Her experience could be a good cautionary tale.'

'She won't talk to anybody about it. She's strong willed,' Dinny sighs.

'So I noticed,' I murmur. I can't stand another silence. I want to ask him about his travels, his life, our past. 'Well, I should be getting back. Getting out of this rain,' is all I can say. 'It was really good to see you again, Dinny. I'm glad you're back. And nice to meet Honey, too. I'll . . . well, we're up at the house, if you need anything . . .'

'It's good to see you too, Erica.' Dinny looks at me with his head on one side, but his eyes are troubled, not glad.

'OK. Well, bye.' I go, as casually as I can.

I don't tell Beth about Dinny when I find her, watching TV in the study. I'm not sure why not. There will be a reaction, I think, when I tell her. And I am not sure what it will be. I am agitated suddenly. I feel like we're no longer alone. I can feel Dinny's presence out there, beyond the trees. The third corner of our triangle. I switch off the TV.

'Come on. We're going out,' I tell her.

'I don't want to go out. Go where?'

'Shopping. I'm sick to death of tinned soup. Plus, it's about to be Christmas. Mum and Dad are coming for lunch, and what are you going to feed Eddie on Christmas day?' Beth considers this for a moment, then stands up quickly, puts her hands on her hips.

'God, you're right. You're right! We need lots of things . . . turkey, sausages, potatoes, puddings . . .' she counts items off on her fingers. Christmas is ten days away yet—we have plenty of time. But I don't say that. 'And decorations!' she cries.

'Come on. You can make a list in the car.'

Devizes is prettied up for Christmas. Little fir trees lean out from the sides of shops and hotels along the High Street, strung with white lights; there's a brass band playing, and a man roasting chestnuts. We wrap our scarves around our ears and window-shop. Back in the world, the pair of us, after the solitude of the manor. It feels good, exciting, and I miss London. Inside each shop, Beth hums along to the carols, and as we walk I loop my arm through hers, holding her tight.

Several hours later and Beth has gone into Christmas overdrive. We have eight different cheeses, a huge ham, chipolatas, crackers, a turkey, and a cake that cost a ridiculous amount of money. We cram it all into the boot, go back for glittering baubles, strings of beads, gold paint, glass icicles. There's a farm two minutes from the manor selling Christmas trees. We call in on the way back, arrange to have a tree four metres high delivered and erected on December the twenty-third.

'It can go in the hallway—they can wire it to the banister,' Beth says.

Perhaps I should not let her spend when she is troubled, like now. I daren't put all the receipts together, add it all up. But Beth has money—money from Maxwell, money from her translating work. More money than I have, certainly, but she lives small, most of the time. All mine is absorbed by London, in getting to work, in rent, in living. Now we have enough food for ten people, when we will be five; but Beth looks happier, her face is less drawn. Retail therapy. But that's not it—she likes to be able to give. I leave her threading garlands along the mantelpiece, with a slight frown of concentration while I put the kettle on.

There's a message from my agency on my mobile phone, about some supply work at a school in Ealing, starting on January the twelfth. My thumb hovers over the redial button, but I am strangely reluctant to press it. But money must be earned, I suppose; life must resume. Literature must be crammed between deaf ears. Unless I live here, of course. No more rent. Would it be worth it for five years, even ten? Trying to live here—just long enough for the legacy to stand. Then we could sell up, retire at the age of forty, once property prices are back up. But if living here makes Beth ill? And if I will always have this feeling of something stealing up behind me? I remember everything else that happened that summer, except what happened to Henry.

We came here the two summers after that year, and our mother watched us closely. Not to protect us, but to assess, to see how we would react. I don't know if I was different. A little quieter, perhaps. And we stayed in the garden; we didn't want to venture farther any more. Mum kept us away from Meredith, who was unpredictable by then. But Beth drew further and further into herself. Our mother saw and she told our father, and he frowned. And we stopped coming.

Outside, the sun sets orange and pink on the horizon. I spray the holly gold, the paint burnishing the dark leaves. It looks delicious. I am hanging it from the banisters and laying it along windowsills when Beth comes downstairs, face creased with sleep. She moves from place to place where I have hung it, testing the paint with her fingertips.

'Do you approve?' I ask her, smiling. I've tuned the radio to Classic FM. They're playing 'Good King Wenceslas'. Beth nods, yawns. I sing, 'Silly bugger, he fell out; on a red hot cinder!'

'You're chirpy,' Beth tells me. She comes over to the windowsill, puts my hair behind my ear for me. So rare, her touches. I smile.

'Well . . .' I say. The words teeter in my mouth.

'Well, what?'

'Well, Dinny's here,' I tell her.

Loving

1902

THE JOURNEY FROM New York to Woodward in Oklahoma Territory was a long one, covering a distance of nearly two thousand miles. State after state rolled out beneath the train, ever westwards. At first, Caroline was awed by the scene beyond the window. As they left behind the familiar towns of New York State, settlements became fewer and farther between. They passed through woods so thick and dark that they seemed to belong to another age, closing the train in for mile after countless mile. They passed through fields of wheat and corn no less vast, no less astonishing, and towns that grew smaller and smaller, as if compressed by the wide expanses of land all around them. Caroline sat back in her seat and studied the landscape with a pull of unease, feeling the once-mighty train to be a mere speck, an insect crawling across the endless surface of the world.

The train arrived at Woodward late in the day, as the sun began to set smeared and orange against the dusty window glass. Caroline had been dozing when the conductor strode past her compartment.

'Woodward! Woodward the next stop!' His shout woke her, sent her heart skittering. She gathered her things and stood up quickly. Corin, was all she could think. To see him again, after so many days! She peered eagerly out at the station as the train squealed to a halt, desperate to catch a glimpse of him.

She climbed stiffly from the train, her skirts clinging to her legs. She looked up and down the wooden platform, her heart in her mouth, but could not see Corin among the handful of people waiting at the station. She straightened her hat nervously, but kept her smile ready, her eyes searching. Woodward looked small and slow. The street leading into town from the railway track was wide and unmade, and the wind had carved tiny waves into the sand all along it.

As the locomotive moved away a kind of quiet settled, behind the rattle of a passing buggy and the creak of the trolley as the station man pit his back against the weight of her luggage. Where was Corin? Doubts and fears bubbled up inside her—that he regretted his choice, that she was abandoned, would have to take the next train back to New York. She turned in a circle, desperate to see him. The station porter had paused with her luggage and was trying to catch her eye, to ask, no doubt, where he should take it. But if Corin was not here, Caroline had no idea. She took a deep, trembling breath and tried desperately to think what to do, what to say to the porter to conceal her confusion.

'Mrs Massey?' Caroline did not at first register this as her name, spoken with a slow drawl. She ignored the man with his hat in his hands who had come to stand to one side of her. He looked to be about thirty, but the weather was wearing his face as it was fading the blue from his flannel shirt. His scruffy hair was shot through with strands of red and brown. 'Mrs Massey?' he asked again, taking a step towards her.

'Oh! Yes, I am,' she exclaimed, startled.

'Pleasure to meet you, Mrs Massey. I'm Derek Hutchinson, but everybody calls me Hutch and I'd be happy if you would too,' he introduced himself, holding out a hand, which Caroline shook tentatively.

'Where is Mr Massey?' she asked.

'Corin was due back in time to come and get you, ma'am, but there's been some trouble with cattle thieves and he was called upon to ride out and see to it . . . He'll be back by the time we are, I'm sure of that,' Hutch said, seeing Caroline's face fall. Tears of disappointment blurred her vision. Hutch hesitated, unnerved by her reaction.

'I see,' she gasped, swaying slightly, suddenly longing to sit down. Corin hadn't come to meet her. In sudden terror, she began to guess at reasons he might have to avoid her.

Hutch cleared his throat diffidently. 'I uh . . . I know it truly was his wish to meet you here himself, Mrs Massey, but when there are thieves to apprehend, it's the duty of the landowners to help one another in that mission. I have come in his stead and I'm at your service.'

'It's their duty to go?' she asked, tentatively.

'Absolutely. He was duty-bound to it.'

'Are you his . . . manservant, then?' she asked.

Hutch smiled and tipped his chin. 'Well, not quite that, Mrs Massey. Not quite that. I'm foreman at the ranch.'

'I see,' she said, although she did not. 'Well. Will we be there in time for dinner, do you think?' she asked, fighting to regain her composure.

'Dinner, ma'am? Tomorrow, do you mean?'

'Tomorrow?'

'It's nearing on thirty-five miles to the ranch, from Woodward here. Now, that's not far, but too far to make a start this evening, I think. There's a room waiting for you at the boarding house, and dinner too.'

'Thirty-five miles? But . . . how long will it take?'

'We'll set out early tomorrow and we should get there by noon time on the second day . . . I had not reckoned on you bringing quite so many boxes and trunks with you, and that might slow the wagon down some. But the horses are fresh, and if the weather stays this fair it'll be a good, smooth ride.' Hutch smiled, and Caroline rallied herself, finding a smile for him in return. Hutch stepped forward, proffering his arm.

'That's more like it. Come with me now and we'll get you settled. You look fairly done in, Mrs Massey.'

The morning dawned fair and the sun was strong as they began the final stretch of the journey. As Hutch helped her into the wagon, Caroline noticed a gun belt buckled around his hips, a six-shooter holstered into it. She tilted her bonnet forward to shade her eyes against the bright light.

It did not take long to pass through Woodward town. They drove down Main Street, which was flanked predominantly by wooden-framed buildings. There were several saloons, several banks, a post office, a large general store, an opera house. There was a bustle of wagons and horses, and a fair number of people going about their business, most of whom were men. Caroline looked back over her shoulder as they left town.

'Is that the whole of Woodward?' she asked, incredulously.

'Yes, ma'am. Over two thousand souls call it home, nowadays, and growing all the while. Ever since they opened up the Arapaho lands to the south, folks have been pouring in, starting to settle and farm.'

'Arapaho? What does that mean?'

'The Arapaho? They're Indian folks. From more northern parts originally, but settled here by the government. This land we're driving through now was Cherokee until recently, although they themselves lived farther east. They leased it to ranchers and cattle folk till it was opened up.'

'But is that safe? For civilised people to live where there are Indians?' Caroline was shocked. Hutch gave her a sidelong look.

'They sold their lands and moved on east. I reckon they've as little urge to have white neighbours as some white folk have to share with Indians.'

'Thank goodness!' Caroline said. 'I could never have slept at night, knowing that such creatures were roaming around outside the window!' She laughed a little, high and nervous, and did not notice Hutch's thoughtful gaze, out over the prairie.

The wagon made slower progress over the open prairie, bumping over knots of sagebrush, dragging sometimes in patches of shifting sand. Occasionally they passed small dwellings, homesteads dug in and knocked together in haste to keep a family safe, to stake a claim, to make a new beginning. But these were far apart, and grew more infrequent the farther they went. As the afternoon grew long Caroline drowsed, swaying on the seat next to Hutch.

'We'll stop for the night soon, ma'am. I reckon you could use a hot cup of coffee and to bed down.'

'Oh, yes! I am rather tired. We must be very far from town, by now?'

'It seems farther in this slow wagon. I have made the journey on horseback in a day before, without even trying too hard. All you need is a good, fast saddle horse.'

'Where will we stop the night? Is there a settlement nearby?'

'Oh, no, ma'am. We'll make camp tonight.'

'Camp?'

'That's right. Don't look so alarmed, Mrs Massey! I am a man of honour and discretion,' he said, smiling wryly at Caroline's expression of wide-eyed bewilderment. It was a moment before she realised he had imagined her scandalised at the thought of spending the night alone with him. She blushed and dropped her gaze, only to find it resting near the waistband of his trousers, where his shirt had pulled a little loose to reveal a small area of his hard, tanned stomach. Caroline swallowed and set her eyes firmly on the horizon. Her first fear had actually been of being outdoors all night, unprotected from animals, weather and other savageries of nature.

Before sundown Hutch drew the wagon to a stop on a flat area where the ground was greener than it had been, and more lush. He helped Caroline down and she stood, unsure of what to do. Hutch unhitched the wagon, took the bits from the horses' mouths and slapped their behinds. With glad expressions and swishing tails, they trotted lazily away to a near distance and began to crop huge mouthfuls of grass.

'But . . . won't the horses run away?' Caroline asked.

'Not far, I reckon. And they'll come miles for a slice of bread, anyway.' Hutch unloaded a tent from the wagon and soon had it built. He spread blankets on top of buffalo hides to make a bed, and put her vanity case inside for her. 'You'll be cosy as anything in there. As fine as any New York hotel,' he said. Caroline glanced at him, unsure if she was being mocked, then she smiled and seated herself inside the tent, wrinkling her nose at the smell of the hides. But the bed was deep and soft, and the sides of the tent belled in and out with the breeze. Caroline felt a gentle calm come over her.

The sunrise woke her, light glowing irresistibly inside the tent. For a moment, Caroline could not remember where she was. She poked her head cautiously out of the tent and was relieved to see no sign of Hutch. The eastern sky was dazzling. Caroline had never in her life been up so early. She stood up and stretched. Her hair was in disarray and her mouth was sour with last night's coffee. She rubbed her eyes and found her brows full of sand. Her whole face, in fact, and her clothes. Rumpled blankets beside the cooling embers of the fire spoke of where the foreman had spent the night.

'Good morning, Mrs Massey,' Hutch called, giving her a start. He was approaching from the green expanse beyond the parked wagon, a chestnut horse held by a halter rope in each of his hands. 'How did you find your first night as a cowpuncher?' he smiled. Caroline smiled back, not really understanding him.

'Good morning, Mr Hutchinson. I slept well, thank you.'

'I'm taking these two to water at the creek over this way, then I'll get some breakfast cooking,' he said. Caroline nodded, and glanced around. 'I put a can of water there, in case you wanted to freshen up any,' he added, smiling again as he made his way past the camp.

By midday the sun was scorching, but Caroline's arm, clutching her dusty parasol, was heavy with fatigue. She gave up and folded it into her lap. Looking up into the vast, fathomless sky, she saw two distant dark spots, circling high above.

'Are those eagles?' she asked, pointing skywards. Hutch followed her gaze, squinting.

'Just buzzards, I'm afraid. Not really many eagles down here on the prairie. If you go up into the Rockies you'll see some beautiful birds. Those are some sharp eyes you've got there, Mrs Massey,' he told her. He looked back out over the horses' ears and sang quietly to himself, 'Daisy, Daisy, give me your answer do . . .' Caroline let her eyes drift to the horizon, then she straightened in her seat and pointed again.

'Somebody's coming!' she exclaimed, excitedly.

'Well, we're not at all far from the ranch now, ma'am. It could be one of our own riders,' Hutch nodded, with a subtle smile.

'Is it Corin?' Caroline asked. She began to tuck wayward strands of hair beneath her bonnet. 'Do you think it's Mr Massey?'

'Well,' Hutch smiled again, as her frantic grooming continued, 'I know of no other man who rides a mare as black as that in this vicinity, so I think it just might be your husband after all, ma'am.'

Caroline was still brushing her skirts and pinching her cheeks, when the rider drew near, and she at last saw Corin for the first time since she'd wed him over a month before. The black horse covered the ground in an easy lope and when at last he reached them Corin pulled the kerchief down from his face to reveal a wide grin. He was as golden and lovely as she remembered.

'Caroline!' he cried. 'It's so good to see you!' He swung down from his horse and came to stand by her foot. There she remained, seated high on the wagon, transfixed with fear and anticipation.

'How was the journey?' When she didn't reply Corin's face fell a little and a puzzled look came into his eyes. This was her undoing. Still lost for words, Caroline surrendered all propriety and toppled herself from the bench into his waiting arms. Behind them, Hutch watched with a laconic smile, and gave his boss a genial nod.

There was a scattering of people around the ranch house when the wagon bringing Corin Massey's new wife finally pulled up outside. They were young men mostly, with worn, dusty clothes, who seemed, nevertheless, to have made some attempts to comb their hair and tuck in their shirts. The men nodded, tipped their hats and murmured greetings as she climbed down from the wagon, and she smiled and acknowledged them politely.

'I so want to take you on a tour of the ranch, Caroline. I'm so excited to show you everything! Unless you're too tired after your journey?' said Corin, swinging down from his horse.

'Oh, I am so tired, Corin! Of course you must show me everything, but first I need to lie down, and then take a bath,' she said. Corin nodded readily, although he looked a little disappointed.

The tall, white house Caroline had envisaged was instead a low, wood-frame building; and although the front had indeed been painted white, prairie sand had blown up against it and given the bottom half a grubby look. Corin followed her gaze.

'A spring wind blew up before the paint had a chance to dry,' he told her, sheepishly. 'We'll paint over it, don't worry.'

'I'll see to Strumpet. You take Mrs Massey on into the house,' Hutch said, taking the reins from Corin.

'Strumpet?' Caroline asked, bewildered.

'My mare,' Corin grinned. 'The most contrary, bad-tempered soul you'll find on these lands, and that's a known fact.'

'Why do you keep her, if she is so unpleasant?'

'Well,' he shrugged, as if this had never occurred to him, 'she's my horse.'

Inside, the walls were bare and no curtains hung at the windows. There was furniture enough but it was placed higgledy-piggledy. An easy chair drawn up to the burner, with piles of livestock journals and seed catalogues beside it, was the only thing that looked to be in its right place. Many boxes and cartons stood around the floor. Caroline turned a slow circle, gazing at all this. When she looked at her husband she could not hide her dismay. Corin's smile faded from his face.

'Now, I deliberately didn't have it all fixed up because there was no point, I thought, until you'd arrived and told me how it should be fixed. We'll get it set up quickly enough, now that you're here,' he explained, hurriedly. Caroline smiled. 'It just . . . it took me longer than I had planned to get the place built . . . I'm sorry, Caroline.'

'Oh, no! Don't be!' she exclaimed, anguished to see him crestfallen. 'I'm sure it will be wonderful—I know just how we should finish it. You've done so well.' She turned and leaned her head against his chest, and revelled in the smell of him.

'Come with me,' he murmured, and led her through a door in the far corner of the main room, to a smaller room where a large iron bedstead dominated. It was draped with a fine, multicoloured quilt, and Caroline ran her fingers lightly over it. 'I had the bed freighted all the way from New York,' Corin told her. 'It arrived right before you did; and the quilt was my mother's. Why don't you try it?'

'Oh, no! I'd dirty it. It's so lovely, Corin,' Caroline enthused.

'Well, I'm dirty too; and I say we try it out.' Corin took her hands and then her waist, and then linked his arms around her.

'Wait! No!' Caroline laughed, as he pulled them both down to land, bouncing, on the mattress.

'We never did get our wedding night,' he said softly. The sun streaming in from the window lit his hair with a soft coronet and threw his brown eyes into shadow. Caroline was very aware of the stale smell of her own unwashed body, and the dryness of her mouth.

'No. But it's not bedtime yet. And I need to bathe . . . and someone might see in.'

'We're not in New York any more, love. You don't have to do as your aunt tells you, and we don't have to do what society tells us . . .' Corin placed his hand flat on her midriff and Caroline caught her breath. He worked each button of her blouse free and smoothed it gently aside.

'But, I—'

'But nothing,' Corin murmured. 'Turn over.' Caroline obeyed, and Corin fumbled slightly as he undid the laces of her corset. Released, the sudden rush of air into Caroline's lungs made her head spin, and she closed her eyes. Corin turned her to face him and traced the lines of her body with the roughened palms she had noticed the first time they met. He kissed her eyelids softly. 'You're so beautiful,' he said quietly, his voice was deep and blurred. 'Eyes like silver dollars.'

Alarmed by the force of the passion she felt, Caroline kissed him as hard as she could. Bathilda had hinted darkly at pain that was to be borne, but the press of Corin's skin against her own was a feeling more wonderful than any she had yet experienced; and the gentle insistence of his touch filled her with a sensation that was so far beyond anything she had felt before that she cried out in astonished joy.

Corin toured his new wife around the ranch in a buggy, since it was too far to walk and she had never ridden horseback before. He had seemed stunned by this fact, but then he'd shrugged and said, 'Don't worry; you'll learn soon enough.'

But Caroline did not trust the animals, and the thought of sitting atop of one did not appeal to her in the slightest. Corin drove her around the various corrals, stock pens and cattle chutes, and the low, roughly built bunkhouses where the line-riders slept. They passed a pitiful-looking hovel, half dug into the ground and then roofed with planks and sod.

'That would have been our home, if you'd come to me much sooner!' Corin told her with a smile.

'That?' Caroline echoed, appalled. Corin nodded.

'That dugout's the very first dwelling I put here when I staked my claim in ninety-three. And I wintered in it twice before I got a proper house set up—I found one out on the prairie and dragged it here!'

'You stole a house?'

'Not stole! No, not that. I suppose it had been put up by some boomer, trying to settle the land before it was legal. Well, whoever built it had moved on. It was just sitting there, so I loaded it on a flatbed wagon and dragged it back here. It was a good little house, but certainly not roomy enough for a family.' As he said this he took her hand and squeezed it, and Caroline looked away bashfully.

'A large family?' she queried, tentatively.

'I reckon four or five kids ought to do it,' he grinned. 'How about you?'

'Four or five ought to do it,' she agreed, smiling widely.

'Here, now; this is the shelter we bring the mares into when they're due to foal.'

'What's that?' Caroline asked, pointing to a conical tent beyond the mare's corral.

'That's where Joe's family lives. See the dugout beside? Joe and his wife sleep there, but his folks wanted a teepee like they'd always had, and so that's what they live in still. They're a traditional sort of people.'

'Why would . . . Joe's family live in a teepee?' Caroline asked, perplexed. Corin looked at her, as puzzled as she.

'Well, they're Indians, sweetheart. And they like to live as they ever have, although Joe himself is more forward-thinking. He's worked the trails for me since the very beginning, when I could pay him only in clothes and five-cent tins of tobacco. One of my best riders—'

'Indians? There are Indians here?' Caroline's heart quickened and her stomach twisted. 'Hutch told me they were all gone!' she whispered.

'Well, most of them have. The rest of Joe's people are on the reservation, east of here, on land that reaches the banks of the River Arkansas. Those that remained here—in Oklahoma Territory, that is—Chief White Eagle leads them. But some went north again a few years back,' he explained, but Caroline scarcely heard this history of the tribe. She could not believe her ears, or her eyes, that here camped on her doorstep were the savages of whose atrocities lurid stories had circulated in the east for decades. Fear froze her to the core. Wildly, she grabbed the reins from Corin and dragged the horse's head around, back towards the house.

'Hey—wait, what are you doing!' Corin exclaimed, trying to wrestle the reins from her as the horse tossed its head in protest.

'I want to go! I want to get away from them!' Caroline cried, shaking all over. Corin steadied the horse and then took her hands into his.

'Now, look!' he said seriously, eyes pinioning hers. 'Listen to me, Caroline. They are good people. People, just like you and me; and no matter what you've heard back east, I am telling you that they don't want to trouble you or anybody else. There's been strife in the past, but now all any of us wants to do is get on as best we can. Joe has brought his family here to live and work alongside us, and that's taken a kind of courage you and I can't understand, I do believe. Are you listening to me, Caroline?' She nodded, although she could hardly credit what he was saying. Tears rolled down her cheeks. 'Don't cry, my darling. Nothing you've been told about Indians applies to Joe. I can guarantee you that. Come along now and I'll introduce you.'

'No!' she gasped.

'Yes. They're your neighbours now, and Joe is a firm friend of mine.'

'I can't! Please!' Caroline sobbed. Corin took out his handkerchief and wiped her face. He tipped her chin up and smiled affectionately.

'You poor thing. Please, don't be afraid. Come on, now. The second you meet them you'll see you've got nothing to be frightened of.'

Clicking his tongue at the buggy horse, Corin turned it again and drove them towards the teepee and dugout. A fire was burning outside the tent, and as they approached a small, iron-haired woman emerged with a blackened pot to place over the embers. Her back was bowed, but her eyes sparkled from deep within the creases webbing her face. She nodded, eyeing Caroline with quiet interest as Corin jumped down from the buggy.

'Good morning, White Cloud, I've come to introduce my wife to you,' Corin said, tipping the brim of his hat respectfully. Caroline's legs, as he helped her down, felt unsteady beneath her. A man came out of the dugout, followed by a young girl, and a middle-aged woman. She said something incomprehensible to Corin, and Corin, to Caroline's utter amazement, replied.

'You speak their tongue?' she blurted out, and then recoiled when all eyes turned to her. Corin smiled, somewhat diffidently.

'Indeed, I do. Now, Caroline, this is Joe, and this is his wife Magpie.' Caroline tried to smile, but she found that she could not hold the gaze of either one of them for more than a few seconds. When she did she saw a stern, dark man, not tall but broad across the chest, and a plump girl, her long hair prettily braided with coloured strings woven through it. Joe's hair was also long, and they both had high, feline cheekbones. Magpie smiled and ducked her head, trying to catch Caroline's eye.

'I'm very pleased to meet you, Mrs Massey,' she said, and her English was perfect even if her accent was strong. Caroline gaped at her.

'You speak English?' she whispered. Magpie gave a cheerful chuckle.

'Yes, Mrs Massey. Better than my husband, although I have been learning for less time!' she boasted. 'I'm so glad you are here. There are far too many men at this ranch.'

Caroline took a longer look at the girl, who was wearing a simple skirt and blouse, with a brightly woven blanket wrapped around her shoulders. Her feet were shod with soft slippers of a kind Caroline had never seen before. Her husband muttered something sharp in their own tongue, and Magpie scowled, answering him with something short and indignant. Joe did not smile as readily as his wife, and his expression seemed, to Caroline, most hostile.

'I have never met any Cherokee . . . people before,' Caroline said.

'Still you have not.' Joe spoke for the first time, wryly. Caroline glanced at Corin.

'Joe and his family are of the Ponca tribe,' he explained.

'But . . . Hutch told me these lands were Cherokee before . . .'

'They were. It's . . . well, put simply, there are many tribes in this country. It was Indian Territory before it was Oklahoma Territory, after all. Joe and his family are a little out of the ordinary, in that they have chosen to adopt some of the white man's ways of living. Most of his people choose to stay on reservation lands. Joe here got a taste for cattle driving and has never looked back—isn't that right, Joe?'

'Got a taste for beating you at cards, mostly,' the Ponca man said, twisting his mouth to one side sardonically.

As they moved away from the teepee, Caroline frowned. 'Joe seems an odd name for an . . . for a Ponco . . .'

'Ponca. Well, his real name, in his own tongue, is just about unpronounceable. It means Dust Storm, or something of that kind. Joe's just a lot easier for folk to say,' Corin explained.

'He does not seem to show you much respect, considering you are his employer.'

At this Corin glanced at Caroline, and a frown shaded his eyes for a moment. 'He has plenty of respect for me, I assure you; and it's respect I've had to earn. People like Joe don't give out respect because you're white, or because you've got land, or you pay their wages. They give it when you can show you have integrity and a willingness to learn, and can show respect to them where it's due. Things are a little different out here than in New York, Caroline . . .' He trailed into silence. Stinging with his rebuke, Caroline sat in unhappy silence. 'You'll soon settle in, don't you worry,' Corin said, in a lighter tone.

A few days later, they took their honeymoon picnic, setting out in the buggy while the sun was skirting the eastern horizon, and heading due west of the ranch for three hours or so, to a place where the land rolled into curves around a shallow pool, fed by a slow-running creek. Silver willows leaned their branches down, shading the water's edge and touching it in places, pulling wrinkles in the wide reflected sky.

'It's so pretty here,' Caroline said, smiling as Corin lifted her down from the bench.

'I'm glad you like it,' Corin said, planting a kiss on her forehead. 'It's one of my favourite places. I come here sometimes, when I need to think about things, or when I'm feeling low . . .'

'Do you come here often then? Do you get low, out here?'

'I did sometimes, when I was first here. Wondered whether I'd staked the right claim, wondered if it was too far from my family, if the land was right for the cattle. But I've not been back here for many months,' he shrugged. 'It soon became clear to me that I never did a better thing than making those choices. Everything happens for a reason, is what I believe, and now I know that's right.'

'How do you know?' she asked, turning to him.

'Because I have you. When my father died, I thought . . . I thought for a time that I should move back to New York and look after my mother. But the second I got back there I knew I couldn't stay. And then I found you, and you were willing to come away with me . . . and if any good thing could come from losing my father, then you are that good thing, Caroline. You're what was missing from my life.' He spoke with such clarity, such resolve, that Caroline was overwhelmed.

'Do you really think that?' she whispered, standing close to him.

'I really think that,' he said, and she stood up on her toes to kiss him.

In the shade of the willow trees they spread out their rugs, unpacked the hamper and unhitched the buggy horse, which Corin tethered to a tree. Caroline sat with her legs tucked carefully beneath her, and poured Corin a glass of lemonade. He lay down easily beside her, propped on one elbow, and undid the buttons of his shirt to let the cool air in. Caroline watched him almost shyly, still not used to the idea that he belonged to her, still not used to his relaxed manner.

'Corin?' she asked him suddenly. 'How old are you?'

'What? You know that!'

'But I don't! I just realised . . . I don't know how old you are. You seem so much older than me—not in appearance, I mean! Well, partly in appearance, but in other ways,' she floundered. Corin smiled.

'I'll be twenty-seven next birthday,' he said. 'There now—are you appalled that you've married such an old-timer?'

'Twenty-seven is not so very old! I shall be nineteen in just a couple of months. But . . . you seem to have lived here for a lifetime already. You're as settled here as if you'd been here fifty years!'

'Well, I first came out here with my father, on a business trip—prospecting for new beef suppliers. My father traded in meat, did I tell you that? He sold to all the best restaurants in New York, and for a time I was destined to go into the business with him. But I knew as soon as I got out here that we were at the wrong end of that chain of supply, and I never left. I was just sixteen when I decided to stay on out here and learn about raising the beeves instead of just buying their dead flesh.'

'Sixteen!' Caroline echoed. 'Weren't you scared, to leave your family like that?' she asked. Corin thought for a moment, then shook his head.

'I've never been much afraid of anything. Until I asked you to dance,' he said. Caroline blushed happily, straightening her skirts.

'It really is hot, isn't it? Even here in the shade,' she commented.

'You want to know the best way to cool down?'

'What is it?'

'Swimming!' Corin declared, pulling his shirt up over his head.

'Swimming! What do you mean?' Caroline laughed.

'I'll show you!' he said, sliding off his boots, kicking his trousers to one side and charging into the pool, as naked as Adam, with a wild whooping and splashing. Caroline stood up and watched in utter amazement. 'Come in, sweetheart! It's the best feeling!' he called.

'Are you crazy?' she cried. 'I cannot swim here!'

'Why ever not?' he asked, swimming the length of the small pool.

'Well, it's . . .' she waved an incredulous arm. 'It's muddy! And it's out in the open—anybody could see! And I don't have a bathing suit.'

'Sure you do! It's right there under your dress,' Corin grinned. 'And who's to see? There's nobody around for miles. Come on! You'll love it!'

Caroline walked to the edge of the bank, unlaced her boots and hesitated. The sun beat down on her, scorching the top of her head and making her clothes feel tight and stifling. She bent down, pulled off her boots and stockings and put them on the bank, then, gathering her skirt to her knees, she stepped in until the water lapped her ankles. The relief of cold water on her clammy skin was her undoing.

'Oh, my goodness,' she breathed.

'Now, how much better does that feel?' Corin called to her, coming over to where she stood. 'Come on, come in and swim! I dare you!'

Caroline looked over her shoulder, as if an audience might have appeared, ready to gasp in dismay at her wantonness, then she undid her dress and stays and draped them over a willow branch. She kept her chemise on, then went back to the edge of the pool. There she paused, mesmerised by the feel of the mud as it squeezed up between her toes. She had never felt anything like it, and hitched up her petticoat to look down, flexing her feet and smiling. When she looked up to remark upon it, she found Corin watching her with a rapt expression.

'What is it?' she asked, alarmed.

'You. Just look at you . . . You're so brave. And so beautiful. I've never seen anything like it,' he said simply.

Caroline had only intended to paddle, but the touch of the water and the thrill of Corin's words made her bold, and she waded in up to her waist, the water swirling the translucent folds of her chemise around her legs. With a nervous laugh she lay back and let the water buoy her up. It felt chilly as it fingered through her hair.

'Come here and kiss me,' Corin demanded.

'With regret, sir, I am far too busy swimming,' Caroline replied grandly, paddling away with an ungainly stroke. With a start, she realised she hadn't swum since childhood, at her family's summerhouse.

'I shall have a kiss, even if I must chase you down for it,' Corin told her. Laughing and kicking her legs Caroline tried to escape; but she did not try very hard.

The sun was setting as they came over the last rise and saw the lights of the ranch house glimmering below them. Caroline's skin felt hot and raw where the sun had singed it, and her dress felt odd without the chemise underneath, which was laid out drying on the back of the buggy. They had made love on the river bank, and the languor of it lingered in her muscles, leaving her heavy and warm. Suddenly, she did not want to arrive back at the house. She wanted the day to last for ever—she and Corin in a shady place on a hot day, making love over and over again, without another thought or care in the world. As if reading her mind, Corin reined the horse to a halt, before turning to her.

'Are you ready to go back?' he asked.

'No!' Caroline said fiercely. 'I . . . I wish every day could be like today. It was so perfect.'

'It truly was, sweetheart,' Corin agreed, raising her hand to his lips.

'Promise me we'll go back there. I won't go one inch closer to the house until you promise me.'

'I promise you we'll go there again. We will go back, and we'll have many more days like today. I swear it,' he said.

Caroline looked at the outline of him in the indigo twilight, caught the gleam of his eye, the faint shape of a smile. She put her hand out and touched his face. 'I love you,' she told him simply.

With a shake of the reins the horse began a lazy descent towards the wooden house below, and with each step it took, Caroline felt a sense of vague foreboding growing inside her. She turned her eyes to the dark ground ahead and was suddenly afraid, in spite of Corin's pledge, that no day to come would be as sweet as that which had just passed.

3

I HAVE BEEN trying to remember good things about Henry. Perhaps we owe him that, because we got to grow up, live lives, fall in love, fall out again. He liked to tell stupid jokes, and I loved to hear them. Beth was always kind, and took me with her, and helped me, but she was rather serious, even as a child. Once I laughed so hard at Henry's jokes that I nearly wet myself—the fear of it abruptly stopped the giggles, sent me scrambling for the toilet with one fist corked between my legs.

He was telling me stupid jokes one day when I was about seven. It was a Saturday. I wasn't really watching what Henry was doing as he reeled out his jokes. I just followed him, prompted him whenever there was a pause: *Say another one! How do you know when there's an elephant in your bed? You can see the 'E' on his pyjamas. What's brown and sticky? A stick.* He had the biscuit barrel and he was cementing two shortbreads together with a thick daub of extra-strong English mustard. I was trying to remember a good thing about him, and now this.

He wrapped the biscuits in a napkin, pocketed them. I followed him across the lawn, demanding more jokes. We went west to the lane, skirted along it, behind the hedge, until we got to Dinny's camp. Henry hunkered down in the ditch, pulled me in with him. At this point only did I think to whisper, 'Henry, what are you doing?' He told me to shut up so I did. A spying game, I thought. Dinny's grandpa was sitting on a folding chair outside his battered white motor home, waxed hat pulled low over his eyes. Asleep, I think. His dogs lay either side of him, chins on paws. Two black and white collies called Dixie and Fiver.

Henry threw the sandwiched biscuits over the hedge. The dogs were on their feet in an instant, but they smelled the biscuits and they didn't bark. They crunched them down, mustard and all. I held my breath.

Dixie made a hacking noise, sneezed, put her muzzle down on one paw and rubbed at it with the other. Her eyes squinted up; she sneezed again and shook her head, whimpered. Henry had his knuckles in his teeth, his eyes bright, intent. Lit up inside, he was. Grandpa Flag was murmuring to the dogs now, awake. He had his hands in Dixie's ruff, was peering at her as she retched and snuffled. Fiver walked a small, slow circle to one side, heaved, threw up a disgusting yellow mess. A sob of laughter escaped around Henry's fist. I was strangled with pity for the dogs, boiling with guilt. I wanted to stand up and shout, *It wasn't me.* I wanted to disappear, run back to the house. I stayed, rocked on my crouched legs, hid my face in my knees.

But the worst of it was that when I was finally allowed to leave, we'd gone a scant twenty paces before Dinny and Beth appeared.

'What have you two been doing?' Beth asked. Henry scowled at her.

'Nothing,' he said. Able to inject a world of scorn into a single word.

'Erica?' She looked at me sternly, incredulous that I should be with Henry, that I should look guilty. But where had they been, without me? They had left me. Henry glowered at me, gave me a shove.

'Nothing,' I lied. I was quiet and sullen for the rest of the day. And when I saw Dinny the day after, knowing that he had been home, I couldn't look at him. I knew he knew. Because of Henry's jokes.

'**R**ick? Can we go now?' Eddie's head appears at the door to my room.

'Sure, Eddie, we can go. Give me five seconds.'

'One-two-three-four-five?'

'Ha, ha. Push off. I'll be down in a mo—I can't go out in my dressing gown.' I was defiantly still in it when I opened the door to Maxwell earlier.

'Not today,' Eddie agrees, retreating. 'It's cold enough to freeze the arse off a penguin out there.'

'Charming, dear,' I call. The frost has cast the trees in white. It's like another world out there—a brittle, albino world where white and opalescent blues have replaced dead grey and flat brown. I am soaring with optimism today. It would be hard not to be. After so many overcast days, the sky seems to go up for ever. And Beth has said she'll come with us—that's how vibrant the day is.

When I told her Dinny was here she froze. I was scared for a minute. She didn't seem to breathe. Then she looked away from me and licked her lower lip with the tip of her tongue.

'We'd be strangers, now,' she said, and walked slowly into the kitchen. She didn't ask me how I knew, what he looked like now, what he was doing here. She was relaxed again when I went to find her, as we made mugs of tea and I dunked Hobnobs in mine. But she didn't eat that night. Not a Hobnob, not the plate of risotto I put in front of her, not the ice cream afterwards.

It's the twentieth of December today. The car steams up as I drive east through the village and then turn north onto the A361.

I take the turning to Avebury. Eddie's been doing prehistory this term. Wiltshire's riddled with it. We park, join the steady trickle of people going along the path towards the stones.

A fine Saturday and there are lots of other people at Avebury, all bundled up like we are, moving in and out of the ancient sarsen stones. Two concentric rings, not as high as Stonehenge, not as grand or orderly, but the circles far, far bigger. We walk all the way around the ring. Beth reads from the guidebook but I am not sure Eddie is listening. He has a stick again. He is swordfighting somebody in his head.

'The Avebury Stone Circles are the largest in Britain, located in the third largest henge. In all, the surrounding bank and ditch and the area enclosed cover eleven point five hectares . . .'

'Eddie, I'm going to test you on this later!' I shout. My voice blares in the still air. An elderly couple turn to look. I want him to listen to Beth.

'The quarrying methods used include antler picks and rakes, oxshoulder blades and probably wooden shovels and baskets . . .'

'Cool,' Eddie says, dutifully.

We pass a tree grown into the rampart, its roots cascading above ground like a knotty waterfall. Eddie scrambles down it, commandostyle, crouches down, clings to it, peers up from three metres below us.

'I'm a woodsman, waiting to rob you,' he says.

'Bet you can't get me before I pass this tree to safety,' Beth challenges.

'I've lost the element of surprise,' Eddie complains.

'I'm getting away!' Beth goads, sauntering onwards.

With a rebel yell Eddie scales the roots, slipping and sliding. He grabs Beth with two hands, makes her squeal. 'I submit, I submit!' she laughs.

We walk out, away from the village along the wide avenue of stones that leads away to the south. The sun shines on Beth's face—a long time since I saw it lit this way. She looks pale, older, but there are blooms in her cheeks. She looks serene too. Eddie leads us, sword aloft, and we walk until our toes get too cold.

On the way back I pull up at the Spar in Barrow Storton for some ginger beer for Eddie. Beth waits in the car, quieter again now. Eddie and I are pretending not to notice. There's a horrible feeling of her teetering, being on the edge of something. Eddie and I hesitate, wanting to pull her one way, scared of accidentally tipping her the wrong way.

'Can't I have Coke instead?'

'Yes, if you'd rather.'

I smile, wincing at the weight as two huge bottles of Coke go into the basket. As we approach the till, Dinny comes in. At once I don't know where to look, how to stand. He has walked right past Beth, in the car. I wonder if she saw him, if she knew him.

'Hullo, Dinny,' I greet him. I smile. He looks up at me, startled.

'Erica!'

'This is Eddie—I mean Ed—who I was telling you about. My nephew—Beth's boy.' I pull Eddie to my side, he grins affably, says hi. Dinny studies him closely, then smiles.

'Beth's son? It's nice to meet you, Ed,' he says.

'Are you the Dinny my mum used to play with when she was little?'

'Yes. I am.'

'Erica was telling me about you. She said you were best friends.' Dinny looks at me sharply, and I feel guilty, even though what I said was true.

'Well, we were, I suppose.' His voice calm and low, always measured.

'Stocking up for Christmas?' I butt in, inanely. The Spar is hardly bursting with seasonal fare.

Dinny shakes his head, rolls his eyes slightly. 'Honey wants salt and vinegar crisps,' he says, then looks away sheepishly.

'Did you see Mum, outside? She's out there in the car—did you say hello?' Eddie asks. A flutter in the pit of my stomach.

'No. I didn't. I'll . . . I will now,' Dinny says, turning to the door, looking out at my grubby white car. His eyes are intent; he moves straight, shoulders tense, as if compelled to go to her.

I can see him, through the glass in the door. He bends down at the window, his breath clouding the air. Beth rolls the window down. I can't see her face with Dinny in the way. I duck; I crane my neck to see. Dinny leans his bare arm on the roof of the car.

'Rick—it's our go,' Eddie says, nudging me with his elbow. I heave the basket onto the counter, am forced to break off my surveillance and smile at the gloomy-looking man at the till. I pay for the Coke, a Twix and some ham for lunch, and rush to get back out to the car.

'So what do you do now? You wanted to be a concert flautist, if I remember rightly?' Dinny is saying. He straightens up from leaning on the car, folds his arms. He looks defensive suddenly, and I notice that Beth has not got out of the car to talk to him. She barely looks at him.

'Oh, that didn't quite pan out,' she says. 'I got to grade seven and then . . .' She pauses, looks away again. She got to grade seven the spring before Henry disappeared. 'I stopped practising as much,' she finishes, flatly. 'I do some translating now. French and Italian, mostly.'

'Oh,' Dinny says. He studies her, and the moment hangs, so I blunder in.

'We've just been to Avebury. Ed was keen to see it because they've been doing it at school. Mind you, once we got there you were more interested in having a hot fudge sundae in the pub, weren't you, Ed?'

'It was amazing,' Eddie assures us. Dinny gives me a quizzical smile.

'So, how long are you staying?' he asks, and he addresses this to me.

'For Christmas, definitely. After that, we're not really sure. There's a lot of sorting out to be done,' I say. 'How about you?'

'For the time being,' Dinny shrugs, even more ambiguous.

'Ah.' I smile.

'Well, I'd better be getting on. Good to see you again, Beth. Nice to meet you, Ed,' he says, nodding to us and walking away.

'He didn't get the crisps,' Eddie observes.

'No. He must have forgotten,' I agree, breathless. 'I'll get some and take them over later.'

'Cool.' Eddie nods. He pulls open the back door with one hand, the other hand fighting its way into the Twix. So flippant. No idea how huge the thing that just happened is, here at the car window. I go back into the shop, buy crisps, and when I get back into the car I start the engine and take us home, and I don't look at Beth because I feel too awkward, and the things I would ask I won't ask in front of her son.

Eddie is lying on his bed, in pyjamas, tethered to his iPod. On his front with his heels swinging over his back. He's reading a book called *Sasquatch!* I leave him. Downstairs, Beth is making mint tea.

'I hope Dinny didn't startle you, appearing at the car window like that?' I say. Lightly as I can. Beth presses her lips together.

'I saw him go into the shop,' she says.

'Really? And you recognised him? I don't think I would have—not just from glimpsing him go by.'

'Don't be ridiculous—he looks exactly the same,' she says. I feel inadequate—that she saw something I didn't.

'Well,' I say. 'Pretty amazing to see him again after all this time, isn't it?'

'Yes, I suppose so,' she murmurs.

Now I can't think what to ask. She should not be this careless about it. It should matter more. I search her face and frame for signs. 'Perhaps we should ask them up to the house. For a drink or something?'

'They?'

'Dinny and Honey. She's his . . . well, I'm not sure if they're married. She's about to have his baby. You could talk her out of having it in the woods. I think he'd be grateful for that.'

'Having it in the woods? How extraordinary,' Beth says. 'What a pretty name though—Honey.' There is more to it than this. There has to be.

'Look, are you sure you're OK?'

'Why wouldn't I be?' she says.

'But you hardly spoke to him. You two used to be so close . . . didn't you want to talk to him? Catch up?'

'Twenty-three years is a long time. We're totally different people now.'

'Not totally different—you're still you. He's still him. We're still the same people who played together as kids . . .'

'People change. They move on,' she insists.

'Beth,' I say, eventually, 'what happened? To Henry, I mean?'

'What do you mean?'

'Well, I mean, what happened to him?'

'He disappeared,' she says flatly, but her voice is like thin ice.

'But, do you remember, that day at the pond? The day he vanished? Do you remember what happened?' I press. And I know I shouldn't.

'How can you ask me that?' Beth demands, constricted.

'How can I? Why shouldn't I?' I ask, but when I look up I see she is shaking, eyes alight with anger. She doesn't answer for a while.

'Just because Dinny's around . . . just because he's here it doesn't mean you need to go raking up the past!' she says.

'What's it got to do with Dinny? I just asked a simple question!'

'Well, don't! Don't keep asking bloody questions, Erica!' Beth snaps, walking away. I sit quietly for a long time, and I picture that day.

We ate lunch in the shade of the oak tree on the lawn. A special little table laid there just for the three of us. Beth, Henry and me. Peanut butter and cucumber sandwiches. A bird in the tree crapped on the table. Henry scraped it up with his knife, flicked it at me. I ducked so violently that I fell off my chair, kicked the table leg, spilled my lemon-ade and Beth's. Henry laughed so hard a lump of bread went up his nose, and he choked until his eyes streamed. He was vile for the rest of the day. We tried everything to lose him. The heat made him groggy and violent. Eventually he was called inside to lie down because he was caught tying a Labrador's legs together with string. Meredith would not stand for the torment of her Labradors.

But he came out again later, as the afternoon broadened. He found us at the dew pond. The three of us by then, of course. I had been swim-ming, pretending to be an otter, a mermaid, a dolphin. Henry laughed at my wet saggy knickers. Have you pissed your pants, Erica? Then something, something. Running. Thoughts of the plughole at the bottom of the pond, of Henry being sucked down through it. That must have been why I said to them, again and again, *Look in the pond. I think he's in the pond. We were all at the pond.* Even though they had looked, Mum told me, the policeman told me. They had looked and he wasn't there. Meredith took me by the shoulders, shook me, shouted, *Where is he, Erica? Mother, stop it! Don't!*

Beth and I were given dinner in the kitchen, our mother spooning beans onto our toast, her face pale and preoccupied. But Beth did not eat. That was the first time, that evening. The first time I saw her mouth close so resolutely. Nothing in, and nothing out.

'**W**hat's with all the crisps?' Beth asks, poking the multipack of salt and vinegar among the breakfast detritus on the table.

'Oh . . . they were supposed to be for Honey. I forgot to take them down to her yesterday,' I say. Eddie is sitting on the bench with his back to the table, throwing a tennis ball against the wall and catching it.

'Are you bored?' Beth asks him.

'A bit. No, not really,' he flounders. The equal pull of honesty and tact.

'Why don't you deliver those crisps to Honey?' I suggest.

'I've never even met Honey. And I only met that bloke once, yester-day. I can hardly go marching into their front yard waving crisps, can I?'

'I'll go with you,' I say. 'Do you want to come, Beth? The camp's just where it always was,' I can't resist adding.

'No thanks. I'm going to . . . to walk into the village. Get the paper.'

'Come on, Eddie. We're going. Boots on, it's pretty muddy,' I say. I take us to the camp the long way, via the dew pond. It's becoming a daily pilgrimage. I pause to walk to the edge, look into the depths of it.

'I think you're a bit obsessed with this pond, Rick,' Eddie tells me gravely. I smile.

'I'm not. What makes you say that, anyway?'

'Every time we come near it you go all Luna Lovegood. Staring into space like that.'

'Well, excuse me, I'm sure!'

'I'm only joking,' he exclaims. 'But it does kind of look the same every time. Doesn't it?' He crouches to pick up a stone, hurls it into the water. The surface shatters. I watch him and suddenly my knees ache, sickeningly, as if I've missed my step on a ladder.

'Come on, then,' I say, turning away quickly.

'Did something happen here?' Eddie asks in a rush. He sounds tense.

'What makes you ask, Eddie?'

'It's just . . . you keep coming back out here. You get that look in your eye, like Mum gets when she's sad,' Eddie mumbles. I curse myself silently. 'And Mum seems . . . she doesn't seem to like it here.' It's easy to forget how clearly a child can see things.

'Well, something did happen here, Eddie. When we were small our cousin Henry disappeared. He was eleven, the same age as you are now. Nobody ever found out what happened to him, so we've kind of never forgotten about it.'

'Oh.' He kicks up sprays of dead leaves. 'That's really sad,' he says.

'Yes. It was,' I reply.

'Maybe he just ran away and . . . I don't know, joined a band or something?'

'Maybe he did, Eddie,' I say, hopelessly. Eddie nods, apparently satisfied with this explanation.

Dinny is standing with a man I don't recognise as the dogs come charging over to us. I smile and wave as if I pop in every day, and Dinny waves back. His companion smiles at me. He's a thin man, wiry, not tall. He has fair hair, cropped very close. Eddie walks closer to my side, bumping me. We move nervously into the circle of vehicles.

'Hi, sorry to interrupt,' I say.

'Hello there, I'm Patrick. You must be our neighbours up at the big house?' the wiry man greets me. His smile is warm and real.

'Yes, that's right. I'm Erica and this is my nephew, Eddie.'

'Ed!' Eddie hisses at me sideways, through unruly teeth.

'Ed, good to meet you.'

I notice Harry sitting on the step of a van behind the two of them. I think about calling out a greeting, but change my mind. Something in his hands again, something the focus of immense concentration.

'Well, uh, this might sound a little odd but we noticed you'd forgotten to get Honey's crisps yesterday. In the shop. So, we brought some over for her. That's if she's not craving pickles this morning instead?' I wave the big sack of crisps. Patrick gives Dinny a puzzled look.

'I know how fed up I get when Mum forgets my food when she goes shopping,' Eddie rescues me. At the sound of his voice, Harry looks up.

Dinny shrugs one shoulder. 'Honey!' he yells at the ambulance.

'Oh! There's no need to disturb her . . .' I feel colour in my cheeks. Honey appears at one of the windows. It frames her face.

'What?' she shouts back, far louder than she needs to.

'Erica has something for you.' I squirm. Eddie edges closer to Harry, trying to see what he's working on. Honey appears, picking her way carefully down the steps. All in black today, hair arrestingly pale against it. She stands at a distance from me and watches me suspiciously.

'Well. Silly really. We got you these. Dinny said you fancied some, so . . .' I trail off. Slowly, Honey steps forward and takes them from me.

'How much do I owe you?' she asks, scowling.

'Oh, no, don't worry. I don't remember. Forget it.' I wave my hand. She shoots Dinny a flat look and he puts his hand in his pocket.

'Two quid cover it?' he asks me.

'There's really no need.'

'Take it. Please.' So I take it.

'Thanks,' Honey mutters, and goes back inside.

'Don't mind Honey,' Patrick grins. 'She was born in a bad mood!'

'Fuck you, Pat!' Honey shouts, out of sight. He grins even wider.

Eddie has got closer and closer to Harry. He is peering at the man's hands, and probably blocking his light.

'Don't get in the way, will you, Ed?' I say, smiling cautiously.

'What is it?' Eddie asks Harry, who doesn't reply, but smiles.

'That's Harry,' Dinny tells Ed. 'He doesn't really like to talk.'

'Oh. Well, it looks like a torch. Is it broken? Can I see?' Eddie presses. Harry opens his hands wide, displays the tiny mechanical parts.

'So, will you be down for our little solstice party this evening, Erica?' Patrick asks.

'Oh, well, I don't know,' I say. I look at Dinny and he looks back, steadily, as if working out a problem.

'The more the merrier, right, Nathan? We're lighting a bonfire, having a bit of a barbecue. Bring some booze and you're most welcome, neighbour,' Patrick says.

'Well, maybe then.' I smile.

'Your dreadlocks are wicked,' Eddie tells Harry. 'You look a bit like Predator. Have you seen that film?' He has his fingers in the torch parts, picking bits out, putting them in order. Harry looks faintly astonished.

'I've got to run. I'll catch you later.' Patrick nods at Dinny and me. He leaves the camp with a springing step.

'Ed seems a good lad,' Dinny says then, and I nod.

'He's the best. He's a great help.' There's a long silence.

'When I spoke to Beth she seemed, I don't know,' Dinny says, hesitant.

'She seemed what?'

'Not like she used to be. Almost like there was nobody home?'

'She suffers from depression,' I say, hurriedly. 'She's still the same Beth. Only she's . . . she got more fragile.' I have to explain, even though I feel treacherous. He nods, frowns. 'I think it started here. I think it started when Henry disappeared,' I blurt out. This is not what Beth has told me, but I do think it's true.

'I would hate to think that what happened then has made her ill all this time,' Dinny says quietly. He knows what happened. He knows.

'Oh?' I say. If only he would go on, say more. Tell me. But he doesn't.

'It wasn't . . . well. I'm sorry to hear that she's not happy.'

'I thought coming back here would help, but I'm worried it might be making her worse. You know, bringing it all back. It could go either way. But it's good that Eddie's here. He takes her mind off things.'

'Do you think Beth will come to the party tonight?'

'Truthfully, no. I'll ask her, if you like?' I say. Dinny nods.

'Ask her. Bring Eddie too. He and Harry seem to be getting on well. He's great with kids—they're less complicated for him.'

I nod, bury my hands in the back pockets of my jeans. 'Are you coming, Ed?' I ask. 'I'm going back to the house.' Eddie and Harry look up from their work. Two sets of clear blue eyes.

'Can't I stay and finish this, Rick?' I glance at Dinny. He shrugs, nods.

'I'll keep an eye out,' he says.

I'm up in Meredith's room. This is the biggest bedroom, of course, with an ugly four-poster bed, heavy with carvings. In here more than anywhere the ghostly remains of her seem to linger. Part of me wishes that I'd come to see her as an adult. That I'd pinned her down, made her tell me where all that bad feeling came from. Far too late now.

Her dressing table is a huge thing—deep, wide, several drawers in columns on either side, a triptych mirror set on a box of yet more drawers. I think Mum should have the jewellery as well as the photos. Lipsticks and eye shadows and blushers in the top right-hand drawer. Belts in the next. Handkerchiefs, hair clips, chiffon scarves. In the bottom right drawer are boxes. I take them out, put them up where I can see them. Most are full of jewellery—dress pieces by the looks of it. One box, the biggest, is full of papers and photographs.

With a prickle of excitement, I sift through the contents. Letters from Clifford and Mary, holiday postcards from my mum and dad. Some photographs too, which I put to one side; and then I find the newspaper clippings. About Henry, of course. Local papers started the coverage. *Lady Calcott's Grandson Missing. Search for Local Boy Intensifies. Clothes found in Westridge woods did not belong to missing boy.* Then the nationals joined in. Abduction fears, speculation, a mysterious hobo spotted walking the A361 with a bundle that could have been a child. Boy matching the description seen lying in a car in Devizes. Police very concerned. I can't take my eyes from it. We never saw any of this, Beth and I. Nobody reads the paper when they're eight years old, and we weren't allowed to watch the news at the best of times.

I had no idea it was such a big story. I hadn't connected, until right now, the reporters milling at the gates with any kind of national infamy. Of course, I realise now why they were there. Children shouldn't just vanish without trace. That's the worst fear, worse even than finding the body, perhaps. Having no answers. Poor Meredith. She was his grandmother, after all. She was meant to be looking after him.

I pick up the pile of photographs and flick through them. Random family portraits and holiday shots for the most part—the sort of thing Mum was after. A small black and white photo of Meredith and Charles on their wedding day—my grandfather Charles, that is, who was killed in the Second World War. Charles wasn't in the armed forces, but he went up to London on business one week and a stray V2 found its way to the club where he was having lunch.

The best shots of their wedding day are on the piano in the drawing room, but in this shot Meredith is twisting to look back over her shoulder, away from Charles. In profile her face is young, painfully anxious. Her hair is very fair, eyes huge in her face. How did such a lovely girl, such a nervous young bride, ever become Meredith? The Meredith I remember, cold and hard as the marble shelves in the pantry.

Only one other photo arrests me. It's very old, battered around the edges. A young woman, perhaps in her early twenties, in a high-necked dress, hair pinned severely back, and on her lap a child in a lace dress, not more than six months old. A dark-haired baby, its face slightly smeared, ghostly, as if it wriggled just as the exposure was taken. The woman is Caroline. I turn it over, read the faint stamp on the back: Gilbert Beaufort & Son, New York City, and handwritten in ink, 1904.

But Caroline did not marry Henry Calcott, my great-grandfather, until 1905. Mary was seized by a genealogy fad a few years back—

traced the Calcott family lineage and sent us all a copy in our Christmas card that year. They married in 1905, and they lost a daughter before Meredith was born in 1911. I frown, turn the picture to the light and try to find any more clues within it. Caroline stares calmly back at me, her hand curled protectively around her baby. Where did this child go? How did it fall from our family tree? I slip the photo into my back pocket, begin to pick through the jewellery, hardly seeing it.

After dinner Eddie escapes from the table to watch TV. Beth and I sit among the dirty plates and bowls. She has eaten a little. Not enough, but a little. When she senses Eddie watching her, she tries harder. I lean back, feel something stiff in my back pocket.

'What's that?' Beth asks, as I pull out the photo of our great-grandmother. She hasn't spoken to me much since I asked her about Henry, and now her voice is stiff. But I know an olive branch when I see one.

'I found it up in Meredith's room—it's Caroline,' I say, passing it over.

Beth studies the young face, the pale eyes. 'Gosh, yes, so it is. I remember those eyes—even when she was ancient, they stayed that bright silver colour. Do you remember?'

'No, not really. What else do you remember about her?' I ask. Beth leans back from the table, pushes her plate away from her.

'Well, let me think. I remember the time she went mad at the summer party—when was it? I can't remember. Not long before she died. Do you remember it? With the fireworks and all the lanterns strung along the driveway to light the way up to the house?'

'God! I'd totally forgotten about that . . . I remember the fireworks, of course, and the food. But now you remind me I do remember Meredith wheeling Caroline inside, because she'd been shouting something about crows . . . what was it about? Can you remember?' I ask.

Beth shakes her head. 'It wasn't crows,' she says. And as she tells me, the scene slides into focus in my mind.

The Storton Manor summer party was an annual affair, usually held on the first Saturday in July. Most of our extended family, people I never see any more, attended, as well as everyone who was anyone in county society. A photographer from *Wiltshire Life* circulated, snapping the more attractive women, the more titled men. Horsey women with flat hair and big teeth, who wore garishly expensive evening gowns in shades of pink, peacock and emerald. The men wore black tie. My dad fidgeted with his collar, his cummerbund, not used to the stiff edges, the layers of fabric.

A whole crew of staff was brought in to cater the party. Wine waiters, cooks who took over the kitchen, waitresses to ferry the trays of hot canapés they produced, calm, implacable butlers who lingered indoors, politely directing people to the downstairs bathrooms and discouraging the curious from peering into the family rooms.

It was one of these workers that Caroline attacked, inexplicably. She had been positioned in her chair on the veranda, near enough to the terrace to hear the music, but still within the shelter of the house. People drifted over to pay their respects. Some of them Caroline acknowledged with a faraway nod of her head. Some she just ignored. And then a waitress went over with a smile, offered her something from a tray.

She was dark, I remember that. Very young, maybe only in her teens. Beth and I had noticed her earlier in the evening because we envied her hair. Her skin was a deep olive and she had the most luxurious black hair, hanging in a thick plait over her shoulder. She might have been Spanish, or Greek perhaps. When Caroline looked up and focused on the girl her eyes grew huge and her mouth dropped open. I was close enough to see that she was shaking.

'Magpie?' Caroline whispered, a ragged breath forming the word so loosely I thought I'd heard it wrong. But she said it again, more firmly. 'Magpie, is that you?' The waitress shook her head and smiled, but Caroline threw up her hands with a hoarse cry. Meredith looked over at her mother, drawing down her brows.

'Are you all right, Mother?' she asked, but Caroline ignored her, continuing to stare at the waitress with a look of pure terror on her face.

'It can't be you! You're dead! I know you are . . . I saw it.' she wailed.

'It's OK,' the girl said, backing away from the old woman. Beth and I watched, fascinated, as tears began to slide down Caroline's cheeks.

'Don't hurt me . . . please don't,' she croaked.

'What's going on here?' Meredith demanded, appearing next to her mother, glaring at the hapless waitress, who could only shake her head, at a loss. 'Mother, be quiet. What's the matter with you?'

'No! Magpie . . . how can it be? I was sure I didn't . . . I didn't mean for it . . .' she begged. Her face was aghast, haunted. The waitress moved away, apologising. 'Magpie . . . wait, Magpie!'

'That's quite enough! There's nobody here called Magpie! For goodness' sake, Mother, pull yourself together,' Meredith admonished her, sharply. 'We have guests,' she said pointedly, leaning forward to speak right into Caroline's ear. But Caroline just kept staring after the black-haired girl, frantically searching the crowd for her.

'Magpie! Magpie!' she shouted, still weeping. She grasped Meredith's hand. 'She's come back! Don't let her hurt me!'

'Right. That's enough. Clifford—come and help me.' Meredith beckoned sharply to her son and between them they manoeuvred Caroline in through the glass doors. Caroline tried to fight them, kept craning her head to look for the girl, kept saying the name, over and over again. *Magpie, Magpie.* It was the first and only time I remember feeling sorry for her, because she sounded so frightened, and so very, very sad.

'Magpie, that was it. Funny name,' I say, as Beth stops speaking. 'I wonder who she thought that girl was?'

'Who knows? She was obviously pretty confused by then. She was over a hundred, remember.'

'Do you think Meredith knew? She was so brusque with her about it!'

'No. I don't know,' Beth shrugs. 'Meredith was always brusque. You should go and have a root around in the attic if it's old pictures and papers you're after.'

'Oh?'

'That old trunk up there—when we came here for Caroline's funeral I remember Meredith putting everything she could find of hers up in that old red leather trunk.'

'I'll go and have a look later, then,' I say. 'You should come up, too.'

'No, no, I've never been that bothered about family history. You might find something interesting, though,' she smiles. I notice how keen she is for me to investigate this distant past rather than our more recent one. How keen she is to distract me.

Longing

1902–1903

AS SPRING BECAME SUMMER, Caroline grew more used to the presence of Joe and Magpie and the other Ponca women, who were Joe's mother White Cloud and widowed sister, Annie. She did not call upon them again, but Corin warned her that it was traditional for Indian women-folk to drop in on one another, and to exchange gifts, and she received several such visits before the Ponca seemed to lose interest.

Caroline dreaded seeing the trio approach the house, and she sat awkwardly through their visits, crippled by nerves, unsure of how to speak to them, or what to give in return for their gifts of honey, mittens and an elegantly carved wooden ladle. In the end she usually gave them money, which White Cloud accepted with a closed expression on her face. When their visits ceased she could not help but feel that she had failed in some way.

She did not get used to the heat, which increased with each passing day. By noon the sun was a flat, white disc that seemed to press like a giant hand on her head whenever she stepped outside. When the wind blew it seemed as hot as the blast from an oven. Caroline took to getting up with Corin, at first light, in order to have some time to exist, some time to live before the heat became unbearable.

Corin drove her back to Woodward to order fabric for curtains, and rugs, and a large mirror to hang above the mantel, and he paid for all of these things with a slightly bemused expression. Caroline chafed with impatience in the intervening weeks it took for the goods to come by train from Kansas City, and she clapped her hands with excitement when they arrived. Gradually, she dragged the furniture in the house into a better arrangement, and she swept and swept to keep the sand out on windy days, until her hands blistered and she gave up in frustration.

It was even harder for her to get used to the work required, on a daily basis, just to keep the household up and running. Each morning there was the water to bring in from the well, the stove to sweep out and re-lay, breakfast to make and then pots to clean, laundry to wash. She had also to tend to her wilting, stunted vegetable garden. Corin had presented her with the seeds proudly, having traded them with a neighbour: watermelons and marrows, peas and beans.

Then there was lunch to prepare, clothes to be mended and then dinner. Caroline was not a good cook. She scorched the eggs and forgot to salt the beef. Vegetables went soft, meat went tough and stringy. Her beans had hard, gritty centres. Her coffee was weak, and her bread refused to rise. Each time she apologised, Corin reassured her.

'You've not been brought up to do it, that's all. You'll get the hang of it,' he smiled, manfully swallowing whatever she put in front of him.

She did not complain of the work, not even to herself. Whenever she caught herself flagging, she pictured Bathilda, smiling in mocking triumph; or she thought of Corin, so full of admiration, calling her brave and beautiful, and how she would hate to prove him wrong. But on the occasions that her spirits did begin to sink, Corin seemed to sense it. He brushed the sand from her hair at the end of the day, singing softly as he pulled the bristles through in long, smooth strokes. Or, as she lay in the tub and rubbed her calluses, he would appear around the bath screen and work his fingers into the tight muscles of her neck and shoulders until she was all but drowsing in his hands; then he would gather her up and carry her, dripping wet, to the bed. In the consuming, blinding joy of his lovemaking, she forgot all other aches.

It was two months before a neighbour dropped by to visit. Caroline heard a shout at the front of the house, as she was glumly examining a sunken honey cake that she'd just taken from the oven.

'Hullo, Masseys!' the shout came again and, startled, Caroline realised it was a woman's voice. She opened the front door, stepping onto the porch with regal grace. Then she gaped. The woman was not only dressed as a man—in slacks, leather chaps and a flannel shirt tucked into a leather belt—but she was sitting astride a rangy bay horse.

'You're home!' the woman said, swinging her leg over the horse's back and dropping abruptly to the ground. 'I'm Evangeline Fosset. Pleased to meet you, and do call me Angie since everybody else does,' she continued, approaching with a smile. A long ponytail of orange hair swung behind her, and although her face was as tanned as Corin's it was also strong and handsome. Her blue eyes shone.

'I'm Caroline. Caroline Massey.'

'Figured you were.' The keen blue eyes swept over her. 'Well, Hutch told me you were a beauty, and Lord knows that man never lies,' she said. Caroline smiled, uncertainly, and said nothing. 'I'm your neighbour, by the way. My husband Jacob and I have a farm about seven miles that way.' Angie pointed to the southeast.

'Oh! Well . . . um . . . won't you come inside?' Caroline faltered.

She cut little squares from the outside edge of her honey cake, where it was indeed more or less like a cake, and served them on a large plate, with tea and water. Angie took a long draught.

'So, how are you settling in? You getting used to ranch life?'

'Yes, I think so. It's rather different . . . from New York.'

'I'll bet it is! I'll bet!' Angie chuckled, a low, throaty sound.

'I've never seen a woman ride astride before,' Caroline added, feeling rude to mention it, but too astonished not to.

'Oh, it's the only way to travel around here, believe me! Once you've tried it, you'll never go back to fiddling around sideways. When I heard Corin was bringing a gal back from the city, I thought, that poor thing! She can't know what she's getting into! Not that I don't love this place. It's my home, although Lord knows Mother Nature can be a bitch around here at times, pardon my language—but really, she can.'

Again, Angie looked at Caroline, and Caroline smiled nervously, at a loss. She poured her guest some more tea.

'The loneliness gets to some women. Not seeing anyone—well, any other women—for weeks at a time. Months, sometimes. It can get to a person, being in the house by yourself all day.'

'I've been . . . keeping very busy,' Caroline said hesitantly.

'As we all do, for sure,' Angie shrugged. 'Kids'll help, when they start coming. Nothing like a houseful of little ones to keep you distracted, I can tell you!' Caroline smiled, and blushed a little. She could hardly wait to have her first baby.

'Corin wants to have five,' she said, smiling shyly.

'Five! My good Lord, you've got your work cut out for you, girl!' Angie exclaimed with a wide grin. 'Well, when you fall, be sure to let me know. You'll want more help then, and advice from an old hand. Just remember where I am, and send word if you need anything.'

'That's really very kind of you,' Caroline said, secretly sure she would need no such help.

When Angie left, an hour or so later, she did not set off in the direction of her home, but towards the corrals where some of the men were at work. Caroline tended not to venture there herself, feeling too shy of the men. But seeing Angie lead her horse over to Hutch, who was overseeing the branding of new calves in the nearest corral, Caroline suddenly felt left out and left behind. She hurriedly removed her apron, grabbed her bonnet and walked quickly in the same direction.

Hutch was leaning on the fence as he talked to Angie. Wondering how to announce her presence, feeling high strung with nerves, Caroline heard her name spoken and stopped instead, stepping sideways so that the shadow of the bunkhouse engulfed her.

'She's none too friendly, is she?' Angie said. Hutch shrugged.

'She's trying her best, I reckon. Can't be easy, with her brought up so soft. I don't think she ever walked more than a quarter-mile at a time before, and I hear from Corin that she surely never cooked before.'

'Shame he didn't set up nearer town—she could have taught class or something. Made better use of those fine manners than she will out here,' Angie said, shaking her head. 'What do the boys make of her?'

'Hard to say, really. She doesn't come out of the house much; she doesn't ride out, sure as heck doesn't bring us lemonade on a hot day,' Hutch grinned. 'Feels the heat a bit strongly, I think.'

'What was Corin thinking, marrying such a green tenderfoot and leaving her out here by herself?'

'Well, I reckon he was thinking she was a fine-looking girl with a good head on her shoulders.'

'Hutchinson, one of these days I'll hear you speak a hard word about someone or something and I will fall clean off my horse. Good head on her shoulders in the city maybe, but out here? Why, she's even setting about the chores with corsets on so tight she can hardly breathe! Does that sound like good sense to you?' Angie exclaimed. Hutch said something that Caroline could not hear and then he turned towards Angie. Fearing she would be seen, Caroline skirted the side of the bunkhouse and walked swiftly back to the house, angry tears smarting her eyes.

Later, at dinner, Caroline watched her husband as he ate the bland food she had given him without complaint. He had come in late from rounding up two stray beeves, arriving at the table ravenous. She watched him and felt a surge of love that was at once wonderful and somehow desperate. He was her husband, and yet she felt as though she might lose him. She had not known that she was failing until she heard Angie Fosset's verdict on Corin's soft new wife. She swallowed her tears because she knew she would not be able to explain them to him.

'Evangeline Fosset came by here today,' she said.

'Oh? That's wonderful! She's such a good neighbour, and always so friendly. Didn't you find her so?' he asked.

'I heard her talking about me to Hutch,' Caroline said. 'She called me tenderfoot. What does it mean?'

'Tenderfoot?' Corin smiled briefly, but stopped when he saw his wife's tight expression, the glimmer in her eyes. 'Oh, now, sweetheart— I'm sure she didn't mean anything bad by it. Tenderfoot just means you're not used to the West, that's all. To the outdoor kind of life.'

'Well, how can I be used to it? Is it my fault, where I was born? Is that any reason to talk about a person, and use names? I'm trying to get along with life out here!'

'I know you are! I know.' Corin took Caroline's hands and squeezed them. 'Don't fret about it. You're doing great—'

'No, I'm not! I can't cook! I can't keep up with all the work! The plants aren't growing . . . the house is full of sand!' she cried.

'You're exaggerating—'

'Hutch knows I can't cook, so you must have told him! I heard him say it!'

Corin paused, and a little colour came into his cheeks. 'I'm sorry, sweetheart. I shouldn't have said it and I'm sorry that I did. But, my love, if you need some help just tell me, and we'll find you some help!' he assured her, stroking her face where tears were wetting the skin.

'I need help,' she said, miserably; and as she admitted it she felt the weight of it lighten on her shoulders. Corin smiled.

'Then you shall have it,' he told her gently, and he murmured soft words to her until she smiled back at him and stopped her crying.

So Magpie was recruited to come into the house and share the housework, and although Caroline was not sure that she wanted the Ponca girl beside her all day long, Magpie came with a ready smile and an ease of doing things that came from being born to it.

Happily, Caroline relinquished the cooking to her and watched as old bones and dried beans became thick, tasty soup; and bread dough rose willingly between damp cloths when left in the sun on the windowsill; and handfuls of herbs picked from the prairie made sauces savoury and delicious. The washing took less than half the time it had previously taken, and came up cleaner; and Magpie did the heavier jobs, like fetching water and carrying the wet linens out to the line so that Caroline, for the first time since her arrival, found time in the day to sit and read, or to start some sewing. Magpie worked with good cheer, and she taught Caroline tactfully, never making her feel inadequate, so it was impossible to resent the girl.

There was a dun-coloured mare called Clara, who had short, slender legs, a compact body, ribs like a barrel, neck a little scrawny. She was in her twilight years and had foaled a half-dozen times for Corin, foals that had grown into fine saddle horses, with just one exception—a colt who was never right between the ears, and could not be broken, and who snapped the bones of several fine broncobusters before his heart finally gave out with the strain of his own fury.

'Clara hung her head all sorrowful the day it happened,' Hutch told Caroline, as she stroked the mare's face tentatively. 'Now, Clara here wouldn't hurt a fly. You could get up on her back, give her a mighty wallop with a stick and she wouldn't even hold that against you.'

'Well! I don't think I'm going to do any of those things!' Caroline laughed.

'Well, sure you are—getting up on her back, that is,' Hutch smiled.

'Oh, no! I thought I was just learning how to put the saddle on today?' Caroline said, a note of alarm in her voice.

'That's right, and that's taken all of five minutes. And what's the point of a horse with a saddle on it if nobody gets up and sits in it?'

'Hutch, I . . . I don't know that I can . . .' she faltered.

'Only one way to find out,' he said gently. 'Come on now, Mrs Massey. There's no way the wife of a rancher can go around not knowing how to ride.' His smile was crooked and warm, and when he held out his hand she found it impossible not to take it.

'I'm not sure about this,' she said, nerves making her voice small.

'In about ten minutes' time, you're going to be wondering what all the fuss was about,' Hutch assured her.

He cupped his hand around her shin and boosted her into the sidesaddle, where she perched, her face pale, expecting at any moment to be cast back into the sand. He showed her how to take her weight in the left stirrup for balance.

'All right now. Comfy?' he asked.

'Not really,' she said, but she found the beginnings of a smile for him.

'Now, give her a little nudge with that heel, and say, "Get up, Clara!" '

'Get up, Clara! Please,' Caroline said, with as much conviction as she could manage, and then gave a little shriek as the mare moved forward.

'OK, now you're riding!' Hutch exclaimed. 'Just relax, she's not going anywhere. Relax, Mrs Massey!' he called, walking beside her with one hand loosely on the rein. 'You're doing a great job,' he told her.

For half an hour or so Hutch escorted her around the empty corral. Clara walked steadily, stopping and starting and turning left and right without the least hint of bad attitude or boredom. Caroline listened to what she was told, and tried to remember it all. Her back and legs were soon aching, and when she commented on this to Hutch, he gave the sidesaddle a disparaging look.

'Well, that's bound to happen when you do something for the first time. But, to be honest, Mrs Massey, you'd be a heck of a lot more comfortable riding astride than you are sat sideways like that . . .'

'Men ride astride. Ladies take the sidesaddle,' Caroline said firmly.

'You're the boss,' Hutch shrugged.

At that moment, Corin came cantering in off the pasture and pulled up at the corral fence.

'Well, now! Look at you! You look fantastic up there, sweetheart!' he beamed, pulling off his hat and rubbing his hot scalp.

'You want to go on over?' Hutch asked, and Caroline nodded. 'Well, go on then. You know how,' he urged her. Cautiously, Caroline turned the mare's head and persuaded her to walk over to the fence.

'That's fantastic, Caroline! I'm so happy to see you up on a horse at last!' Corin told her.

'I'll never be able to saddle her alone—it's so heavy!' Caroline smiled, anxiously.

'Well, that's as may be. But you can just ask any one of the boys and they'll help you with it. There's always somebody around.'

'Can I get down now, Hutch?' she asked.

'I think we've done enough for one day,' Hutch nodded. 'Couple more goes like today and we'll change your name to Annie Oakley!'

Feeling altogether less of a tenderfoot, Caroline listened as Hutch described the best way to dismount, but somehow her foot got snarled up in the stirrup, so she sprawled forward on the descent, landing on her front in the corral sand with the air whooshing out of her lungs.

'Damn! Are you all right, Caroline?' Corin swore, scrambling out of his own saddle.

'Well, that wasn't exactly how it was supposed to go,' Hutch remarked calmly, helping her to sit up.

Caroline climbed shakily to her feet. Her neck was jarred and one wrist badly overbent where it had taken the weight of her fall. She was covered in dust from hair to hemline. She glared at Corin, furious with herself and crippled with embarrassment.

'Why, you look every bit as fierce as Inferno, when you fire up like that!' Hutch said, admiringly.

'And every bit as red, too,' Corin grinned.

'Don't . . . laugh at me!' Caroline bit the words off, frustration and anger burning her up inside. She turned on her heel and stalked away towards the house, shaking with the shock of the fall, her legs jellied by the riding. She was more disappointed than she could bear—to have failed again, to have made herself a laughing stock.

'Ah, hell, Caroline! Come back! I wasn't laughing at you!' She heard Corin call out behind her, but she squared her shoulders the best she could and kept walking.

They saw out the end of 1902 and welcomed in 1903 with a party at the Fosset's farm, to which all of the nearby ranchers, their families and riders had been invited. There were fires burning about the yard, and meat smoking on the griddle, and a mass of people and horses all gathered into this oasis of light and life on the dead, dark plains. Corin's arm was shaken, his shoulder clapped, and they were soon engulfed by the friendly crowd of their neighbours. An accordion, a fiddle and a drum struck up in the barn, and the heat given off by dancing bodies warmed it, filled it with the animal smell of breath and sweat.

Angie's children had made a painted banner out of a ragged old sheet, and it hung above the gate, reading 'happy new yere!' Angie had two girls, aged twelve and eight, and a little boy aged four, who had his mother's red hair. Even as she danced and laughed and talked, Angie kept one eye on this perfect, happy little lad, and when she saw Caroline admiring him, she called him over.

'Kyle, this here is our good neighbour Caroline Massey. Now, what do you say to her?' she whispered to the boy, swinging him up onto her hip.

'Please' t' meetya, Missus Massey,' Kyle mumbled shyly.

'Oh, well I'm pleased to meet you too, Kyle Fosset,' Caroline smiled, taking the hand that wasn't in his mouth and shaking it gently. Angie set him down and he darted away, ungainly on his short chubby legs. 'Oh, Angie! He's just the most beautiful child!' she exclaimed.

'Yeah, he's my little angel all right, and don't he just know it!'

'And the girls too . . . you must be so proud of . . .' Caroline said, but she could not keep her voice steady and had to stop.

'Hey there, now—stop that! This here is a celebration of the new year, and all the wonderful new things it's going to bring. You hear me?' Angie said, significantly. 'It's going to happen for you. You just have to be patient. You hear?' Caroline nodded, and wished she could feel as sure as Angie sounded.

'Mrs Massey? Will you dance with a rough rider like myself?' Hutch asked, appearing beside them.

'Of course!' Caroline smiled, hastily blotting her eyes with her finger-tips. The band played one tune into the next without pause, and Hutch led her in a swaying dance that was almost a waltz, but not quite so.

'Is everything all right, Mrs Massey?' Hutch asked, seriously.

'Yes, of course! Why wouldn't it be?' she said, too brightly.

'No reason,' Hutch shrugged. 'Are you ready for another riding lesson, yet? You did great, that first time we tried it, but I never saw you go back for another try.'

'No, well . . . I'm not sure I'm the world's most naturally gifted horse-woman,' she said.

'There are some people that take naturally to it and others that don't. But I've seen those that once struggled get to grips with it in the end, with practice. But you have to be willing to get back on the horse, Mrs Massey. You do have to get back on the horse,' Hutch said, intensely, and she was no longer sure that he was talking about riding.

'I . . .' she started, but could not think what to say.

'You're going to be just fine,' Hutch said, his voice so low that she hardly heard him.

'Hutchinson, I'm cutting in! That's my wife you're cradling and she's by far the handsomest girl in the room,' Corin announced, taking Caroline's hands and spinning her into his embrace. His eyes were alight with happiness, cheeks flushed from sipping whisky and danc-ing, and he looked glorious, so glorious that Caroline laughed and threw her arms around his neck.

'Happy new year, my darling,' she whispered into his ear, letting her lips brush lightly against his neck, so that he held her tighter still.

In February snow fell deeply, lying in thick drifts and making the world too bright to look upon. Caroline stared at the featureless scene beyond the window in wonder, and stayed close to the stove as much as she could, her hands curled inside the fingerless mittens the Ponca had given her, which kept as much of her skin covered as possible while still allowing her to do the mending.

'Now you are glad to have them,' Magpie said, nodding at the thick mittens. 'When White Cloud gave them to you, I saw in your face you thought you would never need them!' she smiled.

'I should have paid her double,' Caroline agreed, at which Magpie frowned slightly.

'Will you tell a story, while I do this work?' Magpie requested. She was kneeling at the washtub, rubbing the stains out of Corin's work wear on a ridged wooden washboard.

'What kind of story?'

'It doesn't matter. A story of your people,' Magpie shrugged. So Caroline told her the story of Adam and Eve in the Garden of Eden, and of the treacherous serpent, the delicious apple, and the subsequent fall from grace. She put down her sewing as she reached the finale, describing their sudden shame at their nakedness. Magpie chuckled.

'This is a good story, Mrs Massey—a missionary man told this same story to my father once, and do you know what my father said?'

'What did he say?'

'He said this is typical of a white woman! An Indian woman would have picked up a stick and killed the snake and all would have been well in the garden!' she laughed. Caroline, stung for a moment by the implied criticism, soon found herself catching the girl's infectious laughter.

'That's probably about right,' she conceded, and they were still laughing when Corin came in, brushing the snow from his shoulders. He looked at Caroline, sitting by the stove with her sewing to one side, and at Magpie on her knees by the tub, and he frowned.

'Corin? What's wrong?' Caroline asked; but he shook his head and came over to the stove to warm himself.

Later, as they were eating supper, Corin spoke his mind.

'When I came home today, I . . . I didn't like what I saw,' he said.

'What do you mean?' she asked, her heart high in her throat.

'You just sitting there, keeping warm, when Maggie was working so hard—'

'It wasn't like that! I was working at the mending! Ask Magpie . . . I just stopped to tell her the story of Adam and Eve . . .' Caroline trailed off, unhappily.

'I know you're used to having servants, Caroline, but Maggie is no servant. I meant for her to help you in the house, of course, but she does not have time to do everything here. She has her own home to tend to, and soon she won't be able to do as much. You need to help her more, love,' he finished gently.

'She does help me! I mean, I help her too—we share the work! What do you mean, soon she won't be able to do as much? Why won't she?'

'Sweetheart, Maggie's pregnant. She and Joe are going to have a baby. Their first.' He looked away again, his face sombre, and in that expression Caroline read an accusation. Tears sprang to her eyes and she was choked with an emotion a little like ire, a little like grief, a little like guilt. An insufferable mixture of the three that burned in her gut and made a roaring noise in her ears. She clattered up from the table, ran to the bedroom and closed the door behind her.

In a light buggy the journey to Woodward could be made in a day, with a dawn start and a break to rest and water the horse at noon time. Most of the ranch hands and riders accompanied them on horseback, including Joe and Magpie. Caroline watched the Indian girl, who rode a wiry grey pony, and wondered how she could have failed to spot the telltale swell at her middle, the slight deference in her movements.

'Is it wise for Magpie to ride in her condition?' Caroline whispered to Corin.

'I said the very same thing to Joe,' Corin smiled. 'He just laughed at me.' He shrugged. 'I guess Ponca women are a bit tougher than white women.' A few tiny flecks of rain blew out of the sky. Caroline made no reply to Corin's remark, but she felt the sting of it. The implication she heard, whether he had intended it or not, was that she was weak and that she was failing here in the West, as a woman and as a wife.

They arrived in Woodward as dark was falling and took a room at the Central Hotel. Joe, Magpie and the ranch boys melted into the town: to the Equity, Midway, Shamrock and Cabinet saloons, to the brothel run by Dollie Kezer at the Dew Drop Inn, and to the houses of friends. Caroline's back ached from the long drive and she was tired, but she nevertheless urged Corin to lie with her, and she shut her eyes as she felt him spend himself within her, praying that whatever magic it was that made a child coalesce into being, it would happen this time.

Caroline's spirits had soared with the prospect of coming into town for the spring gala day, and for dancing. Woodward, which had seemed upon her arrival from New York to be a one-horse town indeed, now seemed a vibrant hub of life and activity.

The following day dawned fair and the streets thronged with people, cowboys and settlers alike. They formed two thick cords that ran for several blocks along the length of Main Street, undulating where a raised sidewalk ran in front of a shop. The air thronged with the smells and sounds of thousands of bodies and excited voices. Store fronts were strung with colourful bunting and had their doors flung wide open to welcome the opportunity for new custom that day. The crowd was entertained with a roping and riding contest, a mock buffalo hunt, and shooting competitions.

They ate barbecue, fresh peaches, ice cream and honey cakes, and the ladies drank iced tea while the men took beer. Caroline, who had been without ice or refrigeration since leaving New York, found the chilled drink in her mouth to be not far short of heavenly. They caught up with neighbours, and Corin swapped the current prices of wheat and beeves with fellow ranchers; and they ran into Angie and Jacob Fosset, Angie clad in a lurid lilac gown with too much colour on her face. When Corin complimented her, she laughed and exclaimed, 'Oh, I look like a showgirl, I know, but we gals don't get to dress up often enough! And I need a little help to look festive, Lord knows—we can't all be pretty as paint like your wife here, Corin Massey!'

'Well,' Corin told her, 'you look just fine to me, Angie Fosset.' While the men talked, Angie took Caroline to one side.

'Any news, honey?' she asked in a low tone, in answer to which Caroline could only grip her lower lip in her teeth and shake her head. 'Well, I've thought of some things you could try . . .' Angie told her.

In the evening the band played waltzes and polkas, as well as some square dances. Caroline danced with the grace of her upbringing, even though Corin's steps were marred by beer. With buildings all around her, and people, Caroline felt better than she had in months. For a while, the smile she wore was not a brave one, but a genuine one.

But later, as she stood talking to a circle of Woodward wives, Caroline saw Corin across the street, bending down in front of Magpie and putting his hands on her midriff. He seemed to cradle the bulge in her abdomen gently, almost reverently, and while Magpie looked embarrassed she also looked pleased. Caroline caught her breath and blood flooded her cheeks. Corin was in his cups, she knew, but this behaviour was too much. His face was turned away, his gaze was unfocused. Waiting, she realised, waiting for the child to move inside the Ponca girl. And as she witnessed this act of intimacy, she suddenly thought she saw something possessive in her husband's touch—something altogether too interested.

4

It's cold as we walk down towards the woods on the longest night of the year. All three of us. Eddie pestered Beth into coming, and in the end she seemed almost curious. In the clear dark our torch beams stagger haphazardly. The moon is bright and the flowing clouds make it seem to sail across the sky. A vixen shrieks as we get near the trees.

'What was that?' Eddie gasps.

'Werewolf,' I say, matter-of-fact.

'Ha, ha. Anyway, it's not a full moon.'

'All right, then, it was a fox. You're no fun any more, Edderino.'

I am in high spirits. We can hear music now, and raised voices, laughter; and now the glow of the bonfire shines at us between the trees. Beth hangs back. I pull a flat bottle of whisky from my coat pocket, fight to open it with gloved hands.

'Swig. Go on. It'll warm you up,' I tell her, and for once she doesn't argue. She takes a long pull.

'Can I have some?' asks Eddie.

'Not on your life,' Beth replies, as she wipes her chin and coughs. She sounds so real, so there, so like Beth that I grin.

I take a drink myself, feel the fire in my throat, and then we move. There's a moment of nerves as we step into the firelight. The same as before, of being unsure of our welcome. But then Patrick finds us and introduces us to a myriad people. Sarah and Kip—long hair shining in the firelight, Denise—a tiny woman with ink-black hair, Smurf—a huge man, hands like shovels, a gentle smile. Their clothes and hair are bright. They look like butterflies against the winter ground. There's a sound system in the back of a pick-up and vehicles parked all the way up the lane. Children too, dodging in and out of the crowd. Eddie vanishes and I see him a little while later with Harry, threading thick wads of dead leaves onto long twigs and thrusting them into the fire.

'Who's that with Eddie?' Beth asks, a note of alarm in her voice.

'That's Harry. I've met him, don't worry. He's a little bit on the slow side, you could say. Dinny says he's always got on well with children. He seems totally harmless to me,' I tell her.

'Oh,' Beth says, not quite convinced. I see Honey, moving across the clearing, preceded by her enormous bump. Her face is alive this evening; she's smiling, and she is lovely. I feel a small prickle of despair.

'That's Honey, there. The blonde,' I say to Beth. Watching expressions veer wildly across Honey's face, I am sure of it—I have taught girls older than her: she is too young to be having that baby. I feel something close to anger, but I can't tell who or what it's aimed at.

Then Dinny appears beside Beth, smiling his guarded smile.

'Glad you came down to join in, Beth, Erica,' he says.

'Yes, well, thank you very much for having us,' Beth replies, looking around at the party and nodding as if we are at some society do.

'You've got lucky with the weather tonight, anyway. It's been foul,' I say. Dinny gives me an amused look.

'I don't believe in foul weather—it's all just weather,' he says.

'No bad weather, only the wrong clothes?' I ask.

'Exactly! Have you tried my punch? It has a certain . . . punch. Don't take any naked flames near it, whatever you do,' he smiles.

'I tend to avoid punch,' I say. 'There was an incident with punch, I'm told. Although, they might be lying because I sure as hell don't remember anything about it.'

'Beth, then? Can I tempt you?' Beth nods, lets herself be led away. She still looks slightly dazed, almost bewildered to be here. Dinny's hand is on her elbow, guiding her. For a moment I am left alone as he pulls her away, and some emotion scuttles through me. A familiar old emotion, to be left behind by Beth and Dinny. I give myself a shake, find faces that I know and foist myself upon them.

Beth is cooking something for lunch that's filling the ground floor with garlic-scented steam. The windows cloud with it and rain cloaks the outside world so that the house feels like an island. Eddie's gone off into the woods with Harry, and strains of Sibelius's fifth come creeping up the stairs to the attic. Beth's favourite. I take it as a good sign that she has looked it out in Meredith's music collection, and is preparing food that she might even eat. I head for the attic stairs.

On such a wet day it is dark up here, the far reaches of the space hung in shadow. The tiny dormer windows are few and far between and they are crusted up with watermarks and algae.

The leather of the old red trunk is so dry and brittle that it feels sandy when I touch it. I strain my eyes to see inside, dragging it around to face the nearest window. Inside are wads of papers, boxes, a small, dilapidated valise, a few mystery objects wrapped in yellowed newspaper pages, a leather writing case. It doesn't look much, if this is all of Caroline's personal things. Not much for a hundred years of life.

I unwrap a few of the paper parcels. There's a gold face-powder compact and matching lipstick, a silver dressing-table set, the mirror cracked across its face, a curious bone ring, satin smooth, with a silver bell hanging from it that tinkles, startling me in the stillness. I wonder what sets these objects apart, what stopped Meredith selling them off like she did with so many of the other precious things. After a while, I notice it. They are all engraved, CC. I turn the bone ring over in my fingers, looking for the same mark. The script, when I find it on the rim of the silver bell, is small and almost worn away. *For A Fine Son*, it reads.

I rewrap these treasures and put them back in the trunk. The valise is empty, the pink silk lining now in tatters. I take out the writing case instead. Inside are her letters, many still in their envelopes. I flick through, realise that most have been addressed in the same hand—a small, slanting script in black ink. I open one carefully and skip straight to the end. Most of these letters are from Meredith and have a Surrey postmark.

My heart gives a strange little twist. I turn back to the first page of the one I am holding, and read.

April 28, 1931
Dear Mother,

I hope this letter finds you well, and less troubled by your rheumatism than of late? You will be pleased to hear that I am settling in well here, and am gradually becoming accustomed to running my own household—even though I do of course miss you, and Storton. Charles is rather relaxed about the arrangements—his only stipulation is that breakfast be served at eight and dinner at nine! An easy man to please, and I have had the freedom to find my own way of doing things.

It does seem rather unusual to be alone in the house all day while Charles is at his offices. There is a singular quiet in the afternoons here—I often look to my left to remark upon something to you, only to find the room empty! I suppose I ought to make the most of the peace and quiet before it is carried away by the patter of little feet . . . I find myself entirely pulled between two emotions: the thrill of anticipating the birth of your first grandchild, and utter dread of the same event! Were you afraid, when you were first expecting?

I do hope you will come and visit, Mother—I should dearly love to have your advice. The house is smaller than you are used to, but it is nevertheless quite comfortable. Write and let me know if you will come, and when you might like to. In anticipation of our happy event, Charles has sworn me off driving the motor car, but I can arrange for our man Hepworth to collect you from the station at any time—it is a short drive, not at all arduous. Do come.

With much affection, Meredith

In 1931 Meredith would have been just twenty years old. Twenty years old, married and expecting a baby that she must have lost, because my mother was not born for some time after that. I read the letter again, try to re-imagine Caroline as a mother somebody loved, as somebody Meredith clearly missed. The letter makes me sad, and I have to read it again to work out why. It is such a lonely letter. From far below, I hear Beth calling me for lunch. I slip the letter back into the case and tuck it beneath my arm before going down to her.

The rain doesn't stop until Tuesday afternoon, and I am itching to get outside. I envy Eddie, who comes back as it gets dark, hair in damp curls and mud up to the knees of his jeans. At what age do you start to notice the cold and the wet and the mud? About the same time you stop moving everywhere at a run, I suppose.

In the nursery the gap where the linen press stood yawns at me from the wall. I cross to the piles of cloth I evicted from it, start to go through them, putting cot sheets, lacy sleep-sacks, tiny pillowcases and a christening gown to one side. I have no idea if any of it will be any use to Honey and her baby, when it comes. But it is good, heavy linen, smooth to the touch. I catch sight of those pillowcases again, with the yellow stitched flowers. I make a mental note to look the flowers up, identify them, in case that will tell me why they tug at my subconscious so.

'Where are you going with that lot?' Beth asks, as I lug it downstairs.

'I'm taking it over to Honey. It's all baby stuff—I thought she could use it.' Beth frowns.

'What's wrong?' I ask.

'Erica, why are you trying so hard to be friends with them again?'

'Why not? Anyway, I'm not trying that hard. They are our neighbours. You seemed happy to chat to Dinny at the party the other night.'

'Well, it would have been rude not to talk to him. But I . . . I don't think we have much in common any more. In fact I'm not sure we ever knew him as well as we thought we did. And I don't see what purpose it serves, trying to pretend everything is how it was before.'

'Of course we knew him! What's that supposed to mean? And why shouldn't things be how they were before, Beth?' I ask. She seals her lips, looks away from me. 'If something happened between the two of you that I don't know about . . .'

'Nothing happened that you don't know about!'

'Well, I'm not so sure,' I say. 'Besides, just because you don't want to be friends with him any more, doesn't mean I shouldn't be,' I mutter, dragging the bag to the door and pulling on my coat.

'Erica, wait!' Beth comes across the hall to me. 'We can't go back to the way things were. Too much has happened. It's far better to just . . . move on. Leave the past alone,' she says, her eyes sliding away from mine.

'It sounds to me,' I say, steadily, 'that you don't want him any more, but you don't want me to have him either.'

'Have him? What is that supposed to mean?' she says sharply. I feel colour flare in my cheeks and I say nothing. Beth draws in a deep, uneven breath. 'It's hard enough being back here as it is, Erica, without you acting like an eight-year-old again. Can't you just stay away, for once? We're supposed to be spending time here together. Now Eddie is off with that Harry all day long, and you'd rather chase after Dinny than . . . I don't have to stay, you know. I could take Eddie and go back to Esher for Christmas . . .'

'Well, that's a great idea, Beth. Just the kind of unpredictable behaviour that Maxwell is always looking out for!' I regret this as soon as I say it. Beth recoils from me. 'I'm sorry,' I say quickly.

'How can you say things like that to me?' she asks softly, her eyes growing bright, blurred. She turns and walks away.

Outside, I take a deep breath. I drop the bag of linens, suddenly unsure of myself, and sit down on a bench at the edge of the lawn. Perhaps I will take it down later.

I phone my mum in the afternoon, to check that all is well, and ask what time they plan to arrive.

'How is it going there? How's Beth?' Mum asks, in a casual tone that I recognise. I pause, listen for sounds of my sister close by.

'She's OK, I think. A little bit up and down, I suppose.'

'I'm looking forward to seeing you both—and Eddie of course. Is he having fun there?'

'Are you kidding? He loves it! We hardly see him—he's out playing in the woods all day. Mum—could you do me a favour?'

'Yes, of course, what is it?'

'Could you possibly dig out your copy of that family tree Mary drew up? And bring it along?'

'Yes, I think so. If I can find it. What do you want it for?'

'I just want to check something. Did you ever hear of Caroline having a baby before she was married to Lord Calcott?'

'No, I never did. I would doubt it very much—she was very young when she married him. What on earth makes you ask that?'

'It's just this photo I found—I'll show you when you get here.'

'Well, all right then. But any questions about family history ought to be directed at Mary. She did all that research the other year, after all . . .'

'I suppose so. Well, I'd better crack on here—I'll see you very soon.'

For bedtime reading, I prop Caroline's writing case on my knees and read a few more of Meredith's letters from Surrey. Tucked into one of the pockets of the case, I find an envelope addressed in quite a different hand. The paper inside is like dried leaves, and I unfold it with consummate care. Just one page, with one paragraph of script. Far larger lettering than Meredith's, written with emphatic pen pressure, as if in some urgency. The date given is the fifteenth of March, 1905.

> *Caroline,*
>
> *I received your letter this morning and with no slight concern. Your recent marriage and delicate condition are matters to be much celebrated, and no one could be more satisfied than I to see you settled and joined to a man such as Lord Calcott, who is well positioned to give you everything you require for a happy life.*
>
> *To put your current position in unnecessary jeopardy would be foolhardy in the extreme. Whatever it is that you feel you must confess, may I strongly urge you that all matters arising from your previous existence in America should by every means possible remain in America. No purpose can be served by revisiting such matters now. Be grateful for the new start you have been given, and let that be the last word upon it between us. Should you bring embarrassment or infamy of any kind upon yourself or our family, I should have no other choice but to sever all ties with you, however it would grieve me.*
>
> *Your Aunt, B*

The scoring beneath the phrase *remain in America* has all but torn the paper. A heavy, violent strike. In the quiet after I read these ringing words, I see all the secrets within this house lying in drifts as deep as the dust and shadows in the corners of the room.

On Christmas Eve our parents arrive, and their familiar car pulling into the driveway seems a small miracle of some kind. Proof of an outside world. I meant to keep Eddie in this morning but he is up before us and gone.

'We've lost your grandson, I fear,' I say, as I take bags from the back of the car. Perhaps not the cleverest thing I could say. Mum hesitates.

'What's happened to Eddie?' she asks.

'He's got a friend—Harry. He camps here, just like . . . Well. They're always off in the woods. We hardly see him these days,' Beth says, and we can hear that it bothers her. Just a little.

'Camping? You don't mean . . . ?'

'Dinny's here. And his cousin, Patrick, and some others,' I say casually. But I can't help smiling.

'Dinny? You're kidding?' Mum says.

'Well, well!' Dad adds.

'Hmm, well, now you know how we used to feel, I suppose,' Mum says to Beth, kissing her on the cheek as she goes indoors. Beth and I share a look. This hadn't ever occurred to us.

Beth looks like our mother. She always has, but it's getting more pronounced the older she gets. They both have Meredith's willowy figure, the delicate bones of her face, long artistic hands. Meredith cut her hair short and set it, but Mum has always left hers natural, and Beth's is long, unchecked. And they have an air about them, which I lack. Grace, I suppose it is. I take more after our father. Shorter, broader, clumsier too. Dad and I stub our toes. We knock our wineglasses over, bruise ourselves on coffee table edges, chair legs, worktops. I have a huge affection for this trait, since it comes from him.

We drink coffee and admire the Christmas tree that came yesterday and now towers up into the stairwell.

'Bit extravagant, isn't it, love?' Dad asks Beth.

'The house needed cheering up. For Eddie,' she says.

'Ah well, yes, fair enough,' Dad concedes. He's wearing a red jumper, grey hair standing up in tufts just like Eddie's does, and the hot coffee flushing his cheeks pink. He looks jovial, kind—just as he is.

There's a thump on the door, which I open to find Eddie and Harry on the step, out of breath, as ever, and damp.

'Hi, Rick! I came to say hello to Grandma and Grandpa. And I told Harry he could come and see the tree. That's OK, isn't it?'

'Of course it's OK.'

Eddie is hugged, kissed, questioned. Dad proffers a hand to Harry for him to shake, but Harry just looks at it, bemused. He drifts over to the tree instead, crouches down to gaze up into it, as if trying to see it at its biggest, its most imposing. Dad shoots me a quizzical look and I mouth, *I'll tell you later*. We decide to keep Eddie, since lunch is not far off, and send Harry home with a box of Beth's mince pies, which he dips into even as he shambles off across the lawn.

'He seems a funny old thing,' Mum says mildly.

'He's wicked. He knows all the best places to go in the woods—where to find mushrooms and badgers' nests,' Eddie defends his friend.

'Badgers have setts, not nests; and I hope you haven't been playing with fungi—that's really very dangerous!' Mum says.

I see Eddie bridle. 'Harry knows which ones you can eat,' he mutters, defensively.

'I'm sure he does. It's fine, Mum,' I say, to quieten her. 'Old people don't know that wicked means good,' I whisper to Eddie. He rolls his eyes, escapes up the stairs to get changed.

Later on, I show Mum the photographs I've found for her. She identifies the people I didn't recognise—more distant relatives. I show her the one of Caroline, taken in New York with the baby cradled in her left arm. Mum frowns as she scrutinises it.

'Well, that's definitely Caroline—such pale eyes! She was striking, wasn't she?'

'But what was she doing in New York? And whose baby is it, if she only married Lord Calcott in 1904? Do you think they had one before they got married?'

'What do you mean? She was from New York!'

'Caroline was American? How can nobody have told me that before?'

'Well, how can you not have realised? With that accent of hers . . .'

'Mum, I was five years old. How would I have noticed her accent? And she was ancient by then. She hardly spoke at all.'

'True, I suppose,' Mum nods.

'Well, that explains why she was in New York in 1904. So, who's the baby?' I press. Mum takes a deep breath, inflates her cheeks.

'No idea,' she says. 'There's no way she could have had a child with Henry before they wed. She only met him late in 1904, when she came over to London. They married in 1905, soon after they met.'

'Well, was she married before? Did she bring the baby over with her?'

'No, I don't think so. You really would be better off asking Mary. As far as I know, Caroline came over from New York, a rich heiress, married a titled man at quite some speed, and that was that.'

I nod, oddly disappointed.

'Perhaps it was a friend's baby. Perhaps she was its godmother. Who knows?' Mum says.

'Could have been,' I agree. I take the picture back. My eyes seek out Caroline's left hand, her ring finger, but it's hidden in the folds of the child's dress. 'Do you mind if I keep this one? Just for a while?' I ask.

'Of course not, love.'

'I've . . . been reading some of Caroline's letters.' I am strangely reluctant to confess this. Like reading somebody's diary, even after they're dead. 'Have you got that family tree? There was a letter from an Aunt B.'

'Here you are. Caroline's side of things is a bit sketchy, I'm afraid. I think Mary was more interested in the Calcott line—and all of Caroline's family records would have been in America, of course.'

There is nothing on Caroline's side, except the names of her parents. No aunts or uncles, a very small twig to one side before Caroline joined the main tree in 1905. Caroline Fitzpatrick, as she was then.

'In this letter, her aunt—Aunt B—says that whatever happened in America should stay in America, and she shouldn't do anything to mess up her marriage to Lord Calcott. Do you know anything about that?' I ask. Mum shakes her head.

'No. Nothing at all, I fear.'

'What if she had a baby before she came over here and got married?'

'Well, for one thing she wouldn't have managed to get married if she had! Well-brought up girls did not just have babies out of wedlock back then. It would have been unthinkable.'

'But what if she did get married to someone else before Lord Calcott? I found something up in the loft—in the trunk where Meredith put all of Caroline's stuff—and it says *To a Fine Son* on it,' I say.

'It was probably Clifford's. What kind of something?'

'I don't know—it's some kind of bell. I'll fetch it later and show you.'

We have drifted into the drawing room. Mum picks up each photo from the piano and studies it at length. She runs her thumb over the glass of Charles and Meredith's wedding portrait. A futile little caress.

'Do you miss her?' I ask. Normally a stupid question when somebody's mother dies. But Meredith was different.

'Of course. Yes, I do. It would be hard not to miss somebody who knew how to fill a room quite the way my mother did.' Mum smiles.

'Why was she like that? I mean, why was she so . . . angry?'

'Caroline was cruel to her,' Mum shrugs. 'Not physically, or even verbally . . . perhaps not even deliberately; but who can say what damage is done when a child grows up unloved?'

'I can't imagine. I can't imagine how a mother could fail to love her child. But, how was she cruel to her?'

'Just in a thousand and one little ways,' Mum sighs, thinks for a moment. 'For example, Caroline never brought her a present. Not once. Not on birthdays or at Christmas, even when Meredith was small. Not on her wedding day, not when I was born. Nothing at all.

Can you imagine how something like that might . . . chip away at you?'

'But if she'd never had a present, perhaps she didn't expect one?'

'Every child knows about birthday presents, Erica—you've only to read a storybook to learn about them. And the staff used to get her little things when she was small—Mother told me how much they meant to her. A rabbit—I remember her mentioning that. One year, the house-keeper gave her a pet rabbit.'

'That's . . . really sad,' I say. 'Didn't Caroline believe in presents?'

'I just don't think she was aware of the date, most of the time. I honestly don't think she knew when Meredith's birthday was. It was as though she hadn't given birth to her at all.'

'But if she was so awful, why was Meredith so devoted to her? Why did she move back here with you and Clifford when your father died?'

'Well, difficult or not, Caroline was her mother. Meredith loved her, and she was always trying to . . . prove herself to her.'

'But why didn't Caroline love Meredith? I don't understand.'

'Neither do I. Your great-grandmother was a very strange woman. Very distant. Sometimes I would go and sit next to her and try to talk to her, but I soon realised she wasn't listening to a word I said. She would just stare right through you.'

'It's amazing how normal you are. What a great mother you are.'

'Thank you, Erica. Your father helped, of course. My knight in shining armour! If I'd moved back here after my degree, if I'd stayed here long enough to resent them both . . . who knows?'

'Perhaps not everyone is cut out for parenthood. I can't imagine Meredith was the cuddliest . . .'

'No, but she was a good mother, for the most part. Strict, of course. But she wasn't as . . . sharp when we were small, as she was after we'd been living back here for a few years. As Caroline grew frail, she needed a lot of looking after. I think Mother resented that. She did her best for us, but I don't think she got over losing my father, or the disappointment of having life begin and end here. But we turned out OK, didn't we? Clifford and I?' she asks me, her face sad. I cross the room, hug her.

'More than OK.'

After dinner we put all our presents under the tree. Eddie looks like a miniature gent in his navy-blue monogrammed dressing gown, stripy pyjamas and red felt slippers. He checks the gift tags and positions each parcel carefully. We drink brandy, listen to carols. Outside the rain is lashing at the house in waves. It makes me shiver.

Christmas morning passes in a rushed, comforting haze of food preparation, champagne and piles of torn shiny paper. Dad helps Eddie unpack his new games console, and they experiment with it on the inadequate television in the study while we women occupy the kitchen. The turkey barely fits into the Rayburn. We have to poke its legs in, and the tips of them blacken where they touch the sides.

'Never mind. Everyone prefers breast, anyway,' Mum says to Beth. It will take hours to roast and, pleading a slight headache, Beth retires to lie down. She shoots us a mute, angry glance as she goes. She knows we will talk about her now.

Mum and I slide ourselves onto the kitchen benches, link hands across the table, our conversation hanging awkwardly around the urge to talk about Beth. I break the silence.

'I found a load of newspaper clippings in with the photos in one of Meredith's drawers. About Henry,' I add, unnecessarily.

Mum sighs. 'Poor Henry,' she says.

'I know. I've been thinking about him a lot. About what happened—'

'What do you mean, about what happened?' Mum asks sharply.

'Just, that he vanished. His disappearance,' I say. 'Why? What do you think happened to him?'

'I don't know! Of course I don't know. I thought, for a while that . . . that perhaps you girls knew more than you were saying . . .'

'You think we had something to do with it?'

'Of course not! I thought that, maybe, you were protecting somebody.'

'You mean Dinny.' Something flares inside me.

'Yes, all right then, Dinny. He had a temper, your young hero. But, Erica, Henry vanished! He was taken, I'm sure of it. If anything had happened to him here on the estate, then the police would have found some evidence of it. He was taken away, and that's all there is to it,' she finishes, calm again. 'It was a terrible, terrible thing, but nobody is to blame except the person who took him. There are just a few very dangerous people out there, and Henry was unlucky enough to meet one of them.'

'I suppose he was,' I say. None of this rings true to me. Eddie by the pond, throwing a stone, and that watery ache in my knees.

'Let's not talk about it today. How has Beth been?'

'Not great. A bit better now. We went to a party at the camp the other night, and she chatted to Dinny a bit, and she seemed to pick up a little. And now that you and Dad are here too . . .'

'You went to a party with Dinny?' Mum sounds incredulous.

'Yes. So what?'

'Well,' she shrugs, 'it just seems so odd, after all these years. Taking up with him again . . .'

'We're not taking up with him. But we are neighbours now. For the time being, anyway. He's . . . well. He's not really much different, and neither am I, so . . .' For a terrifying moment, I think I will blush.

'He was so in love with Beth, you know. Back when they were twelve,' Mum says, smiling. 'They say you never forget your first love.'

I down the last of my champagne, get up to fetch the bottle, as tears threaten. 'Come on. These spuds won't peel themselves!' I smile.

Losing

1903–1904

THE SUMMER SWELLED and Magpie's body ripened in time with it, seeming to expand by the day as her baby grew. Caroline watched her. She watched, and she wondered, her heart full of suspicions that she went from discrediting to confirming to herself twenty times a day. And more than anything, she was jealous. She felt sick and weak and full of something dark and bitter. And if anything could have driven her from the house and out into the summer sun, it was this.

The wooden house just could not keep out the heat as the thick brownstone walls of New York had done. And, Caroline reflected, when it was hot in New York, it was never as hot as this, and she had never before had to be active in such temperatures. But Hutch's exhortation to her at new year were at work upon Caroline's mind; so one day, which dawned slightly overcast and a little cooler than usual, she decided to get out of the house.

She packed a basket with a ripe melon, some biscuits and a bottle of tonic water, tied the ribbon of her sun bonnet in a bow beneath her chin, and set off for the nearest neighbouring farm, which belonged to an Irish family called Moore. It was six miles to the northwest and Caroline had overheard Corin say that a man might easily walk four miles in an hour. Setting off early, she thought, she would be there in time to take coffee and maybe lunch, and then back again in time to help cook dinner. She told Magpie where she was going, and squared her shoulders when the Ponca girl gave her an incredulous stare.

She walked for an hour, at first admiring the flowers on the horsemint and wild verbena and gathering a posy to present to the Moores, but she was soon slick with sweat in spite of the clouds. Her skirts swung ponderously around her legs, tripping her. She battled slowly up a long rise, certain that from the crest of it she would see the neighbouring farm. She could not. Breathing hard, she saw the landscape roll away into the distance, as far as the eye could see. Putting the basket down, she turned in a slow circle, staring into the unbroken horizon. A hot wind blew, making waves in the long grass that looked, in the distance, like a green and gold ocean.

'There's nothing here,' Caroline murmured to herself. Something rose up in her then, something like panic, or anger. 'There's nothing here!' she shouted, as loudly as she could. Her throat felt raw and dry. She sank onto the prairie and lay back to rest. An endless sky above her, and endless land all around. If she did not rise again, she thought, if she stayed where she was, only wild dogs and buzzards would ever find her. It was an irresistible thought, a terrifying one.

Walking back at last, having never reached the Moores' place, Caroline nearly missed the ranch. She had veered to the north by a mile or more and only happened by chance to see smoke rising from the chuck hut to her right, where a silent Louisiana Negro called Rook would be cooking dinner for the ranch hands. Turning south, Caroline's legs wobbled with exhaustion. Behind her she could feel the vastness of the prairie spreading out, watching, and beyond the ranch the grasslands stretched away to every point on the compass. The corrals, fences, wheat and sorghum fields her husband had mapped onto the land were pitifully small. When she finally reached the house she shut the door and burst into tears.

That night Caroline lay awake, in spite of her exhaustion. The clouds cleared as night fell, and the moon rose luminously full. It was not this that kept her awake, but the new understanding of how vast and empty the land she now lived upon truly was. She felt swallowed up by it: tiny, invisible. The air inside the bedroom was smothering, thick with the lassitude of summer. Beside her, Corin snored softly, his face pressed into the pillow. Caroline rose, took a spare blanket and went outside.

She spread the blanket among the watermelons and lay down upon it. Something scuttled away into the foliage close to her face, and she shuddered. There were no other sounds, though her ears strained to pick up any movement from the bunkhouse, any sign of an approaching ranch hand. Then she pulled her nightdress up until it covered only her breasts, leaving the lower portion of her body bare to the night sky. Her heart beat fast in her chest. Stars scattered the sky. She began to count them, lost her place and started again, and again. Then the door banged behind her and she heard uneven steps, and Corin grabbed her beneath her arms and pulled her into his lap.

'What is it? What's wrong?' Caroline gasped. Painted in greys and blacks, Corin's face was pinched with fear. Seeing her awake and well, Corin let her go, exhaling heavily, and put his face into his hands.

'What are you doing out here?' he mumbled. 'Are you all right?'

'I'm . . . fine. I just . . . it was so hot in the bedroom . . .' Caroline hurriedly pulled her nightdress down.

'But it's just as hot out here! What are you doing—why were you naked?' he demanded. Alarmed, Caroline saw that he was shaking.

'I was moonbathing . . . Angie told me it might help,' Caroline said quietly. She had sneered inwardly at such superstition when their neighbour mentioned it, but now it seemed she would try anything.

'Help with what? Love, you're not making sense!'

'Help a woman to get pregnant. To lie with the moon shining on her body,' Caroline said, shamefacedly.

'And you believed her?'

'No, not really. Not really. It's just . . . why aren't I pregnant yet, Corin? It's been over a year!' she cried. 'I don't understand.'

'I don't understand it either,' Corin sighed. 'But I'm sure these things happen when they're good and ready, that's all. A year is not that long! You're young and . . . it's been a big upheaval for you, moving out here to be with me. It will happen love, please try not to worry.' He tipped her chin up with his fingertips. 'Come back inside now.'

'Corin . . . why were you so afraid just now?' Caroline asked, as she rose stiffly to her feet. 'What did you think had happened?'

'There was a woman, on the other side of Woodward a couple of years ago . . . never mind. I just thought something might have happened to you. But you're fine, and it's nothing to worry about . . .'

'Tell me, please,' she pressed. 'What happened to the woman?'

'Well, apparently she felt the heat badly, like you do too, and she was also pining for her home back in France, and she took to sleeping out in the yard to keep cool, but one night . . . one night she . . .' His fingers grasped the night air, searching for a way to tell her without telling her.

'She what?'

'She cut her own throat,' he said, in a rush. 'Three children waiting for her indoors and all.'

'And you thought I'd . . . done that to myself?' she breathed.

'No! No, love, no. I was just worried for you, that's all.' He ushered her back into the bedroom and said he would wait up until she slept, but soon his soft snores began again, and still Caroline's eyes stayed fixed upon the ceiling.

She wondered. She wondered where Corin went all day. It had never occurred to her to think about this before. He always gave an account of his day over the supper table, but how could she know that he was telling it true? And Corin could, of course, send Joe anywhere if he wanted him out of the way. And Magpie had often already left, by an hour or so, before Corin came in for the evening. There were plenty of times when she had no idea where either of them might be. And the way he had touched Magpie at the Woodward gala. These were Caroline's thoughts as she lay awake, and as she sat at the end of each day, waiting for Corin's return. When Caroline saw her husband, her fears vanished. When she was alone, they flourished like weeds.

Before dawn the next day, as Corin stirred and began to wake, Caroline went on soft feet to the kitchen. She poured him a cup of cold tea and cut two thick slices of bread from yesterday's loaf, which she spread with honey. She presented him with these offerings as he sat up, blinking in the charcoal glow of near-day.

'Breakfast in bed. I always used to have breakfast in bed on Saturdays,' she told him, smiling.

'Well, thank you. How grand I feel!' Corin cupped her face in the palm of his hand, and took a long draught of the tea.

'Corin?'

'Yes?'

'You know, it's been more than a year now since we were wed and we never have been back to go swimming again, like on our honeymoon.'

'I know. I know it, Caroline. It's so hard to find the time,' Corin said.

'Can we go? Soon? I just . . . I want to spend the day with you. The whole day . . . we hardly ever do that! Not with all the work you do.'

'Well, I don't know, Caroline. There's just so much to do at this time of year! We've got the stupidest bunch of beeves as I've ever had on the ranch and they've been wandering off and getting themselves stuck in the creek and caught up in wire and I don't know what else. Maybe in a week. In a week or two . . . how about that?'

'You promised me we would,' she said quietly.

'And we will. We will,' he insisted. Soon afterwards he rose, pulled himself into his clothes, stroked one hand gently over Caroline's hair and kissed the top of her head before going through to the kitchen to make coffee. Caroline sat and listened to the clang of the kettle hitting the stove, and she felt a peculiar weariness wash over her. For a moment, she did not think she had the strength to rise, to see another day through to its end. But she drew in a long breath, and she stood, and began to dress herself slowly.

At the end of September, Joe appeared at the house one wet afternoon, his hat in his hands. Caroline smiled, but she could not help but draw back from him, and she saw a hardening in his eye when she did this.

'Magpie's time is come. She asks for you to go there,' Joe said.

'To go where? Why?' Caroline said, not understanding.

'To go to her. To help the baby,' Joe explained.

Caroline hesitated. She would have to go inside the dugout. However used to having Magpie around the house Caroline had become, she could not help thinking of that half-submerged dwelling as some kind of animal's den. 'I see,' she said quietly. 'I see.'

'In this way, she honours you,' Joe told her solemnly. 'Such work is only for family.'

After a hung pause, pinned by Joe's inscrutable gaze, Caroline went back inside. She squashed her hat onto her hair, took off her apron and felt panic rising like bubbles in her throat. She had no idea what she should do to help. She was not sure that she wanted to help at all.

Outside, Joe showed the first and only sign of impatience Caroline had ever seen any of the Ponca show. He repositioned his hat in his hands and looked over his shoulder towards where his wife lay in labour. Seeing this, Caroline hurried out, turning her face to the ground as they went so that she would not see the terrifying spread of land around them. Ever since her abortive walk to the Moores' farm, she had felt a dizzying horror of the gaping landscape of Woodward County. The expanse of it seemed to pull her thoughts apart, building an unbearable pressure behind her eyes.

Three steps led down into the dugout, and they dropped into a soft, warm darkness lit by a kerosene lamp. There was a strong smell, made up of smoke from the stove, animal hides and herbs. The blood thumped at her temples as she felt all eyes turn to her—Magpie's, White Cloud's and those of Joe's sister, Annie. Joe himself stayed outside. Magpie's face was slick with sweat, her eyes wide and fearful.

'Joe . . . said I should come. He said you had . . . had . . . asked for me to come?' Caroline stammered. Magpie nodded and smiled slightly before her body convulsed, and she ground her teeth together.

'What should I do? I don't know what I should do!' Caroline quailed. White Cloud handed Caroline a small wooden pail, filled with rainwater, and a clean cloth. The old woman motioned dipping the cloth into the water, and then pressed her hand against her forehead, gesturing to Magpie. Caroline nodded and knelt beside the girl, wiping her drenched face with the cool water, afraid, as she performed this intimate duty, that the girl would somehow see into her troubled heart.

In the semidark, White Cloud began to sing a soft monotonous song that lulled them all, lulled Caroline so that she had no idea how much time was passing, whether hours or minutes or days. Magpie heaved against the pain inside her, screwing up her eyes and bearing her teeth, but she did not cry out. On and on these waves came, as the darkness deepened outside; and on and on White Cloud sang, mixing up a pungent drink that she gave to Magpie a spoonful at a time. Then, with a low sound in her throat like a strangled growl, Magpie's baby arrived into Annie's waiting hands, and White Cloud broke off her song with a sharp cry of joy, her wizened face breaking into laughter.

Caroline smiled with relief, but as Annie passed the wriggling baby boy to its mother, she felt a splinter pierce her heart and lodge there. Tears sprang to her eyes and she looked away to hide them, seeing, in a dark corner of the dugout, a pair of spurs on leather thongs. A pair Corin had been looking for and had asked if she had seen about the place. She stared at them, and the splinter wormed its way ever deeper.

Two months later, the baby was chubby and delightful. He was named, in the Ponca tongue, first-born son, but called by his parents and so by everybody else, William. He rode around the ranch in a sling on Magpie's back, gazing out at the world with an expression of mild astonishment in his round eyes. And he slept there in a crumpled little heap, dribbling down his chin, not stirring as Magpie returned to work in the main house, her body not at all fatigued by the child.

Caroline had sent Hutch into Woodward to collect the gifts she had ordered for William from Corin and herself. Magpie had accepted each present with increasing embarrassment.

'Mrs Massey . . . this is too much,' Magpie told her, her eyes troubled.

'Well,' Caroline smiled, as she gave her the ivory pacifier. 'A lovely little boy should have lovely things.' She felt that Magpie could see into her heart—that these were gifts she had wanted to give her own baby, not Magpie's.

And although it hurt her to hold William, Caroline often asked to do so. Like exploring a wound, or pressing a bruise. She cradled him in the crook of her arm and rocked him gently. He was a good-natured baby and did not cry for strangers. He had an array of fledgling facial expressions that melted her heart and eased the splinter from it. But the pain of handing him back to his mother was a little stronger each time; and the only thing harder than this was watching Corin play with the baby, when he came in from working. He grinned foolishly when he managed, by tickling and mugging, to make William smile.

Each time he succeeded he glanced at his wife, to share it with her, but Caroline found it hard to find the smile she knew he wanted. Seeing him love this child that was not hers was almost more than she could bear.

Caroline and Corin sat outside on the porch one fair Sunday afternoon, after a travelling preacher had called by to read a service for all the ranch's inhabitants, and, because of the contentment she read in Corin's face, rocking gently in his chair, she felt a hundred miles from him.

'Corin?' she asked hesitantly. 'Are you awake?'

'Mmm . . .' came the drowsy reply.

'I come into my money soon, Corin. I know I told you before, but I didn't tell you how much money it is. It's . . . a lot of money. We could go anywhere you wanted . . . you won't have to work so hard any more.'

'Go somewhere? Why would we go anywhere?' he asked.

Caroline bit her lip. 'It's just . . . so isolated here—so far from town! We could . . . buy a house in Woodward, perhaps. I could spend some of the week there . . . Or we could move everything closer, move the whole ranch closer! I could . . . join the Coterie Club, perhaps . . .'

'What are you saying, Caroline? Of course I can't move the ranch closer to town! Cattle need open grasslands, and the land nearer town is all given over to homesteaders now.'

'But you won't need to raise cattle any more, don't you see? We'll have money—plenty of money!' she cried. Corin looked at his wife and she recoiled from the pained expression on his face.

'If money was what I was interested in, I'd have stayed in New York. Sweetheart! This life is everything I've dreamed of since I was a boy and I saw Buffalo Bill Cody's "Wild West and Congress of Rough Riders of the World" . . . That was when I decided to come out here with him, when he came looking for fresh suppliers. Ranching isn't just a job for me . . . it's our life, and this is our home, and I can't think I'll ever want to move or live anywhere else. Is that what you want? Do you want to live somewhere else? Somewhere away from me, perhaps?' His voice caught when he asked this question and she looked up, shocked to see tears waiting in the corners of his eyes.

'No! Of course not! Never away from you, Corin, it's just . . .'

'What is it?'

'Nothing. I just thought . . . perhaps I might be happier, to have a little more company. More refined society than I have here, perhaps. And . . . perhaps if I was happier, we might start a family at last.'

At this Corin looked away across the corrals and he seemed to consider for a long time. Caroline sank back into her chair and shut her eyes, sad to her core and exhausted by this attempt to voice her fears.

'We can build. We could use some of the money to double the size of the house, if you like, and get a maidservant, perhaps. A housekeeper to take over from Magpie now that she has William to look after . . . An electricity generator, maybe. And plumbing! A proper bathroom for you, with running water indoors . . . How about that? Would that fix this?' Corin asked. He sounded so hurt, so desperate.

'Yes, perhaps. A bathroom would be lovely. Let's see when the money comes,' she said.

'And I'll take you to town very soon. We can stay the night, maybe even a couple of nights, if you like? Buy you as many books and magazines as we can carry back; and I need to go to Joe Stone's for some new spurs. I've been idiot enough to break my spare pair and I've still not yet laid hands on the original ones . . .'

'They're at Joe and Magpie's place. In the dugout,' Caroline told him.

'What? How do you know?'

'I saw them in there, when I was helping with the birth.' Hating herself, Caroline watched him closely. For signs of guilt or embarrassment, or a telltale blush. Instead Corin smacked a palm to his forehead.

'Lord, of course! I loaned them to Joe, months and months ago! Way out towards the panhandle that day we chased those thieves down— his snapped and since that gelding of his was being a brute, I gave him my spurs. I never thought to ask for them back at the end of that long ride! Why didn't you say, if you saw them, love?'

'Well, I . . .' Caroline faltered. 'I . . . just forgot, that's all. The baby came and that was something of a distraction.' Corin sprang to his feet.

'You clever girl to remember them now! I'll go over and fetch them right away, before we both forget again,' he smiled, and strode away from the house. Caroline watched him go and then she put her face into her hands for all the times since William's birth that she'd pictured the spurs, lying there in Magpie's home; all the times she'd imagined the haste and the urgency with which they might have been discarded there, flung aside by passionate hands in the desire to reach that hidden, adulterous nest of blankets.

After her suggestion that they move to town, and as the second anniversary of their marriage approached, Caroline caught her husband watching her more closely—for signs of malaise. He must have noticed, then, that she was increasingly quiet, but there was little he could do about it. Caroline smiled when he asked after her, and assured him that she was quite well. She did not say that when she opened the door she felt as though she might fall out, might tumble into the gaping emptiness of the prairie.

The four walls of the house became her gaol, trapping her with Magpie and William—two constant reminders of how she failed, day after day. For if Magpie's return to work, her cheery demeanor and the ease with which she coped proved anything to Caroline it was that she would never belong on the prairie like the Ponca girl did. Only cradling William seemed to soothe her. The movement of his small body against hers seemed to fill a dark and gaping hole inside her. But Caroline always had to give the baby back to his mother, and each time she did the hole inside her returned.

One evening, Caroline saw Corin stop Magpie as the girl headed for the dugout. Caroline strained her ears as if she might hear what her husband asked. Magpie answered him in her usual contained way. When Corin released the girl and started towards the house, Caroline turned away and busied herself plating up the meal Magpie had made. Roasted corn chowder, with thick slices of roast beef and warm bread.

Corin was troubled by what Magpie had told him, that much was clear. Caroline felt a stab of resentment towards the girl, but she smiled as she put food on the table, willing him reassured, because she did not know what she would say to him, if he were to ask if she was happy.

What he said, as they settled down to eat, was, 'I do think, sweetheart, that you should learn to ride and come out with me sometime to see more of the land we live on. There's nothing that lifts my heart more than a fast ride over the prairie . . .' But he broke off because Caroline was shaking her head.

'I just can't, Corin! Please don't ask me . . . I tried! The horses frighten me . . .'

'But you were afraid of Joe and Maggie, until I introduced you to them. You're not still afraid of them now, are you?'

'Well, no . . .' she reluctantly agreed. Magpie she no longer feared, of course, but on the rare occasions that Joe came up to the house a knot of tension still clenched in the pit of her stomach. His face looked fierce to her, no matter what Corin said.

'Well, it would be just the same with the horses. That mare you rode—Clara. Why, she's as gentle as a lamb! And the season's changing now, the weather's better . . . .'

'I can't! Please, don't try to force me! I am far happier staying here . . .'

'Are you, though?' he asked. Caroline stirred her soup around with her spoon and said nothing. 'Maggie tells me . . .' He trailed off.

'What? What has she said about me?'

'That you don't want to go outside. That you stay indoors, and you're too quiet, and she has much more work to do. Caroline . . . I . . .'

'What?' she asked again, dreading to hear what he would say.

'I just want you to be happy,' he said miserably. He watched her with his eyes wide and she saw nothing within them but truth and love, and hated herself anew for ever thinking he could have betrayed her, could have passed over her infertile body to make a son elsewhere.

'I . . .' she began. 'I want to be happy too,' she whispered.

'Then tell me, please. Tell me what I can do to make you happy!' he implored. Caroline said nothing. What could she say? He had done everything a man could do to give her a child, but she could not manage it. He had loved her, and married her, and given her a new life, and she could not ask again for him to give that life up.

'We'll go swimming again. We'll have our honeymoon again. This Sunday—we'll go. Hang the ranch, hang the work—just you and me, my love. And we'll make a baby this time, I just know it. What do you say?' he urged. Caroline shook her head. It was too late, she realised. Too late for their second honeymoon swim. She could never go back to that pool, not now. It was too far, the way too open; it was too much for her now, too frightening. But what remained? What else could she suggest?

'Only . . . only promise me you'll never leave me,' she said, at last. Corin put his arms around her and held her tightly with quiet, helpless desperation.

'I will never leave you,' he whispered.

The first hot night of June, Caroline woke in the darkness with sweat slicking her hair to her forehead. She looked beside her at the comforting outline of Corin, edged in grey light from around the shutters. The coyote song that always haunted the night echoed outside. Caroline closed her eyes and tried to shut out the sound. It shook her very soul to hear it. It told her, over and over, of the wilderness outside the walls, of the empty, pitiless land.

Suddenly then, Caroline faced what she had long known but refused to acknowledge. This was where she lived. Here was her husband, here was her life, and this was it. No change, no move; Corin had told her so. And no children. It was two years since she and Corin had been wed and the failure to conceive a child certainly did not stem from a want of trying. She would watch Magpie and Joe raise a brood, she thought, and never have a child of her own. It would be unbearable. If Magpie were to conceive again, she would not be able to have her in the house all day. So, this empty house then, when Corin was away. This empty house in this empty land, for the rest of her life. I will lose my mind, Caroline realised, seeing this fact clearly. She sat up with a cry and beat her hands against her ears to block out the howling and the resounding silence behind it.

'What is it? What's happening! Are you ill?' Corin stirred from his sleep. 'What is it, my darling? Did you have a nightmare? Please, tell me!' he begged, grasping her hands.

'I just . . . I just . . .' she gasped, choking and shaking her head.

'What? Tell me!'

'I just . . . can't sleep with those goddamned coyotes shrieking all night long! Don't they ever let up? All night! Every night! They're driving me out of my goddamned mind, I tell you!' she shouted, eyes wild with rage and fear. Corin took this in and then he smiled.

'Do you know, that's the first time I've ever heard you swear?' he said, releasing her. 'And I have to say, you did a mighty fine job of it!' he grinned. Caroline stopped crying and an odd calm befell her—the numbness of exhausted sleep as it stole in and overcame her in seconds.

The next morning, Corin went out briefly before breakfast and then returned, smiling at his wife with a twinkle in his eye. In silence, Caroline warmed some bean pottage from the night before and made a batch of flat biscuits to go with it, all of which Corin wolfed down with great relish. Before long there was a shout from outside. Caroline opened the door to find Hutch and Joe outside, mounted on their horses with rifles jutting up from the saddles. Joe held Strumpet's reins and the black mare was also saddled.

'I didn't think you were riding out today? I thought you were mending fences?' Caroline asked her husband.

'Well,' Corin said, walking out of the house. 'This is a little extra trip I've decided to take, on the spur of the moment.'

'Where are you going?'

'We're going . . .' Corin swung into the saddle, 'to hunt some coyotes,' he grinned. 'You're quite right, Caroline—there are too many of them living close to the ranch. We've been losing some hens; you've been losing some sleep. And it's a fine day for a bit of sport!' he exclaimed, wheeling Strumpet in a tight circle.

'Oh, Corin!' Caroline said, touched by his efforts for her. The men tipped their hats to her, and with a whoop and a drumming of hooves they were away, leaving nothing but tracks in the sand.

Caroline stood and watched from the window as the first drops of rain began to fall. She listened to the percussion of it on the roof. It took a while for her to work out what was making her uneasy. The rain had come on slowly, out of the northwest, the same direction in which the men had ridden away. They would have seen this rain closing in, and yet they had not returned. There would be no hunting in rain like this, and it was late. Magpie had put a rabbit stew in the stove and had left, over an hour ago. Caroline stood at the window and her unease grew with each drop of rain that fell.

When at last she thought she saw riders coming, the light was weak and made them hard to discern. Two hats only, she could see. Two riders only, and not a third. Her heart beat in her chest—not fast, but hard. A steady, slow, tight clenching that was almost painful. Two hats only; and, as they drew nearer, definitely only two horses. And as they drew nearer still, she saw two horses with dun coats and no black one.

5

ON BOXING DAY I wake up to hear voices in the kitchen, the clatter of the kettle on the Rayburn. I expect I am the last one up. Still full with yesterday's rich food, I go up to the attic in my dressing gown, unwrap the bone ring from Caroline's trunk and take it downstairs with me.

The four of them are at the table, which is properly laid with plates and cutlery, coffee mugs and a huge cafetière, a platter of bacon and eggs, toast tucked neatly into a rack. The four people I care most about in the world, sitting together at a laden table. I lean on the door jamb for a second and wish that it could always be this way.

'Ah! You've decided to grace us with your presence,' Dad beams, pouring me a coffee.

'Cut me some slack, Dad, it's only nine o'clock,' I yawn, sauntering to the table, sliding onto a bench.

'I've been out already, to fetch in loads more wood,' Eddie boasts, smothering some toast with chocolate spread.

'Show off,' I accuse him.

'Ed, would you like some toast with your Nutella?' Beth asks him pointedly. Eddie grins at her, takes a huge bite.

'Sleep OK?' I ask my parents.

'Very well, thank you, Erica.'

'Here, Mum—this is that bell I was telling you about, that I found up in Caroline's things.' I hand it to her. 'The handle looks like it's bone.'

Mum turns it over in her hands, glances up at me incredulously. 'It's not a bell, you dope, it's a baby's teething ring. A very lovely one, too. This is ivory, not bone . . . and the silver bell acts as a rattle.'

'A teething ring? Really?'

'A very old-fashioned one, yes; but that's certainly what it is.'

'Was it Clifford's? Do you remember it?' I ask.

Mum frowns slightly. 'No, I have to say I don't. But I may have forgotten. Or . . .' she reaches behind her, takes the family tree from the sideboard. 'Look at the gap between Caroline getting married, and Meredith being born—seven years! That's rather unusual. There's my great aunt, Evangeline—she died before her first birthday, poor thing.' She points to the name preceding Meredith's, the pitifully short dates in brackets beneath. 'Two babies in seven years is not very many. Perhaps she had a son that died and this ring belonged to that poor little chap.'

'Maybe. But wouldn't he be on the family tree, even if he'd died?'

'Well, not necessarily. Not if he was born prematurely, or was still-born,' Mum muses.

'Perhaps we could talk about something else at the breakfast table?' Beth says quietly. Mum and I button our lips guiltily. Beth miscarried a child, very early on, before Eddie was born.

'What are we going to do today, then?' Dad asks. 'I, for one, feel the need to stretch my legs a bit—walk off some of yesterday's excess.'

'To make room for today's excess, David?' Mum remarks, peering at his plate.

'Quite so!' he agrees cheerfully.

It is brighter today, but grey clouds nose purposefully across the sky and the wind is brisk, penetrating. We take a route through the village, westwards past the little stone church that nestles into a green slope studded with the gravestones of generations of Barrow Storton's dead. In the far corner is the Calcott plot, and in unspoken unity we drift over to it. It is about two metres wide, and as long. A cold bed of marble chippings for our family to sleep in. Henry, Lord Calcott, is in there, and Caroline, with the little daughter she lost before Meredith. Evangeline. And now Meredith has joined them. I shudder, make a silent pledge that I will never lie in this claustrophobic family grave.

'I suppose if Caroline had had a son, he'd be buried here, wouldn't he?' I ask, breaking the silence. Beth sighs sharply and walks away, over to where Eddie is climbing the gabled lich gate.

'I suppose so. Probably. But, who knows? If he was very tiny, perhaps they'd have given him an infant's grave instead,' Mum replies.

'What would that look like?'

'Just like a grave with a smaller stone, usually with an angel on it somewhere—or a cherub,' she says. 'Sometimes there's a special area for the infant graves . . .' Mum sets her gaze to the far corner of the churchyard. 'Try over there—do you see? Under that beech tree.'

I walk quickly to where the wind is seething through the naked beech. There are fifteen or twenty graves here. On the older graves are little cherubs, their features blurred with lichen. There are a couple of newer stones too, carved with teddy bears instead. I scan the names and dates hurriedly, walk away from the sad little party with a shiver.

'Can we go, now?' Beth says impatiently. 'If you're that desperate to know if she had a son, go and look it up in the births, marriages and deaths register. It's all online now.'

'Perhaps she was married before, in America,' Mum says. 'Perhaps the baby in the photograph died there, before she came over.'

To the north of the village is a web of farm tracks and bridleways, dodging through the drab winter fields. We take a circular route, at a brisk pace, falling into pairs to pass along the narrow pathways. Eddie drops back to walk beside me. He is leaving later on today. I look at his sharp face, his scruffy hair, and feel a pull of affection. It gives me such an odd, desperate feeling for a second that I pause to consider how Beth must be feeling. As if reading my mind, Eddie speaks.

'Is Mum going to be OK?' A carefully neutral tone he is too young to have developed.

'Yes, of course,' I tell him, with as much certainty as I can find.

'It's just . . . when Dad came to pick me up last time, before Christmas, she seemed . . . really unhappy about it. She's getting thin again.'

'Look, it's just . . . it's hard for your mum, being back at the manor house,' I say. 'Has she told you about your great-grandma's will? That we can keep the house only if we both come and live in it?' He nods. 'Well, that's why we've come to stay. To see if we would like to come and live here.'

'Why does she hate it so much? Because your cousin was kidnapped—and she misses him?'

'Possibly . . . possibly it's to do with Henry. And the fact that, well, this place is in our past now, and sometimes it can feel wrong to try and live in the past. To be honest, I don't think we'll come to live here, but I'm going to try to make your mum stay for a bit longer at least; even if she doesn't really want to.'

'But why?'

'Well . . .' I struggle for a way to explain. 'Do you remember that time your finger swelled up to the size of a sausage and it was so sore you wouldn't let us look at it properly, but it wouldn't heal up so finally we did look and you had a splinter of metal in it?'

'Yeah, I remember. It looked like it was going to explode.'

'Once we got the splinter out it healed, right?' Eddie nods. 'Well, I think your mum won't . . . heal because she has a splinter. Not of metal, and not in her finger, but she's got a kind of splinter inside her and that's why she can't get better. I'm going to get the splinter out. I'm going to . . . find out what it is and get rid of it.' I hope I sound calm, confident in this purpose—when what I feel is desperate.

'How? Why do you have to be here to do it?'

'Because . . . I think this is where she got the splinter in the first place,' I say.

Eddie considers this in silence for a while, his face marked by worried lines I hate to see.

'I hope you do. I hope you can find out what it is,' he says. 'You will find out, won't you? And she will get better?'

'I promise you, Ed,' I say. And now I must not fail. I cannot let us come away from here without a resolution of some kind. The weight of my promise settles onto me like chains.

Our parents leave soon after lunch, and by tea time Maxwell has come for Eddie as well. Maxwell is grouchy, blotches of overindulgence on his cheeks. I load carrier bags of presents into the boot, Beth watching me blackly as if I am colluding in the theft of her son.

'See you, Edderino,' I say.

'Bye then, Auntie Rick,' he says, and climbs into the back. He is calm, resigned.

'Did you tell Harry you were going today?' I ask, leaning into the car.

'Yes, but you might have to tell him again, if you see him around. I'm not sure how much attention he was paying.'

'OK. Call your mum later on, won't you?' I keep my voice low.

'Course,' he mutters, looking at his hands.

The brake lights of the car gleam red as they pull out of the drive. It's raining again. Beth and I stand and wave until the car is out of sight. Neither one of us wants to turn back to the house. I glance at Beth.

'Eddie's so great, Beth. You've done so well there,' I say, needing to break the silence. But there's a chilly, sad edge to Beth's eyes.

'I'm not sure how much of it comes from me,' she says.

'All the best bits,' I say, taking her hand, squeezing it. She shakes her head. We turn and go inside again, alone.

When she is this quiet, when she is this pale and still, I think of her in the hospital. At least I didn't find her. I've only got Eddie's descriptions, making pictures in my head. She was in her bedroom, lying on her side. He couldn't see her face, he told me. Her hair had fallen over it. He says he doesn't know how long he stood there before going over to her, because he was too afraid of moving her hair, of seeing what was underneath. His mother, or his dead mother. He needn't have touched her at all, of course. He could have just called an ambulance. But he was a child. He wanted to make it right himself. He wanted to touch her and find her sleeping, nothing more. What courage he must have found. To do it—to push back her hair. I am so proud of him it hurts.

She had taken a lot of sleeping pills and then tried to cut her wrists—with a short-bladed paring knife—but the conclusion drawn was that she had hesitated. And while she hesitated the pills sank into her bloodstream and she passed out. The doctors called it a cry for help rather than a genuine attempt, but I knew different.

I clattered into the hospital, waited while they pumped her stomach. Opposite me in the corridor was a window, blinds drawn. My reflection stared back at me. In the greenish light I looked dead. Lank hair, face drooping. I fed money into a machine; it expelled watery hot chocolate for Eddie. Then Maxwell came and took him away.

When she woke up I went in to see her, and I had no idea until I got to her that I was angry with her. Angrier than I have ever been.

'What were you doing? What about Eddie?' These were my first words. Snapping like a trap.

A nurse scowled at me, said, 'Elizabeth needs her rest,' as if she knew her better than I. There was a bruise on Beth's chin, purple hollows around her eyes, in her cheeks. *What about me?* I wanted to add. Hurt, that she would want to leave me. The same feeling as when she ran off with Dinny, snowballing down the years. She didn't answer me. She started to cry and my heart cracked, let the anger run out.

It's been a long time since I spoke to my Aunt Mary, let alone telephoned her. I am still reluctant to, but I have got a ball rolling now. I have started to learn things, started to uncover secrets.

I shift uncomfortably in the chair as I wait to hear Mary's voice. She was always mousy and quiet. It was a shock to hear her scream, to hear her shout and cry and curse in the aftermath of Henry's disappearance. Then when that stopped she was even quieter than before, as if she'd used up all the noise she possessed in that one burst.

'Mary Calcott speaking?' So timorous, as if she's really not sure.

'Hello, Aunt Mary, it's Erica.'

'Erica? Oh hello, dear. Happy Christmas. Well, I suppose it's a bit late for that now. Happy New Year.' There is little conviction behind these words. I wonder if she hates us, for surviving when Henry did not.

'And to you,' I say. 'The reason I was calling, and I hope you won't mind me asking, is that I wanted to pick your brains a little about the family research you did, the year before last.'

'Oh, yes?'

'I've found a photo of Caroline, you see, dated 1904, and it was taken in New York . . .'

'Well, that certainly sounds right. She came to London in late 1904.'

'Yes. The thing is she has a child with her, in the picture. A baby that looks about six months old or so. I just wondered if you had any idea who the baby might been?'

'A child? Well. I can't think. That can't be right.'

'Was she married before, in the States? Only, the way she's holding the baby . . . it just looks like a family portrait to me. She looks so proud . . . It looks to me like it's her baby, you see.'

'Oh, no, Erica. That can't be right at all. Let me just get the file down. One moment.' I hear rustling, a cupboard door creaking. 'No, I've got a copy of her marriage certificate to Sir Henry Calcott here, and it clearly says, in the "condition" column, that she was a spinster. A spinster at twenty-one! Hardly seems an appropriate label, does it?'

'Could she have . . . got a divorce, or something?' I ask, dubiously.

'Goodness me, no. It was very rare in that day and age, and certainly not without it being well talked about. Or mentioned on the occasion of her subsequent marriage. The child must belong to somebody else.'

'Oh. Well, thank you . . .'

'Of course, Caroline was always rather reticent about her early years in America. All anybody could discover was that she had grown up without any close family and had come to England to make a fresh start when she came into her money. She married Henry Calcott very soon after meeting him.' Twice now, she has said his name.

'Yes, it does sound that way. Well, thanks for looking it up for me.'

'You're welcome, Erica.'

There's a pause and I can't quite bring myself to say goodbye, to admit that this piece of information was all I was after, and that I do not want to talk to her. There is so much to say, so much not to say.

'Do you ever think about your cousin, Erica? Do you still think about Henry?' she asks, rushing the words.

'Of course. Of course I do. Especially now we're . . . back here again.'

'Good. I'm glad,' she says, and I wonder what she means. I wonder if she senses guilt, hanging around Beth and me like a bad smell.

'So there's been no news? Of him—of Henry?' Ridiculous thing for me to ask, twenty-three years after he vanished.

'No,' she says flatly. 'I know you never got on. You girls and Henry. I know that you didn't like him,' she says, suddenly tense, offended.

'We did like him!' I lie. 'It's just . . . well, we liked Dinny too. And we kind of had to choose sides . . .'

'Did it ever occur to you that Henry used to . . . act up, sometimes, because you always left him out of your games and ran off to play with Dinny?' she says.

'No. I . . . never thought he wanted to play with us,' I mumble.

'Well, I think he did. I think it hurt his feelings that you couldn't wait to get away,' she tells me, resolutely. I try to picture my cousin this way—try to shape the way he treated us, treated Dinny, in these terms. But I can't—it won't fit. That's not the way it was, not the way he was. A flare of indignation warms me, but of course I can say nothing and the silence buzzes down the line.

'Well, Erica, I really must go,' she says at last, in one long exhalation. 'It was . . . nice to talk to you. Goodbye.'

She hangs up the phone before I can respond. She does not do this crossly, or abruptly. Absently, rather, as if something else has caught her attention. She's had lots of fads and projects in the years since Henry died. Tapestry, watercolours, horoscopes, brass rubbing, Anglo-Saxon poetry. The family genealogy was the longest running, the one she really followed through. I wonder if she did it because she got to say his name, over and over again, when Clifford would not allow her to speak of their son. *Henry Calcott, Henry Calcott, Henry Calcott.* Learning everything she could about his ancestors, the source of each component part of him, as if she could rebuild him.

He's dead. This I know. He was not carried off. It wasn't him, lying in the back of a car in a Devizes car park. It wasn't him, being carried by a mysterious hobo on the A361. I know it because I can feel it, I can feel the memory of his death. I can feel it at the dew pond, even if I can't see it. We were there, Henry was there; and Henry died. I have the shape of it. I just need to colour it in. Because I've stalled. I can't go in any direction until I can fill this hole in my head, until I can work Beth's splinter free. And if I must start in 1904 and work my way towards it, then that is what I will do.

Beth finds me in the study. I am curled up in a leather chair. I stood on the desk to get this book of wild flowers down from the top shelf. Now it's open at a double-page spread of yellow marsh flags. Ragged, buttery irises. I recognised them as soon as I saw them. Marsh flags.

'The rain's stopped. Do you fancy a walk?' Beth asks. She has plaited her hair, put on clean jeans and a jumper the colour of raspberries.

'Absolutely,' I say, all astonishment. 'Yes, let's.'

'What were you reading?'

'Oh, just about wild flowers. There were three old pillowcases up in the press. They had yellow flowers embroidered on them, and I wanted to know what they were.'

'What were they?'

'Marsh flags. Does that ring any bells with you?'

'No. Should it? What kind of bell?'

'Probably a misplaced bell. I'll just get some wellies on.'

We don't walk very far, since the sky is like charcoal on the horizon. Just down into the village and then we cross the tawny grassland up to the barrow. Beth links her arm through mine, walks with a swinging step.

'You seem happy today?' I ask her, carefully.

'I am. I've come to a decision.'

'Oh? What kind of decision?' We've reached the barrow. Beth lets go of my arm, conquers the mound in three long strides and turns to gaze over my head into the distance.

'I'm going. I'm not staying,' she says, throwing her arms wide, girlish, dramatic. She takes a huge breath, lets it out with emphasis.

'What do you mean? Going where?'

'Going home, of course. Later today. I've packed!' she laughs.

'You can't!' The thought of being alone in the house fills me with a dread I can't define. I feel panic sputtering in my stomach.

'Of course I can. Why stay? What are we even doing here?'

'We came to . . . we came to sort things out. To . . . decide what we wanted to do!' I grope for words.

'Come on, Erica. Neither of us wants to live here. You don't, do you? '

'I don't know yet!'

'But . . . you can't want to. It's Meredith's house. Everything about it says Meredith. And then there's . . . the other thing.'

'Henry?' I say. She nods, just once. Short and sharp.

'It's our house, Beth. Yours and mine now.'

'Oh my God, you want to stay.' She is utterly incredulous.

'I don't know! I don't know. Not for ever, perhaps. For a while, maybe. I don't know. But please don't go, Beth! Not yet. I'm . . . I'm not done. I can't go yet and I can't stay here on my own. Please. Stay a bit longer.' On top of the barrow Beth sags. We are quiet for a while.

At length she comes down to me, her eyes lowered.

'I'm sorry,' I say.

'What do you mean, you're not done yet?' Her voice is flat now, lifeless.

'I need to . . . find out what happened. I need to remember.'

'Remember what?'

I stare at her. She must know what I'm talking about. 'About Henry, Beth. I need to remember what happened to Henry.'

'You remember what happened. Don't lie. You were old enough.'

'But I don't. I really don't,' I say. 'Please tell me.' Beth looks away.

'No. I won't tell you,' she says. 'I won't tell anyone. Not ever.'

'Please, Beth! I have to know!'

'No! And if . . . if you love me, you'll stop asking.'

'Does Dinny know?'

'Yes, of course Dinny knows. Why don't you ask him?' She flicks her eyes at me. 'But you know, too. And if you really don't remember then . . . then maybe that's a good thing.' She glares at me. 'Why do I have to stay? You must see that it's bad for me, being here?'

'No, I . . . I think it could be good for you,' I force myself to say.

'What do you mean?' she asks me, darkly. My heart beats faster.

'I mean what I say. You can't keep running from this, Beth! Please! If you would just talk about it—'

'No! I've told you—over and over. Not to you and not to anybody!'

'All I want is for us to be able to leave this place behind, Beth! Look at you—since we've been back it's been like sharing the house with a ghost! You're miserable and you seem determined to stay that way!' I shout.

'What are you talking about?' Beth shouts back at me. 'You're the one determined to keep me here—you're the one determined to make me miserable! I only came here at all because you pressured me into it!'

'I'm determined to get rid of whatever it is that's keeping you down, Beth. And it's here—I know it is. It's here at this house—don't walk away from me!' I grab her arm, stop her. Beth will not look me in the eye.

'If you don't let me go, I might not ever forgive you. I don't know what I will do,' she says, her voice trembling. Startled, I drop my hand from her arm but I don't think this is what she means. I am afraid of what she will do. My resolve wavers, but I fight to hold on to it.

'Please, Beth. Please stay here with me. At least until the new year. Let's just . . . figure this out. Life can't go on the way it has been. This is our chance, Beth—our chance to put things right.'

'Some things can't be undone, Erica. The sooner you accept that the better,' she whispers. Tears are bright in her eyes, but when she looks at me they are full of anger. 'It can't be put right!' she snaps, and storms away from me. I pause before I follow her, find that I am shaking.

It's midafternoon and I am upstairs, wedged onto the windowsill in my bedroom. My breath has steamed up the glass, obscured the view, but I am reading so it doesn't matter. More of Meredith's letters to Caroline. I am surprised that Meredith kept them all—that she stowed them away with Caroline's things, as a record of their troubled relationship. I am interrupted by the doorbell. I make my way to the top of the stairs, pause when I hear Beth open the door, and Dinny's voice. My first impulse is to rush down the stairs to see him, to ease things for them. But I stay still, my hand on the banister, listening.

'How are you, Beth?' Dinny asks, and the question carries more weight than it normally would. More significance.

'I'm very well, thank you,' Beth answers, something odd in her tone.

'Only . . . Erica said that you—weren't happy to be back. That you wanted to leave.'

I can't hear Beth's reply to this. If she makes one.

'Can I come in?' he says, almost nervously.

'No. I . . . I think you'd better not. I'm . . . busy right now,' Beth lies, and I feel her tension, making my shoulders ache.

'Oh. Well, I really just came up to say thanks to Erica for the baby things she took down to Honey. Honey even smiled when I got back— it was amazing.' I smile as I hear this.

'Oh, well, I'll pass that on. Or shall I call her down?' Beth asks stiffly.

'No, no. No need,' Dinny says, and my smile fades. 'Listen, Beth, I'd like to talk to you about . . . what happened. There are some things I think you don't understand—'

'No!' Beth interrupts him, her voice higher now, alarmed. 'I don't want to talk about it. There's nothing to talk about. It's in the past.'

'Is it, though?' he asks softly, and I hold my breath.

'Yes! What do you mean? Of course it is.'

'I mean, some things are hard to leave behind. Hard to forget about. Hard for me to forget about, anyway.'

'You just have to try hard,' she says bleakly. 'Try harder.'

'It's not that simple, though, is it, Beth?' he says, his voice stronger now. 'You can't just pretend nothing happened, you can't wash your hands of it—of me.'

'I don't want to talk about it.' She emphasises each word.

'You may not have a choice. There are things you need to hear,' Dinny says, every bit as firmly.

'Please,' Beth says, her voice meek and afraid. 'Please don't.'

There's a long, empty pause. 'It's good to see you again, Beth,' Dinny says at length. 'I was starting to think I never would. See you again, that is.'

'We shouldn't be here. I wouldn't be, if it weren't for . . .'

'And you'll go again soon, will you?'

'Yes. Soon. After New Year.'

'Never a backward glance?' he asks, a bitter edge to the words.

'No,' Beth says, but the word does not sounds as firm as it should. The cold air makes me shiver and I am shot through with desperation again, to know what it is that they know, to remember it.

'I'll go, then.' Dinny sounds defeated. 'Thank Erica for me. I hope . . . I hope I'll see you again, Beth. Before you disappear.' I do not hear Beth's reply, only the door shutting and a sudden loud sigh.

I stay on the stairs for a short while, listen as Beth goes into the study. I hear the whoosh of a chair as she sits down abruptly, then nothing more. It would be easier, I think, to squeeze truths from the stones of these walls than to squeeze them from my sister.

In frustration, I return to the attic, flip open the lid of the red trunk with none of my usual care, and run my fingers through Caroline's possessions once more. There has to be something more, something I have missed. But once I have taken everything out, I am none the wiser. I stop, sit back on my heels, notice that my hands are shaking. And as I pick up a paper parcel, reach in to put it back, something catches my eye. A tear in the lining paper at the bottom of the trunk, a tear that has left a loose flap. And, half hidden beneath the paper, an envelope. I reach for it, see that the handwriting is not Meredith's, and as I read the letter inside my pulse quickens.

Scrambling to my feet, I rush down to the study. 'Beth—I've found something! Up in Caroline's things,' I tell her. She looks up at me, her face drawn. She has not forgiven me for the things I said at the dew pond.

'What is it?' she asks flatly.

'It's a letter to Caroline—it had got lost. I found it in the lining of her trunk, and it's very old—from before she came to England. Listen to this!' The ink has faded and in places, I can hardly make out what it says, but there is enough here, enough to prove a theory.

'*April the 22nd, 1902,*' I read aloud. '*My Darling Caroline—I received your letter and was much dismayed to hear that you had not received mine—nor the one before it, it would seem! Please rest assured that I have been writing—that I do write, almost every night.*

'*There is so much work to be done here, to ready it for your arrival, that I am ending each day fairly well beat, but nevertheless I think of you every night, I swear it to you.*

'*Please do not fret about your aunt's departure—here you will have all the home and family that you will ever need! I know it troubles you to part on bad terms with her, but surely* . . . I can't make out what it says next. In fact, most of this paragraph.'

I squint at it, then continue. '*I have seen to it that* . . . *It pains me to* . . . *Be patient for just a little while longer, my darling, and before you know it we will be together. I have found a place beside the house where I am going to make you a garden. I remember you told me once how much you would love to have a garden. Well, you shall have one of your very own. The soil here is a little sandy, but many things will flourish in it. And we will flourish here, I know it. My heart reminds me of your absence every day, and I thank God that we will soon be reunited.*

'There's a huge chunk here that I can't make out at all,' I interrupt myself, scanning down the rest of the page. 'Then he finishes: *I long to see you again, and it gladdens my heart to know that you will soon be setting out to journey here to me. Be at ease, darling—very soon we will begin the rest of our lives. Yours always, C.* How about that, then?'

'So, she was married!' Beth exclaims.

'It would seem so . . . nothing actually says that they were but I can't think of another reason, back then, that he would write a letter like that—about starting their lives together and her having a new family and all the rest of it.'

'Where was she travelling to? What does the postmark say?'

I study the envelope. 'I can't make it out. It's totally worn away.'

'Shame. What if she was meant to travel out to marry him and something happened before she got there?'

'But then what about the baby?'

'True. So she lost a husband and a baby before she even came over here. And she was how old at that point?'

'Twenty-one, I think. She'd just come into her money.'

'How amazing—that none of it was on her marriage certificate, or was known until now! I wonder how it was forgotten?' Beth muses.

I shrug. 'Who knows. If she divorced him, maybe she wanted it kept quiet? Mary said that Caroline never wanted to talk about her early years. And remember that letter from Aunt B I showed you—that mentioned things that happened in America staying in America. She was definitely worried about a scandal of some kind. If her husband had died, it would have just said widow on her marriage certificate to Lord Henry. She must have left him. And if her baby died, that might explain why she was always so frosty, so impenetrable.' At this Beth falls quiet.

She has not mentioned Dinny's visit to the house. She has not passed on his thanks to me, and I can't find out if this is deliberate, or an oversight, without letting on that I was listening. But it is niggling me.

'What's wrong?' I ask.

'Erica, why are you so keen to know all this? To know everything?'

'Don't you find it interesting? I want to know why . . . why our family hates the Dinsdales. Hated the Dinsdales,' I correct myself. 'I want to know how Meredith got as cruel as she did. And the answer seems to be that she inherited it from Caroline. And I just want to know why . . .'

'And you think you've found out?'

'Why they hated the Dinsdales? No. I have no clue about that. But at least I think I know why Caroline was so cold. Why, as Mum said, she never loved Meredith.'

'Because she lost a child?'

'Lost a whole life, by the sounds of it. You remember that time, at that summer ball, when Caroline thought she recognised the waitress?'

'Yes?'

'I wonder who she thought it was and why she was so upset by her.'

Again Beth doesn't answer. 'And I can't get those blasted marsh flags out of my head! I'm sure I remember something about them . . .' But Beth isn't listening to me any more.

'Losing a child . . . I can't imagine how that must feel. A child that has had the chance to grow, to become a real person. When your love for it has had years to deepen. I just can't imagine.'

'Neither can I.'

'No, but you can't even begin to, because you don't know what it feels like—you don't know how strong that love is,' she tells me intensely.

'There's lots I don't know,' I aver, hurt.

'We never missed Henry,' she said. 'We saw the search for him and the way it nearly pulled the family apart. In a way, we saw the consequences of . . . what happened. But we never missed him. We were only ever on the edges of it . . . of the pain it caused . . .'

'It was hard to miss him, Beth. He was vile.'

'He was vile, but he was just a little boy. Just a little boy, Erica. He was so young! I don't know . . . I don't know how Mary survived it,' she says. I don't think Mary did survive it, not entirely. For a hideous moment I picture Beth being like Mary. Beth, twenty years from now, every bit as empty and deadened as Mary. For surely that is how it will go, if I do not manage to heal her. If I have got it wrong—if I have made it worse, bringing her here. I do not trust myself to speak.

It's late now and Beth went to bed hours ago. There's a kind of quiet desperation gathering beneath my ribs. If Beth won't tell me what happened then Dinny has to. He has to. Which means I have to ask him. Pitch black outside but I haven't bothered to draw the curtains. I like sitting in full view of the night. I have been staring at the fire as it dies, and thinking. It's comforting to know she is up there. The house gives me an empty feeling. Without her it would be unbearable.

There's a knock behind my shoulder, and a face at the black glass that makes me gasp. It's Dinny, and I stare stupidly, as if he's walked right out of my thoughts. The rain has slicked his hair to his forehead. I open the window and the wind almost pulls it out of my hand.

'I'm sorry to . . . sorry it's so late, Erica. I saw the light. I need help.'

'What's wrong? What's happened?'

'Honey's gone into labour and . . . something's wrong. Erica, something's going wrong and all the vans are bogged in after all this pissing rain . . . We need to get to hospital. Can you take us? Please? It'll be quicker than waiting for an ambulance to find the place . . .'

'Of course I will! But if I drive down to you my car will get stuck too.'

'No, no—just go to the top of the green lane, can you? I'll carry her up to you.'

'OK. OK. Are you sure you can carry her?'

'Just go, please—we need to hurry!' Dinny vanishes from the window, back into the dark. I scrabble for my car keys, my coat, pause only for a second to think I should tell Beth. But she is probably asleep and I can't wait to explain it to her. I shove my mobile into my pocket and run for the car. In the short sprint from the house my shoulders are soaked. My hands shake as I try to find the ignition and I have to stop, make myself calmer. The driveway is potted with puddles and I splash out onto the road, wipers flailing.

There's no sign of them as I pull in at the top of the green lane. My headlights flare on the hedgerow, flood away towards the camp. I trot down the track, slipping. The ground is slimy. I stop at the far reach of the car's headlights and stare into the blackness. Then I see them, making slow progress, and as I lurch towards them Dinny slips and falls onto one knee, fighting to keep his balance with the bulk of the pregnant girl teetering in his arms.

'Can you walk?' I ask Honey, as I reach them. She nods, grimacing. 'Dinny, let go! Let her get to her feet!'

He tilts to the side, lowers Honey's feet to the ground then levers her up. She is upright for a second before she doubles over, cries out.

'Fuck!' she howls. 'This can't be right . . . it can't be right,' she moans.

'Her waters broke discoloured,' Dinny tells me. 'The baby's in trouble,' he says. Honey is still doubled up and now she is sobbing.

'It's going to be OK,' I tell her. 'Listen—really, it's going to be OK. Are you sure you can walk? The car's not much farther.' Honey nods, her eyes tight shut. She is breathing like bellows.

We reach the car and manoeuvre Honey into the back seat. I have mud up to my knees. Honey is soaked to the skin, pale and shivering.

'I'll drive. You help Honey,' Dinny says.

'No! She needs you, Dinny! And it's my car. And the steering is a little snappy in the wet. It'll be safer if I drive,' I shout. I push past Dinny, take the driver's seat, and he climbs into the back. We skid off the verge, slalom down the lane, make for the main road.

I take us to Devizes at a reckless pace, as fast as I dare, squinting into the tunnelling rain. But when I corner Honey is thrown about in the back seat and so I slow down, unsure of what is best. She cries quietly between contractions, as if to herself, and Dinny seems dumbstruck.

'Not far now, Honey! You're going to be fine, please don't be scared! They'll whip that baby out faster than you can say epidural,' I shout, glancing at her in the mirror. I hope I am not lying to her.

'It's not far?' she gasps, eyes on my reflection, pleading.

'Five minutes, I promise. And they'll take good care of you and the baby. It's going to be fine. Right, Dinny?' He jumps as if I've startled him. His knuckles around Honey's hands are white.

'Right. Yes, right. You're going to be fine, sweetheart. Just hang in there.'

'Have you thought of any names?' I ask. I want to distract her. From her fear, from the pain shining her face with sweat.

'Er . . . I think, um, I think . . . Callum, if it's a boy . . .' she pants.

'And for a girl?' I press.

'Girl . . . for a girl . . . Haydee . . .' she groans. 'I need to push!'

'Not yet! Not yet! We're nearly there!' I press the accelerator flat as the orange glow of town grows in front of us.

I pull up right in front of the hospital and Dinny is out of the car before it stops. He comes back with help, and a wheelchair.

'Here we go, Honey.' I turn around to her, take her hand. 'You'll be fine now.' She squeezes my hand, tears rolling down her face, and there is no trace of her attitude. She looks little more than a child. Then the back door is pulled open, and they take her out, and she shouts at them, and swears, and we pile into the building. I follow them as far as I can. At the last set of doors somebody stops Dinny and me.

'Partners only from here, I'm afraid. You can wait back down the hall—there's a waiting room there,' the man tells me.

'You're Honey's partner?' he asks Dinny.

'Yes—no. I'm her brother. She's got no partner,' he says.

'Right. Come on then.' They disappear through the doors, leave them swinging in their wake. Dinny is her brother.

The clock on the wall says ten to one as I sink into a green plastic chair, and I watch as it creeps round and round, wondering how it hadn't occurred to me that Dinny might have a sister. He didn't have one when we were little, so I assumed he still didn't have one. A feeling appears in me, to know it is not his baby. I feel a tentative hope.

Half past three and I am still the only person in the waiting room. My legs are heavy from sitting too long. I am drifting into a kind of daze.

A figure passing the door rouses me—Dinny, walking slowly. I run clumsily into the corridor. 'Dinny—what's happened? Is everything OK?'

'Erica? What are you still doing here? I thought you'd have gone.'

'Well, I was waiting to hear. How is Honey? And the baby?'

'Fine, she's fine,' he smiles. 'It's a girl and she's doing well.'

'That's great! Congratulations, Uncle Dinny,' I say.

'Thanks,' he grins, a touch bashfully.

'So, how long do they have to stay in?'

'A couple of days. Honey lost a fair amount of blood and the baby's a little jaundiced. They're both fast asleep now.'

'You look shattered. Do you want a ride home?' I offer. Dinny rubs his eyes with his forefinger and thumb.

'Yes, please,' he nods.

The weather has not let up. I am light-headed with fatigue. I have to concentrate hard on driving safely.

'You never said Honey was your sister. I didn't realise,' I say.

'Who did you think she was?'

'Well . . . I thought she was . . . I don't know . . .'

'You thought she was my girlfriend?' he asks incredulously, then laughs out loud. 'Erica—she's fifteen years old!'

'Well, I didn't know that!' I say defensively. 'What was I supposed to think? You didn't have a sister the last time I saw you.'

'No, I didn't. She was born well after you left. A late bonus, my mother called her.' He smiles slightly. 'Now she's not so sure.'

'What do you mean?'

'Well, you've met her. Honey doesn't have the easiest temperament.'

'So what happened? How come she's been staying with you?'

'The baby. When she got pregnant Mum wanted her to get rid of it. She thought it would ruin her life, having a baby so young. Honey refused. They had a massive row and then Keith weighed in as well. So Honey flounced out and was told not to come back.' He sighs. 'They're just angry with each other, that's all.'

'Keith's your mum's new husband?'

'They're not married, but yes, to all intents and purposes. He's OK. A bit strait-laced.'

'I can't really imagine your mother with somebody strait-laced.'

'No, well, neither can Honey.'

'But Honey must be used to a more conventional sort of life?'

'She travelled with us until she was seven, when Dad died. I guess it got into her blood. She's never really settled into the mainstream.'

'But now, with the baby . . . surely she can't stay with you for ever?'

'No, she can't,' he says firmly, and I glance across at him.

'What about the father?' I ask cautiously.

"He's a twenty-year-old townie idiot who told Honey she couldn't get pregnant on her first time.'

'That old chestnut.' I wince.

'If I ever catch up with him . . . Honey won't tell me his full name, or where he lives,' Dinny says, blackly.

I cast him a wry glance, smile slightly. 'I wonder why,' I murmur. 'Still, it must be a great way to raise a child—living the way you do. Travelling around, wherever you feel like. No mortgages, no nine-to-five, no juggling with childcare . . . The great outdoors . . .' I venture.

'It's fine for me, but for a fifteen-year-old with a fatherless kid? She hasn't even finished school yet,' he sighs. 'No. She needs to go back home.'

I park in front of the house. The study light I left on blooms out, lighting the stark tree trunks nearest the house.

'Thanks, Erica. Thank you for driving us. You were really great with Honey, back there—you've been great,' Dinny says.

'Why don't you come in? Just to warm up. There's brandy, and you could have a shower, if you want. You're covered in mud,' I tell him. He looks at me, tips his head in that quizzical way.

'I don't think that's a good idea, Erica.'

'Oh, for goodness' sake! It's just a house. And you're welcome in it, now. You're not going to catch convention, just by using the plumbing.'

'I'm not sure how welcome I am. I came up to talk to Beth. She wouldn't let me in,' he says quietly.

'I know,' I say, before I can stop myself. He shoots me a questioning glance. 'I was listening. At the top of the stairs,' I say apologetically.

Dinny rolls his eyes. 'Same old Erica.'

'So are you coming in now?' I smile.

Dinny looks at me for a long moment. 'All right. Thanks,' he nods.

I lead Dinny through to the study. The fire has gone out but it's still very warm. I go to draw the curtains.

'Sit,' I say. 'I'll get brandy.' I creep to the drawing room, fetch the decanter and two crystal tumblers, make as little noise as I can. I shut the door softly. 'Beth's asleep,' I tell him, filling the glasses.

'The house looks just the same as I remember it,' Dinny says, taking a swig of amber spirit, grimacing slightly.

'Meredith was never one for unnecessary change,' I shrug.

'The Calcotts are part of the old guard. Why would she want anything changed?'

'Were old guard. You can hardly say that of Beth and me—I'm an impoverished schoolteacher, and Beth's a single working parent.'

'That must have really pissed the old bird off.'

'Thanks. We like to think so.' I smile. 'Do you want another?' I ask as he drains his glass. He shakes his head, then leans back in his chair, stretches his arms over his head, arches his back, catlike. I watch him, feeling heat in my stomach, the blood pounding in my ears.

'I might take you up on that shower, though.'

'Sure.' I nod, casually. 'This way.'

The room the farthest away from Beth's is Meredith's and its en suite has the best shower. I find new soap, a clean towel, and I turn on a bedside lamp. Dinny stands in the middle of the room and turns, taking in the huge bed, the heavy drapes, the elegant antique furniture.

'This is her room, isn't it? Lady Calcott's?' Dinny asks.

'It has the best shower,' I say nonchalantly.

'It feels a bit . . . wrong, to be in here.'

'I think she owes you a shower, at least,' I say gently.

Dinny says nothing, starts to unbutton his shirt while I hurry from the room.

Creeping softly away along the corridor I hear the shower come on, and I shut my eyes, hoping Beth won't wake up. But even as I think it she appears, looking at me around the side of her door.

'Erica? Is that you?' Her voice is taut with alarm.

'Yes—everything's fine,' I say quietly.

'What are you doing up? What time is it?' she yawns.

'It's very early. Go back to bed, love.'

Beth rubs her face. 'Erica? Who's in the shower?' she asks.

'Dinny.' I look at my feet in my grubby socks, shifting guiltily.

'What? What's going on?'

'It's no big deal. Honey had her baby tonight—I had to drive them to Devizes and we got soaked and muddy and . . . when we got back I said he could have a shower here, if he wanted,' I tell her, all in one breath.

'You've been to Devizes? Why didn't you tell me?'

'You were asleep! And I had to go in a rush—Honey didn't feel right and . . . and it was all in a bit of a hurry, that's all.' I flash her a grin. 'Imagine how Meredith would have gone off—to know a Dinsdale was in her shower!' I whisper, but Beth does not smile.

'Dinny is in the shower and you're waiting outside the room like . . . like I don't know what,' she says.

'I'm not waiting outside the room! I was just going to grab him a clean T-shirt . . .'

'Erica, what are you doing?' she asks me, seriously.

'I'm not doing anything,' I say, but even though it's true it doesn't sound it. 'Are you going to tell me that I shouldn't have invited him in?'

'He's . . . virtually a stranger, Erica! You can't just go inviting in random people in the middle of the night!'

'Not random people. Dinny,' I say firmly. I hold her gaze, see that I have won this argument. She can't explain her objection, not without explaining other things. She says nothing more, turns slowly and shuts the door. I hurry to my room, pull one of the oversized T-shirts I wear for pyjamas out of my case and drop it outside Meredith's door. I retreat to the study, knock back the last of my brandy.

I emerge when I hear Dinny jogging down the stairs. The hallway is sunk in shadows. He pauses when he sees me.

'Erica! You made me jump,' he says, sounding tired, putting one hand up to his wet hair, raking it roughly with his fingers. He smiles. 'That, I have to admit, is a great shower.'

I can't seem to answer him; I can't seem to breathe right. I feel as if I've forgotten how. He reaches the bottom of the stairs, is by my side, and I feel as if I am standing too close to him. But he does not move and neither do I. He tips his head, gives me a bemused look. Gradually his expression changes, grows more serious. I watch a drop of water trickle down his arm, watch the faint scattering of goose pimples in its path. My hand moves without my bidding.

I touch the place where the droplet stops, trace my fingers along his forearm, wiping away its cold trail. The shape of the muscles over the bones. The warmth of his blood beneath the skin. My skin feels raw where it touches him, but I leave my hand on his arm; I cannot move. For a second he is still too, as still as I am, as if I have frozen us both with this uninvited touch. Then he moves away, just slightly, but enough.

'I should go,' he says quietly. 'Thanks for . . . all your help this evening—really.' He sounds puzzled.

'No . . . no problem. Any time,' I say, blinking, startled.

'I'll see you around.' He smiles awkwardly, lets himself out into the bleak early morning.

Lament

1904

CAROLINE FOUND HERSELF outside, found herself soaked and shivering, without even realising she had moved. Water ran into her eyes and through her hair and as the two horses trotted into the yard she splashed over to them from the house. She recognised Hutch and Joe, their hats pulled low over their faces, and as she drew breath to ask she saw the third rider, hanging across the front of Hutch's saddle, bare-headed, the rain streaming from bronze hair gone slick and dark.

'Corin?' she whispered, putting her hand out to shake him slightly. She could not see his face, could not make him look up at her. 'Where's his hat? He'll get a chill!' she shouted at Hutch.

'Mrs Massey, come now, step aside. We have to get him inside the house. Quickly now!' Hutch told her sternly.

'Where's Strumpet? What happened to Corin—what's wrong with him? Tell me!' she asked, frantic now. She knotted her fingers around the horse's reins, pulled its head around, stopped it walking past with its precious cargo. Hutch said something terse, and Joe swung down from his horse, taking Caroline's hands and freeing the reins.

More men arrived, to take the horses, to gather Corin up. Caroline stumbled behind them to the bottom step of the house; she fell, and could not rise again. She could not remember how to walk. Strong hands lifted her and she fought them savagely, as if she could resist what was happening, and make it not so.

They laid Corin down on the bed. Caroline dried his hair carefully with a linen towel, peeled his wet shirt from his torso and pulled his sodden boots from his feet. She fetched clean blankets and covered him thickly. His hands were like ice and she held them in her own, trying to rub some warmth into them when she had none to give.

'He was riding hard after a big dog coyote. It was the last one we were going after, since we'd seen the rain coming in. Strumpet—she always was the quickest. Quick thinking. I never saw a horse and rider move so well together as Corin and that mare . . .' Hutch spoke in a low monotone, his eyes fixed on Corin. Caroline hardly heard a word he said. 'But then, with no warning she just went over. High in the air, heels right up over her head. Whatever she stepped in, and I think it was some sinking sand, she never saw it coming or she'd have avoided it for sure. Corin was thrown down hard and . . . and then Strumpet came down on top of him. It was so fast! Her two legs were broke in front. Joe shot her and we had to leave her out there for the damned coyotes.' He broke off, tears coursing down his cheeks.

Caroline blinked. A dark water stain was ruining the silk squares of the quilt, seeping out around Corin. His right shoulder sat at a wrong angle and his head lolled to the left. Caroline slipped her hands beneath the blankets to see if he was warming up, but his flesh was cold and solid and wrong somehow. She lay her head close to his and refused to listen to the quiet, terrified corner of her mind that knew he was dead.

They buried Corin on his own land, at the top of a green rise some hundred and fifty feet from the house. Angie Fosset and Magpie were responsible for Caroline's attendance that day, and for lacing her into a borrowed black dress that was too big and hung from her thin frame in folds. They also found her a veiled hat with two black ostrich feathers.

'Have you written to his people, Caroline?' Angie asked. 'Sweetheart, have you written to his mama?' But Caroline did not answer her. She had no will left to draw breath, to form words. Angie shot Magpie a dark look, and took the Ponca girl aside for a whispered consultation. They led her up the rise to stand by the graveside as the parson read the sermon to a crowd of ranchers, neighbours and a good portion of the population of Woodward. The sky was tarnished. A warm wind shook the wreath of white roses on the coffin and carried a few sprinkled raindrops onto the congregation.

Hutch, Joe, Jacob Fosset and three other men stepped either side of the coffin, gathered the ropes into their weathered hands and took the strain. The parson spoke again but Caroline turned and stumbled away down the hill. She could not bear to see the weight on those ropes. She could not bear to picture what was weighing that coffin down; and the blackness of the open grave awaiting it appalled her.

'Don't you leave her alone for a second. Not for a second, Maggie. She was lonely enough when Corin was alive, God help her,' Angie whispered to Magpie as she got ready to depart after the funeral.

Angie turned to Caroline, put firm hands on her shoulders.

'I'll be back on Tuesday,' she said sadly, but as she opened the door Caroline found her voice at last.

'Don't go!' she croaked. She could not bear to be left, could not bear the emptiness. 'Please . . . don't go, Angie,' she said.

'Oh, Caroline!' Angie sighed, embracing her neighbour. 'My heart is breaking for you, it truly is,' she said, and Caroline wept.

'I . . . I can't bear it . . . I can't bear it!' she cried.

The heat of high summer was hardly worth fighting now. Caroline did as she was told, and ate as long as Magpie sat with her and forced her to. As she went about the chores, Magpie took to putting William into Caroline's lap. She did this particularly when Caroline had not spoken for several hours, or was not responding to questions. The child, by then ten months old, soon began to wriggle and climb about her person, and she would be forced to take hold of him, steady him, and focus her attention on him. William regarded her with his curious, velvet dark eyes and grinned wetly from time to time; and from time to time Caroline gathered him up and held him close, her eyes shut tight, as if drawing strength from his tiny body.

Throughout the summer, Caroline spent long hours sitting out on the porch, tapping the runner of Corin's rocking chair with her toe and then shutting her eyes. She tried not to think. She tried not to wonder how things might have been if she had not blamed the coyotes for her fears in the night. She stared into the wide, far horizon and let herself be afraid of it. It was the only way she knew to punish herself, and she felt that abject misery was no worse than she deserved.

Some weeks later, Hutch came into the house with a respectful knock. Had Caroline not been so inward facing since Corin's death, she would have noticed the man's suffering, and that he avoided her, shouldering the blame for Corin's accident upon himself. Guilt weighed heavy upon him and grief was ageing him, stamping its mark on him, just as it was on Caroline.

She made coffee for him and noticed that she had finally brewed a good strong cup, not weak, not bitter, not burnt. She pictured Corin complimenting her on it—planting a kiss on her face. Even her smallest triumphs had made him proud. Thoughts like this made her sway.

'Mrs Massey, you know I hate to bother you, but there are things that require your attention,' Hutch said, taking a cup from her.

'What things?' she asked.

'Well, with Mr Massey . . . gone, you're the owner of this ranch now. I know that may sound alarming, but it needn't be. I'll stay here and run it for you. Your husband trusted me with his business concerns, and I hope you can too. But there are things I can't do, and one of those things is pay the hands and riders their wages.'

'Pay them? But . . . I haven't got any money,' Caroline frowned.

'Not here, perhaps. Corin always drew the wages every couple of months from his bank in Woodward, and I can't see that there'll be any trouble in you doing the same.'

'You . . . want me to go to Woodward? I can't,' she refused.

'I'll drive you. We can stay one night only if that's what you want; or you can go visiting some of the ladies while we're there. I think . . .' Hutch paused. 'I think you need to go to Woodward, ma'am. I think you need to see some people. And if we don't pay them, those boys'll go elsewhere. They've had no money for two months now, and that's just not right. And I can't run the ranch without them.'

'All right then, if it's the only way. Corin . . . Corin would have wanted the ranch to carry on.'

The wind was blowing, hot and dry, and a pall of dust sat around Woodward. Sharp grains got into Caroline's unblinking eyes, so that as they travelled down Main Street her face streamed with tears.

'Is this the place?' she asked dully. They had pulled up outside Gerlach's Bank, a large building with a grand, handsome sign.

'This is it,' Hutch said. Do you want me to come in with you?'

'No.' She shook her head. 'I'll be fine. Thank you.' Inside the building it was quiet and cool. She approached the neat young clerk and saw him recoil from the disarray of her face and clothes and hair.

'May I help you, madam?' he asked.

'I would like to make a withdrawal,' she said.

'Do you have an account with Gerlach's, madam?' the clerk asked, making this prospect seem unlikely.

Caroline fixed him with a steady gaze. 'I believe my husband has kept an account here for many years. I am Mrs Corin Massey.' At this an older man appeared behind the young clerk and smiled kindly at her.

'Mrs Massey, do come and sit down. My name is Thomas Berringer. I've been expecting you. Everything has been put in order and you may of course have access to your late husband's account.'

When it came to how much money should be withdrawn, Caroline realised that she had no idea. No idea how much was owing, or even how many young men there were to be paid. She withdrew half of the available funds, and although Mr Berringer looked surprised, he filled out the necessary forms and passed them to her to sign without comment. The date he had written at the top gave Caroline a small jolt.

'It's my birthday,' she said dully. 'I'm twenty-one today.'

'Well, now.' Mr Berringer smiled, looking slightly uncomfortable. 'Many happy returns of the day, Mrs Massey.'

The resulting packet of banknotes was thick and heavy. Caroline weighed it in her hand, unsure of where to stow it. Seeing her predicament, Mr Berringer again beckoned to the clerk, and a cloth bag was found to conceal the money from prying eyes. Outside, Caroline stood on the raised sidewalk and gazed at all the people and horses and buggies. She had once felt so at home amid people. Now she felt at home nowhere, she realised. Seeing a haberdashery, she bought a soft, white crocheted blanket for William, and an open carry-cot made of close-woven straw.

'It'll be cooler in the heat than that leather papoose carrier he has currently,' she explained to Hutch.

'That's mighty kind of you. I'm sure Maggie will be very pleased,' Hutch nodded, stowing the gifts beneath the seat of the buggy.

The men were paid, and the wad of banknotes thinned by barely a third. Caroline returned the remainder to the cloth bag and put it into her vanity case. Her hand brushed something soft and she drew it out. It was her blue velvet jewellery fold, with her mother's emeralds and some other fine pieces inside. She unrolled it and looked at the bright stones, thinking of the last time she had worn them, the night she had first met Corin. When had she thought she would wear them out here? They looked ridiculous in the simple bedroom. She rolled them away and put them back in the case. Then, without thinking, she packed away some other things too—some clean undergarments and blouses, a nightdress with long sleeves too warm for the summer, some hair combs and face powder. She closed the lid and fastened the clasps tightly, wondering where on earth she thought she could go.

Late in August the ranch grew quiet. Hutch, Joe and several of the other men had gone out onto the grass with near a thousand head of cattle for the final weeks of fattening up before the animals would be shipped north, to the meat markets of the eastern states. Many of those men who remained on the ranch were laid low with an illness that passed quickly from person to person, consigning them to their beds.

Sitting on the porch early one morning, Caroline saw Annie, Joe's sister, ride out of the ranch on Magpie's grey pony. She headed east, urging the pony into a brisk canter. The Ponca woman's face, as she passed, was set into deep lines of disquiet. Caroline thought for a while and realised that she had not seen Magpie since the previous afternoon. She stood and walked slowly across the yard.

The dugout was hot and rancid. Magpie lay still on the bed and William mumbled and grizzled to himself in the straw carry-cot Caroline had bought for him. There was an unmistakable smell of ammonia and faeces coming from the baby. With her heart beating fast, she knelt beside Magpie and shook her gently. The girl's face was deep red and dry. When she opened her eyes they had an odd, dull gleam and Caroline drew back slightly, frightened.

'Magpie, are you sick? Where has Annie gone?' she asked hurriedly.

'I am sick. White Cloud too. Her medicines have not cured us,' Magpie whispered. There was a wooden cup by the bed and Caroline picked it up. There was some concoction within, which smelled sharp and vinegary. She held it up to Magpie but the girl turned her head away weakly. 'No more of that stuff. No more of it,' she whispered.

'If you have a fever, you have to drink something,' Caroline said. 'I'll get some water. You have to get up, Magpie. William's dirty . . .'

'I cannot get up. I cannot change him,' Magpie replied, sounding so unhappy that Caroline faltered. 'You must do it. Please.'

'But I don't know how!' Caroline said. 'Magpie, why didn't you send word to me that you were sick?' she asked. Magpie gazed at her, and she read the answer there. None of them had thought she would be any help. Tears welled in her eyes. 'I'll clean him. I'll fetch you water,' she said, wiping her face. She grabbed a pail and headed over to the cistern. 'Where's White Cloud? Where's Annie gone?' she asked again.

'White Cloud is sick too. She is in the teepee, resting. Annie has gone east, to our peoples' lands on the Arkansas River . . . to fetch medicine.'

'The Arkansas River? That's nigh on two hundred miles! It will take her days and days!' Caroline cried.

'Please, clean William,' Magpie said again. Caroline fetched a pail of water and a ladle. It took all of her strength to lift Magpie's head and shoulders so that the girl could drink, but Magpie could manage only tiny sips and found it hard to swallow.

Searching the dugout, Caroline found clean napkins and a towel. She took William out of the carry-cot and went outside with him. The filth she found when she undressed the baby made her gag, and she threw the rags onto the coals of the dying cook fire. The water was cold and William began to cry as she dunked him into the pail. His cries were weak though, and he seemed to tire himself out, falling into a kind of doze. Sitting on the ground, she lay him along her thighs and was stroking his arms, when she realised how warm he was and how flushed his cheeks had grown. Hurriedly, she gathered him up and went back into the dugout.

'Magpie . . . William's very hot. I think he has a fever too,' she said. The Ponca girl's eyes filled with tears.

'I don't know how to help him. Please . . . he will get sick too. You must take him . . . take him to the house! Clean him, feed him. Please!'

'I have cleaned him, see? He will be fine . . . you'll both be fine, Magpie,' Caroline declared.

'White Cloud . . .' Magpie murmured indistinctly. Caroline lay William back in his cot and went over to the teepee. She hesitated outside, afraid to go any farther. She thought of White Cloud's iron gaze.

'White Cloud? May I come in?' she called tentatively, but there came no reply. Breathing fast, Caroline lifted the tent flap and went inside. White Cloud lay crumpled on the ground like so many old rags.

'White Cloud?' she whispered, kneeling beside her and shaking her. But White Cloud did not stir. Her skin radiated heat and her breathing was fast and shallow. Caroline had no idea what to do. She went back outside and then faltered, standing alone with her hands shaking, surrounded by people who had need of her help.

Caroline took William back to the house with her. He was fast asleep, his fist wedged into his mouth. She put him in the coolest, shadiest spot she could find and began to explore the kitchen cupboards, looking for food she could take over to Magpie.

Steeling herself, she went over to the bunkhouses and found three of the beds occupied. The stricken riders murmured in embarrassment when she entered, assuring her they were quite well even though they were too weak to rise. Caroline fetched pails of water and made each of them drink, before leaving a cup of water beside each man's bed. She had been hoping to find somebody able to ride to town and fetch the doctor, but they were too ill. She went back to the house and began to make a soup from dried beans and a chicken carcass. She also fetched a pumpkin from the cellar and cooked it up into a mash for William.

In the night William woke her up with thin cries of distress and she rose, holding him to stop his crying with comforting words and kisses. She laid him back down as he went back to sleep, then sat on the edge of the bed and cried to herself, because it was all she had ever wanted to have a baby sleeping next to the bed, and to comfort it and love it. But this child was not hers, and Corin was not lying beside her, and this tiny taste of how things should have been was so bitter and sweet.

By morning, there was no denying that William had caught the fever as well. He slept too much, he was hot, and was groggy and limp when he woke. Caroline went over to the bunkhouses with the soup she had made, and then to the dugout to Magpie, pausing outside the teepee. She forced herself to lift the tent flap. White Cloud had not moved. She did not move. Not at all. Not even her chest, with the rise and fall of breathing. Caroline dropped the tent flap and backed away, horror squeezing her insides. Breathing fast, she went down into the dugout.

Magpie was weaker, and harder to wake. The whites of her eyes looked grey, and her skin was even hotter. Caroline washed her face with a wet cloth, and ladled more water through her cracked lips.

'How is William? Is he sick?' Magpie whispered.

'He . . .' Caroline faltered, unwilling to speak the truth. 'He has a fever. He is quiet this morning,' she said gravely.

'And White Cloud?' Magpie asked. Caroline looked away.

'She is sleeping,' she said shortly. When she looked up Magpie was watching her, and she could not hold the girl's gaze.

'I don't know what to do. I don't know how to help myself or White Cloud,' Magpie whispered, despairingly. 'We must hope for Annie to come back soon, and to bring medicine.'

'That will take far too long!' Caroline said desperately. 'Somebody will have to go! You can't wait for Annie!' She stood up, pacing the dugout. 'I'll go,' she said in the end. 'I'll go, and . . . I'll take William with me. The doctor can see to him straight away and then come back with me and look after you and everybody else. It's the best way.'

'You will take William with you . . . ?'

'It's the best way. You can't look after him, Magpie! I can do it. I'll take the buggy and that way the doctor will see him this evening. Tonight, Magpie! He could have medicines tonight! Please. This is the best way.' Now that she had decided, she was desperate to start. 'It might be too late, otherwise,' she added. Magpie's eyes widened with fear.

'Please, take care of him. Please come back quickly,' she implored.

'I will! I'll send the doctor to you at once. It will be fine—truly it will,' Caroline said. She took Magpie's hand and squeezed it hard.

She loaded her vanity case, the carry-cot and a bag of William's things into the buggy and drove it as quickly as she dared, steering the horse between thickets of brush as she had watched Hutch and Corin do. The North Canadian was low between its banks and cool droplets of water spun up from the wheels as they took the ford.

Pausing to rest herself and the horse, Caroline lifted William into her arms. He was still hot and cried fitfully each time he woke, but now he was sleeping, and his face reminded Caroline of how Corin's face had looked when he'd slept in his chair. Thinking again, even for a second, that this might be Corin's child stole the air from her lungs. She sat down in the sand with William in her lap, and she studied him. His hair was dark, but his skin was lighter than either Magpie's or Joe's. His eyes, although brown, had a greenish ring around the iris that lightened them. In the furrow of the tiny brow, Caroline thought she saw traces of her husband. She cradled the child to her chest and she wept. She wept for Corin's betrayal, and for the loss of him, and for the perfect, agonising feeling of holding his baby to her.

The doctor took one look at Caroline's frantic face and the child in her arms and ushered her inside. He took William and examined him closely, quizzing Caroline about the symptoms the adults at the ranch were showing and how long the illness had been rife.

'I think he will be well. His fever is not too high as yet, and his heart is strong, so please, try not to worry too much. Are you staying in town tonight? Good. Keep him cool. The main thing is to bring his fever down as soon as possible. Cold wet cloths, changed regularly. Give him three drops of this on his tongue, with a teaspoon of water afterwards, every four hours. It's an antipyretic—it will help break the fever. I believe he will recover quickly. You brought him to me in time. But I must leave for the ranch, for if it goes unchecked this sickness could prove more serious. You will follow on tomorrow, so I can check your child again?' Caroline nodded. 'Good. Are there any others at the ranch as young as this, or any of great age?' the doctor asked as he ushered her from the room. *Your child.*

'There are no other children. White Cloud is advanced in years,' she whispered. 'But I think . . . I think she has died already,' she said, her throat constricting. The doctor shot her an incredulous glance.

'I must leave at once and travel through the night—I can hope to be there by sunrise. A fellow doctor can be found at this address—if William takes a turn for the worse, call upon him.' He handed Caroline a card, nodded briskly, and stalked from the room.

Caroline did not sleep. She fetched a basin of cold water from the hotel kitchens and laid damp cloths gently onto William's skin, as instructed. She checked the clock obsessively, giving him his dose when four hours had passed. By morning she was light-headed with fatigue, but William's colour was better, and his skin was cooler. He ate some rice pudding that the landlady had made for him. Caroline wrapped him in the crocheted blanket, laid him in the carry-cot, put a pacifier into his hands and gazed at him. He could be hers—the doctor had thought so. He could be the child of a respectable white woman—nothing about his person marked him out as a Ponca. Indeed, he could have been hers, she thought. He should have been hers.

Caroline was reluctant to go back to the ranch. The thought of starting back made her feel so tired inside. When she returned she would have to give William back. She thought of Magpie, helpless and sick. She thought of life, stretching on for year after empty year, and all of them without Corin. But when she looked at William she smiled and felt something swelling up inside her. Something that pushed the other thoughts aside and made it bearable to go on. She could not go back.

Across town, plumes of steam rose from the railway track. Caroline walked in that direction, her case in one hand, the carry-cot in the other. She moved purposefully, her mind now empty of thought, because her thoughts were too dark. The platform was wreathed in steam and the hot metal smell that had accompanied her to Woodward in the first place. But this immense, black locomotive was facing the other way. Northwards, to Dodge City, Kansas City and beyond.

'Look, William, look at the train!' she exclaimed, holding the baby up for his first sight of such a thing. William eyed it distrustfully. Then the guard's whistle startled them both and the train exhaled a vast, ponderous cough of steam, its wheels easing into motion. A latecomer ran onto the platform, wrenched open a carriage door and leaped aboard, just as the train began to inch slowly along the platform.

'Come along, ma'am! Quickly now, or you'll miss it!' the man smiled, holding out his hand. Caroline hesitated. Then she took the man's hand.

6

ON MONDAY MORNING, I dress in warm cords and slide the teething ring into my pocket. The bell makes a cheerful little giggling sound. I go to the study, look in the desk drawers for a pen and a pad of paper and stuff them into my bag. Outside is another of those crystal-clear days, painfully bright. I leave Beth on the phone to Maxwell, bargaining for the return of her son.

The sun is low in the sky, inescapable. It stabs at me through the windscreen, lances up from the wet road so that I must drive through a blinding wall of light. I turn gingerly out of the village onto the main road and see a familiar figure walking along the frosty white verge. I pull over, wind down the window and call to him.

'Where are you headed?' I ask. The cold makes my eyes water.

'To the bus stop,' Dinny replies.

'Well, I gathered that. Where then? I'm going into Devizes—do you want a lift?'

Dinny walks over to the car. 'Thanks. That'd be great,' he nods.

'Shopping?' I ask, as I pull away from the verge.

'I thought I'd get something for the baby. What about you?'

'I'm going to the library, to look something up in the births, marriages and deaths index. I've been tracking down a Calcott family secret.'

'Oh?'

'I found a picture of my great-grandma, Caroline—do you remember her?'

'Not really. I think I saw her from afar a couple of times.'

'She was American. She came over to marry Lord Calcott late in 1904, but I've found this picture of her in 1904, in America, with a baby. Nobody seems to know what happened to that baby—there's no record of her marrying before, but I've also found a letter that suggests otherwise.'

'Well, the baby probably died there, before she came over.' He shrugs.

'Probably,' I concede. 'But I just want to check—just in case he's mentioned in the records. If he is . . . if I can prove that Caroline lost a child—another child, since we know she lost a daughter here in Barrow Storton—it might help explain why she was the way she was.'

Dinny says nothing to this. He studies the photo, frowning slightly.

'Perhaps,' he murmurs, after a while.

'I've been trying to find out, you see, why the Calcotts—the earlier Calcotts—had such a bee in their bonnets about you Dinsdales,' I say.

'A bee in their bonnets?' he echoes quietly. 'That's a gentle euphemism.'

'I know,' I say apologetically. I change the subject. 'So, how's Honey doing?' We chat about his sister for a while, until I try to park in Devizes and am met by row upon row of parked cars.

'What on earth is all this?' I exclaim.

'Sale mania,' Dinny sighs. 'Try Sheep Street.' Eventually, I creep the car into a space.

'Do you want a lift back as well?' I offer.

'How long will you be?'

'I'm not sure. An hour and a half? Maybe a bit longer?'

'OK—thanks. I'll meet you back here?'

'How about in that café on the High Street—the one with the blue awning? It'll be warmer if one of us has to wait,' I suggest. Dinny nods, twists his hand in salute and strides away between the packed cars.

The library is on Sheep Street, so I don't have far to walk. It's almost empty inside, with a few people perusing the shelves. Seated at a computer, I search for deaths in 1903, 1904 and 1905, and the names Calcott and Fitzpatrick, in London and in Wiltshire. I skim these results for the deaths of children under the age of two. My pad of paper remains blank. After an hour, I scrawl on it: *He's not here.*

The baby probably died in America. That, and whatever happened to make Caroline leave the man who signed himself C, might even be what made her come over to England in the first place, and could certainly have contributed to her distance, her frigidity. So why can't I let it go at that? What is it that is pulling at a far corner of my mind, begging me to grasp it? Something else—that I know and have forgotten.

I pull the teething ring from my pocket, run my fingers around the smooth, immaculate ivory. Inside the bell, on the rim, is the hallmark. A tiny lion cartouche, an anchor, a gothic letter G, and something I struggle to make out. I turn it to the light, hold it close to my face. A flame? A tree—a skinny tree like a cypress? A hammer? The light bounces from it. It's a hammer head.

I turn back to the computer, search for *American silver marks G.* Several online encyclopedias and silver-collecting guides appear. Searching entries under the letter G, it takes no time at all to find the stamp on the bell. Gorham. An influential silver maker, founded in Rhode Island in 1831. I find the vertical hammer head in the list of Gorham's date marks—1902. This then I have managed to prove— whoever the baby in the photo is, this silver and ivory teething ring belonged to him. He was the fine son it was offered to.

It is slow work, making my way to the High Street, through knots of purposeful browsers, and the café, when I reach it, is full to the brim. I feel a wash of irritation, until I see Dinny already at one of the small tables in the steamed-up window.

'Hi—sorry, have you been waiting long?' I smile.

'No, not long. I got lucky with this table—a couple of old dears were just getting up as I came in.'

'Do you want another coffee? Something to eat?'

'Thanks. Another coffee would be good.'

I buy two big mugs of coffee, and an almond croissant for me.

'Did you find what you were looking for?' Dinny asks.

'Yes and no. There's no record of the baby dying this side of the Atlantic, so I suppose he must have died on the other side of it.'

'Or, the baby didn't die at all.'

'So where is he?'

'I don't know—it's your project. I'm just pointing out one reason why there might be no record of his death.'

'True. But on her marriage certificate, it says spinster. It couldn't have said that if she'd come over with another man's baby,' I counter. Dinny shrugs. I pass him the teething ring. 'I checked the mark on this, though. It's a—'

'Teething ring?' Dinny says.

'Which apparently everybody knows but me.' I roll my eyes. 'It's an American mark—and it was made in 1902.'

'But didn't you already know the baby was born in America? What does that prove?'

'Well, if nothing else, I think it proves that Caroline was his mother. When I showed Mum the photograph she suggested Caroline could have been its godmother, or it could have been a friend's baby, or something. But for her to have kept his teething ring this whole time—she has to have been his mother, don't you think?'

'I suppose so, yes.' Dinny nods, hands me back the ivory ring.

I gulp the hot coffee, feel it bring blood into my cheeks. Dinny casts his eyes back out to the thronging street, seems deep in thought.

'So, how does it feel to be the ladies of the manor? Are you starting to get used to it yet?' he asks suddenly, still looking out of the window.

'Hardly. I don't think we'll ever feel that the place is ours. And as for staying on to live . . . well, the upkeep costs alone would stop us.'

'What about the Calcott riches village rumour has it you've inherited?'

'Just rumour, I'm afraid. The family wealth has been in decline since the First World War. That's why Meredith had to sell off so much of the land, the best paintings, the silver . . . the list goes on. There was some money left, when she died, but it'll be spent on death duties.'

'What about the title?'

'Well, that's gone to Clifford, Henry's father.' As I say his name I raise my eyes, lock with Dinny's for a fleeting moment. 'My great-grandfather, who was also a Henry, changed the letters patent by act of parliament, because he had no sons. He fixed it so that the barony could pass to Meredith, and then revert to male offspring. Her heirs-male of the body, or whatever they call it.'

'So that's why Meredith stayed Calcott, even though she married?

And why your mother is a Calcott too? But how come you and Beth are Calcotts, then?'

'Because Meredith bullied my parents into it. Poor Dad—didn't stand a chance. She said the Calcott name was too important to cast off. Apparently, Allen just doesn't have the same clout.'

'Odd, that she left the house to you girls if the title was going to your uncle,' he muses, swirling his coffee around the bottom of the mug.

'Meredith was odd. She had no say in where the title went, but she could do what she liked with the house.'

'So, after Clifford, it will be . . . ?'

'Extinct. No more title. Theoretically, Clifford could go to court again, and have it pass to Eddie, but there's no way in the world Beth would allow it. She wants nothing more to do with it. Or the house, really. Which kind of makes my decision for me, too—we would both have to live here if we wanted to keep it.' Dinny is silent for a while. I can feel the shape of Beth's reluctance, the reason for it, trying to coalesce in the air between us.

'Not really surprising,' Dinny murmurs at last.

'Isn't it?' I ask. But Dinny shrugs, leans back from the table.

'Why are you here, then? If you know you aren't going to stay?'

'I thought it would be good. Good for Beth. For both of us really. To come back for a while and . . .' I struggle for words. 'Revisit. You know.'

'Why would it be good for her? It doesn't seem to me she even wants to think about it, let alone revisit it. Your childhood here, I mean.'

'Dinny . . .' I pause. 'When you came up to the house to see her, what did you mean when you said there were things she needed to know. What things, Dinny? Something about Henry?' I press.

Dinny looks at me with lowered brows.

'I think she ought to know some things about when we were young. I don't know what she thinks, but . . . some things might not have been what they seemed,' he says quietly.

On Tuesday I drive to West Hatch, squinting into the lazy sun. I drive around the village twice until I see what I'm looking for. In front of a compact brick bungalow, there's a battered old motor home taking up the whole of the driveway. I know it at once. Mickey Mouse's house.

At the door I find my nerves fluttering. Excited rather than scared. The bell makes a soft, electronic *ping . . . pong*. Mo looks smaller, older, slightly denuded, but I recognise her at once. More lines on her face, and her hair a solid, unlikely chestnut colour, but the same shrewd eyes. She looks at me with a steady, measuring gaze.

'Yes?'

'Um, I've come to see Honey? And the baby. It's Erica. Erica Calcott.'

'Erica! By Christ, I would never have known you! You look so different!'

'Twenty-three years might do that to a girl.' I smile.

'Well, come in, come in, we're all in the front room.' She ushers me inside, gestures to a doorway on the left and suddenly I'm nervous about going in. I wonder who *we all* are.

'Thanks,' I say, hands clammy on the plastic flower wrapper.

I find myself the only one standing in a room full of seated people. I glance around, smile like an idiot. Dinny looks up sharply from one end of the sofa, and he smiles when he sees me.

Honey sits next to him, an empty carry-cot at her feet and a bundle in her arms. There's another young girl I don't recognise, with shocking-pink hair and a crystal in her lip. Mo introduces her as Lydia, a friend of Honey's, and an older man, thin and beady, is Mo's partner Keith. There's nowhere for me to sit so I dither awkwardly in the small room, and Honey struggles to sit up straighter.

'Oh, no—don't get up!' I say, proffering the flowers and chocolates, then shunting them onto the table through a clutter of empty coffee mugs and a plate of Rich Tea biscuits.

'I wasn't. I'm passing her to you,' Honey says, flicking her kohled eyelids and carefully manoeuvring the baby towards me.

'Oh, no. No. You look comfortable.'

· 'Don't be chicken-shit. Take her,' Honey insists, half smiling. 'How did you find us?' she asks.

'I went down to the camp first—bumped into Patrick. He told me you were home.' I glance at Dinny, I can't help it. He is watching me intently, but I can't guess his expression. I drop my bag and take Haydee from her mother. A small pink face below a shock of dark hair finer than cobwebs. She doesn't stir as I perch on the arm of the sofa, or as I kiss her forehead and smell the baby smell of brand-new skin.

'She's beautiful, Honey. Well done you! Is she a screamer?'

'No, not so far. She's been pretty chilled out.'

'She'll get the hang of the yelling, don't you worry,' Mo says ruefully, and Honey flashes her a mildly rebellious look.

'I'll put another brew on,' Keith says, levering himself from his chair and collecting empty mugs onto a tin tray. 'You'll take a cup, Erica?'

'Oh, yes please. Thanks.' I can feel eyes on me and I look to my right. Dinny watches me, still. Those dark eyes of his, unblinking. I hold his gaze for two heartbeats and then he looks away, stands up abruptly.

'I have to get going,' he says.

'What? Why?' Honey asks.

'Just . . . things to do.' He bends down, kisses his sister on the top of her head, then he hesitates, and turns to me. 'We're all heading to the pub tomorrow night, if you and Beth want to come?' he asks.

'Oh, thanks. Yes—I'll ask Beth,' I say.

'Raise me a glass,' Honey grumbles. 'New Year's Eve and I'll be at home and in bed by nine.'

'Oh, you'll soon get used to missing out on all sorts of occasions, don't you worry,' Mo tells her brightly, and Honey's face falls in dismay.

'I'll be back later. Bye, Mum,' Dinny smiles, briefly presses his hand to the side of Mo's face and then stalks from the room.

Keith returns with a fresh tray of steaming mugs, and I pass Haydee back to Honey.

'Mo, I wanted to ask you about something—if you don't mind?' I say.

'Fire away,' she says, but there is tension around her eyes.

'Well, I was wondering if you'd tell me again why Grandpa Flag was called Flag? I know someone told me before, when we were little—but I can't remember it properly now.' At this she relaxes.

'Oh! Well, that's an easy enough one to tell. His proper name was Peter, but the story goes, that he was a foundling. Did you know that? Mickey's grandparents found him in the woods one day, in a patch of marsh flags—those yellow flowers, you know them? He'd been ditched by some young lass who'd got herself in trouble, no doubt, so they picked him up and took him in to raise as their own, and called him Peter; but more often than not Mickey's grandma just called him her "baby of the flags", or some such fancy, and the name just stuck.'

'I remember. In a patch of marsh flags . . .' I say, and everything else about the story I remember being told before, except this part. With a tingle of recognition, I realise that this detail is not exactly right. 'Do you know when that was? What year?'

'Lord, no! Sorry. In the early years of the last century, it would have been; but I couldn't say any surer than that. Poor little mite. Can you imagine, leaving a baby out like that? Terrible thing to do.' Mo shakes her head.

'Do you know where they found him? Where in the country, I mean?'

'Well, here, of course. In Barrow Storton. He was a local baby.'

I take this in, and I almost tell them what I think, but I don't. It seems suddenly too big, the incredible, disturbing, idea that I have, and the way it chimes with something Dinny said to me in the café yesterday.

'Why do you ask?' Mo says.

'Oh, just curious. I've been looking into the history of the Calcotts, and what have you, since I've been back. Shuffling through what I remember, trying to fill in the gaps,' I shrug. Mo nods.

'It's always the way. We wait until the people who could answer our questions are dead and gone, and only then do we realise we had questions to ask them,' she says, somewhat sadly.

'Oh, I'm not sure Meredith would have answered any questions of mine, anyway,' I say wryly. 'I was never her favourite.'

'Well, if it's the history of the house you're after, you should go and talk to old George Hathaway, over at Corner Cottage,' Keith tells me.

'Oh? Who's George Hathaway?' I ask.

'Just a pleasant old boy. He ran the garage on the Devizes road most of his life. Retired now. But his mother was a maid at the big house.'

'How far back?' I ask eagerly.

'Oh, right back. You know, they used to go into service at an early age, back then. I think she was only a girl when she started there. Before the First World War, it would have been,' Keith says. 'You know which one Corner Cottage is? On the way out of the village, towards Pewsey? It's the little thatched place with the green gates just there.'

'Yes, I know it. Thank you.' I smile. I leave them shortly afterwards, as Honey starts to drowse on the sofa.

'Come again, won't you? Bring Beth—it'd be nice to see you both,' Mo says, and I nod as the cold outside makes my nose ache.

I go straight to Corner Cottage, which sits by itself on the outskirts of Barrow Storton. The gate is closed, but I let myself in, cross the weed-choked driveway. I knock three times, hard.

'Yes, my love?' An old man smiles at me, keeps the chain on the door.

'Um, hello. Sorry to bother you—are you George Hathaway?' I say, hurriedly marshalling my thoughts.

'That's me, my love. Can I help you?'

'My name's Erica Calcott, and I was wondering if—'

'Calcott, you say? From the manor house?' George interrupts.

'Yes, that's right. I was just—'

'Just a tick!' The door shuts in my face, opens a second later without the chain. 'Never in all my years did I expect a Calcott to arrive at my door. What a turn up! Come in, come in; don't dawdle on the step!'

'Thank you.' Inside the cottage is clean, tidy, warm.

'Come on through. I'll put the kettle on and you can tell me whatever it is that brings you here.' George bustles ahead of me along a narrow corridor, followed by a small, fat, wire-haired mongrel he introduces as Jim. 'Coffee suit you?' George moves with a speed and deftness that belies his years. Neat curls of white hair around a thin face, eyes a star-tling pale green, the colour of a driftwood fire.

'Here you go. Sit down, my love.' He passes me a mug of instant and I cup my hands around it gratefully, slide onto a chair at the table. 'You've moved into the big house, now, have you?'

'Oh, not really, no. We've been here for Christmas—my sister and I. But I don't think we'll be staying on permanently,' I explain.

George's face falls. 'Now that's a shame! Not selling up, I hope? Shame for the place to fall out of the family, when it's been in it so many years.'

'I know. I know it is. Only, my grandmother was rather specific about the terms of her will, and . . . well, let's just say it might be very hard for us to keep to them,' I say.

'Ah, well, say no more. None of my business. Families is families, and they all have their ins and outs, Lord knows, even the grand ones!'

'Perhaps especially the grand ones.' I smile.

'My mother worked for your family you know,' George tells me, pride in his voice.

'I know. That was why I've come to see you, actually. The Dinsdales put me on to you—'

'Mo Dinsdale?'

'That's right. I was wondering if your mother ever used to talk about the time she spent working at the manor?' I ask, sipping my coffee.

'If she ever talked about it? Well, she never stopped talking about it, my love—not when I was a lad.'

'Oh? Did she work there a long time, do you know? Do you know when she started there?' George grins at me.

'It was the length of time she worked there that was the cause of all the natter!' he says. 'She was let go, you see. Only eight or nine months after she started. It was a bit of a source of shame, in our family.'

'Oh.' I can't hide my disappointment, because I doubt that she can have learned much in so short a time. 'Do you know why?'

'Lady Calcott fingered her for stealing. Mother denied it with every breath she had, but there you go. The gentry didn't need proof back then. Off she went packing, with no character reference or nothing. Stroke of luck that the butcher here—my dad—was in love with her from the second he set eyes on her—she married him soon afterwards, so she wasn't without means for very long.'

'Which Lady Calcott was it? Do you know the year your mother was there?'

'Lady Caroline, she was; 1905, as I remember Mother telling me.' George rubs his chin, squints into the past. 'Must have been,' he concludes. 'She married my old man in the autumn of '05.'

'Caroline was my great-grandmother. Would you like to see a picture of her?' I smile. I have it with me, in my bag. The New York portrait.

'Why, yes, look at that! She looks much the same as I remember her!'

'You knew her?' I am surprised at this.

'Not knew her, so much—the likes of her didn't come around to tea with the likes of us. But when I was a lad we used to see her, from time to time. She opened the church fête a couple of times, you know.'

'So, did your mother say anything else about her time working for Caroline? Like why she was accused of theft, if she said she didn't do it?' At this, George looks a little sheepish.

'It's a bit of a wild story, that one. Mother was always very straight, very honest. But most people had trouble believing what she claimed, so after a long old while she finally stopped talking about it. She reckoned she found out something she wasn't supposed to.'

'What was it?' The air expands in my chest, makes it hard to breathe.

'She said there was a baby vanished from the house. She didn't know whose baby it was—it just appeared one day, which was one of the things that made people doubt her. Babies don't just appear, after all, do they? But she swore it—that there was a baby in the house, and that it vanished again, just as quick as it arrived. And about the same time, one was found out in the woods and the tinkers—Mo's people—took it all round the village, asking who it belonged to. Nobody put their hand up, so they raised the child. But my mother could not let it lie—she swore blind to anybody that'd listen that that baby was in the manor house one day, and that Lady Calcott took him out and left him. So, of course Lady C wanted her gone. Accused her of stealing some trinket, and that was that.

'Make of that what you will. Some in the village said my mother cooked this baby story up, to get her own back. But I can't credit her just lying about something like that. Nor stealing, for that matter. She was straight as a die, my old mum.'

George stops, stares into the past, and I realise I am holding my breath. My heart bumps painfully, makes my fingers shake a little. I tap one nail on the blurred baby in the New York picture.

'That's the baby. That's the baby that appeared at the manor. The baby that Caroline dropped out in the woods. Your mother wasn't lying,' I tell him. George goggles at me and I feel the blessed relief of closure, of solving a puzzle, however distant from me it may be.

I tell him what I know, what I have gathered from her letters, from this photo, the teething ring, and the missing marsh flag pillowcase.

And the age-old animosity towards the Dinsdales. And when I am done I feel bone weary but glad. It feels like finding something precious I thought I'd lost, like filling in a huge hole in my past—in our past. Mine, Beth's, Dinny's. He is my cousin. Not two families at war, but one family. At length, George speaks.

'Well, I'm staggered. Proof, after all these years! My mother—if she can hear you from wherever she is, believe me, my love, she's doing a little victory dance right now! And you're sure about all this, are you?'

'Yes, I'm sure. It probably wouldn't stand up in a court of law, or anything, but I'm as sure as I can be. That baby came with her from America, and she kept him hidden while she married Lord Calcott. But then he wound up here at the manor, somehow, and she had to get rid of him. That's the part I'm most in the dark about—where he'd been in the meantime, and if she was married before and had a baby, why keep it hidden? But it's too much of a coincidence. The baby that vanished and the one that was found have to be one and the same.'

I leave Corner Cottage a short while later, promising to go back and visit. 'A new entente cordiale between Calcotts and Hathaways!' George announced, quite delighted, as I left. I hadn't the heart to say I might never be back—to the village, the manor, any of it. Unexpected, the way this thought makes me feel, when for twenty years or more I have lived away quite happily.

The heat and humanity of the White Horse crashes out like a wave when I pull the door open. It's cheek by jowl. Voices so loud, so close. I thread us a path to the bar, searching the crowd for Patrick or Dinny, or anybody else I recognise. It's Harry's dreadlocks that I spot, in the snug room at the back of the pub. I buy two whisky and waters, tip my head and smile at Beth to follow me.

'Hi!' I shout, arriving next to the table. I recognise faces from the solstice party. Denise, Sarah and Kip. Dinny and Patrick, of course. Patrick grins at me, and Dinny smiles, his eyes widening with surprise as they alight on Beth.

'It's the ladies of the manor! Come join us, ladies!' Patrick calls. His cheeks are pink, eyes bright. Harry pats my arm and on impulse I bend to him, kiss his cheek, feel the brush of his whiskers. Dinny stares. There's a shuffling, a bunching together along the horseshoe-shaped bench, and room is made for Beth and me at either end.

'I've never actually been in here before,' I shout. 'We weren't old enough the last time we came to stay!'

'That's a crime! Well, this is your local now, so let's get you acquainted with it. Cheers!' Patrick clatters our glasses together. Cold liquid seesaws out, catches the back of Dinny's hand.

'Sorry,' I say, and he shrugs.

'No problem.' He sucks the whisky from his skin, grimacing. 'I don't know how you can drink that poison.'

'After the fourth or fifth nip you get used to it,' I reply jovially. 'So, how are you getting used to being an uncle?'

'I'm not! I still can't believe she's had a baby—five seconds ago she was a baby herself, you know?' Dinny tips his head wryly.

'Make the most of her when she's tiny,' Beth tells him, her words struggling to rise above the mash of voices. 'They grow so quickly!'

'Well, I do have the best of both worlds, I suppose. I get to have fun with the kid and then give her back when she stinks or starts howling,' Dinny smiles.

'That's always been my favourite part of being an aunt,' I say, smiling at Beth. And so just like that we chat. We sit and talk like neighbours, like nearly friends. I try not to think about it, how miraculous it is; I don't want to break the spell.

'How's your family research going?' Dinny asks me a while later when my body is warm, my face slightly numb. I peer at him.

'Well, what I've found out, basically, is that we're cousins,' I say, smiling widely. Beth frowns at me, Dinny gives that quizzical look of his.

'Rick, what are you talking about?' Beth asks.

'Quite distant—half-cousins, twice removed, or thereabouts. Seriously!' I add, when I am met with scepticism all round.

'Let's hear it, then,' says Patrick, folding his arms.

'Right. We know that Caroline had a baby boy before she married Lord Calcott in 1904. There's a photograph, and she kept hold of the kid's teething ring for the rest of her life—'

'A baby boy who more than likely never came over the water with her, or she would have had trouble remarrying as a spinster, which she apparently did not,' Beth interjects.

'Just hear me out. Then there's a pillowcase missing from one of the antique sets in the house—a pillowcase with yellow marsh flags stitched onto it. Now, Dinny, your grandpa himself told me the story of how he got his name, and your mum reminded me the other day, when I was over there. But I think some of the finer details have got scrambled over the years—Mo said Flag was found in a patch of marsh flags and got the name that way, here, in the Barrow Storton woods which aren't really good ground for marsh flags to grow in. I'm sure I remember Grandpa Flag telling me that he was found in a blanket with yellow flowers on it. It has to be the pillowcase—it has to be!' I insist, as Dinny looks even more sceptical. 'And today, I met George Hathaway—'

'The bloke who ran the garage on the main road?' Patrick asks.

'That's him. His mother worked at the manor house when Caroline first arrived there. She was sacked—ostensibly for stealing, but she insisted, George says, that she was sent away because she knew there had been a baby in the house—right at the time the Dinsdales found Flag. There was a baby in the house and then it vanished. Your grandpa was my great-grandmother's son. I'm sure of it,' I finish.

'That's . . .' Beth gropes for the word. 'Ridiculous!' she finishes.

'Why is it?' I demand. 'It would explain Caroline's hostility to the Dinsdales—she dumps the kid, wants rid of him, and they pick him up and raise him right on her doorstep. Every time they came back here, they brought that baby with them. It must have driven her mad.'

'Answer this, then,' Dinny says. 'She brings the baby over with her. She has him with her while she remarries—for some reason her previous marriage is not recorded, but there's no way she'd have wound up marrying a lord if the baby was illegitimate. So, she keeps the baby until she gets here, to Barrow Storton, and then she dumps it in the woods. My question would be why? Why did she do that?'

'Because . . .' I trail off, study my drink. 'I don't know,' I admit. I think hard. 'Was your grandpa disabled in any way?'

'Fit as a fiddle, sharp as a tack,' Dinny shakes his head.

'Maybe Lord Calcott wouldn't let her keep another man's son?'

'Then he would have just not married her if he minded that much.'

'Isn't it possible,' Patrick begins, 'and rather more plausible, that Caroline's baby died in the States, one of the servants at the manor got herself in trouble, took a pillowcase from the house in a moment of desperation, and got rid of her illegitimate baby?' he suggests cheerfully.

'He has a point,' Beth tells me. I shake my head. 'No. I know it was the baby in the picture. It has to be,' I insist.

'And as for her attitude towards me and mine,' Patrick goes on with a shrug, 'she was just a product of her time. God knows we come up against enough prejudice these days, let alone a hundred years ago! Vagrancy used to be an actual crime, you know.'

'All right!' I cry. 'I still think I'm right. What do you say, Dinny?'

'I'm not sure. And I'm not sure I want to be a Calcott. They haven't been very kind to the people I love over the years,' he says, and his gaze is so direct that I have to look away.

'Well, drink up, cousin,' Patrick says. Conciliatory, but not convinced. The subject is changed, my parade rained upon.

By midnight my ears are buzzing and when I turn my head the world blurs past, takes a while to settle back into the right order. I lean against Harry, who sits up straight and has drunk so much cola that he climbs over me to go to the toilet every twenty minutes or so. There is talk all around me and I am part of it, I am included. I am happy, drunk, blinkered. At midnight the barman turns the radio up loud and we listen to Big Ben, waiting with our breath paused in the gap before the first toll of the new year. The pub erupts and I think of London, of my old life carrying on without me. I find I don't want it back.

Patrick and Beth and several others kiss me and then I turn to Dinny, proffer my cheek, and he plants a kiss there that I can still feel long after it's gone, wonder if it will leave an indelible mark.

Not long afterwards Beth pulls my arm, says that she's going. I want to stay. I want to keep this party going, maintain the false impression that I belong with these people. Beth shakes her head.

'I'm tired. I think you should come too, so we can see each other safely back. You've had quite a bit to drink.'

'I'm fine!' I protest, too loudly, proving her point.

Beth gets up, smiles her goodbyes, starts to pull on her coat and hands me mine.

'We're off,' she says, smiling in general but not meeting Dinny's eye.

I pull on my coat. I am clumsy, can't find the arms. As we turn to go Dinny catches Beth's arm and speaks into her ear.

'Good night, cousin Erica!' he calls as I weave away.

'I'm right!' I insist, tumbling out of the pub.

'Erica! Wait for me!' Beth shouts into the wind as she emerges from the pub behind me. 'That was actually quite fun,' she says.

'Told you,' I say, loud above the buffeting air. 'What were you and Dinny whispering about back there?' I ask.

'He, uh . . .' She looks taken aback. 'He just said to . . . see you safely to bed, that's all.'

'That's all?'

'Yes, that's all! Erica, don't start—you're drunk.'

'I'm not that drunk! You two always had your secrets and not much has changed. Why won't either of you tell me what happened?'

'I . . . I've told you—I don't want to talk about it and neither should you. Have you asked Dinny, then?' She sounds alarmed, almost frightened. I think back, muzzily, realise that I haven't. Not outright.

'What did he really say just now?'

'I just told you what he said! My God, Erica . . . are you jealous? Still—after all this time?' I stop walking, turn to look at her. It never occurred to me that she knew. That they knew, that they noticed me clamouring for attention. Somehow, it's worse that they did.

'I'm not jealous,' I mutter, wishing it were true. We walk on, stumble up the driveway in silence.

Beth opens the front door but I step back from the darkness inside. In the graphite glow of the moon, it looks like a grave mouth. Beth steps in, flicks on a blinding yellow light, and I turn away.

'Come on—you're letting all the heat out,' she says. I shake my head.

'I'm going for a walk.'

'Don't be ridiculous. It's half past one in the morning. Come inside.'

'No. I'll . . . stay in the gardens. I need to clear my head,' I tell her.

'I'll wait for you to come in, then. Don't be long.'

'Don't wait. Go to bed. I won't be long.'

'Erica!' she calls, as I turn away. 'You're . . . you're not going to let it drop, are you? You're not going to leave it alone.' Real fear in her voice now. It sounds as brittle as glass. I am frightened too, by this change in her, by her sudden vulnerability. But I steel myself.

'No. I'm not,' I say, and I walk away from her.

I won't let this evening end until I have something. Until I have remembered something. I stride across the lawn. I know where I am going.

The dew pond is just more blackness at my feet. The stone-and-mud smell of the water rises to greet me. Here I sit in the dead of winter, in the dead of night, a woman with a head full of whisky trying to go back, trying to be a child full of fantasies under a hot summer sky.

I stare at the water, I take myself there. My breathing slows and I notice the cold for the first time, the press of the ground through my jeans. *Have you pissed yourself, Erica?* Henry laughing, Henry smiling that nasty smile of his. Henry bending down, looking around. What was he doing? What was he looking for? What was I doing? I went back into the water. I'm sure I did. It was a diversion—I was trying to break the tension. I turned and took a run up, and made as big a splash as I could. And when I came up . . . when I dashed the water from my eyes . . . had Henry found what he was looking for?

Before I know what I am doing, I am in. I take a run up, I make as big a splash as I can; and then reality comes pouring all around me and my skin catches fire at the cold of the water. The pain is incredible. I have no idea which way is up, no idea what to do. I have no control over my body, which flails and contorts itself. The air has vanished from my lungs. I will die, I think. I am sinking like a stone. The water has no surface, there is no sky any more. And I see Henry. My heart seems to stop. I see Henry. I see him, looking down at me from the bank, eyes wide and incredulous. I see him teetering, and I see blood running down into his eyes. So much blood. I see him start to fall. Then I am in the air again and a gasp rushes air into my lungs; I cry out in pain.

I can see the bank. It tips and blurs in my view as my body threatens to sink again. I try to make my arms work, to kick my legs. Nothing will move as it is supposed to. I can't get air to stay in my lungs. I am flayed alive; I am burning. One hand hits the bank and I can't feel it on my skin, only the resistance of it. I claw at it, force my fingers into the mud, try to make my other hand reach it, try to pull myself out. I struggle. I am a rat in a barrel, a hedgehog in a pond. I am whimpering.

Then hands grab me, under my arms, pulling me further out until my knees are grounded. One more pull and I am out, water streaming from my clothes and hair and mouth. I cough and start to cry, so happy to be out, hurting so much.

'What the fucking hell are you doing?' It's Dinny. His voice echoes oddly in my ears. 'Are you trying to kill yourself?' He is rough, furious.

'I'm . . . not sure,' I croak, and concentrate on coughing again.

'Get up!' he commands. He sounds so angry, and the last of my will leaves me. I give up. Lying down on the ground, I turn my head away from him. I can't feel my body, can't feel my heart.

'Just leave me alone,' I say. He turns me over, stands behind my head and pulls me up by my armpits.

'Come on. You need to warm up before you can lie down and rest.'

'I am warm. I'm boiling hot,' I say, but tremors are starting to come, from my feet to my fingertips, convulsing every muscle.

'Come on, walk now. It's not far.'

A short time later I become aware of myself, of the peeled feeling of my skin, the ache in my ribs and arms and skull. My fingers and toes are throbbing, agonising. I am sitting in wet underwear in Dinny's van. Wrapped in a blanket. There's hot tea beside me. Dinny pours in sugar by the heaped spoonful, instructs me to drink it. I sip it, burn my tongue. I'm shaking still, but less now. The inside of the ambulance is warmer than I'd imagined. The embers in the stove light our faces.

'How come you were at the dew pond?' I ask.

'I wasn't. I was going home when I heard the bloody great splash you made. You're just lucky the wind's blowing in from the east or I wouldn't have heard it. I wouldn't have come. Do you know what could have happened if I hadn't? Even if you'd managed to get out and then lain on the bank for half an hour . . . do you understand?'

'Yes.' I am contrite, embarrassed. There is no trace of the whisky in me now. My swim has washed it all away.

'So what were you doing?' He sits opposite me on a stool. I shrug.

'I was trying to remember. That day. The day Henry died.' *Died*, I say. Not *disappeared*. I wait to see if Dinny will correct me. He doesn't.

'Why would you want to remember?'

'Because I don't, Dinny. I don't remember it. And I have to. I need to.' He doesn't answer for a long time.

'Why? Why do you have to? If you really don't remember, then—'

'Don't tell me I'm better off! That's what Beth says and it's not true! I am not better off. There's a bit missing. I can't stop thinking about it . . . And I know he's dead. I know we killed him.'

'We killed him?' Dinny glares at me suddenly, his eyes alight. 'No. We didn't kill him.'

'What does that mean? What happened, Dinny? Where did he go?'

The question hangs between us for a long moment. I think he will tell me. I think he will. The silence stretches.

'These are not my secrets to tell,' Dinny says, his face troubled.

'I just want things to be as they were,' I say quietly. 'Not things—people. I want Beth to grow up the way she should have grown up, if it hadn't happened. It all starts there, I know it does. And I want for us to be friends, like we were . . .'

'We could have been, perhaps.' His voice is flat. I look up for an explanation. 'You just stopped coming!' he exclaims, eyes widening. 'How do you think that felt, after everything I—'

'After everything you what?'

'After all the time we'd spent . . . You just stopped coming.'

'We were kids! Our parents stopped bringing us . . . there wasn't much we could do about it . . .'

'They brought you here the summer after. And the one after that. I saw you, even if you didn't see me. But you never came down to the camp. My family were turned inside out by the police, looking for that boy. Everybody treated us like criminals! I bet they didn't turn the manor upside-down, did they? I bet they didn't keep looking in the herb garden for a grave.' I stare at him. I can't think what to say.

'At first I thought you'd been forbidden to come here. But you'd always been forbidden before and that had never stopped you. Then I thought perhaps you were scared, that perhaps you didn't want to talk about what had happened. Then I finally hit on it. You just didn't care.'

'That's not true! We were just children, Dinny! What happened was . . . too big. We didn't know what to do with it—'

'You were just a child, Erica. Beth and I were twelve. That's old enough. Old enough to know where your loyalties lie. Would it have killed you to come? Just once? To write a letter?'

'I don't know,' I say. 'I don't know what happened. I . . . watched Beth for all my cues. Even now I can't tell if I knew what we'd done, what had happened. I can hardly remember anything I thought or did in those summers afterwards. And then we stopped coming.'

'Well, no wonder. If you were both acting so vacant, your mother must have thought it was damaging you.'

'It was damaging us, Dinny.'

'Well, there you go. What happened, happened. There's no changing it now, even if you want to.'

'I do want to,' I murmur. 'I want Beth back. I want you back.'

'You're lonely, Erica. I was too, for a long time. Nobody to talk to about it all. I guess we have to take what's due to us.'

'Whose secrets are they, Dinny, if they're not yours or mine?'

'I never said they weren't yours.'

'Mine and Beth's?' He stares at me, says nothing.'But I don't know!' I say quietly. 'Yes. You do.' Dinny leans towards me. 'It's time you went home to bed, I think,' he says.

'I don't want to go.' But he is on his feet. I wipe my face, notice that my hands are red and angry, mud under the nails.

'You can keep the blanket for now. Give it back to me whenever.' He rolls my wet clothes into a bundle, hands them to me. 'I'll walk you back.'

'Dinny!' I stand up, stagger slightly. In the small space we are centimetres apart but that is too far. He stops, turns to face me. I can't think of any words to say. I lean towards him, tilt my head so my forehead can touch his cheek. I stay that way for three heartbeats, until I feel his arms circle me. I lift my chin, feel his lips brush mine, and I lean into his kiss, clumsy with desire. His arms tighten around me. I would halt the world, if I could, stop it spinning, make it so I could stay here for ever, in this dark space with Dinny's mouth against mine.

He walks me back to the manor's front door and as I shut it behind me, I hear a sound that makes me pause. Water running. The sound of it echoes faintly down the stairs. 'Beth?' I call out, my teeth chattering. I make my way to the kitchen. The light is on. Beth is not there. 'Beth! Are you still up?' I shout, flinching from the glare of the lights, my head thumping. I fight to focus my eyes, because there is something not right in here, in the kitchen. Something that makes the blood beat in my temples, dries my throat. The knife block, knocked roughly over and lying on its side on the worktop, and several of the knives pulled out. I cannot breathe. I turn, race to the stairs on legs that won't move fast enough.

Lasting

1904–1905

THE STATIONMASTER AT Dodge City was most sympathetic. He listened patiently to Caroline's tale of her lost ticket and allowed her to pay there and then for her whole journey, from Woodward to New York. She spent the long days of the train ride watching out of the window, at grey storm skies and blistering white skies and china-blue skies so pretty they hurt her head. She thought of nothing, but tested the kernel of grief inside herself from time to time, to see if it would diminish with distance when it hadn't with time.

William, still recovering from his fever, slept a great deal, whimpering fretfully when he awoke. But he knew Caroline and allowed her to soothe him. She sacrificed lunch at the Harvey hotel in Kansas City to shop instead for clean napkins, blankets and a bottle for the baby, hurrying back to the train with her heart fluttering anxiously, in case it left without her. The train was the only home she had at that moment. It was her only plan.

New York was impossibly loud and huge. Heavy with fatigue, and with her mind wound tight with nerves, Caroline hailed a hansom cab and climbed aboard. Her clothes were travel-stained and smelled stale. 'Where to, madam?' the driver asked. Caroline had no idea where to go. She thought briefly of Corin's family, but William squirmed in her arms and she blinked back tears. There was no way she could have carried and borne them a grandson without Corin having written to them about it. And she did not want to be anywhere she might be found. She could not go anywhere somebody might look to find her.

'A . . . um, a hotel. The Westchester, thank you,' she answered at length, naming a place where she had once had lunch with Bathilda. The driver flicked the reins and the horse started forward.

Bathilda. Caroline had not thought of her in months and months. She would not have gone to her, even if the woman had remained in New York, Caroline told herself defiantly. She suppressed the treacherous longing she felt just to see a familiar face, even if it was not a friendly one. For whose faces would remain friendly to her now? She thought of Magpie, waiting in the dugout—but only for a second. The thought was too terrible. She thought of Hutch, of what emotions his face would register when he rode back in from the ranges, found White Cloud dead, and she and William gone without a word. Her insides seemed to writhe around themselves, and pain snapped behind her eyes.

At the Westchester she paid for a room, and enquired after a nursemaid for William, explaining that her own maid had been taken seriously ill and been forced to return to her family's care. One was found without delay, a pug-faced girl with bright ginger hair, called Luella, who looked terrified when Caroline handed William to her. William took one look at the strange girl's garish hair and began to wail. Holding the child awkwardly, Luella backed out of the room.

In the end she did not stay more than a week in the city where she had been born and raised. It no longer felt any more like home than the ranch house, or Woodward. There's nowhere I belong, Caroline thought, as she walked William in his new perambulator down streets she had never seen before, had never heard of before, hoping in this way to reduce the risk of anybody recognising her.

Passing a photographic studio, with a handsome gilt sign that read Gilbert Beaufort & Son, Caroline paused. Inside the cluttered, stuffy shop she recoiled from the vinegar stench of the developing chemicals. Not quite finding a smile for the camera, she commissioned several portraits of herself and William, arranging to have them delivered to the Westchester when they were ready.

Her fingers shook as she opened the package. She had hoped to create something permanent, to prove to herself, in some way, that she existed; and that even though she was widowed, she had Corin's child, the child that was rightly hers, to show for her marriage. She was part of a family. She would have some record of herself and of her life, which she was so unsure of that she sometimes wondered if she might still be lying out on the prairie somewhere, dreaming everything that had happened since. One photo alone had captured a trace of what she'd hoped to see—in one shot she looked like a mother, proud and possessive. She slid this picture into her case and threw the rest into the grate.

On the fourth day she saw Joe. She was walking with William in search of a park or a garden, a green space of some kind to feel a breeze and, she hoped, to calm the child. Fully recovered from his illness and returned to his strength, William was loud and unsettled.

Thinking it was the open prairie he missed, Caroline walked him most of the day, growing increasingly aware of how different the noises and smells and sights must be for the child. This was not his home, any more than it was hers, she realised; but unlike herself, William did have a home. She should take him back. The thought stung her like a slap to the face. Even if he was Corin's, even if he should have been hers, he belonged in Woodward County. But how could she explain—how could she be forgiven? She could see the pain, the accusation in Hutch's eyes, the anger and fear in Magpie's. All the times they had helped her, all the times they had encouraged her. And this was how she had repaid their belief in her. She could not face them. There was no going back.

And then she saw Joe, coming around the corner towards her, his face set into a grimace of hard fury, his black hair flying behind him as he strode towards her, knife ready in his hand to kill her. Caroline went cold from her head to her toes and stood petrified as the man walked past her, the black hair in fact a scarf, the knife a piece of rolled-up paper, the face not Joe's at all but belonging to a swarthy, Mexican-looking man who was late for something and hurrying.

Shaking uncontrollably, Caroline sank onto a nearby bench, the din of the city receding as a strange, muffled thumping invaded her head. In the distance, a passenger liner sounded its whistle as it slid into the docks. The deep blast echoed all around and brought Caroline back to herself, and to William's cries. Swallowing, she stroked his cheek, made some soothing sounds, and then she stood up, turning to cast her eyes southwards towards the docks, the ship, and the sea. Five hours later she was aboard a steamer, bound for Southampton.

Joe was indeed in New York, but not on that very day. He and Hutch arrived two days after Caroline's ship had departed, where they made their way directly to the home of Mrs Massey, Corin's mother. No trace of Caroline or William had been found since she had been seen taking breakfast at the hotel, the morning after she'd left Woodward. Word was sent out with every passing traveller, and to every outlying rancher, to report any sighting of her; and although the ticket-office clerk at the station swore that no fair-haired women carrying babies had bought a ticket for any train from him that day, or indeed that week, Hutch followed a hunch and took Joe and himself to New York, making fruitless enquiries at each station after a Mrs Massey.

Mrs Massey Senior had not, of course, seen or heard anything of her daughter-in-law. She was able to supply the men with Caroline's maiden name and former address, but their enquiries in the city after Miss Fitzpatrick were every bit as fruitless. They retraced their steps, trying the name Fitzpatrick instead of Massey, and then had little choice but to return to the ranch, to where Magpie had fallen into a trance, at times tearing at her hair and making long cuts down her arms with a blade that sent rivulets of bright blood to drip from her finger-tips. Joe let his wife mourn in this way; he was impassive, the rage had burned from him, and his own heart was empty without his son.

Between them, the men raised the money to pay a Pinkerton man for one month, but this was just enough time for the detective to follow the same path that Joe and Hutch had, and he finished the term unable even to say whether Caroline and William had been abducted or had run away. Hutch lay awake night after night, mystified and suspicious at once—scared for Caroline and for the ranch, which, having no owner, no longer had a future either.

Dreading her arrival more with each mile that passed, Caroline took the train from Southampton to London, and upon arriving found a hotel she could afford once the shrinking packet of dollars from Gerlach's Bank had been converted into pounds sterling. William was heavy in her arms and his cries made her ears wince.

Now, so tired she could barely think, Caroline hefted the child higher in her arms and propped him against the smooth marble counter in the hotel lobby.

'I need a nursemaid,' she announced. 'My own has been laid low with some fever.' The man behind the counter inclined his head conde-scendingly at her, twitching one eyebrow at her accent. She knew she was creased and careworn, and that William smelled bad, but these facts served only to make her crosser with the hotelier.

'Very well, madam. I shall make enquiries,' he told her smoothly. Caroline nodded, and toiled up the stairs to her room. She bathed William in the porcelain bowl of the washstand. He stopped crying as she washed him, and made small, happy noises, slapping his feet in the water. Caroline hummed a lullaby until he began to drowse. She held him tightly to her, forgetting everything else but the warmth of him, the trusting weight of him, as he slept.

Later a woman came to the room, announcing herself with a quiet knock. She was plump with pale, frizzy hair and grimy smears on her dress, but her eyes spoke of warmth and intelligence as she introduced herself as Mrs Cox, and they lit up when they fell upon William.

'Is this the little chap in need of a nursemaid?' she asked. Caroline nodded and waved her forward to gather him up from the bed.

'Whereabouts in the hotel do you stay? In case I have need of you or the child?' Caroline asked.

'Oh, I'm not attached to the hotel, ma'am, although I have often been called upon to look after the young children of guests when they find themselves in unusual situations, like you, ma'am . . . I live with my own children and my husband not far from here in Roe Street. Mr Strachen downstairs will always know where to find me, if you need him to. How long will you be needing me to watch him, ma'am?'

'I . . . I don't know. I'm not sure yet. A couple of days, perhaps? A little longer . . . I'm not sure.' Caroline hesitated. Mrs Cox's face fell, but when Caroline paid in advance she smiled again, and was jouncing William merrily on her hip when she left with him not long afterwards. Caroline's heart gave a sickening little lurch as William disappeared from view, but then a vast and numbing weariness pulled at her. She lay down on the bed in her dirty clothes and fell instantly asleep.

The next day, wearing the cleanest, least-creased clothes she could find in her bag, Caroline gave the slip of paper upon which Bathilda had written a Knightsbridge address to a cab driver and let him transport her there with all the quiet resolution of a person going with dignity to the scaffold. The house she arrived at was four storeys high and built of pale, grey stone, clamped into a row of identical houses with red front doors. Caroline rang the doorbell and gave her name to the elderly housekeeper, who admitted her to a gloomy entrance hall.

'Please, wait here,' the housekeeper intoned, and moved away along the corridor. Caroline stood as still as stone. She looked inside her head and found no thoughts at all. Nothing but an echoing space, hollowed out like a cracked and discarded nutshell. *Oh, Corin!* His name rushed into that space like a thunderclap. Reeling slightly, Caroline shook her head, and the emptiness returned.

Bathilda was fatter, and the hair at her temples was a brighter white, but other than that the two years since they had last met had wrought few changes upon her. She was occupying a brocaded couch with a cup of tea in her hand, and she stared at her niece in astonishment.

'Good gracious, Caroline! I should never have known you if you weren't announced!' she exclaimed at last, raising her eyebrows.

'Aunt Bathilda,' Caroline said in a quiet voice, quite tonelessly.

'Your hair is quite wild. And you're so tanned! It's disastrous. It does not suit you at all.'

Caroline accepted this criticism without blinking, saying nothing while Bathilda sipped her tea. She was aware of her heart beating, hard and slow, just like when they had brought Corin home from the coyote hunt. This was another kind of death, but a death all the same.

'Well, to what do I owe this honour? Where is that cow-herding husband of yours? Has he not joined you on this foreign expedition?'

'Corin is dead.' It was the first time she had said the words. The first time she had had to. Tears scalded her eyes. Bathilda absorbed this news for a moment and then she relented.

'Come and sit down, child. I'll send for some more tea,' she commanded, in a softer tone of voice.

Bathilda soon took control of Caroline and seemed happy enough to do so now that the younger woman was meek and no longer defiant. Caroline went back to the hotel to collect her things that afternoon, and moved into a spare bedroom at the pale grey town house. She was introduced to the owner of the house, Bathilda's cousin by marriage, Mrs Dalgleish, who was thin and dry and wore a censorious look.

Bathilda took Caroline to the bank and arranged for her money to be transferred from her parents' New York bank into an English account. She took Caroline shopping, accepting the story that all of her old clothes had been ruined on the ranch. They visited a hairdressing salon, where Caroline's hair was trimmed and curled neatly against her head. And, for the first time in over a year, Caroline's tiny form was tied tightly into corsets once again.

'Well, you are almost fit for society,' Bathilda said. 'You will have to remarry, of course. I know of just the gentleman, and he is in town now, to see the newest girls. A Baron, if you please—land-rich but cash-poor, and in need of an heir. He would make you a lady . . . from farmer's wife to nobility in the space of a couple of months! What a resolution that would be!' she exclaimed. 'But, although he is not as young as once he was, he's known to prefer fresh young things . . . not the world-weary widows of backwater cattlemen. It will be best if we do not mention to anyone your unfortunate first marriage. Can you do that? There's no evidence to the contrary? Nothing you haven't told me?' she asked.

Caroline took a deep breath. Words clamoured to be spoken, and her pulse raced. But she knew that if she confessed to having brought a child with her, this new life Bathilda was building for her would fly apart like a mirage and she would instead have to remain in this agonising present, with no chance of a more bearable future. Caroline shook her head. But when she raised her left hand and worked the wedding ring free, it left a perfect white band on her skin. She kept the ring in a closed fist and later slipped it into the satin lining of her vanity case, next to the photograph of herself and William.

The white band soon faded, kept hidden under satin and kid gloves until it was wholly invisible. Caroline met Lord Calcott at a reception that Bathilda took her to the following week. He was lightly built, not tall, perhaps forty-five years old, and he walked with a slight limp. They met twice more, at a ball and a dinner party, in rooms stuffily heated against the late autumn chill. As they danced he asked her about her family, and her favourite pastimes, and how she liked London. Later he spoke to Bathilda and enquired after Caroline's temperament, her lack of conversation, and her income. After one such evening she accepted his proposal of marriage with a nod of her head and a smile as fleeting as winter sun. He drove her back to Knightsbridge in a smart black carriage pulled by a team of four, and his good-night kiss roamed from her cheek to her mouth, his hands shaking with rising lust.

'Darling girl,' he whispered hoarsely, pushing up her skirts and kneeling between her legs to shove his way inside her, so abruptly that she gasped in shock. *Do you see?* She hurled the anguished thought out, silently, to wherever Corin had gone: *Do you see what has happened because you left me?*

Caroline spent Christmas of 1904 with Bathilda and Mrs Dalgleish, and she arranged to marry Henry Calcott in February the following year. This time her engagement was properly announced, and a picture of the happy couple was published in *The Tatler*. As the wedding approached Caroline began to suffer from a consuming lassitude, and a sickness in the mornings. Bathilda kept a stern eye on these developments.

'It seems the wedding won't come a day too soon,' she commented one morning, as Caroline lay in bed, too dizzy and weak to rise. When the nature of her condition dawned upon her, Caroline was stunned.

'But . . . but I . . .' was all she managed to reply to her aunt. Caroline remained still for several hours, and thought and thought, and tried not to see the clear implications of her pregnancy. For she was every bit as thin as she had been in Oklahoma Territory, if not thinner, and every bit as unhappy, indeed if not more so. The only thing that had changed was the man with whom she lay.

Storton Manor seemed unlovely to Caroline. It was grand, but graceless, the windows too stern to be beautiful, the stone too grey to be welcoming. The driveway had been colonised by dandelions and couch grass, the paint was peeling from the front door and the chimney stack was missing several pots. Her money was much needed, she realised.

The staff lined up to meet her. Housekeeper, butler, cook, parlour maid, chambermaid, scullery maid, groom. Caroline swallowed back a threatened storm of weeping as she pictured the scruffy ranch hands who had lined up for her presentation to her first marital home. And you left them all without a word, she accused herself. She smiled and nodded for each as Henry introduced them, and they in turn bobbed a curtsy to her, or made a short bow, muttering *Lady Calcott*. She took hold of her real name, Caroline Massey, and squeezed it tightly to her heart.

Later, walking around the broad sweep of the grounds, Caroline began to feel a little better; the snowstorm pieces of herself began to settle, just softly, into a kind of order. The air of the English country-side had a sweetness, even at the far end of winter. She was neither too hot, nor too cold. She could see the rooftops and smoke plumes of the village through the naked trees around the house, and it soothed her to know that within a moment's walk there were lives being lived. A swathe of bright daffodils lit up the far end of the lawn, and Caroline walked slowly through them. She meditated on the emptiness of her mind, on the hollow feeling she couldn't shake, but she allowed herself to think, just for a moment, that she was safe and could bear it all.

Henry Calcott was a lusty man, so Caroline suffered his conjugal attentions every night in the first few weeks of their wedded life. She was passive, amazed at how different lovemaking felt when undertaken with a person for whom she felt nothing.

Workmen appeared at Storton Manor and began to tidy the grounds and make repairs to the house, both inside and out.

'Will you be all right, if I go up to town? The men shan't bother you?' Henry asked Caroline, three weeks after her arrival at the manor.

'Of course they won't bother me,' she replied calmly.

'You are more than welcome to come to town with me . . .'

'No, no, you go. I prefer to remain here and get better acquainted with . . . with the house, and . . .'

'Very well, very well. I'll only be a week, I should think. Just a few matters of business to attend to,' Henry smiled, returning to the morning's papers. Caroline turned to look out of the widow at the overcast day. *Matters of business*, she repeated to herself. At one London ball, a thin-faced girl with platinum hair had whispered to her that Henry Calcott loved a game of poker. Caroline did not mind as long as his habit took him to London every few weeks, and left her well alone.

The second day after his departure was a day of steady rain. Caroline sat close to the fire in the drawing room, reading an overblown romance by a woman called Elinor Glyn. Her thoughts were on the child inside her: when she should tell Henry, and why she had not done so already. The parlour maid, a timid girl called Estelle, inter-rupted her reverie with a knock.

'Begging your pardon, my lady, but there's a woman here to see you.'

'A woman? What woman?'

'She wouldn't state her business, my lady, but she gave her name as Mrs Cox. Should I show her in?'

Caroline sat mesmerised with shock. There was a long pause, in which the sound of approaching feet could be heard.

'No!' Caroline managed at last, standing up abruptly but too late, as Mrs Cox pushed past Estelle and stood before Caroline with rainwater dripping from her hem onto the Persian rug. She fixed Caroline with a fiery eye and a determined set to her jaw.

'That will be all, thank you, Estelle,' Caroline whispered.

Mrs Cox looked immense. As she unbuttoned her raincoat the reason for this became clear. William was asleep, warm and dry beneath the coat, in a sling the woman had fashioned from a length of cotton canvas.

'I don't know what you mean by it!' Mrs Cox exclaimed at last, when it became clear that Caroline was lost for words. 'Leaving the child with me all these many weeks . . . I don't know what you can mean by it!'

'I . . .' But Caroline had no answer to give. Her careful neutrality, her passive acceptance of her fate, had written William out of the script. She had distanced herself from all thoughts of him, all responsibility. Seeing him again gave her a feeling like a blow to the stomach, a hard spike of love that was riddled with guilt and fear. 'How did you find me?' was all she could think to ask.

'It wasn't that hard, not with news of your wedding published in all the papers. I waited a bit longer, thinking you'd wanted the child kept safe and quiet while you got wed, but then I saw you weren't going to come for him at all! You weren't, were you? And him such a good, healthy boy . . . I don't know what you mean by it!' Mrs Cox repeated, her voice growing thick. She dabbed at her eyes with a handkerchief. 'And now I've had the expense of bringing him here on the train . . .'

'I can pay you. For the train, and . . . for the time you've had him. I can pay you more than that, even—here!' Caroline rushed to the dresser, withdrawing a purse of coins and holding it out to the woman. 'Will you keep him?' she asked suddenly. Mrs Cox stared at her.

'Keep him? What can you mean? I'm not running a baby farm, I'll have you know! You're his mother—a child belongs with its mother. And look at the life he'll have here!' She gestured at the grand surroundings. 'I've enough mouths to feed and enough bodies to find beds for without taking on another one!' The woman seemed distraught.

Caroline could only stand and stare in desperation as Mrs Cox began to work at the knot holding the sling around her shoulders. 'Here. I've brought him back to you now. Fit and well. All his things are in this bag—all but the carrier, for which he has grown too big, and I could not carry it as well as him to come down here. I hope you'll love him, ma'am. He's a good boy and he deserves to have a mother's love . . .' She seated William on the red silk cushion of a winged armchair. He held his arms up to her and smiled. 'No, lovey, you're staying with your real mam now,' she told him, her eyes again filling with tears.

'Take good care of your boy, Lady Calcott,' Mrs Cox said, and hurried away. William sat quietly for a minute, then he began to cry.

Frantic to hide him, Caroline scooped William up and went quickly via the back stairs to her bedroom. She put him down on the bed and stepped back, clasping her hands to the sides of her head, trying to still her thoughts. Her breathing came in short, panicked snatches. Quickly, she found a pacifier in William's bag of things and gave it to him to distract him. He stopped crying and grasped at the familiar, tinkling object, making small conversational noises to himself.

Gradually, Caroline calmed down. He had grown so much! But then, he was a year and a half old now. His skin was darker and his hair was thicker. His face was beginning to show the high, slanting cheeks and straight brows of the Ponca. How could she ever have thought he was Corin's child? William was Indian, through and through; it would have been obvious even if she had not come to realise that her failure to give Corin a child had more to do with Corin than with herself. Which meant that she had stolen Joe and Magpie's baby.

The enormity of this heinous crime hit Caroline like a poleaxe, and she sank to the floor, cramming a fist into her mouth to stifle uncontrollable sobs. And she could not undo this terrible thing. There was no redress she could offer to Magpie—kind, gentle Magpie, who had been nothing but loyal and friendly, who was missing her child thousands of miles from where he now lay. Thousands of miles that neither she nor William would ever traverse again. It was another world, another lifetime. In bringing him here she had crossed a one-way boundary. In that moment, Caroline did not know how she was going to live with what she had done. She sat slumped on the carpet, and she wished to die.

Half an hour later, the maids and the housekeeper, Mrs Priddy, saw Lady Calcott struggling across the waterlogged lawn, carrying something heavy in what looked like a cloth bag. They called after her, but if Lady Calcott heard them she showed no signs of pausing. She vanished with her burden into the trees at the farthest edge of the gardens.

Caroline kept to her bed for several days. She lay in a state of dread and sorrow, which deepened when she slid her hand beneath her pillow and found William's pacifier there. The one she had given him, to quieten him as he lay on the bed. The one she and Corin had given him as a welcoming gift. She ran her fingers around the silken ivory, cradled the silver bell in her hand. She ought to get rid of it, she knew. She ought not to have anything in her possession that could link her to the child. But she could not. As if some essence of William, of Magpie, of life and love, remained caught up in that one precious talisman, she clasped it tightly in her fists and held it close to her heart. And when Lord Calcott returned from London, she finally delivered the news of her delicate condition with a calm demeanour.

The tinker family did not move on, as Caroline had assumed they would. Instead, a few days later, they brought William to the door, to ask politely if anybody in the household had any idea to whom the child belonged. Caroline saw them coming along the driveway from her position at the drawing-room window. Her heart squeezed fearfully in her chest. She waited as the butler opened the front door, heard muffled words spoken, then the approach of footsteps and a subtle knock.

'Yes?' she called, her voice wavering.

'I'm sorry to disturb you, my lady, but Mr Dinsdale and his wife say they have found a child in the woods and they wonder if we have any idea to whom it might belong or what they ought to do with it?' The butler, Mr March, sounded puzzled. Feeling like she was going to be sick, Caroline turned on the man.

'What can that possibly have to do with me?' she demanded coldly.

'Yes, my lady,' Mr March intoned, making the slightest of bows as he withdrew. So the Dinsdales went away again, still carrying William. Caroline watched them go with increasing unease, and she traced this feeling to the way Mr March had referred to them—*Mr Dinsdale and his wife*. As if he knew them.

'Dinsdale? Ah, you've met our young campers, have you?' Henry exclaimed when Caroline asked him about the tinkers. She put down her knife and fork, her throat too tight to swallow. 'Harmless folk. Now, I know it may seem a little out of the ordinary, but I've given them permission to stay on that stretch of land—'

'What? Why would you do that?' Caroline gasped.

'Robbie Dinsdale saved my life in Africa, my dear—at Spion Kop, some years ago. Were it not for him, I would not be here today!' Henry said dramatically, putting a huge forkful of potatoes into his mouth.

'But . . . they are Gypsies. Thieves and . . . and probably worse! We cannot have them as our neighbours!'

'Now, my dear, I will not have that, I'm afraid. Private Dinsdale stayed with me in our pitiful trench when I was shot, and defended my prone body against a dozen Boer snipers until the Twin Peaks were taken and the buggers pulled back!' Henry waved his knife emphatically. 'He was wounded himself, and half-dead with thirst, but by my side he stayed, when he could have run. All that was left of the rest of my men was a bloody mess like a scene from hell. The war changed him, though . . . He was eventually discharged on medical grounds. Lost a few of his marbles out there. He's much improved now, but he was never quite able to fit back into his civilian life. He was apprentice farrier in the village here, but that soon finished. He couldn't pay the rent and was thrown out of his cottage, so he took to the road. I told him he could stay here as long as he made no trouble, and he never has done. So here they stay.' Caroline studied her plate, fidgeting nervously.

'He took to the road, you say? So they move around the country; they're not often here?' Her voice was little more than a whisper.

'They're here a lot of the time. It's close to both their families, and Dinsdale can get work here and there, mending metalwork and the like. So I fear you will have to get used to them, my dear.' Henry concluded, and Caroline knew that the matter was closed.

She shut her eyes, but she could feel them. She could sense that William was there, not two hundred yards from where she now sat at dinner. If he remained always there to remind her, she knew it would prey upon her, and slowly devour her. She prayed that they would give the child up, or move on, taking the object of her guilt with them.

When her baby was born, Caroline wept. A little girl, so tiny and perfect. The soaring, consuming love that Caroline felt for her daughter served only to show her just how great the ill that she had done to Magpie truly was. The mere thought of being separated from this child of hers was painful enough. So Caroline wept, with love and with self-loathing, and nothing that was said could console her. Henry patted her head, at a loss, and did a poor job of hiding his disappointment that he had a daughter, not a son.

At night she was beset by dreams of Magpie, eyes fever-bright, dying of grief; and when she awoke the taint of her crime made her head throb as though it would burst. The baby was dressed in white lace gowns and named Evangeline. For four months Caroline loved her to distraction, and then the tiny girl died, one night in her crib, for no reason that any one of three doctors could ascertain. Caroline was shattered. What little will to go on she had kept since losing Corin now ran out of her like blood from a wound, and there was nothing left that could staunch it.

Lord Calcott was in residence less and less, and spent scant enough time with his wife for a second child to be conceived—the pregnancy was a long time coming. Caroline feared that nothing would ever again feel as wonderful as holding Evangeline for the first time, but the changing of her body brought with it an anticipation of love that was irresistible, and she succumbed to it. But the boy was born months too soon and had no chance of life. Caroline studied the tiny face in wonderment—that she could still feel loss, that her eyes had tears left to shed. But it was the last of the love she possessed poured into that one long look she took at the dead baby's face. The very last touch of warmth inside her, she passed to him; and then the doctor took him out with the bloody sheets and all was lost.

Caroline's recovery was slow, and never complete. By the time she was well enough to receive visits from friends, and Bathilda, they found her slow and dull, and her beauty much diminished. There were hollows at her eyes and cheeks and touches of grey at her temples even though she was not yet near thirty. People shook their heads sadly and thought twice before adding the Calcotts to any invitation list.

Left alone, Caroline walked a great deal. Around and around the gardens, as if looking for something. One day she went through the woods, to the clearing where the Dinsdales camped.

Caroline waited in the trees, staring at their brightly painted wagon and the pony tethered nearby. Caroline was reminded of White Cloud's teepee, and this, like any thought of the ranch, made her vision swim and her mind close up in misery. Just then the Dinsdales returned from the village. Mrs Dinsdale, whose blonde hair hung in angelic ringlets, had a babe in arms, and holding onto Mr Dinsdale's hand was a sturdy dark-coloured boy of about three years. Caroline's breath caught in her throat. William so resembled Magpie that it was near unbearable to look at him.

She watched them for some time. Mrs Dinsdale put her baby down to sleep inside the wagon, then sat on the steps and called to William, who came running to her with his arms aloft to be carried. She did not call him William, of course. It was some other name that she used, which sounded like Flag.

Watching them, Caroline was so torn apart with sorrow and envy that she did not know how to contain it. But she was so angry too, that this family of drifters should flourish when her own had been snatched from her, twofold. She stared at William and she hated him. She hated them all. No more, she thought, I can take no more. The price she had been made to pay was far too high, and though some part of her thought that this injustice must, somehow, be redressed, she knew that it could not be. She sat down in the shadows and cried quietly for Corin, who could not help her.

7

THE LIGHT IS ON inside the bathroom, tendrils of steam creeping under the door. And the tap still running. With my hand on the door I freeze. I am so afraid, so afraid of what I might see.

'Beth?' I call, too meekly. No reply. Swallowing, I give two tiny knocks then throw open the door.

Beth is in the bath, her hair floating around her, water perilously close to the rim, escaping into the overflow. Her eyes are shut and for an instant I think I have lost her. But then she opens her eyes, turns her face to me, and I am so relieved I nearly fall. I stumble in, sit abruptly on the chair where her clothes are folded.

'Rick? What's going on? Where are your clothes?' she asks me, pushing the tap closed with her big toe. I dropped them and Dinny's blanket in the hallway. I am wearing wet, muddy underwear, nothing more.

'I thought . . .' But I don't want to tell her what I thought. It seems a betrayal, to think that she would do that to herself again.

'What?' she asks, her voice flattening out, growing taut.

'Nothing,' I mumble. 'Why are you in the bath at this time of night?'

'I said I'd wait for you to get back,' she replies. 'And I was cold. Where have you been?' she asks, sitting up. She bends her knees, wraps shining arms around them.

'I was with Dinny. I . . . fell into the dew pond.'

'You did what? What was Dinny doing there?'

'He heard me fall in. He helped me out.'

'You just fell in?' she asks incredulously.

'Yes! Too much whisky, I suppose.'

'And did you just . . . fall out of your clothes? Or did he help you with those as well?' she asks tartly. I give her a steady look. I am angry now—that she scared me so. That I scared myself so.

'Who's jealous now?' I ask, just as tart.

'I'm not—' she begins, then puts her chin on her knees, looks away from me. 'It's weird, OK, Erica? You chasing after Dinny is weird.'

'Why is it weird? Because he was yours first?'

'Yes!' she cries; and I stare, amazed by this admission. 'Just don't get involved with him, all right? It feels incestuous! It's just . . . wrong!' She struggles to explain herself, stretching her hands wide. 'I can't stand it.'

'It's not wrong. You just don't like the idea, that's all. But you needn't worry. I think he's still in love with you,' I say quietly.

I wait to see her expression change, but it doesn't.

'We should go, Erica. Can't you see? It would be by far the best thing. We could go tomorrow.' She fixes me with desperate eyes. 'Never mind sorting out all Meredith's things—that's not why we came here, not really. The house clearance guys can do it! Please? Let's just go?'

'I know why I came here, Beth.' I am tired of tiptoeing around it. 'I wanted us to come because I thought I could make you better. Because I want to find out what it is that torments you. I want to shine a light on it, and show you that it's not so bad.'

'Some things are, Erica! Some things are as bad!' she cries, the words torn from her, terrified. 'I want to leave. I'm leaving, tomorrow.'

'No. You're not. Not until we've confronted this. Whatever it is.'

She stands abruptly, reaches for her dressing gown and shrugs it on. 'Goddamn it, Rick! Why are you doing this?' she swears.

'I . . . I promised Eddie. That I'd make you better.'

'What?' she whispers. I think carefully, before I speak again. I think about what I saw, as the dew pond closed over my head. 'Tell me what Henry was looking for at the side of the dew pond,' I demand softly.

'What? When?'

'At the side of the dew pond that day. The day he disappeared, and I'd been swimming in the pond. He was looking for something on the ground.' I hear Beth's sharp intake of breath. Her lips have gone pale.

'I thought you said you didn't remember?' she says.

'It's coming back to me. A little. Not all of it. I remember jumping back into the pond, and I remember looking up at Henry, and he had been looking for something on the ground. And then I remember . . .' I swallow, 'I remember him bleeding. His head bleeding.'

'Shut up! Shut up! I don't want to talk about it!' Beth shouts again, puts her hands over her ears, shakes her head madly.

'Just tell me what he was looking for.'

'Stones, of course,' she says quietly. 'He was looking for stones to throw.' She slips from the bathroom into the dark of the corridor.

No sleep for me. There's a bright moon tonight, and as the hours spin past, I see it sail heedlessly from one pane of the window to the next.

I feel dreadful when I get up: heavy and tired. My throat is sore; there's an ache behind my eyes that won't go. It was a hard frost last night—Dinny was right about what might have happened if I'd lain about on the ground, drunk and befuddled. Now there's a dense mist, so pale and luminous that I can't tell where it ends and the sky begins.

The thing is, we ran. That day. Beth and I ran. I remember scrambling out of the pond as fast as I could, and we ran. Back to the house, back to lie low, to hide and stay quiet until the trouble started. Or rather, until the trouble was noticed. We didn't go back, I am sure of it. The last time I saw Henry he was by the side of the dew pond; he was teetering. Did he fall? Was that why I got out, so desperately fast? Was that why I told them all he was in the pond—why I insisted upon it? But he wasn't, and there was only one other person there.

There is only one person who can have moved Henry, who can have taken him somewhere else, because I know he didn't take himself. He was taken somewhere so secret and so hidden that twenty-three years of searching couldn't uncover him. But I am close now.

It could be this memory that I've fought so hard to regain that's hurting my head. Henry bleeding, Henry falling. It worries me that I didn't want breakfast. I looked at the food and I remembered Henry and there was no question of eating anything. No question of putting anything into my mouth, of enjoyment or satisfaction. Is this how Beth has felt, for twenty-three years? The thought turns me cold. It's like knowing there's something behind you, following you. Something as dark and permanent as your shadow.

The doorbell startles me. Dinny is there, wearing a canvas coat, his hands thrust deeply into the pockets. In spite of it all my cheeks glow and I feel a wave of something ill-defined. Relief, or perhaps dread.

'Dinny! Hello—come in,' I greet him.

'Hi, Erica, I just wanted to check you were all right. After last night,' Dinny says, stepping over the threshold but staying on the doormat.

'Come in—I can't shut the door with you standing there.'

'So, how are you?' he asks.

'I'm fine, really. I mean, I feel like death, and I'm sure I look like death, but other than that, I'm OK.' I smile nervously.

'You could have killed yourself,' he tells me gravely.

'I know. I know. I'm sorry. That wasn't my intention, believe me. And thank you for rescuing me—I really owe you one,' I say. At this he looks at me sharply. But then he softens, puts out his hand and brushes cold knuckles lightly down my cheek. I catch my breath, shiver slightly.

'Idiot,' he says softly.

'Thanks,' I say. There's a thump from upstairs. I picture a full suitcase, pulled off a bed. Dinny drops his hand quickly.

'Is that Beth?' he asks.

'Beth or the ghost of Calcotts past. I expect she's packing. She doesn't even want to stay for one more day.' I give a helpless little shrug.

'So you're leaving?'

'I . . . I don't know. I don't want to. Not yet. Maybe not at all.' I glance at him. I really don't think I could stay in this house by myself.

'No more Dinsdales or Calcotts at Storton Manor. It's the end of an era,' Dinny says, but he does not sound regretful.

'Are you moving on?' I ask. My heart gives a little leap of protest.

'Sooner or later. I was only really here because of Honey—'

'I thought you said you saw Meredith's obituary?'

'Well, yes, and that. I thought there was a good chance you and Beth might be around.' For a moment we say nothing.

'I'd like to say goodbye to Beth before you disappear,' he says. I nod. 'I didn't get the chance, the last time you went,' he adds pointedly.

'She's upstairs. We had a fight. I don't know if she'll come down,' I tell him. I study his hands. I think of the way he held me, just for a while. I think of his kiss. How I want to keep him here.

'What did you fight about?'

'What do you think?' I ask bitterly. 'She won't tell me what happened. But she has to face up to it, Dinny! It's what's making her ill, I know it!' Dinny sighs. 'You never did get to tell her the things you wanted to, Dinny. But you can tell me instead,' I say. 'I want to know!'

'What if knowing changes everything? What if your sister and I are right and you're better off not remembering?' Fierce eyes lock on mine.

'I want it to change everything! Change what, anyway? She's my sister. I love her and I'll love her no matter what she does. Or did,' I declare adamantly.

'I'm not just talking about Beth,' he says.

'Who, then? What then? Just tell me!'

'I'm talking about . . . you and me.' His voice grows softer.

'What do you mean?'

'I mean . . . whatever this is . . . whatever it might have been, it would all change.' He looks away from me. 'Do you understand?' he asks. I bite my lower lip, feel my eyes stinging. But then I see Beth, in the bath, as she was last night: whole in body, but slipping away. I swallow the hot little flame that Dinny has just lit inside me.

'Yes. But I have to know,' I whisper. I wait for him to speak, but he doesn't.

'Just tell me, Dinny! Beth and I ran off. I don't know what happened, but I know we ran off and left you and Henry at the pond.

And that was the last anybody saw of him and I want you to tell me!'
'Beth should—' he begins.
'Beth won't. Oh, maybe she will, one day. Or maybe she'll try to kill herself again, and this time she'll manage it! I have to get this out of her!' I cry. Dinny stares at me, shocked.
'She tried to kill herself?' he breathes. 'Because of this?'
'Yes! Because she's depressed. Not just unhappy—ill, Dinny. And I want to know what caused it. If you don't tell me then you're just helping keep her like she is—haunted. Just tell me what you did with his body! Tell me where he is!' I plead.
'Erica!' Beth's shout echoes across the hallway. Dinny and I jump, like guilty children. 'Don't!' she cries, running down the stairs to us. Her eyes are wide, face marked with fright.
'Beth, I wasn't going to tell her—' Dinny starts to say.
'What? Why not—because Beth has told you not to?' I snap at him.
'Don't tell anybody! Ever!' Beth says. Her eyes are fixed on Dinny's and something passes between them that I can't bear.
'Beth! Please—Beth, look at me! Look at what trying to keep this secret has done to you! Please, Beth. It's time to get rid of it. Whatever it is, let it go. Please. For Eddie's sake! He needs you to be happy—'
'Don't bring Eddie into this!' she snaps at me, eyes awash with tears.
'Why not? It's his life that this is affecting too, you know! He's your responsibility. You owe it to him to be strong, Beth—'
'What would you know about it, Erica? What would you know about responsibility? You haven't even got a permanent job! You change flats every six months! You've been living like a student since you left home—you've never even had a pet so don't tell me about my responsibilities!' Beth shouts, and I recoil, stung.
'Beth, maybe it would be better just to tell her. She's not going to tell anybody. It's just the three of us. I think . . . I think she has a right to know,' Dinny says, his voice soft. Beth stares at him, her face so pale.
'No,' she whispers.
'Dinny, tell me. Tell me whare Henry is. It's the only way to help her,' I say firmly. Beth's gaze flickers from me to Dinny and back again.
'Stop it!' Beth commands me. She is shaking uncontrollably.
Dinny's eyes are ablaze. He seems torn over something, undecided. I hold my breath and my head spins in protest.
'Fine!' he barks, grabbing my arm. 'If you think this is only way to help her. But if you're wrong, and when everything is different, don't say I didn't warn you!' He is suddenly angry, furious with us. His fingers bruise me; he tows me away from the door and wrenches it open.

'No! Dinny—no! ' Beth shouts after us, as he pulls me outside.

'Ow—stop it! What are you doing? Where are we going?' On instinct I fight him, try to dig my heels in, but he is far stronger than me.

'You want to know what happened to Henry? I'll show you!' Dinny spits the words out. Fear grips my insides. I am so close to finding Henry, so close that it terrifies me. Dinny terrifies me. Such strength in him, in his grip, such an implacable look on his face.

'Dinny, please . . .' I gasp, but he ignores me.

'Erica! No!' I hear Beth's ragged shout chasing us but she does not follow. I look back over my shoulder, see her framed in the doorway, mouth distorted, hands grasping the jamb for support.

Dinny marches me across the lawn, out of the garden through the trees, heading west. We are going to the camp.

My heart pummels inside me. Dinny pulls open the door of the nearest van, not bothering to knock. Harry looks up, startled, smiles when he recognises us. Dinny propels me up the steps into the van.

'What the hell is this?' My voice is shaking, I can't get my breath.

'You wanted to know where Henry was.' Dinny raises his arm, points at Harry. 'There's Henry.'

I stare. My head empties, the plug is pulled. I'm not sure how long I stare, but when I speak my throat is dry.

'What?' Dinny shuts his eyes and puts a hand over them, wearily.

'That's Henry,' he repeats.

'But . . . how can it be? Henry's dead! How can this be Henry?'

'He's not dead. He didn't die.' Dinny drops his hand and the fire has gone out of him. He watches me but I can't move. I can't think. Harry smiles, uncertainly. 'Try not to shout. It upsets him,' Dinny says quietly.

I can't shout. I can't anything. I can't breathe.

'Come on—let's go. Let's go outside and talk,' Dinny murmurs, taking my arm more gently now. I snatch it away and lean towards Harry. I am so scared as I look at him. Scared enough for my knees to sag—there's a hollow thump as they hit the floor. I push stray dreadlocks back from Harry's face, peer into his eyes. I try to see it. Try to recognise him, but I can't. I won't.

'You're wrong. You're lying!'

'I'm neither. Come on, we can't talk about this here.' Dinny pulls me to my feet and takes me outside again.

For the second time in twelve hours I sit in Dinny's van, shivering, stunned, stupid. He makes coffee on the stove. Sipping from the cup he gives me scalds my mouth, and I feel it revive me.

'I . . . I can't believe it. I don't understand,' I say.

Dinny looks both hard and nervous. He sighs. 'What don't you understand?' He says this quietly, in the spirit of genuine enquiry.

'Well, where has he been all these years? How come he was never found? They searched everywhere for him!'

'Nobody ever searches everywhere.' Dinny shakes his head. 'He's been here, with us. With my family, or with friends of my family. There's more than one traveller camp in the south of England. Mum and Dad had plenty of friends to leave him with, friends who looked after him, until it had blown over. As soon as I was old enough to keep an eye on him myself, I did.'

'But . . . I saw him bleeding. I saw him fall into the pond . . .'

'And then you two ran away. I fished him out and I fetched my dad. He wasn't breathing, but Dad managed to get it going again. The cut on his head wasn't as bad as it looked . . . head wounds just bleed a lot.'

'And then? Didn't you take him to the hospital? Why didn't you come and find somebody at the manor?' I ask. Twenty-three years of my life are rewriting themselves behind my eyes, unravelling like wool. I can hardly focus, hardly think. Dinny doesn't answer for a long time. He grips his chin in his hand, knuckles white. His eyes burn into me.

'I . . . wouldn't say what had happened. I wouldn't tell them how he'd got hurt or by who. So Dad . . . Dad thought it was me. He thought Henry and me had got into a fight. He was trying to protect me.'

'But, you could have told them it was an accident—'

'Come off it, Erica. Everyone's always looking to be proved right about us—all my life, people have looked to be proved right. That we thieve, that we're criminals—that we're scum. The social would have leaped at the chance to take me away from Mum and Dad. A spell in juvy, then a proper home, with a proper family . . .'

'You don't know that . . .'

'Yes. Yes, I do. It's you who doesn't know, Erica.'

'Why is he . . . the way he is?'

'Not from the knock on the head. Dad took him to an old friend, Joanna, who used to be a nurse in Marlborough. This was that same afternoon, before anyone knew he was missing. She put a couple of stitches in his head, said he might have a concussion but it was nothing to worry about. We were going to wait for him to wake up, make sure he was OK, then drop him within walking distance of the village and disappear. That was the plan. Joanna looked after him for the first few days. He was out of it for two days straight and . . . then he woke up.'

'You could have brought him back then. You could have left him somewhere he'd be found, like you said. Why didn't you?'

'By then the search was enormous. We were being watched. We couldn't move without some keen copper noting it down. Henry would have told them we'd had him—when he was found, of course. But we thought we'd have a head start to vanish. By the time we realised there was no way we could bring him back without being seen, it was too late. And he wasn't right, when he woke up. Anybody could tell that. Dad took me to see him, since I knew him best, out of all of us. *Just tell me what you think*, Dad said.' Dinny pushes his fingers through his hair. 'I tried talking to him. But he wasn't the same. He was wide awake, but . . . distant. Dazed.'

'But why? You said his head wasn't hit that hard?'

'It wasn't. It was the time he spent not breathing. The time before Dad got to him and got air back into his lungs.' Dinny sounds so tired now, leaden. There's a sparkle of pity, at the core of me, but I can't let it fill me yet. Too many other things to feel.

I've finished my coffee before I speak again. I hadn't noticed the silence. Dinny is watching me, waiting. Waiting for my reaction, I suppose. A defensive gleam in his eye.

'It didn't blow over, you know. Not for his parents. Not for our family.'

'Do you think it blew over for me? For my family? I've had to see him nearly every day since then, wondering if it would have been different if I'd tried to revive him myself . . . If we had taken him to hospital.'

'But you've never told. You've kept him—'

'Not kept him. Looked after him . . .'

'You've kept him and let his family—let his parents think he was dead! You've let Beth and I think he was dead.'

'No, I had no idea what you and Beth were thinking! How would I know? You ran, remember? You ran and washed your hands of it! You never even came to ask me about it! You left him with me and I . . . we . . . did what we thought was best.'

This I cannot dispute. 'I was eight years old!'

'Well, I was twelve—still just a kid, and I had to let my parents think I'd nearly killed another boy. That I'd brain-damaged another boy. At least, that's what I thought I had to do. That's what I thought was right. By the time I realised you two were never coming back, it was too late to change anything. How much fun do you think that was?'

I feel the blood run out of my face when he says this. A memory fights its way through the clash in my head. Henry bending down, surveying the ground, gathering four, five stones. Henry, taunting, throwing names at Dinny, Beth's shrill commands: *Stop it! Go away! Henry, don't!* Henry said, *Pikey! Filth! Dirty Gyppo! Thieving dog! Tramp!* With each word he threw a stone, whipping it from the shoulder with that throw boys are taught at school, but girls never are. A good aim. I remember Dinny crying out as one hit him, grabbing his shoulder, wincing. I remember what happened. And I picture Beth, in the doorway just now, her shout following us, and the terror on her face. *No!*

'I have to go,' I whisper, stumbling to my feet.

'Erica, wait—'

'No! I have to go!' I feel sick.

I rush back to the house, tripping over my feet. In the cold downstairs toilet I collapse, throw up. But with my throat burning and the stink of it all around me, I somehow feel better. I feel justly punished. I feel as if some kind of retribution is beginning. Now I know what has tortured Beth all these years. Now I know why she has punished herself so. Splashing my face in the basin, I gasp for breath. I am cold with fear—I think I know what retribution she might seek from herself.

'Beth!' I call. 'Beth, where are you—I have to tell you something!' I run in and out of all the downstairs rooms, my heart skittering.

'Beth!' My voice is rising, almost a scream. I pound up the stairs, run to the bathroom first then along the corridor to Beth's room. Inside, the curtains are closed, the room in darkness. And what I fear the most is there in front of me. 'No!' I rush into the room. My sister, curled on the floor, her face turned away from me. Long-bladed scissors gripped in her fragile hand, and a dark pool around her. 'Beth, no,' I whisper. I fall to my knees, gather her up; she is so light, insubstantial. For a second I am struck dumb by the pain, and then she turns her face to me, and her eyes are open, focused on mine, and I laugh out loud with relief.

'Erica?' Her voice is tiny.

'Oh, Beth! What have you done?' I smooth her hair back from her face and then I realise. She has hacked it off, all of it. The dark pool on the floor is the severed length of her hair. 'Your hair!' I cry, and then I laugh again and kiss her face. She has not cut herself, is not bleeding.

'I couldn't do it. I wanted to but . . . Eddie . . .'

'You didn't want to do it! You don't want to do it! I know you don't, not really,' I tell her. I pull her further into my arms, rock her gently.

'I did! I did want to!' she weeps angrily. 'Why did you make him tell you? Why wouldn't you listen to me?'

'Because it had to happen. It did. But listen to me—Beth. This is important.' I take a deep breath. 'Beth, Henry's not dead. Harry is Henry! It's true! Dinny told me the whole story . . . he didn't die. They took him off to some friend of theirs for first aid, then they moved him around different camps for years. That's why none of the searches ever found him.'

'What?' she whispers.

'Harry—the Harry your son just spent the Christmas holiday playing with—Harry is our cousin Henry.' In the silence I hear her breathing.

'That's not true,' she whispers.

'It's true, Beth. It's true. I believe it. Dinny wouldn't tell anyone what had happened, so Mickey thought Dinny had done it, and they didn't want him to be taken away . . .'

'No, no, no! None of that is right! I killed him! I killed him, Rick.' Her voice rises to a wail, wanes to a sliver. 'I killed him.' She says it more calmly now, as if almost relieved to let the words out.

'No, you didn't,' I insist.

'But . . . I threw that stone . . . it was too big! I should never have thrown it! But I was so angry! I was so angry I just wanted to make him stop! It went so high,' she whispers.

I can see it now. Finally, finally. Like it was there all along. Girls aren't taught to throw properly. She flung her whole body behind it, let go of it too soon, sent it too high. Henry was already laughing at the ineptness of the throw. He was already laughing when it came back down, when it hit his head with a sound that was so wrong. Loud, and wrong. The sound of flesh breaking, of a blow to the bone. It was that sound that made me sick just now. As if I were hearing it again for the first time, and only now rejecting it. And then all that blood, and his glazed look, and my scramble from the water, and our flight. I have it now. At last.

'I didn't kill him?' Beth whispers at last, eyes boring into my face.

I shake my head, smile at her. 'No. You didn't kill him.' I see relief seep into her face, slowly, so slowly, like she hardly dares believe it. I hold her tightly, feel her start to cry.

Later, I go back to the camp. In the early afternoon, with the sun burning through the mist. I feel something in me pouring out, pouring up. I'm left with a neutral feeling that could become anything. It could become joy. Perhaps. I sit next to Harry on the steps of his van. I ask him what he's doing and although he doesn't speak, he shows me. A tiny penknife in one hand, a half-cylinder shard of tree bark in the other, and patterns scratched into it. He is miraculous to me now. That Henry could grow into this gentle soul. Was he damaged or, rather, was something knocked out of him by Beth's blow? The spite? The childish arrogance, the aggression? All the base things, all of Meredith's legacy, all the hate she taught him. He is a cleanly wiped slate.

I let him keep working. I sit, and he works, and I watch his face. And slowly, familiar things surface. Some of his features settle back into the shapes I knew. Just here and there, just traces. The Calcott nose we all have, narrow at the bridge. The blue-grey shade of his irises. He doesn't seem to mind me watching. He doesn't seem to notice.

'He recognised you, I think,' Dinny says quietly, coming to stand in front of us. 'That first time you saw him in the woods and he stopped you passing by. I think he recognised you.' I look up at Dinny, but I can't speak to him. Not yet. He was right. Everything has changed.

I go up to fetch Beth as the light is failing. She has been lying down for hours. Assimilating. I tell her who is downstairs and she agrees to see him. In the kitchen the lights are on. Dinny and Henry, sitting at the table, playing snap and drinking tea. Dinny glances up as we come in, but Beth looks only at Henry. She sits down, at a safe distance, and stares. I watch and wait. Henry shuffles the cards clumsily.

'Does he know me?' Beth whispers, her voice so thin.

Dinny shrugs slightly. 'There's really no way of knowing. He seems . . . comfortable around you. Around both of you. It usually takes him a while to warm up to strangers, so . . .'

'I thought I'd killed him. All this time, I thought I'd killed him . . .'

'You did,' Dinny says flatly. Her mouth opens in shock. 'You knocked him out and left him face down in the water—'

'Dinny! Don't—' I try to stop him.

'If I hadn't pulled him out, he would be dead. So just remember that before you start judging what I've done, what my family's done . . .'

'Nobody's judging anybody! We were just kids . . . we had no idea what to do. And yes, it was lucky you thought so fast, Dinny,' I say.

'I'd hardly call it lucky.'

'Well, whatever you want to call it then.' Dinny draws in another breath, eyes narrowing at me, but Beth starts to cry. Ragged, ugly sobs, torn out from the heart of her. I put my arms around her as if I can hold her together.

Dinny goes to the window, leans his forehead against the glass. I can't begin to decipher what I feel about Dinny, about this secret he's been keeping. Henry, squirrelled away in England's labyrinth of lay-bys and green lanes, in vans and motor homes and caravans and lorries, a world away from the door-to-door search for him in the neat and tidy villages.

It's too big. I can't see it clearly.

We part some time later, to deliver our respective charges to bed. Dinny goes into the night with Henry; I walk up the stairs with Beth. She cried for a long time and now she's quiet. I think her mind is rewriting itself, like mine had to, and that she needs time.

I pull the blankets up to her chin like a mother would, and she smiles a half-mocking smile.

'Erica,' she says. 'How long have you been in love with Dinny?'

'What?'

'Don't deny it. It's written all over you. How long?' she presses.

'I don't know,' I say shortly. 'I don't know that I am in love with him.'

'Erica!'

'What?'

'I . . . was pleased, when you said you didn't remember what had happened. I didn't want you to remember. You were so young . . .'

'Not that young.'

'Young enough. None of it was your fault, I hope you know that. Of course you know. I didn't want you to remember, because I was so ashamed. Not of throwing a stone back at him, but of running. Of leaving him there, and never telling Mum and Dad. I don't know why. I don't know why I did that! I've never known!'

'It wasn't—'

'It was a thing to be decided on the instant. That's what I've come to think, as I've got older. A decision made in an instant and once it's made you can't go back on it. Do you face up to a mistake, even one so terrible, or do you run away from it? I ran. I failed.'

'You didn't fail, Beth.'

'Yes, I did. You only ever did what I did. I was the leader, the eldest. If I'd spoken up straight away he could have lived.'

'He did live!'

'He could have lived normally! Not been so damaged . . .'

'Beth, there's no point to this. He lived. It can't be undone now. Please stop torturing yourself. You were a child.'

'When I think of Mary, and Clifford . . .' Tears blur her eyes again, spill over. I can think of nothing to say to this. Clifford and Mary. Their lives were ruined more completely than ours. The thought of them settles like lead around my heart.

I am awake before sunrise, and creep quietly to the kitchen. I make coffee, drink it strong and too hot. The little clock on the microwave tells me it's half past seven. The caffeine bustles my brain awake, but it doesn't help me think. How can we not tell Henry's parents that he's alive? How can we not? We can't not. But they will want to know what happened. Even placid Mary, so broken, will want to know what happened. And Clifford will want justice. Justice as he would see it. He will want charges brought against the Dinsdales for kidnapping, for withholding medical treatment. He will probably want charges brought against Beth and me, although these would be harder to bring. Grievous bodily harm, perhaps. I have no idea what charges apply to children. So how can we tell them?

Outside the sky lightens slowly. Beth appears, fully dressed, at ten o'clock. She stands in the doorway with her bag on her shoulder.

'How are you doing?' I ask her.

'I'm . . . OK. I've got to go. Maxwell's dropping Eddie off after lunch tomorrow and nothing's ready. I've got him until he goes back to school on Wednesday.'

'Oh, right. I thought . . . I thought we were going to talk about it? About Henry?' I ask.

She shakes her head. 'I'm just not ready to talk about it yet. Not yet. I feel better, though.'

'Good, good. I'm glad, Beth. Really, I am. I want nothing more than for you to be able to put all this behind you.'

'That's what I want too.' She sounds lighter, almost bright, smiles in readiness to depart, grips her bag convincingly.

'Only . . . I don't know what we should do about Clifford and Mary. What we should do about telling them . . .' I say. Her face falls.

'Right now I have to go. But honestly, Rick, I don't think I should have any say in what happens next. I don't have the right. I've done enough to him. To them.' Little shadows chase across her face again.

'Don't worry about it, Beth. I'll sort it out.' So sure of this, I sound. She smiles at me, comes over and hugs me.

'Thank you, Erica. I owe you so much,' she says.

'You don't owe me anything.' I shake my head. 'You're my sister.'

She squeezes me with all the strength in her willow-switch body.

It starts to sleet from a flat grey sky as we get into the car, and I have just started the engine when Dinny appears from beneath the trees, knocks on the window.

'I was hoping I'd catch you. I guessed you'd be off this morning,' he says to Beth. Just the faintest hint of a rebuke.

'Beth has to catch the next train,' I say.

He flicks his eyes to me and nods. 'Look, Beth, I just wanted to say . . . I just . . . when I said last night that you'd killed him, I didn't mean that . . . that you'd done it deliberately or anything,' he says. 'I used to ask my parents why Henry was such a bastard. Why he was such a bully, such a vicious little git . . . They told me over and over again that when children behave that way it's because they aren't happy. For whatever reason they're full of fear and anger and they take it out on other people.

I didn't believe them then, of course. I thought it was just because he was an evil sod, but I believe it now. It's true, of course. Henry wasn't happy then, and, well, he is happy now. He's the happiest, most peaceful soul I know. I just . . . I just thought you should think about that.' Dinny swallows, tips his chin at us and steps back from the car.

'Thank you,' Beth says. She can't quite look him in the eye, but she's trying. 'Thank you, for what you did. For never telling anybody.'

'I'd never have done anything to hurt you, Beth,' he says softly. My knuckles on the steering wheel are white. Beth nods, her eyes downcast. 'Will you ever come back this way?' he asks.

'Perhaps. I think so. Sometime in the future,' she replies.

'Then I'll see you around, Beth,' Dinny says, with a sad smile.

'Goodbye, Dinny,' she says quietly. He smacks the roof of the car with the flat of his hand and I pull away obediently. In the rear-view mirror I see him standing there, hands in his pockets, dark eyes in a dark face.

Saturday the third of January today. Most people will be back at work on Monday. I will call the Calcott family lawyer, a Mr Dawlish of Marlborough, and tell him he can put Storton Manor on the market. I have decisions to make, now that I can go forward again. There's nothing missing any more, no cracks, no excuses to stall.

I could leave it all—leave the huge tree and all the holly I painted gold. They could stay, gathering dust until the auctioneer has been and gone with all the good stuff, and the house clearance men have been for the rest. But I can't bear the thought of it. That shreds of our lives should be left like Meredith's apple core in the drawing-room bin.

Industry is good. It keeps my thoughts from overwhelming me. Three things only I will keep: Caroline's writing case and the letters within it, the New York portrait and Flag's teething ring. The rest can go. I strip the tree of baubles and beads. I find pliers in a scullery drawer, climb the stairs to where the Christmas tree is fixed to the banisters, and cut the wire.

'Timber!' I cry, to the empty hallway. The tree sags slowly to one side, then flops to the floor. Dry needles cascade from the branches, carpet the flagstones. With a sigh, I fetch a dustpan and brush and set to chasing them around the floor. I can't help conjuring a life for myself with Dinny, picturing staying with him. Sleeping on a narrow bunk in the back of his ambulance, cooking breakfast on the tiny stove, perhaps working in each new town. Short contracts, sick-leave cover. Tutoring. As if anybody would hire a supply teacher with no fixed address. Lying close each night, hearing his heartbeat, woken by his touch.

There's a knock, and Dinny's voice startles me from my reverie. 'Is this a bad time?' His head appears around the front door.

'No, it's perfect timing, actually. You can help me drag this tree out.' I smile, climbing to my feet and wincing.

He hands me an envelope. 'Here. A card from Honey. For your help the other night, and for the flowers.'

'Oh, she didn't have to do that.'

'Well, after you'd left Mum's the other day she realised that she hadn't actually said thank you. And now that the hormones are settling down, I think she appreciates how vile she's been for the past few weeks.'

'She had good reason, I suppose. Not an easy time for her.'

'She didn't make it easy. But it all seems to be working out now.'

'Here—grab a branch.' I open both sides of the front door wide and we grasp the tree by its lowest branches, tow it across the floor.

We abandon the tree on the driveway, brush the needles from our hands. Everything is dripping wet out here, weighed down with water.

I look at Dinny, suddenly shy. I can't give a name to what's between us, can't quite feel the shape of it. 'Come for dinner tonight,' I say.

'OK. Thanks,' he replies.

I've made a meal with the last of anything edible from the larder, the fridge, the freezer. I will throw the rest away. I said he could bring Harry, if he wanted. It seemed only right. I feel I ought to have some part in looking after him, in supporting him. But Dinny sensed this, and he frowned, and when he arrives at seven he's alone.

'Beth seemed a bit better when she left,' I say, opening a bottle of wine and pouring two large glasses. 'Thank you for saying . . . what you said. About Henry being happy.'

'It's true,' Dinny says, taking a sip.

All along, he has known. All this time, all these years. He can't know, then, how I feel now—looking down and seeing I wasn't walking on solid ground after all.

'What is this, anyway?' he asks, turning the food over with his fork.

'Chicken Provençal. And those are cheese dumplings. Mixed bean salad and tinned spinach. Why? Is there a problem?'

'No, no problem,' he smiles, and gamely begins to eat. I take a forkful of dumpling. It has the texture of plasticine.

'It's horrible. Sorry. I never was much of a cook,' I say.

'The chicken's not bad,' Dinny says diplomatically. We are so unused to this. To sitting and eating together. Small talk. The silence hangs.

'My mum told me that you were in love with Beth back then. Is that why you would never say what had really happened? To protect Beth?'

'We were twelve, Erica. But I didn't want to tell on her, no.'

'Do you still love her?' I don't want to know, but I have to.

'She's not the same person now.' He looks down, frowns.

'And me? Am I the same?'

'Pretty much,' Dinny smiles. 'As tenacious as ever.'

'I don't mean to be,' I say. 'I just want to do the right thing.'

'You always did. But life's not that simple.'

'No.'

'Are you going back to London?'

'I don't think so. No, I'm not. I'm not sure where I'm going.' I look at him when I say this and I can't keep the question from my eyes. He looks at me, steadily but without an answer.

'Clifford will make trouble,' I say at length. 'If we tell them. I know he will. But I'm not sure if I could live with myself, knowing what I know and letting him and Mary think Henry's dead,' I say.

'They wouldn't know him now, Erica,' Dinny says seriously. 'He's not their son any more.'

'Of course he's their son! What else is he?'

'He's been with me for so long now. I've grown up with him. I've seen myself change . . . but Harry just stayed the same. Like he was frozen in time the day that rock hit him. If anything, he's my brother. He's part of my family now.'

'We're all one family, remember? In more ways than one, it seems. They could help you look after him . . . or I could. Help support him . . . financially, or . . . He's their son, Dinny. And he didn't die!'

'But he did. Their son did. Harry is not Henry. They'd take him away from everything he knows.'

'They have a right to know about him.' I cannot let this lie.

'So, what—you're picturing Harry living with them, cooped up in a conventional life, or in some kind of institution, where they can visit him whenever they like and he'd be plonked in front of the TV the rest of the time?'

'It wouldn't be like that!'

'How do you know?'

'I just . . . I can't even imagine what it must have been like for them, all this time.' We are quiet for a long time. 'I'm not going to decide anything without you,' I tell him.

'I've told you what I think,' Dinny says. 'It would do them no good to see him now. And we don't need any help.'

He looks sad. I cannot bear this thought, that I am making Dinny sad. I put my hand across the table, mesh my fingers into his.

'What you did for us—for Beth—taking the blame like that . . . it's huge, Dinny. That was a huge thing that you did,' I say. 'Thank you.'

Will you stay?' I ask him, late in the evening. He doesn't answer, but he stands up, waits for me to lead. I choose a guest room on the top floor, in the attics of the house, where the sheets are chilly and the floorboards creak as we cross them. The silence makes us quiet, and the night outside the bare window sketches us in silvery greys as we undress. My skin rises where he touches me, the tiny hairs on me reaching out. I kiss his mouth, bruise my lips against his, drink him in. I want there to be no space between us, no part of my body not touching his. I want to wind myself around him like ivy, like a rope, binding us together. He has no tattoos, no piercings, no scars. He is whole, perfect. The palms of his hands are rough on my back. He coils one through my hair, tips my head back.

'I could stay with you,' I say afterwards. My eyes are shut, trusting. 'I could stay and help you with Harry. I can get work anywhere. You shouldn't have to support him alone. I could help. I could stay with you.'

'And travel all the time, and live like we do?'

'Well, why not? I'm homeless now, after all.'

'You're a long way from being homeless. You don't know what you're saying.' I lean against him. His skin is hot and dry beneath my cheek.

'I do know. I don't want to go back to London, and I can't stay here. I'm at your disposal,' I say, and the absurdity of this statement makes me chuckle. But Dinny does not laugh. 'I don't mean . . . I'm not trying to foist myself on you, or anything,' I add hurriedly.

He sighs, turns his head to press a kiss onto my hair.

'It wouldn't be so bad having you foisted on me,' he smiles. 'Let's sleep on it. We can sort it out tomorrow.' He says it so softly, so quietly that I decipher the words from the rumble in his chest beneath my ear. Deep and resolute. I am awake long enough to hear his breathing deepen, slow down, grow even. Then I sleep.

When I wake up I'm alone. The sky is flat, matt white, and a fine drizzle sifts down through the trees. A rook perches on a bare branch outside the window, feathers fluffed against the weather.

I run my hand across the side of the bed where Dinny was when I fell asleep. The sheets aren't warm. I could have imagined him here with me, but I didn't. I didn't. I won't race down there. I won't be alarmed. I make myself get dressed, eat breakfast cereal with the last of the milk. Today I will either have to shop or leave. I wonder which it will be.

I slip across the sodden lawn. I feel clear-headed today, purposeful. I've got a box of things for Harry. I found them in some drawers in the cellar. A broken Sony radio, some old torches and batteries and bulbs and small metal objects of unknown provenance. They rattle against the cardboard under my arm.

I stand for quite some time in the centre of the camp clearing, while the rain begins to soften the box I carry. No vans here now, no dogs, no columns of smoke. It is deserted and I am left behind—alone in an empty clearing churned muddy by feet and wheels, and me, churned muddy by him. By the getting of him, and now the losing. My long-lost cousin, my childhood hero. My Dinny. I have no phone number for him, no email address, no clue in which direction he has gone. I turn in a slow circle, in case there is something behind me, something that waited for me, or someone.

Legacy

1911–

CAROLINE'S LAST CHILD was born in 1911, long after the occupants of Storton Manor had given up hope of there being a Calcott heir. The little girl was born in August. It was a long, hot summer the likes of which no one could remember, and Caroline sweltered, shuffling into the garden to lie swollen and prone in the shade, drowsing. The heat was such that sometimes, as she hovered on the edges of sleep, she imagined herself back in Woodward County, sitting on the porch and gazing out at the yard, waiting for Corin to ride home.

The labour was long and arduous, and Caroline was delirious by the end. One of the maids, Liz, and Estelle kept the baby those first few days, taking turns to lay cold cloths onto their mistress's skin to cool her. Henry Calcott, who was by then uncomfortable around his own wife, remained at home long enough to see the child safely born, and then quit Wiltshire to stay with friends by the sea in Bournemouth.

Caroline recovered, at length, but when they brought the child to her, her gaze swept over it impassively, and then she turned her face away and would not nurse it. A wet nurse was found in the village and Caroline, who wanted to be sure that the girl would live before she dared to love her, found, as months and then years passed, that she had left it too late. The little girl did not seem to belong to her, and she could not love her.

Meredith was a lonely child. She had no siblings to play with and was forbidden to play with any of the village children that she saw roaming the fields and lanes around the manor house. Henry Calcott kept mainly to town, where his gambling consumed so much money that several of the staff were laid off, leaving Mrs Priddy to keep the house as best she could with only Estelle to help her.

Mrs Priddy was kind to Meredith, letting her eat the leftover pastry scraps and keep a pet rabbit in a pen outside the kitchen door. A tutor came, five mornings a week, to teach Meredith her letters, music, needlework and deportment. Meredith hated the lessons and the tutor both, and escaped into the garden as soon as she could.

But Meredith longed for her mother. Caroline was an otherworldly creature by then, who sat for hours in a white gown, either at a window or out on the lawn, staring into the distance. When Meredith tried to hug her, she tolerated it for a moment and then disentangled the child's arms with a mild smile, telling her vaguely to run along and play.

Mrs Priddy admonished her not to tire her mother out, and Meredith took this instruction to heart, fearing that she was somehow responsible for her mother's persistent lethargy. So she kept away, thinking that if she did her mother would not be so tired, and would get up and smile and love her more. She played alone, watching the Dinsdales in the clearing through the woods. She watched them whenever she could, but she was too shy ever to let them see her.

The Dinsdales had three children: a tiny baby, a little girl with yellow hair like her mother's, who was a few years older than Meredith herself, and a boy, a dark, strange-looking boy whose age Meredith was unable to guess at, who went everywhere with his father and played with his little sister. Their mother was pretty and she smiled all the time, laughing at their antics and hugging them. Their father was more serious but he smiled often too, and put his arm around the boy, or lifted the little girl high into the air to sit astride his shoulders. Meredith watched this family, fascinated, and even though they were happy and bright she came away from her clandestine visits feeling tearful and dark, unaware that she watched them because she envied them and was filled with yearning for her own mother to hug her that way.

One day she made a mistake. Her mother was on the lawn in her wicker chair. Meredith emerged from the woods and was startled to see her there. Her mother did not look up as she approached, but managed a wan smile once her daughter was standing right in front of her.

'Well, child, and where have you been today?' her mother asked. Meredith went right up to her and tentatively took hold of her hand.

'I was in the woods. Exploring,' she said.

'And what did you find in the woods?' her mother asked.

'I saw the Dinsdales—' Meredith said, and then put her hand over her mouth. Mrs Priddy had warned her never to mention the Dinsdales to her mother, although she had no idea why not.

'You did what?' her mother snapped. 'You know that's not allowed! I hope you have not been talking to those people?'

'No, Mama,' Meredith said quietly. Her mother settled back into her chair. Meredith steeled herself. 'But, Mama, why can I not play with them?' Her heart beat fast at her own temerity.

'Because they are filth! Gypsy, tinker villains! They are thieves and liars and they are not welcome here—and you are not to go near them! Not ever! Do you understand?' Her mother grasped Meredith's wrist so that it hurt. Meredith nodded fearfully.

'Yes, Mama,' she whispered.

They are not welcome here. Meredith took these words to heart. When she watched them next her envy became jealousy, and instead of wanting to play with them, and share their happy existence, she began to wish instead that they did not have their happy existence. She watched them every day, and every day she grew crosser with them, and sadder inside, so that it came to seem to her that it was the Dinsdales who were making her sad. Her and her mother both.

On a hot summer's day in 1918, Meredith heard the Dinsdale children playing at the dew pond. She edged closer, and stood behind the smooth trunk of a beech and watched them jumping in and out of the water. It looked like tremendous fun. She leaned out for a better view, and then froze to the spot. The Dinsdales had seen her. First the boy, who had climbed out and was standing on the bank, then the girl, who paddled in a circle to see what her brother was looking at.

'Hello,' the boy said to her, so casual and friendly. 'Who are you?'

Meredith stood, stock still, not knowing whether to stay or to run.

'Meredith,' she whispered, after a long, uneasy silence.

'I'm Maria!' the girl called from the water.

'And I'm Flag. Do you want to come in for a swim? It's quite safe,' the boy told her. He put his hands on his hips and examined her, head tipped to one side. Meredith felt almost too shy to answer him.

'What kind of name is Flag?' she asked, haughtily, in spite of herself.

'My name,' he shrugged. 'Do you live at the big house, then?'

'Yes,' she replied, her words still reluctant to come.

'Well,' Flag continued, 'do you want to swim with us or not?'

'I . . . I don't know how to swim,' she was forced to admit.

'Paddle then. I'll fetch you out if you fall in,' Flag shrugged.

Meredith pulled off her boots, then crept carefully to the water's edge. She slithered the last few inches down the steep bank and gasped nervously as her feet stumbled into the water.

'It's so cold!' she squeaked, scrambling backwards. Maria giggled.

'It's only cold when you first jump in. Then it's perfect!' she said.

Meredith edged forward again and let the water rise to her ankles. With a yell, Flag took a short run up and leaped into the middle of the pool. The splash caused a wave to engulf Maria and soak the bottom six inches of Meredith's dress.

'Now look what you've done!' she cried.

'Flag! Don't,' Maria told him gaily as he surfaced, spluttering.

'It'll soon dry out,' Flag told her carelessly. Meredith climbed out crossly and sat down on the bank.

'Flag—say you're sorry!' Maria commanded.

'Sorry for getting your dress wet, Meredith,' Flag said, rolling his eyes at his sister. But Meredith didn't reply. She sat and watched them swim for a while longer, but her sullen presence seemed to spoil their fun and they soon climbed out and pulled on the rest of their clothes.

'Do you want to come and have tea?' Maria asked her.

Meredith shook her head. 'I'm not allowed,' she said.

'Come on then, Maria,' Flag said, a touch impatiently.

'Goodbye, then,' Maria shrugged, and gave Meredith a little wave.

It took nearly two hours for the thick cotton of her dress to dry out completely, and during that time Meredith kept to the outer edges of the garden where only the gardener might see her. She imagined how it might be to go to tea, to see the inside of the covered wagon, to meet their affectionate mother. But there could be no arguing that this would be a huge disobedience. And that talking to Flag and Maria had been one as well. Just thinking about what would happen if Mama found out about it brought her spirits low again, and when she was called in for tea she made sure that she gave nothing away.

A week later, she was playing in the barred shadow of the tall iron gates when she saw Flag and Maria walking along the lane towards the village. They would not see her unless she called out and for a second she was paralysed, torn between longing to speak to them again and knowing that she shouldn't. In desperation she came up with a compromise of sorts and burst loudly into song—a song she had heard Estelle singing as she pegged the laundry out to dry.

Flag and Maria turned and, seeing her, came over to the gates.

'Hello again,' Maria greeted her. 'What are you doing?'

'Nothing,' Meredith replied, her heart yammering behind her ribs. 'What are you doing?'

'Going on to the village to buy bread and Bovril for tea. Do you want to come too? If we can get a broken loaf, there'll be a ha'penny left to buy sweets,' Maria smiled.

'You have to go to the shops yourselves?' Meredith asked, puzzled.

'Of course, silly! Who else would go?' Maria laughed.

'Suppose you've got servants to run around buying your tea, haven't you?' Flag asked, a touch derisively.

Meredith bit her lip, an awkward blush heating her face. She hardly ever went into the village.

'Do you want to come, then?'

'I'm not allowed,' Meredith said unhappily.

Flag tilted his head at her, a mischievous glint coming into his eye.

'Come on—I dare you. Or maybe you're just scared?' he asked.

Meredith glared at him defiantly. 'I am not! Only . . .' She hesitated. She was scared, it was true. Scared of being found out, scared of her mother's lightning-fast temper. But it would be so easy to slip away and back again without being noticed.

'Cowardy, cowardy custard!' Flag sang softly.

'Don't listen to him,' Maria advised her. 'Boys are stupid.' But Meredith was listening, and she did want to impress this black-eyed boy, and she did want to be friends with his sister. Jangling with nerves, she slipped out into the lane.

They bought a broken loaf and a jar of Bovril from the grocer's, and even though there was only enough left for two small sugar mice, the lady behind the counter smiled at Meredith and gave them a third.

'Not often we see you in the village, Miss Meredith,' the lady said, and Meredith caught her breath. How did the woman know who she was? And would she tell Mrs Priddy? Her face went pale and panicked tears came hotly into her eyes. 'Now, now. Don't look so aghast! Your secret's safe with me,' the woman said.

'Thank you, Mrs Carter!' Maria called brightly, and they went outside.

'Why aren't you allowed to go into the village?' Flag asked as they stopped by the pond to watch the ducks. Meredith nibbled at her sugar mouse, determined to make it last. She so rarely had sweets.

'Mama says it's not seemly,' Meredith replied.

'What's seemly?' Maria asked. Meredith shrugged.

'It means she's too good to go mixing with the hoi polloi. The likes of us,' Flag said, sounding amused.

'So . . . what would happen if your ma found out you was along here with us, then?' Maria asked at length.

'I would be . . . told off,' Meredith said uncertainly. In fact, she had no real idea. She had been told off for even watching the Dinsdales. She swallowed the last of her sugar mouse. 'I should go back,' she said nervously, scrambling to her feet. The Dinsdales got up without argument and they began to walk back along the lane.

At the gates, Meredith slithered back through the gap as quickly as she could and pulled the gate closed. Her blood was racing and only once the gate was shut did she feel a little safer. She held on to the bars for support while she got her breath back.

'You're an odd one and no mistake,' Flag said, with a bemused smile.

'Come and have some tea with us tomorrow,' Maria invited her. 'Ma said you can—I asked her already.'

'Thank you. But . . . I don't know,' Meredith said. She was feeling exhausted by her adventure and could hardly think of anything except getting away from the gates without being seen talking to them. The Dinsdales wandered off and Meredith put her face to the bars to watch them go. As they passed out of sight Meredith turned and saw her mother standing in the upstairs hall window, watching her. Behind the glass, her face was ghastly pale and her eyes far too wide. She looked like a spectre, frozen for ever in torment.

Meredith's heart seemed to stop, and at once she thought desperately about running away to the farthest part of the garden. But that would only make matters worse, she realised in a moment of cold clarity. She made her slow progress into the house, up the stairs and along the corridor to where her mother was waiting.

'How dare you?' Caroline whispered. Meredith looked at her feet. 'How dare you!' she shouted, so loudly and harshly that Meredith jumped, and began to cry. 'Answer me—where have you been with them? What were you doing?' Mrs Priddy appeared from a room down the hall and hurried along to stand behind Meredith protectively.

'My lady? Is something the matter?' the housekeeper asked.

Caroline ignored her. She bent forward, seized Meredith's shoulders and shook her roughly.

'Answer me! How dare you disobey me, girl!' she spat, her gaunt face made brutal by rage. Meredith sobbed harder, tears of pure fear running down her cheeks. Straightening up, Caroline took a short breath and slapped her daughter sharply across the face.

'My lady! That's enough!' Mrs Priddy gasped. Meredith fell into shocked silence. Caroline grasped her arm again and towed her viciously to her room, pushing her inside.

'You will stay in there and not come out until you have learned your lesson,' Caroline said coldly. 'You're a wicked child. No mother could ever love you,' she said; and the last thing Meredith saw before the door closed was Mrs Priddy's stunned expression.

For a week, Meredith was kept locked in her room. The staff were given orders that she was to have nothing but bread and water, but once Caroline had retired, Estelle and Mrs Priddy took her biscuits and scones and ham sandwiches. They brushed her hair for her and told her funny stories. Meredith remained silent and closed off, so that they exchanged worried looks above her head.

No mother could ever love her. Meredith dwelt on this statement for a long time and refused to believe it. She would make her mother love her, she resolved. She would strive to be good and decorous in all things, and would win her mother's heart that way. She would shun the tinkers. Because of them, her mother could not love her. They are not welcome here. She lay listlessly on her bed and felt her old anger at the Dinsdales, her old resentment, well up so that it cast a dark shadow over her heart.

Epilogue

IT WAS A RELIEF, in the end, to have all my decisions made for me. Made by Dinny. What could I tell Clifford and Mary? That Henry was alive but damaged, and although I had seen him many times over Christmas and not told them, I now had no idea where he was? And why would I even try to stay at the manor, with all of them gone? Beth, Dinny, Harry. Henry. But I didn't go far. There was no question of me going back to London. And on the edge of Barrow Storton there was a 1950s two-up, two-down cottage to rent. Two bedrooms, so Beth and Eddie can come and stay. It's on the opposite side of the village to the manor. I can see right across the valley, with the village at its bottom, and one corner of the manor is visible through distant trees.

It makes me very serene, living here. I feel like I belong. I have no sense of there being anything else I should be doing, or working towards, or changing. I am not even waiting, not really. I make a special point of not waiting. I teach in Devizes, I walk a lot. I call in on George Hathaway for cups of tea and biscuits. Sometimes I miss the people I used to see in London—not specific people as such, but having so many faces around me. The illusion of company. I've made friends with my neighbours, Susan and Paul, and sometimes baby-sit for them. The girls are good-natured and they do as they're told, most of the time. I take them on nature walks up on the downs or along the river bank; we make cornflake cakes and hot chocolate while Susan and Paul go to the pub, the cinema, the shops, their bed.

Honey knows I'm here, and so does Mo. I went back to see Haydee and told them where I was and they've both been to visit since. I polished the tarnish from the silver bell on Flag's teething ring and tucked it into Haydee's cot. She grabbed it with one fat hand, crammed it immediately into her mouth. 'It was your great-grandpa's,' I whispered to her. I wrote down my address, told Honey to keep it in case anybody asked for it. She gave me a straight look, solemn, then arched one eyebrow. But she didn't say anything. She's back at school now and Mo comes around with Haydee in her pram. She walks from West Hatch, says the fresh air and movement is the only thing that makes the baby sleep. As I make tea she twitches the blanket over the child and can't keep herself from smiling.

I have the photo of Caroline with her baby in a frame on the windowsill. I never did get around to giving it to Mum. I am still proud to have uncovered the child's identity, to have found the source of the rift between my family and Dinny's. Mum was astonished when I told her the story. I can't prove it all, definitively, but I know it to be true. I've decided to like the fact that I can't fill in all the blanks—why Caroline hid her earlier marriage, why she hid her child. Some things are lost in the past—surely that's why the past is so mysterious, why it fascinates us. Nothing much will be lost any more—too much is recorded, noted, stored in a file on a computer somewhere. It's harder to keep a secret these days, but they can be kept. Harry is living proof that they can be kept. I find I don't mind secrets half so much when they are mine to keep, when I am not excluded.

The manor house was sold at auction for a figure that gave me a sinking feeling inside, just for half an hour, imagining what I could have done with such wealth. Clifford came to the auction but I hid from him, at the back of the conference room, as the figures got bigger and bigger. I could sense his anguish just by looking at the back of his head, rigid on stiff shoulders. I felt sorry for him. A developer bought it and it's being converted into luxury flats, just like Maxwell suggested.

I think about Caroline and Meredith a lot. I think about what Dinny said—that people who bully and hate are not happy people. They behave that way because they are unhappy. It is hard to find sympathy for Meredith when I have such memories of her, but now that she is dead I can manage it, when I try. Hers was a life of disappointment— her one bid to free herself from a loveless home over so soon after it began. It might have been harder still to feel sympathy for Caroline when she chose to abandon one child and then raised another without love. It would be easy to conclude that she just could not love. But then I found the last letter she wrote before she died, and I know better.

It lay undiscovered for weeks in the writing case, after I left the manor. Because she never sent it, never even tore it from the writing pad. It was there, all along, beneath the cover, in her spidery writing. The date is 1983. No day or month specified, so perhaps that was the best she could do. She was over a hundred by then, and knew that she was dying. Perhaps that was why she wrote this letter.

My Dearest Corin,

It has been so long since I lost you that I cannot count the years. I am old now—old enough to be waiting to die myself. But then, I have been waiting to die ever since we were parted, my love. It is strange that the long years I have spent here in England seem, sometimes, to have passed by in a blur. I cannot recall what I can have done to fill so much time—I really do not remember. But I remember every second I spent with you, my love. Every precious second that I was your wife, and we were together. Oh, why did you die? Why did you ride out that day? I have been over it so many times, and I try to change the memory. I convince myself that I ran after you, told you not to go, not to leave me. Then you would not have fallen, and you would not have died, and I would not have had to spend these long dark years without you.

I did a terrible thing, Corin. An unforgivable thing. I ran away from it but I could not undo it, and it has followed me through all the years since. My only consolation has been that I never forgave myself, and that surely this life I have endured has been punishment enough? But no, there could never be punishment enough for what I did. I pray that you do not know of it, for if you did, you would not love me any more and I simply could not bear that.

I wish I could see you one more time, before I die. Part of me believes that there would be some justice in this—that if the world was a fair place, I would be allowed just a second of your embrace, to make up for losing you. No matter what I did in the madness of grief, no matter how I compounded my mistake or how much worse I have made it ever since. I would gladly give myself up to an eternity of torment just to see you one more time. But it cannot be. I will die, and be forgotten, just as you died. But I never forgot you, my Corin, my husband. Whatever else I did, I never forgot you, and I loved you always.

Caroline

I read and reread this letter in the weeks after I found it. Until I knew it by rote, and each word broke my heart a little. Such a vast depth of regret and sorrow. When I feel it take hold of me, when I feel I have absorbed too much of it, I remember Beth. Her crime will not follow her any more. She will not compound it, or let the regret tear at her for ever. The chain has been broken, and I helped to break it. I remember that, and I let it cheer me, fill me up with hope.

I will never know what Caroline did. Why she took her baby and ran to England, why she then abandoned him. One thing I do notice, though, from my many readings of this letter: she does not mention her son. If the child was hers, and Corin his father, why doesn't she mention him? Why doesn't she tell her Corin about his son? Try to explain why she abandoned him? And this abandonment seems inexplicable, really unbelievable, when matched to the love she professes for the child's father. I remember the dark young girl at the summer party—the girl whom Caroline called Magpie. Her hair, as black as Dinny's. I will never know for sure, but this omission from the letter hints at a crime indeed, and makes me doubt the claim of kinship I made to Dinny.

Beth came to stay a couple of weeks ago. She wishes, I think, that I'd settled in a different village, but she's getting used to the idea. She doesn't shy away from this place any more.

I may well settle somewhere else, sometime—soon, or eventually. I'm not waiting, but I need to be where he can find me. Just until the next time he does. And he's got reasons to come back here, after all. More to pull him here than just me, and my desire for him. A mother, a sister, a niece. I think Honey would tell me, if he'd been back.

My happiness at seeing Beth improve bubbles up whenever I set eyes on her. No miracle cure, of course, but she's better. She can split the blame for what happened with Dinny now; she no longer has to think that she and she alone dealt fate to Henry Calcott. The truth of it, the right and wrong, is more diffuse now. She didn't take a life, she just changed one. So no miracle cure, but she talks to me about what happened, and because she's turned around and looked at it, it's not dogging her steps like it used to. I can see the improvement and so can Eddie, although he hasn't asked me about it. I don't think he cares what's changed, he's just pleased that it has.

It takes a while to see somebody differently when for years you've seen them in a particular way, or not seen them at all. I still saw Harry, when Dinny told me to see Henry. And I still saw Dinny as I had always seen him, always loved him. I tell myself that he needs time to see me differently, to see me as I am now and not see a child, or Beth's little sister, or whatever else it is he sees.

There was a legal wrangle over the plot of land where the Dinsdales are allowed to camp. The developer didn't want a load of travellers parking up in the communal gardens of his new flats. In the end that piece of ground was sold to the farmer whose land adjoins it, and he has known the Dinsdales for years. So it's still there, waiting for them. Waiting for him. A beautiful place to camp in the summer, green and sheltered, and unmolested now.

I'm hoping for a hot summer. Weather to bake the bones and excuse this languid life I've adopted. Weather to sneak to the dew pond, to paddle, to swim, to chase its ghosts away. And today a small parcel came in the post for me. Inside, crumbling, was a piece of tree bark with patterns scratched into it. Nothing I could distinguish in the designs, except the name at the bottom—HARRY—in crooked, almost unreadable letters. A declaration, I take it to be, of who he is now, of who he wants to be. And an unspoken message from Dinny, who wrapped it up and posted it. That he knows where I am, and that he thinks of me. For now, I find I am quite happy with that.

Katherine Webb

What was the main inspiration behind *The Legacy*?

History—not the big, well-known stories about wars and politics of years gone by, but the private histories of everyday people, and the ways in which they can influence us in the present day, even if we aren't aware of it. It's also a story about just how deeply we are shaped by things that happen to us, and the people we meet in our childhood.

Do you remember your own childhood clearly?

I have such good memories of childhood, so vivid. It seems as if it was always the summer holidays! I was a bit of a tomboy so most of my memories are of being outside—climbing trees, riding ponies, getting muddy, falling into puddles. My mum's excellent cooking, of course, and running riot with my sister and all my cousins on our grandparents' farm in Devon—so much fun.

How did you set about creating four such different characters as Erica, Beth, Meredith and Caroline?

Erica's voice came to me first, clear as a bell. I knew straightaway who she was, so writing her was effortless. Beth and Meredith were trickier. Although they are very different women, both had been affected badly by events in their own lives, and their mental health has suffered as a result. Caroline is so young when the story starts, I imagined her as a blank page. She has lived a cosseted life and has never had to face up to challenges. Then along comes the biggest challenge of her life. The question I asked was: how will she cope with this?

Which character did you enjoy writing about most?

Erica felt like a close friend by the end of the book, but I have to say I absolutely loved writing the Wild West sections of Caroline's story. I find that era of history so fascinating, and Caroline's journey, both physically and mentally, is possibly the most dramatic within the novel.

What made you decide to set the book in Oklahoma Territory?

I wanted it to be set at the beginning of the twentieth century so that Erica could remember Caroline as an old lady. As I started my research, I realised that by 1905, much of the 'wild' west was wild no longer—towns had spread, railways criss-crossed the land, the vast open grasslands were being fenced in and farmed. Except in Oklahoma Territory, where the area had been set aside for the Native Americans and closed to white settlers until the last years of the nineteenth century. It was the perfect place to send Caroline to really make her feel she was in the middle of nowhere.

Have you ever been to Oklahoma?

No, but I have travelled extensively in the American West, and experienced the vastness of landscapes in places like Wyoming, Montana and Utah. A hundred years ago the scale and emptiness must have been truly staggering.

Did you always want to be a writer?

I studied History at Durham University and after that did a variety of jobs in London, Berkshire and Venice while waiting for my big break! I don't remember ever making a conscious decision to become a writer, but when I told people I was writing a novel, nobody was very surprised. My mum still has stories I wrote when I was very young and I won various poetry and fiction prizes while I was at school and at college. So I suppose the urge to write has always been there, and in the end no other career choice even got a look in.

What gave you the determination to keep writing in the years before you got a publishing deal?

Well, I left myself no option. I put all my eggs in one basket and gambled on the fact that I would one day get published. There was never any question of giving up, even as the number of completed, unpublished books grew, as did the pile of rejection letters! I think I would have kept going even if I never got published—it's just what I do.

Where do you write?

At my desk in the tiny spare room in my cottage in Newbury. I dream one day of owning one of those vast, leather-topped desks that I can spread piles of books and papers over. Right now, there is just enough room for my elbows between the wall and the printer!

The House of
Dust and Dreams

Brenda Reid

*I have loved the far south-east corner of Crete for many years.
Here is where my husband and I restored an old village house
belonging to the grandfather of a friend, some fifteen years
ago. And here is where we come whenever we can.
The villagers have welcomed us, our children, grandchil-
dren and many friends with affection and friendship.
I stopped working as a television drama producer and
started down a different road, to become a story teller. I
became fascinated by the recent history of Crete; especially
the extraordinary resistance to the invasion and occupation
of the island in the Second World War. This was a story that,
without care, was destined to be forgotten.
I imagined a young English woman developing a close
friendship with a Greek woman. I imagined a forbidden love
affair. And wondered how all the players would survive and
be changed by the events in these great mountains.
I hope you enjoy my story.*

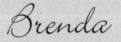

The Island of Crete, Greece

SUMMER 1937

HEAVENLY

I FIRST SAW the old Orfanoudakis house on a warm, sunlit afternoon; the only sounds a lone bullfrog and the cicadas. The village around it was sleeping.

It had taken a week to get to the island from Athens by seaplane and then five hours up a narrow mountain track from the Sea of Crete below. This last stretch was in a donkey cart owned by a fisherman, Petros.

Our companions were his mother, two of his six children and a crate of squawking chickens. When Petros stopped in the village square he pointed ahead to the house, Hugh's family's house; a majestic structure dominating a row of tiny white houses, their windows like mouseholes. I raced up the steps of the wide street and stopped in front of it.

It was dilapidated certainly, but nothing that couldn't be fixed, I felt sure. I turned in delight to Hugh, but he was struggling with our luggage; the sunlight caught a flash of a silver coin in his hand and there was much kissing and hugging and welcoming cries of 'Kalos orisate' from Petros and his family.

'Come and see, it's beautiful!' I cried excitedly. 'It's really old, and just how it used to be, I think, when your grandfather was here.'

'Great-grandfather,' he muttered, gasping for breath.

I was hugging myself with delight and jumping up and down so hard my straw hat fell off and rolled down the street.

And then he was beside me. 'Christ Almighty, Evadne,' he said, amazed. 'We can't stay here, it's a ruin.'

I looked at the shutters along the front terrace. They had no paint left and they were hanging rather precariously. But the front door, open on one hinge, looked welcoming to me and there were crimson geraniums blooming in a stone amphora on the terrace above.

'Oh, Hugh, don't be such an old pessimist; a lick of paint, a nail or two and it'll be fine.'

Hugh sighed bleakly as he set the trunks down. 'This, Evadne, is supposed to be our honeymoon. We've been married for two years and never had a proper time to ourselves, and now are you telling me I must start hammering and painting?'

'Well, Petros said there were no hotels so we'd better make the best of it, hadn't we? Anyway, I bet it's beautiful inside.' To my eyes, it already was.

The steps leading up to the front door were aged and weathered, with brown stringy weeds and yellowing grass pushing up through the cracks. Hugh resisted all my efforts of help and, scarlet-faced with exertion, struggled with insistent determination up step by slow step.

As I crossed the cracked and broken stones of the threshold, a poignant flicker went through me. The day was bright with sun but, inside, the large room was cool and dim. The rays spilling in at the windows on one wall cast an almost romantic light so that, for a moment or two, the room, even with the sagging beams high in the ceiling and the cracked and broken white walls, seemed full of all the dreams I'd ever had and, I believed, all those still to come.

This morning it is the mosquito that wakes me; that insistent, whiny buzz. I stretch my arm across the sheet, but there is only space. Nobody there. I stumble out of bed and up the rickety stairs, hanging onto the rope. From the terrace window I can see the dawn break the sky. I can also see Hugh on the steamer chair outside. His head back, his mouth open and with every breath, a small snore rumples the silence.

It takes only a moment to slip out of my nightgown and into yesterday's dress. It's creased like all the others—there's no proper wardrobe. Thank goodness for stone floors: no boards creak as I creep out of the house. I pause every few steps and listen; the snores are regular.

It is ten days since we came up that mountain path and every day for me has been a delight. The villagers here have opened their arms and their hearts to us. I have, I think, for the first time in my life, a sense of belonging.

At first we were just a curiosity. No one here has met an English person before. They struggled with our names and were quickly defeated by 'Hugh' and 'Evadne' so we became 'You' and 'Heavenly'. I laughed but Hugh said rather crossly, 'They must know Evadne was a Greek goddess!'

I remembered what he had told me—the daughter of Poseidon—but I had seen the blank look in their eyes. 'Apparently not, in this bit of Crete.'

Even so early, I am not alone out here; as I walk up the path, there are several villagers on the way to their gardens at the edge of the village and they greet me cheerfully; *'Yiassou'*, *'Kalimera'*. With every step the sky lightens a little and over in the east I can see the first rays of today's sun. It will be warm in an hour and very hot in three.

The road where our house is leads with wide steps up, up and round and round. Near the top is a *kafenion* called 'Il Piperia', its courtyard shaded by a very old pepper tree from which it takes its name.

This is the only bit of the village that Hugh seems to enjoy.

He sits with the local men as they play cards or backgammon and, spurning the thick, sweet coffee they offer, drinks the local wine or *raki*. I once suggested I accompany him there, but this was greeted with derision: 'Men only, old girl, strictly a boys' club.'

Further on up, the road branches off to the school and winds round to the other parts of the village. Just as Petros described on our journey up here, there is the cluster of houses forming Pano Panagia, the upper village; self-contained almost, sitting atop the rest as if keeping a watchful eye. There is Mesa, the middle part; by far the largest, containing our house at the edge. Further down is Kato, the lower, snugly tucked in at the bottom. I look about me with delight. Two great ribs of mountains enclose this paradise.

By the time we arrived here from the embassy in Athens, I was already in love with the island. And in this village, Panagia Sta Perivolia, and the old house I have just left, I have found somewhere I want to call home.

But yesterday a letter arrived asking Hugh how he wanted to arrange our return travel: by ferry or flying boat? And I don't want to leave.

In Athens and the embassy it seems there is nothing but talk of war and the German Chancellor, Hitler. Here in the village, life is so much simpler; it is regulated only by the sun and the moon, the seasons and the crops. I have tried talking to one or two of our neighbours and I'm sure, given a chance, I could get to know them, be happy here; but Hugh can hardly wait to be back to the endless round of parties and receptions we have left behind. He loves all that.

I am up in the hills now, and it is going to be a very hot day. It crosses my mind that I should have brought my hat, but at that moment I catch my foot on a stone half hidden under a golden clump of briar, and fall. A horrid, clumsy fall that has wrenched my ankle round.

As I try to stand, I fall again; it's sprained, I think.

I manage to get onto all fours and peer round me. I am on one of the ancient goat tracks that pepper these hills and although I can see for miles, there is no sign of anyone. I try to think how long I've been walking: an hour? Longer? And in which direction is the village?

Birds are singing and somewhere, far away, the bells of a flock of goats tinkle.

'Hello, hello. Is there anyone here?' I call.

But who on earth is going to hear that bat-squeak of a sound? I call again for help, this time in Greek, '*Atrape mou!*' and again as loud as I can, '*Atrape!*' and then, sinking back in desperation, 'Oh, damn and bloody hell, won't someone *atrape* me?'

The sun is beating down on me, and the fall has left me giddy and nauseous. There is a tremor of panic and I feel frightened and alone.

And then a moment later, 'Hello!' comes from somewhere and after a pause, 'Where you are?' A miracle. Someone is near and they've spoken in English! I wave my arm in the air as high as I can. 'Hello,' I call again, 'I'm here!' And I can see her now, running towards me. She stops when she reaches me, and looks down in astonishment.

'*Panagia mou!*' she says. I'm not sure calling on the Virgin Mary is going to help me much. But at least she's here.

She is young, probably the same age as me but tiny. Stocky, sturdy but with a lively, twinkly face; with the rosy cheeks of one who spends a lot of time outdoors.

We speak in a mixture of Greek and English and, in spite of the giddiness, I laugh.

'I'm sorry, I don't know your name. And no one here speaks English, so how is it that you do?'

'Anthi,' she says. 'It's short for Rodianthi. I'll explain about the English later. And you are Heavenly, aren't you? Everyone knows you.'

A wave of giddiness sweeps over me and I press my head down between my knees.

'You stay here,' she says. 'I must leave you for a little and get my horse. He is tethered further up the mountain.'

'You will come back, won't you?'

She stands now, very still. 'You don't know me yet, Heavenly, but when you do, you will know I never break my word.'

'You are an angel, Anthi. I hope you and I will be friends.'

It seems to take for ever, but it is probably no more than twenty minutes before she is back beside me. She is on her horse, goats skittering round her.

She pulls her straw hat from her head and tries to tug it over my hair. It is hard; my hair is wiry and wild and in this heat, all over the place.

'Put the hat over your face if it won't stay on your head, you are start-ing to burn.' She clears a large bundle of grasses from the back of the saddle, throwing them down any old how.

'Anthi, I'm sorry but your goats are attacking me!' Even as she quickly moves to shoo them away, one starts to eat my dress and another is hungrily licking my foot.

'I'm sorry about them,' she says as they move away, bells clinking, and we both laugh.

Between us we manage to get me up into the saddle and she jumps up behind me. '*Entaxi?*' she says. 'You are OK?'

'*Entax.*' And I am, just.

ANTHI

WE DON'T SPEAK much as we move towards her house. Heavenly, I think, is in pain and although she doesn't complain, her body is tense in my arms as I hold the reins round her. In spite of her protests I made her keep the hat. She needs lessons in how to dress for this climate. No hat, and her frock, I can see, is fine linen, layered in tiers of palest green and grey, and underneath what appears to be a silk petticoat. Beautiful certainly, costly I am sure, but not appropriate for days like these.

I look at her, this strange and rather wonderful creature they call Heavenly, come to earth in the hills of Panagia. Her hair is a shining golden red and stands out like a halo all round her face in curls and waves. It must be painful to brush. She is a little older than me, I think, but she looks young. The eyes that look back at me from time to time are the colour of fresh spring grass. I can tell her legs are long and her arms, too. In spite of all the finery, I can see that her hands, gripping the pommel of the saddle, are tough hands, working hands.

From the village square and the small hall that serves as our commu-nity centre, we ride up the steps to Heavenly's house. As soon as we turn, I see the tall figure of her husband outside, and as we approach I see the anxiety creasing what is a handsome face. Behind him are the Kanavakis brothers, Spiros and Katis, two of the biggest *raki* drinkers in the village. They look odd in contrast with the tall, fair Englishman;

two swarthy, fat shepherds beside a china figurine. He runs down the steps, gesturing the others to follow.

'My dear, what on earth happened to you?' The three of them struggle clumsily to lift her down.

'I feel very silly,' she says, 'but I tripped over, sprained my ankle, I think, and probably would have died if Anthi here hadn't rescued me.'

He picks her up and carries her up the steps into the house, where she smiles at me as she passes me back my hat. She already looks better, just being in his arms. 'Come on, Anthi, we need a drink, we've earned it!' I tether Astrape and climb the steps.

I think I had been in the old Orfanoudakis house as a child, but for years it has been empty. No one in the village seems to know its story, only that English people owned it and have now come to live in it.

I gasp aloud as I go inside; it seems as if I have entered a cave it is so dark and cool after the heat of the day outside. The room we are in is vast. At one end I can dimly see that there is a wine press and what is probably furniture, but it is piled in heaps in a corner, and what feels like a century's worth of dust rises as we step across the floor.

The Englishman she calls You smiles as he places her carefully on an army camp bed at one end of this great room. 'I can see you are shocked,' he says, 'but my wife insists we stay in this broken-down wreck.'

'Stop complaining and pour some brandy for your guests.'

The Kanavakis brothers bow hastily, giving embarrassed glances in my direction, and back out of the door, muttering goodbye. I think they have had several brandies here this morning and they are off now, I guess, to Il Piperia to have a few more. With their departure I feel curiously alone. There is an unspoken intimacy between this English couple. He is moving around what I guess is some sort of makeshift kitchen while talking over his shoulder to her.

He is a handsome man; his fair hair flops into his eyes and he is clean-shaven. I'm not used to that. But the thing that is really strange are his trousers. They stop at the knee, leaving his lower legs bare. I have never seen a man's bare legs before, and I turn quickly away, feeling myself begin to blush. My husband Manolis takes his clothes off in the dark, or sometimes sleeps in them. Certainly no Greek man would wear such revealing trousers.

I sit beside Heavenly on the floor and You hands us brandy in cups, but I realise I have been away most of the morning. I have duties and must be gone. I gulp my brandy and rise to leave. Heavenly catches my hand. 'Promise me you will come back soon?'

'I will, I really will.'

I ride away across the horizon, blue and sunlit. Seabirds are wheeling inland. I can see the village below, sheltering in the side of the mountain.

I like this Heavenly, I hope she stays. I can't see her house any longer, but I can see the row of cypress trees nearby. They were planted by my great-great-grandfather, and they always make me think of my father; he loved them. I still miss him so much. He would like Heavenly, I know it. I remember now one night, when I was eight years old, I heard him tell my mother I was special—different—not only when compared to my brother and sister but to all the other children in the village. I liked to hear this, so I listened more. 'She could read when she was four,' he said, 'do her numbers when only five. This child will stay at school. Go to the college in Heraklion if we can make it happen. Travel the world. Be a proud woman. Anthi will do better things than any of us.'

But when I was ten my father died and his dreams died with him. My mother and my uncle made what they thought was a good marriage for me and, at sixteen, I was the wife of Manolis Manadakis. At seventeen, I was the mother of Despina; at eighteen, my son Constantinos was born, too soon, after only six and a half months in my belly; then, at twenty-one, my beautiful Voula was born to me.

I am home now and, as I dismount, I feel a soreness between my legs. Manolis was drunk again last night and the memory of his violent thrusting in me still hurts. There must be better ways to show love than to cause this burning?

I am so late home! These long summer days when I don't go to help in the school are precious. I am not used to idleness. I'll finish hiving the bees and then go to collect Despina and little Voula. They have been with my neighbour, Maria, playing with her daughter, Athena. Voula is too young to play but she loves to be with her sister. She will surely be wanting my milk now.

As if she sensed me, I hear a small cry from Maria's house. Quickly I am there and Voula is in my arms, smiling already. I'll take her with me to the bees and feed her there under the olives.

Her soft, warm plumpness is like a piece of heaven in my arms; the milky smell of her, the dark curling wisps of her hair and velvet eyes I could look into all day. I am lucky in my girls; they came into the world laughing and seem never to have stopped. Even Manolis, when he is sober, can only gaze at them, astonished that these little peaches are the product of his angry coupling.

My hat is crammed onto my head and as I bend to Despina, it falls to the ground. I pick it up and as I raise it I can smell a faint, delicious perfume. Heavenly! I remember that red-gold hair of hers, so different to mine. My hair is like a thorn bush. When I married Manolis it was my shining crown; now, it already has streaks of silver—twenty-two years old and hair like my grandmother! As we walk to the bees, I remember how buxom I was on my wedding day; round and firm, just how my bridegroom liked me. But I quickly learned to become what he didn't want—that way he left me alone.

So now I am more like a carrot than a peach—my body is hard, tough. I prefer it this way; muscled from work, and soft around the belly from babies. My body, my hair, my thoughts and my heart, they are mine. This is who I am.

HEAVENLY

'FUNNY LITTLE WOMAN.'

'Oh, Hugh, is that all you can say? If it weren't for her, I'd still be lying on the side of a mountain, burnt to a cinder by the sun.'

Hugh lopes across the room and pats me gently on the head.

'Oh, dearest, please don't get steamed up. I was worried, you know, but I'd no idea where you'd gone.' His eyes are so soft and kind, a pleading in them for understanding, forgiveness. 'Please, let's go home.' He is actually on his knees now, a quiet desperation in his eyes.

'Home? Where's home?' I ask it gently, for his eyes are alight at the very thought of leaving this house, this village.

And here is the problem, and it seems small, just a little difference between us; other times it is as big as the world. I don't want to go back to Athens and embassy life, and Hugh does.

This beautiful old house, its stones soaking in the golden sun over the mountains and the Sea of Crete, is exactly where I want to be. I see it in the future, filled with rugs and hangings, comfy old furniture and children laughing from room to room. I dread returning to our life in the British Embassy in Athens, supposed to be our home.

We arrived there a long year ago, from a short posting in Paris, and I had done everything I thought was expected of a diplomat's wife. I learned Greek. I went to tea parties with the other wives. I took part in endless discussions about hairdressers and dressmakers. In truth

I was bored to within an inch of running away.

Excitement among the wives reached a peak with the abdication of King Edward. They all clustered round the wireless to listen to his speech to the nation from Windsor Castle, twittering like magpies. In fact we had known for days that this was to happen, so I found it hard to join in the thrill of it all.

And then there were the speculations about Wallis Simpson: her hair, her clothes, her shoes, her waistline. I am genuinely sad that I can find so little in common. I would love to have a friend. For one thing, none of them have ever worked. Never earned any money.

When Hugh was asked to come to Crete to sort out some minor demonstrations that were taking place at the tomb of Venizelos, near Chania, it seemed all my prayers had been answered. At first he thought to make the trip alone, but I am afraid I made rather a fuss and he brought me, too.

The King of Greece had asked the British ambassador for help in a potentially tricky situation and Hugh had been entrusted with the task of this political manoeuvring for the king, who had recently returned from twelve years in exile. I was thrilled to think of us, well, me anyway, involved in the real world. This was what I thought we would be doing all the time.

Before we left Athens for Crete, I read as much recent history of the area as I could find. I knew the importance of Venizelos, who had died only a short time ago and was buried on the island of his birth.

I had come to understand the tension in the air when Venizelos was spoken of. He had tried to turn the country into a democracy, but there was strong opposition from the royalists and he had had major battles with General Metaxas, the king's choice of leader. I liked the sound of this Venizelos, but Hugh looked blank when I said so.

'Don't get involved with things you don't understand, darling,' he said.

Actually, I understood more than some of his colleagues, but I couldn't say so; women's opinions are considered of little worth. Hugh's friend, Foxy, for instance, was puzzled that Venizelos had been buried so quickly.

'You'd have thought a chap like that would have a proper lying-in-state,' I heard him say to Hugh as they played billiards one night.

'Dangerous times, these, old boy,' said Hugh, as he cannoned his ball in off the red. (I remembered to stay quiet. Women were only allowed in the games room on sufferance.) 'Don't forget, not so long ago the communists held the balance of power here. The important thing now is to keep them happy. Not keep reminding them what a good chap Venizelos was; all those social reforms he made are enough of a memorial, don't you think? Give him a damn great funeral in the middle of Athens and all hell could break out. It's bad enough having him stuck in Crete, where he's still causing trouble from his grave.'

By the time we arrived in Chania, the trouble was more or less over, so we decided to travel across the island and find this old house that had been in Hugh's family for ages. One of his grandfather's brothers had married a Greek heiress. She had owned two houses in Thessaloniki, and this one in Crete. A couple had lived in it for years, in theory to look after it, but when they died it stayed shut up and falling apart, until now. Hugh having no brothers, it eventually came to him.

After Athens, where life was one seemingly endless round of formality, this island is like arriving in heaven. The villagers are so wonderfully welcoming and kind. There is much poverty outside the cities, but everywhere we go we are showered with gifts—it seems that whatever you have you share with a visitor. And, oh, the beauty of the hills around us! Crete has only been part of Greece for twenty years or so; one coast looking towards the Balkans and the other to Arabian Africa.

'Help me up, and get me out onto the terrace. I'm sure looking down to the sea will make us both feel better.'

Hugh sighed and, helping me to my feet, half carried me outside. It was painful, more than I had expected, but we were now out in the fresh, sweet air. I was on one of a pair of long carved chairs and Hugh was on an upright bench that looked wildly uncomfortable. But even he couldn't resist the lure of the mountains for long and his eyes followed the curve of the crags down to the sea far below. Turning, he gave me a smile, a special Hugh smile and, even though I was hurting, I smiled back at him.

'That's better, isn't it? Could you be an angel and get me an aspirin?'

An hour or so later we were still on the terrace. The pain was dulled and Hugh was dozing.

The first time I saw Hugh, he was asleep. Well, not so much asleep as unconscious. He was on his way to my ward from the operating theatre at the hospital where I was working. Mr Carter had removed his appendix and he was going to be in my care for the next ten days.

'One, two, three, over.' The porters heaved him onto the bed, but his feet wouldn't tuck in tidily. Matron would be there in ten minutes and she'd go wild if the ward, or any of the patients, were in a mess. Hard as I tried, I simply could not get anything right in her eyes.

I was one of the youngest nurses in Greenbridge Hospital. I'd passed all my first-year exams and I loved nursing, but neat and tidy I was not.

Actually, I've never been much good at anything. I grew up in the shadow of my perfect sister. Where I am gawky, she is elegant. Where my hair is ginger and crinkly, hers is silky and auburn. Where my skin throws out freckles at the first hint of summer, Daphne's is creamy smooth with a faint hint of a golden blush.

After my father died, my mother had even less time for us. She was the district organiser for the Red Cross, and a gathering of strangers in a church hall somewhere always had needs greater than ours. She would say, 'For people like us, duty is never finished. My life is not my own.'

I remember it was a glorious spring day when Hugh Timberlake came into my life. Most of the patients on the ward were elderly, and varied from cranky and fed-up to really miserable and whingey. Hugh was none of these. The funny thing was, I hadn't even looked properly at his face and when I did, I could see he was very handsome. He had shaggy hair, fair; a straight nose, quite classical; and his skin was a light gold, as though he spent time in the sun. He was altogether delicious.

I gathered his notes together and put them in a folder at the foot of his bed. Hugh Timberlake: even his name sounded romantic. At the top end of the bed he had started to snuffle a little, so I moved round to bend close and listen to what he was trying to say.

'Sorry, nurse, I think I'm going to be—' And he was, all down the front of my clean apron. I had been so busy looking at his green eyes that I had completely forgotten one of the first rules of nursing: always approach a post-op patient with a bowl in your hand. And now here were Matron and Sister approaching.

'My goodness, what a mess you are, Tyler!' That was me, Tyler. Just like a boys' school, we were all surnames there.

'Sorry, Sister, Matron,' I mumbled. Matron raised an eyebrow and Sister went, 'Tsk, tsk', before moving on.

One of the main things that mattered was always to be clean and tidy, just like the ward. This was the bit I fell down on, day after day. If there was some blood or sick around, it always seemed to end up on me. I also have a real problem with my hair. It is red and jumps out all round my head. Even when I pinned it up with hair clips and squeezed it under my stiff cap, it still sprang out.

Hugh Timberlake was on the ward for a fortnight and for barely a moment of that time was he alone. He seemed always to be surrounded by bevies of pretty girls fluttering round him like butterflies.

One day his mother came to see him. I know because he introduced me to her. She sat beside his bed and held his hand throughout.

'Mother, this is Nurse Tyler.' I blushed bright red. I didn't know he knew my name.

She was charming and smiled warmly at me as she shook my hand, which she held as she thanked me for looking after her son so well. She looked like him, the same green eyes. It seemed that, after Hugh's father died, she had remarried and now lived in Ireland.

'Her husband breeds horses,' Hugh said to me as I changed his sheets the next morning. 'I think he looks like a horse. I can't think what she sees in him. She was devastated when my father died. It was so unfair, he'd survived all through the war and then died of the flu. He was quite a hero: he was a major in the East Surrey Regiment, awarded the George Cross at Ypres. And now she's married to this boring chap.'

'Perhaps she needed company. It must be lonely to be a widow.'

'Do you know, I'd never thought of that,' he said. 'How wise you are. I was away at Winchester, so there was no one for her to talk to.'

When I was on the night shift, he would sometimes persuade me to linger by his bed, and we would share a whispered conversation. Until one night when he said, 'I'm out of here tomorrow, Nurse, and I don't even know your Christian name.'

'It's Evadne,' I whispered. I knew he was smiling.

'It's a lovely name: Evadne, the daughter of Poseidon, the sea god. Did you know that?'

'No,' I whispered back, thinking, *But I'll never forget it now*.

And then I was busy and, of course, when I went in the next evening he was gone, and a grim old vicar had taken his place.

It was about a week later that I went with Maisie, one of the other nurses, for tea at the Copper Kettle in Greenbridge High Street.

We were lingering over a cucumber sandwich when Maisie peered past me and gasped. 'Don't look now,' she said, 'but that patient just walked in. You know, the good-looking one with all the girlfriends.'

I froze, not daring to peek behind me.

He walked past us, and sat at a table across the room. He was alone.

The waitress brought him a menu, but he pushed it aside and I heard him say, 'Just a cup of tea, please. Darjeeling if you have it.' And he flashed the waitress that lovely smile he had. As she scurried away, looking pink and flustered, he caught sight of us.

'He's waving us over,' Maisie whispered, 'what shall we do?' As we dithered, I saw him get to his feet and come over to us.

'Hello, girls,' he said, 'what a lovely surprise. May I join you?'

Before I thought of anything to say, Maisie, blushing furiously, was on her feet. 'Here, have my chair,' she said, 'I've got an anatomy lesson in twenty minutes.' And she was on her way, leaving a shilling on the tablecloth as she went.

I can't remember any of the things we talked about that afternoon. I just know that half an hour went whizzing by in a flash before there was a shriek and a gorgeous girl appeared at my shoulder.

'Hugh, darling!' she squeaked. 'I'm so terribly sorry. Am I unforgivably late?' He was on his feet in a moment and her arms were round his neck. 'Sorry, sorry, angel,' she said. I couldn't hear the rest as I was too busy trying to get up without knocking over my chair.

'Here,' I said, 'have my seat, I have to go anyway.' And, knowing I was blushing horribly, I was on my way to the door.

'Excuse me, miss,' said the waitress as I passed her, 'that's one and ninepence, if you don't mind.'

Somehow I managed to get out of there. Hugh had insisted on paying for Maisie and me, pointing out that Maisie had left a shilling towards the bill, anyway.

I walked along Greenbridge High Street in a daze. How foolish to think anything of it at all. He was merely being polite, talking to me while waiting for his girlfriend. I tried to think no more about him and, as the days passed in sleep and the nights were busy, I concentrated on my next exams.

One day, Sister grabbed my arm as I was coming on duty. 'Got a job for you, Tyler. Helping out the St John brigade tomorrow afternoon.'

I must have looked puzzled.

'There's a garden party at Lady Troutbeck's. Extra pair of hands needed. They usually fork out a good deal for us at Christmas, so Matron said you should go. Pick up two o'clock from the nurses' home. Try and look a bit decent, will you? Clean uniform, including cuffs, and for goodness' sake, comb your hair!'

I was hardly at my best the following afternoon. I knew I'd barely scraped through a rather important viva on fractures in the morning. I'm hopeless at bones and the examiners, two of them, all steely grey hair and grim faces, were clearly unimpressed.

On top of that, the vicar had a bout of sickness in the night, and I'd had to wash and dry my uniform at half past five that morning. It was still damp and creased at five to two, but I had to wriggle into it anyway.

I'd used a dozen massive hairpins and scraped my hair into a sort of bun on top of my head, but as I rushed past a mirror I could see it was already on its way down my neck and would, more than likely, be on my shoulders by the time I got to wherever I was going.

And then, of all things, oh, horrible fate, Mr Hugh Timberlake was standing in the hall. He grinned when he saw me.

I gave a flustered smile while trying to hold up my hair. 'Are you waiting for someone?'

'You,' he said, 'I'm waiting for you.'

I must have looked completely stunned and inanely said, 'Me? You're waiting for me?'

'I believe it's you that's coming to do a spot of first aiding at the fete? Well, I've come to take you there.' He gave an exaggerated bow, and took my arm.

I found myself looking up into his eyes. A faint, exciting scent of cigars and *eau de cologne* emanated from him and gold links gleamed from pristine cuffs, which covered an enticing hint of golden hairs.

'I'm not sure I—' I began, but he put his finger on my mouth and led me in the direction of the drive. Parked there was a low-slung, grey and silver car. 'It's a terrible old wreck,' said Hugh, apologetically.

In a cloud of evil-smelling black smoke, we chugged off out of the grounds of the nurses' home and up Greenbridge High Street.

'Shall I tell you the truth, Evadne?'

I nodded, which was a mistake as the movement finished off the bun for ever, and I felt my hair tumbling down to my shoulders.

'Dora told me the St John ambulance lot were short of people and I suggested she ring the hospital and ask her friend the Matron to let you out for the afternoon.'

I was scrabbling around, trying to get my hair back up and asked, 'Why me?' when I remembered I'd left my cap on my dressing table. I thought I might burst into tears, but he put his hand on my knee —only for a moment—and said, 'Stop worrying about whatever it is you're worrying about and give me one of those big smiles you have.'

'Have I?' I said, astonished, and he laughed.

'You are a funny one, Miss Poseidon. I don't think you have any idea how lovely you are, do you?'

I shook my head, bewildered, and the last few strands of hair dropped down as a huge metal hairpin pinged off and landed in his lap.

The afternoon passed, for me, in a daze. 'Dora' turned out to be Lady Troutbeck; Hugh had been staying with her when he was taken ill and brought into the hospital.

It was only later, after I had joined the two jolly girls at the St John first-aid tent, that I felt more at ease. Together we fanned and gave seats to swooning old ladies gasping for *sal volatile*, or put ammonia on wasp stings, or bandaged the odd child who'd tumbled off the swings or the roundabout.

As the crowds drifted away, our little tent finally emptied. Hugh came in to take me off to be introduced to Lady Troutbeck. She was on the terrace, her young figure exquisitely dressed in a riot of coloured silks and clutching a large, empty glass. She smiled vaguely at me but carried on talking to the group of pretty girls around her.

'Rather too much gin and not enough "it", I think,' said Hugh as he led me to a small table on the now almost deserted lawn. 'Wait here,' he said.

He vanished, to reappear a few moments later with two glasses of champagne. We stayed there for ages, until the sun began to go down, and I suddenly realised the time and leapt up. 'I must get back,' I said, 'I'm on duty in an hour.'

He had been engaging and delightful and, more than anything, he made me laugh. Whether he was speaking about his job as a junior civil servant in Whitehall or his family, everything was a cause for his gentle wit. He seemed so comfortable in himself that, within moments, I had felt relaxed and happy, too. We also talked a little, as we had done together on the ward, of more serious things. He was working hard to pass the Foreign Office entrance exams as he wanted to work abroad in an embassy.

Hugh took my arm as we walked back to his car. 'Dear daughter of Poseidon, when can I see you again?'

'I am on nights for another two weeks . . .'

'Tomorrow afternoon then?'

'Well, I am supposed to sleep during the day or I get—'

'Tomorrow afternoon it is, then. You can sleep in the morning and I will collect you at two.'

As we got into his car he said with a smile, 'By the way, I love your hair down.'

After that I saw Hugh every minute I could escape from the hospital. I was living in a curious world of bandages and decay, and cocktails and dancing. Sometimes, as I wearily crawled into the nurses' home by the landing window, I wondered how long I could last in this confusion before I started dancing through the ward or asked the head waiter at Claridges if his bowels had opened that day.

It seemed as though Hugh had rescued me from a dull and predictable life. The most important thing of all was that I forgot about myself. I no longer stood with my knees bent or my shoulders rounded. I was so busy looking out at the world now that I forgot to look into myself.

This was the greatest gift Hugh gave me—myself. I no longer cared only how others saw me. Through Hugh my confidence grew. He told me I was beautiful. He didn't seem to notice that my hands were the best things about me.

Everywhere we went he knew people. 'You have so many friends,' I said one night as the silver car bunny-hopped me back to the nurses' home. He waved his hand dismissively. 'You haven't met my real friends yet. Well, Dora Troutbeck, now she's a chum.' I wasn't sure why, but a shiver of unease flickered through me. Was it that Dora Troutbeck was the one person who didn't seem to like me? She was always charming and polite, but there was a brittle surface there, in her brilliantly coloured garb. A sugared almond, I thought: pink and cream on the outside, and a tough little nut inside. We visited her house often and it was always full of the glittering people that she and Hugh liked. I dismissed these thoughts, these doubts. I learned to walk tall, to look at the world round me, and lose myself in it.

And not for a moment did I question this, or ask myself if it was what I wanted. Why would I have?

I had never envisaged happiness in my blueprint for the future, never experienced it, so for all this I could only thank Hugh. And when one night under the stars he asked me to marry him, I thought I could know no greater joy and said, 'Yes, please' without another thought.

ANTHI

'IS IT FAR, MAMA?' Despina's question takes me by surprise. I was daydreaming about the Orfanoudakis house and Heavenly. Hoping so much that we should see each other again soon.

'You know when you can see our house from the top of the hill, then we are nearly home.'

'I'm hot, Mama, too hot.' Her voice is little more than a croak. I sigh, but do not answer. Voula is strapped by a shawl to my back and if the rhythm of my walking changes for even a moment she will wake and cry piteously; and that will just be too much because here, a short way from the fields we have left behind us, there is no shade, and I cannot stop and nourish her in the middle of the path.

'Please, Mama, please can I sit on Astrape? Just for a little bit?'

'You know that is not possible. You are too heavy for poor old Astrape. He is loaded down, just as we are.'

We are all carrying home the sacks we have filled with the leaves of the tobacco plants we have just stripped. We left the house at first light, the three of us, while Manolis still slept and, only pausing for some cheese and fruit with bread, we have worked until now. Looking at the harsh sun above us, I think it is about four or five o'clock.

Manolis is tending the sheep today. This means that he will be sitting in the shade of a pomegranate tree in the top pasture with a flask of *raki* beside him. Poor man, how hard is his life! The tobacco will not wait so we have to do it for him.

The seabirds wheel and cry hungrily in the sky, only to remind me that when I get home I must prepare an evening meal and I have picked no *horta* or wild spinach or vegetables today, so it will take even longer.

We have one of the largest farmsteads in the whole of Panagia. That is why my mother arranged this marriage. Me? I would be happy with one garden, two goats and six chickens.

Apart from the wheat and my bees, I must constantly tend my garden crops: lettuce, radish, spring onions, tomatoes, courgettes and broad beans. I am lucky that our garden surrounds our house; most of the villagers must walk each day to their plots on the edges of the village.

Manolis and his brother Stelios own more olive trees than anyone hereabouts and, unusually for this area, many and abundant vines. The red wine they produce each year is rich and strong. Stelios is the treader. Since he was a young man, at the end of each summer, he is much in demand, from as far away as Palio Kastro, to spend a day treading for family and friends. His feet are magic.

I am considered better than many, I think, and one reason why is my horse, Astrape. The only horse around and he is mine. He is my escape. In my dreams I pick up Despina and Voula and gallop away over the hills never to return. We go to India, Africa, the Americas, wherever we choose. But it is a long time since Astrape galloped anywhere and his name, meaning lightning, is now something of a joke. Maybe once he had some speed in those long black legs, but he is a comfortable, middle-aged mount now and safe as a rabbit for the girls.

We pass the priest's house. He is outside, fat and complacent like a squatting toad. His eyes travel over my body as I acknowledge him. Lecherous old goat!

'Good afternoon, Papa Yannis,' I murmur, but he is too busy staring at my breasts to answer me.

My mother thinks he is wonderful and I blame him as much as her for my marriage. I remember well the night when it all started.

My mother had been cooking all day for the celebration of my sister's name day. Ririca favours my mother in looks as well as temperament. She is bony in her youthfulness. Our mother is very protective of her and slaps me hard if she ever catches me saying she has a nose like a clothes pin.

In the evening, all the uncles arrived with their wives and my cousins. The men, as always, sat round the table; the women and children squashed in a corner together. By nine o'clock, the *raki* was sinking lower in the jugs and the laughter was echoing round the walls of our good room. There was a noise outside and Papa Yannis came in, rubbing his hands together and calling greetings to everyone. Behind him was Old Man Manadakis, another fat, ugly creature. I wondered why he should be there. He had no connection with our family— certainly my father had disliked him.

My mother had grabbed my arm and pulled me with her into the kitchen. It was like a furnace; the great oven through the wall had been working for hours, churning out trays of cheese pies, spinach tarts, a great dish of *pastitsio* and the whole of a goat slaughtered in honour of my sister's day. I thought back to my name day. I had had to make do with my two aunts and their daughters coming for coffee and an almond biscuit.

'From now on,' my mother said, 'you will spend time with me in here. You must learn women's duties, and we will start with cooking.'

She marched back into the good room and I made to follow her, holding a tray of honey cakes. Ririca put her hand out to stop me.

'Want to know why you are going to learn to cook?' she whispered, a nasty little smile creasing her face.

'You are obviously going to tell me,' I said.

'You are going to be married to old Manadakis's son.' She was so glee-ful to be able to tell me this that I could have hit her.

'I am thirteen years old, I am not going to marry anybody.'

'When you are sixteen, silly.' She giggled. 'I heard Mama and Uncle Lukas talking last night. That's why the priest has brought him here.'

I was furious; not only that I was to be married, but also that Ririca should know and I did not.

Our mother was calling for us to take the food in, so there was nothing more I could say just then, but I looked very carefully at the man sitting beside Papa Yannis, and tried to remember what his son was like.

I hoped he looked better than his father, who sat like a great drop of olive oil, sweating and greasy.

Late in the evening the Manadakis sons arrived to escort their father home. Just as well, I thought, as he was so drunk he could hardly stand. They carried musical instruments with them, a lyre and an accordion, as they had been playing at a wedding in a village across the mountain that day. There were calls for them to give us music now. They played well; old Cretan songs that Stelios, the younger brother, sang with a clear, true voice.

I looked at him curiously as they played; I supposed he was quite good-looking, in a rough sort of way. He was swarthy, dark, with a fine moustache of golden brown strands, curled at the ends. I barely looked at his brother, who was so much older. At his age he would be long married.

When everyone had left that night, I helped my mother clear all the dishes, plates and glasses into the kitchen. Ririca had gone to her bed long before. Clearly, counting the money and gifts she had been given had exhausted her.

'When is my wedding supposed to be?' I asked my mother, as casually as if asking about tomorrow's weather.

As I knew she would, she looked at me in astonishment. 'What do you mean?' she said.

'Why, my wedding to the son of Manadakis, Mama, what else?' I was pleased I could remain so cool and detached, when part of me wanted to scream and stamp my foot in rage.

'How do you know of this?'

'Ririca told me, Mama,' I said sweetly. I knew this would make her furious, so there was a certain delight in saying it.

Her next words, however, filled me with horror. 'You will marry Manolis Manadakis when you are sixteen,' she said.

'*Manolis?*' I couldn't breathe. Manolis was the elder of the two brothers. She must be making a mistake. 'I can't marry Manolis; he is much, much too old!'

'He is only forty, Anthi, a fine age; why, he's barely older than me.' She was smiling smugly now, having recaptured her advantage over me.

'Then why don't you marry him?' I said, and for a moment I thought she was going to slap me.

'Enough!' she said. 'You will go to bed now and tomorrow, the first thing you do will be to help me clean and clear the mess here. Then you will have your first lesson in cooking.'

'But tomorrow is a day when I help in the school—'

'First things come first. Cleaning and cooking are more important.

When you have time, if you have time, you may continue to help in the school.' She swung round and went through the door, paused, and over her shoulder said, 'That is for now. Perhaps later . . .'

'Yes, what about later?'

'Later will be for your husband to decide.' And she was gone.

Miserably, I trailed after her. In a few, short hours my life had completely changed: my future was decided and all my hopes and dreams pushed away.

Voula is awake now and wriggling uncomfortably on my back. Ahead of me I can see our gate and there is someone sitting on the grass beside it. A drip of sweat drops into my eye, blurring my sight momentarily. But it is her—Heavenly has come to see us!

What wrecks we must appear. She has jumped to her feet and is coming towards us, smiling, the sun catching the gold in the red of her hair and lighting up her face. I am suddenly so happy.

'Here, let me help you,' and she takes the sack swiftly from Despina, who smiles with relief and pleasure. 'What is it? Where are you taking it? Give me another, you look exhausted.' We are drifting towards the fig tree and I drop my sacks and sigh, holding my back to straighten it. At just that moment Voula opens her mouth and wails as if she has been starved for a week.

An hour later, the girls are fed, Astrape watered and some carrots, leeks and barley are simmering with some oil and dill. We are back under the fig tree, working on the tobacco leaves with Heavenly beside us, helping as though she is part of my family.

After Despina has checked each leaf for blight, she passes it to Heavenly to pierce with an awl. I then take it and thread it onto long strings. Later, these will hang out in the sun by the barn to dry until the autumn, when Manolis will press them into bales in a machine Stelios owns. Then he will take them to Sitia and sell them. There is good money to be made from this crop.

Heavenly is bouncing Voula on her lap and singing a funny English song about piggies and horses, and Voula is chuckling with delight.

I feel as if I have found a sudden new happiness. In spite of the heat, everything seems to exist in a glow. The crags of the mountains round us shine golden with the flowers of broom, and kestrels hover above.

Of course, this joyous, dream-like afternoon cannot last.

Despina is suddenly on her feet and running across the garden. 'Papa!' she is shouting, and Manolis comes towards us. He does not walk like a man who has worked all day under the boiling sun as we have, although over his shoulder hangs a dead sheep, its mouth open in a stiff rictus, blood slowly dripping onto his booted foot. He stands in front of us, legs splayed, and stares at Heavenly.

'Papa, is it Easter again? Do we have the roasted lamb?'

He still stands motionless, ignoring his eldest child who is hopping up and down with excitement, and tugging at the loose leg of his *vraka*.

'This is Kyria Timberlake.'

'I know who it is, wife, I have eyes.' And he nods his head slowly in her direction. 'You are welcome.' His voice is so cold it is hard to believe his words. But he is a superstitious man and thinks if you do not offer hospitality to a stranger, the meat you eat will be turned into human flesh in your mouth.

'My wife has offered you refreshment, I hope?'

'Thank you, yes.'

He nods again and abruptly turns and strides to the barn.

There, on the wall, is the cross-beamed post we use as a hanging straight. Expertly, he slings the sheep to fall from this, with the spike at the top through the head.

I see him through Heavenly's eyes. He looks raddled and smells even worse. The once stocky body has spread into fat. His still deep, dark eyes are sunken now in the oily craters of his face. The hairs that sprout on his flabby breasts are greying. I don't know what colour the hairs on his head would be as there are none there. Ever since he came home from Sitia, months ago, with a crop of lice, picked up, I've no doubt, from some whore's pillow, even he could see the sense in shaving it lest he pass them to the girls and me.

'Why do we have a sheep? What happened?'

'Whatever it was, and I don't know yet, it will give us good food for a while, so I do not expect to hear complaints.'

I sigh. I had no intention of complaining.

As if to compound his brutishness, Manolis reaches for the large knife in his belt and, pulling it out, tries the blade along his thumb. A speck of blood appears; it is sharp enough. With one movement he slits the sheep open from the head downwards. The guts rapidly spill out and fall into a slithering pool on the ground at his feet.

Despina and I are used to such a sight; we are farmers and violent death is part of our daily lives, but Heavenly has shut her eyes tight. This is not something she has seen before, I think. I cross to her and take her hand.

She squeezes it. 'I think I must leave you to your family now, and go back to my house. When can we meet again?'

I answer quickly, 'If you invite me, I'll come to see you tomorrow, but I will walk along with you for part of the way now, as I have to check the bees before sundown.'

'Can I come too, Mama?'

'We'll all go, *koritsaki mou*.'

'Wait, wait,' and Despina disappears, returning quickly with a little bundle she must have put together earlier. There is a tattered bit of fishing net, lined with cabbage leaves. Nestling inside are a dozen or so strawberries.

'For you,' she says shyly, as she hands them across to Heavenly, who smiles and quickly reaches down to kiss her. Heavenly looks beautiful today, her hair covered with a straw hat. Her dress is cotton, simple, but still made with the best cloth that surely must have come from Athens.

She called goodbye to Manolis, who paused only to turn briefly and spit a gobbet of phlegm that mingled with the mess at his feet. He muttered something that might have been farewell, but I doubt it.

With Voula, as usual, on my back, we walked along together in a comfortable silence. It felt as though we had been friends for years.

'What do you think was wrong with that sheep?'

I merely shrugged. 'Whatever it is, I don't suppose I will be told. All I know is that my husband will not be happy about it. Every animal in our flock is precious and he will need to watch carefully to see if any of the others show signs of disease. Healthy sheep do not drop dead for no reason. It's also possible that it's meant as a warning to him.'

I was in danger of saying more than I intended when I saw puzzlement on her face.

'My husband is not a popular man in these parts. Oh, certainly, he has his own friends—they all drink together in the *kafenion* they call The Brothers, on the edge of Pano Panagia. But there are not many of them and he makes enemies easily. He is a royalist, and in these parts most people are republicans.'

'Do you mean that someone who disagrees with your husband's politics would deliberately harm his sheep?' Heavenly looked astonished.

'It can happen.' I felt I had said enough, but Heavenly wanted to know more.

'I can't really explain it to you,' I said. 'I will take you to meet my Pappous, my grandfather, one day and he will tell you more.'

Heavenly had lived in Athens and heard and read about our politics. I believed my Pappous would enjoy talking with her. I told her that I did know that General Metaxas ignored the communists completely and it was rumoured that he had imprisoned many of their leaders. Most of the men in Panagia were delighted when the communists gained power, but not my husband and his friends—they still drink happily together in the name of the king.

'I would love to meet your family one day, if you will take me.'

'Oh, I will,' I said eagerly.

We walked on together. Above us, the sky mercifully filtered the last, blistering heat of the sun through the scattered clouds. A kestrel wheeled overhead and Despina, with her keen child's eyes, laughed and pointed upwards.

'Look, it has caught something!'

She was right, we could see, clenched in its beak, a creature of some sort; now certainly dead. The bird flew swiftly up and away.

'He is taking the dinner home to his wife and babies, just as Papa has done for us.'

I could not disillusion my daughter. To her and her sister, he is like every father in the families she knows; the provider, the ruler of the household.

The path divided. Here, at the crooked olive tree, my bees were on the hillside above, and Heavenly's house lay at the other edge of lower Panagia. She hugged each of us in turn and repeated her request that we should visit her the next day. Despina would have gone home with her then, I think, she looked so forlorn at parting with our new friend. Even Voula looked sad as she was kissed. We trudged on upwards towards the hives knowing, all of us, that we had something to look forward to tomorrow.

HEAVENLY

The British Embassy, Athens

My darling girl, I am missing you dreadfully and we have only been apart for a few weeks. Every night I find it hard to sleep; partly the wretched heat, but mainly because I am plagued by doubts that I am doing the right thing. Why did I listen when you begged to stay alone? I should have resigned from the embassy and stayed with you. But you

*know, I think I would have gone mad by the end of another week living
with all those Mr and Mrs Diddlyakis peasants. I think you are marvellous, darling, to be able to put up with them constantly. I would have
lost my temper before long, and thrown them all out or, even worse,
shot them with one of their wretched rabbit guns.*

*The journey back here seemed to go on for ever, making me wish the
flying boat had been a possibility. The crew of this rackety old boat were
mostly a good sort, especially the captain. He was very persuasive with
the raki flask and it was impossible to say no.*

*I know I promised, dearest one, and I will stop all this stuff now that
I am back at the office. Truth is, I am missing you so much that a glass
or two of raki after dinner does make me feel a little better.*

*All is gloomy here, and the general feeling is that this chap Hitler is
going to push everyone one step too far and then anything could happen. I'm sure all that seems very far away to you, there in your little
paradise. But I'll write when I can, and will look forward to a note from
you if you can manage it.*

Foxy and Janet send their love to you, as do I, my angel.

Your adoring husband, Hugh

Hugh is right; sitting here under the stars of this warm summer night,
Athens and that life seem very far away. Have I done the right thing?
I certainly don't feel lonely, but I am missing Hugh. It's so sad that he
can't feel as I do. I love all these 'Diddlyakis' people; they are so utterly
kind to me and I feel so comfortable with them.

It was a bleak day when Hugh told me our time in this little village
was up and we must go back. At first I just accepted it and started to
pack our clothes. But that evening, out on the terrace, under the soft
blue cloak of the sky, I felt close to tears.

'Come on, darling,' he said, 'you know you don't belong here. You go
off for a ramble and damned near break your neck.' He was laughing.

'Oh, how can I make you understand? I feel I belong here more than
I do in Athens. I feel so out of things there. I know the other wives are
nice, but I honestly don't have anything in common with them. I'm sick
of hairdressers tugging at my hair, and I can't possibly want another
frock for at least ten years. And supposing there is a war with Germany,
I'd be much safer here than there, wouldn't I?'

I was clutching rather wildly at straws, but Hugh couldn't disagree.

'Are you thinking you could stay here alone?' he asked.

'Oh, darling, I'd so much prefer it if you stayed too, but I know that's
not possible. You have responsibilities there, and I don't.'

'Well, that's certainly true. I have to get back as soon as possible.'

'You could come back when you get some leave and perhaps then I will have a proper house for you to live in. That's what I should love to do, you know. If I could get some local help to get this house put to rights, I think you would be happy to think of coming here for holidays.'

He looked round the living room and I saw it through his eyes. It needed everything mended and made anew. It was shabby and broken down. Even I could feel its sadness. For a moment I wondered if I was completely mad to think of living here alone. But it was a fleeting thought and, as a ray of moonlight lit up the old beams, I was filled with hope.

Parting with Hugh was desperately sad. It was early in the morning, and he left in the back of Petros's donkey cart; Hugh and several hundredweight of potatoes. We waved until he was out of sight and, as he veered round the corner, I felt tears start to fill my eyes and wondered if he was crying, too. I rubbed my eyes swiftly with the back of my hand and walked slowly back to the house.

I have discovered a tiny little church just below, beyond where all the women go to do their washing at the spring. It is called Panagia Sta Perivolia, like the village. It means The Virgin in the Garden and because it is always empty, I feel I can go and sit there by myself any-time. It is so peaceful.

This evening Anthi is bringing someone round to see what he thinks about repairing the house. Anthi has become a real friend. I love her and her beautiful daughters, although I am not at all sure about her husband, Manolis. I long to ask her how it came about that she married him; I feel sure that it must have been set up for her. That's what happens here; parents arrange suitable matches and a lot depends on dowries and how much land each partner will bring to the union. I find it hard to believe that she chose him for herself. Perhaps she wasn't even consulted—how awful!

Anthi seems as happy as I am that we have become friends, and we see each other most days. She is very different to most of the village women. Of course, they are amazingly kind, but after a few random questions about how we all are, conversation dries up, rather. As if to prove this, my neighbour, Irini, has just been in with some fruits from her garden: lemons, oranges and figs. We sat on the terrace and I tried to have a conversation about the village, some of its customs and about my little church, but she looked rather blank. Clearly anything other than children or food is for men to talk about. She didn't stay long, saying she must get home to her chickens and her children, and scampered away.

It's ages yet before Anthi will be here so I have wandered through the long grass, past the spring and the trees surrounding it and have come to my little church. It is so cool inside, and if I leave the door open I can see down to the sea below. In the distance are two small boats; they are barely moving, the water is so calm.

All my thoughts seem to move towards Hugh. He has done so much for me it is hard to complain, but there is one thing he hasn't done and it troubles me greatly; it is to give me a child.

Tears are brimming up as I think this. Usually I make myself move quickly on to something else, because it is the side of our marriage that is dark, painful, and I feel I must keep secret, even from myself.

The first night we were together, really together I mean, in our suite in the Savoy, was a disaster.

The day had been frantic. Our wedding was to happen at Caxton Hall register office in the middle of London at twelve o'clock. A small affair: just us, Daphne, a few friends of Hugh's, Lady Troutbeck and three girls I called Minky, Mouse and Boo, who seemed to go everywhere with her. I did ask a couple of the nurses, Maisie and another, but they couldn't get the time away. My mother couldn't come. She had something else on, very important, she said. But I'd bet it was just another wretched bridge party or a Red Cross bring and buy sale.

I was sad that Hugh's mother couldn't get there. She had had a fall from her horse the week before and had a badly sprained ankle. She wrote me a letter, which I shall always treasure, saying how very happy she was that Hugh had chosen me, rather than one of the 'flighty London flibbertigibbets' he spent so much time with. 'I know you will make him happy,' she wrote.

My mother had sent the money for a frock, at least, and I raided Harrods with Daphne and chose a floaty, pale blue crepe and lace affair that cost sixteen pounds, more than I'd ever spent on anything.

From the start the wedding was not as I had imagined it.

I got there first, which was not how it was meant to be. Then Foxy, who was Hugh's best man, ran up the steps and said he'd lost Hugh the night before, and this morning he couldn't find the ring, either.

I stood there, looking and feeling completely stupid. I thought I was going to cry but Daphne held my hand very tightly. The registrar was very kind, but said he had people waiting and couldn't hang about much longer.

Hugh arrived looking flustered and unhappy. He hugged me and said he was desperately sorry, but Lady Troutbeck's car wouldn't start and they couldn't get a taxicab, so he'd run all the way from her London flat.

She was there, just behind him, looking even more amazing than usual. She'd dyed her hair jet black and put a lot of white make-up on, with black round her eyes. I thought she looked like a panda, but her friends all cheered and told her she looked fabulous.

I did wonder why Hugh had been at her flat in the first place. He had told me he was having a few drinks with Foxy and some friends at the Savile Club, and then an early night.

We all squeezed inside the small and certainly very unimpressive room that was the actual 'office'. I thought, momentarily, that I was glad Mother wasn't there; she'd have sniffed loudly, with her nose in the air, and made some comment.

You have to have two witnesses in these affairs apparently, and Hugh had chosen Foxy and Jack Timberlake, his uncle, whom I hadn't met.

Foxy was here but where was Uncle Jack?

'I think still stuck in the fleshpots of Calais,' said Hugh. 'So, I've asked Dora to oblige and she said she would. She's a brick, isn't she?'

Of course it was kind of her to step in at such short notice, so why did my heart sink?

We did the marriage bit, which was over so fast I barely caught my breath, and wondered if we were really legally married. But darling Hugh turned to me with such love in his eyes, I wanted to cry again.

Lady Troutbeck cracked her face into a smile and signed the register with Foxy, then swept outside into the crisp October sunshine, smiling warmly at everyone except me.

Hugh took my arm and, leaning over, kissed me and told me he loved me. All the negative feelings I was having melted away as he spoke.

'We'll soon be on our own, Evadne, and I can tell you and show you how dear you are to me.'

He put his arm round me, swept me outside and pushed us into the circle of Lady Troutbeck's admirers.

'Sorry to break up this delightful street party,' he said, laughing, 'but we're going to go and find some champagne, I believe.'

'Aye, aye, Captain,' called Foxy and we all piled into a fleet of taxis that were waiting at the kerb.

Later, much later, we managed to get away from the, by now, extremely noisy crowd. 'Don't go yet, Hugh, just another little drinky!'

'Spoilsport, Hugh! Evadne, let him stay and have a bit of fun.' And more and more calls of the same, so that I felt like the wicked witch snatching poor Hansel into the gingerbread house. But Hugh showed no sign of wanting to stay, and we went off to the Savoy hand in hand.

When we got there, Hugh signed the register, 'Mr and Mrs Timberlake'. I was so thrilled! Then the man behind the desk said, 'Excuse me, sir, but a gentleman is waiting to see you.'

We turned and a man uncurled himself from an armchair and leapt towards us on long, tweedy legs.

'My dear old fella,' he boomed, and clasped Hugh in his arms. 'Where's the party then? Not too late, am I?'

'Uncle Jack, how marvellous! I thought we'd lost you. Evadne, this is Uncle Jack. Uncle Jack, this is my lovely bride.' And my hand was pumped up and down.

'My dear lady, what a delight you are. Hugh, you've done yourself proud, old chap. Let me kiss the bride, eh? Uncle's privilege.'

I was seized in a warm, sweaty grip while thick bristles nibbled at my cheek. I eased myself away slightly and looked at this man. He had beady, blackish eyes, which peered out of pink, jelly-like whites. His hair was dark and thin and combed over the top of his head with oily brilliantine, and a thin black moustache lay across his lip. This was a vain man and I instantly disliked him.

It appeared that Uncle Jack had, indeed, got lost in Calais and missed the boat. But he knew we would come to the Savoy at some point, so had thought he would catch up with us here.

'Time for a little nightcap? Can't send poor old Uncle out into the streets all on his own, eh?'

Hugh looked rather despairingly at me, and I thought I had no alternative but to help him out.

'Darling, why don't you do just that,' I said. 'I'll go up to our room and I'll see you there in a little while.' I turned away quickly. I really didn't want another kiss from this man.

The truth was, I minded quite a lot. I'd looked forward all day to this chance to be on our own and this boring old man had got Hugh, just when I thought I deserved a bit of him to myself.

There was nothing to be done except go upstairs alone and wait. I lay on the vast bed and looked round the sumptuous room. I had never seen anything quite so luxurious. I yawned and, within moments, I was asleep.

When I awoke it was dark. I lay still for a moment before reaching out to touch the sleeping body beside me. 'Hugh,' I whispered. The only response was a great, grunting snore that must have woken him.

'Christ, darling, I'm so sorry.' The blankets and sheets were scrabbled up and away as my new husband sat up and put the light on. I'm glad he did because I instantly realised we were not alone in the room. To my horror, I saw a sleeping figure on the chaise longue at the foot of the bed.

Uncle Jack was snuggled down under Hugh's greatcoat, snorting throatily, dribble running down his chin.

Hugh spent most of the rest of the night apologising. I sat on the huge green brocade sofa shivering. I didn't cry; I felt only despair. He'd felt rather sorry for the old boy. Couldn't turf him out on the street, could he? Thought I wouldn't mind.

There were no words to express how I felt, so I didn't try.

Hugh finally persuaded Uncle Jack to wake up and he staggered off into the corridor, waving a shaky hand behind him.

'Any chance of meeting up for breakfast?' he'd said, just before he disappeared. 'No, I suppose not. Oh well, see you soon. Toodle pip.'

It probably was not the best start to anyone's married life, but somehow, by the end of the next day, Hugh had managed, just, to make me laugh about it.

We left for Paris within the week and I looked forward to a new beginning, a new start, with my beloved Hugh.

I'm not sure what I had imagined embassy life to be like. Paris itself had seemed to be the important thing, with the Eiffel Tower, the Seine, the Louvre and all the places I'd heard of, but life inside the embassy was exactly the same as being in England. Everyone spoke English all the time, except when dealing with the French, who annoyingly made demands on one's time.

We had bacon and eggs or kedgeree or kidneys for breakfast, roast lamb and cabbage for lunch, and steak and kidney pudding for dinner.

I would often escape before breakfast, when I could manage it, and would find a little pavement café where I had café au lait, croissant, or pain au confiture. I spoke French in the markets and shops, and as long as the weather was fine I walked alone among the beautiful streets and boulevards. I haunted the many art galleries and churches when it was not. No one seemed to miss me from the embassy. Sadly, even Hugh seemed happy to let me wander round without explanation.

I turned up for any important lunches or dinners, of course. It seemed there were more cocktail parties than there were days in the week, and Hugh encouraged me constantly to shop for clothes, get my hair done or my nails manicured. I was soon very bored.

There were sometimes beggars on the street, especially gathered on the steps of the many elegant churches and cathedrals. I would give them as much money as I could; it seemed so wicked to me to have my hair done again and again when there were women and children so desperately in need. It was the children who moved me the most and it made me long all the more for a child of my own.

Hugh would laugh when I tried to talk to him about it.

'Bored with me already, darling? Aren't I enough company for you? Plenty of time for kiddies when I'm established. Early days yet.'

But I was unhappy that the lovemaking we indulged in was rare, and deeply unsatisfactory.

And then we were sent to Greece; to Athens, and I hoped and prayed again that this time we could make a real go of things. But it seemed that, apart from the language, nothing changed, not even the food.

Night after night, I would go to our rooms alone, get into bed alone and try to sleep, still alone. It was only ever the lightest of sleeps, for I was instantly awake when Hugh came to bed, often in the early hours.

I remember one night—we had been there for a month or so—when, sad and feeling lonely, I tried to arouse him. I stroked his body gently at first, and then, as I hoped he would do to me, more strongly. I was nervous; this was new to me, to take the initiative like this; suppose it displeased him? But to my surprise and delight, murmuring my name, he pulled me closer to him. I felt him stiffen against my body and the pattern of his breathing changed, he was panting and stroking me in return. I was ready for him; it had been weeks since we had made love, months. He leaned over me but, as his part touched my body, his face contorted and he cried out.

'I'm so sorry, so sorry.' As he turned over I realised he was crying.

'Don't worry,' I said. 'It doesn't matter. There are other nights.'

But I suspected that this was just the beginning of something that was going to trouble us for a long while, because it was not the first time it had happened. We never spoke of it. If I tried to raise the subject of our intimacy, Hugh would look horrified and change the conversation at once. His flat refusal to talk about this left me wretchedly sad. His only answer was to drink more each night and fall into bed, incapable sometimes of even saying good night.

He swore everything would be fine when we got a chance to be alone together. So I had hoped so much that this house, this village, this time away together would be the honeymoon we had not had. But here, in Panagia, we had been alone and he still turned away from me each night.

There was a call, and then a small voice saying my name, 'Heavenly,' and then again louder, 'Heavenly!'

A small, sweet face hovered at the corner of the church door— Despina, Anthi's eldest daughter, was peering into the dark interior.

'Heavenly, are you here?' I jumped up into the light, facing her. 'Boo!' She gave a shriek and leapt backwards, laughing. Hand in hand we climbed upwards through the scrub and weeds to the village, where, outside my house, Anthi was waiting with Voula and a man. This must be Yorgo Babyottis, the builder.

He was smaller and older than I had expected, with a creased face like a walnut and twinkly blue eyes. His moustache was a handsome one and shaped finely over many years.

He held out his wrinkled hand and I grasped it, smiling at him.

We all looked at the vast exterior of the house. I saw the cracks and the roughness of the weathered stones. I felt a sudden wave of nervousness as I looked at the supports of the terrace, perilously close to disintegration. I remembered the days and nights when Hugh and I had sat there; it could have crashed down so easily.

'Come, let's walk round and I'll show you what I'd like to do.'

ANTHI

I THINK YORGO BABYOTTIS was stunned by Heavenly, as were all the people in the village. Coming here from Athens is odd enough, but to have come here to live, from England, is beyond thought.

We walked round her house together, Despina skipping behind. As we saw the scale of the work, I began to get concerned. Yorgo was delighted, I think, although he was trying not to show it. He could see he would be employed on this one job, in his own village, for a long time to come. All Heavenly could see was her dream coming to life.

'Kyria Heavenly,' Yorgo started, 'of course I can do this work for you. I have much experience of such places.'

I looked at him in astonishment. He spent most of his time making coffins for the old people who die in winter.

Although I had brought him to Heavenly, I had warned her that he was a village man, no more accustomed to great renovation work than anyone else here. The men of the households repair their own homes when necessary: a hole in a roof, a simple outhouse to be built, or a new coat or two of thick white isvesti were easily coped with.

Yorgo Babyottis clearly wanted this job, but I could not let my new friend employ him without some serious talking. He was telling her now how he could remake all the windows, doors and shutters.

'But what of the really heavy work, Yorgo?' I said. 'Who will help you?'

Yorgo shifted from foot to foot and looked worried. 'When do you want me to start, Kyria?'

We all turned to look at Heavenly. 'As soon as possible, I think.'

'Excellent,' he said. 'We will wait for Kyria Heavenly's husband to come home and I will agree a price with him.'

Heavenly was still smiling, but it looked a little stiff now—I could see she needed help.

'Yorgo, Kyria Heavenly is an English lady,' I started slowly, 'and in England they do things differently. The ladies deal with everything about the house, so you will expect to get decisions from Kyria Heavenly. Her husband is away at the moment. You will discuss everything with her. Or,' I added hastily, 'with me.'

Heavenly looked pleased that I was helping her with the difficulties of the situation, as well as with the language. Athenian Greek is a long way from the Greek spoken in these villages.

Yorgo finally left. He had at last seemed to understand Heavenly's situation, and said he accepted her as the person in charge of the house. But he looked very doubtful as he walked down the steps.

In passing, he had mentioned his nephew, his sister's boy, Christo, who lived in a village near Sitia and who wanted to be an architect. The boy was trying to earn money to help his widowed mother pay for his training. 'I will speak with my sister,' he said. 'Perhaps her boy can come and help me for a while. Not,' he added hastily, 'that I need much help, but it's good to give a hand to the family from time to time.'

Heavenly had wanted to give Yorgo money straight away. I had stopped her.

'Yorgo, you must give Kyria Heavenly a list of everything you will need money for and how much each piece will cost. Then she will give you some of the money to buy these things. You understand?'

Yorgo agreed. He is not a dishonest man, but with a pocketful of money he would be at risk. A bellyful of *raki* and the first tinker passing through would sell him more ribbons and cloths than bricks and mortar.

As she watched him go, Heavenly said, 'Anthi, I know you feel responsible, but it is my choice, you know, my decision. Mr Yorgo will find me as hard as any man to deal with, I promise.'

She put her arms round me and hugged me. 'Dear friend, trust me.'

Voula woke noisily at that moment, needing food. I picked her up into my arms and, sitting on the army bed, I opened my shift to feed her.

Any shyness I felt at baring my breast in front of another was not there with Heavenly. Sometimes when Voula was unsettled, she held her in her arms and rocked her, singing a song she told me was especially for babies. I liked to see her singing my Voula to sleep.

She is a woman without a child. This puzzles me. Loving babies as she seems to, why does she not have one of her own?

Riding home that day, I thought about my friend and her husband in his funny trousers, who is happy to leave her alone here for who knows how long. Months? Years? If only Manolis would go away for a few months or years, I would be happy!

Before the babies came, our marriage had not been a bad one. Certainly at sixteen, I already had better things to do with my life than devote it to my husband. But he seemed not to mind me continuing to help in the school. As long, of course, as I looked after him and the house. But I had started to enjoy the cooking I had learned from my mother. I especially delighted in the fact that I quickly became better than she. My pastry was lighter, crisper; my roasted lamb and kid were sweeter, juicier; the fruit I picked and dried or preserved in liquor was more delicate, and richer.

This made her furious and she had no sooner forced me into the kitchen than she was trying to keep me out of it, so mean-spirited is she! She taught me to weave and sew instead, and again my slender fingers worked the wools and hemps into pleasing shapes far faster than her fat, stubby ones. The humour I found in all this so delighted me that I begged for more lessons, but she all but threw me out of the house saying, 'Surely you are needed at the school, go, go!'

I was replaced at the oven by Ririca, who thought that as I had mastered these skills with so little effort, so, too, would she. She was hopeless. Stodgy *pastitsio*, those delicious layers of macaroni, cream and meat which was my favourite thing to make, would be thrown for the chickens and goats, along with limp cheese pies and vinegary preserves.

As is the custom, I saw little of my husband before we were wed; certainly never alone. By the time of the ceremony I was thoroughly sick of my mother and her sisters and Ririca squealing and giggling all over our house as they stitched and sewed for my trousseau. I sought refuge with my grandparents whenever I could.

Often, during my visits there, I would sit in front of their fire, watching as my grandfather carved a chest for me, from wood he had gathered from the pine forests. These two old people were the ones I loved more than anyone in the world. Soon I would be the wife of Manolis Manadakis—could I love him even a quarter as much? A tenth? I thought not. I looked at them sitting side by side, their love for each other apparent in every move, every breath. Occasionally, one or other of them would catch my look and smile: their eyes full of the affection they felt for me, the only love in the world I was sure of.

It was my grandmother who prepared me for my wedding night, and told me of the things my husband would expect from me. I was astonished. 'Is it true, Yaya, that men behave just as the animals in the fields?'

'Yes, child. Human babies are born just like all the other creatures.'

I tried to think of this closeness, this intimacy with Manolis Manadakis, but it was hard. I shivered to think of sharing a bed with him.

At first it wasn't so bad. Manolis had some redeeming features, I thought. He had beautiful eyes, dark, velvety brown, which at first looked at me kindly. He even seemed to enjoy my company. Certainly, in the beginning, I laughed a great deal, so glad was I to be out of my mother's house. I loved having my own home and Manolis, his mother being long dead, was happy for me to make any changes I wanted.

His demands on my body were concluded swiftly, with the minimum of fuss. In the beginning it was painful, but it became easier. There was no pleasure for me, but why would I expect there to be?

It was on a cold morning in winter, when I had been to the mill to grind the wheat for our bread, that I first was sick. When this happened again and my breasts became swollen and tender, I knew I must be with child. My grandmother said this was so, and nine months later I was gripped with pains all one day, growing stronger and stronger towards the evening. Manolis fetched Kyria Glykeria and she bustled in quickly.

She was all clean apron and tidy neat with her daughter, Tassia, behind her, smiling vacantly. They set about boiling water, tearing into pieces a fine linen bed sheet my aunt had so carefully embroidered. The pains were fierce, ripping through me until I screamed.

Tassia sat mutely by my side. No one knows her age and she is known to be stupid. Her mother peered under my shift and poked at me with a pad of nettlesoak. I had heard that cloths stewed in nettles, gathered by the light of a full moon, would ensure the safe delivery of a boy. But fifteen minutes later, a beautiful girl was born to me, Despina.

I was soon back to work in the kitchen and the fields, Despina always on my hip or by my side. Manolis seemed fond enough of her, as fond as any man would be for a girl child, I thought.

He was keen to resume our mating, and soon I was pregnant again.

Manolis was delighted. 'This time you will bear a son,' he said, with such certainty that even I thought he was right.

But then, one day, the movements inside me stopped and that night my body, swollen and tender, was gripped with terrible pains. A great flood of my waters, streaked with blood, fell from me and onto the floor. I was not due for another three months. This was too soon. I wept as Manolis, his face stormy and troubled, rode over the hills and through the chill air for Kyria Glykeria.

As before, she brought Tassia, who sat again silently by my side while I sweated and chewed on a length of cloth, trying to stifle my screams.

Soon after dawn the child was born. A son indeed, but already dead as I pushed him out of my body.

Tassia was sent to break the news to Manolis, who was sitting by the fire downstairs. With Kyria Glykeria pressing down on my belly, causing the worst pain I have ever endured, I heard my husband's great roar through the wooden boards. 'No!' he shouted, and again, 'No!'

Tassia slid back into the room, her eyes wide with fear, and resumed her place at my side. The afterbirth came away from me. Kyria Glykeria reached for it quickly and, together with the dead child, wrapped it in a sheet. Drearily I watched from the bed, my hair matted with sweat.

As she moved away, I realised she was leaving the room with her bundle and I whispered, 'Please give him to me.'

She turned in surprise. 'Oh, child,' she said gently, 'best not spend time with the dead. Leave it to me. I'll do what is necessary.'

'He is my child, my son, let me hold him.'

She shrugged and pushed the cloth towards me. I unwrapped him carefully and, my heart full of sadness and my eyes full of tears, I said, 'Hello and goodbye, little man. At least you will never know evil. Have a safe journey, my Constantinos.'

Tassia's eyes were full of excitement and she reached for the little body. I let her take him. She rocked him roughly in her arms but, as she started to sing to him, her mother pulled him away.

'What do you think you are doing?' she said. 'Creatures like this are the spawn of the devil and bad luck will come to us.' She bundled the body up again, and pushed it down to the bottom of her capacious bag.

As she washed me clean I heard the door slam below.

'Your husband has gone to drown his sorrows at the *kafenion*,' she said. 'Who can blame him? Every man wants a son.' I knew Manolis would blame me for this tragedy. I turned my head and wept into the pillow. Tears for my lost little boy, and for the bleakness of my life ahead.

We lived our separate lives under one roof from then. Little Despina would run between us. Mercifully, she didn't seem aware of the scant attention Manolis gave her, but then he was only there to eat and sleep. Occasionally he would take down his lyre from the wall and carry it out to the waiting mule. I guessed on those evenings he and Stelios were playing at a wedding or a feast day in another village. He would return, sometimes days later, stinking of drink and tobacco, his moustache bedraggled and his cheeks dark and unshaven.

In the village, no one spoke to me of Constantinos. This was not a surprise. Bad luck, like bad health, is considered contagious here, so it is pushed away and forgotten.

Then Voula was born, calmly, one winter night after a short labour, already smiling. Manolis was gone for three days after her birth. Another daughter. Another failure.

This is my life. There is much to keep me happy and I am grateful for that. My girls have been my only friends. But now there is Heavenly.

It is a beautiful autumn day, with the memory of summer in the air, as the girls and I ride on Astrape to Heavenly's house.

We move slowly along on the dusty dirt ridge, through vineyards and olive groves. As always here, I can't help looking up. On the top of the mountain stands the little church of St Kosmas and Damianus, now rarely used. My father wanted to be buried there, my Pappous had told me, but my mother insisted that he be buried in the bigger, more splendid church of St Athanasius. She never visits his grave now; my girls and I are the only ones to tend it.

I smile a little as I remember discovering, some time after the event, that she had arranged the burial of my son Constantinos at the little church on the top of the mountain. She, of course, wanted him disposed of as far away from the village as possible. She couldn't know how happy this would make me when I discovered it. St Kosmas and Damianus has long been my favourite, and I felt that the little spirit of Constantinos would watch over us.

Today we are taking a picnic up into the hills to celebrate the last day of freedom. School begins tomorrow, and Yorgo Babyottis is due to start work in Heavenly's house.

I tether Astrape outside her house, and we start to walk up the mountainside. A kestrel hovers overhead as we walk through the heather.

'When Yorgo is busy on my house, do you think it may be possible for me to visit you in your school?'

I was suddenly struck with a thought: 'Not only visit—help teach the children English, why not?'

'Do you think I could?'

'I think it is a wonderful idea. They can have proper English talk, with a real English person!'

I was laughing with excitement. It gave me great pleasure to think of my friend by my side in my school. I was sure Professor Tsimbanakis would agree—he would see what a good idea it was for the children.

After my father died, it was from the professor that I learned a delight in words and language. When school finished each day, I would stay behind and he taught me English. I was a greedy pupil, hungry to learn all I could of the world away from here.

In spite of my father's fancies there was, of course, now no chance I should go elsewhere for learning. No one from these parts went to the university in Heraklion, and as for going even further, say, to Athens, hah! A village girl at such places? What a thought!

My girls will go, though, I swear, whatever else happens. Knowledge will be their wealth, their inheritance from me.

It seemed natural to me back then that I should stay and help the professor with the growing number of children coming to learn. It was unofficial, of course; Kyrios Tsimbanakis had applied many times to the authorities for help, but his requests always went to the bottom of the pile.

And now Heavenly can come and be an unofficial assistant as well. How lucky!

HEAVENLY

Athens, November 1937

My dearest Evadne,

I think of you all the time and miss you painfully. Sometimes I just want to rush back to Crete and be with you, but I must remember my life is here in Athens now. And what a different world it is!

There are worrying things happening. The other day the remains of King Constantine and Queen Sophia, of the old royal family, were disinterred and brought back here for burial in the grounds of their old estate in Attica. Reasonable, you would have thought, as I did. But ever since, there have been rumblings of dissent all around. A nasty fire on the edge of Athens killed many, including children, probably started by the communists. And many other such incidents. There are rumours every day of plots against the government and even here we are seeing increasing signs of poverty. In Panagia no one spoke of this to us, but the disastrous wheat harvest this year has crippled the country. There was a general strike and all the services broke down.

How I wish you were here beside me now, and we could talk about these things. Do you remember how we used to talk, my darling, in your ward at night? We seem to have got out of the habit of that lately. My fault, I know; always something else to do.

But I must be here, to earn the shillings to pay for the bricks and slates for mending broken-down old ruins. And you do seem to be happy there.

I hope it's just that, beloved, and that you are not just happier to be away from me. I long for news of you; your little notes are kept in my bedside drawer and I read them over and over.

Your adoring husband, Hugh

'**O**h, Yorgo, what have you done?' In front of me the small, wrinkled man stood shaking his head vigorously from side to side. He was covered, brows to boots, in grey plaster dust. Well, some dust; otherwise it was flakes, chunks, some hefty slices. It was falling, slowly for the most part, from the ceiling and walls of my living room, onto Yorgo below.

'*Kalimera*, Kyria. I thought we should start quick, quick, not waste time. I finish Kyrios Manos's coffin.'

Then, 'Ah!' He stopped abruptly and ran across to the door, tripping on his ladder, which crashed from where it had been precariously balanced against a beam, bringing down with it most of the rest of the vast ceiling. Only the great beams of oak, a rich brown and majestic, were left behind; a mere skeleton of what had been before.

Ignoring this, he was rummaging now in a sack which was under a heap of rubble. 'Ah, yes!' He stood up, clutching three cucumbers in his filthy hands. He skipped across what was now a building site to stop in front of me. 'For you,' he said, and I think he smiled—it was hard to tell.

I had a ruin of a house to live in, but at least I had three cucumbers. It was impossible not to smile, but at the same time, dismay filled my heart.

Holding the cucumbers, I looked up slowly. 'Why, Yorgo? Was it really necessary to pull the whole ceiling down? Why?'

'To see what was underneath, of course.'

'And what is underneath?'

'It is good. Bamboo, as I thought, and good hemp and sheep wool, all very old, of course, hundreds of years maybe. And there was much else besides. It will be warm in winter and cool in summer. Perfect.'

'And now that you have it down and know this, what happens?'

He looked momentarily puzzled, as though I had asked a stupid question. 'Now, Kyria, we put it back up again.'

Each evening, he walked me round what was still standing of the house. With delight and pride he showed me more and more devastation. Each day I wondered anew if I could live in this wreckage for much longer.

One day, the room I optimistically called my bedroom was piled so high with planks of wood I couldn't see my bed. It was simply too much for me.

'Enough, Yorgo. I have had enough. All I see is my house falling down. Now I want to see at least one sign of it going up again. You cannot work alone like this; you must bring in some men to help you. How am I going to sleep in my bed tonight, buried like this?'

He looked so crestfallen I thought he might cry. Instead, he led me outside to where the old cypress trees stood at the edge of the path to the house.

There was my bed, one leg broken off. Lying on the top, three cats and a kitten were fast asleep. Yorgo pointed to it with pride.

'See, I move it for you,' he said, shooing the cats away. 'No wind tonight, no rain.'

'No, Yorgo. You must mend the bed and bring it back inside. Tonight, I'd better sleep in the kitchen.' This was one room Yorgo had not touched. Yet.

That night I took a chair outside and sat watching the stars. Music echoed round the village, a plaintive melody of ancient sadness, of love long abandoned. This was a low moment for me. The first time I felt both helpless and hopeless. I missed Hugh painfully, and regretted that I had urged him away.

It seemed impossible that I had ever thought that, alone, I could turn this wreck, this heap of old stones, into a home for us. I recalled my excited dreams of warm tapestries lining the walls, children's voices echoing happily through the great rooms. Where was Hugh now? It seemed far more than a few months since he had gone. His letters always left me hungry for more. Yet, what would I be doing there in Athens now? Lying alone in our bed, probably.

Enough self-pity, I told myself. Tomorrow I would help Anthi at the school, and the hope in the eyes of the children would cheer me up.

The village school is a centre of real pleasure for me, and I feel lucky to be here. I have been coming several days each week, and the children, now used to me, seem to like me.

It is a long, low building of soft, grey stone. Its windows at the front are small, as are all the windows here. The sun does not shine in, so in the heat of the summer the rooms inside are always cool. But there is a balcony all round the structure, and in spring and autumn much of the schoolwork is done outside. I love the vista from this balcony, sweeping down to the village below, tucked into the curve of the mountain. The olive trees, with their gnarled trunks—some of them over a thousand years old—give a feeling of solidity and safety. Looking way up above, the little church of St Kosmas and Damianus sits on the highest peak, seemingly offering calm protection to all below.

There are probably thirty children in the school, divided into three groups. The professor, Kyrios Tsimbanakis, looks after the brightest. Anthi looks after the middle group and Kyrios Tsimbanakis's wife, whom everyone calls Kyria Titica, looks after the youngest.

The school has become the centre of the community, along with the church. Mothers leave their babies and toddlers here with Kyria Titica while they work in the fields. Often Anthi's little Voula, who is now beginning to toddle around, will be among them.

I was warmly welcomed into this cheerful group. Education is the most important thing in villages like Panagia, so helping the children to speak English is a valuable service. It was decided that I should have any child from any group who wanted to come to me for an hour or so each day; any child who showed the ability to learn some basic English.

For the first time since my marriage, I feel a real sense of myself again. Here I am, performing a service. The children are a delight to me. Almost without exception, their bright eyes gleam as they rise to the challenge of new words or thoughts in this strange English language. They love to say a whole sentence and receive a 'Bravo!' from me, a woman who but a short time ago had felt totally useless.

There is just one child who bothers me, a deaf and dumb boy. He is the only son of a shepherd, and they live in a cave above the village.

The boy's mother died three years ago. Each morning his father, Manos, brings the boy into the school and each afternoon he collects him. Dimitri is thought to be about ten but neither Anthi nor Kyria Titica can be sure. He has no papers from his birth.

He is quiet, seemingly responsive, but silent. Whether he takes in and remembers any English at all I can't be sure, but Kyria Titica feels he's happy to be here, so he comes whenever he wants.

One morning I arrived at the school before anyone else.

Yorgo had woken me at daybreak with exciting news: he had found some workers to come and help him.

Thrilled as I was at this, I would have been equally excited an hour or so later. I found it hard to go back to sleep, so decided to walk through the early sunshine—dawn was just breaking—to the school.

I was so early it was deserted. But there was a figure curled up in the porch. It was Dimitri.

I ran towards him and he cringed away as I reached down to touch him. He was cradling his head in his arms, but through the torn sleeve of his shirt I could see drying streaks of blood on his arm and a couple of horrible slashes. On his knees, showing through the old cut-down *vraka* that barely covered his legs, there was dark, purple bruising.

I heard a group of children beginning to arrive, Anthi's voice and laughter. I turned quickly; she saw me and I waved her over as urgently as I could without alerting the children to something being wrong.

As soon as she saw the child huddled there, she said, 'Stay here a moment with him. I'll get help.'

She was back almost at once, with the professor running behind. I moved aside, and still Dimitri remained motionless in his corner. The professor picked Dimitri up, as gently as if he were an injured bird, and carried him through the back door of the school building.

Anthi seemed strangely reluctant to speak of the incident, only to say to me, 'It's nothing. We will keep him here for the day, and Kyrios Tsimbanakis will take him to his father later.'

We went into Kyria Titica's room and there was Dimitri, curled into himself on an old army bed, not unlike the ones in my house. Anthi knelt down beside the boy, stroking his head.

'You are a nurse, Heavenly, can you help him?'

I bent down to the motionless figure. Gently, I rolled up the sleeves of his shirt and moved his arms by turn, slowly and carefully, up and down and round. He didn't flinch. I did the same with his legs. When I finished, he instantly curled himself back again into the cocoon in which he felt secure.

'There are no breaks, which is a good thing. The bruises are bad, but will heal themselves. The cuts are quite deep, though; I need to dress them. Wait here with him.'

I went quickly to my desk and rummaged in its single drawer. I had, in the beginning, brought in some simple first-aid remedies, just in case. I had never needed them until now. I had iodine, some swabs and a few bandages. I went back to Dimitri, and Anthi rolled him over to help me. I cleaned the wounds on his legs, and what looked like slashes on his arm. Iodine is painful on such raw cuts, but he did not flinch or moan. He lay still and let me finish.

As I put my old skills back into use, I felt a rising anger in me. 'I can't believe this comes from a natural fall, Anthi. It looks to me as though he has been beaten. Who has done this to him? Is it the father?' I spoke in English so only Anthi could understand.

'No. Not his father, never. I don't know who would do this to a child, but we must find out.'

As I walked home, I looked round the echoing hills. What secrets did they hold? An image flashed into my mind of the dead sheep hanging in Anthi's garden and the swoosh of the knife as her husband, smiling with pleasure, it seemed, had slit the belly open so that the guts spilled out. Death and its companions were no strangers in these parts. Involuntarily, I shuddered.

Reluctantly, I walked up the path to my house—there were voices and some laughter coming from inside.

'*Yiassou*, Kyria,' Yorgo called to me as I walked inside. 'Very soon now the work can be finished. Soon, soon. You are pleased, eh?'

I looked round. Nothing was changed. There was still rubble every-where, the air thick with dust. But today Yorgo was not alone: there were several other men scattered round the room.

Two I recognised as Hugh's drinking companions on the day of my accident out walking: the Kanavakis brothers. I nodded in their direction and tried to raise a weak smile. Another couple of men stood at the far end by the wine press. On top of the rubble on the floor there were now several long planks and a couple of ladders propped against the walls.

As the men realised who I was, they all went into action, moving the ladders around, shifting the planks. One man had acquired a rudimen-tary broom and was briskly sweeping; all *that* meant was shifting the rubble from one bit of the floor to another.

Yorgo stood still in all this activity. He could tell from my face that I was not impressed by what I saw.

'We will get all the work done very quickly, now I have good, strong help, Kyria.'

'I'm sure you are right, Yorgo,' I said, somewhat desperately, 'but they don't actually seem to be doing any building, do they?'

'Kyria, of course not at this very moment! You see this is, just now, the time for lunch. They must have a break.'

'A break from what?'

'Ah, you see, a break from thinking about where to start, who is to do what, who is to be in charge of which job and when.'

I waited as he paused, running out of ideas.

'Much thought is required for a house as big as this. At four o'clock we will start. That is,' he hastily corrected himself, 'we will start again.'

It was hot, I was tired and I simply couldn't argue any more. A battered chair was produced from somewhere and I sank down onto it. Everyone sat on the floor amidst the rubble.

Wine, bread and fruit appeared from various pockets, and from somewhere a half-wheel of cheese and a lethal-looking knife.

We ate together in silence. The wine vanished quickly—three bottles seemed to have emptied by themselves when Spiros Kanavakis spoke.

'How old are you, Kyria?' and another said, 'How old is your husband?'

While I stumbled over the answers to these rather surprising questions, Yorgo said, 'And how old is your king?' I didn't need to answer as the room then erupted into a discussion about the rights and wrongs of a monarchy, and I remembered Hugh saying it was all anyone in Athens seemed to care about.

'About forty,' I said loudly. They stopped arguing and looked at me. 'The King of the United Kingdom is about forty, I think,' I said firmly.

'Why do you come here? Why are you alone? Why does your husband leave you here? What does your husband do? How much does your husband earn?' I was bewildered by this hubbub of interrogation, but I remembered Anthi telling me everyone asks personal questions of each other all the time, especially of a stranger. Yorgo, his eyes twinkling over his great moustache said, 'How much does your prime minister earn?'

I breathed a little more easily. 'Oh, millions and millions of drachmas, I should think, but I don't know for sure.'

'Huh,' said Yorgo, with a shrug. 'I suppose he can afford to eat tinned meat twice a week if he wants to.'

'Probably,' I said, thinking of the tables heavy with food at the embassy banquets. 'At least twice.'

The questions died away and for a while there was silence.

A couple of men left the house and lay down under the cypress trees, no doubt feeling they had earned a rest after the arduous lunch. The others slowly wandered off, uttering promises to help another day.

Yorgo and I were left alone in the middle of the wreckage. I was about to try and force him to make a proper plan, when a sound from the doorway caused me to look up. There was someone there, someone I hadn't seen before.

The room was so dusty it was difficult to see him in detail, but a ray of brilliant sunshine came through the high window at that moment and lit up his face. He saw me at the same moment and smiled. He was about my age.

He was holding two buckets and, as he moved towards me, still smiling, I saw they were brimful of water. As he reached me, he placed them on the floor at my feet and not a drop spilled. He wiped his hand on the back of his *vraka* and stretched it out to me.

'*Kalispera*, Kyria Timberlake,' he said formally, in a low voice. 'You have a beautiful house, and it will be an honour to work on it.'

I took his hand in mine and shook it. It was a strong, warm hand.

He was tall and slender, and the first thing I noticed was that he smelt of the sunshine outside, and fresh grass. That was the moment it struck me that in the village most people smelt of their animals. It was not unpleasant, I was used to it. But this young man smelt oddly different: clean and sweet.

Beside him, Yorgo was bobbing up and down with excitement.

'This,' he spluttered, 'this is the very Christo, the son of my sister. He has come to make your house lovely. He is clever and—'

'Enough, Uncle,' said the very Christo. 'Kyria Timberlake knows there is much work to be done here and I will try and help, but it will not be quick. It must be rebuilt properly.'

I was so grateful to hear these words. This man would not just pull down walls, I felt sure; he would start to build them up.

As if I had spoken aloud, Christo said, 'First we must get these walls and ceiling back up again.' He looked round, his eyes the same piercing blue as his uncle's, and only partially hidden by the little steel-rimmed glasses he wore.

'We shall get these ladders and planks together and make a scaffold, so that we can reach the top and start from there. We must make cement.' And he gestured to the buckets of water.

'But first, would you show me round your house, Kyria, and tell me how it is in your imagination?'

'I should love to do that,' I said.

Together we walked into the adjoining kitchen. As this was almost part of the main room, it was not much better to look at than the living room, but at least the smoke-blackened ceiling and beams were intact. Yorgo hadn't taken his hammer to them yet.

I explained my fears to Christo and he shook his head.

'It's not necessary. My uncle felt it was important to take one room apart to discover its structure.'

'It seems a pity that he chose the biggest room to experiment on.'

'But that is the most important room in the house, from a structural point of view. If that roof is safe, everything else can rest on it.'

'And the bedroom?' I asked, as we moved down the stairs and into it. It was still full of planking. 'Does everything rest on that, too?' He smiled again, and thought for a moment.

'Well, I think this was probably a mistake.'

'I'm glad you say that,' I said, and he raised an eyebrow, questioningly. 'Now I know I can trust you, because I think you are telling me the truth.'

He laughed. 'Perhaps when we look round, I can be truthful about more of my uncle's mistakes, but I hope not.'

'Oh, so do I,' I said. 'I long for this house to be finished so that I can enjoy it properly. Your uncle thinks it is acceptable for me to sleep in my bed under the cypress trees.'

He laughed again. 'Well,' he said, 'I often sleep out under the stars when I come away from the town and into these hills. It is possible to sleep well and deeply. You are quite safe.'

'Do you stay with your uncle here in the village?'

'No, no, I prefer to be independent. I sleep up there.' And he pointed up into the mountains. He saw the puzzled look on my face and smiled. 'In a cave. I promise you it is comfortable, warm and dry. Most of the shepherds here sleep up in the caves, you know. It is not a strange thing to do in this part of the world.'

I remembered Dimitri, the battered shepherd's son from this morning, and told Christo about him. He frowned. 'I think I know this family, Kyria,' he said.

'Can you call me Heavenly? It's what everyone calls me here.'

'My uncle calls you Kyria Heavenly, so it is better if I do the same.'

We walked on through the house.

'I believe you came here from Athens and, before that, England?'

'You know all about me already, I think,' I said.

'There are few secrets here, Kyria Heavenly. Everyone knows everything. Never doubt it.'

'I have no secrets,' I said quickly.

'No matter. They will make something up if there is nothing to tell. This is a simple place; no one writes letters or reads newspapers, so they only acquire knowledge by talking to each other, and then, of course, a little is added and by the end of today, for instance, the village will believe your husband is closely related to your prime minister.'

I laughed at this absurd thought. 'And, of course, eats tinned meat at every meal, I suppose?'

He bowed his head and smiled. 'Of course. They meet in the fields, by the school, in the square and *buzz, buzz, buzz*, little stories are passed round. Sometimes they start as truths, but if an old widow is feeling vindictive or perhaps just mischievous, these gossipy bits will be made up. Then, a much more interesting story comes along, and the last one is forgotten in the excitement of the new.'

While he was speaking, he had athletically climbed onto my wooden boxes. These were all that I had as a wardrobe and chest of drawers. Even though he looked as though he knew what he was doing and had excellent balance, he seemed very precarious. As if he could read my thoughts he called, 'Don't worry, I won't cause harm.' He clambered down swiftly.

'Your ceiling is quite safe here. This room used to house the animals and no one would risk danger for them. They are the most valuable creatures in the household. They'd rather put the grandmother outside in a storm than let an animal suffer. It's good to have this as your bedroom down here. It will be cool in summer and warm in winter.'

He paused and then asked, 'How do you want your house to look, Kyria Heavenly? Do you want it to be very modern? Do you want marble on your floors? Are you fond of wallpapers and paints? Maybe you want to cover these old walls with new *isvesti*, and lose these dirty old stones?'

'Is that how you see me, Christo? As a woman who prefers marble to wooden floors?'

'You must tell me, Kyria; I do not know you yet.'

'I shall not be keeping animals in the kitchen, you can be sure of that, and if my grandmother were alive and came here, she would be treated at least as well as the goats, and she would certainly sleep in the house.'

As I was speaking, he had moved to the wall and was feeling a large stone that protruded into the room. 'Come here, Kyria Heavenly. Touch this stone, what do you feel?'

I let my fingers linger on the rock before I answered him.

'I feel the warmth of the summer sun from outside. I feel the strength of the sea that is so near. I feel that this has been part of this structure, part of this house, for many, many years.'

'Exactly,' he said.

We stepped back and looked at each other.

'I believe we feel the same things, Kyria,' he said.

'Yes, Christo. Will you make this house as beautiful as it used to be? Once upon a time, someone had a dream of how this house would look, even for the animals.'

'Then we must search for that dream,' he said. 'But first, I'm hungry.

Let's find my uncle and see if there is any of that cheese left.'

As we walked back through the rooms I tried to tell him how important it was that I should get this house ready for when Hugh came back.
'I want us to live here, and I think my husband will need persuading.'

Back in the main room, Yorgo was trying to balance one of the ladders against the wall. Christo sprang across to help him. 'Here, Uncle,'
he said, and showed him how it should be done, to make it hold the
scaffold plank.

Within moments, it seemed as though the room had taken on a different attitude. Suddenly, with the addition of this structure, I could see
that building work could begin, that there would be no more destruc-
tion. Soon, the men were carrying hefty buckets of rubble outside.
I stood nearby and watched as they carted them down to the ravine.

'We give these stones back to the mountain where they came from,'
said Christo.

They worked together for the rest of the afternoon. I think Christo
understood how useless I was feeling just watching them for, after a
while, he said, 'Do you want to help, Kyria Heavenly?'

'Oh, yes,' I said quickly. 'Tell me what I can do that will be useful.'

'Oh, no!' said Yorgo. 'It is not suitable work for a lady like you. You
should rest.'

'Rest from what exactly? And where precisely would you have me
rest? I have done almost nothing all day. I want to help. Please let me.'

By the end of that day, the three of us had shifted at least half of the rubbish and the room, full of dust as it was, felt like a different place to me.

I fetched *raki* and water and cut up pomegranates, and we sat in the
fading sun on the terrace drinking together as if we had been doing it
all our lives.

I think the arrival of his nephew had re-energised Yorgo, and he
seemed happy to take second place to this young man, who clearly
knew what he was doing.

'Oh, Christo, you still haven't eaten. You were hungry and in search
of food hours ago.'

He shrugged and waved my protest aside.

'I forgot about food when I started to work. It's always the way. My
uncle will feed me tonight and I shall be fine.'

'Aphrodite is roasting fat pigeons. We shall have a feast.' Yorgo
laughed and rubbed his hands together. He suddenly realised I would
probably dine alone for he looked awkward and said, 'Kyria Heavenly,
perhaps you would like—' but I stopped him before he could go further.

'I have my supper planned, thank you, Yorgo. Remember you have brought me fresh salad every day, and I have eggs and cheese and cakes from Irini. Plenty.'

He sprang to his feet and, shaking my hand firmly, said, 'Until tomorrow, Kyria Heavenly.' And they were gone.

The room suddenly felt very empty.

I ran outside and watched them walk down the mountain away from me, through the gathering mist, Yorgo astride his old donkey and Christo walking alongside. It was a timeless picture, two villagers moving across the horizon of the hills.

As I watched, Christo turned round. I couldn't see the expression on his face, but his glasses glittered in the last rays of the sun. He was too far away, but he waved to me, and hesitantly I waved back.

ANTHI

THERE WAS A HAZE as thick as a bridal veil over the hills as we rode through them this evening. The dying rays of the sun tried to instil warmth into the hour, but I shivered a little. At my back, strapped close with a shawl, was my sleeping Voula. Despina had gone home with Athena. I knew Maria would keep her there until my return.

Ahead of me, Professor Tsimbanakis held Dimitri in his arms as he urged his horse onwards. He had told me not to come but I was curious; I needed to know. If there was danger for one child in the village, perhaps there was danger for them all?

It was rare for Manos not to collect his son. Was something wrong? After all, I was sure he would never raise a hand to him. Also, in the caves the shepherds thought of as home, I would swear no one else would touch him. They are a close-knit community who have lived apart from the village for many years. Coming down only to seek work, they are diligent and honest.

It had taken a long time for people to trust them. Many of them had seen much conflict in their lives. Some had come from Turkey in the population exchange, leaving behind their homes and any hard-won living to return to this island they only knew of as their own.

Some had fought against the Albanians and had ended up here with nothing but the rags on their backs. Most of them, one way or another, came from another life. As a consequence, they thought of themselves as brothers. If you hurt one, you hurt them all.

That is why I was so sure the injuries to Dimitri must have come from within the village of Panagia. Quarrels in these parts were usually simple. They may be long-lasting; years, generations even, but the reasons are straight: among women, almost always the gossip is about the size of a dowry; among men, about property or boundary lines, borders of land. Politics and differences of opinion about royalty can divide whole families for years.

But none of those things would apply to the cave dwellers. What use would they have for an argument about the king, or the ruling of the country?

I shook my head and gently kicked Astrape on for the last half mile. There was no sign ahead of the professor, or his precious passenger.

A faint scent of wood smoke in the soft mountain air told me I was approaching the caves. It sharpened as I pushed upwards, and Astrape whinnied and shook his head.

I tugged him to a halt by a pine tree twisted from the wind, next to the professor's horse, tethered roughly to the trunk.

I went onwards alone. I could hear the professor's voice, although he was speaking low and gently. Cautiously, I stepped forwards and into the entrance of a cave.

The flickering light from an oil lamp showed the rough interior. It was simple but quite large, and in the chill evening air I could feel warmth from inside. The professor was lowering Dimitri to the ground and I could dimly make out the huddled figure of his father on a blanket, under an overhanging rock. As I watched, Manos reached out an arm to his son who whimpered painfully as he stretched to touch his father. I could see, even from where I stood, that Manos's arm was bruised and bloody as well.

'You'd have done better to leave him in the school tonight.'

'Did you bring him down this morning?' The professor's voice was soft.

'I did. I could do nothing for him here. I see you have dressed his wounds. Thank you.'

'We have indeed. The Englishwoman who comes to the school was a nurse. Do you want to tell me what happened here last night? I assume it was last night?'

Manos didn't answer immediately, but paused and looked round in the flickering gloom of the cave. I must have moved at that moment for he suddenly saw me and called, 'Who is it? Who are you?'

I stepped forwards into the light.

Holding Dimitri tightly in his arms, Manos stared at me and I saw that not only his arm, but also his face, was bruised and swollen.

'What are you doing here?' he said.

'Please, you know who I am,' I said gently. 'You know how I care for Dimitri in school; I was worried about him.'

Still he was silent. He was angry and suspicious for sure. Kyrios Tsimbanakis did not look pleased that I was here. He spoke under his breath: 'Perhaps this is men's business, not the place for you.' I was stricken. He was right. Of course I should not be here and I turned to leave at once.

Manos spoke and I paused. 'Perhaps it's no one's business but my own.'

The professor spoke again. 'We are only here to try and help.'

'Perhaps we don't want your help,' was the reply.

'But Dimitri needed help, didn't he?' I looked from one to the other.

'If you think I beat up my son, you are wrong. And if I did, it is not for you to chastise me, gossip about me.'

Unwanted here as I was, I had to speak.

'Oh, please, we would never believe that, and certainly would never let you or your son be the subject of rumour or gossip. It is because we know you would never harm Dimitri that we came. And it is clear that you yourself have been beaten. Is there nothing we can do?'

He laughed harshly. 'You?' he said, and looked away.

There was a long silence and I saw that Dimitri had fallen asleep, safe now in his father's arms. It broke my heart to see his battered little face, the painful cuts now drying into scabs. He is a child who cannot speak in his own defence, and never will be able to.

'Come, Anthi, we'll not bother them further.'

It was as the professor turned that Manos finally spoke again, rocking the sleeping boy gently in his arms.

'It's not the first time we have felt threatened here. Ever since the sheep started to go missing, some in the village have turned against us. We are the obvious targets. We have little, but down there,' he pointed savagely, indicating the bottom of the mountain, 'something goes missing and it must be us who have taken it! An animal dies strangely, and we must be responsible. It's a rough justice there now. Ever since the mayor died, it has been every man for himself; there is no one to speak for us.'

A picture suddenly came to me: sheep! A violent memory of my husband slaughtering the beast, the innards slithering out. I didn't know there had been others. I felt cold to my very centre, and a sharp stab as if a knife of ice was seeking my heart.

I opened my mouth but no words came. My throat was as dry as a bone bleached by the mountain sun. 'And Dimitri?' I finally managed.

He looked at the boy, sleeping in his arms, and stroked the top of his head. 'They came last night and he got in the way. Simple as that.'

He fell into a stubborn silence, making it clear he wished us gone. We turned to leave. We had no place here now.

We didn't speak until we had reached our horses. Darkness had fallen while we were in the cave and there was a strong, chill breeze now blowing. I pulled my shawl closer round Voula and shivered.

We parted ways at the bottom of the mountain path; Professor Tsimbanakis to his village over the next hill, and me to my home in Pano Panagia. He took my hand briefly and warmed it in his strong grasp.

'Titica and I will take them something tomorrow. Dimitri must have clean bandages. Titica will ask Heavenly to show her how to dress the wounds.'

'What do you think really happened there, Professor?'

'Don't look for trouble where there is none. You heard what he said. Leave it at that. I told you not to come.'

'One of the sheep he spoke of came from our flock, not stolen, I agree, but an unnatural death. Manolis is not a man to forgive and forget. Do you think—'

'You have always had a powerful imagination. Let this matter rest now. Accept what Manos has said and get on with your life. Look to your children.' And he was gone.

I need to talk to someone who knows the village and the villagers well. Someone who cares about the cave dwellers and who doesn't assume they are thieves or sheep-stealers. I distrust my husband so completely, he is the first person to my mind to be involved in evil-doing.

Away across the hill, the faint voice of the cantor echoes from the church. Of course, today is the day of a big memorial ceremony for Andreas Mamadopolous, the mayor. He was a good and powerful man in Panagia and there was much grief when he died. Today it is the special ceremony that takes place ninety days after death, and my grandparents will be there. My Pappous was a very close friend of Andreas, and there are many here who want him to be the next mayor. He, like Andreas, is seen as an honourable man. I must ask him to seek justice for these people.

As I urge Astrape forward, I look up to the heavens. There is the brightest of the stars, the evening star, always the first to shine.

I stood at the back of the church with the other women and looked round. The church was packed—Andreas had been a popular man and the whole village had come today in his memory.

I scanned the faces, looking first among the men. Manolis was not there. But there was my Pappous, dressed as usual for such an event in his old blue flat hat with the red scarf draped across his shoulder. With his proud silver moustache he could have been a visitor from another century. And there, at the back with the women, was Yaya. I caught her eye and she smiled.

The priest, Papa Costas, himself an old friend of Andreas, chanted the closing words of the service; I had got there just in time.

Everyone milled round the entrance and some took my hand or kissed me in welcome. My grandmother bustled close to me and took my cold fingers in hers. Her dear hand was warm and rough to the touch. I took it up to my face and saw her fingernails were blackened. 'Elderberries,' she said, by way of explanation. 'There will be some preserve for you for later.' She reached her hand up behind me and murmured some endearment to Voula, who was stirring now and cooing. 'Here, let me hold her for you, Anthi. She is heavy and you look tired.'

Voula chortled in Yaya's arms—she loved her great-grandparents and it was a while since she had seen them.

'Will you come back to the house with us, Anthi?'

'Of course, Yaya, I need to ask Pappous's advice.'

She looked at me shrewdly. 'Are you in trouble, child?' she said, her brow now creased into a frown.

I smiled. 'Of course not. But if I were, where else should I go for help?'

She nodded, reassured. 'Come, we shall take some of Irini's memorial bread and get Pappous away from those wicked friends of his; they would have him down to Il Piperia and we should not see him until midnight.' But she was smiling and I knew she spoke in jest.

The scent of acacia was strong and sweet in the air, and fought for precedence with the lavender and rosemary that grew in profusion round the door. Pappous fumbled for the key they kept under a stone in the porch. I felt a momentary anxiety for Despina, but I knew she was at home, and would light the lamps and wait for me.

'I have heard this sheep business talked about in Il Piperia. It was a hard winter, food is scarce, money is almost non-existent and that makes simple people behave in ways they might avoid in more prosperous times.' Pappous threw another log onto the already blazing fire and sat back. He was drinking his usual *raki* and I was sipping a hot cordial Yaya had made from wild berries gathered on the mountain.

'Cretans have always been fighters. If they can't take arms for the defence of their country, they'll find something else to rage about. But I tell you, if war comes as they say it will, everyone will want Cretans as friends, certainly not enemies.'

'War, Pappous?'

'I listen to the wireless set Fanis has installed in Il Piperia and I'm sure war is not far away.' He paused, puffing at his pipe. 'Years ago, this village was not the happy place it seems to you now. Families fought against families, as they did all across this island. We were Cretans, not Greeks—we still are!' The strong *raki* slipped down his throat in a single gulp and he held out his glass for Yaya to pour him another, which she did. 'You know, my friends and I grew up believing violence was normal in a village. When our fathers went off for a day's hunting, we almost expected them not to return in the evening. As children we played revolutionaries and soldiers. Our guns were sticks, but we all longed for the real thing. We never knew about sides. We copied what we saw our fathers and uncles and neighbours do—shoot each other. We never questioned why. And nobody told us, so when we were older and got real guns, we were ready to go and shoot anybody.'

Yaya had lit the lamp by now, and excited moths were ramming the glass of the shade again and again.

'Pappous, I need to ask you something.' He looked at me quizzically. 'Can you not do something for these poor cave dwellers? It seems so unfair they should be considered target practice for the village men, who have nothing better to do.'

Of course, he knew what I was thinking and said at once, 'Child, I am too old now to take on the responsibilities of Andreas Mamadopolous. There will be a mayor before too long. I hope, a younger man. Until then I do what I can, of course. I'll ask around and see what I can find out.' He seemed momentarily lost in thought and puffed hard on his big pipe. I love the smell it makes, that pipe. It is a ripe autumn smell that makes me think of log fires burning, warm wine and a wonderful *stifado*. This is a stew that my Yaya makes better than anyone in the village. Its rich scent of rabbit and juniper filled the air now and I could see she was ladling a dish full for me to take home. My mouth watered as I thought of eating this later, but I must remember why I had come. I must tell them of my fears that Manolis may be involved in this revenge.

As I knew they would be, they were horrified.

'You can do nothing about this, child,' Yaya said at once. 'You must forget this nonsense. It cannot concern you.'

But it is to Pappous that I look for an answer. His eyes are creased in what I think is anger and I am right, for when he finally speaks, his words are like sparks that shoot from the fire and burn as they land.

'She can do nothing about this on her own, Giorgia, but she must know the truth. We must all know the truth. This is our family as well, our name that will be associated with this. It is a bad time, little one, when neighbours, friends in a village, take arms against each other. It was always easier to give in to the invaders. That way you stayed alive. If you fought, as any true Cretan did, mostly you were punished. Your house burnt down, your sheep or crops destroyed. Our family, your family, Anthi, stood against the Turks. My father and I fought side by side on this mountain. In my life I have seen many die here. One time, eight men from Panagia were shot as they lay sleeping. One, who had dug his land daily with my mother's father, was killed by a neighbour of them both. A bullet in the head. BANG!' His shout caused Yaya and me to shudder.

'It is not wrong to remember the truth. Be proud to be a good Cretan, and that means caring for the poor and helpless in our community. Men, women and children who are, for one reason or another, unable to defend themselves. I will walk home with you. It is a dark night and I prefer you not to walk alone.'

I smiled. Even with my own baby here, and her sister waiting, he still saw me as a child myself. I found the thought comforting, and, as I knew he would, he did not dismiss me as being over-imaginative.

Pappous sat on his donkey and rode ahead through the outskirts of Panagia. The closer we got to my house, the more apprehensive I felt.

'He may not be here.' I said quietly.

'Child, do not fret. I am an old fool, I know, but I will do nothing to cause your husband's alarm. I shall certainly ask around, with discretion, to see what I can discover, but confrontation without informed knowledge or proof is not the way of a good soldier, don't worry.'

As we crossed the hill, the dim light from our lamp shone through the windows, and I knew the house was not empty.

We tethered our animals and walked through the half-open door. The very first thing I noticed was that there was no sign of Despina. Manolis was in his usual place by the fire. He did not stir as we came in and I saw quickly that the *raki* jug at his feet lay on its side, empty. My grandfather called out a greeting and, at his voice, Manolis slowly turned his head and peered at us blearily.

'Where is Despina?' I asked.

'Excuse me, wife's grandfather.' It was as if I hadn't spoken. 'I am not feeling quite myself tonight. I have not eaten yet and my hunger is great. You see, your granddaughter has other things to occupy her, instead of minding her house and her family. You are aware from her words that she doesn't even know the whereabouts of her eldest daughter, who could be lost on the mountain, for all she cares.'

Fury swept through me at his words, but it would not have done me any good to have answered him. Voula was in full cry and needed my urgent attention. I swiftly crossed the room and sat in my nursing chair in the dark corner at the back.

My grandfather ignored Manolis and was now coldly refusing his offer of alcohol.

'Not even a glass of my best wine?'

'I will take nothing. I think your wife needs you to tell her where Despina is.'

Manolis poured a glass of the rich, ruby-coloured liquid for himself. He shrugged. 'The raising of the children is my wife's duty. Perhaps the child is with one of our neighbours?'

My grandfather's eyes were like black ice as he turned to me.

'Where is she likely to be, Anthi?' he said. 'I shall go and fetch her.'

'Thank you. I think she will be with her friend Athena, the daughter of Maria and Michaelis. They came from school together.' Without another word, Pappous turned and left the house.

Manolis spat in the fire and watched the flames spurt up before he stood and spoke to me. 'Why is Stephanos Karanakis here? He is not the most preferred of visitors in my house.'

'He is my grandfather, Manolis, and will be welcome wherever I am.'

'You forget something, wife: this is my house and visitors are only welcome here with my permission. He is a dangerous man in Panagia, and well you know it. He has always been known as an agitator, a communist.' And he spat on the fire again.

'At least he is a man of honour. A kind man who does not attack innocent people and children.'

I had walked over to him as I spoke and Manolis turned and smacked his fist into my face. I reeled back in shock and pain, clutching my baby tightly in my arms. She began to cry.

'You are hysterical, Rodianthi, and don't know what you are talking about.' His voice was like snake venom, creeping into my heart.

My face burnt and stung, like when one of my bees had taken against me. He had taken his hands to me before, but never with such violence.

'You won't silence me, Manolis. Beat me as you choose, I will speak out.'

His face was ugly in his rage and he was breathing hard. I think he would have hit me again, but my Pappous was standing in the doorway.

'She is not there. Michaelis said she walked home with Athena but he saw her wave and come on in this direction. He assumed she had come here, to her home, to you.'

My heart thumped wildly and my voice was little more than a tremble. 'Did you not see her, Manolis? What time did you come home?'

Despina is eight and a sensible child. She knows her way round the village as well as anyone older and wiser.

He shrugged. 'What does it matter? She is not here and that's it. She'll come back. I'll go to the other end of the village and look. And I'm telling you, if I find her, she will have the biggest thrashing of her life.'

Pappous and I looked swiftly at each other. Both of us realised that Manolis was incapable of finding a scorpion in a coffee cup in his state. The *kafenion* he visits is the only place his steps will take him. As if to prove his lack of intent, he slumped again into his chair and drank deeply from his glass.

'Come, Anthi,' said Pappous, 'we can do nothing standing here. We must go through the village. We shall find her in no time at all.'

Pulling my shawl round Voula and myself, I hurried with my grandfather to the door.

'You can leave the baby here, if you want, I shall not eat her.' Manolis paused, belched loudly and continued, 'even though I am near to starving. Thanks to you, wife.'

I did not answer but silently put my grandmother's dish of rabbit stew on the table. Pappous pulled the door shut behind us.

The night was full dark now and, coming from the warmth of the house, I shivered in the blackness.

'Come, onto the donkey with you. I shall walk beside.'

Gratefully I sat in the hard, worn, old saddle that had moulded over the years to fit my grandfather's rear. For half an hour or so, we walked the rocky paths of the village. We were the only people abroad in the foggy night. Others were warm in their houses with their animals, or already sleeping.

From somewhere ahead, through the thickening mist, I heard the sweet sound of a woman's voice. She was singing a song I recalled from my childhood—it was Yaya's voice.

'Is it my wife?' Pappous said, and then louder, 'Is it you, Giorgia? What are you doing here singing, and so late? What is wrong?'

She was still invisible through the damp mist, but she answered, 'Stephano, I have Despina here. With me.' It was Yaya! My daughter had gone to my grandmother. I jumped down from the donkey and she ran into my arms, weeping.

'Don't cry. You are safe. We are together now, nothing is wrong.' Pappous ruffled his hand across Despina's head.

'I don't know why she came to us, but I am pleased that she thought to do so. She was greatly distressed when she arrived, but I could not get her to tell me why. She hasn't spoken. She missed you by moments, and I knew you would worry, so I thought I must get her back quickly.'

'I am so grateful. Despina, come with me now.'

Yaya was flushed, and mopping her face. Pappous put his arm round her and she seemed happy to have his support, for she leant against him, almost collapsing.

'Thank you, Yaya, and thank you, Pappous. I will find out what has happened here.' Despina's tears had almost stopped, but she was trembling like a feather in the wind. I rubbed her head. 'My darling child, it's all right, you are safe. Pappous, you must take Yaya home, we will all come to see you tomorrow. I can only apologise for the lack of welcome you received in my house.' Both my grandparents hugged me and I felt the warmth and security of their unquestioning love.

Pappous and I helped Yaya onto the donkey. Her clothes felt damp from the misty air and, knowing we could run to warm ourselves, I wrapped my shawl round her in spite of her protests.

'Until tomorrow. We have unfinished business I shall not forget. Take care of yourself tonight.' And Pappous lowered his voice: 'You must not rile your husband in any way; his mood is ugly with the drink. Do not put yourself at risk any further.' As he spoke, his hand gently stroked my swollen, bruised cheek.

I put my hand on his arm. 'It's since the stillbirth of our only son— I can do nothing right for him.'

'*Sto kalo*, child,' he said. 'Take care of yourself.'

The children fell asleep quickly and I lay with them. I was deadly tired but sleep was far away. I was trying to make sense of the day behind me. Manolis was still in his chair by the side of the fire. He had not looked at me, feigning sleep when we returned. But it was obvious that he was awake, for his fingers were moving through the rough black coat of the dog lying at his side.

Despina had clung to my skirts desperately all the way home. From time to time, a great hiccuping sob would shake her body. But she would not speak a word.

This really worried me; she is normally full of chatter, but there was something alien in her silence tonight, as though she was afraid. And she shook all the harder as we walked into the house.

She wanted nothing to eat, even Yaya's stew, which usually she would gobble down.

When we were upstairs I questioned her gently, 'Was Papa here when you came from school?'

She was looking blankly into the far corner of the room and seemed unable to answer me. Her eyes looked bruised with tiredness.

'Did you do something naughty to make Papa cross?'

She was in bed now and buried her face in the sheet, pulling the cloth round her tightly so that she had made a cocoon for herself, and not even her face looked out. Within moments she slept.

As I lay with both my girls, worried and unhappy, I was thinking that something was wrong and I could not understand what it was.

The only relief I had was to hear Manolis's snores. Tonight, at least, I would sleep alone. But it was hours before my stiff body could relax.

I awoke long after the rest of the village and, quickly jumping from my bed, I could hear Voula sobbing from somewhere in the house. My body was slow today and my yawns seemed never-ending, but I got myself together and forced myself down the stairs, thinking to see Manolis snoring.

Not so; he had started the fire and was walking Voula round the room, rocking her in his arms. He looked awkward and clumsy. 'This baby needs her mother,' he said, pushing her into my arms. Despina sat at the end of the table eating a chunk of bread and drinking water.

I quickly quietened Voula at my breast. 'Will you have some fruit with your bread, Despina?'

She shook her head. Her eyes had not looked up once since I had come down the stairs. Manolis walked round the table towards me and looked at Despina closely.

'She has not spoken this morning,' he said, and he shrugged.

It was as though my child, my sparkling, laughing Despina, had been taken, and another put in her place.

'Speak to me, Despoula, my dear one.' And rising, I moved round and held her in my arms. Despina was rigid. I stroked her hair back from her brow. She didn't respond to the touch. I wanted to weep as this changeling child rejected my advances. I looked up helplessly at Manolis, but his face was stony.

I took my shawl from the hook under the *iconostasis*. 'Come, we will take Astrape this morning and ride to the school.' This was normally a great treat for them and Voula laughed. But this morning there was no answer from Despina and her eyes were blank, but she did rise and allowed me to push her gently forwards.

'**A**way in a manger, no crib for a bed . . .' The voices went on but they were getting ragged now and there was laughter. Heavenly was here.

'Listen, Despina. You know who is here today? You can go and join in. They are singing the English Christmas song Heavenly taught you.'

This morning she didn't jump down and run in to school as normal, but clung to the saddle as if she would never move again. 'Come, Despina, Voula and I will come with you.' There was suspicion in her eyes, but at least she moved to get down from the horse. She clutched my skirt as we went in at the door.

'Despina! How lovely. I thought you might be ill.' And Heavenly held out her hand to her. There was a moment of stillness and then Despina moved forwards and took it in hers. She looked round the room and I knew she was afraid that her friends might laugh at her.

She was a different child this morning and anyone could see it.

Heavenly looked at me, unspoken questions in her eyes. She had seen my bruised face, but there was nothing I could say. She nodded to me and, taking Despina with her, moved across to rejoin the children. But within seconds Despina was back, clutching my skirt again.

She was beginning to seriously worry me. Why would she suddenly stop speaking? What had sent her reeling back to babyhood overnight? My arm went round her, and I uttered a silent prayer to the Virgin. There was no question of leaving Despina here without me.

Professor Tsimbanakis was at the door. There were questions in his face, too, as he saw me, but he would not ask in front of the child.

'I'll be here as usual tomorrow. You will stay if I am here, won't you, my darling?' Her face was bleak but she nodded.

Outside, the sky had cleared, but the mountains seemed to tower against a threatening, violent darkness. I felt afraid as I rode home through the village. I am not a woman who feels fear. But today I felt the first threads of it weave their way through my blood. With all that I have known in my short life, I have never felt so vulnerable as I do now.

I looked down at my firstborn child, just there in front of me on Astrape's saddle, and circled her small body with my arm. Then I felt a pat on my head and a sweet cooing. Voula was gently stroking my hair. Her tiny hands came to the front and, as she patted my cheeks, I knew I was weeping. Here was the root of my fear, in my girls. And I don't know what is happening to us.

HEAVENLY

Athens, December 1938
My dearest Evadne,
I think we must be living in two separate worlds, you and I. I have to admit I read your letters about the building work going on in the house with some horror, although this chap Christo seems to know what he's doing, which makes a change, but is it necessary for you to work with them? The thought of you banging away with a hammer is an amusing one, I agree, but not really suitable for a diplomat's wife.

Your life in the school sounds interesting enough but I hope, my love, you are not working too hard. I like to think of you having lazy days in the sun, not rushing round a class full of smelly brats. Do you have to keep going there? If you are bored, I can ask Janet to send you some silks and whatever bits and pieces needed to make a tapestry. You may enjoy that. I hate to sound stuffy, darling, but I keep wondering where you get your hair done and things like that. Who does your laundry? Don't tell me you go to that spring place with all the village women!

Meanwhile, life feels very unsettled here. The Germans seem to be full of good intentions and are offering help with the Greek defence programme, but can one really trust them?

I can't remember if I told you that Dora T arrived here on the twenty-fourth and is staying in the Residence. I must say, it's wonderful to have her here. She's en route to Egypt. That's where everyone is heading. She's taken a house there with some chums. In the UK, they are all worried about war in Europe.

There's a lot of talk here of northern Crete being a particular hot-spot. I know you are down in the south-east, my love, but I worry that I could look after you better if you were here with me. At the first sign of trouble, those villagers you are so fond of will rush out to fight. I know I've asked before and you never seem even to think about it, but please consider coming back. There's a flying boat once a week or so to the islands. My darling Evadne, I love you and miss you so very much, please take great care of yourself until we are together again. It seems such an irony that I agreed to you staying on the island because it would be safer and now it only looks like trouble!
Your loving husband, Hugh

The letter was accompanied by a rather bleak card, showing an unsmiling Greek royal family. Christmas has come again. Last year it had passed as a day like any other. There was little to celebrate; the winter was a harsh one.

This year, Manolis was off with his brother, so Anthi asked me to go with her and the girls to her Pappous and Yaya. I think it was in my honour that Yaya had cooked a roasted hare with red wine and sage. I was touched and had a lovely day. I taught them all to sing 'Away in a Manger', although they were puzzled why lying in a stable was so strange to the infant Jesus and his parents—they share their houses with their animals even now.

I left to walk home at the end of the afternoon and suddenly felt very alone. And at home I read Hugh's letter again. I sit very still as I read, wrapped in many layers, for the night air is chill in these, the last, lingering days of the year. The lamp gutters low, creating a soft glow. I feel a sadness come over me as I read. It seems that I hardly know the man who wrote these words. And he certainly doesn't seem to know me!

In the days and the weeks and the months that have drifted past since we were together, his life in the embassy has gone on as before, whereas I feel I have embraced a new life in this village. How could he know me as I am now, thinking my days should be taken up with tapestry? I write to him regularly of my work at the school and here in the house. I thought they were rather jolly letters because I so want to share with him the pleasures of my life.

I tried and failed to find a flicker of jealousy that he is to have a high old time showing Dora Troutbeck the high spots and nightclubs of Athens. I feel only grateful that she will keep his thoughts away from my return.

I have a melancholy ache now, that so easily we seem to have become different people, with separate dreams and hopes for a future that lies way beyond any recognisable horizon.

I think back to when everything began to change for me here. It was the day that I found the boy Dimitri huddled in the porch and Anthi couldn't or wouldn't tell me what was going on. That was the day little Despina changed from a lively chatterbox into a silent and reserved child. But that was also the day I met Christo. I smile. Everything began with Christo.

For a start the house began to look as though one day I might live there comfortably. Working alongside Yorgo and Christo, I have learned skills I never thought to have! Christo showed me how to lay a tile on a roof so that it stays there. It's very unusual to have a tiled roof on a village house. Yorgo couldn't believe it could be done. 'They will fall off!' he kept saying. But, slowly and patiently, Christo showed us both how to do it and we are now, Yorgo and I, experts in the fine craft of tiling.

I learned how to chip away at a stone with the right hammer (and to do it slowly and carefully) so that it was a thing of beauty in a wall and not just a support. He taught me how to rub up a stone so that it reflected glints of light to make it shine like a lamp, and he taught me how to polish wood with the wax from Anthi's bees so that it would keep clean and dry, even when left, by mistake, in the rain.

In the beginning I made many mistakes like that. Yorgo would say 'Po po,' and look at me helplessly, but Christo would say, 'It is from the mistakes that you will learn perfection.'

One day I realised, to my surprise, that my clothes were all too loose on my body. The work I am doing, some of it quite physical and tiring, and the diet I am living on now, all simple fresh food, make the pounds I had gathered at banquets in Athens fall away. Hugh was also right to wonder about my hair. It now either stands out round my head, or hangs down my back, it is so long! Occasionally I keep it tidy in a head-kerchief like the village women.

Once or twice a week, I wait for dark and walk down to the spring to bathe and wash my hair. There is never anyone there and the clear crystal water sends the day behind me into the past with a quick gasp as the first icy drops hit my body.

I go down to the spring on other days, too, for Hugh was right again; I join the village women to do my laundry. I have learned so much there: not only how to use a pumice to scrub away a stain but all the gossip. Who is planning a liaison or a marriage, how the progress of a dowry was coming, or a trousseau. Who is ill and with what, and which herbs were being cooked to make a linctus or a poultice. The women have discovered I was a nurse and call me in to help them with a sick husband or child, or to give advice on pregnancy or childbirth.

I have quickly become absorbed in village life. I am no longer a novelty, a curiosity among them. They accept me. They are still so kind, bringing me gifts of eggs, lemons and cakes or sweetmeats, sometimes a dish of olives steeped in brine, or the pungent green oil from the first pressing of their olives.

But while this kindness and generosity is shown me in great profusion from the villagers I am beginning to think of as friends, I no longer look round me only through spectacles tinted rose-pink. I know there are many sides to these hills. All is not always well in these clustered dwellings along the rocky paths. A quarrel can spring up from nowhere, and suddenly one family will not be seen speaking to another. A father and son will fall out over a shooting incident or a proposal of marriage.

Occasionally a wife will appear with a bruise on her face or arm. No one speaks of these things.

The shepherds who live in the caves above have a harder life than most. I sit on the terrace at night, wrapped warmly against the chill, and see the lights of fires outside the caves. Which one did little Dimitri and his father Manos sit beside? Which one had Christo lit and sat next to after his day working on my house?

I am at the school for two days at least, as well as helping with the restoration here. It is good to have the entirely separate life of the school, but each day I hurry home to see the day's progress. Christo shows me where he wants me to look. He peers over his wire-framed spectacles and watches my reactions as I admire the work.

One day I told him his painting was good, and he told me, smiling, it had been done a couple of hundred years ago. I didn't mind making a mistake in front of him. It was the first time he didn't call me the more formal 'Kyria'. It was also the first time I noticed how very blue his eyes are in his sun-darkened face.

As he turned away from me, he caught his arm on a piece of rusty iron. It ripped the thin cotton of his shirt and as he looked down at it he saw, as I did, that it had cut lightly through his skin and a line of blood droplets had sprung up. His arm trembled and he held it stiffly away from his body in an urge to control the shaking. His face was white, ghostly. 'Here, let me—' I started to say, but he pushed me roughly away and went quickly outside where I heard him retch repeatedly. I looked across to Yorgo who shrugged and said quietly, 'Just like his mother, she could never stand the sight of blood.' Before I could speak Christo was back with us, wiping his hand across his mouth. Colour was returning to his cheeks, his sleeve was buttoned tight over the wound. He never referred to it.

From the day little deaf and dumb Dimitri appeared huddled in the corner of the porch at school, Anthi seemed to change. And it was some time after that before she reappeared at the school.

There was nothing strange in that; she mostly only worked two or three days a week. On the days she wasn't there the children would all work together with the professor or Kyria Titica, but this time, Despina did not appear either.

I walked over to her house once or twice but it was deserted, and if she was working in her fields, I did not know which ones to try. Eventually I decided I must see her: I was worried.

From first light it was a terrible day; the worst I had ever seen here.

Rain poured down in sheets; thunder resounded through the hills, forks of lightning lit the dark clouds.

In the main room we kept the shutters closed against the torrents. There was a pleasant intimacy working by lamplight with Yorgo and Christo. We talked little.

At midday we paused and sat for a little looking out of the lower doorway at the street that had turned itself into a river. The terrace above, now made strong and safe, sheltered us.

'We really need more time for the new struts to dry and weather,' said Christo, frowning and shaking his head.

'I used old wood,' said Yorgo, 'deliberately, in case this happened.'

'You see,' Christo said to me, 'an old carpenter has his uses after all.'

'Not so old,' Yorgo replied. 'Aphrodite tells me we shall have a new baby in the spring.'

I could see him puff up with pride as he spoke.

'Congratulations,' I said, and he beamed.

'Did you need another baby?' asked Christo, and Yorgo chuckled.

'Well, we like the ones we have well enough, but Aphrodite wants a boy. She's in charge of all of that sort of thing.'

The rain had stopped as we talked and now the wind blew strongly.

'There you are,' said Yorgo, pointing outside, 'the wind will dry it all in no time.'

'I hope so,' I said, and got to my feet. 'I want to go to Anthi's house.'

'You can't go alone in this weather, you'll be blown away. I'll take the donkey and walk with you.' Christo had acquired his own animal from somewhere. He knew I was about to protest, so he quickly added, 'I'll call at your house, Uncle, and pick up the other saw we need for the beams.'

The rain had turned to a drizzle, but we were fighting the wind all the way along the beaten track to Pano Panagia. The journey, which usually took twenty minutes, took an hour. Christo insisted I sit on the donkey while he walked beside and guided us along the path. It was hard to speak and even harder to hear.

Around the last of the bends, the donkey stumbled and fell to one knee. Of course I fell with him; both of us hard up against Christo who staggered slightly. Then, holding me tightly round the waist with one hand, he shoved hard on the animal with the other and within moments we were all stable, upright and safe again.

I laughed to conceal my embarrassment. 'You are a hero, thank you.'

'Should I let you fall next time? Here, up again.' With what felt like a great heave, I was back on the animal and moving onwards. There was no other soul in sight. Houses we passed were shuttered fast against the outside world.

'Heavenly!' It was a great shout that ripped through the air and I turned quickly, looking from left to right. It was Anthi, and she was hurrying towards us from one of the fields. Voula was stumping along next to her, but Despina walked slowly after her, her eyes to the ground.

Anthi looked tired and drawn. Despina, now clinging to her mother's skirt, was still gazing at the ground. She hadn't spoken or shown any sign that she knew who I was.

Anthi looked at Christo. I mumbled an introduction and they briefly smiled at each other.

Christo knew that Anthi was a good friend to me but Anthi, to my surprise, could barely mumble a greeting in return. This was far from the Anthi I knew.

Christo broke the awkward silence and said, 'I will leave you with your friend.'

I jumped down from the donkey and promptly fell flat on my face, on the dirt and grit of the path. Everyone rushed to help me up, but as Anthi bent to grasp my arm, Voula, who had been skipping up and down, lost her balance and tumbled down, too.

Christo pulled me to my feet and we all started to laugh. It was only a moment but it had broken the awkwardness and, to my relief, even Despina gave a small half-smile.

Later that day, I walked back along the same path alone. The storm had cleared hours before and all was calm now. Anthi had insisted I leave while there was still some light in the sky and I trod the familiar track, thinking about the things I had learned that day. I was horrified by what Anthi told me she had discovered with the professor in the cave. But it was the unspoken words that affected me most. When she told me about the brigands, or whatever they were called, who had harmed that innocent family, her voice had quivered and she was trembling.

When I asked her who they were, she shook her head in such vigorous denial that it seemed to me that she did indeed know, but was not going to tell. Which meant her husband Manolis was implicated, or why not tell me? Other names would mean little to me.

I hurried back to the house. I wanted Christo to tell me what was going on. He was the only person I knew to ask. I had an instinctive feeling for his truthfulness; he knows everything about these hills.

Ahead of me was the house. A figure on the terrace was silhouetted against the skyline: Christo. He had waited for me to come home.

I found myself smiling for the first time that day. As I approached, he came down the steps and peered into the gloom.

'Is it you, Heavenly? Are you safe and well?'

I smiled. 'Yes, thank you, I am safe and well.'

I spoke to him about the things I had learned from Anthi and he looked sad and thoughtful. I had joined him on the terrace at first as he seemed in no hurry to get back to his cave, and then we had lit a fire in the living room and sat before it on a pile of blankets.

'You come from a country which has only once, I think, been at war with itself.'

I nodded. 'Certainly not in my lifetime.'

'Here, war and fighting is second nature to us. My grandmother, and before her my great-grandmother, always said every Cretan male child born will come out fighting; it is then up to the women in his life to teach him peace. This is why every traditional song that we have sung for generations tells of the same thing—always they are about the one perfect woman, the mother.'

I nodded again. 'Anthi told me some of this,' I said, and laughed. 'Even her own brother, who couldn't wait to leave home, still sings songs in praise of his mother.'

'The Greeks are ready for war,' he said, 'and especially here in the biggest of the islands. We are ready, always, for invasion. And it will come. What no one yet understands is from where it will come.'

'This is what I hear from Athens,' I said.

'The Cretans are the masters of being invaded; it has happened to us so many times we are always ready. But we don't always fight in regular armies. We get together in groups, small groups, and the hills that surround our villages are the best hiding places. This is what is happening here, now, I think. It is possible Manolis is involved in something, but also likely that it was a simple fight about a missing animal. Manolis is known as a hothead. He is not a popular man.'

'Poor Anthi,' I said. 'It must be awful to be married to a man like that.'

'She has two lovely children for compensation.'

'Daughters are not the same thing at all. She told me she is considered by her husband to be a failure because she has not given him a son.'

'Then the man is a fool. His daughters are beautiful.'

There was a wonderful stillness about him as he spoke. His gaze never left my face. I found this most extraordinary in a man. Usually they look anywhere but in my eyes directly. It is too revealing. But he had none of this anxiety, and there was a confidence in his words that, although spoken quietly, told me of the truth in him.

'I hate war, detest fighting. I prefer to save my energy for repairing your house, and think of my studies for building things up, rather than destroying, pulling them down. But I will be ready, and so will my friends, to fight any real enemy that tries to take us.'

Only the sharp crackles of the newly chopped log he had thrown on the fire broke the silence.

'Time for me to go back to my cave,' he said, 'although it is hard to take myself away from this fire, and . . .' He stopped quickly and shook his head.

'Sometimes I sleep right here,' I told him.

He laughed. 'You do no more than most of the shepherds.'

'I wondered about that,' I said. The fire flickered and I saw the flames reflected in his eyes. We had eaten bread and fruit and slices of cheese his aunt Aphrodite had made. He had showed me how to soak the sun-dried tomatoes that Anthi had given me in olive oil to soften them and release their sweet, sticky juices into our mouths. He poured a little wine into the only two glasses I owned and I told him that in England people said 'Cheers' when they toast each other.

He told me that he had wanted to speak English well since he was a child. We were speaking in English now. It was a pleasure and a relief to me to use my familiar tongue. I had even started dreaming in Greek.

'When we are together here, why don't we speak in English? It would be good for you and I should love it.'

'We must be careful. There is nothing more pleasing to the village women here than something to gossip about, and if we are speaking a different language to them, they will invent what they think we are saying, and it might not always be good.'

I answered without thinking, 'Does it matter? Do we care?'

'We have become friends and friendship between a man and a woman is unknown here. They will presume our relationship to be more.' I was just taking this in and considering what it could mean, when he spoke again: 'Also, I don't want my uncle Yorgo to feel excluded, isolated. However,' he said slowly, looking at me now, 'when we are alone together, like this, perhaps . . .?'

Quickly I leant across and threw another log onto the embers. My back was to him, he could not see my face. I knew I was blushing. I was trembling inside, but something made me say, 'Do you think we shall have other evenings like this then? Alone together?'

There was a long silence before he answered. 'Yes, I should like that. But right now I think you should move, or you may fall over and set fire to your hair.'

I turned back to him and, of course, as I did so, I hit my elbow, not badly enough to hurt, but enough to cause him to laugh.

'That is three knocks today. This is not good for you, all these tumbles, you will hurt yourself.'

I brushed myself down. I was wearing a long skirt I had made from a thick curtain I had found in an old trunk in one of the rooms. It was brightly coloured and warm, but attracted the dust, and bits liked to cling to it.

At the moment it was covered in warm ashes.

'You noticed my falls?'

'Of course I did.' And then into the silence he said, 'I notice everything about you.' Before I could react, he was on his feet and had moved to the door. 'Thank you for the food. Sleep well. May the angels watch over you tonight.'

Yorgo and Christo will be here soon. Last week Akis, the blacksmith from the forge in Aghios Georgios, was here with them, and the doors now all have proper fastenings to close them to the elements. It is a huge, childish pleasure of mine to open and close the shutters and doors, just because I can.

Now it is eight o'clock, but there is no sign of them. They are always here before this time and we start our day by taking coffee together.

Anthi has taught me well how the Greeks like their coffee, and it is certainly different to Hugh's drink, which was bitter and tasted burnt. I felt rather guilty when I threw his percolator away.

Wrapping my long curtain skirt round me for warmth, I walk outside and gaze along the path up through the village.

Christo said I looked like a sparkling firework in this homemade skirt. I think I am considered to be so eccentric here that my wearing window dressings surprises no one.

The early morning sunshine sends an arrow of warmth through me and here comes Christo now, urging his donkey along the path towards the house. He sits on the donkey like a jockey, leaning forward, a crop in his hand. Through the thick serge of his *vraka,* the muscles of his thighs look so strong. His shiny mountain boots encase his leg from the knee down. Does he clean them at night in his cave?

'No coffee. I must leave at once. Yorgo tried to come back with all the supplies alone from Sitia, Aphrodite told me, and of course he had an accident and they are scattered all over the mountainside. He left at dawn to retrieve them. I must go and find him. Will you wait here for Andreas? I have asked him to come today to measure for the windows.'

I take my coffee onto the terrace. The wind cannot make up its mind this morning; some moments it whips up the dust underfoot, and then there will be an hour or two of calm. Across the horizon down to the sea, clouds are tossing round in the sky, but it is still the same azure blue of a summer's morning.

I think back over the last weeks. I feel Christo and I have become good friends, but there is a caution between us. I cannot bring myself to speak of Hugh or think of Hugh. I know that I am pushing away all thoughts and memories of him.

At night, in the darkness, it is then that I allow thoughts of Christo to swim round in my head. Even as I feel a warm glow at these moments, I am frequently overcome by a wave of guilt. For I think of him in ways that should be reserved for my husband. I know it is wrong of me to think of him in this way but oh, it can send me to my own private heaven! Sometimes, when we sit by the fire in the evening, I am afraid he will feel the heat from my body and know it for what it is.

At last I see he is coming back, his donkey loaded with all the stuff Yorgo had tried to bring alone.

There is no sign of his uncle. I run down and together we bring everything inside. I stand alone in the middle of the main room for a moment, catching my breath.

Christo comes in quietly. I can feel his presence even before I see him. I know, as I turn, that we are standing too close together. Our eyes meet, interpreting our separate thoughts, and I can sense the knowledge we have of each other.

His eyes scan my face. I hesitate, my heart beating furiously in my chest. I know I shouldn't touch him, but I want to put my arms round his strong body, know I want to rub my cheek into his beard. I want everything and then more.

We turn away from each other at the same moment and when he speaks his voice is tight. 'Heavenly?' he says. Then again, 'Heavenly? What is it that you want? What can I do?'

But I can't speak, and we stand separate but together.

'Yia, Christo, yia, Kyria.' It is Andreas, and as quickly as it had come, whatever was in the air vanishes. Within moments, I am making coffee and they are discussing life. I put the coffee and a plate of Irini's biscuits on the table.

It was the middle of the day before Andreas left us. He had to go to Sitia and buy glass. I had to thrust my energy into doing something, so I began to clean up the house. After a while, I threw the broom down in frustration and swore aloud. It was pointless. All I was doing was moving the dust and woodchips from one place to another.

I wanted to weep.

Such a short time ago, my life had seemed perfect. Hugh was busy in Athens and I was content to be here. I took pleasure from my friendship with Anthi and her lovely daughters. My days at the school were a delight and gradually this house was becoming a home. I saw it all now through my tears as though all the goodness had been stripped away.

Yes, Hugh was happy in Athens, but if I was there or he here, would our physical life be a growing thing of ugliness between us? I remembered the nights of loneliness. And the days! Oh, those dreary days. Would I still be wandering from shop to shop, party to party?

I sit on the floor before the fire, which I had lit to warm me, and drop my head in my hands. And then there was Christo. What was happening to me?

I am forced to admit that I am a married woman in love with someone who is not her husband. I cannot lie to myself. I can make my head think of other things. I can exhaust my body with working, but I still ache for Christo each day in my heart and in every bit of me. I can hardly bear the thought of a day going by without seeing him. Whichever way I turn it will be wrong; follow my heart and I will always be guilty, follow my head and a lonely path lies before me. Tears fill my eyes.

As if he had sensed all or any of this, I heard him call softly. And then he was beside me. I was trembling. He paused and looked at me. 'Are you all right? You look strange, flushed.'

I couldn't speak. I couldn't be sure when I opened my mouth which words would fly out. Slowly I nodded my head, and he sat down beside me.

'It's too late to think of working today. It is already dark and you look as though you have had enough.' He threw a log on the fire and stirred the embers until it caught and strong flames were warming us through.

'Shall I tell you a story?'

I nodded.

'I will tell you about another uncle of mine, one who went to London, England.' I looked at him through my drying tears and he reached out his hand and took mine as he told me. His hand was firm and warm, and I worried that he would feel the trembling in mine.

'Many years ago, long before I was born, my Uncle Stephanos ran away to England, to London. He was thirteen and, coming from here, knew nothing of the ways of the world. First he worked as a waiter in a restaurant. For years he saved all his money, living on scraps he found in the kitchens. One evening, the owner of the restaurant, who was also the cook, fell and sprained his ankle. So Stephanos said he would do the cooking for that night. He had never cooked anything in his life before, but for years he had stood beside his mother in the kitchen and she would let him mix the flour and the eggs for the pastry, stuff the herbed mixture of meat and rice into the vine leaves, or taste the juniper in the *stifado*.

'That night in the restaurant he made only Greek dishes. He made a big tray of moussaka. He made *gemisto*: large, glistening tomatoes and zucchini filled with a meat mixture, sprinkled with olive oil and *rigani* and baked. And that night in the restaurant, he sweet-talked the customers into trying this new and very foreign food.'

By now I was enthralled. 'What happened?' I asked.

'That was the first night that everything from the kitchen was sold.'

I smiled. It was all he needed to encourage him to continue.

'Better than that, people came back for more. Before long, he had a reputation across that part of London and there were queues every night. Gradually he saved enough to open his own restaurant. He took a great risk, as Greek cooking was unknown in those days. He eventually had several restaurants, all over London, and he was a very rich man. Perhaps you know his restaurants?'

'London is a big city. What are they called?'

'Ilios. Each one is called Ilios—sunshine.'

I sat very still. Yes, I knew these restaurants. Hugh had taken me there the first time we left Greenbridge and went to London. Christo was right; the food was excellent.

Hugh, Hugh, Hugh. Now he was here in the room with me. If I closed my eyes I could see his face.

'Is something wrong ? You are very white.'

I jumped up and, moving very fast, was suddenly on the other side of the room.

'Nothing wrong, nothing at all. It's a lovely story, thank you for telling me.'

I was in the dark corner beside the wine press. I could see his face only by the light of a sudden flame. He was puzzled and, getting up, moved across to me.

'Have I upset you? Telling you a story about England? I am so sorry, it was thoughtless. I have made you homesick for your friends, your family.' He was beside me now, very close beside me, and his voice faltered, 'And homesick for your—'

I knew what he was going to say and I couldn't bear him to. I had to stop him and the only way I knew how was to kiss him. So I did.

It seemed as though it were the most natural thing in the world. His lips were soft and gentle. His hands rose and caressed my cheek, my brow. He gently pulled the comb from my hair and his fingers wandered through my tangles, smoothing them. He pulled away from me, but only for a moment, and then his arms were round me and his kiss was strong and sweet and seemed everlasting.

My fingers were moving across his back when he pulled away and looked at me. 'Heavenly, Heavenly,' he said, 'that is what you are to me.'

My breath was fast and hard and while my head was thinking, *This is too bold, too soon*, my heart and my body were urging my hands onwards, and I was undoing the lacing at the top of his shirt. It was rough hemp and as it parted I felt the intoxicating silkiness of his skin against my hand. He raised his arms and pulled it over his head. Then he took my hand in his and walked me back to the fire. Still standing, his body close to mine, he looked into my eyes and said, 'Are you sure?'

I nodded. 'I am sure, quite sure.'

Together we sank to the rugs and his hands were moving more strongly now and tugging at my skirt. Released of all our clothing, I gasped as his firm body moved over mine. His fingers reached down softly and his lips kissed my breasts. He paused to say, 'So beautiful, my Heavenly,' and I trembled with a pleasure I had waited for all my life.

ANTHI

SLEEP IS an elusive thing that only babies and drunks seem able to do easily, in this house at least. My body is so exhausted each night that I drop sometimes wherever I am and sleep like the dead. But only for a couple of hours and then my dreams haunt me and I wake fast, my heart thumping in my chest. Then I lie until dawn in silent wakefulness. Despina is often there beside me these nights. Sometimes I think she has woken me by stroking my face, as if she wants me to share in her own sleeplessness.

She used to sleep fast at night. I could barely wake her for the morning. That was before—oh, everything good was before.

Despina is growing fast, but it seems to me sometimes that inside her child's body beats the heart of an old woman. It is as though she knows too much of the world. There is suspicion in her eyes. She jumps and turns at the slightest sound, she rarely smiles. She talks again, but very little, not like before, and she will do anything to keep close to my side.

'It's just a phase. She is growing up. She will grow out of it.' Everyone has said so: Professor Tsimbanakis, even Heavenly. But I am beginning to find it hard to remember the child who laughed every day.

Voula is tottering round and I can see in her face, her sweet, round, apple-cheeked face, the woman she will one day become. She is a solemn little girl, not given to constant laughter as Despina was. She is thoughtful, watchful and then, when she has decided who you are, and whether you are a good thing to have in her day, her face will suddenly crease and a rich, sweet chortle will emerge from her rosy lips.

'Are you coming to the school today, Mama?' Despina asks.

'No, child, but Athena will come for you, so wash your hands and face and get your books. Heavenly will be there today, I think.' And she smiles and something of the old Despina is there as she skips away.

The spring sun is already beating warmly on my back as we take the laundry loaded on Astrape to the spring. Aphrodite is there ahead of me and greets me with a loud welcome.

'There were some women from Pano Panagia here earlier and they said something about war. And Yorgo heard some talk of it in Tres Petromas last night.'

'Did Yorgo remember anything more?' I ask, and she laughs.

'When he has taken drink Yorgo doesn't know whether it's Wednesday or April.' She doesn't mention Manolis, so neither do I.

'Your English friend, Heavenly, wouldn't she have some idea? Her husband sends her news from Athens, doesn't he?'

'I'll ask her,' I say.

Heavenly's house is just a little way above the spring and there is silence from there as I walk closer.

I pause a little before we arrive and look round at my beautiful hills. So quiet, so peaceful, only the ring of goat bells and the cries of birds, dots in the sky as they fly past. Is this peace to be shattered soon? Men crowd nightly into Il Piperia to listen to the news from Athens, but they rarely share it with their wives. Manolis, however, would sooner be seen in his grave than go to what he considers to be the haunt of communists. He has his own sources of information, I'm certain, and he would laugh at the thought of telling me anything.

Voula is impatient, clapping her hands together, calling, 'Helly, Helly.' But Heavenly is nowhere to be seen.

Then suddenly I hear her laugh. No one in Panagia laughs like Heavenly. It starts from deep inside, and pulses fast and rich as it reaches her throat.

It is answered by a man's rich echo. Someone is happy. I tether Astrape and wait a moment. Oddly, I have a sudden notion of intimacy from inside. The closed door seems to divide us into two worlds. It seems wrong to interrupt without warning.

I'm rescued by a shout and Yorgo appears at the end of the path.

'*Yia*, Kyria,' he calls up to me, a full bucket clanking in each hand, 'you are well today?' And Voula answers him for me, '*Yia!*'

In the house the laughter has stopped, and seeing the door is open a little, I step slowly inside.

Christo is at the top of a ladder and at first I fail to see Heavenly. She is standing against the ladder on the furthest side, one foot raised carelessly on a rung. I'm sure the purpose is to steady it, but her skirt is pulled up and a long tanned leg looks oddly naked from where I stand.

Her head turns in my direction and I see the sun catch her face and light it up. She is flushed and smiling. I have never seen her look as beautiful as she does at this moment.

Above her, Christo smiles down and, after greeting me, asks her to pass him another brush.

It is several weeks since I have been here and in that time something has happened, something that has changed them both. It's barely a moment before I guess what it is. There is an aura, almost tangible around them, and they seem to shine. It is the sun, I tell myself. But I don't believe it.

Flustered, I make my way into the kitchen and offer to make some coffee. Heavenly moves forward. 'Here, let me.'

'No, if you don't mind, let me do it for you.'

'Of course, if you'd like to.'

She has gone back into the living room where I can see Christo smiling to see her again, as if she has been away a week.

Yorgo is in and out of the room with his buckets, singing softly to himself: songs telling anyone who wants to know how much he loves his mother. He seems oblivious to the electricity that sparks between Heavenly and Christo. Yet I know I am not imagining it. Intrigued, anxious, I stay longer than I mean to. They seem not to notice I am here, so absorbed are they in each other.

The house is changed now every time I see it. Christo is a craftsman, just as his uncle is, and between them the house is slowly regaining its ancient majesty. The stone floor in this room is painted a warm red, contrasting brilliantly with the richness of the old rugs that had not seen daylight since the Orfanoudakis family lived here. And downstairs, where the animals lived, is being transformed into rooms, each opening onto the lower terrace.

Christo and Heavenly chat to each other, occasionally including Yorgo, or even me, for a moment's questioning: the angle of a stone, the slope of the floor. But while Yorgo nods in agreement, or I shake my head, it is simply politeness.

Yorgo leaves at noon to take lunch with Aphrodite and whichever of his children are around. I wait for a moment and then say in a rush, 'I must go home. See, Voula now needs more food than I can give her from . . . from me . . .' I falter, suddenly embarrassed. That's what it is like here today. I no longer feel at ease with them both, as I do when I'm alone with Heavenly.

Taking Voula by the hand, I mutter goodbye and move towards the door. But Heavenly is there ahead of me.

'Stay,' she says. 'Why not take some food with us? We have plenty.'

'Oh, no,' I say, too quickly, 'I must go home now and Voula must sleep. Thank you.'

'But I have so much to tell you. I desperately want to see you alone and talk to you. So much is changing in my life and I need, want, to share it with you.'

'I can see,' I say, more coldly than I mean to. 'I am not blind or foolish. The changes are written clearly on your face. And . . . and him.'

'Oh, dear God, is it that obvious?' And she flushes bright pink. But she is so happy, it's hard for me to be angry with her.

'My dear friend, you must take care. You know how gossip flies through this village, and there are already questions about the way you work in the house with the men.'

She looks astonished. 'Is that true? I only help here on the days when I am not with you at the school. I can't just sit around and watch them. I would go mad, and I am learning so much.'

'I think it's not only about house-building you are learning.'

She looks straight at me, her eyes shining with truth. 'I am in love with him, and I believe he is with me. I have never in my life felt such happiness before this. Don't tell me to stop because I don't think I can.'

'And Hugh? Your husband? Am I to forget you are married? As you seem to have done.'

Her face changes, taking on a look of great sadness.

I take her hand in both of mine. 'Be careful! This is not Athens or London. If the women here see you appear to discard your husband so easily, they will fear for their own, and turn against you. You are an outsider with different ways to us. They watch you closely and a woman who spends time alone with two men in her house is a feast for someone who hungers for trouble in a dull round of work and children.'

She looks not only stricken, but totally shocked. 'I mean no harm. I love this village and all my neighbours. I have felt so free here and I think I have at last found out who I am and how I want to live.'

Tears now freely pour down her cheeks. I have frightened her beyond words and I am filled with guilt.

I hug her to me. 'I meant only that you must take care. Be watchful of yourself. Your happiness shines from your eyes and anyone who looks at the two of you together will jump to the most obvious conclusion. Be on your guard. I think Yorgo is oblivious to anything except his family and his work. But your neighbours are used to wandering in and out of your house as if it were their own. They will see the glances, the unspoken words before you even think them.'

She rubs the drying tears from her face. 'I know what you are telling me is right. I suppose I have been a careless idiot. Only tell me that you understand? Tell me that you forgive me. I have fallen so in love I hardly know myself. I barely tolerate each moment without him, longing for the sight of him again.'

A wedge of sun shines down between us but I feel only chill. 'There is little I can say to you. This love you speak of is unknown to me and I suspect to most of the women here. Our marriages are arranged for us as transactions; land changes hands and we smile and dance through a ceremony that has little to do with our feelings. We survive: that is all I ask each day. Love is something I reserve for my girls. All I can say to you is, take care.'

Truly, I feel a great shaft of pain shoot through me as I speak. Envy. How I long to feel even a little of something like this.

Her fingers grip mine tightly.

'From now on I will look at Christo as if he is the ugliest man I have ever seen.' And she pulls a face full of such disgust, I can only laugh.

Although I leave Heavenly's house with laughter, it lasts only a moment. 'She must be so careful,' I find myself repeating as Voula and I ride home.

I had reached Yorgo and Aphrodite's house when I was called to a halt. Yorgo had run out of his door and was waving me down, calling, 'Kyria Anthi, stop, stop!' Aphrodite, holding her youngest child in her arms, was behind him. 'It is true. Everything the women from Pano Panagia at the spring said is coming true!'

'What do you mean?'

'War! There is going to be a war!'

A cold wave of fear rippled through me and I gripped Voula tightly in my arms. 'Tell me what you have heard, what is happening?'

'Guns, all our guns. We have to take them to the square this afternoon. The general has ordered it. It is the same in every village.'

'Your Pappous,' Aphrodite nodded at me, 'he is to be in charge for now. He is sending Michaelis, and anyone else he can get hold of, round the village, upper, lower and middle, and we are all to gather in the square with our weapons at five o'clock. Tell anyone you pass and we shall see you later in the square.'

Heavenly. I must tell her what is happening. I head back to her house.

Voula wailed when she realised we were going in the wrong direction for food, but cheered up when she saw we were back at Heavenly's house.

A little later she was sitting on a cushion at Heavenly's feet, munching happily on a piece of apple and a rusk dipped in milk. We are waiting for Christo, who had gone straight up to Il Piperia when Michaelis called with the summons.

We didn't have to wait long. We heard him as he ran up the steps.

'It is not war,' he said, 'yet. But Metaxas is taking a precautionary measure. With the army in Albania, if defence is needed here, there will be no weapons for the volunteers or the conscripts to fight with. There is no need to panic.' Heavenly looked dubious.

During the afternoon I felt more relaxed in their company. They were so happy together and they included me so warmly, it was impossible to feel otherwise.

Heavenly, proud of the new skills she had learned, didn't mind that I took over her kitchen and provided cold lemonade or sliced fruit while she skimmed and smoothed a wall with white *isvesti*.

It is impossible to miss the importance of the gathering at five o'clock. Half an hour before, there started first a trickle and then a constant stream of villagers along the pathways and tracks leading to the village square. They came from their firesides, their gardens and fields.

When the girls and I arrive in the square it seems as though the entire population of the island is gathered there. Every wall has become a seat for the older villagers. Babies and children are in their parents' arms or on shoulders. Games of football and cup-and-stick start, and girls whizz themselves deftly in and out of skipping ropes or jumping hoops made from large twigs.

There is one thing in common with everyone gathering here: most adults, and even one or two of the children, have a gun. A rough assortment: battered, rusty and creaking in movement, hauled out of attics or cellars or taken down from walls.

A large table is being dragged along from a nearby house and several pairs of hands lift it onto the stone platform in front of the old village hall, creating a focus for the activities. There is a buzz in the air; nothing so exciting has happened in Panagia for years.

At the back of the platform sits Manolis's brother, Stelios, the grape treader. In his hand the lyre that I know he can play exquisitely. Beside him, the fiddler known as Pipos and his son, on a small drum. Cautiously, and at first rather tunelessly, they begin to play a traditional song and one or two of the younger women, careless of the solemnity of the occasion, link arms in a dance.

'Do these idiots think it is a party?' The thick nasal twang tells me the priest, Papa Yannis, is here. If he is, then Manolis will not be far behind.

In front of the platform is a growing heap of weaponry. While some are reluctant to part with anything until absolutely necessary, others throw their weapons down swiftly and casually carry on their conversation.

Coming down the hilly path from Mesa Panagia is my Pappous. Sitting astride his donkey and firmly looking ahead, he comes to a stop at the front of the gathering and slips easily to the ground, his every movement that of a much younger man.

A growing hush sweeps over the crowd like a breeze. Pappous is hoisted onto the platform by his friends; he looks magnificent in my eyes and I feel so proud to be his granddaughter. By his side is the old Turkish *yatagan*, the magnificent sword that is usually hung over the fireplace in his house. It had been captured by his great-grandfather in the war against the Turks over a hundred years ago.

Pappous raises his right hand in the air and the last whisper dies away. 'People of Panagia,' he says, and his voice carries to the far reaches of the square. 'I am here today instead of my dear friend Andreas Mamadopolous. A man we all loved, admired and respected. I make no pretence to be able to take his place here fully. But until we have been appointed a new mayor, I will do as I can. Most of you know that these are dark times for our country. There is much unrest across the whole of Europe and especially among the Balkan nations. We none of us know from where will come any attack. But clearly our leaders in Athens and our recently restored King believe there is danger for us. We must help. Every one of us must give up our own weapons for the greater good of Crete.'

'I'll keep mine and shoot any enemy that comes near me!' comes a shout from the crowd. Others cheer and call, 'So will I.'

'It is not an option for you to keep your gun, Kyrios Matalous. If it is not surrendered by the end of this week, there will be only punishment for you and anyone else who chooses to turn their back on patriotism.

'Here, see,' and his hand waves the heavy *yatagan* over his head and rests it down atop the weaponry already there. 'Do as I do,' he says and a cheer rises from the crowd at his gesture.

I see that Christo is here now, but no sign of Heavenly. I am relieved, as they should not be seen in public together, and no one would expect her to have a weapon to relinquish. Manolis is also here. I duck my head down to speak to Voula and hope he does not see me. He would expect me to be at his side.

The pile of weapons is growing smaller as Michaelis and his friends have started to gather them up and carry them for safekeeping inside the old village hall. They are to be locked and guarded there until the prefecture in Lasithi has time to collect them and dispatch them to where they are needed.

'I'm hungry, Mama!' Despina says, and Voula claps her hands at the thought of more food. I sigh, for it is the middle of the Lenten fast and hard for me always to find enough to eat for the girls without breaking it. My family expect me to adhere strictly to the rules as they have always done: no oil, meat, fish, eggs, milk or cheese. How are we to nourish our children without the simplest essentials?

Manolis pretends to keep the fast and the laws of Lent, but I know that he eats with his friends elsewhere, for he comes home reeking of garlic and wine.

When we get home, I prepare a dish of greens with a stew of lentils and beans with potatoes, tomatoes and herbs. I say a quick prayer to the Virgin for forgiveness as I liberally splash in olive oil.

My girls eat hungrily. There is barely enough left for Manolis when they are finished, so I must make do with some forbidden bread soaked in the juices. But really I am too disturbed to think of food for myself just now. Heavenly today has shocked and frightened me. I don't think she has any idea of the real danger she is in. And this man, this Christo. Oh, yes, I can see he is charming—he has certainly charmed her. But he is Greek. He will tire of her and move on to another after the novelty of the conquest has worn off—they all do.

The slightest hint of scandal and people like Papa Yannis will look for her to be driven out of the village. And nothing any of us can do will help her.

HEAVENLY

Athens, Easter 1939
My dear Evadne,
I cannot begin to tell you how awful it is here now. War, war, war is all anyone speaks of and our letters are now being xxxxxxxxxxxxxxxxxxxxxxxxxx so I shall be brief. I can tell you that it seems to me now that you are in the best, the safest place. The Italians now appear to xxxxxxxxxxxxxxxxxxxxxxxxxxxxxxxxxxxxxxxxxxx.
The Embassy insists that we must stick to the Orthodox Lenten fast. So I am now stick-thin and hungry most of the time. However, thank goodness for Foxy, who has managed to find a nightclub or two that defies the protocol and we can get a steak or a good chop, but at a price!
The stock of decent French wine here is terribly depleted and all we can get on most days is some local stuff.
I have the great honour of spending a little of each day with the royal family. Naturally we are worried about their safety so I think xxxxx xxxxxxxxxxx.
I've a nasty feeling that everything I write is pretty suspect.
I send you all my love, darling, take great care of yourself,
Your beloved husband, Hugh

In many ways it is something of a relief to me that Hugh's letters are censored. For the last weeks the very thought of him stirs appalling guilt in me.

I have never known such feelings. I couldn't imagine before that it was even possible to feel like this. Such love, such longing, such desire! How does anyone live with such depths of passion?

I know the need to keep everything utterly secret. When she is here, Anthi watches us both like an eagle hunting a mouse. We have learned to avoid even a glance when anyone is around. I can feel my face blush when he comes within touching distance.

We have been lovers now for two months and four days. At first we would snatch moments alone together here. We encouraged Yorgo to leave early each evening, saying he should spend more time with his children, his wife, even his animals. Profuse with his thanks, he would at first reluctantly, and then speedily, depart. We fell on each other as soon as he was down the path. As if starving, we would touch, kiss, taste and inhale each other.

As the sun stayed later over each day's sky, we had to decide between the danger of his lingering, when any of my neighbours might enter at will or, as on many days now, whether I should go out later in the evening and walk alone up into the hills to visit him in his cave.

Sometimes, passing one of my neighbours on these evenings, I feel the need to invent a reason for my late journey; a visit to the church, a need for some air or, and this one I was especially proud of, drawing a view, a waterfall or an odd-shaped tree to send to my husband in Athens.

It was when Anthi guessed that Christo and I had become more than good friends that I realised the danger I was in from the gossips around me. Night after night, I wake from frightened dreams of being pursued by a crowd of angry villagers and told never to return to the place I now love more than anywhere I have been in my life.

When Christo learned how I was tormenting myself, he took it upon himself to put my world in proper perspective for me.

We were lying in his cave on a thick and beautiful rug that had belonged to his great-grandmother. Our lovemaking had been more frantic than usual that night and I found myself weeping uncontrollably. His strong arms held me tightly, his fingers stroking a gentle rhythm through my hair, his lips taking up the tears as they fell.

'Heavenly, Heavenly,' he said. 'Why so sad? Please tell me what's wrong. Has someone upset you? Is there word from Athens?'

I sniffed, blew my nose, and rubbed my tears away roughly with my hands. I could not bear to think of Hugh as I was lying in Christo's arms.

'No, nothing from Athens. It is me, I am what's wrong. I am just so afraid. Suppose we are discovered and I am forced to leave? I could not bear that. I belong to you so completely that I cannot live without you.'

'My dearest love. Are you thinking anyone is interested in us?'

I nodded. 'That is what the women do here, they gossip. Of course they must see us and see what I feel for you. What else?'

He could see that I was genuinely afraid. 'Listen to me. Every day I am out in the village. I am known and trusted here. Believe me, they have far more to worry about now than to give us more than a passing glance. They care for the weather, the crop yields, the tobacco subsidy, the tomato harvest, their olives. On top of all that now, they worry about the war that is brewing on their doorstep. They listen to the radio each night in the *kafenion*, as many of them as can get inside, to see what is happening in Albania.'

I smiled. Of course he was right. 'Anthi says we are in danger, we must be careful every moment. Are you saying she is wrong?'

'No, she is right to be concerned. We must take care. We must keep our lives to ourselves, of course. But if we behave with discretion, as we do, and be quiet with our love, then Panagia will get on with its life and we can get on with ours.'

Inside I knew it was my guilt that plagued me. I was afraid, not really for my neighbours, but for Hugh. I had met and married Hugh because I thought I had fallen in love with him. I had been a sad and lonely person and he had come into my life; picked up this ugly duckling and offered her life as a swan.

My actions over these last weeks, months, astonished me. I had given myself so completely to Christo. But what of my love for Hugh? Where had that gone? If I could discard him so easily and replace him with Christo, was I merely a fickle woman with feelings of no depth?

It is the week after Easter and I call to see Aphrodite and Yorgo and their children to take them some of the cheese that Irini has made for me. I know any additional food will be well received because Yorgo's cousin and his family are visiting.

Their house is quiet.

Usually when visitors are here there is music, dancing and laughter spilling through the windows and doors. Tonight there is just a lonely, echoing silence. Aphrodite opens the door and hugs me.

'Welcome. Have you seen Anthi? Or Christo?'

I shake my head.

'Then you won't know what has happened. Sotiri and his family have not come. There is no word from them, and they should be here by now. We heard that they left their home in Tirana days and days ago. Something must be terribly wrong. Yorgo has gone to Il Piperia to see if there is some news on the wireless set.'

I try to offer reassuring words, but it is difficult to know what to say.

A familiar voice speaks behind me and I spin round, unable to prevent myself smiling at my lover.

'Aphrodite,' he says, merely nodding acknowledgment at me. 'Yorgo not back yet?' There is no need for her to answer. 'He left Il Piperia ahead of me; I thought to come straight here to you.' He shakes his head. 'It's not good news, I am afraid. On Good Friday, Italy landed troops in all the Albanian ports and marched on Tirana. Within twenty-four hours, they had completely occupied the country and declared it part of Italy.'

Aphrodite draws in her breath sharply and begs the Virgin Mary for help. Tears are forming in her eyes. Her girls, sensing there is something wrong, flock round her, hanging onto her skirts and whimpering, 'Mama, Mama, what's happening? Where is Papa?'

Yorgo finally appears home late, as he had stopped everyone he met to pass on the news. Many people round here have relatives in Albania. He is not alone when he comes in: Aphrodite's aunt, Yanna, is with him, a plump woman who carries with her always the sweet smell of baking bread mixed with the scents of lavender and acacia blossom that grow in profusion round her tiny house in Kato Panagia.

The soft white skin of her face is creased, and damp with tears. As Aphrodite gathers her in and pours a large glass of what I take to be brandy, Yorgo says quietly to me, 'She has three boys, all in Albania. She has heard nothing from them for weeks.' He is shaking his head sadly.

I feel a slight tug on my arm and turn round to see Christo. He looks so serious. 'I will take you home, Heavenly; this is a place for family tonight. You and I should not be here.'

I am about to protest, to tell him I will leave and perhaps he should stay, but he is already moving to the door with my sleeve still caught in his grip, so I can only go with him. Once outside, having called a hasty goodbye, he says, 'This is a bad day for many here.'

'I will go home. I can feel you would like to be somewhere else just now, not worrying about me.'

His smile is brief. 'I will go back to Il Piperia and see if I can help in some way there.'

The days lengthened slowly again, and while the news from abroad filtered gradually through to us, all of it bad, at least the promise of a better year for food came in with the sun, offering survival at least.

One afternoon, when the girls were resting after their lunch, Anthi and I sat under the shade of a flowering almond tree that grew at the top of their garden. In the distance seabirds called to each other, that long, sad sound they make. The silence between us was comfortable and slow.

'Do you think there will be a war?' Anthi suddenly looked anxious.

'Yes, I am afraid I do, at least across a lot of Europe. Whether it will affect Greece, I can't tell you. Even if it does, it is not certain that it would affect Crete. Hugh can't say much in his letters, but he seems to imply that this is the safest place to be.'

'My Pappous feels that we would not have had the collection of arms unless it was intended to use them.'

'Christo agrees with him about that. His friend from Sitia, Kotso, has convinced him that there is no doubt of war. He says that across the rest of the country, villagers are preparing for invasion. Whether from Italy or Germany, he seems unsure.'

Christo is spending more and more time with Kotso and tells me he thinks him well informed. I like him very much. He is small and chunky with stocky, well-muscled legs. He is always smiling and seems to find humour in everything. I suspect he has guessed that Christo and I are lovers, but he is relaxed when we are all together. What I didn't tell Anthi was that he has persuaded Christo to help form a band of young village men. They are to operate together in secret in the hills and could, at a moment's notice, be ready to fight any enemy.

I shivered as if there were a sudden chill: war, fighting, hate; I long for the wonderful peace I found in these hills when I first came here.

'Oh, I wish we could do something!' Anthi suddenly spoke aloud. Often between us it was as though we shared each other's thoughts.

'I do have an idea,' I said.

'Tell me.'

'Well, why don't I teach the children simple first aid?' She looked puzzled. 'It would help us to feel we were actually doing something, rather than sitting wringing our hands like the other women.

'Then, I'm thinking, we could all help if the war did come as far as here. Of course,' I added quickly, 'of course it won't, we know that, but there are always accidents of one sort or another, and how terrific if the children were able to offer proper help.'

Anthi merely gazed at me. 'Is there something you know and are not telling me?' She spoke quietly.

'No, no, I swear, but it is something I could easily do. So could you if I showed you how.'

There was a moment, and then she picked up on my excitement.

'Yes, that's a really good idea.' She was smiling. 'I shall speak to the professor next week.'

Luckily, Professor Tsimbanakis thought it a good idea, too, and found a little money from his government allowance that would pay for a few cloth bandages and surgical spirit. Water, with the addition of red ink, made an excellent substitute for blood. The children loved this especially, and at first were bleeding profusely every day, and limping round the school with supposedly broken limbs. But they soon settled down and began to take it seriously.

I ran the first-aid group after school twice a week. The first rush of excitement settled into a small group of stalwarts who confessed to me that being doctors or nurses was what they wanted to do when they were grown up. Many days I took this ragged collection outside and down to the little cobbled square to bandage each other.

Sometimes they persuaded one of the old men who sat on the benches there, in the shade of the ilex tree, sipping their daily ouzo, to be patients. There was no shortage of willing volunteers who would sit with an arm or a leg in the air while telling their 'doctor' or their 'nurse' how they had come by the old scars that most of them sported.

I learned much of Panagia's recent hostile history in this spot during these warm days, with the sound of the cicadas chirruping.

For a while, Christo and Kotso thought this was really something of a joke: children learning to dress wounded soldiers? What nonsense! But it was the children who refused to listen to their laughter that soon convinced them to take it seriously. Marina, daughter of the blacksmith, and Despina, had emerged as the natural leaders and came to me after school one day when Kotso and and another friend were teasing them without mercy.

Kotso was lying on the ground groaning, his head in Andros's lap. 'Help me,' he called, 'my leg has fallen off, nurse. Please sew it back on.'

Despina pointed to them and said to me, 'Please, can you make them stop?'

'Even if I do, little one, they will only come back tomorrow,' I said.

One of the old men, sitting hunched over his glass, waved his stick in the air and said, 'They have nothing to do all day, lazy *malakas*, but to come here and torment children.'

There was no answer that I could make to this, but I knew that while Kotso and his friends may have had their days free, their nights were busy locating and clearing old mountain tracks and hideaways disused for years.

'Please, Heavenly,' Marina said, 'why don't you ask our parents to come and we can show them what we are doing.'

'And anyone else who thinks we are just playing,' added Despina, looking directly at the laughing Andros.

And so, on a day when the sun shone blindingly down, a motley collection of adults: parents, aunts, uncles, pappouses and yayas walked or struggled slowly up through the wooded mountain paths to the little church of Saint Kosmas and Damianus, built a hundred and fifty years ago to house the holy relics of a long-forgotten priest. It was the professor, I suspect urged by his wife Titica, who suggested that we could set up our own little clinic in this church at the top of the mountain.

'It is mostly unused,' he said, 'except one day a year in October, when it celebrates the name day. And it is most suitable. Kosmas and Damianus were two brothers who healed the sick and needy and charged nothing. It will need cleaning, but I am sure the children will help.

'I will need to get permission, of course,' he continued, 'from the diocese, but I think Papa Costas will be happy to support us.'

Permission had been swiftly granted, and the children and one or two of the mothers had swept and dusted, rubbed and polished, and washed and scrubbed every inch of the inside of the church.

I had asked that Christo make Kotso and Andros come. He had not been easy to persuade. 'I know Yorgo is going,' he said. 'If I come too, that is several hours lost when we could be working on the roof.'

I wondered for a moment if he was staying away for fear of being exposed to the sight of blood.

'Oh, all right, Heavenly. I'll threaten Kotso and Andros with a flogging if they do not come to your demonstration.'

ANTHI

THE STRAGGLING LINE of people climbed slowly up the mountain path for the first-aid demonstration. My Pappous was in front with Yaya on the donkey behind him. Children ran round impatiently on and off the path. Their parents, mostly mothers, tried and failed to keep them in any form of order. Not many fathers had been persuaded to appear. They should have been working the fields but, with wives safely occupied elsewhere, I had no doubt the *kafenions* were full.

A great shout tore through the air, stilling the laughter. We had our first casualty: Vilandis the baker had tripped on a rock and the wicker tray of bread on his head had shed its load over the scrub and sandy path. His oaths were scattered to the sky as he tried to decide whether he minded more his flying loaves or the gash bleeding through his flax breeches. The villagers had no such problem: flying bread was fair game and, within moments, it had all disappeared into pockets or baskets.

The air inside the church was cool and sweet. The professor stood at the front, at Papa Costas's invitation, and there was a respectful quiet, broken quickly by Vilandis who limped painfully forwards and lowered himself down onto a bench. He groaned and said, 'I am a true patient today—so here you are, mend my leg.'

The children giggled and looked to Heavenly for guidance.

'Right,' she said, 'Despina and Tika, this patient is for you. What are you going to do?'

The two little girls skipped forwards, glowing with pride that they had been chosen to be first.

'Shall we wash his leg?' asked Tika.

'Yes,' said Heavenly, 'that's always the first thing to be done, isn't it? Vilandis, do you wish to remove your breeches yourself or shall the nurses do it for you?'

Vilandis stammered, 'Oh, it's not so bad, I think I'll wait . . .'

But Heavenly was swiftly on him, rolling up his trouser leg gently, and exposing the angry red gash on his skin.

'Yes,' she said, tucking strands of her hair back, 'this wound needs urgent attention before poison sets in.' At the word 'poison', one or two of the older women crossed themselves. Despina and Tika had filled a vessel with cool, fresh water and, with swabs of clean cotton, were gently bathing the wound.

I was proud of them. They did not flinch or hesitate, although this was certainly the first real blood they had seen since the lessons began. Heavenly smiled at them and whispered something, at which Tika took the dish of dirty water outside and Despina pulled a wad of clean cotton from one of the boxes of dressings we had brought up the hill. Dribbling antiseptic on the cotton, she swabbed the wound clean.

Within moments Vilandis was standing again, his breeches tidied and a smile on his face.

'I reckon you were born to be nurses, you girls,' he said. 'This leg feels better already.' And turning, he walked back to sit beside his wife.

Standing in a huddle at the side, Christo had indeed persuaded Kotso and Andros to come, and Kotso now volunteered for treatment 'for a very severe headache'.

There was laughter as he moved to the front.

'Less *raki* at night would cure that,' shouted some wit. Meanwhile, Dimitri had slowly and thoughtfully started to bind Kotso's head with a large white bandage.

Kyria Titica was passing round cups of cool lemonade she had brought, and the demonstration continued until every child was winding bandages and fitting splints and tourniquets, and it seemed there were more patients than in the hospital in Sitia.

Suddenly, there was a disturbance from a group of women sitting under the big window at the rear of the church.

'Why do they need all this modern stuff: gauze and antiseptic?' someone called out. 'We don't have money for that sort of thing here.' One of the women from Kato Panagia was on her feet, a tiny but aggressive widow I knew as a troublemaker. 'We have always done well enough with poultices we make ourselves from leaves and berries, and they are free!' Around her a couple of her cronies called out their agreement.

'Did you never lose someone close to you to infection and disease?' the professor asked. For a moment there was a hush.

'I did,' said one woman rising to her feet; a gentle-looking woman, her face like fresh kneaded dough. It was the widow Kariakis, a sad, lonely woman who cared as best she could for her three daughters. 'My husband and my sister died from green leg. The doctor came too late to save them; he cut off both their legs. What use was that? They were dead by the end of the week.'

She was wiping her eyes roughly; the memory had stirred her feelings. There were murmurs of sympathy from all round and there was a flutter as most of the women crossed themselves hastily.

'And my sister-in-law,' called someone, 'died from child-birth fever. How could you help with that?'

Heavenly stood tall and firm now, and looked round her. She was a commanding figure, her eyes fiery and determined. 'Of course we cannot perform miracles, but we can certainly try to improve things.' Her face was flushed, but only I could see how nervous she was.

'There will always be a need for home cures and remedies,' she said. 'No one can deny the value and strength of wormwood, or barberry, and I am sure there are many more, but I intend to have all modern drugs and dressings sent to us from Athens. There is no reason why, simply because Panagia Sta Perivolia is a mountain village in a remote part of Crete, we should suffer from a lack of knowledge that is freely available in the rest of Greece.' There were cries of approval from many in the church now. She had touched a weakness that they well knew: the feeling they were not a part of civilised Greece.

The professor thanked us and then added, 'I am pleased to thank our very special friend, Kyria Heavenly. She has come from many miles away to share her knowledge with our small community. Thank you, Kyria, from everyone in our village.' He clapped and within moments most people had joined in. I could see Heavenly was scarlet with embarrassment, but she busied herself with the children in a demonstration of how to bandage a sprained ankle.

By the end of the afternoon some were beginning to shuffle towards the door, when a shadow fell across the porch. I felt before I saw a new, cold presence. Two men stood there; my husband and his friend, Papa Yannis. A ripple of dislike and fear was almost tangible in the church, I thought, but there were one or two calls of welcome as some stood aside to let them pass through.

Manolis's shaved head was hazy with grey stubble, and a strong odour of sweat and tobacco came from the damp, soiled vestments of the priest. The professor stepped forwards to greet them; Papa Costas right behind him, his clean robe putting the fat priest to shame.

'Is it October the ninth already, Costas?' puffed Papa Yannis, wiping his sweating brow. 'Are we celebrating St Kosmas's day so soon?'

The arrival of these two men had changed even the very air. I'm certain it wasn't just me that felt it; all the mamas, the pappous and yayas, everyone was now shuffling towards the door.

Heavenly moved to my side and I felt the comfort of her hand as it slipped into mine.

'Despina!' Manolis's voice rang high to the beams. He had spotted his daughter but she didn't move, just stood with her head down. 'Home,' he said. 'Now!' he commanded.

I called, 'I'm coming, Despoula,' as I saw she was looking helplessly round for me, her eyes now dull and downcast. 'Do as Papa says, I shall be right behind you.'

Beside the stone font at the front of the church, beside the icons, beside the sand for holding the candles, the talk between Papa Yannis, the professor and Papa Costas was of sacrilege; the disgrace in using the sanctified church as a meeting place, an extension of the schoolroom.

The priest waddled towards the door as quickly as his sweating bulk would allow, calling over his shoulder, 'This is not the end of it, Costas.'

I was going, too, to catch up with Despina, when I saw the curtain to the altar was moving, yet there was not a whisper of a breeze. I pulled it aside and there was Dimitri crouched on the floor. He seemed terrified so I took his hand. 'Come, Dimitri.' I knew what was wrong. There was only one thing that would terrify him like that. 'The man,' I said, indicating someone tall, 'with the priest?' And I drew in the air a fat, round man.

He nodded quickly and pulled back from me. 'Come, Dimitri, we will find your father. I saw him here earlier. Papa? Yes?' He nodded again. I patted his head gently. 'Wait, wait here.' He seemed to understand so I ran outside into the hot air calling, 'Manos!' and, oh, thanks be to the *Panagia*, the all-Holy Mary, there he was. Quickly I explained, and without a word he ran back into the church, reappearing a moment later with Dimitri in his arms.

'Thank you, Kyria Anthi,' he said. 'My child will never be at peace while those *malakas* are around.' I felt only shame. He spoke of my husband. I started to apologise but he cut me short: 'Not your fault. But your mother must have no value for you to marry you to that animal. I wish you good day.' He turned away.

I stood, looking after them with an icy heart, the brim of tears close in my eyes. I felt a gnawing sadness. He spoke of my husband and I felt nothing but shame.

Voula had gone home with Pappous and Yaya. I knew she was safe with them, so I started to run down the mountain path towards home.

I went through our gate and immediately I could hear Despina crying. Inside there was no sign of Manolis.

We did not see him for three days and none of us missed him—even the goats seemed happier.

HEAVENLY

BRITAIN HAS DECLARED WAR on Germany and Hugh's letters are so heavily censored that only a few inane words survive. Often I find myself wishing the house wasn't finished and Yorgo and Christo were still here each day.

The atrocious heat of the summer took many of the older villagers, and it seemed each day there was another funeral. The still, hot days of autumn called me to walk the nearby hills. Everyone prayed for rain, but each morning dawned hot and clear. For me, in the old Orfanoudakis house that looked down to the clear mountain spring, time moved differently than it did elsewhere. These days ceased to be measured by the seasons, the crops and the harvests. Hugh's letters, sporadic and censored as they were, gave me some insight into where the world was heading and it was impossible not to be afraid. Even Christo, my untroubled lover, seemed always to wear a frown these days.

Nightly he went to Il Piperia and would tell me a little of what he had gleaned—it seemed there was trouble across most of Europe. He was spending a lot of time each day with Kotso and Andros. Sometimes strangers turned up in the village looking for him and he would then disappear for a day or more at a time. There was never an explanation, but I knew they were working secretly to prepare what they could in case the war did come this far.

Looking back, it seems extraordinary to me that we were so ill-prepared for any war that would come. Most people here believed that Crete was their country and Greece was somewhere else. The village had itself to look after. There was enough to concern us all every day. Failing crops, lack of food, even, it seemed, a shortage of wood for fires, so over the winter those old people that had survived the unrelenting heat of the summer began to die from the cold.

The shepherds fared worse. Out on the hillsides there were several deaths just in the course of one night. An unexpected blizzard took six, their bodies lying hidden in crevasses and under rockfalls until spring.

This far south it was unheard of to have to face weather like this. The women spent most evenings in prayer, believing they must have angered the *Panagia* in some way.

Christo and Andros were now openly recruiting any of the village men they could to join them. They had a makeshift camp in a cave in the hills, far, far up and somehow Christo had acquired a two-way wireless set. He was rather mysterious about where it had come from and I didn't press for an answer. He proudly showed it to me one night, but it only made crackling noises. Frustrated, he hit it with his fist and loud Greek music filled the cave. It was impossible not to laugh and Christo took my hand and led me in a dance. I was filled with a happiness I hadn't felt for weeks. We whirled and twirled to the music, dipping and gliding until we fell to the ground in a heap, gasping. We lay exhausted, panting for breath, and then we were kissing deeply and passionately and we pushed our clothes off to one side and made love. We hadn't made love like that for a long time. Usually our stolen moments together were quieter and gentler.

As no one ever went near the little church of St Kosmas and Damianus on the mountain top, Christo suggested we keep it as the 'hospital' we had created for the first-aid lessons, in case there ever was really a need. I didn't argue, although in my heart I still found it difficult to believe that here, tucked away in the mountains, we would be bothered by invaders. What did we have to offer? Foolishly I didn't think of the food and sustenance that any army would need, or the very ownership of the land.

And then one morning a letter from Hugh arrived, and this time it was not just about the weather or his lavish embassy dinners, but contained a phrase to really puzzle me, and more, confuse and worry me.

I had woken feeling slightly sick. The night before, Irini had brought me in a dish of her rabbit stew. It had tasted rich and gamey and, sitting alone, I had eaten every morsel, together with a glass of Yorgo's red wine. I think I had indulged myself too freely and this morning I was paying for it.

I couldn't say when Hugh had written this letter, but it was carried up the mountain from Sitia as usual by a man from the offices that governed our region in Lasithi. It could be days, weeks, or even months old, and told me little that I didn't know already.

Until the last paragraph.

'Darling,' he had written, 'at last I can tell you that I may be with you sooner than we hoped. I can say almost nothing for fear of interception, but I have been requested to arrange the safe passage to Crete of an important package.'

Oh, how I wished then that I could speak to him. I hated hints and mysteries like that.

'I may be with you sooner.' Did that imply that he would be coming here, to Crete? To this village?

I decided to talk to Anthi. I jumped to my feet but, as I went towards the door, a wave of nausea swept over me and I staggered to the cushions to sit down again. I forced myself to breathe in slow, deep, cool breaths until I felt well enough to read Hugh's words again. I think I must have slept a little, for when I opened my eyes I could tell from the shadows that it was later. I felt better, stronger, and pushed myself to my feet. I would walk to Anthi's house and hope the fresh spring air would clear my head.

But as I reached the path, I realised I still felt so weak that I had to clutch hold of a hanging branch to steady myself. Several deep breaths set me to rights and I walked slowly onwards.

ANTHI

DESPINA IS SILENT again.

Three days now and she has not spoken. Inside I feel sad and desperate. If she would answer me only, I could bear it. But she just nods or shakes her head; and that just the smallest gesture. I believe her face shows fear. Her eyes dart round the room, looking for what? Oh, my happy, laughing child, come back to us. Sometimes I hold her close to me, burying my face in her hair, telling her I love her. But she stands rigid in my arms.

This morning I have tended the bees and checked the goats' feet for infection. I had heard from a woman at the spring that there is a different kind of hoof rot around, and many goats are affected by it. I have fed and watered the chickens and sent Despina off to collect any eggs. A stew is already bubbling in the pot and the house is beginning to smell of the garlic and herbs I have put in with the meat. Now I must go up into the fields. Walking, of course. I keep Astrape out of use as much as possible to let him rest.

Along the path uphill I saw that the figure coming towards me was Heavenly and, as always, I started to smile. But she was not smiling and we only exchanged a quick greeting before walking onwards together. It was impossible not to notice how pale she looked.

'I'll come to the fields with you,' she said, and even Despina almost smiled.

'What's wrong, Heavenly? You look like a bowl of milk. Are you ill?'

'Oh, it's nothing.'

By the fields, I spread myself at the edge, our lunch basket and stone water jar marking out the space. Despina placed herself by the hedge alone and kept her gaze averted.

Heavenly looked at her and then at me with her eyebrows raised, questioning. I put my finger against my closed lips and shook my head.

Voula laid herself down with her head on my leg, thumb in mouth.

'Tell me what is wrong,' I said, quietly.

'I think Hugh may be coming back. Look at this letter.' And she handed me a scrappy piece of paper with thick black ink crossing through much of it. I read the few words that were visible.

'See, he says a package? What do you think he means by that? I can only think that he means he is on his way here.'

I nodded slowly. 'Maybe.'

'My head is so muddled and my heart is split in two. I'm sorry, I had to talk to someone about this, and try and make sense of my feelings. And there is only you.'

'Is this the reason you are so pale?'

'No, I think Irini's rabbit stew didn't agree with me.'

I looked down at the paper again. I had no idea what it could mean, except that her husband was coming here.

'What am I to do?'

'You will do nothing, I think, but wait and see what happens.'

I looked at her again, closely. She was drawn and ashen-faced. This letter had disturbed her more than she would admit. I realised that it was some time since I had seen the old Heavenly, the woman who laughed and sang and danced and was always happy. I knew these were worrying times for all of us. Not that you could tell that from a casual glance at the villagers. Their attitude was to shrug and water their gardens, pick their produce and get on with their lives.

Heavenly sat, her shoulders hunched, beside Despina who, locked inside herself, seemed not to notice.

'You look so tired, are you sure you are not ill?'

She shook her head.

'Is it your monthly time come round?'

An intimate question. I would never ask it of any other woman.

She closed her eyes, suddenly motionless.

'Heavenly, I only wondered—'

But she raised her hand, silencing me. 'What day is it? What month?' It was a whisper.

'It is October, early, I don't know the number. It's about the middle of the week, I think. Why?'

But as soon as the question was asked, it was clear to me why it mattered. She was shaking her head, her expression one of panic, fear. I took her by the shoulders.

'Why? Tell me. When is your monthly due?'

'I don't know, I can't remember. I haven't . . .' and she turned to me, her face like stone. 'I haven't had my monthly for ages. I thought perhaps it was just worry; about the war, about my home, about Christo, about Hugh . . . You don't think my sickness is, is . . .'

What could I say to her? This was no time to be kind or gentle or reassuring. Just looking closely at her now, I knew with complete certainty that she was pregnant. There is something in the eyes, the skin, the features. There was not a glimmer of doubt in my mind. How could I not have seen it earlier?

'Tell me, are your breasts tender, enlarged?'

She didn't answer but, just like Despina, nodded mutely.

'You were a nurse, surely of all people you must understand what is happening to your body?'

She nodded again. 'It's true. I am carrying a child.' She sounded puzzled, uncertain, but she looked up at me, her eyes deep and sparkling, and there was no way she could sound unhappy. A smile was playing round the corners of her mouth; wonderment, as if she had been given a much-longed-for gift.

'Do you want to keep it or lose it?' I said coldly. 'You have no time for indecision about this. You are pregnant with the child of a wandering mason. And your husband is on his way here. What do you want to do?'

I could only be brutal, for part of me wanted to weep and if I was a true friend to her, this was no moment for celebration.

'I don't know. Tell me what to do.'

'How can I do that? This is trouble, serious trouble, and you must decide now.'

She was lost to me for a moment. I could only think she was away in her head somewhere. A place where there are no problems. A place where neighbours, friends and husbands, smiled warmly on a new life and never, ever asked questions.

I clapped my hands together loudly, furiously, so that even Despina looked at me in astonishment. Voula rolled over in her sleep and settled into a new comfort.

Heavenly slowly turned her head to me and repeated, 'Tell me what to do.'

I hesitated and said, 'Let me think for a moment.' Even I was undecided on how to advise her. I knew she longed for a child; she was born to be a mother. There is so much love inside her, but, I am certain, not this way and not now.

'Right,' I said, 'go to your house and rest. Don't think about this just now. You are not feeling good; rest and sleep is what you need and don't speak to anyone of this. Do you understand? Not anyone.'

She looked at me, her eyes vague and slightly puzzled. 'I must tell Christo,' she said simply, as though we were speaking of the weather.

'No, not Christo, especially not Christo.'

Her face clouded with disappointment. 'Why can't I tell him?'

'I think this, this happening, has made you lose your mind, your sense. In a moment you will be telling your neighbours.' Where had my wonderful, admirable, sensible Heavenly gone? My own mind was a whirl of anxiety and concern for her. 'Promise me, my dear friend, you will just go to your house now and rest and speak to no one.'

She sighed. 'Of course, if you say so.'

She was obviously depressed with this conversation and rose to leave. I rose, too, and hugged her to me hard.

'I love you, dearest friend, so trust me for the moment. I will come and see you tonight or tomorrow, and we will make a plan.'

At last she smiled. I gathered my girls to me and we set off in the opposite direction. The crops must wait for tomorrow. There was absolutely no doubt in my mind what was to be done. She could not keep this baby.

But now was not the time to persuade her to think of anything sensible. She was strong, young and she would produce a fit, healthy child, unless I helped her. I shuddered at the thought of what I must do.

I took the girls to Pappous and Yaya. They were so happy to see them. Yaya was worried about Despina's silence and as I helped her wash the wild greens for salad, she asked me about it.

'There is nothing I can say. This is the third or fourth time she has descended into this state and she will speak to no one.'

'Poor child,' said Yaya. 'It is as if she has a devil inside her that takes her words away.'

Pappous was quieter than usual, and I asked him why.

'The news from the wireless last night in Il Piperia is very worrying, Anthi. The fighting in Albania is getting closer and closer to Greece. Yesterday, a port very close to the frontier was blown up and the Italians are saying it was the work of the British or the Greeks. This sort of thing is just the excuse the Italians need to attack Greece.'

'But how could they prove it?'

Pappous laughed. 'You think they need proof? If they decide that the Greeks need teaching a lesson, BOFF! In they come with all their weapons ready and that's it.'

Yaya rolled her eyes. 'Enough, enough! We have the children with us, a rare treat, and you spoil it with all this talk of war.'

'Can the children stay with you a little this afternoon?'

'Of course, child. Despina can help me with my needlework while Voula rests.'

Despina visibly brightened at the thought of sewing with her grandmother and within moments they were together on the balcony. Pappous was already rocking in his chair, his pipe alight, Voula curled on his lap, her thumb firmly in her mouth.

I needed to be alone to do what I had to do for Heavenly.

First I went home and collected Astrape, who seemed suddenly lively at the prospect of an outing alone with me.

The paths we rode slowly through that afternoon took us out of the village and up into the hills above. I passed ground scorched and burnt from recent fires and bare, sad olive trees in fields that were only dry earth scattered with a sparse few weeds. On the sides of the hills, thin sheep scrabbled for any blade of grass they could find.

It took half an hour to reach the group of hovels I was looking for. The small cluster of dwellings in the curve of the hill showed little signs of life at first, but as I paused and waited a moment, a boy ran out through a broken doorway and, thumb in his mouth, stared at me.

'Kyria Glykeria, is she here?' He didn't answer, just continued to gaze at me. 'Her daughter, Tassia, do you know her?' He nodded and pointed to the first house in the dilapidated and crumbling row.

I climbed down from Astrape. He was so tired, there was little point in trying to find a hitching post, so I left him untethered and, with the child still staring after me, walked towards the midwife's door.

It creaked open as I approached and the wrinkled, brown hand that had pulled it propped it back so that I could glimpse the interior.

The first thing I noticed was the smell. A rank, thick odour of stale bodies struggled against an over-sweet aroma of cooking flowers or fruit.

'What do you want?' She wasn't going to waste time with polite conversation. I was about to answer when a small cry came from inside and, clutching my arm, she pulled me over the threshold and into the darkness.

There were no windows here. A thin candle, guttering in the breeze that came as the door opened, threw little light.

'What do you want?' she wheezed again as she sat down beside another shadowy figure, close to the thin flicker from the hearth. It was from this person that the cry had come and, as I looked, Glykeria's daughter Tassia held up a thin bundle of rags. She shook it and said, 'Baby, baby,' with a fond smile.

'Why are you here?' Glykeria said, and before I could answer, she rose from her stool and poked me in the stomach with a sharp finger. 'Nothing in your belly, then. No little dead boy for your mother to bury in some forsaken graveyard?'

I closed my eyes against the memory of my only son and pushed her dirty hand away from my body.

'It's for a friend that I need help.'

'Too proud to come herself, then?'

'No, no, she lives near Sitia,' I lied. 'Too far to travel.'

Kyria Glykeria is not only the midwife here; she also makes potions from herbs to hasten on the monthly bleed.

'What will you give me?'

My mind raced frantically. What could I give this hag? Food of some sort, she'd want food.

As if she heard she said, 'You have plenty of sheep.'

If I slaughtered one of our sheep, Manolis would know at once and that would be the end of our marriage. I didn't care, but it would quite possibly be the end of my life as well.

'I will give you a goat,' I said. I had no idea how I could do that, but it would be less obvious a loss than one of Manolis's precious sheep.

'*Ne!*' She nodded, satisfied, and I immediately thought I should have bargained harder. Offered some honey, maybe, or some eggs, but in my heart I knew she would settle for nothing less than several weeks' supply of good meals.

With the promise now of succulent meat, she got to her feet with surprising alacrity and reached for a rusty iron pot lying on its side in the hearth.

'Angelica, pennyroyal, cotton root . . .' As she spoke she was plucking at dried herbs, hanging in bundles above the fireplace. These all went into the pot. She pulled a lethal-looking knife from a pocket and grabbing Tassia's arm, quickly making a small slit near her wrist. Blood instantly surged up and holding the arm of the whimpering girl high, she dripped it onto the herbs in the pot. Glancing up she saw the look of horror on my face and muttered aloud, 'Virgin blood.'

She reached for more dried-looking twigs and these were pushed into the pot. 'Stop your snivelling,' she said to Tassia, who was sucking on her wrist, 'and get me some night primrose and some tansy.'

The girl scampered away through the door.

'What are you waiting for?' Glykeria said to me. 'You'll get nothing without payment.'

I nodded at the pot. 'When will it be ready?'

'An hour, two hours, maybe, and then it must be drunk fresh. So you had better bring me your goat as quick as you can, hadn't you?'

I was back within two hours, one of my young goats on a piece of string behind me.

Glykeria appeared in her doorway, in her hand a small hessian sack. She seemed cleaner than before, more like the midwife who had attended my births. I felt only relief; there was no need to go back inside that stinking house.

She snatched the string away from my hand and handed me the bag. By its shape and weight it held a bottle. 'Your friend must drink this before tomorrow's dawn. It will ripen the womb and she will lose whatever she has hidden inside.'

She turned away and dragged the goat behind her, into that foul kitchen. Gently kicking Astrape round, I rode off again into the hills.

Each of Astrape's tired steps seemed endless as we struggled through the darkening twilight. I dismounted and walked beside him. There was a breeze in the evening air. October is a lovely month with the last lingering days of summer, but there are chill moments that surprise.

It seemed like hours had passed, but the sinking sun told me that, in reality, it was only about forty minutes since I'd left Glykeria. At last I could see the wisp of smoke from Yaya's chimney.

She was standing in the doorway with Despina and Voula hugging her legs. Voula clapped her hands and laughed when she saw me, but Despina's eyes were as blank and empty as when I left her.

'I hope they didn't cause you trouble, Yaya?'

She shook her head. 'Never,' she said as we turned to go inside, whispering, 'but Despina has not spoken to me. I tried, but,' and she shrugged her shoulders, 'nothing.'

Sitting on the table, as though awaiting my arrival, was a dish of steaming *pastitsio*. My mouth watered as I smelt its rich fragrance and I realised I had not eaten, except for coffee and some rusks early that morning. Seeing my face Yaya said, 'You will eat with us before you go?'

The three of us were seated, waiting, before she reached for a spoon to serve us. 'Where is Pappous?'

'They came for him early, to go to the *kafenion*. You must eat now— I can see you are hungry. I will eat with him later.'

'For cards?'

'No, no.' She was shaking her head, no longer smiling. 'Worrying times,' she said, cutting deep into the *pastitsio* and placing the full plates in front of us. The garlicky steam rose deliciously and even for a moment, Despina's eyes seemed brighter.

We were wiping our plates with bread, scraping them clean, when Pappous came in. His step was heavy and there was no smile in his eyes, even for Voula who clapped her hands together at the sight of him.

He stood, silent, in the centre of the room.

'Here,' he said slowly, 'here is everything that is good, precious in my world.' His mood was transparent. Things must be wrong, bad.

'The Italians have invaded our country.'

Wise Yaya had already poured him a *raki* and he drank it in one gulp, holding out his glass to her for another.

'Early this morning, apparently, they crossed the border. The army has been mobilised, what is left of it. It is war.'

He sank down into his big chair by the flickering flames of the fire and swung Voula onto his lap. 'Of course, we will fight back. There is already talk of casualties in the far north.'

Yaya crossed herself three times and I hastily crossed myself, too.

Through the open doorway the sky had darkened now to the colour of tarnished silver and I made to leave. They did not try to stop me; their thoughts were elsewhere that evening.

I think I expected the world to have changed in some way with this news, but outside everything was as before.

Overhead a hawk shrieked. I knew the sea glinted below, even though I couldn't see it, and from the path as we slowly passed along it I soon saw Heavenly's house in the distance. She was sitting on the terrace, her outline lit by the shadowy lamp.

Voula waved and shouted, 'Helly, Helly!' but Heavenly was lost in her own thoughts and didn't turn. We were almost at her door before she realised we were there and rose slowly to her feet.

I let the girls go ahead. Voula's stubby little baby legs beside the skinny, slow limbs of her sister.

I looked at my friend and, for a moment, saw her as I had the first time; that coltish girl lying so awkwardly on the ground. The time she'd been here had served her well, only softening and rounding the edges: that girl was now a woman. Her smile was warm and wide as she reached down, clasping Voula in her arms.

A chill that had nothing to do with the weather flashed through me. How was I to persuade this woman with so much love to give, not to welcome motherhood?

HEAVENLY

I HAD SAT ALONE for much of the day, imagining the baby growing inside me. My mind felt numb; unlike my body, that seemed to be fizzing with excitement. I knew that I must think clearly about all the alternatives, all the problems, but I told myself that, just for one day, I could revel in the excitement of a child growing in my body. My body, my child.

I hadn't admitted it to Anthi, but I knew Christo was coming here today; he had promised. I kept looking at my watch.

Nine. Five past nine. Twenty past nine and, at last, I heard the soft footfall outside and the next moment he was here. I ran in from the terrace in a flurry. Heart beating too fast. Then I made myself go slow, in a calm way, and smile gently.

'I'm sorry to be late.' And then I was in his arms and there was no time. It had stopped now we were together. It always does.

The temptation to tell him my news was all but unbearable, but in fact he had come here only to tell me what was happening throughout Greece, and that he had no time to spare for me tonight.

'I must leave again at once,' he said. 'Kotso and Andros are waiting for me in the Kanavakises' barn. We are trying to raise some interest from the villagers in what is happening today.'

'Tell me.'

'The Italians have declared war on Greece. They are supposedly angered by Metaxas's decision to allow the British to build military bases in Thessaly, and there is some ridiculous talk of a Greek spy they caught. If they are determined, and they are, and their army advances across the Greek borders, as they have done, what more do we need?'

'What can we do here?'

'Nothing. Just now we are helpless; we can do nothing but wait to see what happens next. No one can see a reason for Crete to be attacked just now. But I still feel we should be on our guard, prepared to help how we can.' He gave a bitter laugh. 'You should have seen the men tonight in Il Piperia. Once they had heard this they turned the wireless set down as the news was distracting them from their cards! Only old Stephanos Karanakis insisted we continued listening.'

He cupped my face in his hands. Roughened and blistered as they are from work, they were like silk to me and I nuzzled my cheek into his fingers. He reached to kiss me, but I gently pushed him away. 'We can be seen here on the terrace.'

He sighed and stepped back. I was about to tell him of my letter from Hugh—at least I could share that part of my news with him—but he was already moving to the steps, down to the inside of the house.

He paused before he left, looking up at me from the steps. 'You understand my anxiety, don't you?'

'Of course I do.'

And with a wave behind him he was gone.

So Greece is at war. What will happen now? The people here may think only of Panagia and their crops, their harvests and their animals, but I grew up in England. I was an infant when my country was at war, always afraid that the next piece of news would be of the death of someone we knew: a neighbour, a cousin or a friend killed in action.

I was deep in these thoughts, rocking myself gently in my chair when, with a 'Helly, Helly!', little Voula was struggling up the steps and running to me. I was so happy to see her. Like any child she has a wondrous innocence that radiates from her, offering pure love. I held her to me with one hand, reaching out my other to her sister. Slowly Despina took, it but her grasp was limp and her head turned away.

'Shall I make us coffee?' It was Anthi calling from inside the house.

'Can I have a mountain tea?'

'It's your house, you can have whatever you choose.'

We were all back inside now and Anthi had a pan of water set over the ashes, which she had brought to life with Yorgo's old bellows.

'I'll join you in a *dictamus*,' she said, 'but why no coffee for you? You seldom drink this village tea, you tell me it tastes like stewed bird's nests.'

'I haven't a taste for coffee today. I realise that for the last week or so it has nauseated me.'

Anthi turned away, saying, 'Well, you know why that is, don't you?'

Of course! I could only smile as I thought of the baby inside me, rejecting coffee and showing me it preferred *dictamus*.

Despina had wandered over to the corner of the room to the old wine press, and was already unwrapping the brightly coloured scraps of velvet and silk I keep there for her. Her grandmother has taught her to sew and with tiny, neat stitches, she patches together many pieces of the soft cloth to make a usable length. Before she became silent she told me, whispering, that she was making a skirt for her mother, 'like yours, she loves these coloured things you wear. It's a secret, a gift for her name day'. But Anthi's name day has been and gone, the skirt is not finished and her daughter is silent still.

Voula had toddled over to join her now and with care was stretching out each piece of cloth, smoothing it down and making separate little piles according to colour. We sat at the opposite end of the room, Anthi and I, sipping at the hot mountain tea.

'Have you heard the news?' I asked.

'You mean about the Italian invasion?'

'Yes, what else?'

'We came here from my grandparents and my Pappous gave me the word from the wireless set. How did you hear?' She gave me a strange look, eyebrows raised. 'Oh, no, don't tell me, Christo was here. Say you didn't tell him about, about—'

And I cut her off sharply. 'Of course I didn't mention the baby.'

'Hush, keep your voice low, the children . . .'

'I'm sorry,' I said quickly, my hand over my mouth.

'I told you earlier, no one must know, no one.'

'If you could guess just from looking at my face, don't you think my neighbours can do the same?'

'I think none look at you as closely as I do,' and she turned away, her cheeks reddening, 'and none care as I do.'

I put my hand out and took hers in mine. It's like Christo's, rough and hardened from the work she does. Calluses blister on her palms, but it's a dear hand to me, and a reminder, always, of the differences in our lives. Even when I worked on my house with the men, each night I would rub cream or oil of some kind into my fingers.

Anthi was watching her daughters now, as she took a hessian-wrapped package from under her skirt and handed it across to me. 'Take this,' she said. I held the package in my hand, curious. 'You must drink it tonight before you sleep.'

'What is it?' I opened the rough sacking and took out the flask inside. It was almost full with a dark, greenish-brown liquid. Taking out the cork stopper, I sniffed and immediately held it away from me. 'It stinks. Are you trying to poison me?'

'It's what the women use here when their monthly bleed is late.'

I held the bottle out to her. 'Take it away, I don't want it. I don't know where you acquired it from, but if it has cost you money I will give you money. I know what this stuff is and I know what it does, and I don't want it anywhere near me.'

She knew I was angry, very angry. I raised my eyes a moment to look at her daughters but they were oblivious to any tension from this end of the room.

'Please, let me help you. You don't seem to realise the trouble you are in.' She held the bottle of vile liquid out to me again. 'Many women use this here. It's not dangerous, it's not a poison; it just helps to put right any little mistakes.'

I sat back. I had to try and make her understand.

'This is not a "little mistake" as you call it, my dear friend.' I put my hand across my stomach. 'This is my baby. My baby and Christo's baby.'

'And how are you going to tell the village? You think they will believe in a virgin birth?' She was kneeling in front of me now, and crossed herself three times. 'They will be delighted to have a whole new piece of gossip and then they will start to wonder who the father is. They will, of course, suspect Christo first, then perhaps Yorgo Babyottis.'

My face must have expressed the horror I felt as she said this.

'Oh, yes, believe me. Yorgo has been here for months, often alone with you. Then they will look for any errant husband who has spent too many nights late and drunk in the *kafenion*.'

'Oh, stop, please, stop.' I knew tears were pouring down my face now and my heart was beating fast.

She was scarlet with emotion and breathing heavily. 'Oh, *Panagia mou*, how can I make you understand?'

'Dearest friend, I know what you are saying to me. I know in some ways you are right, but I have to make this decision for myself, don't you understand? Allow me just a little time to be happy with my body, please, please. I have longed for this moment for so long, thinking I would never be a mother. From the moment I married Hugh, I have looked with envy at every woman with a swollen belly. I look at Voula and Despina and long for them to be mine, to feel that love, that special love, that I know you have for them.'

There was a sudden yell from the end of the room and Voula ran to us, sobbing. She was clutching a piece of emerald silk tightly in her fat little fist, saying, 'Mine, mine.' Anthi was on her feet, her arms open to her child, consoling her. Despina stamped her foot and, with her hands on her hips, stared towards us. We could see the fury she was feeling.

'I must take them home, they are exhausted. Take this,' and Anthi handed me the bottle again. 'Of course, you are right, it is your decision,' her voice was flat now, 'but I would be no friend to you if I didn't help you to make the right one.'

I held the bottle as if it would scald me. Roughly I wiped my eyes with the back of my hand.

'Thank you. I understand all you say, but leave me to think. Perhaps tomorrow . . .'

But with her girls clasped to her side, Anthi was out on the steps now, her face turned away from me. 'Tomorrow is too late. The medicine will only be effective for a very short time. You must make up your mind.'

'Please, don't leave like this. I need you to be my friend.'

'I am your friend, I will always be your friend, whatever you do. But don't throw away your life for a moment's thoughtless pleasure.' And then she was gone.

I sat for hours alone on the terrace. The cooling wind had died and the evening sky was clear, the air warm. Large moths batted fleetingly across the surface of the lamp and a night bird sang a lonely song.

I put Anthi's bottle on the top of the terrace steps and sat back and looked at it. Of course I was afraid. When I was doing my training as a nurse I saw young girls and women desperate to end an unwanted pregnancy. The results were always dreadful, whatever they did. Some did it with a bottle of gin and hot baths. Some took pills or potions from helpful chemists eager to exploit a girl in trouble. Some pressed thin wooden sticks or knitting needles into themselves. Sometimes their bleeds were induced, but always in great pain, and in the end they usually lost what they were carrying sooner, or worse, later.

But however much I filled myself with fear and dread I knew that

Anthi was right. To keep this child was madness. And how would I keep it? I would be forced to leave the village, I had no doubts of that. And where would I go? With Greece at war how could I live in the wild, a pregnant English woman used only to the finer things in life? If I could by some miracle get myself to Athens, what then? I could no longer trust that Hugh would be there. And if he was? What would he say to my arrival with the bastard child of a Cretan builder inside me?

There were no choices, no decisions for me to make.

I picked up the bottle, shook it gently. A residue already forming at the bottom spread in an oily fusion through the liquid.

I took out the cork and without a moment's pause I put the bottle to my lips and drank, drank it down.

ANTHI

MANOLIS HAD BEEN AWAY again and had come back silent and sulking. He booted the door open, came into the house and kicked his dog. He had no words for any of us. Voula tried to climb on his lap saying joyfully, 'Papa, Papa.' But he pushed her aside. Despina sat in a corner with a schoolbook and didn't look up.

It was two days since I had seen Heavenly. I felt I must leave her alone just now, although my mind was desperate with anxiety. I saw Aphrodite this morning at the spring and asked her, casually, if she or Yorgo had seen her. She shook her head, although she added, 'Yorgo has to collect a saw from Heavenly's house, so he may go there tonight.'

She was carrying her youngest child strapped on her hip as she worked through her laundry. It was a boy with a shock of dark hair sticking up all round his face. He smiled as I stroked his soft brow. Even I could feel an empty broodiness in my belly, so I knew well what Heavenly was feeling.

That night it was dark when I heard a tap at the door and the soft call of my name. Manolis had gone out hours before and as usual had given me no clue where he was going or when he might return.

I opened the door and Yorgo Babyottis was standing outside, peering nervously behind me.

'My husband is not here just now, come inside.'

He shuffled across the threshold looking around him. 'You are well, Kyria? And your children?'

'Thank you, all is well here. Will you take a *raki*?'

'Oh, I don't plan to stay, but if you insist, a very small one.' And he was sitting in Manolis's chair, his feet stretched out to the dying embers of the fire as if he lived here.

'A *raki* glass is a *raki* glass, Yorgo, not smaller or larger.' And I poured him one. Funny how he changed when he realised Manolis was away from here. 'It is, of course, a pleasure to see you, but is there a reason for your visit at this hour?'

'That is a fine piece of wood you have there,' he said rather unexpectedly, looking across to my bridal chest.

'My grandfather made it.' I really didn't want a conversation about my furniture just now. 'Is there something you want with me?'

'Ah, yes, Kyria.' He was not to be hurried.

I breathed audibly; surely he could see my irritation? Polite conversation would drive me to despair very soon but it was likely he would start chatting about my children and animals if I tried to hasten him along.

'You keep a beautiful home,' he said, slowly looking round. 'Your husband is indeed a lucky man.'

He was sipping from his empty *raki* glass, having drunk the contents down in one, so I reached for the flask and filled it again.

'Thank you. Is there something special that brings you this way tonight?' I tried a last desperate measure. 'Perhaps it is my husband you wish to see? He will be here very, very soon.'

He was on his feet at once, draining the glass and moving towards the door. 'No, it is you my wife told me to see. I had to pass by Kyria Heavenly's house tonight, to collect some tools, you see, and I told Aphrodite and she said I must come and tell you. She is clearly unwell.'

'Aphrodite is ill?'

'Not Aphrodite, of course, let me be clear, she is in fine health, but your friend. In fact she could hardly stand, she is so weak. I found my tools, it was my good saw, you know, I use it whenever I make a coffin and tomorrow I have to prepare the wood for old Peridakis, he who lives up in the mountains. Only seventy-three—'

I had grabbed my shawl, wrapped it round me, and was halfway out of the door. I paused only to say, 'I'm sorry, I was wrong, my husband won't be home until much, much later. You are quite safe here. In fact, I would be glad if you could stay for an hour in case the children wake. I'll be back soon, I promise.'

I couldn't hear whether he agreed to stay or not, as I was already running through the yard, the garden and along the road.

I was panting as I arrived at Heavenly's house. The door was unlatched. I called her name as I ran in, but there was only silence. I went straight down to the bedroom. It was dark; I guessed the lamp had long emptied.

'Heavenly,' I whispered, 'it's me.' Still silence, but I could see through the shadows her shape lying on the bed.

There was a strong smell of sickness and I almost kicked over a bucket as I approached. A quick shaft of unease ran through me. Heavenly's bedroom is always sweet with the scent of wild flowers.

'I'll find a candle.' I went quickly back upstairs, taking the pail with me. In one of her ramshackle cupboards was a packet of candles and a heavy silver cigarette lighter. It must be one her husband had left. I ran outside and emptied and cleaned away her vomit.

With the candlelight downstairs, I could see her clearly. She was hunched round herself like a baby. Her face was chalk-white and her eyes, closed as they were, deeply shadowed in purple.

Oh, *Panagia mou*, what have I done to her?

HEAVENLY

I REMEMBER ANTHI COMING. I remember her being here and I remember her leaving. And then, the utter silence of the house bore down upon me, silent as thought, and I drifted again into sleep. But within barely an hour I guessed, I was awake and burning with fever—my bed was on fire.

I tried to move my lips, but my mouth was parched and I drank deeply of some water Anthi had left me. I slept again.

When I woke it was daylight. I think I was still feverish but not with the same fierce fires of the night. My head throbbed and I ached in every joint. I felt so weak and thirsty, and underlying that was a tight wad of anxiety. A contraction caused me to lie rigid, motionless, but it was fainter, less sharp than the night before, and faded away almost immediately.

My memory is hazy and I cannot precisely recall the sequence of what happened next. I think I slept or dozed for most of that day.

Once, when I awoke, Anthi was there. Was that yesterday or last night? Her girls were with her. I know she washed the floor and I think the branch of sweet briar that fills the room with a scented freshness was placed beside my bed by Despina, who stroked my head gently with a cloth and was imitated move by move by her sister. They both smiled a little as my eyes flickered open. I must have slept again, and when I woke in darkness, the house felt still and empty.

I lay for I don't know how long between sleep and wakefulness, but I think it was the sound of scratching on my bedroom window that pulled me back fully into the world. I turned my head in the direction of the sound and said feebly, 'Who is it?'

By answer there was only the soft whisper of my name, 'Heavenly, Heavenly.' It was Christo. He came down and sat beside me on the bed, taking my pale, shaking hand in his strong, brown one and, for the first time in ages it seemed, I felt safe.

'How . . .' I started to ask, and 'Anthi,' he answered. 'She is a true friend and she came here to look after you every day.'

'Every day?' My voice was a whisper. 'How long have I been unwell?'

'Most of the week,' he replied, and my mind raced with all the questions I needed answering.

Christo lay beside me on the bed and I welcomed the closeness of his body. His arm stretched over my middle and his hand stroked me exactly, I imagined, where our baby lay. Unless, I thought bleakly, Anthi's potion had killed it.

Tears filled my eyes. I was weak from the fever and felt only like weeping. Christo lifted his head from the pillow, sensing my sadness, and gazed at me with concern.

'What?' he asked. 'Why? Why so sad?'

'Oh, I'm just weak and silly,' I said, 'ignore me.'

He laughed then. 'That is the one thing it is impossible for me to do. What can I do? How can I help you? Perhaps I could give you a bath to make you fresh? Would you like that?' And all at once that was what I wanted more than anything else just then; to lie in clean, scented water and soak the remains of whatever it was out of my body. I knew I was too helpless to do it alone. 'Could you wash my hair?'

Christo stood, stroked my cheek and said softly, 'I will do anything for you.'

As I pulled myself upright I asked, 'What is happening with the invasion, the war; is there news?'

'Later,' he said, 'I will tell you what I know later.'

With his arms round my shoulders he managed to get me out of the bed. The sheets betrayed me with the sour odour of sweat and sickness, and I shuddered involuntarily as I smelt my unclean self.

Christo caught my eye and smiled. As though he could read my thoughts he said, 'I love the scent of you. Everything about you is wonderful to me. I am lucky that you trust me with this intimacy.' And with his arm firmly round me, we made our way to the bathroom.

In the warm, sweet water, I luxuriated and thought that I may never move again.

First, Christo had run back and forth with pans of hot water. He had rebuilt the fire and I knew the flames would be burning fiercely under the large zinc jars of water. Then he knelt beside the bath on the floor and, with the olive oil soap one of Anthi's neighbours made, his hands slipped slowly and easily over every bit of my body, leaving each part soft and clean. He took a cloth and slowly swept it over my face.

'Lie back now,' he said, and I slid lower into the water.

My hair floated out and round me like seaweed. He held each strand gently in his fingers and threaded a different, silky soap through it. The sweet fragrance of the rose petals in the soap filled the room and carefully Christo massaged my scalp clean.

'Come,' he said, 'time to get out before you are cold.'

I could barely make it back to the bedroom and I did so only by clutching onto his arm and going very slowly. Each step an achievement. He had changed the soiled linen on the bed and bundled it into the corner. 'I will wash these tonight,' he said and, feeble as I felt, I managed to laugh.

'You will give everything away if you are seen washing my sheets. I will ask Anthi to help me later; there is plenty of spare linen here.'

As soon as I lay on the bed, my eyes closed and, within moments, I slept again.

As before, I had no idea of time passing and when I awoke it was again dark, and Christo was standing by the door. 'Are you coming or going?' I asked him through dry lips.

'Neither. I am simply here. Yorgo came an hour or so ago with some broth from Aphrodite. Do you think you can manage that?'

I felt suddenly hungry. Surely a sign I was getting better?

Christo went to the kitchen and reappeared shortly after with a steaming bowl in his hands. It was delicious, and I managed to swallow all the savoury goodness of it.

As I sank back down again in the sweet-smelling sheets, my eyes began to close. I was exhausted from the effort involved in eating and talking. As I did so, I noticed that Christo had one of his large hammers in his hand. 'What is that for?' I asked, puzzled.

He looked at it himself. 'Oh, the hammer,' he said. 'Well, every time Irini or one of your neighbours comes to see how you are, I bang at a wall. They know I am not a doctor, so why else am I here?'

I smiled. 'Do they come often, then?'

'Your kitchen is like a market! They always bring a gift every time they visit, but it seems everyone in Panagia cares about you and has been by to send you greetings.'

My heart was full and I blinked away tears at the generosity of my friends and neighbours; these very people who had so little themselves, as the summer's sun had baked and burnt every drop of much-needed moisture away.

I slept yet again and this time when I awoke it was to see Anthi sitting beside my bed. I reached to hold her hand in mine. Hers felt cool and strong and I know my hand was moist and shaking.

Her face was suddenly stricken. 'Oh, my dearest friend, I am so sorry to have made you so unwell, can you forgive me?'

I smiled weakly by way of answer and, reaching to the floor, she brought up a cloth and a bowl, and bathed my face with cool water.

'You have been ill for many days. I have been so worried about you. Tell me what has happened?'

'I thought I should lose everything inside me, I was very sick, vomiting so badly I thought it would never stop.' My head sank back on the pillow and I closed my eyes. 'I wonder when I will know if the purge has worked,' I said quietly.

She sat very still on the side of my bed. 'What do you mean?'

'I mean, when do you think I will have bleeding?'

'Are you saying there is no blood yet?'

'Oh, no, none. I had great cramps for hours, but no blood.'

'There should have been blood immediately. It can't be possible that you have been so ill but have resisted the final outcome.' She looked desperate now, my dear friend.

'I'm sorry, Anthi.' I felt my eyes closing again with a great weakness, and within moments I was asleep again.

All events at this time run into each other, and days fall into nights and nights slip into sunrise. And here again, Christo is with me.

'Would you like to go to the terrace?' he asks. 'It's a beautiful evening.'

'If you will help me,' and together we make our way slowly, arm in arm, like an elderly couple. It is a balmy, soft kind of night, more like spring than October.

Christo tells me news from the outside world. Sometimes, a man comes to listen to the wireless set in his cave. He's hazy about the details. But the man is not Greek, he's English, and the news he receives comes straight from the Greek High Command.

'I was wrong about the Greek army being fragmented and weak,' Christo tells me. 'They are fighting hard in the north and have forced the Italians back across the Albanian border. There are many dead, many casualties but, they say, the will is strong. There is also news of the British. They are in Greece, here in the north of Crete, and have created a strong base in the bay around Souda. Your navy will help with our defences there.'

'And my home in England?' I ask. My brain feels as weak as my body, but I need to know. 'Do you have any news from there?'

He shakes his head.

A sharp lurch of nausea makes me suddenly aware of my condition.

Christo looks at me, a question in his eyes. 'What is troubling you? Aside from this wretched sickness, you are not yourself.'

'There is something I must tell you,' and I tell him about Hugh's letter and what I believe it to mean.

His face betrays nothing of what he might be feeling, but he slowly drops my hand and I see a new distance in his eyes. Gone, with the soft crack of my words, is the easy intimacy we shared.

Oh, what have I done? Anthi has tried many times to warn me, to wake me up to what I am doing and I refused to listen. So carried away was I in the wonders of this new love that I have created a scorpion's nest of lies and deceit. I have behaved so carelessly with lives and feelings, including my own, and now the man I love more than my life is broken. And the man I married is coming back and I am carrying a child who can never know his father.

I barely notice that Christo is on his feet.

'I must leave you.' Without another word or glance he is gone, and I stand alone on the terrace, watching him ride away into the hills.

What did he mean? '*I must leave you.*' Leave me just now, for a short while? Or does Hugh's return mean he is gone for ever?

I have heard no word from Christo and each morning, with the sickness, comes a longing and a sadness that I try and cheer with a hope: perhaps today he will come?

He never does.

In spite of myself, each night I fall into a deep sleep, my dreams vague and troubled.

It was on one such night when a sound bruised the air and I was quickly awake. My heart was racing, my eyes wide with alarm. It was a voice, two voices, then laughter, loud, ragged and indistinct. They were here, close by my house, too close.

I swung my legs over the side of the bed and slowly got up. It was Yorgo's voice, Yorgo and a second man. There was more laughter, and then a loud pounding on my door. I ran up the stairs as fast as I was able calling, 'Wait, wait.' I opened the door hastily. Yorgo and the other, who had been leaning on it, fell into the room and landed in a pile at my feet. One rose, and one lay helplessly, still giggling. Yorgo, upright, stood straight by clinging onto the wall beside him. The stink of alcohol from the pair of them was so fierce I reeled back.

'Kyria,' muttered Yorgo, 'Kyria, look who I have here. A present for you.' And he started to giggle, too. 'A present! Get up my friend,' and he staggered to lift the recumbent figure at his feet. Yorgo wore his old grey jacket and patched *vraka*, but as the other finally rose to his knees and looked blearily round through his tangled hair, I could see immediately that his garments, although the same peasant clothes and mended, patched and filthy, were of a superior quality.

'Come on, You,' said Yorgo hauling on one arm to raise his companion upright. His face was streaked with grime and sweat and his hair hung greasily over his brow, but I knew in a moment's clarity that this was, of course, Hugh, my husband.

Every part of me stopped, rigid. Not just my arms, clasped by my hands in front of my body, not just my legs, stiffly refusing to let me move forward to offer help, but my face, in a rictus of a half-smile, my eyes, dry but unblinking, my mouth half-open in a protest.

Looking at my husband now, for the first time in, how long? I felt nothing. As he managed with great difficulty to get up, to stand and lurch towards me, I instinctively backed away from him. Yorgo grabbed his arm to steady him, saying rather piteously, 'This is You, Kyria Heavenly. I found him in Il Piperia.'

'Thank you,' I said, 'Perhaps you should leave him here now and go home to Aphrodite. It is late and she will be worried.'

'Of course! You will want your reunion.' With a suggestive chuckle, he pulled the door open and staggered back through it, into what remained of the night.

Hugh looked vaguely round him, his eyes puzzled. 'Is this the same old house?' he managed to ask, then, 'God, I'm tired,' and before he could fall again, I took him firmly by the arm and pushed him slowly ahead of me and down the stairs.

There, he saw the bed in front of him, tumbled forwards to fall on top of it, groaned and passed out.

For the rest of the night I sat on the terrace.

By first light Yorgo, and anyone else who had been in Il Piperia the night before, had spread the word of my husband's arrival. My neighbours made one excuse after another to visit me, each one peering round me trying to catch a glimpse of him. They needn't have bothered. He was dead to the world, until long after the sun was high in the sky.

Eventually, from downstairs, the loud snores stopped and I guessed that Hugh was awake. I was as nervous now as the gauche schoolgirl I had once been. Slowly, cautiously, my heart beating fast, I went down the stairs, but, dark as the room was with the shutters closed, I could see nothing until my eyes were accustomed to the gloom.

He was just getting out of bed. His back was to me and it was a while before he heard me and turned round. His face had aged and he was much thinner than I remembered.

'Hello, Evadne,' he said. 'Dear daughter of Poseidon. Oh, it's so good to see you, come here and let me hold you.' And he stretched out his arms to me. But I couldn't move. I looked at this man, once so familiar to me, and he was a stranger. He glanced down at himself, smiled wryly and said, 'Don't worry, I'll clean myself up and then we'll see, eh?'

I managed to force a smile to my lips, but I knew I couldn't make it reach my eyes. 'We have a bathroom now,' I said, over-brightly.

'Do we?' he said. 'A bathroom? Fancy that.'

That day is frozen in my mind, each moment fixed, unmoving, like a tableaux. We didn't know, I think, either of us, how to treat the other so we skirted round like two cats, stalking.

Like a puppet, I walked Hugh round the house and saw everything through his eyes, fresh as he was from the lavish richness of embassy design. He tried, I think, at first, but couldn't completely hide his immediate disappointment, and as we slowly went from room to room together, even I began to feel the colours I had so lovingly chosen seemed garish and brash. The old furniture that I found traditional and comfortable, happily given by neighbours, seemed coarse and old-fashioned. The painted floors that I loved for their simplicity seemed, today, rough and plain. He didn't need to use words: a slight sniff, the way he ran his fingers over tables and chests, was enough for me to feel sad and embarrassed.

When we got to the bathroom, so simple, so unostentatious, he asked, pointing to the bath, 'Do you wash in this?' I saw the scratches and marks on it. All were the remains of its long, slow progress on the back of a donkey up the mountain. I remember how many times it had fallen and poor Yorgo had to keep getting one of the shepherds to help him reload it. He, Christo and I had laughed so much that day.

I nodded in answer to Hugh, and was about to tell him with my usual pride that it was the only one in the village, but I thought that would be of no interest to him.

The biggest shock to him, clearly, was his wife. He tried, I could see he did, but it was impossible for him to disguise his distaste at my appearance. My skirt, the one I was so proud to have made from old curtains, he pointed to and said, 'Village fashion, is it?' It was not said unkindly, but I knew he was thinking of all the fancy frocks I had left behind; the silks, laces and fine linens he had bought me.

At one point he touched my hair and, I think, almost flinched— I knew it felt rough and untamed, too long to control. A fast image flew through my mind of Christo lovingly washing it in the bath. Shaking a little, I lifted my hand to it myself and felt its wiry coarseness.

He stretched his arm out to me, silently inviting me to take his hand and gingerly I held one of his fingers, but only for a moment, and then I moved away from him.

'Why don't you use the bathroom, and I'll try and find some fresher clothes for you?'

'I feel I must apologise, for turning up here like this. I must admit, I thought you would be pleased to see me, but I suppose my arrival last night was rather inauspicious. I lost my bearings, you see, and went into that place up the road for directions. Old whatsisname insisted on bringing me here himself. Sorry about that, bringing a stranger in with me, and a drunken one at that.'

'Yorgo is as familiar to this house as I am. He was the senior workman, in charge of the renovations. I wrote to you about him. He is a fine carpenter; all the wood you see here is his craft.' *Oh, stop!* I said to myself. I sounded so pompous and over-defensive.

'Oh, good, jolly good,' he said. 'Well, I'll take a bucket of water from the kitchen and go and sort myself out.' And whistling cheerfully, he walked away. I watched him go. He was moving round the house as if he had lived here for years, taking it all for granted as he called out, 'Chuck me a towel, will you?'

Of course he left the bathroom door open; why would he close it? There was only me here, his wife. As I took a towel from the press, he called to me again, 'Any chance of some soap? Or do you use some sort of plant or something, here?' and he laughed.

Averting my eyes from his long, naked form standing, dripping water on the floor, I pointed to the wooden ledge over the bath. 'There is the soap, actually. It's hardly Harrods' finest, but one of my neighbours makes it from olive oil and flower petals. I like it.'

'Of course you do, darling. You love all this village stuff, don't you?'

Suddenly the emotions I had kept bottled up inside for weeks welled up all at once and I found I was shaking with rage. I didn't want him here. I didn't want him walking round the house as if he belonged here, as if it was his! I didn't want to face the savage truth in this; turning on my heel, I walked out of the bathroom.

'Oh, Evadne,' he called after me, 'didn't I leave some clothes here? Be an angel and fish something out for me, will you?'

An hour or so later he returned to the terrace. He certainly smelled fresher. I had left an old suitcase of his outside the bathroom door and he had retrieved some crumpled shorts and a shirt.

'That's a bit better,' he said, smoothing himself down. 'Any chance of some breakfast?' he asked as he sprawled on one of the old chairs.

'Of course,' I said quickly, jumping to my feet. Inside I put a pan of water on the fire and then I remembered that I had thrown out his percolator. I made the coffee as I now took it, thick and sweet like the Greeks. I put some of the hard, Cretan rusks on a plate with a glass of fresh water, arranged them all on a tray with three of Irini's little cakes, and took it out to him.

He took one of the cakes and bit into it, but left everything else.

Well, go without, then, I thought miserably to myself.

'I really am sorry about last night. I didn't mean to arrive in a state like that. It was rather foggy and then there was a light and it was that Pepper Tree place and they were all so kind and I'm afraid I rather let them overwhelm me with their hospitality. You know what they're like here, of course you do. Frankly, I was exhausted and that *raki* went straight to my head.'

My rage had subsided into a seething ache now, a knot of tension under my ribs. Somehow or other I had to get through this.

'How long are you staying?' As I said it, I realised how antagonistic that sounded. He sighed, and I added, 'I mean, how long can you stay?'

'Only two or three days, I'm afraid, and the really bad news is that I can't take you back to Athens with me.' He looked at me. 'I'm so sorry. I want to do that more than anything, but it just isn't possible this time.'

I tried to show disappointment, but inside I was jubilant. Surely even I could cope with a couple of days.

He settled comfortably back in the chair and started to tell me how and why he was here. The war was escalating daily and it was expected soon that Athens would be taken.

'I'm here to find a safe hiding place for the royal family,' he said, obviously thrilled to have been entrusted with this important task. Even I could see it was an honour and said so. He flushed, smiling. 'It was too good to be true, to come to Crete, and the perfect opportunity to see you.'

'Why Crete?'

'Well, no one thinks the Germans will bother with Crete. It's too far from the seat of power, Athens.'

'In the village everyone hopes and prays that to be true, but they don't really believe it. They think Crete is the centre of the world.' I laughed, and my laughter sounded shrill to me, like coins in a tin can. 'Mind you, I'm not sure how thrilled they will be. There's little love lost for the royal family in these villages.'

'This must remain a complete secret. No one must know, understand? Why do you think I dressed as a peasant? I was chosen because my Greek is better than any of the others, and I could travel undercover.'

He started telling me about the base the British had created at Souda Bay: 'Miles away from here in the north, but we wanted people to see our presence, feel the security the British will bring. That's the most likely place for the King. The Prime Minister, Tsouderos, will be with them.'

He reached across and took my hand. 'I so want you to be back with me, I miss you terribly. I thought at first this was the opportunity to get you out of here, but it's far too dangerous a journey for you at the moment. I came over from the mainland on one of the last flying boats, but I'll probably go back on a ferry.'

I couldn't help but feel there was something odd about my husband, treating this whole thing as a lark. Perhaps, I thought, that's how people like him cope with the horrors of war; all a bit of a jape, an adventure.

'Not a word of this outside these four walls, old girl.' I nodded agreement. 'But how about this for a tale? We've got two-way radios set up in one or two key villages across the island, and one of them is at the very top of Panagia! They each have an operator and, you won't believe this any more than I did, but the chap here is young Bingo, Foxy's brother!'

My mind buzzed. That must be the man Christo had spoken of.

'I don't think you met Bingo, did you, darling? We were all at school together. Of course, Bingo's younger than Foxy and I, but in spite of being a squit he was a good sort, even then. And the best thing is, it meant I had a perfectly legitimate excuse to come over to this side of the island. Which meant I had the best possible reason to find you.'

I was smiling and nodding and trying hard to show interest, but then I managed to ask what I really wanted to know.

'Tell me, what is happening in England?'

'It's not good. Hitler is determined to conquer Britain, but don't worry, Mr Churchill is equally determined to keep him out.'

He told me some of the things he knew that had happened; the Germans had occupied France, and my mind filled with pictures of the little streets and markets of Paris that I had walked daily. He told me that Goering had sent hundreds of bombers to try and destroy London, but now, it seems, many people have built shelters in their homes or gardens and those that haven't go down and sleep in the underground train stations at night.

'Your old hospital at Greenbridge and your family will be fine; they're out of London and the Hun don't seem interested in anywhere outside the cities. Well, airfields and that sort of thing, naturally.'

'You say that, but your friend Lady Troutbeck lives near Greenbridge and you wrote and told me she was going to Egypt.'

He laughed. 'Oh, good old Dora! Any excuse for a trip abroad and she's off. Don't take her as typical. Anyway, let's not go on about all this gloomy stuff. I'm sick of war talk. Now I'm here with you and the sun is shining, let's forget about all that, just for a bit, eh?'

He was smiling like a child on Christmas morning. Except that I was the present at the foot of the tree. His arms were round my shoulders and he pulled me to my feet. I made myself meet his gaze. It felt so deep, so penetrating. It seemed to look through me, right to my soul and I felt he must feel me cringing inside, so I willed myself to smile, forced myself to show happiness and he kissed me.

As his lips forced mine open, I couldn't help but cough. The breath issuing from his mouth was so tainted by fumes of the *raki* that I almost doubled over, gasping.

He laughed again as he pulled back from me. 'Oh, sorry, the one thing I couldn't find was a toothbrush. Do I stink still?'

I nodded, relieved that he had said it before I had to.

'Do you think old Diddlyakis will find my bag in the café and bring it round? I'm stuck without it.'

'I'll walk round and get it for you,' I said, grateful for any excuse to get out of there.

'Let's go together,' he said, but at that moment some god or other must have woken up and smiled in my direction for I saw below several villagers coming along the path towards the house.

Papa Yannis hadn't waited long before feeling he could pay a visit, and he and Manolis waved stiffly as they saw us.

'You stay here,' I said hastily, 'and entertain these people. It's you they want; they wouldn't be here to see me.' And thanking the *Panagia* like a village woman, I fled through the house and out of the door.

But my departure was unnecessary as Yorgo was the next to arrive with what I took to be Hugh's bag; a rough hessian sack tied at the neck with a worn piece of string. He saw Papa Yannis and Manolis and, thrusting the bag at me, scuttled back the way he had come.

The villagers all came by during the morning; sometimes, entire families. Of course they all brought some gift to welcome Hugh and mostly these were small bottles of wine or *raki* or a few onions, cakes or eggs.

Hugh knew the rules of Greek hospitality and poured glasses of *raki* for all the men, each time filling a glass for himself. In the kitchen, I chopped fruit and shelled nuts to provide the *meze*. At least it gave me something to do.

When the last visitors left, I finally felt that my house was restored to me. Hugh was quite drunk again and had propped himself in the doorway.

'Go and rest, I'll wake you later.'

'Good idea, old thing.' As he staggered down the stairs he called up to me, 'I gather that chap you took on to do the house is a bit suspect.'

I stood rigid as he spoke, unable to move or speak. He went on, 'Bit of a communist, by the sound of it. The priest and the bald chap were telling me.'

There was a great belch and a thud, and I guessed his body had hit the bed, and then silence. I slowly breathed life into myself again but I knew I was in great danger of weeping and I longed for solitude. I left the house and walked to the little church of Panagia Sta Perivolia.

Inside, its cool walls welcomed me and within moments I felt the calm I always experienced there. Then, exhausted, I sat down and, within moments, slept.

When I got back to the house Hugh was awake and sitting on the terrace. He looked relaxed and at home. He smiled to see me and held out his hand. I took it in mine, and settled down beside him. We sat in silence for a little and, with my new-found calmness, I knew I would feel guilt when he was no longer here. What a hell of a mess I had made for myself.

'Are you hungry?'

'Ravenous. What will you make for lunch? I poked around a bit in the kitchen and you seem to have plenty of provisions.'

'That's the neighbours,' I said. 'Oh, I wish you could understand how good every one is here. How kind to me. I was unwell recently, nothing serious, and they came with food every day, did the laundry, made delicacies to tempt my appetite. Anthi, of course, my friend, was the kindest of all. You remember Anthi? She saved my life when I fell over and twisted my ankle, before you left.'

He laughed. 'Oh, do you mean that rather dumpy little woman? She's your friend, is she?'

I was nodding and smiling now. 'It's only she that has made my life here so memorable, so liveable. She got me teaching at the school— I wrote to you about it, remember?'

And once I started it was impossible for me to stop. My life in the village here was a subject that would never tire me and I told Hugh all the details. How I got the house finished, how well the children were learning English, how they loved it. And the first aid! I told him about the little clinic hospital we had made of the old church. 'In fact,' I said, 'if you think of going up the mountain to find your friend, you could look in and see it.'

He nodded and got to his feet. 'Tell you what, we'll both go when you've cooked us up some of that stuff. I've spent too long away from you to want you out of my sight for a single moment.'

I went to the kitchen and started to prepare a stew of chopped aubergines, courgettes and tomatoes. Irini had brought me some of the dry Cretan bread a day or so ago. I thought if I soaked it in Anthi's rich green olive oil and seasoned it with salt and pepper and put it on a pretty plate with some local cheese, Hugh would find it irresistible.

We were both on the terrace, the tray of food before us, when Hugh said, 'You are pleased to see me, aren't you?' He was peering at me under a fringe of hair and I remembered that wistful look he did so well; it had always irritated me, just as it did now.

Briskly I said, 'Of course I am, why would I not be?'

'Oh, I don't know. You seem to have your own life sorted out here, teaching and all that stuff. I can't help wondering where I fit into it.'

'Let's take each day as it comes,' I said, knowing I sounded rather desperate. 'After all, I can't come back to Athens with you, you said so. Probably just as well I have something to occupy me here.'

He had hardly touched the food; it was getting cold as he sat there and even I could see it must now look unappetising. I piled everything back onto the tray and carried it into the kitchen.

He followed close behind me and when the tray was safely on the table, I felt his arms slide round me, his lips nuzzling into my neck.

I could smell the fumes of his breath. He pulled me round to face him and started to stroke my breasts. They were so tender, the slightest brush against them caused me to wince.

'I had forgotten how firm and wonderful you are; let me love you.'

And before I could speak, he was pulling me with him down the stairs and towards the bedroom. His hands were tearing at his clothes. Age and mildew served only to render the fabric of his shorts to shreds as he tugged at them.

My heart was pounding inside me. The moment I had dreaded was here, and I must act as though I was happy to be part of this desire.

I was slow to remove my clothing: my old curtain skirt and a grubby chemise. My fingers were numb and I fumbled with every fastening. I felt his fingers digging into my shoulders, lifting me onto the bed. He was rough, eager and pushed aside any clothing that was reluctant to come off.

Shutting my eyes tight I tried to think of something else, anything, but I failed. He was my husband and he was here in his house and his bed. I loved you once, I said to myself, when I knew of nothing else.

Hugh, never one to waste time on readying me for his pleasure, tried at once to push himself inside me, but too late; he gasped hoarsely and shuddered. He rolled onto his side with a cry and, curled round like a baby, buried his face in his hands. I could hear him faintly muttering, 'Sorry, sorry, sorry.'

In spite of my relief, I could only feel sad. His face was streaked with tears as he looked up at me, and I stroked his back and across his shoulders. I tried to speak, but my throat had shut tight.

Fiercely rubbing his hands across his face, he sat up.

'I can do it, you know, it's not always like this. I was just too eager today. You know, not seeing you for so long, and you are such a beauty.'

His eyes ran over my body but I got to my feet at once and clutched my skirt round my nakedness. I felt raw, exposed, as his eyes continued to travel over me. 'I think whatever it is you live on here must do you some good. You've really rounded out, you know.'

It was as though he was talking of the shape of a horse. Stepping into my skirt and pulling my blouse over my head, I felt composed again, only wondering at his 'I can do it you know.' He must have taken other lovers. I felt nothing.

The man he called Bingo looked remarkably like Foxy, just younger. He leapt to his feet when we stumbled our way into the cave. 'How wonderful to see you! I heard through this thing'—he banged his hand on the box receiver—'that you were coming. My brother got word to me. Oh, God, it's good to see a human being.' He looked past Hugh in my direction. 'Oh, sorry, madam, no disrespect intended.'

'None taken.' But I didn't smile.

Hugh was hugging him and chuntering on about his journey. I stood awkwardly, glancing round me. I knew every corner and shadow of this place so well. In the few weeks since I was last here, Bingo had taken occupation thoroughly. He was explaining now to Hugh how hospitable the villagers were to him.

'I'm sorry, Heavenly—you are Heavenly, aren't you?' Bingo turned to me. 'I kept meaning to come and find you but I heard you were unwell. I trust you are better now?'

There was a sound of voices behind me. Voices I knew so well. I felt my heart pound harder, faster, and I couldn't move, couldn't look round as Bingo called, 'Hey, come in, you chaps.' And to Hugh he said, 'I'm sure you want to meet this young man, the one I've displaced. He did all the work on your house. This is his home, this cave.'

Christo and Kotso walked in then. Without a glance in my direction Christo shook Hugh's hand, saying, 'I hope you are happy in your house. It was a pleasure to restore it.' He spoke in Greek and so Hugh replied in Greek, with a certain formality, nodding and thanking him.

Turning to me, Christo said, 'I hope you are recovered, Kyria?'

I couldn't trust myself to speak, so nodded briefly.

I wanted to see love in his eyes; I wanted to see the sadness of his missing me, I wanted to see everything there that had ever been between us. But his eyes were those of a stranger; polite, empty.

It was a mistake to have come. How could I have been so stupid to lay myself wide open to this torture? But I knew why I was here; I had longed to see him. I had thought just a glimpse of him would be enough. But this price was too high.

I managed to say, 'I'll get a little air,' and stepped outside.

Behind me, I heard Hugh say, 'The way up here is rather tough for these frail creatures,' followed by laughter. Christo could do everything I could not. He was easy now talking to Hugh about the house, the village, the villagers, the impending war, all in his casual, easy style. Beside him, only Kotso looked pained, uneasy.

After what seemed an interminable time, Hugh joined me outside and with much jocularity we left the cave and set off downwards.

As always I found any journey on the mountain glorious, the air so fresh, clean. There was a cool breeze in the late afternoon air and I pulled my shawl tight round me.

Hugh was full of good humour as we walked down, and told me over and over what a decent chap Christo was. He had obviously forgotten all his earlier reservations and went so far as to tell me I had chosen the workmen well.

I was exhausted when we arrived at the house and longed only for my bed. But I had a husband here now and although I escaped downstairs telling him I had a headache, he looked so disgruntled that I suggested he walk up to Il Piperia and find some rather more cheery company than I could offer.

He did just that and didn't return until two in the morning. By then he was well past the stage of thinking of romance, after the flask or so of *raki* he must have consumed.

ANTHI

I HADN'T SEEN HEAVENLY for days, but I heard her husband was back. Everyone knew that and perhaps it was as well to leave her alone to cope as best she could. The laundry had piled high and Manolis had no shirt he considered clean enough, so it had to be done. Astrape was loaded down with the dirty linen and we all walked beside him.

It was Voula who made me think to call past Heavenly's house. As we made our way to the spring she called, 'Helly, Helly, we are coming.' Looking up at me she giggled, and I thought, why not?

We were hardly at the path that led to her house when Heavenly ran out to greet us, and she was hugging us all with such delight, it was as though we had parted a year ago.

'You are well again,' I said. 'Have you any news for me?'

Of course I wanted her to tell me her bleed had started, but she was chatting to the girls and ignored my question, saying only, 'Everything I have is clean, thanks to you, but I'll happily come with you to the spring. It's good to get out of the house.'

As we approached the crooked pines that edged the path downhill, we heard the laughter of the women at the spring. They were all excited to see Heavenly and dropped their laundry to cluster round her, giggling and gabbling. Aphrodite, who was busy washing her baby's undercloths in the stone bowl at the end of the row reserved for those things, called over her shoulder, 'You'll be doing this next year . . . washing baby clothes.'

There was raucous laughter at this remark and a lot of amiable chat aimed at Heavenly: her husband's return, his short trousers, and even comments on his fine legs. When we had finished and turned to walk away, Aphrodite had the last word. 'You still look tired, after your illness. Get home and rest—besides, you'll need all your strength for your husband.'

Back on the path, the girls ran ahead and I was glad of the chance to speak to Heavenly alone. 'The *Panagia* must smile on you, my friend. You are surely blessed with all the luck in a single day that the rest of us would be happy to see in a lifetime.' She looked puzzled so I said slowly and clearly, 'Now the village expects you to be pregnant. Surely you see? Aphrodite has answered all your problems.'

Her face cleared at once. 'They think I will carry my husband's child? Is that what you are saying? That I can pretend this,' and she stroked her belly, 'is the result of Hugh's return?'

I was nodding with excitement. 'It's the answer to everything for you.'

But instead of her smiles, there were tears. 'Oh,' she said, 'how can this be Hugh's baby? Tell me, how can I make it happen?' She told me then what she had never told me before, that her husband is not able to make sex with her. He has almost never been able to. 'That is one of the reasons why Christo has changed my life. He taught me all the things I never knew I could feel: passion, desire, tenderness. Everything that is felt between a husband and wife, lovers.'

'I wouldn't know.' I was blushing now like a schoolgirl. 'I've always believed that what you describe was for men to feel. Women suffer what they are given and bear the children. I'm not the one to ask if there is anything more than that.'

My mind was busy and full of thoughts as we continued our journey back to Heavenly's house.

When we arrived, there was no sign of her husband, just a note pinned to the door telling her he had gone up the mountain again.

'He leaves tomorrow,' she said as we followed her in. 'You have tonight, still, dear friend. You must prepare for him, as you would for '. . . for your lover. Bathe yourself, smell sweet, wash your hair, put flowers on your bed, anything. Give him warm, sweet wine, just a little, not a lot. And love him as you have never done before.'

'I know what you are saying. I will try and do what you say, I promise. I loathe deception but maybe . . .'

'Loathe deception? It is a little late now to worry about such niceties.'

She winced at my words. 'I will come and find you later tomorrow, when Hugh has gone. Wish me luck.'

That night I slept uneasily. I thought of Heavenly trying to coax her husband into making love to her. What an irony! I longed only for peace from mine. It is some months now since he bothered me at night. Did he go with prostitutes when he went to Sitia? I could not care less.

Voula was fretful and I had to rise and go to her more than once. Despina slept peacefully on. At about three o'clock I took Voula downstairs and, cradling her in my arms, tried to talk her back to sleep while not waking Manolis, who was snoring in his chair by the fireplace, his dog at his feet. The night was stuffy and airless. A low-lying mist gave an eerie silence to the world. Like everyone, I longed for the freshness of a rainfall, craved the coolness of a breeze on my skin.

'Poor Voula,' I said, 'I think you have a painful ear. Will it help you to forget it if we feed the baby goat?'

Thumb in mouth she nodded, and we went into the garden and down to the goat hut at the end, past the vegetables. I keep this ramshackle old wooden building as a kind of nursing shed for any of the animals in need.

It was fresher out here and Voula slid to the ground and ran to find the baby goat and its mother. The kid was bleating pathetically, the mother stretched out lazily beside it, ignoring its pleas.

I guess we were there for half an hour or so, and my little one had surely forgotten her earache and fell asleep in my arms as we walked through the garden back to the house. I paused for a moment before going in. The clouds that had earlier fogged the sky had mostly cleared and the stars shone so bright again, it was like a sky full of candles. There was the evening star, the brightest of all, directly over the roof.

There was no sign of Manolis in his chair. His dog lay across the foot of the stairs and growled as I pushed past it. Slowly, I went up the stairs and into the girls' room where Voula slept alone these nights. She didn't stir as I laid her on her bed and pulled the blanket up to her chin.

And then, what sound was that?

A whisper of a gasp, was that it? Was it Despina? Was there a low, hoarse, breathy noise? A rhythmic sort of murmur? Or was I imagining sounds where none should be? But I felt strange, uneasy and a shiver ran through me.

Silently I crept along the few steps of the landing and paused at the door of my room where Despina slept now. It was closed. I clearly remembered leaving it open lest she woke. Slowly, gently, I pushed at the worn wood panel of the door and it swung silently open.

I could not move as I saw what was happening there, what had caused the noises I had heard. For a moment I froze, even my eyes unblinking, and then I flew like the wind across the room to the bed, grabbing Manolis by the collar band of his jerkin, pulling him off our daughter and throwing him to the floor. I do not know where my strength came from. I knew by instinct to be silent, lest Voula hear.

'You animal,' I hissed, as I reached down and pulled Despina into my arms. Her eyes stared up at me, almost blindly. Her nightgown was pulled up, exposing her thighs and the lower half of her body to the moonlight. Her budding womanhood was bruised and reddened.

Over my shoulder I saw my husband scrabble to his feet and leave the room.

'Oh, my baby, my little Despoula.' I rocked her in my arms. Our tears mingled as they fell. 'My baby, my baby.'

I heard a slam from downstairs. Manolis had gone.

I bathed her as gently as I could with the cool water in the basin. There was no blood. The time for that was clearly well past. How long had she suffered this, my baby?

HEAVENLY

I REACHED ACROSS and slowly, tentatively, touched Hugh's arm. He was awake and reached for me within a minute.

The first part of the evening I had spent so deep in the planning of how to seduce my husband that eventually when we lay in the bed, he went to sleep almost at once. I had prepared a meal that I thought he would like—goat begged from Irini, roasted on a bed of autumn fruits—and he ate it greedily. The wine I served was from Anthi's Pappous; rose-tinted and fragrant, it was the best of last year's harvest.

I bathed and washed my hair and dressed in one of the last frocks I had that had come to the island with me: pale, ashes-of-roses silk. Although the moths had made a start on it, it was mostly intact. Thank the lord it fitted, just. The little rounding of my belly had been compensated for by the weight I had lost during the sickness.

He had eaten the kid eagerly and asked for more. 'You have become a fine cook,' he said. 'I suppose needs must here, eh? No servants around. I must say I would miss that side of embassy life; no one to clean your shoes or press your clothes. There's a lot to be said for it.'

He rose from the table and reached out for my hand to lead me out onto the terrace.

If we were looking for romance, this was indeed a wonderful night for it; the air soft as a whisper, the filmy gold light of the moon and the sky full of stars. In the distance I heard the call of a night bird and the last cicadas of the summer crickety-cricking away.

We sat for a while in silence and then Hugh started to speak of the early days of our courtship. He remembered so many little things, details I had long forgotten: the Copper Kettle, the films we saw, the meals we had often snatched between my shifts. He made me laugh tonight, just as he used to do. He said, 'You have probably long forgotten all these silly things, but lonely nights in Athens are when I think back to all that fun we had together, just the two of us.' He turned to me, his smile as jaunty and flirtatious as it used to be. And looking in his eyes I saw all the love he had given me over the years. Impulsively, I reached out, took his hand and held it to my face, shielding my eyes lest he see my tears.

'The sun here has brought your freckles out and added some, I think.' I tried to smile at him. 'The truth is, it was one of the things I loved about you, your freckles. And your hair. And how you used to fall over or trip up at the slightest thing.'

I looked at him in surprise. 'But they were all the things I hated about myself.'

'I know. But they were some of the things that made you so different from all those other girls. What did you call them?' I opened my mouth to tell him and he put his fingers on my lips. 'No, don't, I've got it, the Minky, Mouse and Boo girls. Don't cry,' he continued, 'no need to be sad. When all this . . . this nonsense is over, this stupid war, we'll have each other again, we'll be together and get on with whatever life has dealt us.' And then we left the terrace and went down the stairs to bed.

For a long while in the bedroom we lay together holding hands, I think each of us lost in our own thoughts, and then slowly I realised he had fallen asleep. I was instantly wakeful; I gently stroked his arm and he woke at once and reached for me. Within moments he was touching me and my body responded automatically—I wanted him.

But he stopped, too soon, and eagerly mounted me, calling my name aloud, pushing insistently, trying to enter me. But, once again, he couldn't wait.

I put my arm across his back and I stroked him up and down, up and down. He accepted my comfort and took my other hand, kissing it softly, saying again and again, 'I'm sorry, I'm so sorry.'

Poor Hugh; such a brave-talking figure of romance and here, between ourselves, he was enfeebled and helpless.

We lay for the rest of the night mostly sleepless, side by side. There was nothing to be said, so we didn't speak.

The mechanics of preparing for his departure took up most of the morning. He dressed himself again in his villager's clothes that I had washed and dried in the sun. I gave him bread and fruit, some wine and a flask of *raki* and then suddenly he was ready. We were both so awkward with each other. I was full of sadness, with reasons more numerous than I could say, and it was with a voice breaking with emotion that I said goodbye.

'Take care,' I said, and pushing me slightly back from him he said, 'I love you, Heavenly. Try and remember that. I've never loved anyone else and I miss you desperately.'

And he was gone and I was alone and all that I could think at that moment was that, for the very first time, he had called me Heavenly.

ANTHI

IT WAS WEEKS before I saw my husband again. I learned he was staying with his brother, Stelios.

Despina's recovery was slow. Still there were days when she didn't say a word. I tried to speak to her about her father, about what had happened, but that only served to lock her further away. It was obvious she wanted to bury it somewhere deep inside. What didn't change was that she seemed never to leave my side. She became my shadow, and soon I didn't even notice that any more.

The rhythm of my life was as usual. The sun came and went, sometimes it rained, sometimes it was dry. Winter came in slowly that year and crept away again, and it was spring almost without our noticing.

Heavenly knew there was something wrong. We had come to know each other so well, she and I, that I couldn't hide any secret from her. In the first days, when all I felt was a terrible icy rage, I stayed away from her. School had started again and we met there, but I avoided going to her house, and she kept away from mine. From time to time she gave me a quizzical look and sometimes even a hug in passing. I was grateful for that. And then one day she said, 'Remember I am your friend. You have been so wonderful to me. I will always be here for you.'

She was increasingly obviously with child. All looked at her, but few spoke. Until one day Aphrodite at the spring, said, 'So your husband didn't come from Athens for nothing, I see, Heavenly.'

She blushed and smiled, but didn't answer. Walking home together, I asked her, 'Was it successful, your seduction?'

Her face crumbled. The smile had gone and she closed her eyes tight against the world. 'No, everything was as always with Hugh.' She stroked her hand across her swelling belly. 'This is Christo's child and I have a few months to enjoy that, and then I don't know what I will do.'

But then Manolis was back and I could think of nothing else. He walked in one night as though nothing had happened. Sat at the table and banged a knife up and down. He was waiting for food. My mind raced; supposing I refused him? Say I ignored him completely and left him to do his own cleaning, cooking? Tend his crops and fields and sheep and goats, what then? He would throw me out of the house, that's what. And my girls?

I felt sick to my heart as I realised he now had a use for them, so he wouldn't let me take them, would he? I couldn't bear it, so I gave him food. I washed his clothes and I tended his flocks and looked after his garden and waited on him as I always had, but inside I knew I must find a way out of this. And soon.

Despina and Voula and I all shared the one bed now. Sometimes I could hear him moving about in the night. I smelt the burnt tang of his tobacco in the air. In the mornings smeared, greasy dishes littered the table, smelling of strong wine and cheese.

One morning Yaya was busy baking when we arrived at her house. Voula ran straight to her to dip her finger into the bowl to lick the dough she was making. 'Not for you, little one,' said Yaya gently, pushing her fingers away. 'These are for the funeral gathering later,' she said. 'Did you know the widow Bigorakis died last night?' She shook her head. 'Not many will mourn her passing; she was a miserable old witch.' She crossed herself hastily three times. 'Forgive me, *Panagia mou*, but I speak the truth.'

She took a bunch of green tansy from the side table and, clearing a space, started to arrange the plant for chopping. Pulling off the bright yellow, button-like flowers, she put them to one side. 'Tansy biscuits,' she said. 'Not many remember now, but we always used to make these for a funeral. Dangerous stuff, tansy—if you eat too much before the funeral, you will end up sharing the box with the corpse.'

'How much is too much?'

She indicated the flowers she had cast aside. 'If I used all of those with all of these,' and she pointed to the reddish stalks she was chopping finely, 'it would be enough to kill a strong man. Stop, miss!' and she pushed Voula's hand away again.

Within minutes the tray of moulded biscuits was in the oven but with her words, my mind was far away.

Later, we walked across the hills towards home and it seemed everywhere we went I saw those same yellow flowers of tansy. To my mind, the air was heavy with their scent. Did everyone know how dangerous it was? In my garden, I stood and looked at them and my mind filled with dark thoughts. I shivered, although the day was warm, and ushered the girls inside.

In the house I made a vegetable stew; there was not much meat around, no one was killing. Waiting for Easter. As I was chopping the root vegetables, my eyes kept going to the open window.

'Shall we take Heavenly some eggs, Mama?' It was the most positive idea Despina had had in weeks, and I agreed at once.

We met Heavenly on the road to her house. She was coming to see us.

'I must walk every day,' she said, 'or I'll be as fat as a pie.'

So together we walked. The girls were carrying the eggs in their aprons so our progress was slow, but we did arrive eventually and sat on Heavenly's shady terrace.

She fanned herself with a leaf. 'I have five more months and twenty days to call this baby mine. After that, when it is born,' she shrugged, her face stricken, 'I have no idea what I will do.'

'I wish I lived here, I hate our house,' said Despina suddenly. 'Can we live here with you, Heavenly?'

'And me, and me!' said Voula, jumping up and down.

'You can stay here whenever you like. I would love to have your company, you know that.'

And then a thought came creeping into my head and for a moment

I shivered. 'Perhaps just for one night then,' I said hesitantly.

'Oh, yes, yes,' said Voula.

'Of course,' said Heavenly and Despina looked at me, a smile whisking over her closed little face.

'Tonight?' she said. 'Oh, please, Mama.'

'Tonight, tonight, yes!' giggled Voula.

'Is Manolis home just now?'

'Yes, but it won't bother him whatever we do. I'll go and—'

'. . . get some things,' Heavenly finished the sentence for me. 'We'll be fine while you're gone, won't we, girls? You can help me do some cooking, for our supper.'

They were pushing her towards her kitchen as I left.

I pulled a few of the girls' things together when I got home. I went to the hearth and stared at the cast iron pot on its heavy iron hook, the lid covered in embers. The vegetables inside were almost cooked.

It was as though I was in a dream. My head was in a whirl and my hands were shaking. I stood there as the sky slowly darkened.

I don't know how much time had passed before I left the house, ran through the garden, along the path and, breathing heavily, finally arrived back at Heavenly's house, the warm feeling of safety sweeping through me.

HEAVENLY

MANOLIS MANADAKIS DIED on the day the Germans entered Athens.

Well, that was the day his body was found. He had been missing for two or three days. But as his movements were never consistent, no one could be quite sure. The night Anthi and the girls stayed with me was the last time anyone remembered seeing him alive.

I heard that he was found at the bottom of a ravine, less than a quarter of a mile from his house. Yorgo, who of course made a coffin for the burial, was eager to tell me the details.

'Nasty business,' he said. 'They saw him in the *kafenion* the night he went missing. Sick he was, terribly sick, and not in his right mind.

Talking gibberish.' He shook his head. 'They reckon he was taken bad, lost his footing on the way home and fell down the path. Of course,' he crossed himself three times and lowered his voice, 'I'm sorry to say he wasn't much liked round about. He had his own little group of royalist friends, including Papa Yannis, but not many others.'

I sat out on the terrace knitting; Aphrodite had shown me how and given me wool she had gathered from her goats, washed in the spring water and spun into fine soft yarn.

There had been only one short note from Hugh since he had left. I knew that he had arrived back in Athens safely, little else. It sounded as though it had been a hard journey, with many escapes.

Anything I knew about the progress of the war came from the wireless set in Il Piperia. Yorgo knew that I was always hungry for news so he came here most days to give me bulletins.

I guessed the royal family were in Crete now. Was Hugh with them?

After Hugh left, I had very little sickness, but I was tired all the time. I wanted to sleep and sleep. And then, just at the time I calculated I was three months pregnant, I started to be full of energy all day, every day. And then Christo came.

I was sitting where I always sat these days, on the terrace.

It was one of those glorious spring days when everything seemed full of the promise of good things to come. I was knitting. I didn't hear him arrive, or come in through the house. Suddenly he was there in front of me, standing very upright and his eyes met mine and it was as if I could see in them everything there had ever been between us; all the love, the laughter, the tears.

I whispered his name. 'Christo?'

'Am I welcome here?' he said.

'Do you need to ask?'

'Yes, I think I need to ask.' And he took a step backwards, away from me. 'I want you to know I am here to bring you news of the war. Unless you know all that is happening from your husband?'

'I know almost nothing,' I said.

'I understand from my uncle's wife that you have every reason to be very careful of yourself.' He was turning away from me now, his eyes flickering round the terrace.

'You understand only a little of what is true, then.'

At last his eyes were still, looking at me, slightly quizzical. 'Are you saying you are not with child?' And then he looked away from me again. 'I apologise to you, I have no right to ask any questions, especially not of such intimacy.'

'Look at me, please,' I begged. 'I cannot bear you to look away from me, speak to me like that, as if . . . as if we are strangers.'

He turned his head towards me just a little and I moved in front of him, close. He could not avoid me now. I could feel his breath, the warmth of his body. I willed him not to step away from me. He stayed.

I lifted my hand just a little and touched him. 'You are not wrong,' I said quietly. 'I am carrying a child, and I am careful with myself because this child here,' and I took his hand in mine and lifted it to my body, 'is *our* child. Yours and mine. And nothing is more precious to me than this.'

I waited for him to ask me how I knew it was his. But he didn't. From the moment I told him, he believed me.

Later, of course, when we sat by the fire together, when night had fallen and a spring chill shivered the air, we talked.

We spoke of his family and mine. As he lay at my feet, his head in my lap, he told me for the first time of the sadness of his sister. The irony not lost on either of us, her longing for a child and her seeming inability to bring one to term.

He spoke of Bingo in his cave. How he had come to really like and admire the young man, his determination to be in the front line of any action and his frustration at staying in the backwater of Panagia. He didn't mention Hugh's visits there. He was keen to give me such news of the war as he had. He told me of brave villagers dying in the north of Greece as they struggled to fight the advancing German army. He is convinced that Crete will be invaded.

Bingo is involved in some new secret intelligence and has promised to share any news with Christo and Andros. 'We shall resist, we are ready to fight here whether it is the Italians or the Germans who come.'

We sat in silence for a while. For me it was joyous to simply be with him again. Night fell and through the open terrace door we could see the stars, then the moon, full and rich. We made love and it was just as it had always been. He was so careful of me, so gentle, tender.

'How will we . . . ?' I stopped him asking any questions that began with 'How'. Or 'When'. I have no idea how we are going to cope with any future life together as a family; so best not to speak of it. I know we should, we must, but not just now, not yet. He was so kind to me, gazing at me with such love in his eyes.

'Every moment of every day I will be with you in my heart. You and this, this . . . little person of ours here.' And he stroked my growing belly. 'I will be gone sometimes when I must, when there is no choice, but I will always come back to you.'

ANTHI

THERE WAS SUCH a lifting of my heart that I had to fight to keep myself from smiling every day. I wished I could pretend to feel any of the grief I should show. If I looked at Voula, I could catch her sadness, her bewilderment, and that helped. The poor little girl was barely old enough to understand her beloved Papa was dead. Despina simply said, 'What will happen to his dog?'

Manolis's brother Stelios came as soon as he heard the news and I sent him to Papa Yannis's house, to view the body. When Manolis was found, at the bottom of the ravine, I hoped at first that he had simply got drunk, stumbled and fell. It would not be the first time someone had died that way. But I could not fool myself for long. They told me he had nothing to drink in the *kafenion* that night, that he was ill already when he arrived there, complaining of stomach cramps.

Papa Yannis took the body. It was so badly mutilated it would not be fit for the children to see. I think he was genuinely upset by the events; certainly he wept enough for both of us. Stelios and my mother helped him wash and prepare the body for the burial.

My mother immediately took charge. There is nothing like a death to bring out the worst in her. She provided the grey hemp shroud he would be wrapped in; does she keep a supply of them, always ready?

She came to tell me the coffin would be sealed and there would be no viewing of the body.

I was cleaning the house when she arrived. She exclaimed and snatched the broom from my hand. 'What are you doing? You must never do this so soon after a death, you will sweep his soul away!'

Voula, thumb in mouth, silently followed her round the house as she closed windows and pulled the shutters together. She emptied all the vessels and jars of water, throwing it across the yard before she refilled them.

'Thanks be to the *Panagia*,' she said, 'that he died on the twelfth of the month. One more day and she would never take him.'

She opened the cupboards, sniffing in jars and containers. I said nothing. She was such an interfering old witch! Sometimes it was hard for me to be polite to her, even after all this time.

'We must talk about your future, and what you are going to do.'

'I shall manage well enough alone, thank you.'

'Huh, you say that now but you'll be complaining soon enough. Take those beads off, too, you are in mourning, remember.'

My hand went to my neck and a necklace of carnelian pieces that my Yaya had given me on my name day.

'You know nothing of customs, do you? You have always gone your own way. Well, there will be plenty of talk if you forget the rules now.'

The next day, the day of the funeral, was one of those grey days when the darkness never seems to lift entirely. At first light I took the girls to spend the day with Yaya. Pappous was to accompany me to the service and together we went to Papa Yannis's house.

At noon, the bells started to toll in the church and a thin line of mourners stretched silently outside the priest's house.

I looked quickly round. Although Manolis was liked by few when he was alive, nonetheless it was the duty of everyone who knew him even slightly to attend his burial, and most of Kato Panagia was there. I kept my head down and pulled my kerchief forward to hide my face. Pappous thrust a large, white linen square into my hand. I looked at him with curiosity.

'For your tears,' he said quietly. I nodded quickly, wiping my eyes and blowing my nose loudly.

As is the custom, Pappous walked with the other village men at the rear of the small procession, just ahead of my mother, my sister and me.

My mother was one of the few who wailed noisily with grief, but as we got to the church several others joined her.

Papa Yannis was cantor and intoned the prayers for the dead as we approached Manolis's family plot. Just before the coffin was laid into the freshly dug pit, the priest placed a piece of stone on it with the words, 'Jesus Christ conquers' etched into the surface.

There were no flowers for the grave, but Voula had picked some wild blossoms that morning and I threw them on top of the coffin as it was lowered, clumsily, into the grave by six village men.

Stelios wept silently at the side of the pit and fell to his knees whispering prayers, presumably for his brother's soul.

At last it was over. Outside the church everyone washed their hands and shook them dry as they exchanged news and gossip, their grief quickly forgotten.

My mother had prepared the funeral feast although these were lean times. When we got to her house I quickly scanned the table where a few biscuits and cakes were spread out, with some of Stelios's wine and *raki*. There were no tansy cakes here.

I watched them eat and drink and chatter together as I stood next to Pappous, drawing strength from his presence; they were quickly emptying their glasses and coming back for second measures.

My mother bustled over to me. She was dressed, of course, in deepest black. I reached to my neck as she approached and boldly pulled out my beads to sit comfortably under my own black collar.

The rich amber of the carnelians caught a ray of light from the door and it seemed they glowed. 'Ignore me if you want, you wilful girl. You'll be grateful enough when I find you a new husband. You will need help come the winter.'

'You did harm enough for one lifetime with the husband I have just buried, so don't bother yourself further, thank you.'

I pulled on Pappous's arm and we turned towards the door, when Papa Yannis bumbled over to us, a large glass half-empty in his hand.

'Anthi, dear Anthi,' he said, 'a sad day for all of us. Manolis was a wonderful friend of mine and I am sorry to raise the subject of money at such a time, but we must be ready for what comes next.' He glanced at Pappous, trying to hide his dislike of him and failing miserably.

I knew it was mutual and Pappous pushed me through the door ahead of him, saying over his shoulder to the priest, 'I will see that you are paid for everything today, but now is not the time to start harassing widows with small children to look after.'

And we were gone.

HEAVENLY

I DIDN'T GO to Anthi's husband's funeral. In my condition it was easy to be excused and Anthi told me to stay at home. She seemed a different woman now, relaxed and calm. I warned her she must be careful. Nobody liked Manolis, but they expected to see his widow grieve. It was Despina I was most worried about. In so many ways she was back to normal, but it was strange that she seemed to accept the death of her papa with no tears.

I never asked, never let my thoughts, my doubts ever come to the surface, but certainly each day that passed I felt a little shiver of wonder at the convenience of Manolis's death.

But then everything was swept out of all our minds: deaths, births, nothing mattered, except what was happening to our island.

It was a glorious morning in May, a day when rightly we could expect a cloudless blue sky filled with singing birds, butterflies, the puff of a dandelion clock. Instead, at early dawn, while the red rising sun hovered over the horizon, a cry ran through the village: 'Umbrellas! Umbrellas! Come and see!'

And the weeks and months the Cretans had spent in denial were over, finished.

These were not umbrellas but parachutes carrying German airmen, hundred after hundred after hundred, and then more. All the morning the air was filled with the evil sound of the first bombs, swiftly followed by the terrible sad wailing of injured men, women and children. Dogs barked, animals ran wild with fear.

We should have known, should have been prepared.

All that day and the next I sat on the terrace. Anthi came with her girls and we sat there together, not speaking. Even the children seemed to understand that something momentous, something terrible, was happening on our very doorstep.

It took just eleven days for Crete to be occupied.

It was said that never had a people struggled so fiercely against an aggressor. Christo told me this. I hardly saw him; he and Andros and their compatriots from Panagia and nearby villages were part of the strongest resistance movement in Greece: the National Solidarity group, which offered food and relief to villages up and down the country besieged by the occupying forces that were looting and destroying wherever they went.

And all this with so few weapons! The arms amnesty that General Metaxas had declared had left the people of our province, and others, with so little for our own protection. But our village men fought with sticks and stones and the branches of trees, anything they could lay their hands on.

The men gathered every night in Il Piperia and listened to the radio. Everyone now was hungry for news. War was everywhere, and war was bombs and killing. Women were not allowed in to listen; it was all about aggression, death and fear. War was unpredictable and ugly. Not suitable for women and children. This enraged Anthi.

'Even Pappous tells Yaya and me to get on with other things! While our island is invaded, we are expected to speak only about tomatoes and chickens, I suppose.'

They learned from the broadcasts that the royal family and the prime minister and most of his government had fled from the capital and, escorted to safety by the British Embassy in Athens, it was suspected they had sheltered for a while in Crete. Their island! Although most of them despised the royals in peacetime, come the war all that was forgotten.

Apparently Hugh had been singled out for mention in one bulletin. Of course I was proud.

But, overall, I felt a sense of despair. Crete had been taken, occupied, and in spite of the incredible bravery of every Cretan, there was no longer a feeling here of safety. Now there was an underlying horror that was felt by every man, woman and child: what will happen tomorrow? How long will we be left alone in peace?

As it turned out, it was three weeks, two days and a few hours. Twelve o'clock on a warm and sunny morning, cocks crowing, the song of birds nearby. Yorgo and his cousin Petros were preparing to set off for a day's hunting; the children had come from the school, running homewards with grubby, smiling faces. The square was unusually full that day, that time. And then through the narrow streets of Kato Panagia came the sound of marching feet.

I had strolled to the square to meet Anthi and her girls. We were planning a picnic. And then we all heard the regular clack-clack-clack-clack of boots on stone, and we froze to the spot.

Dust rose in a cloud that made it difficult to see how many there were, but it seemed at least a dozen men or so were coming down the hill in formation, two by two. At the front, I saw immediately, were Kotso and Bingo. They were tied to each other, roughly round the ankles, and were stumbling, nearly falling as they walked. They looked proud and unafraid. Every time they tripped, the soldier behind pushed his rifle harshly in the back of one or other of them, and his fellow soldiers laughed and jeered.

No villager moved. Not a muscle twitched; everyone had, it seemed, taken root where they stood.

'Kalimera!' shouted an officer in front. As the dust settled, I saw he had some medal or other on his grubby uniform. 'Kalimera,' he shouted again. Angrily, he stamped his foot and said, in heavily accented Greek, 'Answer me when I speak to you, when I wish you good morning, villagers.' And then he swore in Greek and you could hear a faint, shocked intake of breath from one or two people in the small crowd.

'*Kalimera*,' whispered a few voices.

He merely nodded in response. And then spoke rapidly to his men.

None of us understood, but it was soon clear what he meant as two soldiers stepped forward and, roughly shoving everyone aside, started tying Kotso and Bingo to the cross that stood in the square. The cross that was there to show anyone and everyone how many Panagians had died at the hands of the Turks in the early years of the century.

From the back of the square there was a sudden disturbance and one or two heads dared to turn to see what was happening. Coming to the front murmuring, 'Excuse me, excuse me,' to anyone in his way, was Anthi's Pappous. He was a magnificent sight. He was always a hand-some, imposing figure, but today he shone with the air of a man in command. In his hand he held the blue and white tissue-thin cotton of the Greek flag. He held it open and, tattered and old as it was, it moved just a little in the faint breeze. A brave and magnificent gesture from a proud man.

I could just see his wife, at the back of the crowd, anxiously watch-ing his every move.

Within moments he was at the front and facing the soldier with the medal. He was no taller than him but, even so, he outmeasured him in every way. He was our general, our leader, and I'm sure everyone there could feel it.

With authority he spoke: 'How may we assist you?'

Ignoring his words, the man with the medal instead spat on the ground at his feet, then smiled around him. 'We are looking for trai-tors here.' And idly he raised a booted leg high and savagely kicked Kotso and Bingo, once, twice.

Tears sprang to my eyes as Bingo whimpered, like a child in pain. Beside me Anthi gripped my hand, hard. Instinctively we both felt that I was in great danger at this moment, because of who I was.

Clearly they were hunting the English, these men, and in Bingo they had found the only one I knew of for miles.

Anthi's Pappous stood tall and unmoving, although I could see his hands clench and unclench. 'Who are you?' he said evenly, his voice clear and calm. 'And on what authority are you here?'

The officer spoke. 'Aah, poor old man. Have you not heard that your village, your country, now belong to us?' And he laughed in his face.

That was too much for Pappous. He had fought and survived many occupations of his country; he would not be humiliated by this piece of trash. It was written in his eyes. And with no thought for his own safety, he raised his arm and waved his flag high in the air.

'Crete is Cretan,' he said, 'and always will be so!'

Later Anthi and I would talk of this moment endlessly. We both felt the terrible inevitability of what happened next.

Furious, the officer turned and spat out the order to his men, 'Take him! Now!' and two soldiers rushed forward and grasped Pappous by the arms.

There was a horrified murmur from the villagers and one lone cry rose from the back, 'No, Stephanos, no!' Then Anthi's Yaya was trying to push her way through to be with her husband. Her friends and neighbours acted together with one thought—to stop her—and they held her back. Anthi looked at me for a moment, desperation in her eyes, and without another thought I pushed her away from me towards her grandmother. Everyone cleared before her and she was beside her Yaya in a breath, holding her, whispering into her hair, comforting her in any way she could.

Voula, beside me, shrieked, 'Mama,' and I gathered her to me at once. Despina reached out for her sister and between us we held her tight.

The officer looked around, a small smile playing on his thin lips. 'Kneel!' he said. But Pappous didn't move; he held his head high, staring straight ahead.

'Kneel, kneel!' said the officer furiously and when nothing happened he looked at the two soldiers holding him and said, 'He will kneel, now!'

The two men shoved and kicked Pappous forcibly to the ground.

And as I drew in my breath, the officer pulled out his pistol and shot Pappous twice in the head.

Mighty creature that he was, Pappous slowly and soundlessly crumpled into a heap and, without a murmur, I think he had died before I could breathe out.

A terrible wail rose from the crowd. I have never before heard, and hope never again to hear, such a sound; such pain, such feeling.

On the cold, grey stones of the base of the cross a thin stream of blood dripped slowly downwards. Kotso and Bingo were spattered where they were tied.

'Silence! Silence,' shouted the officer in command, and the crowd gradually stilled and hushed. There was just one lone cry now, Anthi's Yaya, her voice ragged with grief: 'Stephanos, my Stephanos.'

'I hope this will make you understand who is in charge here now.'

But we knew that whatever happened, whatever they did, there was no victory for these soldiers today, not here, not now. They could kill and destroy the bodies, but the spirit of men such as Pappous would never be crushed.

ANTHI

IT TOOK THOSE MONSTERS but five minutes to leave the square. They dragged Kotso and the wireless operator with them.

As I looked slowly down at my Pappous, I remember thinking there seemed such a small amount of blood from such a great man. But as I stood there, it spread slowly out from beneath him: a dark crimson stain.

My thoughts then were only with Yaya. Surrounded by her neighbours and friends, I took her from the square and home. Behind us, every man of the village who had been there surged forward to carry Pappous, my beloved brave and noble Pappous, to his home.

Heavenly waved just once in my direction and I saw that she had gathered Voula in her arms, and had taken Despina by the hand, to take them home with her. I knew they would be safe with her.

Apart from her first shout as Pappous was taken, and her cry of pain after he fell, Yaya had not uttered a word or a sound. What was there for her to say?

The path to their house was shaded and cool as a breeze whispered through the olive trees. Our steps were slow, measured. Yaya and I walked arm in arm as though we had walked for hours, exhausted. We paused as we entered their house. He was everywhere here. That was his chair by the table, on it the cushion she had made as part of her dowry forty years ago, still bearing the imprint of his body. His thick winter coat hung on a nail from the door. On the wall, the photograph of them on their wedding day looked proudly down. He was smiling, his arm round his beautiful, shy bride. His son, my father, the only other face on the wall, and next to them all the *iconostasis* with the nubs of burnt-down candles.

None of us in the room that day was prepared for this. The rituals of death, although familiar to us all, seemed inappropriate here, now.

Yaya glanced quickly round and seeing so many neighbours gathered in her little room looked at me for help. 'Anthi, will you, can you . . .?'

I felt only the need for privacy here and, as I turned to look at the gathering, they took the message clear in my eyes and slowly left us alone.

There were mutters of '*Mono Theos, mono Theos.*' Hard to believe in a god if this was his will, I thought.

Forlornly they drifted away. I knew they would return later to grieve with Yaya, but for now they all knew she needed only her family.

We sat side by side, she and I, waiting. We knew that the men would carry Pappous back here and we must attend him. I reached across and took her hand in mine. The papery-dry hand clutched my fingers and I stroked it softly. I knew no other comfort.

Outside we heard the sound of the men coming up the path to the house. They were singing quietly as they walked, an old Cretan lament. The words were lost to me but not to Yaya, who whispered along with the men as they carried Pappous into his house for the last time.

Yaya and I washed him with fresh water and dressed him in his best shirt, his neatest *vraka*. His boots bore the shine of the morning's polish. We had cleaned his head of the blood; in his forehead two small holes that he would carry to his grave tomorrow.

Yaya lay beside him on the bed. No tears now, just her arm over him as if to protect him. There was nothing left to protect him from.

I crept away and sat through the night at the table until the chill grey dawn came and the first cock crowed.

The funeral was a very different affair to the burial we had given my husband. Yorgo had stayed up all night to make the coffin and it seemed like a work of art. He had carved his name, *Stephanos*, simply at the head, but he had used the finest wood. He had oiled and polished it, and it gleamed golden in the rays of the rising sun.

As we led the procession to the church, it seemed the entire village had come to join us. Even the strongest men were openly weeping.

I had urged Heavenly to stay at her house today—she had to remember she was in danger. I held the hands of my girls as we walked along beside Yaya. She alone was silent. She would shed her tears in private.

Even though the coffin was open, I knew the body inside was not the Pappous I remembered. This body was merely trying to imitate him; my Pappous would live on in all of us here.

Papa Costas officiated at the funeral. The small, white-washed church was filled to the rafters with the mourners. The priest spoke warmly of Pappous's love of the countryside and his understanding of traditional ways. But it was outside, afterwards, where the villagers waited in line to embrace Yaya, that his fierce patriotism was spoken of.

I heard, 'He was a true Cretan,' said over and over again.

We stood round the grave, the open coffin resting on three strong boards. Panos, one of his closest friends who had played *prefa* with him every night for as long as I could remember, stood on the edge, looking down into the coffin. His hat clutched in his shaky old hands, he sang a *rembetiko*, a mournful, sad dirge of love and loss.

We stood on the damp soil looking down to the bright, sunlit sea below. He had never left this island he worshipped; only rarely had he left this village, and nor did his only son, my father. As the boards were removed and the coffin lowered into the new-dug earth, I vowed to give my daughters everything I had never had—the chance to travel and learn away from home.

HEAVENLY

CHRISTO COMES TO ME now only under cover of darkness. His face betrays his tiredness and it seems he has aged ten years in a moment.

'They have taken Bingo and Kotso over to Sitia,' he told me the first night he came. 'Bingo was captured on the hillside a good half-mile from the cave. At least they didn't discover the wireless. So I try and tune in at least once a day.' His dear face was furrowed into a frown. Suddenly I forgot what his smile was like. Would I ever see it again?

When he left, Despina and Voula ran to me. They were still shy in his presence and mostly hid behind the furniture when he was there. We sat on the floor, all of us huddled together, and we were still sitting like that in the evening when Anthi came. We gave the girls food and then put them together in my bed. They slept within moments.

Anthi is here such a short while each time; she stays with her Yaya. I have offered them both room here but she always refuses and I understand why. It is important for Yaya to live in her own home where she had lived with her husband all the years of their life together.

These last nights I have slept in a pile of cushions and blankets, sometimes in the living room and sometimes in my bedroom. Often little Voula cries herself to sleep and Despina holds her. They share their grief. It is a private thing.

The days all run into each other now and I think it is the same for everyone. We no longer seem to notice rain or sun; birds sing into the

empty air. Flowers bloom and fade, grass grows over paths once tram-
pled daily. Except for necessities, everyone stays in their homes.

From time to time the soldiers come. They need food and they take
what they want, no questions asked, no answers given. We have never
seen Pappous's murderer again. The soldiers stroll through the village,
their guns stuck in their belts, their uniforms scruffy. They steal what
they can find: eggs here, flour there; always wine and *raki* or brandy
when it is to be had.

I stay in the house. My only exercise: walking on the terrace each
day, back and forwards. I am big now with my child; I am sure it is a
boy as he kicks me fiercely, especially when I am resting. I talk to him
sometimes. Softly I whisper stories I remember from my childhood and
I'm sure he is soothed by them. I'm sure by the time he is born he will
know them by heart. But I make my thoughts stop there; I still don't
know what I will do when he is born.

One evening Anthi said, 'I saw Aphrodite today, she came to me at
Yaya's. She said she spoke on behalf of all the women in Panagia. They
want us to know, you and me, that they care for you like a true woman of
the village and you are safe here. They will never speak out against you.'

I was moved almost to tears by her words. 'I have no right to expect
their trust.'

'Maybe not, but you have it. What happened here has shocked
everyone to their roots. If any good is to come of it, let it be that it has
united us. We have a common enemy now; there is no place or time for
bickering or petty quarrels. Even with my mother and my sister.' She
paused and almost laughed. 'They came to pay their respects to Yaya
and to drink her coffee and eat the cake I had made, of course—double
helpings, mind you—and they wanted to tell us that they appreciate
your kindness to my children and they will never reveal your presence
here. If what has happened serves to unite my family in my favour, then
I will start to believe in miracles.' Then she laughed like the old Anthi.
'But not if it means she expects me to behave like a daughter. That
would be too much after all this time!'

We sat in silence for a while. The sky was peppered with stars, so
many there was scarcely room for the dark to come through. I stroked
my swollen belly.

'Christo will come to see you later,' she said. 'He will tell you that
I have asked him to take me with him when he goes out with the
andartes at night. They are going to hunt out and finish the *malakas*
who came here. And I want to be part of it.'

She raised her hand in the air as she saw the look of doubt on my face. 'No, don't even think to try and dissuade me. Christo has already spent hours doing that. I know every possible objection.' She stood up. 'I am a woman. They think I am too feeble, weak. But all over Greece women are fighting alongside their men. Christo let me listen to a report on the wireless set and it made that much clear.'

I sighed. I knew Anthi in this stubborn mood. And Christo knew, as well as I did, that if she was intent on going with him, nothing would stand in her way.

'What of your girls? What will become of them, if you are not here for them?' I couldn't say the words 'if you are killed' aloud.

'I've thought of that, too. Aphrodite and Yorgo will add them to their family and I trust you and my Yaya to make sure that in the years ahead they will have all the things I didn't. The only thing I really worry about is that if I am not around, my mother will try and make some kind of marriage for them. Run away with them! Take them with you to Athens or England. Give them a proper chance of life away from here.'

I hugged her to me. Her arms tight round me, I knew she was weeping silently into my shoulder. She pulled away, scrubbed her eyes with her crumpled sleeve. 'I must do this, you understand, don't you? I must. I can't just let Pappous die like that, like an animal, for nothing.'

Silence. Staring into our separate darknesses we sat there. Behind us stretched the past; the shared warmth and love of our friendship that had grown so strong, meant so much, I believe, to us both. Ahead of us, a future holding we knew not what.

I had to be strong. This woman had done everything for me, given me a life and helped me to learn to love. In all the time we had been friends, she had asked nothing of me. My own future without her flashed before me for a moment. What would I do? How would I bring the child I was carrying into the world without her beside me, without her wisdom, her knowledge? But I knew this was not the moment to raise my own doubts and fears.

'I understand. You must go, and take my love and my friendship with you. We shall hardly miss you before you'll be here with us again. Running our lives as you have always done. Go now!'

I watched from the top of the stairs as she whispered her goodbyes to her girls. They were deeply asleep, sprawled across my bed, the only sound the contented suck of Voula's thumb. She kissed them both and came back up to me.

'Will you look after Christo for me?' I asked tentatively.

'Do you need to ask?' she said.

We hugged and then, without a backward glance, she was gone.

ANTHI

I HADN'T BEEN COMPLETELY truthful with Heavenly. Christo had done more than try and dissuade me: he had forbidden me. I knew that he had recruited Andreas to the *andartes* and I reminded him of this. He had laughed. 'Andreas is six and half feet tall, a giant of a man. Look at you! What will you do, travel in his pocket?'

I begged, 'I am small, yes, but I am strong, too. My size means I can get into spaces you and Andreas can't.'

In the end I suppose my persistence wore him down. Reluctantly he agreed to let me go. I knew the mission was to try and bring back Kotso, and even Bingo. Of course that was important, but I had another reason, too, and Christo knew it.

'None of us has quite the spirit of revenge that you have. But don't let it spoil your judgement. You will do only as I say. There can be only one leader. If Kotso were here it would be him. But . . . well, let's hope we can get him back.'

In the last of the fading light before darkness set in, we left the village. Behind windows and doors, closed in spite of the heat, we knew we were watched. Since the occupation, there is no trust here.

I didn't know where we were going, and what our weapons were, if any, I could only guess. Christo carried on his back a rough straw pannier, and it rattled: maybe they were in there? But I knew it also contained a couple of water jars and a zinc bread-box.

Christo says, 'The less you know, the safer you are.'

Dusk came quickly, enveloping the olive trees with strange purple hues, but we all knew the terrain well as our animals grazed here.

When I had first arrived at the cave before we set off, there had been almost a feeling of shock as the two men looked at me. I was wearing a pair of Manolis's old *vrakes* and I knew in normal times this would not be acceptable: a woman in man's clothes? Outrageous!

We ate together, sitting on the floor in Christo's cave. Andreas spoke of the north of the island, 'My sister lives there, in Galatas.' He paused. 'Well, perhaps I should say, lived. Who knows if there is anything still standing there.'

'I'm sorry to tell you, but they say there is almost nothing left,' said Christo quietly.

Andreas bowed his head, crossing himself quickly, his eyes closed. He is built like a mountain. I have only ever seen his ruddy face smiling, until now.

'She had three children. Two boys I've never even seen.'

Christo put his hand on his shoulder. 'I'm sorry. I heard the city fought bravely alongside the British and the Australians who had come from Souda to help them. Many of the enemy were killed.'

'But not enough, eh?'

'No, my friend, I fear not enough. They passed through and burnt Chania almost to the ground. Well, that's what I heard.'

At last it was time and we set off in the early hours of the morning, creeping through the undergrowth in a line. No one spoke. We stayed close together as Christo had told us and slowly, slowly, we moved forwards, upwards.

By halfway through the fourth night our life had taken on a certain rhythm; we moved onwards by night and rested by day.

We were far from home and it was my turn at the front. I caught Christo's eye as I turned to see where he was, and he nodded reassuringly. He had urged me forwards earlier: 'You go ahead, and I'll follow with Andreas. Keep to the goat path across this hill and follow it round to the left when you get to the other side. You will see where we are to go. We are heading for the sea.' He smiled briefly and continued, 'We are going a little way towards my home village, which is on the stretch of land along from Sitia. The Italians have made a camp about a mile from there.'

The path was steep and uphill just there, and I was soon winded, sweat matting my hair into knots. Behind me Christo stopped. 'All well?' he asked. I nodded, gulping down deep breaths of air. 'We'll pause here,' he said. 'Take some water and rest a little. We have one more village to pass through and then down to the beach. We need to keep our strength for then.'

I found it hard to sleep during the day. When I closed my eyes I saw Despina and Voula sleeping peacefully in Heavenly's big bed and I felt a great ache in my belly. Was I doing the right thing? Would all this really make any difference? It wouldn't bring my Pappous back. As I thought of him and his great courage I wanted to weep. But it was time to move on.

Then at last, a village.

It was dusk. We crept forwards in the half-light, finding our way to the edge of the houses as Christo had taught us to do.

The silence of this village was eerie; just one lone, pitiful howl from a dog. Nothing stirred as we moved slowly through to the centre. Every home seemed empty, and shutters creaked and swung open. From one house, a wisp of smoke rose into the air, but not from a chimney.

Christo paused and behind him we stopped. A sudden breeze sent a terrible smell in our direction.

'Death,' said Christo softly. 'That's what we can smell here.'

We moved forwards, looking in through every door with an appalled fascination. Some houses were empty as we thought, but not many. Bodies were lying everywhere in grotesque mimicry of life. The stink of death hung over everything, overpowering our senses, nothing moving or living.

In one hovel an old couple lay side by side in bed, butchered as they lay sleeping. In another a whole family of men, women, children and even a tiny baby were gathered together in their kitchen, lying in a heap on the floor—all dead.

In the village centre, set apart from the houses, bodies were piled together in, and spilling out of, a water trough. Christo bent over them. I think he feared to find Kotso or another of his friends slaughtered there.

We walked together to the end of this village. Neapolis, it was called; a common enough name hereabouts, but one that would mean only desolation to me for the rest of my life. In front of me, suddenly, Christo paused and then he turned aside and doubled over, vomiting. Retch after retch until surely his guts would follow. He straightened up slowly, panting, his hands quivering like leaves in a breeze. I reached out to him by instinct and he waved me aside. Ignoring us, he walked as firmly as he could onwards. His lapse had never happened.

Daylight was breaking on the far horizon. Over that terrible place the birds sang as sweetly as ever, a goat rang a lonely bell and another glorious summer day dawned. We walked onwards, huddled together. For a short moment there was no thought of our need to hide, the birdsong broken only by the terrible sound of Andreas weeping.

At the first stand of trees we came to, Christo stopped. He was ahead of us by several paces. I sensed he needed to separate himself. We didn't speak; what was there to say? He sat down, his back against an olive tree. Dumbly we sat, too. We were exhausted but no one slept.

It was later that day, when we were getting ready to move on again, that Christo said, 'Do you want to stop now, go home?'

We shook our heads.

'There's no shame if you do. This is not to admit failure or defeat.' He looked around. 'You have seen here what is happening all over Crete; villages taken, every living thing killed and abandoned. It is worse in the north. The bulk of the occupying army is there. Down here, for the most part, the Germans leave their Italian lapdogs in charge; they are pretty feeble and just steal our food, interested only in their own survival. Occasionally they feel the need to prove themselves and take a village, as they did in Panagia.'

It made no sense to me, and I said so. Christo shrugged. 'It's called war; they can do what they like with us, they are in charge now. But believe me, everywhere they go, they are met with fierce resistance. Everyone says they have never before found an enemy as brave or strong as the Cretans. They will wish they never came to this island.' His laughter was just a crack in the empty air.

I thought of my two girls and shivered. I don't think any of us will forget what we saw today.

Christo waved us to a stop on the edge of a small olive grove. There was a shack beside it. I guessed it was an overnight hut for the goatherds or shepherds in spring at birthing time.

We sank into the shade and I drank deeply from a water bottle before passing it to Andreas. 'We will meet Kotso here if he has managed to gain his freedom,' said Christo. His casual words gave no sign of the dread he must have felt.

But there was only the empty silence of birdsong and the wind rustling through the olives.

I could feel my eyes closing as I relaxed. Andreas, on one side of me, slumped low, his head in my lap, his eyes lidded. My mind was drifting when I realised Christo was on his feet, listening. There it was again. I had thought it was birdsong, but it was a distinct whistle.

Kotso had found us.

He looked awful. His eyes were hooded and drawn with exhaustion. He walked with a limp and I could see bruises wherever I saw skin.

He said he and Bingo had been dragged across the island to the small encampment we would see later. They had been questioned daily.

'Every time it seemed that we'd persuaded them that we knew nothing,' Kotso told us. 'But every morning they would start the same questions over and over again. The only use we had was that we knew the terrain. Well, I did anyway. They used me as a guide. They seemed convinced that Bingo had information on the whereabouts of the king and the prime minister. They gave him a very hard time.' At his words

I thought of Heavenly—she knew his family. 'I escaped only yesterday.'

I discovered then that it wasn't just affection for his friend that had made Christo come to find him. Kotso led us to another shack, this one sturdier. Empty now, its roof was in shreds. But under a metal plate in the floor that Andreas heaved up, there was a cellar. 'Anthi, you are the only one who can get through this.'

I scrambled down into the evil-smelling space and as my eyes grew accustomed to the dark, I could see a rough canvas sack in the corner. This was what they wanted, and I pulled it over and hauled it up before wriggling out.

It was guns. There were four, one each. Christo made us clean them, handle them, look through the sights. We had all handled guns before. The rabbits and wildlife we ate had been shot with something like these—hunters' guns. I held one, ready for use. It felt strange; partly right, but it was also the unknown feeling of holding a weapon intended to kill a man.

But, overall, I felt exhilaration. I was so close now to why I was there.

In the middle of that day Kotso shook me awake. My sleep was crawling with dreams and I was happy to leave them behind.

We heard the faraway rumble of battle and a lone Stuka flew low across the sky. Then we heard the cry. It was a terrible scream of pain, and my blood turned to ice in my veins; it barely seemed human. We could see the beach at the edge of the cliff and there was somebody there.

'We will be dead at once if we move now,' said Christo in a whisper. 'That's what they want us to do. We must wait for dusk.'

So we waited and, as evening began to fall, followed Kotso down the steep goat path, inch by inch, until we gathered in the shadows at the base of the cliff. It was Bingo lying there. He was still alive, I thought. His hands were tied behind his back, his feet bound. He was covered in blood, fresh and bright from the cuts and slashes they had inflicted in many places. They had given him no chance.

'Into the caves quickly,' Kotso said, 'they have put him here as a lure. They know we will come to find him.'

Christo swiftly lifted Bingo's head and gave him water.

It was a long time until sundown. We hid behind rocks and in crevices, our bodies cramped and sore. No one slept. Kotso and Christo took turns to look out, and to move out to give water to Bingo, but aside from that far rumble of battle and the occasional plane, nothing.

It broke my heart to ignore Bingo like this. But as the last rays of the sun disappeared over the horizon, we knew we were not alone on the beach. Softly, stealthily, from the other end of the bay they came. Two uniformed men. They were armed and, as they neared Bingo's body, I saw their faces. One was the killer of Pappous, a face I would never forget. They moved silently, looking round. One raised his foot and kicked Bingo over.

The four of us rose as one, took aim and fired. With barely a cry they dropped like stones in a pond. Christo pulled Bingo behind a rock and I know that Kotso dragged me away. I was shaking from head to foot. I expected to feel jubilant. We had achieved what we set out to do, hadn't we? I could tell Yaya I had taken vengeance for Pappous' death. But all I felt was a dreadful, sad weariness. Somehow I felt diminished by yet another senseless killing.

Almost immediately we were on a long march away from the beach, as we knew that after our gunshots the place would soon be swarming with soldiers.

Later, after we had all slept an exhausted, anticlimatic sleep, Christo said, 'It is time for you to go home. You and Andreas have families, responsibilities. You have both been part of a day you can be proud of.'

We didn't argue. As we made ready to leave, Christo took me aside and said quietly, 'You proved your worth.' And then he added, 'I'm glad you came.' And he hugged me.

The carnage we had seen, and the sorrow we felt, made everything else seem so simple and unimportant. Coming slowly through Panagia, I took a deep breath of air. It was late in the day and the sun fell thick along the edge of the mountains.

I felt as old as these hills myself, and even the thought of being home with my girls again could only raise a whisper of pleasure. Andreas, too, was lost in his thoughts.

It was as we were coming down the path that I saw Heavenly. Her face broke into a great smile as she saw me.

'Oh, my friend,' she said. 'You're home.'

I ran to her, falling straight into her arms. She held me tight, saying, 'There, there,' as if to a child.

As I rubbed my tears away on my sleeve she was looking round. 'Christo? He's not with you?'

'He's safe. He will be back soon.'

'Your girls are fine. They're with Yaya. She has been wonderful.'

With a single wave, Andreas moved on up the path. I linked arms with Heavenly and together we walked to her house. She was bulky with the child and moved heavily.

Doors and shutters were closed tight as we passed, just like before. In spite of the heat, no one here risked exposure. I was sad to see my friendly village closed and changed. The only sounds of life were dogs howling and thin chickens scrabbling for scraps. This was what war did; filled everyone with fear, and drove them away from each other.

We went directly to Heavenly's house and I heard the laughter of my girls and my Yaya's voice saying, 'Mix and rub, that's what you do, mix and rub in your fingers until it looks like crumbs. That's right.' She sounded almost happy.

'Being with the girls has helped her grief to heal,' Heavenly said, 'and she's turning Despina into a fine cook.'

She paused, puffing a little. 'Oh, my dear friend, it's so good to have you back.'

We walked up the steps and Heavenly put her finger to her lips. 'Guess who is here?' she called, and Voula ran out of the door first.

'Is it Pappous come back?' she shrieked, her voice high, excited.

A flood of disappointment and sadness flowed through me, but it lasted only a moment, for when she saw it was me, she ran towards me, her arms open wide.

'Mama, Mama!' she said, her voice a squeak of excitement. I hugged her and lifted her high in the air, burying my face in the sweet, girlish scent of her hair, her skin.

Despina stood in the doorway, quite still and quiet. 'Mama, welcome home,' she said. She looked older than her years and her voice was low. But then our eyes met and she smiled.

I realised what the events of the last year had done to our children. I would see later that all the children in the village had seen things that no child should. They seemed to have lost their childhood, their innocence, overnight. And that hideous image behind my eyelids reminded me that Despina had suffered more than most and there were things she would never forget.

'Come, Mama, come and see what we have cooked for you.' Voula was tugging at my hand. It was that moment they all saw what I was wearing—Manolis's old *vrakes* and Voula shrieked with excitement: 'Now you are Mama and Papa, too!' she said.

Yaya appeared in the doorway behind the girls, smiling at first, and then, as she cast her eyes down my body, she gasped and covered her mouth with her hand.

'Oh, *Panagia mou*, my child,' she said, 'What is this?'

I had shocked her. Suddenly I was like a child again myself, incurring her wrath.

I blushed. 'Forgive me. It seemed the best . . .' My voice tailed away.

She was shaking her head. 'You must do nothing, nothing, to make them notice you. Walk through Panagia like that and everyone will stare, and if the army is patrolling and see you, that is the end. Besides, you are a widow now, you seem to forget that.'

She was dressed in deepest black and would do so for the rest of her life. But those cheerless, drab shifts are not for me.

The next day I learned Yaya's lesson the hard way.

I was with the women at the spring. There were maybe five of us, six, no more. Andreas's wife, Marina, was among them. She told me that Andreas hadn't spoken since his return.

'He sits in his chair all night, Anthi,' she said. 'He ignores the children. Every time I pass him, I rub his shoulder, his back, all the things he likes me to do, and nothing.' She lowered her voice. 'He weeps. All the time, his eyes fill with tears and he doesn't even brush them away. Slowly, slowly, they fall down to his lap. I tell you, it is a terrible thing to see a man like Andreas cry.' Her own voice was breaking. 'This bloody, bloody war. Why do they come here? What have we got?'

The other women were nodding; it seemed everyone had a story of horror they had seen. It was at that moment that we heard the sound of heavy footsteps approaching. Our men never come here. We stopped, our hands in the sinks wringing out the clothes, scrubbing. We kept our heads down and nobody spoke.

Soldiers had arrived. 'Stand up, women,' barked one, who seemed the leader. 'Come over here. NOW! Make a line.' He spoke bad Greek in a thick, heavily accented voice, hard to understand.

We shuffled quickly to do as were told but we were stumbling and clumsy. They had guns, these men, and although they had uniforms of a sort, they were stained and dirty. Collars open. They looked like rubbish with unshaven chins and greasy hair. Soldiers of the Cretan army would be ashamed to be seen turned out like that. Curiously, that thought gave me strength; I felt superior.

The leader shouted something; it sounded like an order, but none of us could understand. He repeated it, furious that, in front of his men, we couldn't tell what he was saying. Then he pushed forwards and, seizing the nearest woman roughly, tore her blouse from her body.

It was Marina. She screamed and tried to cover her bare breasts.

He waved his arms in a gesture that included all of us. 'You and you, all of you,' he shouted.

We looked at one another in fear. What did they want with us to make us undress? I could think of only one thing. My hands trembled and I could see from the corner of my eye we were all filled with the same thought.

'Quick, quick!' yelled the one in charge, his rifle pointed at us. We moved, slow and clumsy, until we were exposed, half-naked. I closed my eyes so as not to see my friends' and neighbours' shame. We had never seen the like before, and next to me Marina was muttering a prayer under her breath. Her breasts were full and proud before her. Myrto, older than the rest of us, was openly crying and trying to cover her sad breasts that drooped to her waist.

'The shoulders!' screeched the leader, and this I did understand. 'Look at their shoulders. Have they carried guns that cut into them?' and the men walked up and down the line peering at us.

But it was not only our shoulders under examination there. The soldiers stopped in front of each woman, and it was the young ones who interested them the most. They could not resist squeezing breasts and pulling nipples.

They kept us standing like that for half an hour or so in the full heat of the morning. I glanced sideways; we were all sweating, and Myrto looked as if she were about to faint. I knew I was the only one who had been near a weapon, but for such a short time that it had left no traces.

And that was it. That was all they wanted to know; had we carried rifles, were we *andartes*?

They cleaned their boots in our sinks and used our linen, lying carelessly there, to wipe them. Then they were gone.

As they disappeared under the cypress trees I spat on the ground. '*Malakas*,' I said to their backs, and one by one the women took it up. '*Malakas, malakas*,' and they spat as I had done.

HEAVENLY

THERE IS A CURFEW now, the same all over Greece. Enough resistance fighters have been tracked to the hills and fought back. They travel by night; darkness their only cover.

For days there has been no word from Christo. Exhausted by the worry, my pregnancy and the heat, I can't sleep. I sit on the terrace watching the moon and stars, listening to the cicadas and the bullfrogs, trying to plan for a hopeless future.

When Anthi was back, we went together to the little chapel on the hill, St Kosmas and Damianus, and cleaned it again. The only thing I knew for certain was that it was the place for my baby to be born, away from the eyes of the village. We swept and tidied. I took blankets and sheets there, and the dwindling remains of my medical supplies. Despina and Voula came with flowers and decorated it with twigs and branches and old bits of ribbon and lace. It became a little more cheerful in moments.

And then Christo came back to me. He came under cover of the night and I could see he was exhausted. Just as Anthi had creases round her eyes now and lines of anxiety round her mouth, so Christo looked in some lights like an old man. It was as if his youth had been stolen away.

We lay on my bed and he told me some of the things he had seen. I guessed he gave me a censored version. His eyes were closed as he spoke, but he told me these things would be part of his life for ever now.

'In the centre of the island,' he whispered hoarsely, 'I saw a village burnt to the ground. Men, women and children shot and chucked into pits roughly dug from the earth by their killers.' He kept stopping and clearing his throat, and his hands trembled ceaselessly. 'At the very hint that anyone was harbouring one of the *andartes*, their house would be flamed and whoever was inside lined up and shot. Those bastards even raped the women.' He was whispering now and I strained to hear. It seemed important to know. 'In front of their men and their children. How do children ever recover from that?' His voice was tight with emotion and anger.

I stroked his head but there was no comfort for him tonight.

'They won't defeat us, Heavenly. Cretans have always fought back harder than anyone in the world, I think. Not everyone gave up their guns or their old hunting rifles, thank the *Panagia*, and those that have them are determined to be rid of yet another *malaka* trying to take over our island, our Crete.'

'Who are they all, these fighters? Where do they come from?'

'They are all mountain boys who have lived in the hills shepherding their family flocks since childhood. There are hundreds and hundreds of them all across the island. They'll do anything, whatever is needed. And I tell you, Heavenly, it's not only the men and boys. It's the women, too! I think anyone who is not running the home is out there. One night I was following a group crawling through gorse and when we got clear, I saw the leader was an old woman—she must have been ninety. She had a great curved knife tucked into a belt, ready for action.'

I was pleased that he had stopped trembling. Speaking of his *andartes* had cheered him.

'In between fighting, they are messengers carrying information from one group of our friends, our supporters, to another. British, Australian and New Zealanders can only operate with this undercover help.'

He stroked my belly and within moments he slept. There seemed little peace in that sleep. He cried out often.

'Hush,' I whispered to him and stroked his brow, damp with sweat.

We woke with the birds; their sweet calls like a murmur of close friends nearby. Christo left before sunrise. He turned to me, took my hand and said quietly, 'In all the horror I have seen, and I know all the tragedy that must lie ahead, there is one thing that keeps me sane, my Heavenly. It is you and this,' his hand caressed my belly, 'the child of our love, here. I never lose sight of that. It is what I live for now.'

And he was gone again.

I knew we would meet later at dusk in the hospital chapel. He and Kotso had brought Bingo and a New Zealand boy, a soldier, back with them. They were badly in need of medical attention.

I found Anthi and the girls on the path. She had seen Kotso, learned what was happening and come to help. The doors and shutters were open, but there was a smell of sickness inside our little hospital.

I could only remember the day when we had come with the children and their families and played at being nurses and patients. The memory was oddly shocking in the face of the reality that greeted us.

The two men were lying on the makeshift beds. They were filthy. They had travelled without stopping across the country. No place or time for bathing or clean clothes. They were alive, but barely so.

Anthi sent the girls to prepare bowls and pans of clean water. We had no means of heating it so it would have to be cold. I looked quickly at the New Zealander. He would survive, and I sent Anthi to clean him up.

I went to Bingo's side and knelt clumsily there. His dear boy's face was cut and bruised, his hair matted with dry blood. His eyes were puffed and swollen and he could barely open them. When he saw me, his poor face tried to crease into a smile.

'Hello, Nurse,' he said. 'Excuse me if I don't get up, will you?'

I put my hand gently on his shoulder. 'Don't think of it,' I said. 'We'll get you mended and then we'll work on your manners.'

346 | Brenda Reid

'That's the ticket,' he whispered through cracked lips.

He was having difficulty breathing; gasping for air and wheezing. I feared pneumonia had already set in. He had needed help long before this. I wasn't at all sure how much I could help him and the thought made tears well up.

Pull yourself together, Tyler, I thought.

'Nurse,' he said, 'Nurse, I'm cold.' He was shivering with the rigors of his fever.

'It's Heavenly, Bingo, remember?'

'Nurse, nurse, so cold, nurse.'

He didn't know me.

I called Despina over with some water. She crept towards me on tiptoes, trying hard not to spill a single drop.

I wasn't sure how much to involve her, how much to protect her from the darkness of this young man's condition. But as soon as she was with me she knelt down beside him. I watched her for a moment. She soothed his coarse hair back from his face with fingers so gentle. He closed his eyes and I could feel a calm move through him. Quickly I took one of the strips of clean linen that Anthi and I had prepared and wrung it out in the water.

'Good girl,' I whispered, 'you remember perfectly what to do.'

I glanced across quickly towards Anthi and the other lad. He seemed peaceful and cleaner already. Her hands moved quickly, efficiently. Beside her, Voula looked across to her sister and, seeing what she was doing, moved her hand across the New Zealander's forehead in the same movement. Her free hand was raised, her thumb firmly in her mouth.

As slowly and carefully as I could, I washed Bingo's face. Looking down, I knew I would have to cut his shirt off and see the rest of the damage underneath. As though she knew what I was thinking, Despina gently started to undo the buttons. Her fingers were so quick and dextrous. His chest was soon revealed to us and I flinched, but she seemed not to notice the wounds. She eased the sleeves back and looked at me. I nodded and she was up and moving like a gazelle, crossing the floor to the pile of linen in the corner.

We worked on together like that, squeezing the water through the cloths. Every few minutes she would lift the zinc pan up and stagger across the chapel with it to the door, chuck it outside and fill it again from the tap on the wall.

But the fever raged through Bingo, and however much we bathed him down with cool water, nothing would cause this heat to leave him.

He was drifting in and out of consciousness and his skin had the blueish tint of death.

I tried to lift his head but I couldn't persuade his lips to stay open long enough to get him to drink.

I stretched my aching back up and out, but I had to stand and walk, and move around.

I went over to Anthi and the other young man. 'This is Jack,' she said.

He looked up at me. 'How d'you do, nurse,' he said. 'Am I in heaven already, or are you angels living down here these days?'

Anthi had done a good job of cleaning him up and although bruised pretty badly, he looked considerably better than when we had started.

I smiled when I saw that Voula was curled up at his side, fast asleep.

'She's like one of my puppies,' he said, his hand now stroking her hair as she lay. 'We just had a litter when I got called away. My old mum cursed, but I said to her, "Mum, I gotta go and give old Mr Hitler a good seeing to, so you'll have to get 'em going on your own."'

While he was speaking, Anthi had pulled back the blanket covering him and I saw his legs. One was mashed up badly and she had cleaned that, too. There seemed to be no sign of infection, however, and I knew if we kept it clean, with luck, it would heal. I nodded and she covered him again. He had drifted into sleep so Anthi stood up and stretched her own aching back, looking anxiously across to Despina who was now singing softly, sweetly, to Bingo.

'She's fine, Anthi,' I said. 'She's doing a good job.'

Jack slept on for most of the afternoon. Sleep was the best cure. I yawned and Anthi persuaded me to rest, too. Nothing would make Despina leave Bingo's side.

I must have dozed but jerked awake at a cry. Swiftly I rose and was at Bingo's side at once. As I sat down heavily beside him, I saw he was struggling in desperation for each agonising breath. The rattling in his chest grew louder and his breathing was laboured.

'What can I do?' Despina looked up at me, her eyes reflecting pain.

'Nothing more than you are doing now, little one.'

Death was not kind. It came slowly. His eyes flickered open for a moment and he reached out with his hot, dry hand. She took it in hers and stroked it tenderly.

He struggled, gasping for a breath, smiled a moment. 'Lovely roses, Mother,' he said, and breathing deeply just once, he was gone.

'Has he died?'

I answered her gently. 'Yes, he has.'

'Everybody here dies now,' she said bitterly, and ran outside.

A day or so later, in a troubled sleep, I was woken by cramps. They started gently but, within moments, were insistent enough to wake me thoroughly. I had been lost in a dream and at first I didn't know who or where I was. Was it night? Day? At that time sleep washed over me at all hours. The sun was high on the horizon, so I guessed it to be about five in the afternoon.

I was living in Christo's cave. It was no secret. I had given up toing and froing from my house to the hospital. I needed my energy just to live and help any of the sick and wounded that were brought to us.

The day I left my house was one of those perfect days. Early sun from across the mountains, a soft breeze; a golden, precious day.

That morning, I walked slowly round the house that I knew now as home. I remembered that first day I'd seen it. How instantly I had fallen in love. How I knew I wanted it to be in the years ahead with our children, Hugh's and mine, running round and through it.

Now there I was, gross in my belly with Christo's child and no thought of my future at all. Tears of sadness filled my eyes for this house, where I had grown up.

This was where I had left Evadne. This was where I'd found Heavenly.

I lay for a little, drifting and dozing, but the cramps this time were growing stronger and my belly was tightening and seemed to be pulling me down. I stood up and that simple movement released a flood, a torrent that fell from me. It soaked my night shift and left me standing in a puddle of water. So, it was time.

I had to think quickly: what should I do? New-found independence I may have had plenty of, but I didn't want to bring my baby into the world alone.

Anthi and Christo, I needed them both and, as if my prayer had been heard, there was a soft whistle from outside. Christo! Not waiting for an answer he came in, gently calling my name.

'I'm here,' I said.

I hadn't moved and he stood in the entrance, taking in what was happening. Crossing over to me, ignoring the puddle, he put his arms round me and nuzzled softly into my hair. 'Is it now?'

'Can you help me, Christo? Can you really be with me?'

He looked momentarily puzzled. 'Do you doubt I can help you?'

He had never voiced his feelings about blood; I had never asked. I thought it was private, for him alone to know. Anthi had told me of what had happened when they were away. How he had vomited. 'It was terrible there,' she'd said, 'we were all frozen with horror. But Christo seemed, somehow, to take it more personally. I don't know.'

Now he looked at me and slowly nodded. 'It's natural you should be worried. But I've thought about this moment and all I feel is excitement. In all the horror that is going on—something good, something beautiful, will come out of it. My child, our baby, and I will be part of its arrival with you.'

The pains were stronger now, regular, about every five minutes.

'I have a mule here. Anthi is at the hospital. I've just come from there. It's quiet today, not much happening there or anywhere. I think everyone is trying to get the last of the harvest in before the threatened storms come.'

He half pushed, half lifted me into the saddle and I winced at the hardness beneath me. I saw his hand shaking as he grasped the reins.

Our journey up the mountain took twice as long as usual and every movement, every jolt, sent another spasm through me. I couldn't help the groans that fell from my lips.

Christo looked at me, fear in his eyes. 'Is it bad? What can I do?'

Between contractions I managed a smile. 'Nothing, it is normal. Don't worry.'

At last, the small bell-tower of the whitewashed church was in sight.

'Mama! Mama! Come quickly, Heavenly is here and she's injured!' Standing in the doorway, Despina was the first to see me.

'Despina, take the reins,' I heard Christo call through the haze that seemed to fill my mind and, before I could speak or look round, I was lifted high in his arms and carried in through the door.

ANTHI

CHRISTO STAYS BESIDE HEAVENLY, but I think it is hard for him to see her in pain. I remember my own times and, try as I might to think only of Voula, little Constantinos keeps coming to my mind. Not a day passes without my thinking of him, imagining how he would look.

Mercifully, the worst heat of the day is over. A tiny breeze scented with sage and wild thyme whispers in and she takes great gulps of that air as though it were a soothing drug. We are alone. Christo and two villagers took the last of the injured away yesterday. No more Bingos, no more dying; well, not yet, not here.

Heavenly is living in Christo's cave. It's closer and she is in the hospital most days. It makes sense: in fact, it was Aphrodite's idea, and so the women at the spring could only agree. Heavenly can do nothing wrong in their eyes; they know how hard she works with the *andartes*.

Jack, the New Zealander, was one of the last to leave. He mended well and stayed around to help us. Voula adored him, following him like a shadow, and even Despina smiled more when he was around.

She taught him backgammon with the set Pappous had made her. In return, he showed her conjuring tricks. He made us all laugh and Heavenly, and even Yaya, said it was a long time since they had seen me looking so well.

'Even happy,' said Heavenly. Well, it's a long time since anyone paid me a compliment, especially a man. Jack's blue eyes used to crinkle into a smile when he called me 'Angel'.

'You two are Heavenly and Angel,' he had said one day, and it stuck. 'Heavenly carries the baby and you, Angel, carry the world on your shoulders.'

I tried to tell him that I had always done it. 'It's the life,' I said, 'I'm used to it being this way.'

'Well, not when I'm around. You're too pretty to do all that stuff.'

He was a brave man. He had little fear for his own safety and Christo said he was a good runner for the *andartes*. He seemed as at home in the mountains as he must have been in his own country.

'You would love it there, Angel.' Voula was asleep beside him, her head in his lap and his hand stroking her hair. He had strong hands.

'I've worked with animals all me life,' he said when I commented on them. 'A thousand sheep and counting. One day at a time, Angel, I know.' I had often said this to him, many times when he told me of his dreams. 'But I can only hope. Let's get this ruddy war over, get them dirty Krauts back where they belong, and who knows, eh?'

Jack went down to stay in one of the caves by the sea. His New Zealand regiment, the 22nd Battalion, had left Souda Bay to return home. 'Probably thought I was dead,' he said cheerfully. Yaya gave him some of Pappous' *vrakas* and an old sailor's cap. He grew a fine beard, mostly black, but speckled with grey, and he passed for a fisherman.

'As long as no one expects me to open me mouth, I'll do. See you later, Angel, I'll be back.'

I missed him dreadfully.

But still the war went on. Those who had thought that it would only take three weeks, three months, for the Hun to be sent back home, all 'finished by the olive harvest', were not so cocky any more. We coped with it at first as though it was a bad dream.

So when one night a small convoy of casualties—five or six lice-ridden men on stretchers, with appalling wounds, moaning softly, dismally, for their mothers or their wives—arrived silently in Panagia, brought from God knows where by the *andartes*, then the reality came to us.

Suddenly everyone was very quiet and came slowly out of their houses to look at them, these shadows of men. The women clasped their hands together tightly, biting their lips. I think everyone felt helpless and ashamed as, for sure, they were all glad it was not their husband or son lying there.

It took hours to get them up the mountain to the chapel. How much quicker, someone said, to keep them in one of the village houses. 'And have them dead by the end of tomorrow,' Christo had replied. We knew he was right. The enemy sent patrols frequently and with no warning, foraging for food. No, the chapel and the nearby caves were the only places with any chance of safety.

It was such a trek to get up there, so far they had been ignored.

Word of a little makeshift hospital had spread like a fire through the *andartes* in this part of the island, but none knew where it was. It was a closely guarded secret. Somehow Christo had acquired a large box of medical supplies and he and Yorgo lugged it up the mountain, disguised by straw on one of Yorgo's donkeys.

I came up here most days. I thought my girls had seen enough sickness and death to last them for ever, but Voula seemed not to notice and Despina wanted to help. And she did. She bandaged efficiently and was not bothered by the sight of a bloody wound.

Aphrodite and Yaya, even Irini, offered help, but we kept them away. With many of the men away with the *andartes*, the women now did all the men's work as well as their own.

A loud cry from across the room and Heavenly is nearly there, I think. I push Christo away from her and take his place. 'No place for a man,' I say, and laying a kiss on her damp forehead, he reluctantly goes to sit outside the door. So it's just Despina and me. She is pale with fatigue, but will not leave, and her eyes sparkle at the miracle happening in front of her.

'Aahhhh.' Heavenly's face is a mask of freckles and crinkles as she strains to push. She is panting with exhaustion, but even in the throes and indignities of childbirth she is beautiful.

'Harder, harder,' I tell her. 'Nearly there.'

'Look, Mama, look.' Despina's eyes are wide with wonder—there below is the very top of the head just coming into the world. There is a whisper of damp, dark hair and with one final great cry from Heavenly, the baby slithers wetly out and into mine and Despina's clasped hands.

'You were right, it's a boy!'

There was a roaring yell from this new little person. His eyes opened milkily and through long, black lashes he blinked at us all as he took his first breaths.

Heavenly couldn't wait. She grabbed hold of the wet, slippery, blood-stained little chap and put him naked to her breast, laughing and crying all at once.

Christo ran back inside and gazed down at his son and his lover. We were all weeping together with the joy of the moment.

Constantinos she has called him. 'For you, my dearest friend, Angel.'

And so we have a Constantinos with us now. He is a beautiful, healthy baby and he is surrounded by love.

But even then I have to ask, have to know, even through the great joy you can feel in the air of this little hospital, this church: what now for Heavenly? What now for Christo, the father, unacknowledged though he is? And what now for Constantinos?

HEAVENLY

CONSTANTINOS IS TWELVE WEEKS old today and a chubby, healthy baby. His eyes are blue, just like Christo's, and his black hair is tipped with auburn through the curls. Of all the things to inherit, he has my hair! When I bathe him and wash it, it dries to a frizz just like mine. His smile is like his father's: it seems to light up the air around him.

It was too dangerous to take him to the village, so we moved between the cave and the hospital. Constantinos was always on my hip or my back. Anthi had brought me the length of strong, brightly coloured linen that her Yaya first wove to strap her father to her back and then passed to Anthi for Despina and Voula. All that time ago, when I first met Anthi, that was how I remembered her.

But mostly my Constantinos was in my arms. I couldn't bear to put him down. Although I did, of course, when I was nursing any casualties, mostly *andartes*, that had found their way to us.

All of them paused when they saw my baby son, fingered him under his chin or gave him their thumb to clutch tightly, which he did happily. Then, in spite of their pain, every one of them smiled.

'I think he is better than all our medicines,' Anthi said. 'He is the future. It is for all the baby Constantinoses everywhere that they are fighting.'

Voula came most days and just sat beside us smiling. She seemed as bewitched by Constantinos as I was. He loved to play with her fingers and she had been trying to teach him to suck his thumb. But this was not for him. He pulled it out from between his lips and blew a bubble or two instead to make us smile.

I thought I knew love. I had loved Hugh and oh, my Christo, how I love him. But nothing in my life had prepared me for this magic, here and now; my baby, my son, my Constantinos.

Sometimes I caught myself forgetting to breathe, so carried away was I by the thrilling intensity of my love for this little one, and a moment of dizziness would bring me sharply back to earth. I took in the soft, damp, warm sweetness of him with a gulp of air. Grown inside me, inseparable, he was me.

That day I knew would be the most difficult and painful day of my life: I had to say goodbye to Constantinos. Christo was coming at daybreak and then I knew I would never, could never, see him again.

How could I do this thing? I didn't know if I could bear it. But the only thing I could give my son was a life, so I had to do it.

I remembered from Greenbridge the girls who came to have their babies and leave them for the orphanage or adoption. Matron said it was easier for them never to see the baby at all and they were always removed and placed in the nursery within minutes of their birth. And I remembered the pain of those poor girls, who would weep piteously through the nights, begging to be allowed to hold them, just once.

Never to see Constantinos, never to hold him, never to feed him from my breast, would that have been easier than this?

The only people from the village who knew that Constantinos lived, apart from Christo and me, were Anthi and her girls. Together we cared for him up the mountain, in the cave. Despina and even Voula knew and understood that our Constantinos was a secret baby. Despina, of course, understood secrets. Anthi had finally told me of the horrors that sweet child had known. As for Voula, this war and the terrible things she had seen had aged her beyond her childhood years.

Christo and I had talked long into many nights and this was what we had decided for our son.

Anthi wept when I told her, but I think they were tears of relief as well as sadness. It was she who had warned me from the beginning of the impossibilities of any alternative. If he lived here with me, if we survived the war, we should have to leave when it was over. This was Hugh's house and Hugh knew he had no child.

If I left with him now and took him away from there, how would we live and where would we go? Imagine, an Englishwoman and a baby in the wilds of the Cretan countryside? The enemy was everywhere. We would be captured and killed without a moment's thought.

Could I take him to England? I have asked myself that many times. But there would be no place for him. All I had there was my mother and she would not even have allowed me through the door with the bastard child, as Anthi said, of a wandering stonemason. Besides he was Cretan, like his father, and I would be denying him everything I now believed important. I wanted him to grow up in this wonderful island. Its history, his inheritance. I wanted to give him the sunshine to light his days. I wanted to give him the warm Aegean sea to swim in. And I wanted him to run in the olive groves and reach up into the cypress trees, and love this place as Christo did and as I did. And if I kept him I could give him none of that.

He was going to be brought up in a village along the sea, past Sitia. It was not far in distance, but the two mountain ranges between us could be crossed only with great difficulty. His mother was going to be the happy wife of a fisherman there. He would be her only child and her brother, his Uncle Christo, would see him every day and watch over him for the rest of his life. At his baptism Christo would be his godfather and would never leave him.

Christo's sister and her husband longed for a child. But she had suffered many miscarriages and seemed unable to conceive. Her friends in her village would be told she had taken in an orphan of the war.

The day after Constantinos was born, Anthi had gone down to the spring. All the village women were gathered there. 'More for their mutual comfort than to do the laundry,' she said. There had been another raid at dawn the day before, another lesson to be taught to the villagers. This time the savages were from the German army. Christo had heard that they thought the Italians, who were the bulk of the occupying force around this end of Crete, were too soft on us! Soft? Was Pappous's death a game? So this was as much to shake them up as us.

They had marched into the village square and three men had been bound hand and foot, lined up outside the community centre and, in the very place Pappous had died, shot by a firing squad.

One of them was Andreas. 'He died for nothing,' said Aphrodite, weeping. 'What lesson do we learn from this?'

'Only that none of us is safe,' Anthi had said, tears falling from her eyes.

Andreas's wife Marina was a shivering wreck of a woman these days, and could barely find tears enough to weep. 'The things he saw happening on this island had almost killed him already,' she said. 'I think he was happy to die.'

So although they expressed their sympathy for me when Anthi told them my child had not survived, they were so occupied with their own grief that they could spare me barely a thought. 'A quick prayer to the *Panagia* and a promise to light a candle for you, no more. It's the Cretan way,' said Anthi. 'They are so rooted in old superstitions they think they will catch bad luck if they come too close. No, Constantinos will be safe.'

Now, as I wait for Christo to come by, my breasts are aching and tender. But I must ignore them and wait now for the milk to dry up; they are no longer useful.

Christo's sister has found a wet nurse in her village. A woman she knows and likes, who has plenty of milk for two. Sophia, that will be Constantinos's mother. A lovely name and I try hard not to resent her. I must think only warm and good thoughts of her, for Constantinos and Christo's sake.

One thing I don't know, oh, Christo, my love, and have asked him not to tell me, is if he will come back here when he has settled his son in his new mother's arms. If I am truthful to myself, I think that if he is to be the godfather to Constantinos he has promised to be, he will stay over there.

And I know I have to return to being Hugh's wife. I must think of him as my future. I try to remember the morning he left. He called me Heavenly and I hope that with my help he can change. I will think of how I loved him when we met and that has to carry me on to the future. But just now I can barely think of life without the two of them, my son and my lover.

The night has been long and every moment with Constantinos I try to capture another memory to hold with me for ever: his birth, his smile, the tiny blister on his lips from sucking, the sweet almond scent of his hair and that wonderful, extraordinary feeling of him feeding at my breast. But now I hear the steps of a mule and in the low moonlit dust of the mountain path I can see Christo approaching. And now he is here.

We kiss and for a few precious moments I hold him tight in my arms. And then I hand him our baby, Constantinos, already wrapped in a shawl and sleeping peacefully.

And then they are gone.

I stand on the mountainside in the chill air of dawn and watch them ride away. Christo in the saddle with one hand resting protectively on our baby in front of him.

I have to be strong. I have to be brave. There will be no tears. There will be no tears. I stand still until they are far out of my sight and then I turn, alone, each movement a knife in my heart.

It was time for me to say goodbye.

Saratoga, near Auckland
New Zealand

JANUARY 1972

ANTHI

I KEEP IN TOUCH with Panagia Sta Perivolia when I can. Aphrodite writes to me and tells me that she and Yorgo will come and visit one day soon. But she has been saying that for years and always something comes up with one of her children. I know that they have busy lives. One is a heart surgeon in Athens, even!

I have a happy life here. We live on Jack's family sheep farm. His father died some years ago and his brothers wanted to live elsewhere so my Jack keeps it going. I work beside him, and there's a lot to do. We employ over twenty drovers and plainsmen and he says it's time I relaxed more. But he's said that ever since the day we met so he should know by now that I just shrug and say, 'It's the life,' and keep going. I find it impossible to sit and do nothing. I read a lot but never during the day; that would feel like a sin.

We have three children. Despina and Voula, of course, but we also have a son. Jack said I should call him Constantinos, Costas, but I couldn't. That is all far away in the distance, now. Besides, there is another Constantinos, isn't there?

My son's name is Stephanos, after Pappous, of course, but everyone calls him Stefan, which is fine. He started to go to agricultural college in Tasmania but got fed up after three months and came back here. 'I'll work beside Dad,' he said. 'I'll learn a whole lot more that way.'

My girls have done well, achieving everything I ever dreamed of for them. Despina is a Professor of Medicine at Harvard University in America. From those days in our little hospital she longed to be a doctor; it was natural to her. She comes home to us here once a year. She is a serious young woman, well, not so young any more. She is not yet married. It doesn't surprise me.

Voula is a teacher in Auckland. She loves her work, but has somehow found time to have four children, all girls. She married a paediatrician, a Cretan, Yannis, who came here from Heraklion to study, met Voula and never went home. They come here, all of them, every year for Christmas and Easter. I love the girls dearly and Jack spoils them terribly. Jack has given them a pair of fine horses that we keep stabled here for them. They live happily alongside the farm horses and my own stallion, Astrape. I couldn't resist calling him that.

Voula and her family go back to Crete every couple of years, but mostly to the north of the island. I sometimes wish she would go over to Panagia, just to visit, but why would she? Panagia is a place only of memories for her, and so many of them sad.

And what of the old days?

Jack managed to live the life of a fisherman until the war ended. He came up to Panagia when he could and we gradually got to know each other better. I, who thought never to look at another man in my life, began slowly to realise that the pleasure I got from Jack's visits was becoming greater, and was more than simple affection between friends. I missed him when he left each time and counted the days until his return. The girls clearly loved him, too. So when Yaya died just after the war, there was nothing to keep me there. Well, there was, of course: my mother and Ririca. But they didn't care for me, they never had, and moved to live in Chania. I assume they live there the life of two miserable old women. Whether they are alive or dead, I have no idea.

At first it was hard to leave the village, but I had always promised myself that I would give my girls a better life, away from there, so for their sake I left. If I'm honest, it was for my sake, too.

After the war, Panagia, like all the villages that survived, would never be the same again. The Germans surrendered to the British; they couldn't face the Greeks, I heard. When all Europe had fallen, Britain and Greece had been left facing the enemy alone. It seemed impossible to believe that 6,000 on both sides had died, along with Pappous, Andreas and Bingo. And more, too numerous to mention. But we who were there will never forget them.

It seems that the spirit of hope and love, that Pappous had always taught me was the future, was killed along with all the casualties. For barely had we pushed the last German off our land than Greece dissolved into civil war and once again brother fought against brother, father against son. All that sadness, all that pain, and nothing changed.

And then there is Heavenly. Ah, my dear, my beloved Heavenly. She came to our little hospital just about every day and went home most evenings, back to Christo's cave. I went over there once and found her sitting in the entrance gazing up at the stars, her cheeks wet with fallen tears. She was holding one of Christo's cushions to her belly, and wrapped round it one of baby Constantinos's shawls. I hugged her to me and something inside her seemed to give way, to spill over, and she cried and cried until I thought her heart would break.

Christo did not come back to Panagia. I knew that he wouldn't. He had told me so. He could not bear to be with Heavenly knowing that she would have to return to her husband at the end of the war. But also he had promised Heavenly he would be there for their son. And he was.

Whether she ever recovered from the loss of so much love in her life I never really knew. She seemed able somehow to keep herself going day by day. There was a constant stream of casualties needing our care. Kotso was still running the *andartes* in and around our hills, and so she and I continued to work side by side at the hospital. I know she had aged considerably by the end of the war and grief and pain were etched in fine lines on her face.

Hugh came back, something of a hero. Of course, she went with him back to Athens. They were there for some years and then they went to Thailand. I had many letters and postcards from her and I treasure them.

The one that surprised me and, I suppose, pleased me the most came from Panagia. She and Hugh had had a child, William. It gave her a reason to stay there for some of the time while William grew up in the village. Eventually, of course, he went away to England to Hugh's old school. And then later she had a daughter whom she called Angel.

'She named her after you,' Jack said, but I told him not to be so silly.

She continued to send me photographs and news and gossip from the village. Everyone there had long forgotten her first pregnancy. I think they had forgotten she was English! So she could stay happily in Panagia as much as she was able.

And then, two weeks ago now, came the letter from Aphrodite.

'I don't know if you know this,' she wrote, 'but dear Heavenly died on September 21st. She had, it seemed, been ill for a year. Hugh, William and Angel were with her. She was buried in the morning in the little chapel of St Kosmas and Damianus at the top of the mountain. Remember it used to be your hospital during the war?

'A sad day that one, because in the afternoon we had to go over to Sitia for the funeral of Yorgo's nephew, Christo. He died unexpectedly of a heart attack. I know you knew him well when he lived here. He never married.'

I wept for days. I felt I had lost half of my soul. I had always loved her so much. And Christo's world was empty without her.

I try to be positive. I try to look forward, for somewhere there is Constantinos and, of course, William and Angel.

It is the life.

Brenda Reid

Can you tell us a little about yourself?

I am an only child and grew up in the exciting London of the fifties and sixties—the heady time of jazz clubs, coffee bars, Carnaby Street, the King's Road, Mary Quant and Biba. My childhood was very happy but I would have liked siblings who might have shared with me the great handicap I thought I had—being very tall. I am now a tall and ill-coordinated woman who seems to fall over or drop things too easily: just like Heavenly in my novel. But I made her beautiful to compensate.

    I went to a girls' grammar school in London and then to the Central School of Speech and Drama, which I loved. My contemporaries there were Judi Dench and Vanessa Redgrave. When I left Central and looked for work, my six-foot height stopped that happening. So I quickly married the first tall man who asked me and had three tall children instead. But shared height isn't necessarily the best foundation for wedded bliss so, sadly, I divorced—and fell in love with the short man who lived next door, and who made me laugh, instead. I have been married to David, very happily, for thirty-one years and between us, we have five much-loved children and ten grandchildren.

You worked at the BBC. What did you most enjoy about your time there?

I worked as a script editor and then as a producer. I especially loved finding and working with new talent. I worked on Daniel Day-Lewis's first film, Ralph Fiennes's first film, and I gave a chance to a young and beautiful actress with a three-line part—her name was Penelope Cruz. Anglia Television then made me an offer that was hard to refuse, and I became their Head of Drama for five years.

Where did the idea for *The House of Dust and Dreams* come from?

Life rather changed its course for us when David and I went for a holiday in Crete in 1980. We loved it: the landscape, the food, the climate and, most of all, the people. So, year after year we returned, always to the same place—a small harbour town and resort in the south-east of the island. My work had stopped being exciting and challenging because Anglia, along with all the other television companies, was making less and less drama. So I stopped. We sold our apartment in London—the children were now all living their own happy lives—and we bought instead a crumbling old ruin of a house in a mountain village in our favourite part of Crete. The house we bought was the Orfanoudakis house in *The House of Dust and Dreams*. It belonged to a dear friend in Crete—it was his grandfather's house. The friend, Iannis, was the project manager for the house renovations and, working with local builders using the stone of the surrounding mountains, he made our house into the beautiful, comfortable, traditional house it is today.

I started to write *The House of Dust and Dreams* while sitting on our terrace here—it's where I write most happily. I learned stories of the past from old people in the village, but my book is a work of fiction and does not represent our village. I write most mornings here, while all around me are the sounds of village life—the chatter, the laughter, the arrival of the trucks selling vegetables, bread, fish or cheese. I write in the early evenings, and that's when the trucks selling clothes, shoes or chickens arrive in the square below. We don't have any shops here.

What would be your perfect Greek meal?

My favourite Greek meal would be eaten beneath the big pepper tree, in one of the only two tavernas. It would be stuffed courgette flowers to begin and then roast chicken and potatoes cooked in the Greek way with oil and lemon. Or maybe *stifado*; a stew of beef or rabbit with onions and plenty of cinnamon, cloves and juniper. To finish, it would be slices of icy watermelon and figs and copious bunches of grapes from our vine. With this feast, I would drink local white wine and water fresh from the village spring. Perhaps an ouzo to begin with and a *raki* with honey to finish—but not every night!

Are you working on another novel?

I am just finishing my second book, *Heavenly's Child*, but which child I'm not telling you! It is set in the same house in the same village, though this time in the late sixties and early seventies, when Greece was ruled by a military regime.

Finally, what three words do you think best describe you?

I asked David for three words to describe me and he said, kindly, 'Elegant, vivacious and generous of yourself.' I would, of course, add, 'Very tall'.

Sweet

Misfortune

By Kevin Alan Milne

Not long ago, I was eating lunch at a Chinese restaurant and when I cracked open my fortune cookie at the end of the meal, there was a message inside that read, 'All of your dreams will shortly come true.' As I sat there staring at the tiny message, a story was born in my head about a self-described realist and her one-of-a-kind 'misfortune cookies'.

To me, 'Sweet Misfortune' is about life's greatest quest: learning to find happiness, even when all of our hopes and dreams seem to evaporate. Experience and observation suggest that everyone, no matter how rich or poor, will suffer through difficulties. None can escape heartache, sadness, or loss; but mixed in with the hardships and 'misfortunes' there are equally splendid moments of joy and love that make it all worthwhile. And perhaps, it is only in consequence of what we have endured that we are able to look back and appreciate—or even recognise—all of our good fortune. Call me crazy, but life (as near as I can tell) is sweet . . . so take a big bite!

Chapter 1

Have patience: rainy days will soon return.

September 21, 2009

SOPHIE JONES KNEW EXACTLY what the squatty little bus driver was going to say, long before the Gig Harbor Express to Tacoma lurched to a halt in front of her stop on Harborview Drive. She anticipated the woman's words, the disappointment-laden inflections, and even the accusatory facial expressions. Every nuance of what was about to transpire was, to all intents and purposes, a foregone conclusion. As the bus's door swung open with a hydraulic wheeze, Sophie entertained herself by rehearsing the pending exchange in her head. *Again? Oh heck, girl! What's wrong with you? Leave that thing at home!*

Sophie stepped slowly from the kerb and up onto the bus, simultaneously closing the extra-large black umbrella that rested on her shoulder. She half-smiled at the woman behind the wheel but felt instantly silly for trying to be nice. What was the point, since there would not be so much as a courtesy smirk in return?

Knowing what was about to happen, she began counting down.

Three . . . The bus driver scrunched up her face, then drilled into Sophie and the umbrella with her eyes. Two . . . She let go of the steering wheel and folded her arms across her torso. One . . . A sigh, a disappointed shake of her head, and then . . .

Zero.

'Again? Oh heck, girl! What's wrong with you? Leave that thing at home! It's a beautiful Monday morning.'

Sophie chuckled softly as she leaned the umbrella nose-down against a safety bar and paid the fare. She found it mildly amusing that the driver was so predictable.

'And if it rains?' Sophie replied, completely unaffected.

'You see any clouds today? We ain't had a dang sprinkle in a week, thank Jesus Almighty and knock on wood.' She thumped the thick metal steering column with her knuckles.

Sophie shook her head in dismay. The driver was right about the weather. The morning sky was an unblemished blue and the forecast called only for sun. None of that mattered to Sophie. 'Expect the worst,' she quipped, trying again to force a smile.

'I know you do, girl,' the driver baulked. 'That's your problem.'

The woman said something else under her breath while Sophie found a seat. Sophie ignored her. Even on the best of days, it was way too early in the morning to get riled over the offhand remarks of bus drivers. But this was not the best of days.

For Sophie, this day was the single worst day of the year, like an annually recurring nightmare that she couldn't escape. If it weren't for the fact that she had a business to run, she'd have gladly gone back to bed and slumbered the day away in peaceful oblivion.

If only, Sophie thought, as she shuffled along the aisle to her favourite seat at the rear of the bus. As usual, she had the elevated rear bench to herself. While the bus rumbled along she stared out at the lush green landscape whistling by, watched as several eager boats left the harbour for a day in the Sound. She studied the tall cable supports of the Narrows Bridge, which connected Olympic Peninsula to Washington's mainland. On most days, those sights would be enough to distract her from the bitter realities of life.

But this was not most days.

For Sophie, this was a day for regrets, and nothing could quell the sense of heartache and disappointment that this particular date evoked each year. A day for self-loathing, she told herself, as she wedged the enormous umbrella into a space between her seat and the floor heater. My own personal pity party. I can be as miserable as I want on my—

'Happy birthday, Sophie!'

Jumping at the verbal intrusion, Sophie gasped audibly before the familiar female voice registered in her mind. 'Holy crow, Evi! Are you trying to give me an aneurysm? What are you doing here?' Sophie consciously ignored the stares of the handful of commuters who'd craned their necks to see what was going on.

'I thought I'd surprise you! Looks like it worked.' Evi smiled as wide as she could and added a wink for good measure while sprawling out on the vacant seat one row up.

Sophie glared back at her with mock contempt. 'Brilliant,' she deadpanned. 'I have one friend in the whole world, and how does she show me that she cares? By sneaking up on me, making a public scene and reminding me what day it is.'

Evi was still beaming. 'Like you need any reminders,' she teased. 'And for the record, I didn't sneak up on you. I got on the bus two stops before you did, but you were so self-absorbed when you got on that you walked right past me. I was even waving!' She stopped to wink. 'But forget it. It's your birthday, so I forgive you.'

'Yes, my birthday—the worst day imaginable.'

'Oh, shut it,' Evi countered cheerfully. 'We both know that the worst day was forever ago.'

Evi was a short brunette with an infectious smile, an easy laugh and skin a beautiful bronze. Her hair and smile were from her mother, her skin colour came from her Latino father, whom she'd never met, and her laugh was simply how she'd learned to deal with life's complexities. She was also one of the few people in the world whom Sophie trusted implicitly. Much to Sophie's chagrin, her friend's name, Evalynn Marion Mason, had six months earlier been lengthened to Evalynn Marion Mason-Mack, the hyphenation the result of marrying Justin Mack, a friend of theirs since college. Sophie was glad for her friends— but their union made her worry that life was quickly passing her by, a feeling that was amplified when Evalynn announced two months later that she was pregnant.

Outwardly, Evi and Sophie were as different as night and day. Evi was short and Sophie was tall. Evi's hair was straight, brown and bobbed, while Sophie had golden locks that flowed gracefully past her shoulders. And whereas Evi was gregarious, Sophie was more reserved. Everyone assumed that their friendship was built solely on the principle that opposites attract, but Sophie knew that it was much more than that. They were more like sisters than anything else, and they depended on one another in ways that people who grew up under more normal circumstances didn't understand. For as different as they might have appeared to outside observers, the pair had at least two things that stitched them together like a patchwork quilt: tragedy, and their African-American foster mom.

Sophie exhaled slowly. 'You know I hate my birthday.'

'Yep.'

'You should have just stayed in bed with your hubby this morning and left me alone to sulk.'

Evalynn tried mimicking the bus driver's sassy derisiveness to lighten things up. 'Girl, what's wrong with you? You know I ain't leaving you 'lone on the day you turn twenty-nine! Heck!'

'Stop! You're embarrassing yourself.'

A single giggle escaped Evi's enormous grin. 'No, I'm embarrassing you. It's what I do best.' She poked her friend gently in the ribs. 'Oh, c'mon. Smile, Soph! I don't want to spend the whole day with you if you're going to be a grouch.'

Sophie raised her eyebrows questioningly. 'The whole day?'

'I took the day off, and I'm going to help make the chocolates. I don't want you to have to be alone today.'

'Wait. You're coming to help make the chocolates, or to eat the chocolates? Last time you "helped", as I recall, it was tough to tell what your true purpose was.'

Evalynn smacked her on the shoulder. 'You know I love those peanut-butter truffles. Just have me work on something else and I'll be fine. Anyway, I've got other plans, too, that don't involve filling moulds and dipping cherries. I made some special arrangements for this afternoon that I think might help you forget it's your birthday.'

'Arrangements? I don't like the sound of that. What sort of arrangements, Ev?'

Evalynn winked. 'Sorry, it's a surprise. My lips are officially sealed. You'll just have to wait until later.'

The next bus-stop was the park-and-ride on Kimball Drive, where nearly a dozen passengers boarded. Among them was a tall man wearing a navy blazer and khakis. His wavy brown hair curled playfully, and his blue eyes twinkled. If she hadn't already given up on men, Sophie might have been inclined to give him more than a casual once-over. She chided herself for even thinking such things.

Most of the new passengers took the first vacant seat they could find, but the unfamiliar man scanned the bus's interior for just the right spot. He pretended not to notice Sophie looking at him. With a computer satchel in one hand and a bus map in the other, he made his way down the aisle towards the rear.

Sophie turned her head ninety degrees and looked directly out of the window, pretending to be very interested in the passing scenery.

'May I sit here?' he asked courteously a few seconds later, pointing to the empty half of the elevated rear bench.

Sophie continued staring out of the window. 'It's a public bus,' she said coolly. 'But what's wrong with the empty seats up there?' She pointed with her eyes to the vacant seats he'd passed by.

The man smiled graciously and sat down, laying his computer bag across his lap and unfolding the map. 'The view from up here is infinitely better.' He looked right at Sophie as he spoke.

Sophie straightened slightly in her seat, her mind turning briefly to thoughts of her former fiancé. She paused to mentally compare the two. The guy now sitting beside her was, she conceded, easy to look at. Tall. Good-looking. Confident. But he was no Garrett.

'Suit yourself,' she said. 'I've only got one more stop anyway.'

The man continued smiling. 'Well, in that case, maybe you can help me out. I'm new here. Just moved up from Oregon over the weekend, and I'm trying to figure out the transit system. How many stops are we away from downtown Seattle?'

'A lot,' she replied. 'Back where you got on, you should have waited for the next bus.'

'I see.' He nodded quizzically. 'So basically, I'm lost.'

'Afraid so.'

He didn't let it faze him. 'In that case, I'm glad I made my way all the way to the back seat. As long as I'm lost, and likely late for my first day on the job, at least I got to meet you.'

Now it was Sophie's turn for quizzical glances. 'Wait a minute. Is this, like, your shtick? Ride the bus with a map and pretend to be the new guy in town so you can pick up unsuspecting women?'

He grinned. 'If it is, is it working?'

'Absolutely not!' retorted Sophie, sounding quite appalled.

'I'm joking,' he said, chuckling. 'Actually, I'm really not the pick-up-strange-women type.' He caught himself. 'Not that you're strange, but . . . you get what I mean.'

Sophie didn't reply. What's the use? she wondered. He can flirt all he wants, and it won't make a bit of difference. I'm through with men. Another image of Dr Garrett Black popped into her head.

Pulling her umbrella from beside the seat, Sophie said, 'Well, welcome to Washington. Now, my stop is coming up, so if you don't mind I'd like to get by.' She turned to Evalynn. 'Ready?'

Evalynn nodded, and the pair stood up.

The man let Sophie scoot by in front of him. 'Listen,' he said. 'Can you at least tell me how to get to Seattle?'

'There are lots of women on the bus. I'm sure one of them will help.'

He didn't say another word.

As soon as they were on the sidewalk and clear of the bus, Evalynn poked Sophie again. 'Are you crazy? That guy was adorable!'

Sophie shook her head. 'I've told you before, I'm perfectly happy without a guy in my life.'

'Could've fooled me,' Evalynn mumbled under her breath.

The pair continued chatting as they walked the remaining blocks to Sophie's store, although Evalynn carried most of the conversation. Sophie kept an open ear as she moved along, her umbrella perched on her shoulder, but her mind was lost in memories of birthdays gone by. At the forefront of her thoughts was the most important birthday of all, exactly twenty years earlier, which proved to be a day that changed the course of every single day thereafter.

In Sophie's mind, it would for ever be remembered as the day her life shattered.

Chapter 2

You have a good memory weighed down by bad memories.

September 21, 1989

JACOB BARNES rubbed his face on the sleeve of his coat, trying in vain to wipe away the dizziness from his eyes. He felt as though he might faint at any moment. His mind raced to piece together details of the last fifteen minutes, but he was too foggy to recall exactly how he'd got to his current position along the side of the road. After steadying himself against a lamppost, Jacob tugged angrily at his silk tie, which suddenly felt like a noose round his neck. The front of his Italian suit was soaked through, but he figured that was just the result of standing around in a daze in the steady downpour of Seattle's infamous liquid weather.

'Dear God,' he said aloud, once his mind was clear enough to focus on the world around him. He squinted hard to sharpen his focus as he surveyed the scene. Jacob was never known for having a strong stomach, so what he saw before him, combined with his own fuzzy recollection of how it transpired, made him want to vomit. He fought to control the urge.

'It's all my fault,' whispered a terrified little voice from nearby.

Jacob's eyes darted round, searching for the voice's owner. A few paces off, sitting alone on the kerb near a fire hydrant, was a young girl. She, too, wiped her face on her sleeve, but only to hide the evidence that she was crying. But it didn't matter; it was raining hard enough that she could have wiped all night and her face would still be wet. Her nose and lips were bruised and swollen, and a gash on her cheek sent a trickle of red cascading past her jaw and onto her neck. The white blouse she wore also bore flecks of crimson.

The girl wrapped her shivering arms round her legs to protect them from the rain and the unusually cold September wind. 'I . . . I just wanted a p-piece of chocolate,' she sobbed. 'Just o-one piece.'

Jacob felt woozy. He shifted his position against the pole, hoping that would be enough to keep him from passing out again. 'You think you caused this?' he asked in a voice more gruff than intended. 'What has chocolate got to do with anything?'

The girl answered his first question with a nod, then she began rocking slowly back and forth, carefully studying the commotion down the street. Jacob followed her gaze—the steady whirring of sirens, lights spinning and blinking, flares glowing with bright red brilliance, police officers darting here and there while trying to guide traffic, fire-fighters barking out orders, ambulance drivers, broken glass, bent metal, and blood—so much blood. The sights and sounds and smells of the horrific scene filled his senses to overflowing. The girl turned again to look at him, but still said nothing.

Just then a policewoman and a young paramedic came running over. It occurred to Jacob that he and the girl were far enough away from the accident that they might have been mistaken for onlookers by the first wave of emergency personnel who'd arrived earlier.

'Sir,' the paramedic said to Jacob, looking very worried, 'let me help you sit down.' He quickly placed his tackle box of first-aid equipment on the ground, then wrapped a giant arm round Jacob's midriff and lowered him to the kerb. 'Can you do me a favour? Raise your left hand above your head and keep it elevated while I get you some bandages. Can you do that for me?'

Jacob was confused by the paramedic's request. 'Why? I'm fine. Can't you see that? Help that kid—she looks a little banged up.'

'Sir, have you—'

'It's Jacob.'

'Fine. Jacob, you're in shock. I think you've probably lost a lot of blood, and I want to make sure you don't lose any—'

'Blood? From where?' Another jolt of queasiness coursed through Jacob's body. 'Is the blood from my head? My face?'

'Jacob!' shouted the paramedic, his voice like ice. 'It's not your face. Look at your hand!'

Squinting through the pouring rain, Jacob focused on his hand. The sight sent another rush of nausea throughout his abdomen. All four fingers on his left hand were gone, severed where they met the palm. 'I . . . I think I need to lie down,' he groaned.

While the paramedic attended to Jacob's hand, Jacob diverted his attention to the little girl and the policewoman. From his position he could hear everything they said. The officer's name was Ellen, and she started by dabbing gently at the girl's face with a cotton swab while making small talk. Then she sat down next to her on the wet kerb. The girl kept stealing glances at Jacob's mangled hand.

'Everything's gonna be fine, sweetie. Just fine.' Ellen paused to look at the carnage, as if wondering if anything could ever really be just fine in the wake of something like this. 'Now, can you tell me your name?' she asked cautiously.

The child looked up at her with a vacant stare, as though she were trying to process the words. Then she nodded and whispered quietly, 'Sophia Maria Jones.'

'Wow, that's a beautiful name. Sophia Maria.'

The girl swallowed. 'I go by Sophie.'

'Then Sophie it is. How old are you, Sophie?'

'Eight. No—nine.'

'Wow,' replied the officer soothingly, 'that's a great age. I remember when I was nine. When was your birthday?'

A new, giant tear formed at the inside corner of Sophie's eye and spilled onto her cheek. 'T-t-today,' she said, choking on the word.

'Oh, I see,' Ellen said softly. 'Were you celebrating your birthday tonight?'

She nodded.

'Sophie, were you in one of these cars?'

Another nod.

A lump formed in Jacob's throat as he continued listening. He hardly noticed the paramedic who was working swiftly above him, wrapping his injured limb with a gauze bandage.

'Can you tell me which one?' Ellen coaxed, looking up once more to survey the wreckage. A blue Datsun rested on its side fifty paces away, just in front of a late-model station wagon that had damage to its front. Neither would ever be driven again, but the passengers at least had walked away. The other four cars involved in the accident—a Volvo, a small pick-up, a Mercedes sedan and a UPS delivery truck—were spread out along the four-lane road. The pick-up had been struck on the passenger side and flipped over completely, hitting the Datsun in the process. The Volvo had suffered the most damage, having been hit head-on by the UPS truck.

Sophie watched as emergency workers used a hydraulic machine to pry off the Volvo's crushed door to retrieve the lifeless body of a victim trapped inside. On the ground, near the rear of the same car, crews carefully draped a blue sheet over another unfortunate person they had pulled from within. Twenty yards farther down the road, an ambulatory team worked feverishly on the bent and broken body of the UPS truck driver.

'Can you tell me which car you were in, sweetie?' Ellen asked.

Sophie looked sadly at Ellen. She lifted one hand and pointed to the Volvo. 'There. That's my mommy,' she whispered, as two fire-fighters gingerly lifted the limp body of a slender woman in her early thirties from the hole in the passenger side, where the crumpled front door had been only moments before.

Officer Ellen Monroe wanted to cry, but she knew that wouldn't help. Instead, she swooped up Sophie in her arms and tucked the girl's head against her shoulder, then carried her to the far side of a row of ambulances where the view of the accident was blocked.

'Looks like you got your hands full,' said another officer, as the pair approached. 'Anything I can help with?'

Ellen grimaced. 'Can you put in a call to *double-S* for me? I got a hunch we're going to need 'em.'

'Double-S?'

Ellen didn't want to say the words Social Services in front of the girl. She shot the man a look that said, Use your brain, idiot!

'Ah,' he said, finally catching on. 'Of course. *Double-S*. I'll get them on the horn right away.'

Ellen set Sophie down gently on the back end of an ambulance and found a blanket to wrap round her. 'You're gonna get through this, kiddo. You know that, right?'

Sophie only smirked.

'Well you are. There are lots of people who are here to help.' Ellen changed the subject, hoping to keep the girl from shutting down. 'Earlier, when I first showed up, I thought I heard that man say something to you about chocolate. Do you like chocolate? 'Cuz I happen to have a Kiss right here in my vest. You want it?' She reached into her pocket and pulled out a Hershey's Kiss. Sophie's eyes acknowledged the treat with interest. 'Here. It's all yours.'

Sophie popped it into her mouth, then relaxed noticeably.

Works every time, thought Ellen. 'So tell me, Sophie, what was this cute little nine-year-old doing tonight to celebrate her birthday? You have such a lovely outfit on. Did you go out for dinner?'

'Uh-huh.'

'Cool. Where did you go? Someplace fun, I bet.'

'A Japanese place. We only go there for special times.' Sophie looked down at her hand and then clenched her fingers tightly.

'You got something in there you want to show me?' Ellen motioned to Sophie's tight fist.

'I don't want you to see it.'

'OK,' she replied casually. 'That's cool. So, did you have fun at the restaurant?'

'Yes.' She paused. 'They cook it on the table. The chef made a burning volcano out of onions. That was my favourite part.'

'Wow, Sophie. That sounds like a great time. So after dinner, then what?'

'Dad said we had to go, because of school tomorrow.'

Dang! That must've been her dad under the sheet. 'Just you, your mom and your dad?'

'And Grams. She lives with us, ever since Grandpa died.'

Her grandmother too! 'I see. So you all headed home together?'

'Yes.' Sophie clenched her hand tighter.

'And then . . . did you stop anywhere else?'

Sophie looked up the street. 'I wanted to. But Dad . . . he was in a hurry to get home, I guess. I told him the wish of my heart was to get a piece of chocolate at that candy store up there.' She pointed. 'They have the best chocolate in town. At least Mom says they do.'

'I'll be sure to try it sometime. What happened then?'

'Dad said no chocolate tonight, because we already had dessert at the restaurant. But I told him it was the wish of my heart.'

Ellen raised her eyebrows at the use of that phrase again. 'How do you mean?'

'Well, the wish of my heart was to get some chocolate. I showed him'—Sophie raised her white-knuckled hand—'I showed him so that we would stop.'

'You showed him your hand?'

Sophie shook her head. 'I showed him what's in my hand. He told me at the restaurant that it would come true. And then . . . Then a horn honked. He didn't have time to turn back round.' The last words were barely audible. Sophie's head sagged between her shoulders. 'It's all my fault,' she said, crying once more.

Just then the other officer returned. 'They're on their way,' he said quietly, trying not to intrude.

'Thanks, Pete.'

Ellen rubbed Sophie's shoulder and arm a little harder. 'It's all gonna be OK, Sophie Jones. I promise you that. One way or another, it's going to be OK. And it's not your fault.'

Sophie wrapped herself tighter in the blanket and looked down once more at her clenched fist.

'Can you show me now what you're hiding there in your hand?'

Nodding, Sophie slowly peeled open her fingers. Inside her hand was a crumpled slip of paper from a fortune cookie. Ellen leaned in closer so she could read the message, and then she understood.

Happiness is a gift that shines within you.
The wish of your heart will soon come true.

'It's not true, is it?' Sophie asked. 'None of it. Fortune cookies aren't real, are they? My dad lied.'

Ellen didn't know what to say that wouldn't further damage the girl. 'Well, they do come true,' she fibbed. 'Eventually.'

Sophie's eyes opened a bit wider, but her expression was one of doubt. 'Really?'

'Sure.' Ellen shrugged. 'Your dad wouldn't lie to you, now would he? And I wouldn't, either. It will come true.'

Sophie took a moment to weigh Ellen's words. 'OK. Then the new wish of my heart is to have my family back. That's my wish!'

Ellen felt like her heart was being ripped out of her chest. For the first time ever on the job, she allowed the emotions inside her to spill over in the form of tears. 'Oh, sweetie, I'm so sorry,' she cried. 'I know that's your wish. That's my wish too. But . . . but . . . '

'But I can't have that wish, can I?'

Ellen breathed out a long, painful sigh, then brushed away the tears that were running down her own face and tucked a wisp of hair behind the girl's ear. 'I'm afraid not, sweetheart.'

Sophie wadded up the paper and threw it on the ground. It landed in a current of water running along the gutter. She watched as it floated away, carrying with it all her hopes and dreams. Part of her wanted to chase after it, to pick it up and dry it off and pretend everything was OK. But it wouldn't be OK, and she refused to kid herself. Her parents were gone, her grandparents were gone, and there was nobody left in the world to love her. Her mind flashed back to the wreckage—the UPS truck driver, the cars flipped, the man with the missing fingers, her parents' lifeless bodies. 'It's my fault,' she whispered to herself again. 'All my fault.'

Chapter 3

Something you lost will soon turn up,
but some lost things are better left unfound.

September 21, 2009

SOPHIE'S STORE WAS LOCATED in a small retail space on Commerce Avenue, marked by a sleek, brushed-nickel sign that protruded horizontally from the building just above the entrance. The laser-embossed lettering read CHOCOLAT' DE SOPH, followed by a much smaller cursive subscript: *Confections of the Heart.*

The interior of the store was decidedly upscale. Several large post-modern paintings hung on the walls, their colourful patterns providing enough visual interest to keep the clean, contemporary décor from getting stale. Four Austrian crystal dishes for holding free samples of fudge sat atop an etched-glass display case. Matching granite tables stood in opposite corners near the bay windows, providing space for patrons who wished to sit and enjoy a warm drink while nibbling on Sophie's rich chocolate creations.

The morning hours passed as they always did, with Sophie quietly rushing from one task to another. There were nuts to chop, moulds to fill, butters to melt, creams to stir and a thousand other tasks to complete before the doors opened at 10 a.m. Also, Sophie had to make sure that Evalynn stayed clear of the peanut-butter balls in the refrigerator until they were firm enough to dip.

Evalynn, for her part, offered little noticeable help. Most of her effort was spent fingering the chocolate creams to determine which one she liked best. Sophie didn't mind. Even though she would rather have been alone with her thoughts, she appreciated her friend's gesture; Evi's presence had helped lighten her weighty emotional load.

With nearly everything ready, Sophie grabbed a pen and a handful of narrow slips of paper from her small office and sat down to complete her morning preparations. Writing out those unique fortunes had become her favourite part of the job, and it was probably the main reason her business had stayed afloat in a slow economy.

'Any specific theme today?' asked Evalynn.

'Nope.' Sophie tapped the pen while pondering what to write.

'You aiming for mild disappointment or full-blown heartache?'

'Sshh. Neither. The goal is reality, nothing more.'

'Can I help you write them?'

'Nope.'

'Well then, can I at least have a truffle?' she asked hopefully.

With a hint of a growl, Sophie hissed, 'Be quiet! I can't think. Just turn your mouth off for a few minutes. Please.'

'I'll take that as a yes,' whispered Evalynn, as she started for the other room, where a tray of fresh truffles was on display.

Fifteen minutes later, satisfied that she had enough slips of paper filled out to meet the day's demand, she gathered them together and joined Evalynn in the front of the store.

'How'd you make out?' asked Evi.

Sophie handed her the small stack of tiny slips. 'See for yourself. And when you're done, would you mind sliding them into the fortune cookies? I have to clean up in the back before we open.'

Morning sales can be notoriously slow, even for the best chocolatiers, so it didn't surprise Sophie that nobody was beating the door down when she turned on the neon 'Open' sign that hung in the window. Chocolat' de Soph opened promptly at ten, but the first customers didn't arrive until ten thirty.

Shortly after eleven the lunch rush started, and sales began to pick up. As always, the big customer draw was Sophie's Misfortune Cookies, each of which included one of her unique handwritten prognostications of gloom and doom. By design, Misfortune Cookies weren't the best-tasting treat in the store. After the cookies had been bent and baked to the traditional fortune-cookie shape, they were dipped in unsweetened chocolate. The resulting taste was shock-and-awe on unsuspecting mouths. When she dreamed up the odd cookies eleven months earlier, Sophie figured they'd be a short-term gimmick. But to her great surprise, the bitter morsels had gained enough local fame to keep them flying off the shelf.

Just prior to two o'clock in the afternoon, while Sophie was ringing up a husband and wife who seemed perfectly giddy to find out from their Misfortune Cookies that their car would soon break down and that others talked about them behind their backs, Evi tapped on her watch and mouthed, 'It's almost time!'

Sophie's brow furrowed tightly as she remembered the arrangements her friend had spoken of earlier. She handed the couple their change and waited for them to exit before turning back to her friend. 'OK, Ev. Spill it. What's the big surprise?'

Evalynn said, 'I told you, my lips are sealed.'

'Tell me when, then. It better not be until later in the day.'

Evalynn glanced beyond Sophie towards the door, then began tip-toeing towards the kitchen. 'Oh, I'm guessing, right about . . .'—she ducked out of sight as she called over her shoulder—'now!'

At the same moment, the bell that hung from the front door jingled slightly. Sophie kept her back to the door, unwilling to face whatever surprise had just entered her store. Her stomach churned with dread as her mind raced to deduce what kind of surprise would arrive with such obvious punctuality at precisely two o'clock.

She turned reluctantly. Before she made it all the way round she closed her eyes in a final attempt to delay the inevitable. After a few shallow breaths, Sophie forced one eyelid up, just a crack. Then she gasped, and both eyes shot wide open.

'What the—' Her face flushed instantly. She tried to gather her composure before uttering, 'Oh. Crap.' It wasn't exactly what she intended to say, but she delivered the words with as much grace and poise as could be expected, then followed up eloquently with, 'I think I'm going to be sick.'

'Sick? Maybe you should see a doctor.' He held a dozen long-stemmed roses peppered with fresh lilies, and he had a perfect mouth. He was half a foot taller than Sophie, strong jawed and well proportioned. Everything about him—the thick, dark hair, the dimples, the timbre of his voice—was just as she remembered.

Sophie felt an urge to smooth her hair and straighten her blouse, but she resisted. 'I see one. That's my problem.' She paused. Her eyes wandered round the room, hoping to find something more worthy of her stare than him. 'Umm. Why are you here?'

He took a couple of steps forward so he could close the door behind him. His sympathetic smile remained fixed in place. 'Can we back up a sec? Maybe start with a simple greeting, like "Hello"?'

She folded her arms and bit her lip nervously. 'Do we have to?'

'No, but I'd like to,' he said with a wink.

Sophie recalled how she used to love those winks. Now she wasn't so sure. 'Fine. Umm. Hello . . . Garrett. You're—here. Uninvited, I might add. Welcome.'

'Hi, Sophie,' he replied softly. 'Happy birthday.' He held up the flowers and started stepping closer, slowly, like a mouse moving in to inspect a trap. 'You look great. How've you been?'

Sophie didn't respond immediately. Looking down briefly at the display case, she caught a glimpse of her own reflection in the glass, and what she saw jolted her. No longer was she a confident, independent business owner. She was a teenage girl, a starry-eyed kid dreaming of the day that she would fall in love. She looked once more and saw the same girl, a few years older, in college, feeling like she might never find someone. Again the reflection changed. Now she was moving from one bad relationship to another, all of them ending in heartache. Then, as if by a miracle, in the blink of an eye she was showing off an engagement ring to Evi, holding Garrett's hand, making wedding plans and sending out invitations. Sophie squinted once more, but the image faded away.

'I've been better. Now back to my original question. What are you doing here?'

Garrett kept inching forward until the only thing standing between him and Sophie was the glass display case. He looked at her and his demeanour softened even further. The curve of his dimpled smile flattened into a solemn, serious line. 'I've missed you, Soph.'

It took only a second for Sophie's mind to list all the possible reactions to such an incredible statement: cry, walk away, run into his arms, scream hysterically, vomit, panic, faint, call the police, throw the nearest bowl of fudge in his face, all of the above, or . . .

Sophie laughed. A single, simple, 'that's just about the stupidest thing I've ever heard' kind of a laugh. She then glanced out of the window to make sure no customers were about to enter the store. Only then did she yell as loud as she could. 'Evalynn Marion Mason-Mack! Get in here right now!'

Evi poked her head round the wall that hid the kitchen from the rest of the store. She curtsied playfully. 'You screamed, my lady?'

Sophie yanked her into full view by the sleeve of her shirt. 'Explain,' she commanded, motioning to Garrett, who was smiling.

'Hey, careful with the pregnant lady,' joked Evalynn.

'Explain, now.'

'Oh, c'mon, Sophie. I just thought . . . you know, that maybe you could use a little extra spark for your birthday.'

'A spark?' she howled. 'This is an explosion! Or an implosion. Either way, what were you thinking?'

'Well, I . . .' stammered Evalynn, 'I see your point, I guess. But . . . what spark burns brighter than an old flame, right?'

Sophie wanted to scream again, but she held her tongue. 'So this was your big surprise? Twenty years since the worst day of my life, and to celebrate it you invite over the guy who's responsible for the second worst day of my life? Brilliant.'

Evalynn shrugged. 'Well, when you put it like that, I suppose—'

'Wait a minute, ladies,' piped Garrett, wearing his serious expression again. Sophie imagined that was the look he used when he had to give patients bad news. 'Sophie, I contacted Evi a few days ago when I made up my mind that I was coming to see you. She didn't seek me out. In fact, she told me flat out to leave you alone. But when she couldn't change my mind, she chose to come today as well, just in case you needed her.'

Sophie turned to Evalynn. 'Is that true?'

Evalynn nodded apologetically and went to the back.

'And I know very well,' Garrett continued, 'that I hurt you. I won't make excuses, but you should know that what I did hurt me, too. Your second worst day happens to be my very worst day, and that's why I came today. There were things I wasn't ready to tell you back then, but I feel like you need to know the truth.' Garrett held out the flowers and looked deep into Sophie's eyes.

She reluctantly took the bouquet, glaring at him as she did so. 'Are you out of your mind? Usually I ask that the nuts get delivered to the back door, and yet here you are. Garrett, I really don't think we have anything to talk about. It was almost a year ago, for crying out loud. You left. You had your reasons. End of story.'

Garrett's face sank. 'You won't indulge me for one little date to sit and talk, so I can tell you what—?'

'I thought you just came to talk! Now you want a date, too?'

'Sophie,' Garrett said, 'listen. What I have to say to you is important. Can you give me just one evening to say what I need to say, so both of us can have some sort of closure?' He paused, begging with his eyes. 'Please?'

She shook her head sternly. 'No. Not going to happen.'

'Just one date,' he pressed. 'I know I should have handled things better than I did, but is it too much to ask for an hour of your time to say what should have been said before?'

Sophie ignored him. 'If you don't mind, I have a business to run here.'

Garrett looked like he'd been punched. He stared longingly at the beautiful woman who'd stolen his heart. But he'd taken her heart as well, held it in his hands like a treasure, and then, when she least expected it, dropped it like a rock and stomped on it. 'Well as long as I'm here,' he said, 'can I at least buy some chocolates?'

'I won't turn away a paying customer,' she responded flatly.

He scanned the full length of the glass display case. 'Anything new since the last time I was in?'

A mischievous grin played at the corner of Sophie's mouth, but she tried to hide it. 'Actually, yes. These right here are the top sellers,' she said proudly, pulling a basket of chocolate-dipped fortune cookies from behind the counter. 'Believe it or not, you were the inspiration behind them.'

'Really?' he asked, sounding both doubtful and flattered at the same time. 'They look delicious. How much?'

'Three dollars.'

'OK, one of those. Plus half a dozen truffles for the road.'

Sophie gathered the chocolates and boxed them up, but left the Misfortune Cookie out on a napkin. She knew it was cruel, but she hoped he would eat it before leaving the store so she could watch his reaction. He didn't disappoint. Garrett pulled out his wallet and handed her some cash, then grabbed the cookie and took a bite. Sophie watched expectantly as his teeth closed round it.

Garrett's initial reaction was one of calm deliberation. He allowed several seconds for his taste buds to make sense of the new experience. Then his eyes grew big and his lips puckered.

'Sophie that's . . .' he sputtered. 'It tastes like baking chocolate.'

Sophie scrunched her face into a deliberate pout. 'Oh, you hate them. I'm crushed.'

He wiped a piece of the bitter brown from his lip. 'You really sell these to people? I mean, they pay money for them?'

Now, for the first time since he'd entered the store, she flashed a genuine smile. 'Isn't it great? I call them Misfortune Cookies. Only real die-hards eat them. Most people buy them to read the fortune.'

Garrett broke off another chunk of cookie so he could get at the small slip of paper tucked inside. His eyes scanned the message. Then he read it aloud, his voice questioning every word. '*Your job seems secure now, but have patience. Nothing lasts for ever!* That's the most depressing fortune cookie I've ever read.'

'Well, buy some more,' she replied with a twinkle in her eyes. 'I'm sure you'll find one that can top it.'

His mouth hung open. 'You're telling me that people come in here just to get fortunes like this? Why would they do that?'

Beaming, Sophie handed Garrett his change. 'Evi thinks people like them because they're unique. But my hypothesis is that people just want a dose of reality now and then. Life stinks, you know. It's as bitter as that chocolate, so why pretend like it's not, right?'

Garrett stared at her, not knowing what to say. 'Wow,' he finally managed. 'I guess Evalynn was right. You aren't happy, are you?'

Sophie's smile disappeared. 'She said that?'

He nodded.

She shrugged. 'Well, maybe she's right.'

'How long have you felt that way?'

'Oh, don't go trying to make a diagnosis, Doctor. You're a podiatrist, remember, not a shrink. Besides, what is happiness anyway? I'd say that people who think they know what happiness is are probably just making something up to feel better about themselves.'

Garrett frowned. 'You don't honestly believe that, do you?'

She tucked a loose strand of blonde hair behind her ear. 'Why not? The things that people attribute to happiness are just fleeting. Take our relationship, for example. It's like your fortune said—nothing lasts.'

'I think you're wrong.'

Sophie studied his face for a long time. Privately, she couldn't deny that she still enjoyed looking at him. It gave her butterflies the way he was able to look at her like she was the only other person on the face of the planet. 'Then tell me, Garrett. What is happiness?'

He considered her question. 'To me? Hmm. Right now I'd have to say that happiness is being completely honest with the people you care about.'

The comment caught Sophie off guard. She smoothed her apron. 'Meaning what, exactly?'

'Meaning that for the past year I've been living with a secret, and it's killing me. I can't be happy until you know the truth about me.'

Sophie retreated in surprise. 'Oh crap,' she gasped. 'There's a truth about you? What is it? No, wait! Let me guess.' Her mind was reeling. In the wake of her unceremonious dumping, Sophie had considered the possibility that maybe there were things Garrett didn't want her to learn about him. Now those thoughts came flooding back. 'You were cheating!' She wanted to cry.

'No, I could never—'

'Then what?'

Speaking more softly than before, he said, 'I told you. I need to sit down with you where we can really talk. It's complicated, and it deserves your full attention. One date, that's all I ask.'

Just then the bell on the door jingled lightly, and a young mother with two small children entered. Garrett backed away from the counter and sat down on one of the empty stools near the window.

While the mother helped the kids pick their goodies, Sophie considered what Garrett had said. He's cruel, she thought. Yanks happiness away from me, and then shows up out of the blue and accuses me of not being happy.

Dropping her hands to her side, Sophie glanced at the display case.

At first she saw the children's faces from the other side, licking their lips as they evaluated each chocolate. Looking harder, her own reflection took shape once more in her mind. There she was, a smiling little girl, laughing and playing on her father's lap, then giggling as her mother tickled her toes. Sophie's eyes watered, causing the image to shift. Now she was a few years older, old enough to remember every detail of the accident. Everything felt wrong, because she knew it was all her fault. Sophie blinked and the image vanished. Happiness is fleeting, she reminded herself.

'Garrett,' she said, after the family was gone. 'Listen. Whether or not I'm happy is no concern of yours. You left, remember? You don't get a say in my life. And as far as this awful *thing* goes, that you want to share with me? I'd rather not know.' She paused, watching him. 'I think we should leave the past alone. All right?'

Garrett sat quietly, staring at the floor. After several long moments he stood up and spoke. 'Sophie, just for the sake of argument, what if you're wrong? What if lasting happiness does exist? What if we had it right there in our hands and I blew it?' He took a slow step towards her. 'What if there's still a chance that we could have that?'

'There's not,' she insisted.

'What would it take to get you to agree to one date? What I have to tell you isn't just about me, Soph. It's also about you.'

Sophie tapped her fingers lightly on the counter, watching the man who had once treated her like she was the sun, the moon and the stars all rolled into one. Right up until the day he walked away.

'Tell you what,' she said. 'I'll make a deal with you.'

Garrett's eyes perked up. 'What sort of deal?'

The kind of deal you have no chance of winning, she thought. 'Well, ever since Evalynn got married, she keeps telling me that I need to find a man so we can better commiserate. Last week she even tried to get me to place a personal ad in the newspaper.'

Garrett chuckled. 'Like, "Single white female seeking . . ."?'

'"Seeking anything but a foot doctor." Yes, something like that. Anyway, I told her I've always thought those people are just looking for a fling. They're not really searching for lasting happiness. But since you brought up happiness, and you're so sure that it exists, how about you try to find it for me?'

Garrett's brow narrowed. 'How?'

Sophie's grin expanded. 'The newspaper! There are ads for everything else in there. Why not one for happiness?'

'I don't get it. You want me to run a personal ad for you?'

'No. A want ad. Something simple, like, "Wanted. Happiness." You run that in the *Seattle Times*, and if you can get, say, one hundred people to respond with something intelligent, then I'll consent to a date.'

Garrett studied her. He knew the likelihood of anyone responding to an ad like that was slim at best, 'You really don't want to hear what I have to say, do you?'

'Eleven months ago, yes. Now? Not so much. But hey, at least I'm giving you a fighting chance, right?'

He frowned, looking slightly dejected. 'Sure. So are there any other stipulations to this deal that I should be aware of?'

Sophie tapped her fingers again on the glass while she thought. 'Ummm . . . yes. You can't recruit any of your friends, patients or anyone else to send in responses. And everything has to go to the PO box I have for business stuff. I don't want any nutjobs showing up at my house or here at the store hoping to make me happy.'

He kept his gaze fixed on her. 'And what will constitute an "intelligent response"?'

Sophie laughed. 'Whatever I decide when I read them. Obviously, I only want rational, thoughtful statements of happiness. Nothing creepy. And most importantly, nothing that fleets.'

Garrett made a little snorting sound through his nose. 'I have to get one hundred responses, and none of those things count?'

'Those are the rules if you want a date.' Sophie was pleased with her idea, and her ruthless smile showed it.

Garrett, on the other hand, was obviously frustrated. It had taken him eleven months to build up the nerve to share his secret with Sophie, and now she was shutting him down. He turned and walked to the door, his shoulders sagging. He paused a moment, as if considering stopping right there and telling her everything he wanted to say. But he must have thought it was too complicated, because then he kept going. At the door he looked back over his shoulder. 'Goodbye, Sophie.'

Part of Sophie wished that she hadn't been so hard on him. After all, it wasn't like she didn't silently wish that she were still his. But she refused to let her heart get crushed again. 'Goodbye, Garrett.'

His eyes scanned Sophie from head to toe, taking in every detail. 'I'll be sure to stop by periodically to see how the responses are coming. But if we never reach one hundred,' he added softly, 'please know that I always loved you, Soph. Even if I was a coward and a jerk, my feelings for you never changed.'

Sophie didn't allow herself to cry until after he was gone. 'Me too,' she whispered, once the door had closed.

Chapter 4

You'll never really be happy. How sad.

ALTHOUGH SOPHIE encouraged Evalynn to go home to her husband on three different occasions after Garrett left Chocolat' de Soph, her friend didn't budge.

'You're stuck with me until we get off the bus in Gig Harbor.'

'I'm not riding the bus home,' Sophie muttered.

'Whatever,' Evalynn said, thinking she was teasing.

Sophie showed her disappointment with a frown: after so many years, Evalynn should have known without being told. 'Because there's something else I need to do tonight.'

It finally registered. 'Oh, yikes! I'm sorry, Soph. Of all the insensitive things. You're going to the cemetery, aren't you?' Evalynn paused, watching Sophie's expression tighten. 'Do you want me to come with you this year? I mean . . . can I?'

Sophie relaxed her face enough to smile. 'You've done enough already. Really. This is something I need to do alone.'

Evalynn smiled back, then gave Sophie a hug that said, It's going to be all right. But inside Evi was thinking, When is it going to be all right? It's time to get over the past and move on. It wasn't for lack of understanding that Evalynn felt that way. Like Sophie, tragedy was something she knew a thing or two about, having lost her mother to a prison sentence when she was eight. It was their mutual lack of family that ultimately brought the pair together as children and forged an inseparable bond between them. But for reasons Evalynn didn't fully understand, Sophie's scars ran deeper than her own.

Evalynn released her grip on her foster sister. 'Are you absolutely sure? You don't always have to go alone, you know.'

'I'm sure.'

By the time the evening help showed up at the store at five o'clock, in the form of a redheaded college kid named Randy, Sophie was wearing thin emotionally. Usually she would stay for a while after Randy arrived to get a jump on preparations for the following day, but the September sun was already starting to dip, so time was becoming a critical factor.

Hailing the first cab she could find, Sophie made her way north to Seattle. She couldn't bring herself to visit the cemetery more than once a year, but she knew the route by heart.

Traffic along I-5 was, predictably, a nightmare. By the time the cab pulled up in front of Evergreen Washelli Cemetery on Aurora Avenue, the sun had dropped low on the western horizon. Sophie paid the fare and got out quickly.

Inside the cemetery's fenced perimeter, she followed the main road as it curved round to the east until the road split near the base of a famous World War One statue called *The Doughboy*. From the statue she took the path to the left, heading north over and round several small hills lined with tall cedar trees.

Sophie stepped off the main road for the final hundred yards, zigzagging round shrubs and graves until she reached a row of birch trees at the top of the rise. She reached a point where the hedge no longer blocked the view of her parents' burial spot and stopped dead in her tracks. A man was there, squatting down in the grass, looking at the handful of graves at the precise location to which she was heading. The man's back was turned to her.

Sophie wondered what the odds were that the only other person in the cemetery happened to be visiting a grave next to her parents. Not good. The thought of being alone with a strange man who happened to be hovering over the tombstone of her dead family gave her a chill. Turning slowly, she tried to slip away undetected.

She made it only three paces.

'Hello! Don't go! I'm leaving now.' It was definitely a man's voice, but there was a strange, singsong quality to it. Something decidedly . . . unique.

Sophie spun back round.

The man was short with broad shoulders, and he wore dark sunglasses. He walked towards her, smiling, and she noticed a peculiar skip in his step. 'Really,' he continued, 'I'm done here.'

Sophie watched the man as he approached. He was younger than she was, maybe twenty years old. Under different circumstances she might have felt terror, but something about his demeanour told her not to worry. As he got closer, she noticed that his head was a bit larger than normal, his face slightly more rounded. She wanted to see his eyes, but they were hidden behind mirrored lenses. Sophie swallowed the lump in her throat. 'Did you find what you were looking for?' she asked tentatively, when he was a few steps away.

He grinned but didn't stop, or even slow down. 'I was just passing through,' he said with a little laugh. 'Had something to do for my dad.' The man smiled even wider, shoved his hands deeper into his sweat-shirt and continued walking right on by.

Sophie watched the stranger with curiosity for several more seconds. She was contemplating the unusual pitch of his voice—a tempered lisp that rang out like a melody—when another movement behind her caught her attention. It was an arm, waving.

'Sophie! Wait up!'

She didn't need to hear anything more than her name to know who the voice belonged to. Sophie watched as Evi hurried past the curious young man and continued up the hill to where she stood.

'I thought I told you I wanted to be alone.'

'Did you?' Evalynn asked.

'Don't play dumb.'

'Fine . . . here's the thing. Justin thought I'd be out late, so he invited some friends over to watch Monday-night football. I'd have been a fifth wheel, so I hopped in the car and drove up.' She paused just long enough to watch Sophie's expression tighten into a frown. 'I figured this way you won't have to pay for a cab when you're done.' She smiled mischievously. 'You can pay me instead.'

The muffled laugh that escaped Sophie's mouth helped lighten her mood. 'Not on your life. But I'll be happy to buy us both something to eat on the way. I'm starving and I really feel like drowning my sorrows in a greasy plate of onion rings and a chocolate shake.'

'Sounds perfect. Now, can we go see your parents?'

Sophie led Evalynn to a headstone on the far side of the hedge, beneath the boughs of an aged cedar, which marked the final resting spot of Thomas and Cecilia Jones. The engraving read,

Husband and Father
Wife and Mother
Loved their daughter and each other fully and for ever.

'That's sweet,' whispered Evalynn after reading the inscription. 'Tell you what, I'll just hang back a bit so you can do your thing without me hovering.' She stepped away.

'No need,' Sophie said, waving her forward. 'Believe it or not, this will be a quick stop.'

Evalynn watched with curiosity as Sophie reached into her handbag and pulled out a small chocolate box. Opening the box, Sophie picked up one truffle from within and placed it carefully on the top of the gravestone. Then she reached once more into her bag, this time finding a small slip of paper and a straight pin. She knelt down in front of the headstone, then gingerly poked the pin through the paper and stuck it into the centre of the truffle.

Before standing, Sophie did one final thing that perplexed Evalynn. A flat, smooth stone, perhaps two inches in diameter and half an inch thick, lay near the corner of the gravestone. It was clearly not there by accident. The rock was translucent agate with brilliant flecks of silver and burgundy peppered throughout. Sophie marvelled at its beauty. Then she picked it up, dropped it in her bag and jumped up off her knees. 'Let's go,' she said.

'What?' Evalynn queried, surprised. 'That's it?'

'I told you. Quick stop. I'm all done.'

'The chocolate? Do you leave one every year?'

Sophie nodded.

Glancing once more at the gravestone, Evalynn asked, 'What's with the paper you stuck on it? Is that an annual thing too?'

Sophie shook her head. 'That's a new addition this year. After . . .' She stopped, biting her lip nervously. 'After the whole thing with Garrett, I think my perspective on life changed a bit. The note is just my way of sharing what I feel.'

Evalynn smiled sympathetically. 'That's good! You need to express it one way or another. Do you mind if I . . .?' She hinted with her eyes at the paper.

Sophie shrugged. 'Knock yourself out.'

Evalynn knelt down and read the words aloud. '*You will take a chance in the near future, and win.*' Evalynn snapped round and looked at Sophie, who was now smiling contentedly. 'Sophia Maria Jones! I thought you said this was your way of expressing how you feel. How does this express your feelings about your parents?'

'I said it expressed how I feel, but I didn't say it's how I feel about them.'

'What is that supposed to mean?'

Sophie looked around and squinted at the setting sun. 'Think of it this way. Right now, today, it's beautiful outside, sunny and warm. But what about tomorrow? I expect that by then that fortune will be gone. Ruined. And the truffle? A hungry squirrel or raccoon will likely scarf it down by dawn. So the fortune and the piece of chocolate are just little reminders that eventually, hopes and dreams just disappear.' She looked down and silently read the inscription below her parents' names. 'It's the story of my life. Everything fleets.'

Evalynn watched her without speaking.

For a moment Sophie refused to look at her best friend. Finally she looked up and saw the concern on Evalynn's face. She let a sigh escape. 'This is why I come alone. I don't expect you to understand, Ev, but it works for me. OK?'

Part of Evalynn wanted to shake some sense into Sophie, while another part of her would have liked to make Garrett Black pay for what he'd done to her heart. But Evalynn simply gave a nod and a wan smile. 'OK, Sophie.'

Together they made their way back down the hill to the road, neither of them speaking as they walked.

Five days later, the cellphone on Sophie's night stand started vibrating, yanking her from another restless night long before she was ready to wake up. She squinted at the screen to check the time—6:26—then stared at the number of the caller, debating whether or not to answer.

'This is my one day off,' Sophie groaned, as she reluctantly picked up. 'You're horrible for calling at this hour.'

'Couldn't be helped,' replied Evalynn cheerfully. 'Justin and I are heading out early today, but before we leave I wanted to let you know that you should go pick up a copy of the *Times*. I think you'll want to check out page G4.'

'What's on page G4?' she asked groggily.

'Well, do you want me to spoil the surprise?'

'Ev. It's o'dark hundred hours. Tell me whatever it is you've found, so I can go back to sleep.'

'OK fine. Two words. "Wanted. Happiness."' She drew the words out slowly and clearly, articulating every syllable.

There was a long moment of silence. Then Sophie groaned. 'He actually placed the ad?'

'Yep.'

'I totally expected him to ditch the idea. There's no way he'll ever get a hundred responses.'

'I guess he thinks otherwise.'

'Great. Well thanks for waking me up with such wonderful news, Ev,' Sophie deadpanned. 'You're a real pal.'

'Ciao, Soph!'

Sophie put the phone back and pulled the covers up over her head, but after tossing and turning, and finding it impossible to go back to sleep, she rolled out of bed and made her way to the bathroom. Then she threw on a sweatshirt and jeans, slung an umbrella over her shoulder and went for a walk in the morning sun.

There was a small shopping plaza round the corner from her house with a drugstore that sold newspapers from vending machines out front. One dollar and fifty cents later, she was thumbing through the *Seattle Times*.

She found section G, turned to page four.

Sophie grunted when she saw the ad halfway down the second column. She tried hard to force a frown, but found resistance in the form of a smile that kept playing at the corner of her mouth as she read, and then reread, the want ad.

Wanted: Happiness

Please help me find what I've lost. Send suggestions to PO Box 3297, TACOMA, WA 98402 (Lasting happiness only, please. Nothing that fleets.)

'Garrett Black,' she said aloud, shaking her head. 'Don't get your hopes up. Everything fleets.'

Chapter 5

You will soon fall in love. Caution: when people fall,
something usually breaks.

October 2007

'You DIDN'T,' Garrett groaned into the phone. 'Please tell me you're joking.'

Olivia DeMattio was on the other end of the line at her home in Seattle, and she sounded as giddy as a schoolgirl. DeMattio was her married name—second marriage, the first having ended almost before it began. Although Olivia liked the sound of her married surname, she'd always disliked her first name. Her husband of sixteen years, Ken DeMattio, sometimes called her Liv. Friends at the police station usually called her Livie, unless they were on patrol, in which case she answered to 'Dispatch'.

Garrett never called Olivia by any of those names. To him she was simply Mom.

'Oh, c'mon, Garrett. Don't pretend like you're not interested.'

Garrett waited before responding. 'It just feels an awful lot like a blind date, and you know how I hate those.'

'Why is it a blind date? Because she doesn't know who you are? Pfft.

Even if it were a blind date, a blind date is better than no date, right?'
Olivia paused. 'Who knows, the two of you might end up finding
something you didn't know was missing. I mean, we already know you
have a lot in common.'

'Incredible. You just jumped from a blind date to . . . what? A missing something-or-other with a woman I've never even met?'

'So you're going to turn down this opportunity?'

Garrett pulled the phone away from his ear long enough to tell his
head nurse that he'd be right there. 'Fine,' he said reluctantly into the
receiver, after the nurse was out of earshot. 'I'll go. Don't count on
anything coming of it. I'm only going out of curiosity.'

'Whatever you say, Garrett.'

'Good. Now, does this Sophie know anything about me?'

'Just what I've told Ellen at work, which isn't much.'

'Is there anything else you can tell me about her?'

Olivia paused to think. 'I saw pictures today.'

'And?'

Olivia snorted. 'You'll have to wait and see. Just remember to take a
look at what she's got on the inside.'

He knew what that meant. As a kid, whenever the subject of girls
came up, Garrett's mother often told him that 'the real gems of the
female race are often disguised behind imperfect exteriors'. Olivia herself was no beauty queen, and Garrett was pretty sure she considered
herself to be one of those hidden gems.

'Don't worry,' he promised. 'I'll be nice, no matter what she looks like.'

'You're a good boy, Garrett.'

'Got to run. Can you just email me the details for this date?'

'It's seven o'clock this Friday. You can remember that without an
email. But she doesn't want you to pick her up, so I need you to tell me
where you'd like to meet, so I can pass it on to Ellen.'

'Fine. How about the Space Needle? I've only ever gone up there for
the view, but I hear the restaurant is great.'

'I think that'll be nice. You make the reservations, and I'll let Ellen
know you'll meet Sophie in the gift shop at seven.'

He checked his watch, noting that his next patient had already been
waiting for five minutes. 'How will I recognise her?'

Olivia let out a little laugh. 'Just look for a hidden gem who's all
alone, and that'll probably be her.'

Garrett sighed into the phone. 'One date only,' he reminded her.

'Talk to you later, Garrett.'

The phone clicked off.

Friday came much faster than Garrett Black wanted it to. He toyed once or twice with the idea of calling his mom and telling her he was sick in bed, but he feared that she'd send one of her detective friends to check out his story, and then there'd be hell to pay.

At a quarter past six he left his office in Tacoma, and by five minutes to seven he'd found a parking space a few blocks south of the Space Needle. He walked the remaining quarter-mile to Seattle's most recognisable landmark, a towering 605-foot structure built as the centrepiece of the 1962 World Fair.

Checking his watch once more before entering the gift shop at ground level, Garrett saw that he was already two minutes late. Inside, he scanned the dozens of people who were wandering round eyeing souvenirs, but the handful of women who fitted the somewhat homely image he'd contrived in his head of a diamond in the rough were either already with a man or had children hanging onto them.

Continuing his search for Sophie Jones, Garrett made two full loops round the doughnut-shaped store, but still didn't find anyone who fitted the bill. 'I hate blind dates,' he muttered.

As he passed the elevators for the third time to start another loop, someone tapped him on the shoulder. Turning to his right, Garrett found himself face to face with one of the most striking women he'd ever laid eyes on. He'd already noticed her on the previous loops, but had purposefully diverted his gaze out of fear that he'd be caught ogling. She was nicely dressed in slacks and a V-neck sweater. The woman's blonde hair fell a little past her shoulder in thick, wavy locks, her lips and dimpled cheeks formed a cute smile, and her bright blue eyes sparkled and smiled all on their own.

'You look lost,' she said.

'Oh,' he replied, stammering. 'No. I'm . . . I'm looking for someone. Supposed to meet a girl . . . a woman, actually.' Idiot.

Her smile grew. 'Well, can I help you out?'

'No. I'm fine. I'm sure she'll turn up sooner or later. Hopefully sooner, because we have dinner reservations in one minute.'

'What does she look like?' she asked, grinning.

'Good question. But I don't have a good answer. This is sort of a blind date, as pathetic as that may sound.'

She nodded. 'That does sound pathetic.'

'Even more pathetic is that my mom was the one who set me up.'

'Ouch.'

'I know.'

The woman bit her lower lip and twirled a tuft of hair round her finger. 'I have a great idea,' she said after a few seconds. 'Why don't you go to the front desk and have her paged? That'll save you both the effort of finding each other.'

He looked at his watch, then nodded. 'Save time, too. Thanks.'

The main desk was just a little way back, near the elevator. The woman followed Garrett up to the counter.

'Can I have someone paged?' he asked the young lady standing behind the desk.

'Of course,' the receptionist said. 'What's the name?'

'Sophie Jones.'

'Thank you. One moment please.' The young woman leaned in towards a small microphone. 'Sophie Jones to the front desk. Sophie Jones to the front desk, please. Your party is waiting.'

People all through the store stopped to listen to the announcement. Then they continued about their business.

The blonde woman next to Garrett snickered, but her snickering quickly grew to a giggle, then escalated to outright laughter.

The receptionist and Garrett both stared at her, dumbfounded.

'I . . . am . . . so . . . sorry!' she managed to say between fits of laughter. She extended her hand. 'I'm . . . Sophie Jones.'

Garrett's jaw dropped as they shook hands. 'But you . . . I mean you're . . . you're Sophie?' She wasn't anything close to the diamond in the rough that he'd envisioned. She was much better.

She nodded, still giggling. 'I figured it was you when I first tapped you on the shoulder. But you never said who you were looking for, so I just played along.' She wiped away a tear from her eye. 'I really am sorry. But thank you for that. I needed a good laugh.'

'Glad I could oblige,' Garrett said, still stunned that this woman was his date. He thought back to his mother's advice that he should look hard at what she had on the inside, and it suddenly seemed all the more prudent. It would have been very easy with someone as attractive as Sophie to be taken in on looks alone.

Since they were already running late, Sophie and Garrett caught the next elevator to the Space Needle's restaurant, five hundred feet up and just below the topmost observation deck. A waiter named André was ready to seat them as soon as the elevator doors opened.

'Careful,' André said, as the pair stepped into the dining area. 'The floor moves.' He led them halfway round the O-shaped restaurant to a black granite table beside the Needle's outer window. As they walked, André explained that the restaurant spun continually in a circle, making a complete rotation at least once per hour so that patrons could enjoy a 360-degree view of the surrounding landscape. After a few other facts about the history of the structure, he handed each of them a menu and then he left to fetch drinks.

Once they'd placed their orders, Sophie took a pen from her bag and scribbled some words round the edge of a pink packet of Sweet'N Low that she'd grabbed from a basket on the table. When she was done, she placed it on the windowsill next to the table.

'What's that for?' Garrett asked.

'Souvenir,' she remarked. 'It's kind of a tradition here. I wrote our names and the date on it, plus where we're from. Everyone in the restaurant will see it in the window as they pass by, and some will add their names to it just for fun. Some might even write a message. So thirty or forty minutes from now, when we've come full circle, I'll have a little memento of our visit.' She paused. 'Would you like one?'

'Sure. Just not pink. A white sugar packet would be great.'

Sophie made a few scribbles on a sugar packet and placed it in the window. At the rate they were spinning, the Sweet'N Low was already ten feet away. 'There you go. Years from now, you'll have something sweet to remember me by.'

'After announcing your name over the intercom, I don't think I'll be forgetting you anytime soon.'

She bit her lip and smiled. 'I really am sorry,' she said. 'Tell you what. Why don't we start over with some basic introductions?'

Garrett cleared his throat. 'Hi, my name is Garrett. Umm . . . Garrett Black. And it's a pleasure to meet you.'

'OK, my turn. Hello, I'm Sophie Jones. You may have heard of me. They announced my name over the loudspeakers earlier.'

Garrett shook his head and laughed. 'Very funny. Tell me, Sophie Jones, how is it that you and I ended up on this date tonight? Was it more the doing of my mother or yours?'

Sophie's brow furrowed and her smile dimmed slightly. She took a drink of water before answering. 'I think they were equal partners in crime. If they didn't work for the police department, I'd say we should have them arrested. But . . .'

'But?'

'Nothing. It's just that . . . Well, she's not really my mother. Ellen is my foster mom.'

Idiot! 'Oh? How long have you known her?'

'Since I was nine.'

Garrett pondered briefly what to say next. Moving on to a completely different subject might come off as insensitive, he thought, but digging into her past right from the get-go carried the same risk. 'I know this probably doesn't fall under the umbrella of get-to-know-you questions that you had in mind, but . . . do you mind if I ask how you came to live in a foster home?'

Sophie took another drink of water. 'My parents died.'

'I'm sorry. That must've been incredibly hard for you. I lost my dad when I was twelve. My parents divorced when I was a baby, so I wasn't real close to him, but still it was tough.'

Sophie relaxed, suddenly feeling like she had an ally. She allowed her easy smile to return. 'Let's not dwell on the past. There must be better things than that to discuss, right?'

'Right,' he said with a nod.

Not long after that André showed up with the first course of the meal, tomato bisque. As they ate, Garrett learned all the typical first-date information about the stunning woman who sat across from him. Things like where she went to high school, what she studied in college and what she did for a living.

'A chocolatier?' he said, when she told him about her store. 'I can honestly say that I've never known a chocolatier before.'

'I wish I could say that I've never known a doctor before,' she teased. 'But a foot doctor? Honestly, how many problems can there be with feet that we should need specialists to work on them?'

He chuckled at her sarcasm. 'Just wait until your arches collapse, and see if you don't go running to the nearest podiatrist.'

While André cleared a few dishes, Garrett took a moment to glance at his watch. By his calculations, their date was probably halfway over, and he found himself already disappointed that his evening with Sophie Jones would eventually come to an end.

'Can I borrow your pen?' he asked Sophie.

She handed it across the table. He took one more sugar packet and quickly wrote a few words across the top.

'I'll be right back,' he said, then stood and walked partway round the restaurant, and placed the sugar in the windowsill beside an empty table.

'What was that all about?' she said, when he returned.

'One more souvenir,' he responded. 'I want to make sure it gets back to us before we leave, so I gave it a head start.'

She gave him another funny look, but mostly she was just looking at the way his dimples danced when he smiled. 'I see.'

Several minutes later, Sophie's Sweet'N Low came into view again, and a few minutes after that it was within her reach beside their table.

'Three names,' she said proudly, after picking it up. 'Two from Spokane, one from Portland.' She flipped it over. 'Oh, and a message on the back! "Saccharine causes cancer!"'

They both laughed out loud.

'I'm not sure that's been proven,' Garrett quipped, 'but it's funny anyway.'

It wasn't much longer before Garrett's first sugar packet arrived. He let Sophie do the honours. 'Darn,' she said, pretending to be upset. 'You got more signatures than me. Two from Spokane again; same ones as mine. One from Seattle, and three from California.'

'But no messages?'

Sophie flipped it over and burst out laughing.

'What? Don't tell me someone thinks sugar is a carcinogen, too.'

'You really want to hear it?' she said.

'Of course. I like a good laugh.'

'Very well. It says, "Hey Blondie, ditch the dork. We have an extra seat at our table." Signed, Rodney and friends.'

Sophie started laughing out loud again as she handed it across the table. Then she looked past Garrett and waved politely.

Garrett felt blood rushing to his face. Spinning round, he saw that the culprits—three men in their fifties—were practically falling off their chairs and laughing hysterically.

'I'm sorry,' Sophie said. 'For what it's worth, I disagree with their assessment. You really don't strike me as dorky.' She smiled warmly, then turned her attention once more to her plate of food.

Garrett's second sugar packet arrived at the table just as they were finishing dessert. They could both see from where they sat that it was filled with handwritten words.

Here goes . . ., Garrett thought.

Sophie picked it up and studied both sides. Finally she spoke. 'I take it you're planning a date with someone?'

He grinned. 'As a matter of fact, I am.'

Sophie was smiling, which he found encouraging. 'So this sugar-packet survey is intended to help you plan your next date?'

'That was the general idea, yes. Are there any good ones?'

Sophie read the question Garrett had written at the top of the sugar packet. '"Ideas for a second date?"' She looked up at him. 'And I quote, "Three Bs: Bowl, Bar, Beer."'

'That could be Rodney,' joked Garrett.

She snickered. 'Next up, "Dinner Cruise on Puget Sound". Sounds nice. "Hike Mount Rainier". Yikes, not this time of year. And finally,

"Spend an entire evening gazing at the stars". I'm sure a woman wrote that one.' Sophie looked up from the sugar in her hand and smiled.

'Why is that one from a woman?'

'Because it's the only suggestion that is even remotely romantic.'

'Ah. So romance is important?'

'Romance is everything. I'm willing to bet your ladyfriend wants a man who's tender and thoughtful and does all the little things that are important. A truly romantic man must be willing to do whatever it takes to win the lady's heart.'

'Romance sounds daunting,' he commented, still wearing his giant, dimpled smile. 'So if I had to pick something from this list for my next date, you'd definitely go with stargazing?'

She winked. 'Definitely.'

André showed up then with Garrett's credit card and a receipt, and thanked them for coming. He led them to the elevator, and forty-three seconds later they were back down on Planet Earth.

'Sophie,' Garrett said, before they reached the main exit of the souvenir shop, 'I want to apologise for not planning more for tonight than dinner. It just seemed like a safe bet for a blind date.'

'It was great,' she said, sounding like she meant it. 'Are you going to let me know how that second date turns out with your special someone?'

'I'd be happy to. How can I get a hold of you?'

Her eyes twinkled as she pulled out another pink packet of Sweet'N Low that already had her address and phone number on it. 'For you.' Garrett wasn't sure when she'd had time to write that information down without him noticing, but it was clearly premeditated. 'So when do you think you'll be going on that date?'

Garrett could feel his heart thumping against the inside of his chest. 'Tomorrow night,' he stated nervously. 'If she's available.'

Sophie smiled coyly. 'I'm sure she'll make herself available.'

Reaching once more into her bag, Sophie found the sugar packet with suggestions for a second date and handed it to him. She placed it in his palm in such a way that their hands cupped together briefly. His heart pounded faster.

'Thanks,' he said, too nervous to come up with anything more intelligent to say.

'Good night, Garrett,' said Sophie pleasantly, biting her lip and smiling at the same time.

As she started to walk away, Garrett scanned the words on the sugar packet. He flipped it over, quickly reading both sides twice. Then his heart really started to thump in his chest. 'Sophie!' he shouted, but the door had already closed behind her. He ran to the exit and stepped out into the night. 'Sophie!' he called again.

She turned and smiled like she knew what he was going to say.

'It doesn't say, "Gaze at the stars".'

Grinning mischievously, Sophie walked back to where he stood. 'Really?' She took the sugar from his hand, wrote on it with her pen and then placed it back in his palm. 'Well, now it does. Good night, Garrett Black.' She winked.

'Good night, Sophie Jones.'

Chapter 6

Trust your intuition. It's bound to be right sooner or later.

IT WASN'T HARD for Garrett to find Sophie's house the next day in Gig Harbor. She lived on the main street that coursed along the harbour's shore. The home was a small bungalow built in the 1940s, but the slate-blue siding looked less than a decade old, while the crisp white trim round the windows gave it a classic charm. He showed up at seven thirty wearing a light jacket and slacks.

Sophie met him at her front door in a thick winter parka, a wool scarf and mittens. They both took a moment to evaluate the other's choice of clothing.

'You look warm,' Garrett said, smiling. 'Er—I mean, you look great. And warm.'

'It's chilly out, and I thought we might be spending some time outside. Is that not the case?'

He chuckled and pulled a small packet of sugar from his pocket. 'Actually, I was going through these ideas for a second date,' he said brightly, holding up the sugar, 'and even though I liked the idea of gazing at the stars, I'm afraid it's too cloudy for that tonight. So I chose the next best thing.'

'Which is?'

'The three Bs! Bowl, bar and beer.'

Her face dropped. 'You're joking, right?'

'Yes,' he replied, beaming. 'But it really is too cloudy outside for stargazing, so I've made some other arrangements.'

She flashed a generous smile. 'I see. And do I get to know what those arrangements are? I'm not a huge fan of surprises.'

Garrett rubbed his chin thoughtfully. 'Well, I can tell you there will definitely be dinner. And there will also be an activity. But beyond that, you'll just have to wait and see.'

A few minutes later they were on the interstate heading back across the Narrows Bridge towards Tacoma, and a few minutes after that they were on I-5 heading north towards Seattle.

After taking an exit just north of downtown, Garrett slowed the car, retrieved a black sleeping mask from his glove box, and handed it to her while he continued driving. 'Would it freak you out if I asked you to put this on?' he asked. 'If you see where we're going it'll spoil the surprise.'

She looked at him sceptically. 'Yes, it would freak me out.'

'Trust me,' he said reassuringly.

Sophie sighed, then reluctantly pulled the mask over her eyes.

'Can you see?'

'Not at all.'

'Excellent.'

A few minutes later, when the car was stopped and the engine turned off, Sophie asked if she could take off the mask.

'Not yet,' he told her.

Walking round to the passenger side, Garrett helped Sophie out. Then he took her arm and guided her into a nearby building.

'Where are we?' she kept asking, once they were inside.

Garrett didn't offer any hints as he led her through the building. They walked up a flight of stairs, down a long hallway, and through a set of doors. Finally, he told her to sit down carefully. He helped lower her to the ground, onto a large blanket. She felt disconcerted by the complete lack of sound. There were definitely no other people around, and she started feeling like this wasn't such a good idea.

Garrett could see the worry in the lines round her mouth. 'You ready to take off the mask?' he asked, as he sat down next to her.

'Very.'

'OK, then. We're here. Take it off.'

Sophie carefully reached up and broke the Velcro seal on the elastic band that surrounded her head. She squinted to adjust to the new light as the mask came loose.

Only . . . it was still very dark.

She looked all round the strange, bare room. There appeared to be only one continuous wall that surrounded them like a dome, curving to the centre of the room. In front of her on the ground were two empty plates beside a couple of small take-out boxes.

'Go ahead, Vance,' Garrett said, craning his neck back towards the door. A few seconds later the lights dimmed even further.

Sophie studied Garrett's face as the room darkened. He was staring back at her with boyish glee. As their surroundings faded to near pitch-black, a subtle flickering began to emanate from the dome. Sophie turned her head in every direction and watched with amazement as thousands of tiny lights burst to life. And then she understood. 'Stars!' she exclaimed. 'Oh my gosh! I haven't been to a planetarium since fifth grade! How did you arrange this?'

'I know a guy,' he said, smiling. 'Vance is a patient of mine, and he runs the Pacific Science Center. I gave him a call last night, and he said we could have the whole place to ourselves.'

'It's amazing,' she said, taking it all in.

'I'm glad you like it.'

Sophie shifted her weight on the concrete. 'Shouldn't there be chairs in here?'

'Yeah, sorry about that. They're remodelling.'

'Chairs or not, this is incredible. I can't believe it.' She looked around at the growing constellations. 'Thank you so much for this.'

Garrett smiled in the darkness.

The remainder of the evening was spent doing exactly what Sophie had requested: gazing at the stars. While they stared at the expanding universe around them, they also did a great deal of talking, mingled with mouthfuls of pad thai and coconut rice.

During the conversation, Garrett learned that Sophie had a special affinity for astronomy. She could easily name and identify the twelve zodiac constellations. When Garrett asked what, specifically, she liked most about the stars, her answer intrigued him.

. Lying on her back on the hard concrete floor, she kept her eyes focused on the twinkling lights overhead. 'Looking at stars is a glimpse of history,' she said dreamily. 'Some of the things we can see in the sky are millions of light-years away. The Andromeda galaxy, for instance, is two and a half million light-years from earth, and that's a relatively close one.' She took his hand in hers and pointed to a faint blur that made up one of the points in Andromeda. 'We're living in the present, but in a very real way we're staring at the past. Everything in the universe has a past, but stars don't try to hide it. They just keep shining, for everyone to see.'

Garrett studied those sections of Sophie's face that were illuminated by the mock starlight. 'Andromeda. That's Greek, right?'

'Very good. She was a princess in the mythological kingdom of Aethiopia. She also went by a different name. The Chained Lady.'

'Oh yeah? What do you suppose she was chained to?'

Sophie's eyes locked onto Garrett's. 'The past.'

Though Sophie looked away almost immediately, Garrett couldn't help but continue staring at her. Everything about her captivated him. The subtle shift in her voice as she talked about Andromeda made him wonder if she somehow viewed herself as a modern Chained Lady, tied to some hidden past. Perhaps understanding her in the present means looking at her past.

Looking at her profile, Garrett wanted to learn as much as he could about this woman. He wanted to take every opportunity to see her in the present, with a hope of getting a glimpse of that past, all while keeping an eye towards making himself a part of her future.

For Garrett, a blind date spinning round the Space Needle followed by an evening gazing at faux stars from a concrete floor was more than enough time with Sophie Jones to realise that his original plan to meet her only once was very shortsighted. Curiosity had given way to infatuation, and now he wanted to spend as much time with her as possible. Ten minutes after dropping Sophie off at her house at the end of their second date, he decided it was time to ask her out again. He pulled into an empty parking lot and took out his cellphone and sent her a quick text message.

U free tomorrow? he typed.

Sorry. I have 2 work. My 1 employee is going out of town.

Mind if I drop by your store then?

Garrett expected a quick response, but it was several minutes before Sophie's reply came, and the curtness of her answer caught him off guard.

Yes . . . I mind.

Hoping she was joking, Garrett quickly thumbed another brief text:

So that's a definite no???

Yes . . . sorry.

Garrett stared at the words. He'd been so sure that Sophie had enjoyed herself on their previous dates that he couldn't believe she simply didn't want to see him again. Then again, he thought, I'm no expert on women. After five minutes debating whether or not he should send another text message, Garrett decided just to leave it alone. He threw the car into gear and drove home.

Lying on her bed an hour later, Sophie stared at the last note she'd sent to Garrett. Yes . . . sorry. She wished she'd conveyed the message more delicately. It wasn't that she didn't want to see him again; just not so soon. Sophie had had relationships before that started out fast, but they always fizzled out just as quickly, and that was something she wanted to avoid with Garrett.

For the next thirty minutes she stayed sprawled out on her bed, phone in hand, hoping that Garrett would send another note, but nothing came. Then she caved in and crafted a message of her own.

Hey Garrett! Where'd you go??

Garrett didn't waste any time responding.

Just sitting here trying to figure out what I did wrong. :-(

SOOOO sorry! I can be lame, I know. But I want 2 see u 2. PLEASE come by the store tomorrow. U can help me make fudge!!

Fine. But only 'cuz I'm a sucker for fudge.

Perfect! G'night!

Garrett dwelled nervously throughout the next day on what Sophie was going to say, but when he showed up at Chocolat' de Soph that evening, he quickly learned that his worry was unwarranted. As soon as he walked in the door Sophie gave him an affectionate hug, then sat him down on a stool near the window.

'Do all customers get a hug?' he asked coyly. 'I'll have to come here more often.'

'It's why I'm still in business,' she shot back with a giggle. Then she sat on the stool next to him and got more serious. 'Listen, about last night. It was nerves. I don't exactly have a great track record with . . .' There were several ways she could have finished the sentence. A lousy track record with handsome men? With opening up my heart? With commitment? 'With trust,' she said finally.

He looked at her funny. 'You don't trust me?'

She chortled lightly, patting him on the knee. 'No, it's me that I don't trust. I have a bad habit of ruining relationships, so when you said you wanted to see me again so soon, I got nervous, that's all.'

'I think I follow.'

Sophie tucked a lock of hair behind her ear. 'It's kind of ironic. Out of fear of driving guys away, I drive them away anyway.'

Garrett let out a little snicker. 'Stop. Any guy would be nuts to let you drive him away.'

Sophie liked the sound of Garrett's voice. It was confident and strangely comforting. She also liked the way his dimples sank into his cheeks when he smiled and spoke at the same time. 'That's what the last guy who came to my store to help make fudge said, and do you know where he is now?' She watched his face to see if he had an answer. 'Me neither!' she laughed.

Garrett smiled, finding Sophie's self-deprecating humour endearing. 'You know what my mom always says about relationships?'

'Avoid them at all costs, because they can only bring heartache?'

'Close,' he said happily. 'She says that every relationship will be a complete failure, right up until the one that isn't, and that's what makes all the failures a success—that you're able to get past them to find the right one.'

Sophie grinned playfully. 'And do you believe dear old Mom?'

'I do. As bitter as the failures can be—and I should know, because I've had a lot of them—I still hold out hope that the right person will come along. And that'll turn the bitter into sweet.'

'Ahh,' she said, gently teasing. 'You're not just a romantic, you're a hopeless romantic.'

'A hopeful romantic,' he countered. 'There's a difference.'

She returned his gaze, trying to read what he was thinking. 'Just remember what I said about me and trust, OK? Consider yourself warned, Garrett Black—the more I see a guy, and the more I like him, the more likely I am to do something to mess it up. It's inevitable.'

Garrett stood up and stepped closer, gently touching her arm. 'I'll take that as a challenge.' He smiled, looking directly in her eyes. 'Now, are you going to show me how to make chocolates, or what?'

She tipped her head and stood too. 'Chocolates it is. Follow me.' Sophie led Garrett to the kitchen and taught him a few basic tricks to making fudge. Then they moved on to truffles and dipped fruit. For the rest of the evening they worked side by side making all sorts of confections. When the bell on the front door rang, Sophie would help the customers, but the rest of the time they spent talking, joking and otherwise enjoying themselves in the kitchen.

By the time the store closed at nine, Sophie was pretty much finished with the preparations for the following day. The only thing still simmering, in a double boiler, was a new concoction she had been tinkering with. It was a melted brew of dark chocolates, sweetened condensed milk, crème de menthe and an assortment of creams, butters and sugar. While Garrett stacked pots on a counter, Sophie dabbed a finger into the chocolatey mix, then licked it clean.

'Come try this,' she said, motioning at Garrett to join her next to the stove. 'I've been working on a new recipe, and I need an opinion.' She dipped a spoon in the pot, then lifted it to his mouth.

He leaned in and took a slow bite.

'So?'

Licking his lips, Garrett replied, 'It's good.' And then, without thinking, he leaned in even closer. Sophie didn't resist as he gave her a single, gentle kiss. 'No,' he said, as he pulled back. 'It's more than good. It's probably the best I've ever had.'

Sophie laughed. 'The new recipe? Or . . .?'

Garrett beamed. 'Both.'

As much as Sophie didn't want to rush things, she and Garrett were, by anyone's standards, hooked on each other. After their first kiss at Chocolat' de Soph, they spent as much time together as they could. On most days after work, Garrett would pick Sophie up at her store and drive her home. Then they'd enjoy the evening talking, walking, eating, laughing, whatever filled the time.

For the first few months of their relationship, Sophie made a point of telling Garrett that both of them could date others. It was her way of making sure he knew there was an easy way out, if he needed one. Although she hoped things would continue going well, in the back of her mind Sophie always expected that sooner or later he'd take the way out. Each time she mentioned it, Garrett would remind her that unless she had plans of calling it quits, she was stuck with him.

In January, fourth months after meeting in the lobby of the Space Needle, Garrett took Sophie for a day trip to Cannon Beach, a quaint town on the Oregon coast. The weather was too cold to enjoy the ocean water, but searching rocky tide pools for starfish followed by a bowl of clam chowder at Mo's restaurant was a perfect way to spend a winter Sunday. As he guessed she would, during the three-hour drive to their destination Sophie casually asked him how much longer it was going to be before he found some other pretty woman that he liked more than her.

He sighed out loud. Garrett had to admit that the constant questioning of his loyalty to her was beginning to wear thin. 'C'mon, Soph,' he said. 'Do we have to go there again?'

'I'm just being practical,' she said flatly. 'All good things must come to an end, right?'

Garrett reached out and took her hand. 'No. That's completely wrong. Why can't you just accept that I don't want anyone else?'

She looked at him for a long time, then shrugged. 'I don't know.'

He tried to smile. 'Well, one way or another, we have to figure that out. Because I'm not going anywhere.'

She squeezed his hand. 'It's just hard for me to imagine that what we have won't eventually vanish. It's like it's too good to be true.'

Garrett took his eyes off the taillights of the car in front of them long enough to see that the look on her face matched the sadness in her voice. 'Your parents?' he ventured.

Sophie nodded almost imperceptibly.

'So, you think because you lost your parents, that all relationships are somehow going to end up the same way?'

She shrugged. 'I assume so. Starting with their deaths, relationships in my life have felt very . . . temporary. After that, I had several foster families, and they all went south. One of my foster parents even died.'

Garrett reached over again and squeezed her leg. 'Well you don't have to worry about any of those things with me, Sophie Jones. I'm just the guy who's falling in love with you.'

The comment took Sophie by surprise. Not only was it the first time he'd used the 'L' word, it was the way he said it that really pricked her ears. There was no hidden agenda in the words. She didn't even get the impression that he expected her to reciprocate the gesture, which was good, because she wasn't prepared to admit to loving him, even though her heart said that was exactly what she was feeling. Instead of saying anything, Sophie unclicked her seat belt so she could stretch far enough to kiss him on the cheek.

'Careful,' he said jokingly. 'I lose my mental and physical faculties when your lips are near my face, so if you're going to kiss me while we're moving, at least keep your seat belt on for safety.'

Sophie poked him in the ribs, then took his hand in hers, interlocking their fingers. There were lots of thoughts running through her head. A few of them were the same old worries that Garrett might eventually run for the hills, but mostly she was thinking about how much she cared for the man who, she'd just noticed, had hands that fitted with hers like a glove.

Chapter 7

When offered the dream of a lifetime, SAY NO!
Remember, it's just a dream.

FOR SOPHIE, the trip to Cannon Beach with Garrett, and in particular his unexpected expression of love, was a turning point in her willingness to accept that their relationship had a chance of withstanding the cruel test of time. After that, she even found herself dropping hints that she felt the same way about him.

Valentine's Day was the busiest day of the year at Chocolat' de Soph, which meant that Sophie had to work all day long, even after Randy arrived. It took both of them working nonstop just to keep up with the tidal wave of customers looking for last-minute goodies to share with their loved ones.

The next evening, however, Garrett surprised Sophie with a post-Valentine's date that more than made up for the lack of romance the previous day. Picking her up at five thirty, they drove north to a private airstrip near Sea-Tac Airport, where they boarded a small prop plane that Garrett had chartered. The pilot flew them round Seattle for a while, then veered west, landing thirty minutes later on a narrow runway in a remote section of hills north of Mount Rainier.

When Sophie asked why they were landing, Garrett grinned. 'Aren't you hungry?'

The runway, Sophie learned, was maintained by a restaurant. In decades past, the site had been an old logger's lodge. But when the logging company went out of business, a group of entrepreneurs scooped up the property and turned it into a gourmet, hunter-style restaurant, catering almost exclusively to small-aircraft enthusiasts. In the ten years since opening, the establishment had become a regular hot spot for flight clubs all over the Pacific Northwest.

The pilot read a magazine in the restaurant's lobby while Sophie and Garrett dined.

'You've got to be kidding!' Sophie said, when she saw the prices on the menu. 'It's like a weeks' worth of groceries for one meal.'

'I'm trying not to look at the prices,' he chided. 'I bet people who can afford to own their own plane don't bat an eye at the cost.'

'Either that, or they know that the safety record of small planes justifies an expensive meal, since it may very well be their last.'

Garrett chuckled. 'You make me laugh, Soph. I think that's what I love most about you.'

The timing may have been a bit awkward, but without even thinking about it Sophie blurted out, 'I love you, too.'

Both of them sat in stunned silence.

'Whoa,' Garrett managed eventually. 'Did you mean that?'

Sounding as surprised about it as he was, she said, 'I guess I must have.' She paused, biting her lip nervously. 'Is that . . . OK?'

He smiled warmly and reached across the table to hold her hands. 'It's perfect.'

She smiled back. The way Garrett was looking at her, Sophie felt an odd sense of vulnerability, but it was balanced out by an even odder feeling of safety and assurance that he wouldn't hurt her. This is what it's supposed to feel like, she told herself.

The rest of the evening was as enjoyable a time as Sophie could ever remember having, though the specifics about what made it so wonderful were sketchy, even to her. The only concrete details she could recall the following day were the rough landing back at Sea-Tac airport and the smooth kiss good night in Gig Harbor. 'I know we did a lot of talking, but I don't have a clue what either of us said,' she told Evalynn by phone the next evening. 'I think emotionally I was so overwhelmed by what I'd told him about how I felt, that that's all I could think about for the rest of the night. Everything beyond that was a happy blur.'

Two weeks later, Garrett attended a week-long podiatry convention in New Orleans. It was the first significant time he and Sophie had spent apart since meeting almost six months earlier.

Garrett returned from Louisiana on Saturday, March 8. Sophie was still working when his flight arrived, so he told her not to bother coming to the airport. Instead, he wanted to see her immediately after work for dinner. He wouldn't say where they were going, but he did let her know that she should dress up.

Sophie carried a dress with her to work, and as soon as Randy arrived for the evening shift, she slipped into the privacy of her office to put on the dress. Garrett arrived in a suit ten minutes later.

'Well, don't we look dapper tonight,' Sophie said when she saw him, then gave him a quick hug and kiss to say hello.

'Dudes,' Randy said jokingly, 'I'm trying to work here! Take it outside.'

After driving north for forty-five minutes in traffic, Garrett produced the infamous black mask that he'd made her wear on their second date. 'How would you feel about putting this on again?'

She laughed. 'What's with you and blindfolds?'

'It's the element of surprise that I like.'

'OK,' she said, smiling. 'I trust you.' As she fastened the strap round her head, Sophie pondered what it meant that she could say those particular words to him and really mean it. She didn't know how, but, somehow he'd managed to show her that love and trust are inseparable.

Five minutes after Sophie put on the blindfold, she and Garrett arrived at their destination. Garrett got out of the car, gave the key to an attendant, and then helped walk Sophie to the front doors.

Once inside, he told her she could take off the mask.

As she let the mask fall from her face, Sophie knew immediately where they were. 'The Space Needle!' she said, looking to her left and right. But Garrett wasn't there. She turned quickly round to look behind her, but he wasn't there either.

Perfect, she thought half-jokingly. Just when I was beginning to think he might stick around, he vanishes into thin air. Just then, a woman's voice echoed throughout the souvenir shop over the sound system: 'Sophie Jones to the front desk. Sophie Jones to the front desk, please. Your party is waiting.'

Sophie couldn't help but break into a huge grin as she made her way to the reception desk. There, next to the young woman who'd paged her, was Garrett, holding a single red rose.

'It's our six-month anniversary,' he said, as he gave her the rose. 'I thought it might be fun to go back to where it all started.'

'You're nuts,' she said, beaming. 'But it's very sweet.'

Taking her arm in his, Garrett redirected Sophie to the elevators. 'We're a few minutes early, but I bet if we head up they can get us seated.'

After getting a table five hundred feet above ground level and hearing the usual spiel of Space Needle facts from their waiter, Sophie and Garrett pulled out pens and wrote their names on sugar packets, then stuck them on the window's ledge. While they waited for their food, they swapped stories about the previous week, each happily telling the other how glad they were to be back together.

By the time Sophie and Garrett were through with their main course, the restaurant had spun back to where the sugar packets rested against the window. Garrett was closest, so he grabbed the first one, looked at it long enough to see that five people had signed it, then handed it to Sophie. A moment later he plucked the second sugar packet from the windowsill and checked it for signatures.

'Weird,' he said, flipping the small white package over and back in his hand. 'Nobody signed this one but me.'

'Nobody wrote anything?'

'Well, someone wrote a question on the back, but they didn't give their name or where they're from.'

'What's the question?'

'It just says, "Will you?"' he said slowly, then handed it across the table. 'Here, take a look.'

Sophie took the packet and held it in her hands, noting that it was thicker—and heavier—than the other one she'd just read. A puzzled look crossed her face. 'I think there's something in it.'

'Well, open it up. Now you've got me curious.'

Sophie tore gently on one end of the packaging, then dumped the contents onto a plate. In the middle of the pile of sugar was the most dazzling diamond ring she'd ever seen. The sight of it caused her to gasp 'Holy crow!' as she picked it up and dusted it off.

Garrett was smiling sheepishly. 'How about you remind me what that question says on the back?'

'Oh,' she replied, picking up the empty paper wrapper again. '"Will you?"' she read.

Garrett hesitated a few seconds, watching her study the ring with giddy fascination, waiting for her to catch on. 'So? Will you?'

'Will I what?' she responded vacantly. But a moment later a light bulb flickered to life in her brain. Her eyes shot up to meet Garrett's. 'Oh . . . my . . . gosh,' she said. 'Did you just . . .?'

'If you're asking if I just proposed, then yes. Will you marry me, Sophia Maria Jones?'

'Oh . . . my . . . gosh,' Sophie repeated, more stunned than before. Then she started to ramble. 'What? That's huge! How can we? I mean . . . we've only been dating for six months. Do you know me well enough? Do I know you well enough? How could we . . .?'

Garrett just chuckled. 'I know this may seem a little sudden, but I know I'm in love, and I know you are too. Why wait?'

'Well, because . . . things could change.'

'I'm nervous about it too—marriage is a big step. But I've never been happier since I met you, and I want you to be more than just the beautiful woman I'm dating. I really want you to be my wife.'

Sophie held the ring up and examined it more closely. 'I can't believe you left this on the window for forty-five minutes.'

'It was in my pocket the whole time,' he explained. 'I swapped it with the other one while you were reading yours.' He reached out and grabbed one of Sophie's hands. 'So, what do you say?'

'I'm thinking,' she assured him.

'Well, don't think,' he replied, grinning. 'Just go with your gut.'

She snickered. 'My gut is churning. I think it's saying it wants to vomit. Are you sure I should trust it?'

'No, better not. Let's pick something a little higher in your torso. What does your heart say?'

Now Sophie sat back in her chair and looked out at the lights of the Seattle skyline. When she spoke, her voice was steady, but cautious. 'It says . . . that guys like you come along once in a blue moon.' Her gaze remained fixed outside.

'OK, now at least we've picked a trustworthy organ. Is it saying anything else?'

Sophie turned and faced Garrett again. 'Yes. My heart still wants to make sure that you're not going to break it.'

Sitting up in his chair, Garrett took a moment to watch Sophie. She was the most beautiful woman he'd ever known, inside and out. Funny, intelligent, caring, witty—everything he'd ever wanted. 'Soph,' he said softly, 'I honestly love you more than I thought I could love anyone. I can't promise you that we won't experience difficult things in our life. But I can promise you that I will never break your heart.' He smiled. 'Tell that to your heart, and see what it says.'

Sophie tilted her head to the side, as though she were weighing something in her mind. 'It says yes,' she said finally.

'Yes what?'

She held up the empty sugar packet with Garrett's handwritten proposal. 'Just "yes".'

Sophie slid the ring onto its intended finger. *Just like Garrett*, she thought. *A perfect fit.*

October 25 was the date that Sophie and Garrett set for their wedding. It gave them seven months to prepare, which Garrett thought was more than enough time to plan and make all the arrangements. For Sophie, however, it felt like a tight schedule, especially with the demands on her time running Chocolat' de Soph.

By the end of the first week of their engagement, she'd already made a comprehensive list of things that needed to be done. When she showed it to Garrett, he read through it several times, shaking his head at the level of minutiae.

As much as possible, they tackled the massive to-do list together, setting aside time each week to scratch off a few more items. The magnitude of the effort made time fly, and before either of them knew it, it was September, just four weeks from the big date.

Sophie's birthday fell on the third Sunday of that month. She was glad it was a Sunday, because it meant that she didn't have to go to work. She could relax and enjoy her birthday with Garrett.

'I have a surprise for you today,' she told him over brunch.

'But it's your birthday. I'm supposed to be doing the surprising.'

'Well, it's not so much a surprise as a birthday tradition I want to share with you. Can we go for a little drive this afternoon?'

He agreed, so a few hours later they got in the car and Sophie directed him to the Evergreen Cemetery.

'This is your big surprise?'

'Tradition,' she said, smiling.

They parked the car and got out at the base of a small hill, and then walked hand in hand the rest of the way to a large hedge near the base of an old cedar tree.

'Here it is,' Sophie said, pointing, once they'd reached the gravestone of Thomas and Cecilia Jones.

Garrett carefully read every word engraved on the marker. Sophie noticed that his jaw muscles tightened dramatically. 'They died on your birthday,' he said solemnly. 'I never knew that.'

Sophie shrugged. 'It's not something I like to talk about.'

'That makes the whole thing all the more tragic.'

'It's definitely made my birthdays more . . . significant, that's for sure.' She paused and looked at his face. 'You know, I don't usually like sharing this with anyone, but facing the past doesn't seem quite so daunting when I'm with you. Thank you for that.'

He gave her a gentle squeeze, but kept his eyes on the grave marker. 'Yeah . . . sure.'

Sophie brushed off his sudden introspectiveness. Everyone she'd ever told about her parents' deaths had reacted oddly when they learned that her birthday was their death day, so why should he be any different? Allowing him a chance to ponder, she dug into her bag for the box of chocolates. She set a chocolate on the grave, then she picked up the beautiful round stone that was resting on the lower left corner of the gravestone and dropped it in her bag.

'What's the chocolate for?'

'Just a little reminder,' she said softly.

'Of what?'

Sophie stood back up and wrapped her arms round him. 'If you're nice to me, maybe someday I'll tell you.'

'How about the stone? Are you going to tell me about that?'

She stretched up on her tiptoes and gave him a quick peck on the lips. 'Yep. You've earned at least that much.' Then she kissed him a little longer.

With her eyes closed, Sophie didn't see that Garrett was still looking at the gravestone.

After leaving the cemetery, Garrett's mood perked back up, for which Sophie was very grateful. They spent the remainder of the afternoon walking around the Pike Street marketplace in Seattle, and getting an early shish kebab dinner from a street vendor.

Afterwards, they began driving back south towards Gig Harbor. But after crossing the Narrows Bridge, Sophie reminded Garrett that she still needed to explain what she did with the stone that she'd taken from her parents' graves. They took the first exit past the bridge, then doubled back along a little road that meandered eastwards through a residential area. She told him to stop along the side of the road near a pathway that split the property line between two homes.

'What are we doing here?'

'From here, we walk,' she said. Sophie grabbed the stone from her bag and exited the car, then started walking. Two hundred yards down the path, they came to the shore of the Narrows, the stretch of water that separated the Washington mainland from the Olympic Peninsula. The Narrows Bridge loomed overhead.

Sophie had to speak loudly to be heard above the noise of passing cars. 'Do you know what's out there?' she asked, pointing to a spot in the water beneath the bridge.

'No clue,' he said after scanning the surface for a hint.

'When I was in second grade my dad brought me here. He had a fascination with suspension bridges. Anyway, he told me all about the old Narrows Bridge. When it opened to the public in 1940, the old bridge was considered state of the art, an engineering marvel.'

'What happened to it?'

'Four months after it opened, it collapsed. The wind blowing across the Narrows caused it to start pitching and rolling. They say cars on it at the time felt like they were on a roller coaster. After too much twisting, the whole thing broke apart and fell into the water.'

Garrett scratched his chin. 'Amazing. But why is that important to you now?'

Sophie pursed her lips. 'It was a tragedy of epic proportions. An entire bridge—the best of its kind—gone, just like that. But the reason

I come here is because of what happened after it fell. First, engineers learned a ton about how not to build suspension bridges. Plus, believe it or not, the old bridge, which is now a hundred and eighty feet below the surface, has become the world's largest man-made reef, providing a home for countless sea animals.'

Wrapping an arm round her shoulders, Garrett said, 'I think I understand. Something good came out of something bad. Is that it?'

She nodded.

'Then why do you come here with the stone from the grave?'

'For this.' Sophie ducked out from beneath Garrett's arm and flung the stone as far as she could across the water. It skipped seven or eight times, before sinking beneath the surface. 'When I turned ten and found a stone on my parents' graves—on the first anniversary of the accident—I thought it looked like a good skipping stone. I asked Ellen to bring me here, because it reminds me of my dad. Anyway, I made a wish back then that like the old bridge, something good could come out of my tragedy.' She stared out at the ripples moving along the surface where her stone had struck the water. 'I come back here every year and make the same wish.'

He nodded, 'Still waiting for it to come true, aren't you?'

Sophie grimaced. 'Yep.' She took Garrett's hand in hers, and together they made their way back to the car, both of them quietly lost in their own thoughts.

Chapter 8

Sharing too much of yourself with loved ones can have dire consequences.

EIGHTEEN DAYS before the wedding, they drove up to 13 Coins, a restaurant in Seattle known for its live jazz and blues music. It was the place Sophie had chosen for the rehearsal dinner. The manager wanted them to come in to taste the dessert offerings.

By the time they were finished sampling custards and fresh tarts, they were ready for something slightly more filling. Garrett punched some buttons on his GPS to find a listing of restaurants to choose from in the area. 'What are you in the mood for, Soph?'

'You decide. I'm up for anything.'

'You sure?'

She put her hand on his leg, squeezing just above the knee. 'Positive. Surprise me.' She paused and smiled. 'Just no blindfolds.'

'You got it.' He pushed a couple more buttons, found a restaurant and started driving.

The female voice gave periodic instructions, easily navigating the roads to a Japanese restaurant exactly six-point-three miles away.

'I know this place,' said Sophie, as she climbed out of the car.

'Oh yeah? Have you been here before?'

She bit her lip nervously as memories flooded her mind. 'A long time ago,' she said, her voice trailing off.

The restaurant was hibachi-style, with several highly skilled chefs who cooked the meals on the table right in front of the customers. Garrett thought it would be fun to try, but he could tell by Sophie's demeanour that something wasn't right.

After the hostess sat them at a table with a group of four other people, he quietly asked her what was wrong.

'This is the place,' she confided. 'It's where my parents took me for my ninth birthday. We had our last meal together here.'

Garrett rubbed her back. 'You want to go somewhere else?'

She let herself smile. 'You're sweet. No, I'm fine,' she said, looking round the room. 'Actually, it feels kind of good coming here. Maybe I shouldn't have avoided it for so long.'

Their chef came a few minutes later and began his culinary show. It was entertaining, but the food wasn't as good as Sophie had remembered. 'Maybe they're under new management,' she told Garrett. 'After all, it's been almost twenty years.'

At the end of the meal, the hostess returned with a fortune cookie for everyone at the table. 'I thought fortune cookies were Chinese,' remarked Garrett, as he took his cookie.

The hostess bowed her head politely. 'Asian fortune cookie,' she said in a Japanese accent. 'China like cookie, Japan like fortune.'

Garrett laughed. 'I see. I'll have to remember that.'

Garrett was still chuckling when they got back into his car. Sophie was more contemplative.

'Before we go home,' she said, 'do you mind if we head up this street a little ways?'

'Sure. What's up?'

'Just something I want to show you.'

Several blocks farther up the road, Sophie directed him to turn left onto a busy four-lane arterial street which they continued on for another mile. She stiffened as they passed the chocolate shop Sophie had been so adamant about stopping at on her ninth birthday. She clenched her teeth.

A hundred yards beyond the candy shop she told Garrett to get into the right lane. She saw the fire hydrant that she'd sat next to in the rain; it was approaching quickly along the sidewalk.

'Slow down!' she instructed. 'We're here.'

'Where is here?'

She hesitated before answering, keeping her gaze on the yellow hydrant. 'The accident.'

There was no place to pull over, but Garrett slowed to a crawl.

'Right here?' he asked.

'I sat right here next to the fire hydrant, just watching everything happen around me. The ambulances were down there, and our car was in the middle of the road,' she said, pointing. 'I remember there was a UPS truck right up here, and the driver was ahead of it on the ground.' Garrett remained silent as she shared the details she could remember— the number of ambulances, the flares along the road, the police officers waving cars round the pile-up.

When she stopped talking, Garrett was still quietly looking out at the road. 'Garrett?' He looked at her. 'What are you thinking?'

'Just . . . wow,' he said softly. 'That must have really been something.' He kept looking at her. 'I'm sorry you had to go through that, Sophie.'

She smiled softly and touched his arm. 'Let's go home.'

'You all right?' Sophie asked Garrett after kissing him good night. 'You haven't been very talkative since we left the restaurant. You're not having doubts, are you?'

He smiled faintly and wrapped his arms round her. 'No. It's just— seeing where your parents died touched a nerve. Makes me sad that you've carried those memories with you all these years.'

Sophie kept him in the embrace, afraid that if she pulled back right then he might see in her eyes that there were worse things about the accident that she'd carried with her, which she hadn't shared with him. 'Thank you,' she whispered.

When they let go of each other, Garrett gave Sophie another little kiss. 'I'll see you tomorrow, Soph,' he said, and then went and got in his car.

While driving to his own house in Tacoma, so many thoughts were running through Garrett's mind that he missed his exit. After passing it, he told himself he could just as easily take the next exit a mile farther, but he drove past that one too. After all the Tacoma exits were distant blurs in his rearview mirror he stopped kidding himself. Garrett wasn't going home. *Not yet.*

Ellen was drifting off to sleep when she heard the doorbell ring. Jumping out of bed, she threw on a robe, then poked her head into the hallway and yelled, 'Knock once if friend, twice if foe.'

There was no knock in response, only the chimes again from the doorbell. Ellen grabbed her gun from her night stand and carried it with her to the door, just in case.

'Hello?' she asked. 'Who's there?'

'It's Garrett Black,' came the reply. 'I'm sorry to bother you at this hour, Ellen, but I need to talk.'

Ellen quickly unbolted the door and let him in.

'What's going on, Garrett?' she asked after she'd relocked the door. 'Is everything OK?'

'It's fine,' he said, but his fragile smile said otherwise. 'I really am sorry to bother you but . . . Sophie took me by the accident site tonight—the place where her parents died.'

Ellen watched him briefly before speaking. 'I see. I guess she must really love you. She has never—ever—taken anyone there.'

'I know,' he said softly.

'So what's wrong?'

'Even while we were there, Soph didn't give me a lot of details. I'd like to get a better sense of what she actually went through.' He paused momentarily. 'I want to know more about it, so I can share the emotional burden a little bit. Does that make sense?'

Ellen smiled. 'It makes perfect sense,' she said. 'And frankly I'm relieved. It sounds like you care for her as much as she does for you.'

He nodded. 'I do. Ellen, I know you were there that night. Can you share what you remember?'

'I can do better than that. If you promise not to tell anyone, I'll let you see a copy of the police report from that night. It's got every detail imaginable.'

'Has Sophie read it?'

She shook her head. 'I made a copy in case she ever came looking for details, but in all these years she's never asked.' She motioned to the sofa. 'Have a seat. It'll take me a few minutes to find it.'

Garrett did as instructed, but after she left he got up to look at the pictures on the wall. He'd been to Ellen's on several previous occasions but had never really had a chance to study them. Most were of Sophie and Evalynn growing up—school pictures, prom, graduation. But a small one was of a young black couple holding hands. He recognised the woman as Ellen and guessed the man was her husband. Garrett knew that Ellen had been married, and that her husband had died, but that was all he'd been told.

While he was looking at it, Ellen came back in the room. 'Found it,' she announced.

Garrett turned. 'Ellen, is this . . .?'

'My husband, Rick. Yes, that's him.'

'He was a policeman too, right?'

She quietly nodded.

'Sophie said he was killed in the line of duty.'

Ellen nodded. 'Has Sophie ever told you what I used to tell her about there being purpose in everything, even the bad things?'

'Yes, she's mentioned it. Though to be honest, I don't think she shares your view.'

'I know. Someday I hope she will. Being a mother to Sophie and Evalynn has been such a blessing. But I'd never have known the joy of it if I hadn't lost Rick. Sophie was my silver lining.'

'Why is that?'

'It's . . . complicated. Do you have time?'

He nodded.

'OK. Rick and I met in the police academy, then we got hired onto the same precinct as rookies. We were both twenty-one at the time. We got married a year after we met, and when we decided it was time to start a family . . .' She hesitated. 'I found out that I couldn't. Apparently I'm not plumbed correctly for bearing children. Anyway, it was a huge disappointment. So we weighed our options. We knew adoption was one route, and we considered it. But because of our jobs we also knew that good foster homes were in high demand. We felt that we could offer the foster system a great place to bring kids that needed a little extra love. We were in the process of getting qualified when Rick died.'

Garrett looked at her curiously. 'How does that relate to there being purpose in tragedy?'

Ellen's eyes met his. 'Some might chalk it up to coincidence, but I see more than everyday chance in the fact that Sophie became an orphan on my first night back on the job after becoming a widow. I believe it was meant to be.'

He cleared his throat. 'How so?'

'I'd been on leave for two months, just trying to cope. It was hard losing him. I'd been working a double shift, covering for someone, so Rick had already left the precinct and gone home while I was still out on the beat. Near the end of my second shift I was listening to the radio chatter, and there was a call for all available units to an address in Seattle where an off-duty officer had been shot.' Ellen paused and stared at Garrett. 'It was *my* address.'

Garrett gasped. 'Oh my gosh, I'm so sorry, Ellen.'

She smiled stoically. 'I got there as fast as I could, but it didn't matter. He was already dead. Turns out he'd arrested a guy earlier that evening, one of a handful that had robbed a store. I guess one of the kids that got away at the store was waiting outside the police station when Rick left work, and followed him home. Shot him right in the doorway when he opened up, unarmed.'

That explains Ellen's nervousness about answering the door, Garrett thought. 'Geez. I don't know what to say. And I don't know how you're able to find a silver lining in that.'

She shrugged. 'After the initial trauma of losing him, and after I'd found a new place to live, I decided I still wanted to go through with being a foster mom. I went back to work, and that very night I met a little girl who needed a mom. During the months following Sophie's accident I kept making calls, letting the state know I was willing to care for her if the need should arise. Then one of her other foster situations fell apart when the husband died, and lo and behold, Social Services brought my silver lining right to my doorstep.' She paused. 'I lost Rick, but I gained Sophie, and later Evalynn. It's been everything to me.'

Garrett nodded that he understood, but he didn't say anything.

After a few moments of quiet, Ellen handed Garrett the police report. 'Sorry, I'm talking your ear off. You still interested in this?'

In listening to Ellen's tale, he'd almost forgotten about it. 'Oh. Yes.' He flipped open the manila folder. It contained a ten-page report that included statements from eyewitnesses, details about the cars involved and the damage they'd sustained, names and ages of the people in each car, and an assessment of fault that said simply, 'inclement weather, slippery roads, poor visibility'.

Garrett skimmed through the first few pages in under a minute. Then he slowed down, giving his full attention to the remaining pages, reading each sentence very carefully. He felt his face going flush and hoped that Ellen didn't notice. When he was done, he closed the folder and handed it back to her.

She tipped her head. 'You have a better sense of things now?'

He nodded. 'Yes. Thanks. And thanks for sharing about your husband. Sophie really is lucky to have you.' He stood up. 'I better get going now so you can get some sleep.'

She walked him to the door. 'Good night, Garrett.'

A strange sadness filled his face. 'Goodbye, Ellen.'

The next evening Garrett called Sophie after work and explained that he needed to put in extra hours at the office. Due to one thing or another, they hardly saw each other that entire week. Sophie missed him, but she reminded herself that soon she would get to see him every day for the rest of her life. Besides, they still talked every night on the phone before going to bed.

After going to bed early on Saturday night, Sophie was confused when her phone rang at one thirty in the morning. It took several moments before she was alert enough to recognise that it was Garrett's ring tone that she was hearing, and not a dream.

'Garrett?'

'We need to talk, Soph,' he said. His voice sounded strangely distant, and it sent a warning chill down Sophie's spine.

'Now?'

'It can't wait.'

'Umm. OK. I'm listening. Are you all right?'

There was a brief silence on the phone before Garrett said, 'I'm in my car out front. Can you come down?'

For Sophie, panic was already setting in. And dread. Whatever it was that Garrett wanted to talk about, she knew in her gut that it wasn't good. 'I'll be right there,' she whispered.

Although it was drizzling outside, she didn't think to put on a robe or shoes; in her rush to find out what was going on she went downstairs in her satin pyjamas and marched out to his car barefoot.

She was shivering when she slid into the front seat of his car, but she forced an optimistic smile. 'This is a pleasant surprise. Good morning, handsome.'

Garrett's hands seemed riveted to the steering wheel. His face wasn't without emotion, but neither was it the look of someone who was happy to see her. As he turned his head, the light from Sophie's porch illuminated his face enough for her to see that he'd been crying. 'Two hours,' he said numbly. 'That's how long I've been sitting here deciding what I should do.'

'What on earth is going on, Garrett?'

He turned away and whispered, 'I'm sorry, Soph . . . It's over.'

Sophie wanted to vomit. She cupped her hand over her mouth. 'What?' she finally managed. 'Us? We're over, just like that? Garrett, whatever it is, I'm sure we can work it out.'

As she spoke, the rain and wind outside picked up, pelting the car in heavy waves.

'I'm sorry, Sophie,' he said again, pulling his eyes from the steering wheel to look at her. His voice was much more sympathetic now. 'If there were a way to avoid this, I would, but . . . some misfortunes just can't be fixed.'

'At least tell me why,' she demanded.

He shook his head. 'Does it matter? It's over, Soph. You told me long ago that good things don't last. Maybe you were right.'

The impact of what he was saying—the reminder that everything she'd ever loved had ended badly—moved her to tears. 'You lied to me!' she wailed. 'You said that I could trust you!'

'Don't worry about the wedding arrangements,' he said, as Sophie continued to sob. 'I'll make sure everyone is notified.'

She heard him, but refused to look at him or respond in any way.

There were plenty of things he wanted to say to comfort her, but he knew if he said too much it would just lead to more questions. Questions that he wasn't willing to answer. 'I need to go.'

'So that's it? You're calling it quits and leaving, just like that?'

He tipped his head in response.

Sophie opened the door and stepped out into the rain. By the time she shut the car door behind her she was soaked. But instead of running inside, she just stood there, barefoot, and watched as Garrett pulled out of her driveway and drove out of her life.

Once his taillights were out of view, she walked back inside. Dripping puddles across the floor as she went, she marched straight for the couch in the living room and, without bothering to dry off, flopped down, curled up in a ball and cried until dawn.

'**O**pen this door, Sophie!' yelled Evalynn for the tenth time.

'Go away!'

'Like hell! I'm just going to keep knocking, yelling and ringing the doorbell until you let me in!' Evalynn pushed the doorbell five times in quick succession, then started pounding again.

Sophie gave in and opened the front door. She stood there looking very pale. Her eyes were puffy, her hair was a rat's nest, and it appeared as though she'd been wearing the same pyjamas for days.

'Hi Sophie,' Evalynn said softly.

'I just want to be left alone. Why is that so hard to understand?'

'I know. But you've already sequestered yourself for what—three days now? Enough is enough. Can I come in?'

Frowning dramatically, Sophie muttered, 'Fine.'

Not long after, Ellen showed up in her squad car.

'You should have called me, Sophie,' Ellen told her while they hugged.

Sophie pulled back. 'I know. I just . . . didn't want to face the reality of it.'

Ellen hugged her again. 'I know, Sweets. I know.'

Halfway through her shift downtown, Ellen had got a direct call from the police dispatcher, Garrett's mother, telling her the terrible news. Olivia was mortified, especially because Garrett wouldn't provide any reasons for what he'd done, only saying that Sophie had nothing to do with it and that it was his own fault.

As soon as Olivia hung up, Ellen started calling Sophie's cellphone, but it went straight to voicemail. Then she called Evalynn, who was just getting off work. Ellen filled her in on what she knew, and told her to go straight to Sophie's house as quickly as possible.

Sophie related the details of how she was dumped by Garrett.

'And he wouldn't say why?'

'Nope. He said it was better for both of us if he didn't elaborate.'

'Pfft,' Evalynn snorted. 'Maybe better for him.'

Sophie sighed. 'Yeah. That's the thing that's been eating me up. I mean, sure, the whole thing sucks. And yes, I wish I wasn't going through this. But not understanding why? It's just unfair. I've been trying to call him ever since, but he won't answer.'

'We should go to his house,' said Ellen, as she stood up. 'Right now. You deserve better than to be left in the lurch like this.'

'No! Ellen, it doesn't matter. I knew from the start that it would end this way. I want you to take me to the store.'

'Huh?' replied Ellen.

'Chocolat' de Soph. I need to get ready for tomorrow.'

Evalynn protested. 'Soph, you're smack-dab in the middle of a full-blown personal crisis. Work can wait.'

She shook her head adamantly. 'I can't let it stay closed another day. Besides, I think it'll be therapeutic.'

'Making chocolates is anything but therapeutic,' countered Evalynn. 'If you were eating chocolates, then maybe I'd agree.'

'Just get me there. I have a new recipe I want to try, in honour of Garrett.'

'You're going to make something sweet, in honour of him?'

'Not exactly,' replied Sophie quietly, the wheels already turning in her head about what ingredients to use for her new 'treat'.

When they arrived at the store, Evalynn volunteered to stay and help Sophie with preparations. Ellen stayed just long enough to remind Sophie that everything was going to work out just fine.

'God is at the helm,' she insisted, 'even when you think your ship is sinking. Just keep trusting that the Captain knows more about where you're heading than you do, and eventually you'll get where you need to be.'

Sophie laughed. 'If God's steering this boat, I'm jumping ship.'

'Give it time, Sweets,' Ellen counselled softly. 'Give it time.'

After Ellen was gone, Sophie put Evalynn to work on fresh batches of fudge, while she embarked on her new creation. An hour later, just after 11 p.m., Sophie had her first full batch of fortune cookies. The only things missing were the fortunes.

She sat down at her desk and pulled out a piece of paper, which she cut into narrow slips. Then she started filling the slips with words. The first one, she thought, was a gem. *Some people are lucky in love. You aren't one of them.* The second one made her smile, too. *Your life will fall apart in the blink of an eye. Don't blink!*

After that, the words kept flowing until every slip had a unique misfortune. She slid them into the cookies and took them on a tray to show Evalynn, whose mouth was full of peanut-butter dough.

'Care to try?'

Evalynn swallowed. 'Chocolate-covered fortune cookies? I hate to break this to you, but I'm pretty sure that's been done before.'

'Not like this,' she said, smiling. 'They aren't fortune cookies. They are Misfortune Cookies. I think you'll notice the difference.'

Evalynn shrugged and picked one up. Watching her friend's expression as she bit into it, Sophie knew the recipe was a success. An instant later Evalynn was spitting the cookie out. 'It's horrible!'

'Like I said, in honour of Garrett. Which message did you get?'

Evalynn pulled out its paper. '*Like the cookie in your hand, your love life will eventually crumble and leave a very bad taste in your mouth.*' After reading it, Evalynn frowned. 'It's . . . depressing.'

'See,' Sophie said, grinning again. 'Regular fortune cookies are too over the top with optimism. But these? A healthy dose of reality for those of us who've been round the block enough times to know that happiness is just an illusion.'

'I don't know that I'd go that far,' protested Evalynn.

Sophie just shrugged. 'I would.'

Chapter 9

Accept something that you cannot change.
The way you look, for instance.

October 2009

THE POST OFFICE that housed Sophie's PO box was located just five blocks away from Chocolat' de Soph—close enough, but up a steep enough hill that she didn't bother going more than once a week. It had been a full three weeks since Garrett placed the want ad in the *Seattle Times*, and, just as expected, she'd received no responses on her two previous trips to the post office.

As she finished her ascent up the hill on her weekly mail run, Sophie caught sight of a homeless man waving his arm on the opposite corner of the street. She gave a quick wave back, caught her breath while waiting for the signal to change, and then paced across the intersection to where he stood.

'Hello Sophie! How's my favourite customer?' The man cackled lightly. His greasy, greying hair hung in thick clusters, dangling past his forehead and ears, and curling up at the back above the collar of his red flannel shirt. Smudges of dirt covered the weathered skin directly below his eyes, while the rest of his face was covered with a thick beard that was tied beneath his chin with a rubber band. He held a cardboard sign that read: *Vietnam changed me. You can change me too. GOT SPARE CHANGE?*

'Is that what I've become to you, Jim? A customer? You make this sound like nothing more than a business transaction.'

Jim had met Sophie nearly a year earlier, not long after Garrett dropped out of her life. She'd been on her way to send a small package of Misfortune Cookies to a man who owned a novelty shop in Portland and who was looking for potential new products, when Jim stopped her on the street to ask for food or money. Without any cash on her at the time, she told him he could have a Misfortune Cookie, but that he probably wouldn't like it. He took her up on it anyway, thanking her over and over for the kindness.

As it happened, Jim's taste buds didn't work so well, making him the only person Sophie had ever met who ate a Misfortune Cookie and loved it. He also loved the messages inside, and he swore that he kept every one of them, and that one day they would all come true. After that initial encounter he kept a close eye out for Sophie, and eventually figured out that Monday was mail day, and so he planted himself there each week and waited for her to show up.

'Well I ain't out here for my health,' he said wryly, his voice cracking as he spoke. 'What do you call this, if it ain't my business? I'm luring customers with my uncommonly good looks and charm, just like you drive 'em into your store with the taste of your delicious cookies.'

Sophie chuckled. 'Most people think they taste awful.'

'Exactly! Just like I'm no beauty queen, but somehow I still got people giving me cash.'

She shook her head. 'You're something else.'

Jim scratched at his head and let out a hoot. 'Ha! Precisely what my wife said before she walked out on me.' He paused, moving his hand from the top of his head to the back of his neck, where something else apparently itched as well. 'Well, enough small talk. You got another little something for me today?'

Sophie reached into her bag, retrieved a Misfortune Cookie wrapped in a napkin and handed it to him. 'It's all yours. Made fresh this morning.'

Jim licked his cracked lips as he accepted it from her, then he lifted it to his mouth and took a small bite, savouring it. After a couple more small nibbles he retrieved the paper inside. 'Hell yeah!' he hollered after silently reading it. 'Another good one. Says me and the tyres on my car will both be bald very soon.'

Sophie shook her head again. 'And why is that a good thing?'

He stopped and stared at her. 'Why do I always gotta explain this to you? One day these fortunes are gonna come true. What a blessing that'll be. Bald tyres or not, I don't got a car now, so sounds like things'll be turning round for me any day now.'

'Always the optimist.'

He smiled, showing the purple gums where teeth should have been.

There were only a handful of items in the box when Sophie opened it. But to her surprise, unlike standard junk mail, three of the letters had handwriting on the front. She opened one and was floored to find that it was a response to the Happiness want ad. She quickly tore into the other two letters to discover that they, too, were happiness letters.

As she walked slowly down the hill towards her shop, Sophie read the brief notes, still surprised that anyone would respond to the ad. Back at the store she tucked the letters in the top drawer of her desk and then took over for Randy at the register.

Not long after that, the phone near the register rang. 'Chocolat' de

Soph,' Sophie said, as she lifted the receiver. 'Can I help you?'

'Hi, Sophie. How are you?' said Garrett.

'I was fine until a few seconds ago,' she said.

'Oh c'mon, lighten up. I'm just checking in to see how my ad is doing. Any takers yet?'

'It drummed up a response or two, but nothing to speak of.'

'Really?' Garrett sounded very excited. 'So there actually are happy people hiding out there. Was it just one response, or two?'

Sophie cleared her throat. 'Three, actually. They just came today.'

'Three! That's great.'

'Hooray,' she said with mock enthusiasm. 'But keep in mind that just because three letters showed up doesn't mean they will count towards the hundred. They have to be thoughtful, lasting examples of happiness. Since I'm the judge of that, they probably aren't.'

The phone was silent for several moments. 'So even if I get a hundred worthy responses, you're going to nix them all.'

She laughed. 'Not all of them. That wouldn't be fair. But enough to keep putting you off, yes.'

'In that case,' he responded, 'I think it's only reasonable that I get to read the responses too. If I'm going to put out the money for this, I need to know that you're giving these things a fair shake.'

Now it was Sophie who was silent. 'You're seriously going to keep running the ad?' she finally asked.

'Hey, you made the rules, Soph. I'm just playing along. But one way or another I need to sit down with you and explain why I did what I did, and if this is what it takes, then so be it.'

Sophie sighed. She knew she was being stubborn, but didn't the pain he'd caused her justify putting him off for as long as possible? 'It's your nickel,' she said at length.

'I'll be over in a little bit to read the first three letters. See you, Soph!' He clicked off before she could object.

True to his word, ten minutes later Garrett showed up at Chocolat' de Soph, wearing blue medical scrubs and a big smile. Sophie was in the back gathering her things, hoping to get out before he arrived. Closing the front door behind him, Garrett waved cheerfully at Randy, then made his way back to Sophie's office.

'Leaving so soon?' he asked, as he poked his head in the room.

'Yes,' she replied, picking up her umbrella, 'but apparently not soon enough.'

Garrett just kept smiling. 'Well, don't rush off just yet. I want to see the letters you got today.'

Sophie set the umbrella back down and opened the desk drawer. 'Fine. Here.' She handed him the three envelopes.

Taking a seat on the front edge of Sophie's desk, Garrett began reading the letters. After he'd read all three he went back and studied each more carefully. One included a hand-drawn picture, another had a four-by-six photo, and the third was simply a letter. None of them was very long, but it was several minutes before he was through.

'Well,' he said, 'two out of three's not bad, right?'

Sophie let out a derisive laugh. 'Two? I wasn't going to count any of them towards the hundred.'

Chuckling, Garrett tossed one of the letters on the desk. 'I knew right off you wouldn't count that one. I just don't think killing other living things for sport qualifies as lasting happiness.'

'No,' she agreed. 'And I nearly gagged when I first looked at the picture of him standing next to that dead moose.'

'So we're agreed on that one,' he said with a laugh, then held out the other two envelopes. 'But how come you're tossing out these?'

She crossed her arms and stood up, separated from him by the desk. 'The letter from the woman is too generic. All she really said is that happiness is watching your kids grow up, which isn't true.'

He tilted his head to the side. 'Why not?'

'Well, first, what about the people who can't have kids? That sort of happiness would exclude them. And kids are, potentially, fleeting, sad as that sounds. If your kids don't make it to adulthood, then you've watched them die. Is that happiness?'

'You're tough,' he said softly. 'How about the other one? From the little girl?'

'Oh geez,' she said, 'A crayon drawing of a cat? Really?'

'Well to a kid, a pet can bring happiness, can't it?'

'It's a cat, Garrett. As in shedding all over the furniture and coughing up hair. Does that sound like happiness to you?'

Garrett smirked. 'So that's a definite no?'

Sophie nodded. 'Now then, is there anything else I can do for you? I really want to catch the next bus back to Gig Harbor.'

'No,' he said, smiling as he turned to leave. 'Go catch your bus.' He paused momentarily, then asked, 'When are you checking the PO box again?'

She cocked her head to the side. 'Next Monday. Why?'

Grinning playfully, Garrett turned on his heels and whispered, 'Perfect. I'll see you then.' He quickly darted out through the office door before she could put up a fuss.

'**W**here have you been?' Evi demanded when Sophie finally answered her cell. 'I've been trying to get hold of you for an hour.'

'Sorry,' Sophie said apologetically. 'I just turned my phone back on a few minutes ago. Garrett kept calling earlier and I was tired of listening to his ring tone, so I shut it off. What's up?'

'I take it you haven't seen the evening news?' Evi asked.

'You know I avoid it. Half of what they report is just plain depressing.'

Sophie heard Evi laugh. 'Too true. Listen, I'm picking you up in ten minutes. There's some depressing news you need to see.'

'Is it something . . . bad?' Sophie asked reluctantly.

'Not bad, just—hold on a sec. *Justin! Don't change the channel until you're sure it's recorded!* You still there, Soph?'

'Yep.'

'OK. I'll be there soon.'

With a heavy sigh, Sophie mumbled, 'Can hardly wait.'

Not quite ten minutes later, Evalynn's car pulled into the driveway and she honked for Sophie to come out. Shortly after they were in Evi's living room, where the TV was paused on a commercial.

'Have a seat,' instructed Evalynn.

'Hey Sophie,' said Justin a few seconds later, as he walked in and plopped down in an empty armchair. 'Did Ev tell you yet?'

'Not a single word.'

Justin rubbed his hands together. 'Ooh, then you're—'

'Shut it,' Evalynn said. 'Just let her see for herself.'

Evalynn sat down next to Sophie and pointed the remote at the screen. 'Here we go,' she said, as her thumb pressed 'Play'.

After the few last words of the commercial, the screen jumped to the seven o'clock news broadcast—now almost two hours old—zooming in on the primped face of the Channel 2 anchorman.

'Welcome back to Channel 2 News,' he said confidently, maintaining a polished smile. 'I'm Kip Waverly. For tonight's news of local interest, we go now to Lori Acres in Tacoma. Lori?'

A chill shot up Sophie's spine as the man mentioned Tacoma.

The scene cut to a sharply dressed woman in her late twenties, perfectly manicured, standing outside Sophie's post office. 'Thank you, Kip,' she said. 'In these challenging economic times it can be easy to lose sight of the fact that behind the numbers, there are people, ordinary people in pursuit of happiness.' Lori paused dramatically. 'But what happens when that dream no longer seems possible? When happiness feels like an unachievable pursuit? Some of us might lean on family or friends for support. Others turn to religious mentors. But how many of us would turn to the public at large? At least one individual in the greater Seattle area is yearning for a glimmer of hope from others.'

Sophie dug her fingers into the couch as the correspondent held up a copy of the *Seattle Times*. 'Thanks to one of our viewers, who tipped us off to a most unusual advertisement, I can report that a desperate cry for help has been issued to all of us. For several weeks an anonymous ad has been running in the *Seattle Times*. Allow me to read its brief—yet poignant—plea.' Lori paused again and lifted the paper. '"Wanted: Happiness. Please help me find what I've lost. Send suggestions to PO Box 3297, Tacoma, Washington, 98402. Lasting happiness only, please. Nothing that fleets."'

'Wow,' piped Kip from the newsroom. 'I'd never have thought to turn to the want ads to find happiness.'

'Wow indeed, Kip. I'm standing outside the post office where our anonymous advertiser's PO box resides, and where, hopefully, he will receive the answers that will help him get through this difficult time. If you wish to write a response to this ad, you'll find the address at our website. Let's let him know that happiness is alive and well here in the heart of the Puget Sound. Reporting live from Tacoma, I'm Lori Acres. Back to you, Kip.'

'Thank you Lori.' Kip nodded thoughtfully, and then turned to the camera. 'And to the nameless person who created that most unusual want ad, if you are watching, may I add that our thoughts are with you, and we hope you find what you are looking for.'

Evi clicked off the television.

Sophie sat staring at the black screen. '"Thanks to one of our viewers",' she said. 'No doubt in my mind who that was.'

'You think it was Garrett?' Evi asked.

'Of course. What a conniving little—oh, he makes me mad.'

Justin chuckled. 'It's actually quite brilliant.'

Sophie turned her phone back on and saw that she'd missed ten calls and six new text messages from Garrett. She dialled his number.

He answered after the first ring. 'Did you get my messages?' he said immediately, sounding slightly panicked.

'How could you do this?' she groaned. 'Even if nobody knows it's me, it's still hugely embarrassing! That news lady talked about the ad like it was the work of some despondent lunatic who's hanging on by his very last thread. Unbelievable!'

'Listen to my messages, Sophie. I'm as surprised as you are. I tried to call you as soon as I saw it, but I couldn't get through.'

'What if they find out it's me?'

'Nobody is going to find out it has anything to do with either of us. I've already called and cancelled the ad, and I made it clear that if anything is leaked they'll have a painful lawsuit on their hands.'

Sophie paced round Evalynn and Justin's living room. She breathed out slowly, trying to calm herself.

'Sophie,' Garrett said softly, 'I swear it wasn't me. You know, there are a lot of people out there who read the newspaper. Any one of them could have decided to share it with the media.'

Sophie wanted him to be the culprit, wanted another reason to hate him after everything he'd done. But she knew he was telling the truth.

'Sophie? Do you believe me?'

'I'm still deciding.'

'So . . . our deal. It's still on?'

'Fine,' she said reluctantly.

'Well, thanks for calling. Even when you're yelling at me, I enjoy hearing your voice.'

She wished he could see her rolling her eyes. 'Good night.'

''Night, Soph.'

The next morning, Sophie put in the paperwork to forward all of her mail from her post-office box to Chocolat' de Soph.

Several days passed before the post office processed Sophie's request. With the media attention the ad had received, she knew the next wave of responses would be larger than the first.

She couldn't have imagined how much.

The postal worker who pulled up in front of the store on Saturday afternoon came inside first to ask if there was someplace special Sophie wanted him to deposit her mail.

'You can just leave it here on the counter,' she told him.

The man chuckled dryly. 'I don't think that's gonna work. You got room in the back, maybe?'

'Yeah . . . oh . . . umm, sure. The back would be fine.'

The man nodded, then went out to his mail van and opened the tailgate. Sophie watched with disbelief as he stacked four plastic bins full of mail on a dolly and wheeled them through the door.

'Holy crrrow,' she said slowly, as he rolled past her to get to the kitchen. 'It'll take me days to get through all of this.'

The mailman gave another dry laugh. 'Not done yet.' After setting the stack against the wall near her office door, he went back out and filled his hand truck twice more. 'That's the last of it,' he told her after he was through. 'Good luck, ma'am.'

She nodded vacantly, but her eyes remained glued to the stacks of mail in front of her. The mailman let himself out.

Several minutes later she heard the bell on the front door ring, followed by Randy's familiar steps pacing through the store. He stopped walking as he came into the kitchen.

'Dude!' he exclaimed. '*Dude!* You got some serious postage.'

Sophie ran her fingers through her hair. 'Tell me about it. How am I ever going to read all of this?'

Randy shrugged. 'If you need help, I'll do what I can.'

Approaching the nearest stack of bins, Sophie dug her hands into the letters, scooped some out, and then let them slip through her fingers like enormous grains of sand. 'You know what? I'll take you up on that. Let's make sure we're all set on candy to cover the rest of tonight and tomorrow, and then we'll dig into this nightmare.'

While Sophie was in the back sprinkling cashews on a fresh batch of caramel apples, Randy was counting cash in the register to do a quick inventory against sales for the day. He lost track of the count when the phone rang.

'Chocolat' de Soph,' he answered. 'This is Randy.'

Sophie came barrelling round the corner. 'If that's Garrett,' she whispered, 'I don't want to talk to him.' He'd been leaving messages on her cellphone to see if more mail had arrived.

Randy stuck the phone under his armpit to cover up the receiver. 'It is,' he whispered back. 'What should I say?'

'Anything! I don't care, make something up.'

Clearing his throat, Randy extracted the phone from beneath his arm and pressed it to his ear. 'Yeah, sure. Understood. The only thing is, she can't really come to the phone right now, 'cuz she's, like, swamped with mail from that want ad. Bummer, right?'

'No!' Sophie shouted, not caring that Garrett would probably hear her. 'Anything but that!'

Randy's eyebrows shot up at Sophie's rebuke, but he couldn't respond to her right away because Garrett was apparently speaking again. A few seconds later he said, 'Yeah . . . OK. I'll . . . yep, I'll let her know. Later.' Then he set the phone back down on its base.

Randy didn't speak right away, but he didn't have to. His expression said it all.

'He's coming here, isn't he?' Sophie said.

Randy nodded.

Sophie frowned, then went back to finish her preparations for what was shaping up to be a very long night.

'I think I'm on the cusp of winning this little game we've got going,' Garrett said.

Sophie pretended she didn't hear him. Although given the flood of responses, she knew that he was probably right. They had made one pile for the definite nos, another for maybes, and then one for the responses that had real promise.

For the next hour she, Garrett and Randy waded through letters, patiently sorting them into piles. Not surprisingly to Sophie, few of the responses had to do with true happiness, but rather leaned towards what she described as 'momentary fits of pleasure'. A woman from Louisiana described happiness as 'a Harley, a helmet and a tank full of nothing to do but ride'. Another wrote that happiness is 'a week on Bermuda's pink sandy beaches'. No one was surprised at the number of letters that mentioned family, but Sophie dismissed them, offering her own lack of living relatives as proof that families are too temporary to meet her criteria.

'I assume,' said Randy at one point, 'that hour-long massages are not going to count, right?'

'No,' confirmed Sophie. 'Massages are definitely out.'

Randy's eyes lit up. 'Sweet. Then can I keep this coupon? A spa in Seattle sent you a complimentary one-hour session.'

Sophie smiled and held out her hand to take the coupon. 'It's not happiness, but that doesn't mean it's not extremely enjoyable.'

Randy went home first, which left Sophie alone with Garrett longer than she would have liked. But the more time they spent alone, the more she remembered how much she enjoyed his company. On more than one occasion she caught herself admiring his dimples. She quickly scolded herself in each instance for the lack of self-restraint.

Around eight, Garrett and Sophie each opened one last letter, scanned what was written, and then dropped them on the 'No' pile.

'Mine was from a guy in Pennsylvania who said happiness is a roll of toilet paper when you're lost in the woods,' quipped Garrett. 'Yours?'

'Waking up every morning next to the same man for thirty-six years . . . and counting.'

He gave her a look. 'You don't think that qualifies as happiness? I'd give anything to have . . . someone . . . that I could rely on to be there every day, and to have that kind of love and trust for so long.'

'Oh, really,' she fired back. 'Well I'm sorry to remind you, but you could have had that, and you walked away from it.'

He dropped his gaze. 'I know.'

'Anyway, I think you're misinterpreting what she wrote. If you boil it down, all she really said was that happiness is "waking up". And I'm not really a morning person, so . . . no, definitely not.'

Garrett chuckled. 'You're a hard nut to crack, Sophie Jones.'

She crossed her arms and shot him a look, 'Hard to crack, maybe. But of the two of us, I'm not the nut.'

He laughed again, then looked at the piles of mail. 'What now?'

Sophie followed his attention to the mounds of envelopes on the floor. The largest, by far, was the 'No' pile, followed by a lot of maybes. Those deemed promising were fewest in number, but Sophie guessed even that stack totalled over two hundred.

'I'll take these home and see how many pass muster.' She straightened and put a rubber band round the smallest pile of letters. 'And I guess I'll take some of these as well.' She sighed as she grabbed a thick handful of unopened letters from the bin.

Garrett looked at his watch. 'The last express to Gig Harbor has already left,' he said. 'Can I give you a lift?'

Sophie really didn't want to be alone with Garrett in the car. The last time she'd sat in a car with him had been in her driveway on the night he nixed the wedding and drove away. Still, if he took her there might still be time to go to her foster sister's.

'Fine,' she said unenthusiastically. 'But can you take me to Evi's instead?'

He smiled generously. 'Of course.'

Sophie turned away and began gathering her things. 'Oh, stop flaunting your dimples,' she muttered quietly to herself.

Chapter 10

Happiness rightly eludes you.

ON THE DRIVE to her house, Sophie dialled Evi's number on her cellphone. She hadn't talked to her foster sister for a while and was sure Evi would want to be involved in the letter sorting.

Soon she was seated on the couch in the Macks' living room with Evi and Justin, going through the letters she'd brought. Regardless of length she read the notes aloud in their entirety, gave Evi and Justin a chance to weigh in, and then made her final decision. The first letter to meet Sophie's highly subjective criteria was from a man in Wichita, Kansas, who offered sound reasoning, backed by examples from his own life, to support his claim that happiness is 'the consequence of exercising one's right to choose between good and bad, and choosing the good'.

After thirty minutes, only a handful of letters had received Sophie's reluctant stamp of approval, and she was gaining confidence that she'd be able to coast guilt-free through the stack.

By five minutes to ten they had started on the stack of unopened mail. She grabbed the top envelope from the pile, noting that it had been sent from Bellevue, Washington, about thirty minutes northeast of Tacoma. Of all the envelopes she'd read, this one was by far the lightest. Ripping the top seam, she carefully tipped the envelope up at an angle, sending its contents fluttering onto the floor.

There was no mistaking the small, rectangular shape of a fortune-cookie message.

She knew right off that it wasn't from Chocolat' de Soph because she'd always written hers by hand and this one was typed. The paper was wrinkled and worn, and the letters were smeared. With a sense of foreboding, Sophie picked it up and read the message, gasping as recognition set in. She flipped it over and froze. As she stared at the back of the fortune, a small tear trickled down her face.

Sophie brushed it away and closed her hand round the paper. She then looked up at the perplexed faces of Justin and Evalynn.

'Soph? What's wrong?'

Sophie's gaze narrowed on Justin. 'I need to talk to Evi alone,' she said in a hoarse whisper.

'Of course,' he replied, standing up immediately. 'I'll be just down the hall if you need anything.'

'I need you to be totally honest with me, Evi,' said Sophie, once Justin was out of sight. 'Do you know how my parents died?'

Evalynn shot her a confused glance. 'Of course. A car accident.'

'I mean did Ellen ever mention to you that . . . someone was partially to blame for the accident?'

'No. Sophie, what are you getting at?'

Sophie glanced down at her clenched fist. In her mind, she recalled having clutched the paper like that once before. 'I want to tell you something, but you have to swear not to tell anyone else.'

'I promise.'

Sophie took a deep breath. For the next twenty minutes she retold the sequence of events on the night of her ninth birthday that led to the deaths of her mother, father and grandmother. She gave extra attention to her role in causing the nightmare.

When she was done, Evalynn scooted over and put her arms round Sophie in a giant hug. 'You can't blame yourself for what happened. It wasn't your fault, Sophie.' She pulled back. 'If you've held this inside for so long, why are you telling me now?'

Sophie pursed her lips. 'Because,' she replied slowly, staring once more at her hand, and letting her fingers fall open, 'somebody out there knows it.'

Evalynn took the fortune from Sophie's hand and read the message. '*Happiness is a gift that shines within you. The wish of your heart will soon come true.*' She looked up. 'It was twenty years ago—how can you even remember it? Maybe your message was just similar. This could just be a coincidence.'

Sophie rolled her eyes. 'The only thing coincidental is that it got back to me by way of Garrett's stupid happiness want ad. But this is my fortune from that night. It's the same piece of paper!'

Evalynn gave Sophie a look of doubt. 'How can you be sure?'

'Flip it over,' Sophie said, her voice ringing with dread.

Evalynn gasped when she saw what was written on the back. In faded pencil were the words, *Sophia Maria Jones, September 21, 1989.* 'No! This is some sort of a joke! It has to be.'

'If it is, I don't see the humour.'

'The only person you told was Ellen. Do you think she had something to do with sending this to you?'

Sophie shrugged. 'I don't know. I mean, I'd like to think that she wouldn't, but who knows?'

'She was there, and she was the only person who even knew you had it. Plus, it came to your PO box, and only a few of us knew the responses were coming to you.' Evalynn checked her watch, then grabbed Sophie by the hand and stood up. 'C'mon, Sophie.'

'Where are we going?'

'For your sanity, I think we need to go pay Ellen a little visit.'

You OK?' Evalynn asked, as she and Sophie got out of Evi's car in front of Ellen's apartment on Seattle's east side.

It was ten minutes to eleven, and the cold evening wind was starting to whip around. Sophie zipped up her jacket and nodded.

Both Sophie and Evalynn had keys to apartment number 309, but since the clock was encroaching on Ellen's typical sleep schedule, they chose to ring the bell.

There was a small delay before a faint, 'Who is it?' came from one of the back rooms. 'Knock once if friend, twice if foe.' That was Ellen's standard response whenever someone arrived unexpectedly. It was her way of stalling to make sure her firearm was nearby.

Sophie knocked three times.

The deadbolt clicked as it was twisted, and the door flew open.

'Both of my chickadees!' Ellen grabbed Sophie in a giant hug and pulled her into the apartment, then did the same with Evalynn. 'What on earth are you girls doing here so late at night?'

The three women moved together through the living room to the kitchen and took seats round the small dining table. Ellen glanced nervously between Sophie and Evalynn, as though she sensed that the news they'd come to share so late at night was not good.

Sophie ran her hand along the table's wooden surface. She could still make out engraved letters and words from where she and Evalynn had pressed too hard with their pens while doing homework as teenagers.

Invariably, thoughts of her youth rewound all the way back to the day she first arrived at the home of Officer Ellen Monroe. Sophie recalled how hard it was raining outside; even harder than the night she'd first met Ellen on the side of the road in Seattle. The water fell in heavy sheets. The social worker had an umbrella for herself, but didn't offer to share, so by the time Sophie dragged her suitcase from the back seat of the social worker's car to the front door of the apartment building, she was drenched from head to toe.

Sophie remembered the reluctance with which she carried her suitcase up the stairs to the third floor. The social worker was in a bit of a hurry, but Sophie took her time. It was already her fourth trip to a new foster home in the short span of five months, and she was in no hurry to meet her next 'family'.

The first home she'd been placed in was intentionally brief; just a week or so to allow her caseworker time to find a good long-term match, perhaps even an adoptive situation. When no such match was found, Sophie was moved to the home of a single mom named Marion Mason. Social Services eventually figured out that the woman was using the money to support a drug habit, so seven weeks after arriving there, Sophie and the woman's own biological daughter—a precocious little girl named Evalynn—were delivered to new locations throughout northern Washington.

Sophie landed with some very nice empty-nesters, the Bards, who took in children from time to time out of the goodness of their hearts.

Unfortunately for Sophie, the husband's heart was good only in the metaphorical sense; Mr Bard suffered a major heart attack right around the two-month anniversary of Sophie's arrival.

Later that night, in the middle of a rainstorm, Sophie's caseworker showed up and told her to pack her things. They eventually pulled up in front of Ellen's building. After a slow climb to the third floor, a dripping, shivering Sophie knocked on door 309.

'Knock once if friend, twice if foe,' called a friendly voice from within. Sophie knocked once and a moment later the door opened. There, to Sophie's very pleasant surprise, was a familiar face staring back at her. Ellen, the police officer who'd first approached her in the aftermath of the accident, was standing in the doorway, beaming. She scooped Sophie up in a hug. With Ellen's big, black arms round her, Sophie's heart felt warmer than it had in months.

'I have a secret,' Ellen said, smiling, as she squatted down to Sophie's level. 'Don't tell anyone, but it's three knocks for family. OK? If you ever have to knock, that's your number now.' Sophie nodded as Ellen hugged her again.

Evalynn arrived about a month later, right after her mom was sent to prison on multiple drug charges. Since then, the black woman, white girl and half-white Latina had been, in principle, a family.

'Sophie?'

The question from the other side of the table drew Sophie back to the present. She tilted her head and tried to smile. 'Huh?'

Ellen smirked nervously. 'You seem troubled, Sweets. Was there something you wanted to talk about?'

Sophie nodded. She unzipped her bag and pulled out the envelope from Bellevue.

'Ellen,' she said, sliding the envelope across the table, 'who lives in Bellevue?'

A look of confusion settled in Ellen's features. 'Bellevue? I don't know anyone in Bellevue. Why? What is this, Sophie?'

'Open it up.'

Ellen slid two fingers into the envelope and let the small paper fall out. It landed with the handwritten words facing up. 'What the—?' she said, as she read the name and date. There was no question that she knew what day that was. A light bulb seemed to flip on in her mind, like she'd just figured out what she was holding. She turned the paper over and gasped. 'Sophie,' she said, 'I swear to you, I don't know anything about this.'

Sophie pounded her fist on the table. 'Then who, Ellen? You were the only one. The only one who knew about that fortune!'

'I don't . . . I mean . . . I'm just as surprised by this . . .' Ellen was caught off guard by Sophie's outburst and was fumbling for the right thing to say. 'Sophie, I've never mentioned that fortune to a single soul. I can't imagine how it ended up in your mail, let alone coming to the PO box, but I swear, I had nothing to do with it.'

A moment of silence gave Evalynn an opportunity to speak up. 'Thanks, Ellen. It's good to hear it straight from you.'

Neither Sophie nor Ellen spoke.

'Now that that's settled,' Evi continued, 'I think the key is to figure out who sent it, and how they got it. It's sort of spooky.'

Ellen picked up the envelope again. 'I agree, Ev. And I think that's something I can help with. Give me a few minutes to make some calls.' She stood up and left the kitchen.

'You OK?' Evalynn asked, once Ellen was out of the room.

'I'm fine,' Sophie replied, chuckling sardonically. 'I haven't yelled at Ellen like that since she did a background check on Tom Potter before the homecoming dance our sophomore year.'

Evalynn laughed. 'Poor Tom.'

As promised, a few minutes later Ellen strode proudly back into the kitchen. 'Got it!' she announced.

'That was fast,' said Sophie.

'This one was easy-peasy. The return address on your envelope is the home of one Jacob Barnes. Ring any bells?'

Evalynn and Sophie both shook their heads.

Ellen grinned. 'Well, it did for me. As soon as my guy downtown said the name, I knew who it was. But just to be sure, I checked a copy of the police accident report that I keep in my desk. He was listed as one of the people who sustained injuries.'

'Jacob Barnes,' Sophie repeated, familiarising herself with the name. 'So if this Jacob Barnes was there, then he must have found my fortune after I tossed it. But how did he know that it was my fortune? It could have been anyone's.'

'It's tough to say,' remarked Ellen. 'But at least we know he was there, which explains how he got it.'

'I'm no detective,' quipped Evalynn, 'but I think we need to take a little trip to Bellevue. Sophie, are you game?'

Sophie nodded.

'Ellen?'

Ellen winked. 'Me and my nine-millimetre would be happy to give you a police escort.'

Chapter 11

*If good people have good luck, and bad people have bad luck,
why is it that you have dumb luck?*

EVALYNN AND SOPHIE picked up Ellen shortly after lunch on the following Saturday, which was the first day that worked with all of their
schedules. Justin had purchased a plug-in GPS unit for Evalynn on her
last birthday, and the device's female voice directed them off the interstate after twenty-five minutes. From there it was almost a straight shot
up 150th Avenue to a development full of beautiful homes at the top of
the hill near Saddleback Park.

'Wow,' Ellen commented. 'Jacob Barnes is doing well.'

Evalynn slowed the car and pulled to a stop near the kerb. 'You sure
you're OK doing this, Sophie?'

Clutching the envelope that had been sent from the house across the
street, Sophie tried to smile bravely. 'It's not meeting Jacob Barnes that
has my stomach in knots. It's more the thought of facing my past. It's
just weird, you know? After twenty years, to suddenly find out that
some stranger has known all along that I played a part in the accident.'

'You don't know that's what he's thinking.'

'Why else would he have sent that fortune back to me? He must have
somehow figured out I was the one who placed the ad.'

Ellen reached forward and rubbed Sophie's shoulder. 'I've told you
since you were nine that you can't blame yourself. Maybe meeting Mr
Barnes will finally help that to sink in.'

'Maybe,' Sophie said, but she sounded doubtful.

With Ellen leading, the trio got out of the car and crossed the street.
Sophie tried to ignore the woman in the house next door watching
them from her front window as they walked up the drive.

Ellen marched straight up to the door without any hesitation and
rang the doorbell. Sophie and Evalynn stood a few feet behind her.

Several moments later, a stout little man with a large round face
opened the door. He had almond-shaped eyes and a grin that stretched
from one ear lobe to the other. 'Hello,' he said with a funny accent.
'Visitors. I love visitors. I don't get too many of them, though.' He
paused before adding another, 'Hello.'

None of the three women needed to be told that the young man staring back at them had Down's syndrome. His happy demeanour put them instantly at ease. 'Hi,' Ellen said. 'We're looking for Jacob Barnes. Is he around?'

The man scratched at his thick blond hair. 'Is it really important?' he asked, smiling. 'He's my dad. Maybe I can help you instead. I'm Alex.'

Sophie was watching the man intently. Something about him felt strangely familiar. 'Alex, have we met before?' she asked.

He shrugged. 'I don't know. Have you ever shopped at Albertsons? I work there.'

Sophie chuckled. 'Maybe that's it.'

Ellen laughed, too, as she opened up her police badge that was clipped to her hip. 'Alex, my name is Officer Monroe, and I work with the Seattle police department.'

He seemed fascinated by the badge, reaching out to run his fingers over its shiny surface. 'Cool. A cop.'

'My friend here,' Ellen continued, pointing to Sophie, 'got a letter this week that has something in it that came from your dad.'

Alex stared at Sophie quizzically. 'You're the one looking for happiness? Cool.'

'So you know about what was sent?' Sophie asked, holding up the envelope in her hands.

He looked at it briefly. 'Uh-huh.'

Sophie exhaled. 'I'd like to talk to your father. Is he home?'

'Nope.'

'Will he be back soon?'

Alex's bright smile dimmed a little. 'Nope.'

Evalynn spoke up. 'Do you know where he is? If it's not too far, maybe we could pay him a quick visit.'

Alex scratched his head again. 'I know where he is. I don't know the address, but I could take you there.'

Sophie wasn't sure how she felt about involving Jacob's son. Before she could make up her mind, another person showed up at the house.

'Can I help you?' asked the woman, as she walked up the front steps. 'I'm Meredith Sloan, from next door.'

The hawk from the window, thought Sophie.

Ellen smiled. 'No, we just came to visit Mr Barnes.'

Meredith's demeanour shifted. 'Well, I'm not just Alex's neighbour. I'm also paid to look after him and help with his . . . special needs. So if there's something specific that you require, I'm probably the right person to work with.'

Sophie stepped forward. 'I was in an accident when I was a little girl, and Jacob Barnes was in it too.'

'Ah,' Meredith said. 'The accident that took his fingers.'

An image flashed in Sophie's head of a man lying on the ground staring up at his hand while a paramedic worked to stop the bleeding where his fingers had been severed. 'Yes,' Sophie replied softly, 'that's the one. We came today looking for a little more information about the accident, and Alex said—'

'They want to go visit my dad,' Alex interjected.

Meredith looked puzzled. 'You want to visit Jacob?'

All three women nodded. 'If it wouldn't be a bother,' said Sophie. 'Alex says he knows how to get there.'

Meredith searched the faces of the visitors. 'But I don't see what you're going to learn at the cemetery.'

'Cemetery?' Sophie blurted out, trading worried looks with Ellen. 'Is Jacob Barnes . . . dead?'

Now Meredith looked confused too. 'You didn't know?' she said. 'He passed away a few months ago. From leukaemia.'

'Of course not . . . we . . . I mean, I got a letter in the mail and I just assumed . . .' She turned to face Alex again, and a new wave of recollection set in. 'Which cemetery?' Sophie asked.

Alex looked to Meredith for the name. 'Evergreen,' she said. 'It's up there off—'

'Aurora Avenue!' said Sophie excitedly. 'That's where I saw you! About a month ago, on my birthday. Sunglasses, right?'

'I always wear sunglasses there,' Alex acknowledged.

'In case he cries,' Meredith said under her breath.

Sophie remembered the brief but odd encounter with Alex in the moments before Evalynn showed up that night. Sophie stepped closer to Alex, who was still standing in the doorway of the house. Her expression was serious, but her tone was soft and gentle. 'Alex, when I saw you, you weren't visiting your father. You were staring at the grave of my parents. What were you doing there?'

Everyone was silent, waiting for Alex to reply. 'Reading,' he said, matching Sophie's quiet voice. '"Husband and Father. Wife and Mother. Loved their daughter and each other fully and for ever." It's very nice. I memorised it. Dad showed it to me every time we went there. He said he met that daughter once.' He looked at Sophie, his face shining with an innocent happiness. 'I guess you must be her. Sophia Maria Jones.'

Everyone on the Barnes front porch stood in awkward silence.

Everyone, that is, except Alex. 'Are we still going to visit my dad?'

he asked. 'Or do you want to come inside my house?'

'That's a good idea, Alex,' Meredith said, taking a small step towards the door. 'Maybe we should all go inside and sit for a bit. Would you ladies care for something to drink?'

Evalynn and Ellen both looked to Sophie for direction. 'That would be fine,' Sophie said politely. 'Thank you.'

The house was spacious, with vaulted ceilings and an open floor plan. In the living room, the walls were lined with full bookshelves. The only empty space was a cabinet on the far wall, which was only half full.

'Wow,' Sophie said, impressed. 'Someone likes to read.'

'Me!' Alex exclaimed proudly. 'I've read every book here.'

'You're almost out of shelf space,' commented Evalynn. 'What are you going to do then?'

Alex gave Evalynn a funny look. 'Get more shelves,' he said finally, without a hint of irony.

They all laughed in unison. For her part, Sophie was beginning to feel relieved. She'd been dreading facing Jacob Barnes. Had he held deep animosity towards her? Was his life in shambles because of her selfish impatience as a child? But in place of the grumpy old man that she imagined she'd be meeting, there was Alex, with his happy disposition and innocent friendliness.

Meredith went to fetch refreshments, while the rest of the group took seats in the living room. Sophie and Evalynn shared the leather sofa, Ellen sat in the love seat, and Alex plopped down merrily in a thick suede recliner.

Once everyone was settled, Sophie was the first to speak. 'Alex, I'm really sorry to hear that your father passed away. Just meeting you, I can tell I would have liked him.'

Alex fidgeted with his fingers, but kept smiling. 'Are you going to ask a lot of questions about him?'

'I'd like to ask a few, if that's all right with you.'

He scratched nervously at his ear. Then, without saying a word, he got up from his chair and shuffled over to a curved console in the entrance. In the top drawer was a pair of dark sunglasses. He put them on and then returned to the recliner. 'OK.'

Sophie smiled warmly. 'OK, you said your dad took you to the cemetery to visit my parents' grave. How often did you go?'

'Every year. The day after my birthday.'

'Oh? When is your birthday?'

'September twenty.'

Sophie made eye contact with Ellen on the love seat. 'That's . . . the day before my birthday. So you went to the cemetery every year on September twenty-first?'

Alex leaned forward slightly in his chair and nodded. 'On my birthday we always had a big party. Dad said the day I was born was the very, very most important day of his life. And the next day was the very most important one—just one "very".'

Evalynn smiled.

'Did he ever talk about the accident?' Sophie asked.

Meredith returned from the kitchen a few moments later with coffee and an assortment of herbal teas. She set everything on the coffee table and invited them to help themselves.

'What was your question?' Alex asked Sophie.

'The accident that your father and I were in. Did he talk about it much? Maybe when you guys went to the cemetery?'

He shook his head. 'Nope. Dad just said it was a day he would never forget. Mostly we just went there to take the stones.'

Sophie sat up as she recalled the beautiful stones she found annually on the corner of her parents' gravestone. 'The stones on the grave? That was you and your dad?'

'Uh-huh.'

'Is that what you were doing there two weeks ago?'

'Yes. Dad told me before he . . . left, that it would be nice to keep taking stones each year. Now I leave them for Tom and Cecilia, Jacob and Katherine, but not on the same days.' Alex fiddled with his sunglasses. 'A few years ago we figured out that if we went late enough in the day, we would find a piece of chocolate waiting there for me. Dad said that was my treat for taking the stones.'

Ellen stopped stirring her cup of tea. 'Who is Katherine?'

Alex didn't respond.

'Maybe I can field that one,' offered Meredith. 'In fact, since your family was obviously important to Jacob, perhaps a little history is in order.'

Evalynn and Sophie fixed themselves tea while Meredith spoke.

'Jacob and Katherine Barnes were both lawyers,' she continued. 'Partners in a big firm downtown. When Katherine became pregnant they started searching for a full-time nanny.' Meredith smiled and took a sip of her tea. 'They chose me just a week before he was born. Unfortunately,' she glanced at Alex, as if looking for permission to continue, 'it was a difficult labour. There were *complications*. Katherine didn't make it.'

The room was silent, except for the sound coming from Alex, who was fidgeting again with his ear.

'And you've stayed on all these years?' Ellen asked.

She nodded. 'The workload varied, depending on Alex's needs and Jacob's schedule. But Alex has always been such a joy to be around, I couldn't think of a better job. Eventually I got married and started my own family, but I've always been able to balance my own life with the Barnes's needs. Once Jacob developed leukaemia, he purchased the house next door so my family and I could be closer, basically to avoid having to move Alex to an assisted-living home once he was gone. I'm still technically an employee—I'm paid monthly from a trust—but I hardly feel like one. Alex is family, and that'll never change. My whole family adores him.' She paused and looked at Alex, grinning proudly. 'Everybody adores him.'

Alex slid fingers beneath the rim of his glasses to rub at his eyes.

Sophie stared at the tea in her cup. She thought about the old paper fortune she'd wanted to discuss with Jacob. Then she looked at Alex, considering all that he must've gone through in his life, starting with the loss of his mother, struggling with a disability, and losing his father to a terminal illness. A new sense of guilt coursed through her for the additional pain that she'd caused this family.

Without thinking about it, Sophie took a giant breath. She looked at Alex and Meredith. 'This wasn't exactly why I came here today, but now that I'm here, I want you to know the truth. I . . . am to blame for the accident twenty years ago.' After explaining how she had distracted her father, she pulled out the old fortune-cookie message and held it out for them to see. 'This was my fortune from my ninth birthday. I threw it away that night at the crash. Somehow Jacob found it.' Sophie took another moment to breathe while Meredith examined the fortune. 'I can only assume that he overheard what I told Ellen, and then kept it all this time so he wouldn't forget who was responsible for crippling his hand. I know I should have apologised to Jacob while he was still . . . around. But until this moment, meeting both of you, I never had the nerve. I'm very sorry.'

Everyone let the words settle before making a sound. Meredith was the first to speak. 'Ms Jones, thank you. But honestly, I'm sure that Jacob did not blame you for what happened to his hand.'

'Then why keep the paper all this time? And why write my name on the back of it?' She turned to Alex. 'And as a sidebar—who mailed this out last week, anyway?'

Alex raised his hand. 'I sent it. I saw the thingy on YouTube about the newspaper ad, and I wanted to help. Dad always told me that happiness is a gift, and so I thought his paper might help someone—you, I guess—find it. Sorry.'

'Oh, don't be sorry,' Sophie said, smiling warmly at Alex. 'I'm actually really glad you sent it. Of all the things that people sent me, this is my favourite, because it led me here to meet you.'

Alex adjusted the glasses that covered his eyes, but nothing could cover his giant smile.

'And as for why he kept that fortune all this time,' Meredith said to Sophie, 'maybe he liked the message. Perhaps it gave him hope or lifted his spirits.'

'Can I ask something?' said Evalynn. 'I'm still curious about the stones on the grave. Is that like a religious thing?'

Meredith chuckled. 'I don't think anyone would ever label Jacob Barnes as a religious man. But he had faith. He believed that he would see Katherine again. When I asked about the stones he always said "Rocks and memories last for ever". I think the stones were just his way of memorialising the woman he loved.'

Sophie looked puzzled. 'Why put them on my parents' grave?'

Meredith just shrugged. 'I don't know. Alex, any ideas?'

He shook his head. 'I just know we took them, put them on the graves, and then he would tell me about Sophia Maria Jones.' His voice trailed off, and he looked to be thinking very hard.

'Alex?' said Meredith. 'Is everything OK?'

A few seconds later Alex yanked his sunglasses from his face. There was excitement in his eyes. 'I'll be right back!' With that, he jumped up and ran down the hallway, returning a couple of minutes later looking slightly dejected. 'I can't find it,' he announced.

'What were you looking for?' Meredith asked.

'I remembered. When he was sick, Dad said he was writing a letter for Sophie. Said he would put it in my favourite place, and told me that after he . . . you know—after he . . .'

'Died,' Meredith said softly.

'Uh-huh . . . after that, he said if I found it I should mail it to her, and that maybe someday she'd come knocking on the door.'

Sophie waited a few seconds to see if he was going to say more, and then remarked, 'Well, then, looks like I'm early.'

Meredith asked Alex where he'd looked for the letter.

'In my room,' he replied. 'My favourite place is my bedroom. I looked everywhere in there but I couldn't find it.' He turned to Sophie. 'I'm sorry, I don't know where it is. But I'll keep looking.'

'Thank you, Alex. That's very nice of you. Can I give you my phone number, in case it turns up?'

His eyes lit up. 'Yes! I like to talk on the phone. Can I call you?'

'Of course,' she said with a slight giggle. 'If you ever want to talk, just give me a ring.'

Sophie wrote down her cell and work numbers and handed them to him.

The group chatted for a few more minutes before Ellen decided it was time to go. Sophie kept stealing glances at Alex during the conversation, marvelling at his genuine optimism. Fitting, she thought, that he should respond to a want ad for happiness. Lives by himself, lost both of his parents, and he still manages to keep a smile on his face.

Evalynn turned on the ignition and let the car idle. 'Where to now?' She was looking at Sophie in the other front seat.

But Sophie was still staring out of the window at the home of Jacob—and Alex—Barnes. Alex was waving from the front door. Sophie smiled and waved back.

When Sophie didn't answer Evalynn, Ellen spoke up from the back seat. 'You know what I think, Sweets? I think that did you a boatload of good. And it really is unbelievable that that fortune made it back to you. One might almost go as far as to say it's—'

'Here we go,' mumbled Sophie.

Evi laughed.

Ellen ignored both of them. '*Divine Providence*. Gotta be.'

'Oh yeah,' retorted Sophie sarcastically, turning again to look out of the window. 'God made Alex get on YouTube and then forced him to reply to the want ad. I'm sure stirring up my past is at the top of His omnipotent list of things to do.'

Evi chuckled once more.

'Laugh if you want,' commented Ellen, 'but I'm telling you, this is Providence.'

Sophie and Evalynn let the debate die. Evalynn put the car into gear and pulled into the street.

Once they were clear of the Barnes's neighbourhood, Evalynn said, 'Now would someone like to tell me where we're heading?'

'I want to see your copy of the police report from the accident,' Sophie told Ellen. 'You said you still have it, right?'

'Yes,' she replied. 'Mind if I ask why?'

Sophie turned round. Her expression was calm, like things had suddenly become clear. 'Because you were right. Going there today was good for me. I should have done it a long time ago.' Right then, Sophie's phone rang. She flipped it open. 'Hello?'

'Hello! Is this Sophia Jones?'

'Alex?'

'Yes! It's me. I'm calling. Hi!'

'Alex, Is everything OK?'

'Oh. Yes. But after you left I remembered some things.'

Sophie shot a look to Evalynn, thinking perhaps she was about to learn more details about Jacob Barnes. 'Really?'

'Yep! I remembered that there are lots of reasons to be happy, and I wanted to tell you, so you don't have to have an ad in the newspaper any more.'

Sophie smiled. 'I see. That's very thoughtful, Alex. Can I put you on speakerphone so Evalynn and Ellen can hear too?'

There was a pause, and then Alex said, 'OK.'

Sophie pushed several buttons on her phone. 'OK. Fire away,' she said, thoroughly amused.

For the next two minutes Alex rattled off a litany of things that to him were happiness. The three women sat and listened gratefully. Happiness, he told them, is watching the sun break through clouds, or watching it rise in the morning. 'If the sun didn't come up tomorrow, I think I'd be pretty sad. And,' he added, 'it would be really dark.' He also explained that happiness is eating dinner with your family and talking about what happened during the day. Then there was waking up in the morning.

'Waking up in the morning?' Sophie asked, making sure she'd heard him correctly.

'Of course. When was the last time you didn't wake up in the morning?'

Everyone in the car laughed. Then they all thanked him for calling and sharing his thoughts. Sophie reiterated that he was welcome to call her any time he wanted.

'I'll call if I find the letter.'

'Thank you, Alex.'

'Bye, Sophia Jones!'

Sophie smiled at the phone. 'Goodbye, Alex.'

Evalynn took her right hand off the steering wheel and poked Sophie. 'Somebody's got a new boyfriend,' she joked.

'Yes,' Sophie responded proudly. 'I think you're right.'

'So are you going to tell us why you want to see the police report?' asked Ellen from the back seat.

Sophie twisted round and smiled at her. 'The best part of meeting Alex had nothing to do with what he told me. It was what I told him. Simply acknowledging my role in the accident and apologising for it was . . . liberating.' The look of resolution returned to her face. 'I want to put this behind me once and for all. So if there's anyone else in the report that warrants a visit, I want to know.'

Ellen nodded. 'It's in my desk at home.'

Fifteen minutes later, Sophie and Evalynn sat at Ellen's kitchen table while their foster mother retrieved the police report.

Sophie spent a good twenty minutes quietly poring through the report, familiarising herself with the names of people in the other cars and reading their accounts of what happened.

When she was done, Sophie slid the report towards Ellen.

'Please don't tell me you want to contact everyone who was in the accident,' Ellen said.

'No, but one family does deserve a visit.'

Ellen frowned. 'The family of the other guy that died?'

With a nod, Sophie said, 'Tim McDonald. He was a UPS driver, and he died from his injuries a few days after the accident. I just . . . Reading the report was good for me. I think they might like a read of it too. And I can explain a few of the details that didn't make it into the report. To me, it's important that they know.'

Ellen sighed, 'I'll go make a few calls, see if I can track down the family.' She picked up the report and left.

Ten minutes later Ellen retuned holding a yellow Post-it note. She dropped the police report on the table and then stuck the note to it. 'The closest living relative is Tim's mother, Lucy McDonald. She lives on the other side of the state, in a little suburb of Spokane called Millwood. There's the address.'

'How many hours is it from here to there?'

'About eight hours round trip,' Ellen answered.

Sophie grinned. 'Looks like I'm definitely going to have to brush up on my driving.'

'Let Evi go along. That's too much time behind the wheel for you. Besides, you don't even have a car.'

Sophie tapped her fingers on the table while considering what she wanted to do. When she'd turned sixteen, Ellen had forced her to get her driver's licence, but Sophie hated it, mostly because she was afraid that she might cause a collision like the one she'd experienced as a child. So although she knew how to drive and had a licence, she'd never owned a vehicle. 'You're right. It's high time I got a car.'

'And you'll let me come along?' asked Evalynn.

'It's up to you. But if you do, you'll have to help me finish going through all that stupid mail. One of us can read letters while the other is driving.'

Evi grinned. 'Great . . . sounds like a thrilling road trip. I'll read letters, then you'll dismiss them and throw them out of the window.'

Sophie laughed. 'Exactly! Hey, whatever it takes to avoid a date with you-know-who.'

Chapter 12

Your lingering melancholy is intertwined with your outlook on life.

DURING THE NEXT WEEK, Garrett called almost daily to see how things were going with the mail. Though Sophie had taken a hiatus from the piles of letters, she promised him that she would give them proper attention during her Sunday trip.

'Oh?' he asked. 'Where are you going?'

'None of your business.'

'Well, who are you going with?' he pressed.

'A friend,' she said, and left it at that.

'Not a guy friend though, right?'

Sophie was laughing inside. 'Does it matter?'

'Well . . . no,' he stammered. 'It's just . . . mind if I ask what the purpose of the trip is?'

'Let's just say I'm going to meet someone's parents.'

Garrett became very quiet. 'I see,' he said finally. 'Well then, have a good time . . . I guess.' He hung up.

When Friday rolled round, Sophie left the store as soon as Randy arrived. With less hesitation than she'd expected, she went to a pawnshop in Tacoma and rid herself of the engagement ring that Garrett had given her. When the deed was done, she walked out with a wad of cash, which she promptly spent on a seven-year-old Ford Explorer at a dealership two blocks away. It wasn't the prettiest car, but the price was right and it felt safe to drive.

Sophie eased the Explorer out of the car lot very slowly, and for the entire ride home she never came close to reaching the speed limit. Safety first, she told herself, when faster cars honked at her.

After work on Saturday she spent several hours driving around, just to make sure she felt comfortable behind the wheel. The more she drove, the better she felt, but her speed remained slow.

'You drive like an old woman,' commented Evalynn the next morning, after Sophie picked her up for their drive to Millwood.

'Well, that's a sexist thing to say,' observed Sophie.

'And ageist, too. It's the truth. If you don't pick up the pace we won't get there until next week.'

With white knuckles clenching the steering wheel, Sophie pressed harder on the gas, but still didn't keep up with traffic.

After an hour on the road, Evalynn demanded that Sophie take the next exit so they could switch places in the car. Sophie gladly obliged and was relieved to take over opening the responses to the want ad from the safety of the passenger seat.

Halfway through the drive Sophie's cell began ringing. She picked it up to find Garrett's picture staring back at her.

'Hello?'

'Hey, Soph! It's Garrett.'

'What do you want?' She sounded completely disinterested.

'Just checking to see how your trip is going. You're travelling today, right? Who'd you say you're with?'

'I didn't,' she replied flatly.

'Oh, that's right,' he said, amused. 'Well, how are the letters coming? Are we getting any closer to our date?'

'I'm going through them now, but it's still not looking good.'

'Well, there are a lot of crazy people out there who wouldn't know happiness even if they were talking to it on the phone.'

'Huh? What's that supposed to mean?'

'I'm just having fun, Soph. But seriously, what's the tally at now? Seventy? Eighty?'

'Twelve,' she chirped, sounding a bit smug. 'Hold on, Garrett, someone else is calling in.' He heard the line click off. Thirty seconds later it clicked back on. 'I have to take this call. I can't leave him waiting too long.'

'Him? Him who?'

'His name is Alex.'

There was a long silence. 'And how do you know Alex?'

'Oh, our paths crossed recently, and we just sort of hit it off. He's the sweetest guy in the world.'

Garrett felt his temperature rising. 'Seriously? You're seeing him? I could've sworn you said you were done with men.'

'Sorry, Garrett. I can't keep him waiting any longer. Bye.' Sophie clicked off.

Lucy McDonald lived at the end of a dusty road on a one-acre parcel near the edge of town. The home had all the charm of an old country farmhouse, but if there had ever been a working farm there, it was long since gone. The edge of the property was lined with thick maple trees that had already lost their leaves for the winter.

After four hours of driving, Evalynn turned into the McDonalds' drive. As they pulled to a stop Sophie scanned the windows along the house, looking for any indication that someone was home. Her stomach did a somersault when she saw that two lights were on.

'You want to come in with me?' Sophie asked.

'Really? You sure you want me there?'

Sophie exhaled to calm her nerves. 'I could use the support.'

Both women got out of the car and made their way to the large covered porch. Sophie rang the bell, and moments later the door swung open. Standing in front of them was a little old woman, slightly hunched, and smiling. 'Can I help you?' she asked.

'I hope so,' said Sophie. 'Are you Lucy McDonald?'

The woman winked. 'Last time I checked.' Her words came out slow, but were clear and articulate. 'Have we met?'

'No, ma'am.'

'You sure? I swear I've seen your face somewhere.' She waved a bony finger. 'I have a real knack for faces . . .' Lucy's voice trailed off as she studied Sophie's hair, then her eyes, followed by her mouth and chin, and finally back to her eyes.

Sophie tried to ignore the examination. 'I'm sorry to bother you, Mrs McDonald. My name is Sophie. I was hoping I could talk to you about your son, Tim. Do you have a few minutes?'

'Tim? Oh my. Dear Tim. You know he's passed on, don't you?'

Sophie grimaced. 'Yes. That's what I wanted to talk about.'

'Well then,' she cackled, 'don't just stand out there in the cold. Come in. Come in.'

Lucy led the way through the house to a sitting room. A small fire burning in the fireplace made it feel cosy. Lucy held on to the armrests of a tall chair to lower herself down to sit. Evalynn and Sophie sat on a burgundy-coloured Victorian-style sofa.

'Did you know Timmy personally?' she asked, but then immediately answered her own question. 'No, you're too young.'

'You're right, I didn't know him. But I saw him once. On the day of the accident.'

Mrs McDonald's expression had been all smiles up to that point, but the smile quickly deflated in a heavy sigh. 'I see,' she said.

Sophie cleared her throat. 'At the accident, actually. Before he was taken to the hospital.'

Lucy nodded, and then turned to Evalynn. 'You too?'

Evalynn shook her head.

Fixing her eyes once more on Sophie, Lucy said, 'He was a good boy. Had his struggles, like everyone, I suppose. But he was a good boy.' Her face curled up and she shook her head gently. 'How was it that you saw him? Did you see the accident happen?'

Sophie grimaced. 'From very close range, I'm afraid. I was in one of the other cars. After it happened I saw the paramedics working to help your son.' She paused. 'I know it's been a long time since it happened, but I'm really sorry for your loss.'

Lucy may have been old, but she was sharp as a tack. 'Well, I can't imagine that you drove all this way just to tell me that you saw my son on death's door.' She leaned forward in her seat. 'I'm not one for pussy-footing. What's really on your mind, Miss?'

Sophie handed the old woman Ellen's police report. 'I came across this recently. It's the report from the accident, and I thought you might like the official account of what happened that night.'

With a cock-eyed glance, Lucy said, 'That's sweet, dear. But you didn't have to go to the trouble.' She took the report from Sophie and flipped through it. After scanning the parts about her son, she looked up and said. 'It says just what they told me back then. You really came all the way out here just so I could see this?'

'Well . . . not quite. Lucy, I don't know the right way to say this. I guess I could start by pointing out that the term "car accident" can mean different things. Mechanical failures sometimes cause accidents, or poor weather, like the report says there.'

Lucy cackled again. 'Now you're not just pussyfooting. You're beating round the bush. What's the punch line, dear?'

Sophie glanced momentarily at Evalynn, whose wide eyes and pursed lips encouraged her to press onwards.

'OK, here's the deal. Although everyone chalked the accident up to the rain, I want you to know the whole truth about what happened. That night, a person made a costly mistake. A person who's always felt terrible about what she did.'

Now Mrs McDonald closed one wrinkled eyelid so she could narrow her focus. 'Don't tell me you think you were responsible,' she said dismissively, guessing at Sophie's unspoken implication.

'But,' stammered Sophie, 'I was.'

'Oh really? You were a little girl. How old back then? Seven?'

'Nine.'

'Well, there you go. Nine-year-old girls who aren't driving the car don't cause accidents.' She raised an index finger again and pointed. 'That's a fact, mind you, so don't try to argue.'

'But—'

'Shush! No arguing!' She smiled. 'Sophie, I miss my son. Loved him like every mother loves her child. But I don't hold anyone responsible. It was an accident in the rain, end of discussion.'

'But I—'

'Shush,' she said again, smiling.

Evalynn chuckled. Sophie tried to frown but it didn't stick.

'Now then,' continued Lucy, 'I just can't stop thinking that I've seen you somewhere. Are you sure we haven't met before today?'

Sophie was in the middle of telling her that she'd never previously been to Millwood, when Lucy's wrinkled eyes lit up.

'Good Lord! What did you say your name was?'

'Sophie.'

'Sophie, or Sophia?'

Sophie stared back at the old woman nervously. 'It's Sophia,' she responded slowly. 'How did you know that?'

'Good Lord!' Lucy repeated. 'By golly, I was right!' She extended a hand. 'Help me up, dear. I need to show you something.'

Sophie and Evalynn stood up together, and Sophie took Lucy's arm. Lucy led them back to the kitchen. She pointed to the refrigerator. 'There,' she said, using her hand to direct their attention to odds and ends affixed with magnets to the refrigerator door.

Sophie didn't speak. Her eyes were glued to a sage green envelope right in the middle of the mess. She paced slowly forward.

'What the heck?' Evalynn whispered, when she saw what Sophie was staring at.

When she was close enough, Sophie lifted the magnet and ran her hand over the seal on the back of the envelope, remembering how its embossed doves felt to the touch. She already knew what the envelope contained, but she pulled out the contents anyway.

Inside was a picture of her and Garrett, taken more than a year earlier, along with an invitation to the wedding.

'Who sent this to you?' Sophie asked, her voice shallow.

'I have to believe that you did. Or perhaps it was Garrett,' Lucy replied with a twinkle in her eye.

'But . . . why? Do you know Garrett?'

'Sophie, dear, I don't just know Garrett. I'm his grandmother. Tim McDonald was his father.'

Sophie covered her mouth with her hand.

'We don't talk much, he and I, but I send him a birthday card every year, and once in a while I'll get something from him. I was so pleased when I got that announcement. I was looking forward to the wedding. Then a week or so before, he called me and said it was cancelled. I haven't heard anything from him since then.'

Sophie's mind was reeling as Lucy spoke. Garrett had hardly told her anything about his father. He said there wasn't much to tell, because his father had never played much of a role in his life. The fact that he'd grown up with his mother's maiden name had never been a topic of discussion. Her thoughts raced back to all the times Garrett had asked Sophie about the accident. She recalled the consternation on his face when he'd learned that her parents died on September 21, 1989; it was the same look of worry that flashed across his eyes when she pointed out where the accident had taken place.

Her face went white. 'Oh my gosh,' she whispered, as she fit the pieces together in her head. 'He knew.'

'Soph, you don't know that,' Evalynn said.

Sophie glanced at Lucy, and then stared blankly at Evalynn. 'Yes. I do.' The grimace that formed on her face was just a symptom of the nausea she suddenly felt in her stomach. Locking her eyes onto Lucy's, Sophie said, 'You can't tell him, Mrs McDonald. Please promise you won't tell Garrett that I was here. If I decide he needs to know, I'd rather he hear it from me.'

On their ride back from Millwood, Sophie managed to convince herself that Ellen must have known more about Lucy McDonald—and, by extension, Garrett and his family history—than she'd ever let on. How could she not? She'd been on the scene the night Tim McDonald died. She'd kept a copy of the police report for decades. She even worked with Garrett's mother at the police station. Those thoughts began festering the moment they'd pulled out of Lucy's dusty driveway.

Sophie could hardly contain her emotions when she and Evalynn reached Ellen's apartment and rang the doorbell.

'Knock once if friend, twice if foe!'

Sophie knocked loudly three times.

'Sophie? Ev?' Ellen opened the door. 'I thought you were spending the day out near Spokane.'

'We're back,' Sophie said abruptly.

'Was the woman not home?'

'Oh, she was home all right,' snapped Sophie. 'And she had a little surprise waiting for us.'

Ellen could read the emotion in Sophie's voice. 'Let's sit and talk, Sweets.' She motioned to the empty seats in the living room. 'Now then, what's got you all worked up?'

Sophie's response came out as an explosion. 'I know you like to meddle in our lives, but this is going too far!'

Ellen took half a step backwards. 'Sophie, I have no idea what you're talking about.'

Sophie clenched her fists. 'Just answer me this, and I swear if you lie to me you'll never see me again. When did you first learn that Garrett was Tim McDonald's son?'

Ellen's hand shot up and covered her mouth. 'The UPS driver? That was Garrett's father?'

Sophie and Evalynn exchanged puzzled looks. 'You mean you didn't know?' asked Sophie suspiciously.

'On my life, I swear I had no idea. I mean, I heard it mentioned way back when that he had a son, but that was all I knew. The detectives on the scene handled those details, notified the family. I swear, Sophie, I had no idea that there was a connection to Garrett.'

Sophie sat down on the couch and slumped back, holding her stomach with her hands to quell the sick feeling that was forming there once more. 'Well, Garrett knew,' she said with a groan.

Ellen sat down beside her. 'How?'

'I think he started piecing it together when I took him to the cemetery and he saw the date that my parents died. Then a week before he dumped me I showed him where the accident happened, and even pointed out the spot where I'd seen the paramedics working on the UPS driver. He couldn't have not known. Tim died when Garrett was twelve, so I'm sure he knew what his dad did for a living, and how and when he died.' She paused. 'Finding out that our parents died in the same accident must've flipped him out.'

Ellen clasped a hand over her mouth again. 'He read the report.'

Sophie sat straight up. 'What! When?'

'About a week before . . . I'm so sorry, Soph. I should have told you before. He came by one night and said he wanted to read it to better understand what you'd gone through. I thought he was being sweet. And it was far enough before he called things off that I didn't think it was related.'

Ellen's words hung in the air.

Sophie flung herself back against the cushions. 'He knows,' she lamented. 'That has to be why he called off the wedding. It says right in the report that the first cars to collide were the Volvo and the UPS truck. So he knows that my family killed his dad.' She groaned loudly. 'Rain or not—*accident or not*—he knows who struck who.' She paused, wanting to double over and puke. 'I don't blame him for leaving. I'd have probably done the same.'

Ellen touched Sophie gently on the leg. 'No, you wouldn't have. You'd have talked to him about it. And you'd have worked it out.'

Sophie let out a painful laugh. 'I doubt it.'

Ellen spoke with her motherly voice, and she smiled warmly. 'Do you remember what I said after he left?'

'You mean the whole "God is steering the boat, and everything has a purpose" bit?'

'Exactly! Maybe we're seeing that unfold right before our eyes. What are the odds that you would grow up and fall in love with someone who shared the same tragedy as a child?'

'Not great, I guess.'

'Not great? The odds are so infinitesimally small that it's not worth speculating.' She paused. 'It's Providence, Sweets.'

Sophie laughed. She wouldn't allow herself to believe it.

'You have to talk to him,' Ellen added.

Sophie knew she should do exactly what Ellen was suggesting. Part of her even wanted to, if only to come clean so she could get on with her hopeless, tragic life and forget all about him. But this wasn't just a faceless stranger that she would be confronting, like Jacob Barnes or Lucy McDonald. This was the boy who'd lost a father twenty years ago, who grew up to become the man who'd stolen her heart. This was Garrett. 'I know,' she said, as tears began to trickle down her cheek again. 'But I don't think I can.'

For more than an hour that night Sophie paced her living room nervously, eyeing the cellphone on the coffee table. Periodically she would pick it up, stare at it and then set it back down. It occurred to her that she was experiencing the same trepidation that had kept Garrett away for so many months. Sometimes living the lie is easier to bear than confronting the truth, she thought.

Sophie twirled her hair with one hand while biting the nails on her other. Then, grabbing the phone in one swift, fluid motion, she dialled and shoved it against her ear. She focused on controlling her breathing as she listened to it ring.

It kept ringing. And ringing. Nobody answered.

Sophie flipped her phone shut in frustration and dialled again. This time he answered on the fourth ring.

'Sophie?'

'Garrett! I just tried calling.'

'Can I call you back, Soph? I'm sort of in the middle of something. I've got someone on the other line.'

Sophie needed a moment before she responded. 'Work-related?'

'No, Soph. Listen, can I call you back in a little bit? I think another five or ten minutes with her and we'll call it a night.'

'Her?' Sophie said immediately, flummoxed.

'I'll call you back. Don't go anywhere.' The line went dead.

Sophie stared at her phone. She knew she had no claim on him, but the thought of Garrett spending time with another woman didn't sit right. How could he walk into her store one month ago and swear that he'd never stopped loving her, and now suddenly he's loving someone else? Sophie closed her phone and threw it against the couch, then went and sat down next to it.

Ten minutes later, her phone rang. She answered immediately.

'We need to talk,' Sophie said curtly.

'I figured,' he said with a chuckle. 'Why else would you have called, other than to talk?'

'Funny. But I mean . . . I want to have the conversation you've been pestering me to have.'

Garrett spoke softly into the receiver. 'You mean our date?'

'Yes.'

He chuckled again, louder. 'Wow, do I sense a bit of jealousy here? As soon as you hear I'm talking to another woman, suddenly you're ready to give me a chance?'

'That has nothing to do with it,' she asserted firmly. 'Let's just get together. We need to talk. In person.'

'Hmmm,' he said thoughtfully. 'I don't know how the woman I was talking to would feel about that. Can I bring her along?'

'Absolutely not!'

'Then I don't know, Soph. I'm not sure it's such a good idea.'

Sophie could hardly believe what she was hearing. 'But just a month ago you were dying to have this discussion with me.'

'I know,' he replied coolly. 'And I'm willing to. Just not right now. Why don't we just stick with our deal and get together as soon as you've found one hundred acceptable responses.'

'You're serious?'

'Of course.' He paused. 'I want you to admit that happiness really does exist out there. So you show me one hundred happy letters, and then we'll talk.'

Sophie felt her face heating up; this wasn't at all how she'd expected the conversation to go. Was it the woman he'd been talking with on the phone that suddenly made him less interested in their date? It galled her that she cared, but she did. 'Fine. Forget it. We don't need to talk. I was trying to do you a favour, but never mind.'

'You OK, Sophie? You sound a bit out of sorts.'

'I'm great,' she lied. 'Goodbye, Garrett.'

Sophie slammed her phone shut and threw it against the couch for the second time. Then she laid down next to it and allowed her emotions loose in a flood of tears.

Chapter 13

No matter what your past has been, your future is bleak.

SOPHIE TOSSED AND TURNED all night. Images of Garrett schmoozing on the phone with hordes of faceless women littered her dreams, causing her to wake up periodically in a cold sweat. The third time she woke up she decided it wasn't worth going back to sleep, so she crawled out of bed and got ready for work.

When Sophie arrived at Chocolat' de Soph an hour later and started her preparations, her Misfortunes seemed to come much easier than normal. Her final message, she decided, was specifically for Garrett. '*Sure, there are other attractive fish in the sea,*' she read aloud to make sure it captured what she was feeling. '*Too bad you're swimming in a shallow pond full of piranhas.*' A wry grin crept across her face as she slid the paper into a cookie.

After the store opened, but before any customers arrived, Sophie got an unexpected call on her work phone.

'Chocolat' de Soph,' she said.

'Sophie?' asked the distinctive singsong voice. 'Is that you, or is that someone else?'

'Alex?' Hearing his voice relaxed her, and brought a peaceful smile to her face. 'How are you? Aren't you supposed to be at work right now?'

'It's break time. I can call anyone on break time.'

'I see. So what can I do for you?'

'I found the letter to you from my dad.'

Sophie cleared her throat. 'Are you sure it's intended for me?'

'Yep. It has your name on it. Sophia Jones. And it has a note on the outside, telling me that when I find it, I should mail it.'

'Where did you find it, Alex?'

'*To Kill a Mockingbird*.'

'The book?'

'Uh-huh. I should have thought of that when you were here. My bedroom is my favourite room, but that book is my favourite place. I really like its happy ending. I read it at least one time every year. Dad knew that. I think that's why he put it there.'

'Wow. Did you read the letter?'

'Nope. It's closed.' He paused. 'Do you want to come get it?'

Sophie thought briefly. 'I'm afraid I can't come over this week. Would you mind putting it in the mail?'

'OK,' he said. It was several seconds before Alex said anything else. 'Sophie, have you found your happiness?'

'Sadly, no,' she answered with a sigh.

'That's what I thought, because even though I can't see your face, I can tell your voice isn't smiling as much as other days.'

'You're very perceptive, Alex. But even if it doesn't sound like it, I promise my heart is smiling right now from talking to you.'

There was another long silence before Alex said, 'My break is over, Sophie.' He said goodbye and clicked off.

Sophie glanced at the clock as she handed a customer a skewered apple, loaded with a semisoft mixture of white chocolate, milk chocolate, caramel, chopped cashews and crumbled biscuits.

'Beautiful,' he whispered, salivating as he felt the weight of it.

She checked her watch. It was already five minutes to five, which meant the mailman was officially late. Normally, she wouldn't care when the mail arrived, but it had been three days since she'd talked to Alex, and as each day passed Sophie grew more and more nervous to see what Jacob Barnes had written in his letter.

Jacob was the only other person from the night of the accident who would have had any inkling about her involvement. Though Alex's caregiver Meredith was certain that Jacob didn't harbour any ill feelings towards her, Sophie couldn't help but worry that maybe she was wrong. Why would he bother writing a letter, she wondered, if not to blame or accuse? The thought had her on edge.

When the mailman finally arrived and dropped off a box of mail inside the front door, Sophie was busy passing out samples to a family with five kids who wanted to taste everything in the store before making a decision. By the time they had made up their minds, there were another three customers waiting in line. Sophie breathed a giant sigh. Jacob's letter would have to wait, if it was there at all.

Randy arrived shortly after and picked up the box of mail while Sophie was ringing up a woman in her eighties who mentioned how her great-grandchildren were going to love the peppermint truffles in their stockings on Christmas morning.

'Well, then,' Sophie said, 'Merry Christmas.'

The woman smiled happily and waved goodbye.

'Randy?' Sophie called to the back once she was gone. 'Where'd you put the mail?' She was glancing out of the windows as she spoke, and saw a familiar Mercedes pull up in front of the store.

'Oh, crap,' she muttered.

Sophie scrambled to the back of the store and pulled off her apron. 'I'm leaving early, Randy. Where's the mail?'

Randy looked up from a vat of fudge. 'On your desk, like I said.' He cocked his head at an angle. 'You OK?'

'I'm fine,' she lied. 'But, if a certain someone happens to come in the store in, like, the next thirty seconds, do your best to stall him long enough for me to slip out the back.' Thoughts of Garrett had been festering ever since she found out that he was seeing another woman. No, she was not fine. And she didn't even have words for how what she'd learned about his father made her feel. With all of those emotions swimming round in her head, the last thing she wanted right then was to talk to him.

Randy nodded and then went up front to tend the register. Sophie hustled to her office, threw on her coat, and was rifling through the box of mail when she heard the front door open.

'Hey, Randy,' she heard Garrett say.

'Wassup, bro?'

'Is Sophie around?'

Sophie stood motionless, listening. There was a long pause before Randy said, 'She's here, but like, in the john . . . or something.'

'Oh,' Garrett said diplomatically. 'I guess I'll just wait.'

Sophie grinned, pleased that he'd bought Randy's lie. Quietly she sorted through the mail. The letter from Jacob Barnes was near the bottom of the box. She left the rest of the letters on the desk, grabbed her bag and umbrella, then tiptoed out of the back door.

Sophie had figured out that owning a car and driving to work had a few benefits, such as being able to sleep in longer in the morning. This morning she'd needed extra time to wake up, and so she drove her Explorer from Gig Harbor to Tacoma and parked it in a nearby garage.

Sophie popped open her umbrella and walked to the parking garage. By the time she paid the fare to leave, she assumed that Garrett had long since left her store. She pulled out onto the road, making a hard right turn, then hung a left at the next light. A few minutes later she was cruising along the highway, headed home, at her maximum rainy-day speed of forty-five miles per hour.

As usual, plenty of cars were annoyed by her tempo, but the only ones that bothered to honk were those that got stuck in her wake. She ignored them. Sophie was almost at the Narrows Bridge when one pulled alongside her.

Unlike other cars, this one didn't pass. It just stayed there, keeping pace. Sophie was sure that the driver was staring at her, but she refused to turn and look, because that would require diverting her focus from the increasingly wet road ahead, so she just kept driving.

A few moments later Sophie's phone began ringing inside her bag, playing Garrett's ring tone. He must have finally figured out that she wasn't in the bathroom, but even if she hadn't been driving right then, she wouldn't have answered, for the simple reason that she didn't have anything to say to him.

The phone went quiet. A few seconds later it started up again. Sophie wondered how many times he'd call before he got the hint.

After the ring ended for the second time, the car in the next lane, which was still keeping pace, started honking loudly. Sophie glanced over at it out of the corner of her eye.

The sight of Garrett's dimpled face staring back at her sent her into an instant panic. She gasped in surprise, but as she did so she inadvertently punched the accelerator, causing her to leap forward. The sudden shift in speed scared her, so she instinctively hit the brakes.

Then things went very wrong.

The car behind Sophie, who'd been stuck on her bumper for almost two miles, followed her lead when she sped up. It was still on her tail, accelerating quickly, when her brake lights flashed.

Sophie felt the car jolt as she was hit from behind. The next thing she knew she was sliding down the road out of control, tyres screeching, heart pounding and mouth screaming. Her Explorer crossed over into Garrett's lane. He slammed on his own brakes, resulting in another rear-end collision between him and the car behind him. Eight other vehicles also got caught up in the melee, stacking up end to end in one loud, momentous crash.

When Garrett's car finally came to a stop, the only thing on his mind was Sophie. Her car was thirty yards farther up the road, just shy of the bridge, wedged snugly at a ninety-degree angle between another car and the guardrail. He threw open his door, ran to the shoulder and darted up the highway to her.

The passenger door was unlocked when he got there. He yanked it open to find Sophie hunched behind the steering wheel's deflated air bag, with her head buried in her hands.

Garrett exhaled, relieved to see that she wasn't seriously hurt, at least not outwardly. 'Sophie, are you OK?'

She kept her face covered, hiding her tears.

Not knowing what else to do, Garrett reached out and put his hand on her back. She flinched, then dropped her hands from her face and sat up, wiping her nose on the back of her hand.

'I'm fine,' she said finally.

'You sure?'

She nodded.

Garrett turned to look out through the car's rear window. 'Listen, I should go and make sure everyone else is OK. You gonna be all right here for a little bit?'

'I'm going with you. I need . . . to see what I've done.'

Garrett helped her out of the car, and together they went from car to car to check for injuries. Most of the people were out along the shoulder talking, trying to sort out what had happened. One man was complaining of minor back pain, but everyone else seemed fine. Only when they were sure that nobody needed immediate medical attention did Garrett and Sophie make their way back to the Explorer to get out of the rain.

'Well, at least everyone's OK,' ventured Garrett, once they were back inside.

Sophie stared through the window towards the Narrows. She didn't even acknowledge that she'd heard Garrett.

'Soph? You alright?' He touched her gently.

When Sophie was ready to speak, her words came in whimpered spurts. 'You . . . should have . . . told me.'

'Told you what?' Garrett drew his hand back.

Emotionally, Sophie had reached her capacity. For a full year she'd struggled with not knowing why Garrett had abandoned her. And for nineteen years before that she'd been hampered by the loss of her family. Now to find out that the two greatest tragedies of her life were inexorably connected? Adding all of that to the immediate stress over the accident she'd just caused was too much. Sophie's emotions erupted. 'You should have told me!' she repeated, this time screaming the words.

From the look on his face, that wasn't what he'd expected her to say in the immediate aftermath of a ten-car pile-up. He took Sophie's hand, gently interlocking her fingers in his.

Sirens were already starting to scream in the background, but Garrett tuned them out, squeezing her hand tenderly. 'Talk to me, Sophie. What did I know that I should have said?'

With a menacing glare, Sophie let out a little laugh. 'Oh . . . I don't know,' she said sarcastically. 'Maybe you were right not mentioning it.' Tears started falling, and as they cascaded down her face her emotions hit another crescendo. 'Or maybe,' she barked, raising her voice sharply, 'you just didn't know how to say that you were completely disgusted by the fact that my family killed your father!'

Garrett's face went white. 'How do you know that?'

'So that's it!' she shot back, angry and sad and ashamed all at once. 'Well guess what! You don't even know the whole story! It was me! I caused the accident! So if you want someone to blame, you're looking at her!'

'What? That's not true.'

'Yes.' Her head fell into her hands again. 'It is. No matter what anyone says, it doesn't change the facts. If I hadn't done what I did back then, my parents would still be alive. And so would your dad.'

Garrett was flustered. 'Sophie, is that what you've thought all these years? That the accident was somehow your fault?'

'It was,' she snapped defiantly. 'I was there. I know what happened! And there are things that weren't in the police report that you know nothing about.'

He sat quietly. 'I could say the same thing,' he said eventually.

Sophie stared at him. 'What are you talking about?'

Looking over his shoulder, Garrett saw that police cars were pulling up in the space between his car and Sophie's, and he knew they'd have plenty of questions. 'I'll explain everything, just as soon as we're done dealing with . . . this.' He motioned to the line of cars behind them. 'I've got to go find my insurance papers.'

Everyone on the scene did their best to expedite the accident cleanup. Tow trucks were on the scene within minutes and began hauling away cars. A female officer spent less than two minutes talking to Garrett about how the wreck started. He'd only given a brief overview of what he'd seen before she cut him off. 'Let's cut to the chase. In your opinion, was anyone being reckless?'

'Reckless? No. Overly cautious, perhaps, but not reckless.'

As soon as the officer was through with him, a tow truck backed up and hauled his vehicle away. The officer left to talk to Sophie, who was standing beside her car under an umbrella.

Garrett followed, listening as she asked Sophie the same set of questions. He had to bite his tongue when he overheard her say, 'It was all my fault, Officer. It always is.'

The officer gave her a look. 'But you got hit from behind, right?'

Sophie nodded.

'Well then, according to the law, it's not your fault.'

'But—'

'But,' she interjected before Sophie could object, 'it's too cold for debate. Do you have someone coming to pick you up?'

Sophie started to shake her head, but Garrett heard the question too, and said, 'I'll give you a lift, Soph. A rental car is on its way.'

She nodded.

The officer moved on to the next car, and Garrett joined Sophie under the umbrella. They watched from the shoulder of the road as the tow truck winched her car up off the ground. It was starting to pull away when Sophie realised she'd forgotten something.

'The letter!' she shouted as she handed the umbrella to Garrett and took off running after the truck. 'Stop!'

The driver didn't hear her, but he saw her in his rearview mirror and stopped. She retrieved the letter, then jogged back to Garrett.

'What was that about?' he asked.

Sophie considered trying to explain it, but she didn't want to get into another convoluted conversation before finishing the one they'd started twenty minutes earlier.

'Nothing,' she said. 'How long until your car shows up?'

'I don't know. Fifteen minutes. Maybe longer with this traffic.'

Pursing her lips, she said, 'Great. That should be plenty of time for you to finish what you were saying before.'

He grimaced. 'Before I do, how did you find out my dad was in the crash with your family?'

Sophie's mouth curled slightly in a tiny, smug smile. 'I figured it out on Sunday when I met Grandma McDonald.'

Garrett's mouth dropped open. ' But . . . how did you find her?'

'It all started with our want ad.' She paused, trying to think how to bring up Alex without giving too much away. 'One of the guys who responded sent me something that really touched me. I decided I wanted to meet the person who sent it.'

'So you just showed up at his house?'

'Yeah, I went to see him. It turns out we had a lot in common.'

'So that's—'

'Alex? Yes.' Sophie watched his face, and was pleased to see that he seemed disappointed. 'Anyway, we hit it off right away, and he sort of motivated me to put my past behind me once and for all. I figured the best way to do that was to talk to the other family who lost someone that night.'

Garrett ran his fingers through his dark hair and sighed. 'I'm such an idiot. If I could turn back the clock, I'd have told you this on the night I broke off our engagement. I just didn't know how to say it. And I convinced myself that you knowing the truth would have been harder to swallow than losing me.' He shrugged. 'Plus, I figured I was going to lose you either way, so I chose the way that saved me having to explain it, and saved you having to know the bitter truth.'

'Garrett,' she intoned softly, 'in the words of your grandmother, what's the punch line?'

He let out a quiet hoot. 'The punch line, Sophia Maria Jones, is that you didn't cause the accident that night. I did.'

'That's cruel! What are you doing? Making fun of me?'

'I'm being serious, Sophie. I didn't know how to say it to you before. Knowing the effect that the accident had on your life, it made me sick to think that I'd caused you so much pain. I knew telling you would break your heart, and I knew that I couldn't go the rest of my life hiding something like that from you. So I left.'

'You're beyond nuts. You weren't even there.'

He sighed again. 'True. But I wasn't far.'

She folded her arms across her torso. 'Explain.'

'My father always made it clear not to contact him while he was at work.' Garrett kept his eyes locked on Sophie's. 'However, he said if there was an emergency, I could call the UPS receptionist, and she could patch me in to his radio if it was important enough.' He paused, lowering his eyes briefly. 'On the day of the accident, I got in a fight with my mom. I said things to her that I regretted afterwards, and one of those was that I wanted to move out and live with my dad. He'd never really been a part of my life, but I was getting older and I desperately wanted to feel like I had a father, so I called the receptionist and asked her to put me through. I told her it was an emergency—it seemed like one at the time. I told her to keep trying, that he had to call me back immediately.' He stopped talking and looked at her expectantly.

'And?' she asked. 'How does that tie you to the accident?'

'I thought you said you read the report?'

'I did,' she shot back.

'Did you happen to read that bit about the UPS driver holding a CB radio in his hand when they pulled him from the wreckage?'

'Yes,' she said. 'But that doesn't mean anything.'

'Maybe not to you, but to the kid who'd been pestering to talk to his dad immediately, it means a lot. After reading about the CB in Ellen's file, I tracked down that old UPS receptionist. It took a private investigator nearly a week to find her.' He paused.

'And?'

'And she said she remembered talking to him that night on the radio. He was annoyed and wanted to know what the emergency was, and of course I hadn't told her, because I knew he wouldn't think it was important enough. But she was a mother herself, and started arguing with him. And then she said he stopped responding. She found out later it was because of the crash. So just like I said before, I caused the accident. Not directly, maybe, but if I hadn't called . . . who knows? Maybe he wouldn't have been so distracted, and things would have ended up differently for your parents.'

Sophie's eyes were now very wet. 'I don't know what to say,' she admitted. 'You're . . . you aren't making this up, are you?'

Shaking his head slowly, Garrett exhaled. 'I'm sorry, Soph. I should have told you last year. I just didn't know how to.'

Just then a car pulled up. The driver rolled down the passenger window. 'Are you Mr Black? I'm from Enterprise Car Rental.'

'I sure am. Thanks for coming. Can you drop my friend off in Gig Harbor?' The driver agreed, so Garrett opened the door and he and Sophie both climbed in.

The Enterprise driver had lots of things to say—mostly questions about the accident—but when he quieted down, Sophie posed a question to Garrett. 'When you decided not to tell me last year, was it because you thought the news would be hard for me to hear, or hard for you to say?'

He thought about how to respond, and then said simply, 'Yes.'

'So breaking my heart was a better option than swallowing your pride? I meant that little to you?'

His shoulders slumped. 'After two decades I'd just learned that I was partially to blame, not only for the death of my father, but the loss of your family as well. I figured your heart would break no matter what I said.'

'So you took the easy way out,' she deadpanned.

'Like I said, if I could turn back the clock, I'd have done things very differently. I was stupid.'

'Yes. You were.' Sophie turned away and looked out of the window. Garrett kept quiet, allowing her time to think. 'You didn't give me a chance to decide how I felt about it. You decided alone.'

When they got to Sophie's house, Garrett walked her to the door. 'Soph,' he said before she turned the handle, 'I'll never forgive myself for not being honest about what I knew. It was selfish of me, and I'm sorry.'

She shifted her weight. 'We really are something, aren't we? Both of us feeling guilty for the same accident. You know what Ellen would say about that, right?'

'Divine Providence, Sweets, so help me God,' he replied in his best imitation of Sophie's foster mom.

'Exactly. But then I'd have to remind her that Providence would have brought us together on a more permanent basis.'

Garrett frowned. 'Good point.'

'Divine intervention can only get you so far, I guess.' Sophie shrugged, turned and opened the door, then stepped inside.

Garrett waited for her to turn back round. 'So . . . that's it then?'

'I guess so.' She looked straight at him, regretting that they'd let everything between them crumble. But it was a moot point now. He'd moved on, and there was nothing she could do about it. 'Good luck with . . . what's her name? From the phone the other night?'

Garrett's mouth tightened. 'Jane.'

'Jane. Well. I wish you two the best. Whatever happens, it can't turn out any worse than we did, right?'

Turning on his heels, he quietly said, 'Goodbye, Sophie.'

'Goodbye, Garrett,' she whispered back. Sophie closed the door, locked it, and then leaned against it for support. It had been a long day, and she was ready for it to be over.

Chapter 14

What you thought was happiness wasn't. Time to move on.

LYING ON HER BED an hour later, Sophie recounted everything that had happened since leaving work. Because she blamed herself all these years for causing the accident, she could understand why Garrett blamed himself as well. But he hadn't trusted her enough to tell her the truth, hadn't given her the opportunity to forgive him. But if she had known it was his father who was killed, could she have admitted to Garrett it was her fault?

The accident that took her parents accounted for less than a minute of her life, yet the effects of that moment had caused her a lifetime of pain. Like Andromeda, she was forever chained to her past.

As she was replaying everything that Garrett had said again in her head, she remembered that she still hadn't read the letter from Jacob Barnes. Reluctantly, she got up and found the letter in her bag, then sat down and opened it. Reading the date in the top corner of the letter's first page, she noted with some dismay that it had been written just a few days before Jacob passed away.

With a stomach full of butterflies about what it was going to say, she started to read. By the time she reached the end, her emotional levees were in ruins, with tears running freely down her face. For the first time since she was eight, Sophia Maria Jones felt completely unfettered by her past. And utterly sick over her future, a future that should have included Garrett Black.

August 17, 2009

Dear Sophia,

With any luck, you don't remember me at all. But I cannot forget you. How could I? It is the agony of remembrance that now compels me to write to you. I could not leave this world without putting down on paper all of my thoughts and feelings concerning our brief encounter so many years ago.

My name is Jacob Barnes. Believe it or not, you and I shared a few words and a small patch of sidewalk together in the aftermath of a horrific accident on your ninth birthday. I lost four fingers that day, but I know you lost much more than that. I'm so sorry for your loss.

Please know that I've wanted to seek you out for years. I should have done so a long time ago. At first I told myself that you were too young to understand. As you got older, I convinced myself that too much time had passed to dredge this up. Neither excuse was true; I was simply a coward.

I've tried to keep tabs on your welfare, to make sure you were getting along OK. Last year I saw in your local newspaper that you were to marry Dr Garrett Black. Congratulations! Hopefully married life is treating you well. My heart leapt for joy when I saw the photo of you and him. The smile on your face told me that you've somehow managed to deal with the weighty burden that you were left with on the night we met. Which burden? The burden of guilt for causing the accident that claimed the lives of your family.

Sadly, that burden should have never been yours to bear. It rightfully belonged to me.

I hope someday you have the chance to meet my son, Alex. He is the greatest joy I've ever known, and, regrettably, my guilt and shame are inextricably tied to him. Allow me to explain.

Alex was born just before the stroke of midnight on September 20th, 1989—less than twenty-four hours before our collision. His mother, Katherine, and I had put off having children longer than most first-time parents. My wife was forty-three when she became pregnant. The entire pregnancy went off without a hitch, right up until labour began.

Then everything turned sour. My wife started haemorrhaging badly while she was pushing, but the baby was far enough into the canal that they had to focus on getting the baby delivered before they could do much for her. They worked as fast as they could to bring Alex into the world, and then they turned immediately to my Katherine's needs. We all breathed an enormous sigh of relief when they were able to stop the bleeding and stabilise her.

The doctors took Alex to run some tests on him, but I was too caught up in the worry over Katherine to wonder why. For the next four hours I sat next to my wife in her hospital room. She seemed fine. However, while I was watching her, all of a sudden she looked up at me in a panic. She gasped a few times, closed her eyes, and was gone. No goodbyes. No I-love-yous. She never even had a chance to hold our son. I learned later that a blood clot from the earlier bleeding had gone to her brain, shutting down her vital organs in one quick stroke.

Needless to say, I was in shock. I spent the day in a stupor, filling out paperwork, trying to wrap my head round the fact that she was gone. It wasn't until six at night that I finally asked for my son. An entire team of doctors responded to my request. The head of paediatrics explained that my new baby had some chromosomal abnormalities.

When I heard the words 'Down's syndrome', I panicked. And though they tried to get me to hold him, I refused. My head was spinning. How could I raise a child like that on my own? I, who had just lost the love of my life, how could I endure the burden of a child with special needs?

I'm not proud of those feelings, but they pale in comparison to the shame of what I did next.

I left. I simply walked out of the hospital. I was mad at everything: mad at the doctors for letting my wife die, mad at the world for the injustice and, sadly, mad at my new son for his genetic make-up. In a rage, I went to my car and I drove away. I didn't have a clue where I was going; I just wanted to drive, and I wanted to drive fast.

The weather that night was ridiculous. I should have slowed the first time my car hydroplaned, but I didn't. When I saw a UPS truck in my lane, it upset me. Suddenly I was mad at the driver for slowing me down. Since I couldn't get round it on the left due to oncoming traffic, I flew alongside it in the right-hand lane, then swerved in front of it as I passed. Just to show the UPS driver that I owned the road, I tapped my brakes as soon as I got in front of him. When I touched the brake pedal, my car hydroplaned again, and I slammed the brakes even harder. Worried he was going to rear-end me, I looked quickly in the mirror and I saw that instead of hitting me, he'd swerved to the left. He missed me, but hit your car head-on.

The accident was entirely my fault. If not for me, your family would still be alive. The driver of the UPS truck, too.

After the first impact, I lost control of my car. It caught an edge and rolled twice. I probably lost my fingers when they were pinched between the road and the car when my arm swung out through the shattered window. Who knows. It doesn't matter anyway. Four fingers is a small price to pay for my carelessness . . . one finger for every person that died.

I recall sitting in my car once it came to a stop, feeling utterly sick for what I'd just done. I couldn't get out of my door, but the rear window was popped completely out, so I shimmied through it. I ran back up the road to your car. What I found was a little girl—you—in the rear seat, crying. I pulled you out and carried you a safe distance away along the side of the road, setting you down next to a fire hydrant. That's when I passed out.

Sometime later I came to. I was foggy, unsure what was going on. You were there, still crying, and you were saying that the accident was your fault. While I was getting my hand worked on, I learnt that your name *was Sophia Maria Jones. An officer took you to an ambulance, and a few minutes later I was escorted to one nearby. That's when I saw you throw away your fortune. It floated right down the street near where I was sitting. It was wet and in a tiny ball, but I picked it up and read it. I kept it as a reminder of whose life I'd ruined.*

At first I resisted when the ambulance team tried to take me back to the hospital I'd just left an hour before. Looking back, I believe it was Providence, drawing me back to my responsibilities as a father. When I got there, my thoughts kept turning back to you. I imagined what your life was going to be like without parents, and I decided that I could not inflict that same fate upon my own son too. I called the doctors upstairs and had them bring Alex down so I could hold him in the ER. Once I had him in my arms, I never wanted to let go.

So why am I writing this letter now? Even now I cannot bring myself to face you in person. I've wanted to apologise for what I did at least a million times; not only for causing the accident, but for knowing that you believed it was your fault and not correcting that notion. I shouldn't have allowed you to carry that guilt all these years.

I have come to love my son Alex like no son has ever been loved before. He is a rare gift. Instead of being a burden, he has been my greatest joy. Each time I told myself that I needed to apologise to you and tell you the truth about what happened, I found myself unable to own up to it, because doing so would have forced me to admit to two disgusting truths. First, that when he was born, I left Alex parentless— if only for an hour—because I thought he was less than perfect. How insanely wrong I was! And second? that I would never have had the joy of raising Alex at all if not for the accident that claimed the lives of your family. I'd have just kept right on driving and never looked back. It's cruel, isn't it? Your horrible loss was my incredible gain.

I've never been a particularly religious person, but that hasn't stopped me from thanking God every day for that accident that sent me back to my son. And those same prayers have always included the one unending 'wish of my heart': that someday God will make right what He allowed me to mess up in your life.

I'm so sorry for everything. I wish you and your husband every happiness in the world. Hold on to each other, and live each moment as if it were your last. Someday it will be. Later rather than sooner, I hope, but as long as you've lived well, how long you live won't really matter.

God bless,

Jacob P. Barnes

PS: If you're ever feeling discouraged, I encourage you to meet Alex. He can lift spirits like nobody else!

PPS: Each year on your birthday Alex and I place stones on the graves of your parents. I hope you'll let him continue the tradition. I'd like to be able to say there is some profound meaning to it, but that's not the case. To me, it seems like too many things in life are temporary. The stones are just reminders that not all things dissipate so quickly. Some things, in fact, last for aeons . . . maybe even for ever. My love for my wife and son, for instance, and I'm sure the love you have for your parents as well. And, hopefully, the love you feel for your new husband. God bless, Sophia Jones.

Setting Jacob's letter down on her night stand, Sophie wiped her tears on her sleeve and then immediately called Ellen.

'You're not going to believe the day I've had,' she said as soon as her foster mom answered.

'It's late, but try me.'

For the next thirty minutes Sophie shared in great detail the ongoing saga of her and Garrett, starting with him showing up unexpectedly at Chocolat' de Soph, followed by the accident. Then she explained his claim of responsibility for the accident that killed their parents, and ended with a reading of Jacob Barnes's letter.

'Good Lord,' Ellen said slowly when Sophie was done. 'If you don't see something more at work here than dumb luck or happenstance, then you're as blind as a bat, and I feel sorry for you.'

'Ellen—'

'Don't "Ellen" me. I've been saying right from the beginning that something good would come out of that accident. Mr Barnes saw the good of it in his life, and I hope you recognise it too.' She paused to let Sophie speak, but there was only silence on the phone. 'You were meant to be with Garrett, Sweets. It's been twenty years in the making, but now's the time. So are you going to keep sitting there moping about the past, or are you going to do something about the future? Remember—God's steering the boat to shore, you just need to paddle.'

'It's not that easy, El. He has a girlfriend, Jane.'

'Do they share a history that started two decades ago?'

'Probably not,' said Sophie tenuously.

Chuckling, Ellen said, 'Then I have just one more question. Do you still love him? In the end, that's all that really matters.'

While Ellen was speaking, a text message popped up on Sophie's phone. It was Garrett. A gust of hope filled her lungs, and a grin spread across her face. 'Ellen,' she said, 'I gotta go. I'm going to try putting my paddle in the water, and see what happens.'

'That's my girl! Love you, Sweets.'

Sophie pressed a button to open Garrett's message. It said,

FYI: I stopped by your store on way home, let Randy know you're OK. He said a bunch more letters arrived today. I took a peek.

And???

100 letters. All of them are from your guy, Alex.

What??

Yep. I read a handful. He's very optimistic. U R lucky.

At first Sophie wasn't sure how she should respond, mostly because she didn't want to continue letting him think that Alex was anything more than a friend. That prompted an idea.

Can I call U? she typed.

She didn't have to. Five seconds later, her phone rang. 'What's up?' Garrett asked. 'Thumbs out of practice?'

'No,' said Sophie. 'I just wanted to say this to you in person.'

'Uh-oh.'

She took a deep breath. 'OK. Don't freak out, but . . . I'm getting married.'

There was a prolonged silence. 'Wow . . . Soph. Don't you think maybe you're rushing things?'

'Nope. Not this time.'

'Well . . . are you sure you love him?'

'More than I ever thought I could love anyone.'

'Ouch. That stings,' Garrett mumbled. 'Well, I guess you know what you're doing then. So . . . congratulations . . . or something.'

'Thank you,' she whispered. 'Hey, I know I've been a pain about all of the want ad responses; I want to apologise. And I'd still like to read what all of this mail says. Do you think you could come by the store sometime and help me finish going through it?'

'Of course. Just tell me when.'

'How about tomorrow night. Is eight thirty too late?'

'That'll be fine, Soph,' Garrett said. 'I'll see you tomorrow.'

'Great,' she replied. 'Good night, Garrett.'

Biting her lip, Sophie hung up. 'Well, this should be interesting,' she stated out loud to herself. 'I guess I'd better get baking.'

Chapter 15

Between the sun and the rain, there are rainbows.
That's where you'll find the pot of gold.

IT WAS RAINING OUTSIDE the next day when Sophie walked out to the bus-stop, but she didn't care. In fact, unlike previous rainy days, she welcomed the moisture as a way to wash away the past and start anew. As she paced along the street without an umbrella, the water pelting her face made her feel strangely alive. She smiled and strode confidently onwards.

The bus driver was surprised to see Sophie step onto the bus with dripping hair and a bright smile. 'Oh, heck,' she grumbled, 'hell must'a froze over when I wasn't lookin'. What's gotten into you, girl? Don't you know it's droppin' cats and dogs out there?'

Sophie paid the fare. 'Without a storm now and then, how would we ever appreciate sunny skies?' She didn't wait for an answer, but just walked to the rear of the bus and took a seat.

Chocolat' de Soph was always busy before Thanksgiving, but this day was especially hectic. In addition to a last-minute order of pumpkin truffles for a corporate party, Sophie was scrambling to complete something special for Garrett before he showed up that night. Plus she lost an hour in the afternoon because she had to make a trip to the auto repair shop where her car had been towed.

After the evening rush, Sophie focused every spare second on her newest creation, wanting it to be just right. It took multiple rounds of failures before she got the cookies just the way she wanted them, but she was pleased to have them done to her satisfaction by the time she turned on the 'Closed' sign in the window at eight o'clock.

For the next half hour Sophie cleaned the kitchen until a series of loud knocks echoed through the store right at half past the hour.

Tucking a strand of hair behind her ear, Sophie glided round the wall that divided the front of the store from the kitchen and waved at the face peering back at her through the window.

'Hey, Sophie,' Garrett said as she opened the door for him. A cold wind blew in from the street as he entered.

'Hi.'

Garrett looked at her like he wanted to say something, then his face changed. 'Well, let's get started on the mail. I probably shouldn't stay too long . . . you know, Jane might start to think something's up.'

'Understood,' said Sophie, wanting to cringe, but maintaining her composure. 'But before we start, can you spare a minute for something else? I have a new creation I'd like you to try.'

'Sure,' he told her with a dimpled half smile. 'I'd love to.'

Sophie led the way to the back of the store, to a small counter. Sitting on the counter was a plate with two chocolate-dipped treats that looked suspiciously like Misfortune Cookies, with the exception that instead of having only dark chocolate exteriors, they also had thick stripes of white that curved all round in an ornate zebra pattern.

Garrett frowned. 'Misfortune Cookies? Umm, no thanks. I've still got the aftertaste from the one you gave me in September.'

Sophie tilted her head and grinned. 'The recipe is very different. Seriously, Garrett, trust me.' She picked up the cookie that was closest to the front of the plate. 'First, try this one.'

Sceptically, Garrett took the striped cookie and sniffed it.

'Chicken,' she said, egging him on. 'Just eat it.'

'Fine. But if this is a trick . . .' He lifted it again and hesitantly bit into the chocolate shell, then closed his mouth and chewed. He smiled just before he swallowed. 'Wow, Soph! That was . . . I don't even know how to describe it. Uniquely delicious. I can still taste the bitter chocolate from before, but mixed with the sweet it's a completely different experience.'

She curtsied playfully. 'Thank you, kind sir. Glad you approve.'

'So why the change?'

'It just felt right,' she said matter-of-factly. 'I think my perspective has changed. Yes, life can have many bitter moments. But those are tempered here and there by sweet bursts of happiness, which make the whole experience more palatable.'

'I'm impressed. Have the fortunes changed as well?'

'Sort of. Now each cookie has two slips of paper—one positive, and the other, well, the same as before. I guess you could say you get the good with the bad. Read yours,' she told him, grinning.

Garrett carefully pulled two slips of paper from the cookie, and read the top one aloud. '*You have a knack for hurting those you love. Be grateful they still love you.* Ouch. Thanks for the reminder. I take it that's the bad one?'

Sophie nodded as Garrett pulled the second paper closer to read. He noticed that the second fortune was typed, not handwritten, and was printed on paper that felt old and wrinkled. Some of the ink was even smudged. '*Happiness is a gift that shines within you. The wish of your heart will soon come true.* Sophie, is this the fortune you told me about that came with the want ad responses?'

She took a deep breath and nodded. 'It's the fortune I got the night my family died. I just thought . . . your dad died that night too, and you might like to share in my good fortune.'

He nodded appreciatively. 'Thank you.'

'Now try the second cookie,' she said, taking another deep breath to quell her nerves.

Shrugging, Garrett set down the remnants of the first cookie and picked up the other one, then he took a bite and smiled as before. 'Tastes the same.'

Sophie tried to force a smile, but the knots in her stomach were making it difficult. All she said was, 'Hmm.'

Cracking off another piece of the black-and-white cookie, the cookie broke completely in half, and something shiny and metallic fell out onto his palm. 'What in the world is this?'

Sophie held onto the counter to steady herself. Her moment had arrived. *Paddle for shore, or sink trying,* she told herself. Taking a final, extended breath, she said, 'That, Garrett Black, is an O.'

'I see that,' he chuckled. 'It looks like something from a car.'

Grinning awkwardly, she said, 'It's the O from the rear logo on my Explorer. You know, the one I killed yesterday. I had the guy at the auto body shop pop it off for me today.'

'But why would you do that? And why is it in this cookie?'

Paddle faster! 'Because . . . really, it belongs to you.'

'The O?'

'The car.' *Breathe. Just breathe.* 'Did I ever tell you how I paid for that?'

'Uh . . . no.'

She forced a chuckle. 'See, when I was absolutely sure that we were through, I took the engagement ring you gave me down to a local thrift store and turned it into cash.'

Garrett swallowed. 'You hawked the ring to buy a car?'

'Uh-huh.'

With a look of stupor, he glanced down once more at his open palm, and then back up at Sophie. 'So why the O?'

Sophie willed herself to keep looking him in the eyes. 'Well, no matter what happens, when the insurance check comes, I want you to know that I'm handing it all over to you. It's your money.'

'You don't have to do th—'

'Let me finish,' she interrupted. 'It's your money, and I'm giving it back. But I chose the O . . . ' Her voice trailed off as she took the chrome letter from his hand. 'I chose the O because out of that entire car—which used to be a beautiful ring—it was the only shiny part I could squeeze into a cookie and still, well . . .' As her voice trailed off, Sophie stuck her pinky through the centre of the O, and then carefully slid it all the way to the base of her hand. 'It's too small for my ring finger, but close enough.'

Garrett's eyes nearly popped out of his head. 'Sophie, what are you—'

'Hear me out, Garrett. The first cookie that you opened tonight had two fortunes. The first one meant that even though you hurt me, I understand why you did what you did, and . . . I still love you. And I don't care that you've met this . . . Jane. I know she can't love you as much as I love you. The second message is really for me more than it is for you. My father promised me when I was a girl that I'd get the wish of my heart.' She gulped for air. 'Garrett, there's no way I could have ever known that while I sat there crying along the side of the road, that the ultimate wish of my heart—and the greatest fortune of my life—was sitting at home wishing he could get through on a radio just thirty yards away from me. You are the wish of my heart, Garrett Black. My happiest moments are when I'm with you, and I'd love nothing more than to take the good with the bad, with you, for the rest of my life.'

Garrett let a moment or two pass, listening to the sound of Sophie's rapid breathing. 'Are you done?' he asked finally.

She nodded reluctantly, unable to read the expression on his face.

'Good.' In one swift motion he wrapped his arms round her and kissed her. It felt just like the first time they'd kissed.

'What about Jane?' Sophie asked, when she came up for air.

Garrett leaned back and laughed. 'Jane's her middle name. Olivia Jane Black DeMattio.'

Sophie gasped. 'Your mother?'

He chuckled again. 'All I said that night was that I was on the phone with a woman. I didn't say with whom. If you thought I meant a pretty young woman, then good! I was jealous, and I wanted you to be too.' As he said that, his smile dimmed slightly, and his brow furrowed. 'What about Alex and the wedding?'

Standing on her toes, Sophie kissed him again. 'I said I was getting married. I didn't say to whom. If you thought I meant Alex, that was part of my plan.' She winked. 'I guess it worked.'

'So is there even a guy named Alex? Who sent those letters yesterday?'

She giggled. 'Yes, Alex is very real, and the fact that he sent those letters is so sweet. Alex Barnes is very special to me. He just has this innate ability to make me smile and laugh, and to remind me of all the things in life that there are to be happy about.'

'But you're not in love?'

'Oh, I do love him. But it was never what you thought.' Sophie unwrapped herself from Garrett's embrace and went to her bag and found the letter from Jacob Barnes. 'Here, you need to read this. It's from Alex's father. Not only will it tell you what makes Alex so special, but it also clears up a few of our past, umm, *misconceptions* about the accident that killed our parents.'

'Huh?'

'Just read,' she said, and then gave him another little kiss.

Garrett grimaced. 'Not yet.' He reached into his back pocket and pulled out a folded piece of notebook paper. Every line was filled on both sides. 'It's my own list of happiness. I figured since your dream-boat, Alex, was able to come up with one hundred different things that make him happy, then I could too. You'll notice as you read that every single one of them is about you.'

Small tears started to form at the corner of Sophie's eyes. 'And when were you planning on giving it to me?'

Garrett winked. 'Well, according to you on our first date, a truly romantic man will do whatever it takes to win a lady's heart. So I was getting all geared up to crash your wedding. I was going to march right up to the front like they do in the movies and read my list. Then, assuming Alex hadn't already taken a punch at me, I was going to profess my undying love.'

She kissed him again. 'And then we'd ride off into the sunset?'

'Yeah,' he said softly, 'something like that.'

'I'm glad to know you're still a hopeless romantic,' she joked.

'Hopeful romantic,' he corrected. 'There is a difference.'

With Garrett by her side, Sophie read his list of happiness, and smiled.

Garrett read Jacob's letter, and cried.

Then they embraced and ate the last few pieces of the new Misfortune Cookies, grateful to share every bittersweet bite.

Kevin Alan Milne

After graduating from high school, Kevin Alan Milne, pronounced 'Miln-ee'—
'breaking every "silent-e" rule that you ever learned in first grade'—attended a
public event with his parents where recent graduates were asked what they
wanted to be when they grew up. When it was his turn to stand at the
microphone and give his response to the crowd, Kevin addressed himself
directly to his parents. While many of his peers had predicted their success as
future doctors and lawyers, Kevin told his parents honestly that he had no clue
what career he wanted to pursue. 'I'm sure at that moment they wanted to
slink beneath their chairs,' he says. But he wasn't finished with his answer.
'Eventually, I'll figure out how to earn a living,' he continued. 'But if you really
want to know what I'll be when I grow up, I can tell you: I want to be just like
my dad . . . and if I'm even half as good at being a father and husband as he
is, I think everything else will work out just fine.'

During his undergraduate college days, Kevin Alan Milne studied anything
and everything that caught his interest, including political science, German,
journalism, communications and philosophy. Not surprisingly, he changed his
major nearly a dozen times, finally settling on psychology. In graduate school,
he focused on just about the only subject he hadn't yet studied—business—

and earned an MBA from Penn State University.

After landing what he thought was his dream job in the business world, Kevin soon realised that the corporate environment was less exciting than he had anticipated. He found himself functioning on autopilot to complete tedious activities and yearned for mental stimulation. 'It was then that I committed myself to writing a book, something I'd dreamt of doing for as long as I could remember, and I did it the only way I knew how: I sat down at the computer and started typing.' He worked feverishly whenever he had a free moment and the eventual result was his first novel, *The Paper Bag Christmas*, which was published in 2008. This was followed, in 2009, by *The Nine Lessons*, which is an inspirational story about life and fatherhood, set around one of the author's passions: golf.

Sweet Misfortune is Kevin Alan Milne's third novel and the idea came from a fortune cookie. A big fan of Chinese food, Kevin has always made it a point to open his fortune cookie after a meal. He takes his fortunes with a pinch of salt, but if he gets one that he particularly likes, he'll tuck it away. 'One of the most enjoyable parts of writing this book was coming up with the downbeat fortunes,' says Kevin. 'I had a lot of fun with that. Most of them came naturally out of what was happening in the story. It was fun to take the good fortunes and flip them upside down. See what the world is like from a pessimistic view.' While Kevin does not consider himself a glass-half-empty guy, he can relate to the character of Sophie, describing himself as 'a little cynical' and 'a realist'. But he points out that he's actually more like Sophie at the end of the book, when she cheers up and discovers true happiness.

Kevin married Rebecca in Washington DC in 1995 and they now have four daughters: Mikayla, Kamry, Mary and Emma, and one son, Kyler (aka 'the boy'). They live in Kevin's hometown of Sherwood, Oregon, and the author loves watching his children grow and thrive in the area which was his old stomping ground. Kevin still maintains his business career by day, while writing novels during his 'free' time, although as the father of five, free time is nearly impossible to find. His favourite role, however, is that of family man. That's his personal definition of lasting joy and happiness. 'Jobs have come and gone since high school,' he says, 'but along the way nothing has been quite so satisfying—or scary or challenging or downright frustrating—as marriage and parenthood.'

It seems that from an early age Kevin Alan Milne had the foresight to understand that a happy family life plays a large part in the secret to everlasting happiness. He had witnessed it in his own family while growing up, and wanted to emulate it when he became an adult. His hopeful prediction 'to be just like my dad' has come true, as has his dream to become a writer. 'One wife and five kids later, I'm certainly living the dream!' he says.